Life in Peacetime

THE ITALIAN LIST

Life in Peacetime

FRANCESCO PECORARO

Translated by Antony Shugaar

LONDON NEW YORK CALCUTTA

SERIES EDITOR

Alberto Toscano

Seagull Books, 2019

Originally published as *La vita in tempo di pace*

© Adriano Salani Editore S.r.l.–Gruppo editoriale Mauri Spagnol S.p.A.,
Milan, 2013

First published in English translation by Seagull Books, 2018
English translation © Antony Shugaar, 2018

ISBN 978 0 8574 2 482 2

British Library Cataloguing-in-Publication Data
A catalogue record for this book is available from the British Library.

Typeset by Seagull Books, Calcutta, India
Printed and bound by Maple Press, York, Pennsylvania, USA

*It's always night,
or we wouldn't need light.*

Thelonious Monk

*Out of all the countless possible universes, there must certainly be
one in which the world is configured as it appears in this book.*

For Nicola

CONTENTS

1

Prologue

15

29 May 2015, 9.07 a.m.

33

Monsoon

67

10.14 a.m.

87

The Sense of the Sea

149

11.05 a.m.

165

Sofrano

252

2.32 p.m.

265

Bridge and Door

346

3.48 p.m.

362
The Unmoved Mover

431
4.42 p.m.

451
The City of God

525
5.16 p.m.

543
Bomb Crater

572
7.47 p.m.

588
Epilogue

Ivo Brandani was tormented by a relentless sense of catastrophe. He saw it lurking in every undertaking that involved a transformation of reality, in every building (which can collapse), in an aeroplane in flight (which could plummet), in an automobile at speed (which can veer out of control), in an electric socket (which can short-circuit), in a pot on a burner (danger of fire), in a glass of water (it can spill), in a fresh egg (which can break): everything that stands up can fall, everything that works can stop working. In fact, sooner or later it certainly would, that much was certain. But how could he stave off *that* catastrophe? It was an event in the far distant future, it shouldn't have mattered to him. And yet it did.

No one ever really knew who those peoples were, nor where they'd come from, nor exactly when, nor why. All that was known was that they were an ethnic secretion of Central Asia. Someone had gone so far as to claim that they were nothing more than Greeks who had changed their religion and customs. What was known for certain is that a couple of centuries after their first appearance on Mediterranean shores, they had taken Constantinople. And for him this was simply unacceptable. For that matter, since 29 May 1453, in every generation of humanity, there have been people unable to accept the fall of Byzantium. Engineer Ivo Brandani was one of them.

We all expect nothing more from technicians than the kind of robust pragmatism and positivism that allows the ignorant, along with the purest intellects, to take a plane, drive a car across a bridge, board a train or a ship, with reasonable confidence they're not going to die in the undertaking. Technicians ensure that such things exist as houses, bridges, aeroplanes, trains, tunnels, rockets, satellites and space stations, automobiles, computers and so on, and we want them to resemble their inventions, we expect perfect conformity with the objects of their attention. We want them to be detached and painstaking, neutral when it comes to matters political while we imagine them to be difficult to deceive because of their propensity to check and double-check, unwilling to put greater reliance on words than deeds. We want technicians to be unsophisticated, better still if slightly ignorant. In short, we trust them more implicitly if they seem remote and a little obtuse, if we see them carrying a pulp mystery rather than a book of poetry. We don't expect an engineer to fall prey to the kind of obsessions and resentments that inhabited the mind of Ivo Brandani.

The first time he went to Istanbul for work, he chanced to enter a small mosque that stood against the city walls overlooking the Sea of Marmara. On the map it was marked as Küçük Ayasofya Camii, which when translated into English means Small Ayasofya Mosque, but in his guidebook it was called the Church of the Saints Sergius and Bacchus. This was a Byzantine church later transformed into a mosque, which, in spite of its fifteen centuries of age, the Koranic inscriptions scattered over the whitewashed plaster walls and a likely cleansing of all and every earlier image and mosaic, still seemed to be in a good state of preservation. 'It's fifteen hundred years old! Fifteen hundred!' Ivo kept telling himself, trying to wrap his mind around the concept. That's what he always did when he was working to grasp magnitudes not easily pictured: 100,000 tons, 400 cubic kilometres, 300,000 kilometres a second . . . 'The floor plan,' the guidebook said, 'and in general the building's entire structure, take their inspiration from Hagia Sophia.' Brandani immediately had the sensation that something wasn't right; then, after climbing up to the matroneum and leaning out over the balcony, he felt something akin to physical revulsion, a pain like that you feel when someone digs their fingers into the back of your ears: there they were, before his eyes, the Surrender, the Overpowering, the Overpowering, the Expropriation, the Cancellation, the Substitution . . . From up there he could clearly see the twist that had been imparted to the building's axes of symmetry, the cultural uprooting that that church and the city as a whole had undergone. The directional stripes to guide the faithful in their prosternations, impressed upon the sky-blue carpet that covered the entire floor, were arranged so as to point towards Mecca, a direction that was indicated by the niche of the *mihrab*, with a placement that was entirely independent of the church's bilateral symmetry, confirmed by the incongruous location of the *minbar*, or pulpit. The surrounding building didn't count, it was a purely contingent shell that had been repurposed, all that mattered was the faraway centrepoint from which all Islam emanated—the Kaaba. There was a certain poetry to all this but that church hadn't been built to accommodate it.

Brandani was soon able to forget that sensation of irreparable loss that had been so piercing there and then, until it re-presented itself many years later, while he was reading about the events surrounding the fall of Byzantium in a book by Stefan Zweig, an Austrian writer about whom he knew very little, in fact nothing at all. A friend had given him a copy of Zweig's *Decisive Moments in History*: on page thirty-five, the account of *The Conquest of Byzantium* began with these words:

> On 5 February 1451, a secret messenger comes to Minor Asia and brings the oldest son of the Sultan Murad, the twenty-one-year-old Mehmed, the news that his father has died.

Zweig had chosen that event, the death of Murad, as the beginning of a chain of cause and effect which little more than two years later would lead to an unthinkable cultural transplant.

Starting from that account, Ivo Brandani had done his own research and had determined just how novelistically inaccurate Zweig's version was; he had also learnt of the existence of many chronicles and accounts that were roughly coeval with the taking of Constantinople, some of them legendary, such as the one that spoke of a door that had never existed before but which suddenly opened in the walls to accept the defeated emperor of Byzantium and save him from death. He liked the thought that Constantine XI Palaiologos was still there, bricked in like a mummy in a niche, or temporarily consubstantiated with the rest of the wall, awaiting the day of his city's liberation to re-emerge into the open air and light of day. This predisposition to hospitality on the part of the city's masonry structures on the day of the catastrophe manifested itself as well towards the Archbishop of Constantinople who, at the very instant that the Turk was bursting into Hagia Sophia, was said to have vanished, absorbed directly into the massive if tottering walls that still support the church.

Since then—that is, from the first time he read that account—whenever he happened to wake up in the middle of the night, bewildered and clammy with sweat, and had to get out of bed to change his damp T-shirt and take a pee, afterwards, back in bed, he often thought of the Fall of Constantinople and couldn't get back to sleep for the consternation and rage that filled him.

What could it really matter to him, after all these centuries? Even he never knew. In that sense of devastation without remedy that filled him from time to time, the taking of Byzantium was most likely nothing but an effigy, a symbol of something else. Perhaps it was the final sense of catastrophe that came to him from having observed too many abrogations of things that had once seemed to him to be unfailing and everlasting. Perhaps what tormented him was the sense of unhealability attendant upon that event, which struck him as the consequence of mistaken calculations and decisions, of instances of irresoluteness and betrayals, the prevalence of narrow interests that were trivial and insignificant in the face of such gravity of consequence.

And if he allowed the Fall of Constantinople to assault him by night, then it was goodbye sleep: he'd have to get up, make a cup of tea and have a few cookies, sit down in front of the TV, turn the channel to a network broadcasting documentaries and wait for sleep to return. That was providing that worries about work didn't come charging in, things for which he was *responsible*, capable of reawakening his Inner Enemy, which lay constantly in ambush, ready at the blink of an eye to torture him bloody with a cascade of scolding and upbraiding.

Zweig reports that on 29 May 1453, the forces of Mehmed II el-Fatih conquered Constantinople, penetrating the city through a postern gate in the second ring of walls, inexplicably left open. They called it the Kerkoporta, the Circus Gate, and it was little more than a hole in the wall. From there the Turks flooded the city, eating away at the defensive forces from within. The defenders might well have carried the victory that day had they not let themselves be seized with panic at the sight of the enemy popping up behind them, inside their home, like a parasite blackening the pure white sheets of your own bed . . .

But the story, at least as Zweig tells it, isn't true, or at least not entirely. A great many authors report that Mehmed's terrible, gigantic cannon, built especially for that siege, had opened a breach in the walls on a line with the Gate of St Romanus, and that it was through that gap that the Turk had penetrated the city.

'For that type of wall, cannons were a real problem—what they would have needed were proper bastions designed especially with artillery in mind,' Ivo had thought for years, 'they could have held them off if their walls had been several yards thick, and if they'd had real defensive cannons of their own. The Middle Ages were over, that kind of fortification was no longer adequate, they ought to have imitated the defences of Rhodes, there the walls held out for the duration of the siege, the city was taken because in the end the knights capitulated . . . There was no escape from the Turks, that was their world and they wanted it all for themselves, plus they were unbeatable, or practically . . .' Sometimes he'd identified with the besieged populace to such an extent that he let a wave of panic sweep over him when he saw the enemy suddenly rounding the corner, lusting for blood, filthy, foaming at the mouth, bloodstained, charging down streets where he'd loitered with his friends since he was a boy, when Byzantium still lived in the illusion that it actually reigned over something and its inhabitants believed they were safely protected by impregnable walls.

To track back down even the slimmest causal rivulet, to destructure the chain of events, reducing them each to their particular constituent units: that's what Ivo Brandani would have wanted to do, if he'd been capable, to identify the exact point of no return, if in fact it existed, the point, that is, past which

Constantinople would have fallen regardless. In short, could it be possible to retrace in scientific terms the threshold of ineluctability of the event?

'If you had a superpowerful computer, you'd need to upload even the most negligible of facts . . . but no, not even . . . Too much has already been lost, nowadays we know hardly anything about any of it, and after all reality is always so different from the most painstaking, scrupulous and well-documented reconstruction—90 per cent of any event is inevitably lost . . . We know almost nothing about what happens, even at the moment that it is happening . . . It's in the very instant of an event's occurrence that things become muddled and the unknowing begins, the travesty . . .'

Brandani was convinced that to reconstruct was the same as foreseeing, it was simply a matter of proceeding in the reverse direction: therefore the same degree of inaccuracy, the same unknowability of everything that had happened as well as all possible future catastrophes.

Given the profession he practised, a catastrophe for which he could be considered *responsible* was the outcome most greatly feared, the thing that often kept him from sleeping at night. But retirement was near: once work is finished, once responsibilities fall away, a man can no longer be answerable for something that doesn't depend on him. And yet the shared responsibility for what might prove to be poor construction of some building or structure he'd worked on—there were so many—would in any case remain a weight on his shoulders for decades to come.

'Away, away, away . . . I should already have gone away, I ought to have retired years ago, at this point it's useless to try to hold out—the tension, the boredom, the effort, this constant travelling . . . That's enough, I can't keep it up . . .'

Someone had cried: 'The city is taken!' That desperate shout must have echoed deafeningly, even before Constantinople was truly overwhelmed: the forces arrayed in the city's defence still greatly outnumbered those few invaders who had managed to penetrate first the outer shelf of armour and then the last exoskeleton of Byzantium. From there, from that primeval sense of horror that assails us when we realize that something has infested us, dismay spread in seconds to the defenders and many of those who had until then displayed great courage and valour took to their heels towards the port, seeking safety aboard the ships. The Muslim infestation was rapid and terrifying. The majority of sources speak of a blind and irreversible violence that in short order reduced the city to a blood-soaked wilderness. After three days of sack and plunder, there were few left alive in Constantinople.

Horror and panic, that's the gist of it. It's the first reaction to the discovery that something has invaded us, that a creature has penetrated our inviolable corporeal enclosure. An unseen and unseemly animal is using us as its *abode*, drawing its sustenance from us, growing inside us, reproducing in our cavities. On that twenty-ninth day of May, it was panic that caused Constantinople's fall, it was the ancestral horror for the savage, hostile organisms that had succeeded in worming their way into the city's innermost and most intimate veins. The city would have fallen eventually anyway but perhaps not that day, not without the infiltration of the enemy through a portal forgotten and left unlocked in the aftermath of a sortie.

To infest peoples settled in other places is always the objective of every conquest; first destroying their physical defences, then penetrating into their social and productive tissues, but still leaving them alive so as to be able to gradually suck away their resources. That is a concise statement of the historical nature of conquest, Brandani thought to himself. The heroes, the first conquerors, are nothing more than a vanguard sent on ahead with the mission of piercing the defences of the host organism, in order to allow the subsequent penetration of rank after rank of parasites. Parasitism is life that *inhabits* other life, it is the predominant form in which the biosphere manifests itself, yet it is the most secret to our eyes. And so, even as the Turks in arms were attacking the defences of Byzantium with the intention—that is, with the ineluctable *historic need*—to conquer the city and subjugate it, in their bodies, just as in the bodies of the city's defenders, and in the bodies of the animals, whether beasts of burden or meat, which both parties to the struggle were using, as well as in the bodies of all the animals, whether mammals, reptiles, insects or fish in the Bosporus, and in those of all the creatures lying hidden on the silty seabed of the Golden Horn as well as in the bodies of the inhabitants of the Sea of Marmara and all the other seas and oceans on the planet, millions, indeed billions of parasites of every genus and species, of every degree of insidiousness and pathogenic capacity, continued on with their everyday existence, entirely unaware of the unprecedented historic event in which they were participating.

The apocalyptic contact of human bodies in battle, the spattering of breath and bodily fluids, the vast fetid quantities of human and animal faeces scattered everywhere, within and without the walls of Constantinople, the fevered and dramatic contamination of everyone with everyone else, were surely all perfect breeding grounds for the multitudes of parasites capable of seizing the moment to leap from body to body, through the excrement and blood of every species and all the other living species present and involved in the event.

While Byzantium battled the Turk to fight off subjugation, amoebae and viruses and bacilli, worms, protozoa, fungi, arthropods such as lice and crabs, the whole vast population of parasites, deaf and blind to all stimuli save those that come from the universe of living creatures, put into practice all and every strategy they possessed to contaminate the greatest possible number of organisms. Their spores were already swimming in the high-pressure blood being pumped by the hearts of the combatants, as well as in the blood being shed in spurts into the well-trodden dirt, on the stones of the walls, on the paving stones of the city. They were bobbing blindly in a single dense red ocean that was coagulating into a drying crust, tempting and delicious for hungrily lapping dogs, inside which they found shelter, protection and the assurance of a future.

Battle was one of those moments in which the entozoic environment, which consisted of the fluids and tissues of living things, presented itself with a characteristic of accentuated continuity: it was blood on blood, shit on shit, and it was easy for the parasites to swim through it (that is to say, to flail their flagella, pedicels, appendages or tails, for those species endowed with appendages), until they were able to find new places in which to plant roots and claws and beaks, cellular paradises to invade and, in time, to kill, exactly the same thing that, on another order of physical magnitude, the Turks were doing to the city of Constantinople, under the command of Mehmed II, el-Fatih, the Conqueror.

There are two hundred species of parasites that can infest us. The world, as they conceive it, coincides completely with the human organism, where they live their whole lives and where they find all that is good and bad in life, food to eat and an environment suitable for reproduction. Among the infestant species, we should mention protozoa and nematodes and cestodes and arthropods capable of leaping from one organism to another, from one species to another, passing through life phases in an unfettered environment, tough, difficult phases, as moments of pure waiting, lying in ambush, before being able to swim again in some new fluid or to nest slumbering in the tissues of some creature: life feeds on life, which feeds on life and so on. Ivo Brandani, inasmuch as he too was a living being, was likewise up to his neck in this same logic, reaping the benefits at the same time that he paid the consequences.

The biosphere is an infernal continuum of species structured like so many Chinese nested boxes, one within another, one atop the other's back, one upon the epidermis of the next, one subjugating the other to its own vital necessities. This is no different from what *Homo sapiens* does with cattle, swine, poultry, rabbits and horses, camels, yaks and reindeer, that is, with all domesticated species. Then what was the conquest of Byzantium after all, if not an everyday episode of a planetwide way of life, an ordinary uptick of overpowering and subjugation, in which ecto- and endo-parasites, of all shapes and sizes, human and otherwise, took part? What was to Ivo Brandani's mind an inconceivable transplantation of civilization was actually an apocalyptic and promiscuous mixing of species and peoples within and without the walls of Byzantium, within and without the bodies of the combatants, in a seething churn of infections and infestations, as blood was spilt and heroes died, one piled atop the other, in heaps. Lice, tapeworms, amoebae, plasmodia, tics and worms slithered through the dust of the battle-field or more simply mixed in with, it in the form of eggs, or infective cysts expelled in faeces, swarmed over the skin of the combatants, through their pubic hair, in their filthy heads of hair, feeding on flakes of scalp flesh, dead cells, intoxicated by the aroma of *Homo sapiens* in the expectation of finally being able to return to the tepid world of human blood and lymph, of shit, both Christian and Muslim, whether of believers or nonbelievers, the shit of the slave, the outlaw, the mercenary, the whore, the priest, the prince, the vizier, the Palaiologos emperor, and even the sultan himself, Mehmed II the Conqueror.

Perhaps some ancestor of the *Naegleria fowleri* that was to kill Engineer Brandani passed through here. Perhaps the fatal amoeba came from the stagnant waters of Central Europe, nesting in the organism of a professional soldier who would die of it before long, in his tent, never able to see the wonders that were already being told, the great church of Hagia Sophia, built almost a thousand years earlier. Or else it had already burrowed into the tissues of a North African mercenary or a black slave tending the sultan's horses.

Naegleria fowleri: an amoeba, a pulsating gob of spit, microscopic, deaf and blind, that squats in the slime at the bottom of puddles, even in hot-spring pools, and remains in a state of slumber until the water rises above 70 degrees Fahrenheit, whereupon it activates and floats to the surface in search of the first organism suitable for infestation. That's how it makes its way into the nasal mucosa of someone swimming, for example, and then penetrates the olfactory bulbs, spreading from there to the brain, where it only needs a few days to kill you. Millions of generations of this amoeba transited from one organism to another, stopping over inside small freshwater snails and utilizing their faeces to deposit spores in the filthy muds of African waterholes, and from there, with the warming and churning of the sediments at the bottom, they'd come to the surface, remaining in suspension in open water until a specimen of some species, say a mammal, perhaps a human, much larger and warmer and more comfortable than a snail, happened along . . .

We know of amoebic cysts that are scattered into the wind along with the dust of dried-up ponds, dust that's swept away by the gusting air along with its guests, shapeless and freeze-dried, until they wind up lodging in the nasal mucosa of some animal. The nose is the main doorway to the brain of the greater creatures; *Naegleria* adores the cerebellum, it burrows tunnels the way mice do in cheese, it multiplies into hundreds of thousands of specimens, rapidly infesting them, chewing them to tatters, reducing them to a sort of purulent mucus.

Homo sapiens, who considers himself to be outside and above the teeming welter of insignificant and repellent lives, who confers upon himself an unworldly soul and a superterrestrial fate, is himself too a universe in which to survive and proliferate. And that is all he is for other species of amoebae, which can infest in their thousands the twists and turns of our intestine, ulcerating its walls, cutting lesions into the tissues until they collapse, charging through the breach and penetrating everywhere, liver and urogenital organs, utilizing us as a source of nutrition, as a habitat in which to reside for a century of centuries, world without end, all the times of the past that have endured, all the future times that shall continue.

Herod 'was eaten by worms and died'. Ivo had known this since he was a child, from years previous to those of the Bomb Crater. That was something that was written in ink on paper, a divine punishment for the Slaughter of the Innocents. Of everything that he had heard and read in the sacred scriptures of religion, that was what had struck him most: Herod 'was eaten by worms and died'.

'That could happen to me too, I could be eaten by worms and die . . . maybe I'm already full of worms . . . maybe they're already burrowing away inside me . . .' A nightmare that lasted for decades, after *that thing* in the potty. That had been the beginning, they'd tried almost right away, the worms, and they'd even succeeded, but something had gone wrong, maybe it had been the pain and the fear of that time when he'd fallen straight back, between two pieces of furniture, with his ass plumb into a burning brazier. 'Fear makes you get worms,' Ersilia, the imperturbable, had said, stony-faced.

War too produces worms. To be born just after the Second World War for Ivo Brandani had meant suffering an attack of worms: beaten back! *Beaten back?* When, at the parish church, they'd told him about Herod and how it had all turned out, he was never quite sure what to think. And that was only the beginning of the vital torture caused by the hypodermic inoculation of the cycle of sin—redemption—new sin—new redemption and so on. A baleful sequence that they scrupulously installed in his skull, a mental parasite that ought to have operated for the rest of his life—at least this was the plan. At first, the torture functioned as intended: 'I managed to avert a terrible thing, a horrible death like Herod Antipas . . . That was a punishment visited upon him directly by God, for his horrible sins . . . I've never committed horrible sins but I do have to cleanse my conscience on a continual basis . . . The uninterrupted flow of my sins . . . My thought-sins, my lies . . .'

Many years later, reading about *Ascaris lumbricoides* in a pamphlet that taught how to ward off tropical infections, he'd recognized it: it was the *potty worm*. Who, if not *him*, could have possibly killed Herod in that way?

'Herod died of an infestation of roundworms, which immediately exited his corpse, issuing from the tyrant's mouth, nose and already gaping anus, in squirming clumps across his sumptuous deathbed . . . God!' Parasites that flee their host's lifeless body, twisting in the open, dry air, before dying in their turn. Like the tiny monster that emerged from the mouth of that fish in its death throes and slithered across the scalding hot rocks along the shore, where it ended its life in a bid to reach the water whose presence it might perhaps have sensed, perceiving the molecules of humidity suspended in the air. Ivo had stayed to watch it, crouching by the waves, smoking the cigarette he loved best, the after-fishing cigarette. At the time he was a cold, uncaring killer of fishes, he observed with indifference the chain of overpowering force, confident he rested at its summit. That is, provided one of those parasites wasn't already inside him, encysted somewhere just waiting to reawaken. *Ascaris lumbricoides*: an evolutionary genius about

20 centimetres in length, it was one of the filthiest things Ivo had ever seen (in photographs, it must be said), as he learnt that there were roughly a *billion* people infested with these nematodes and their kin, so it really wasn't all that unlikely for a person to get one and, after all, unless he was remembering wrongly, that *thing* in the potty had resembled it closely. As he read more extensively, he learnt that in the phylum of nematodes there are more than a hundred thousand species, twelve of which are exclusively parasitic to humans, nesting in the intestine, the muscles, the liver, the lungs and the kidneys, swimming through the bloodstream, infiltrating the heart, slithering under the skin, everywhere. After ingestion—dirty hands, contact with faeces, inadequate hygiene—the initial cyst descends into the small intestine, burrows through its walls, and from there introduces itself into the veins of the liver, which transport it safe and warm to the right chamber of the heart, from there to the lungs and from the lungs into the bronchi, all the way up into the trachea, and from there to the pharynx. Once in the pharynx, according to a script that always unfolds identically and in accordance with necessity, it is swallowed again, diving back down into the small intestine where it finally takes root and matures, often, though not always, succeeding in occluding it. Once dead, the host is abandoned. So it was for Herod Antipas: it became necessary to burn his body in order to purify the world of such absolute sinfulness. For Brandani nothing could get closer to the image of a cold and inexorable Evil—extraneous to all that's human, indifferent to our existence—than a parasite immersed in a perennial gustatory/olfactory coma. 'Due to the criminal indulgence of God, who allows its existence inside the body of a child who played in the dirt of Africa, who drank river water, who fell asleep at the mercy of hematophagous insects, with their inevitable bloodsucking apparatus, likewise infested with parasites . . . Lest the chain, so painstakingly crafted in the context of Intelligent Design, be broken. How ridiculous is the paradigm that envisions us as "the lords of nature",' Brandani would say to himself over and over again after these readings, 'how ridiculous are those who see "Creation", the reality-outside-us, as a universe at our service.

While it is us who, with our own tissues, our flesh, our blood, serve as pasturage for thousands of species, billions of specimens . . . Distinguished in what way? Special how?'

In all likelihood, Ivo Brandani inhaled *Naegleria fowleri* during an inspection of a vast area of farmland along the banks of the Nile, in the Delta region. They'd called him from the City in the North and told him, 'as long as you're in Egypt anyway', to go take a look at a site where the Egyptian administration planned to build a major water-treatment plant. Ecocare was interested in landing the contract. They wanted him to gather some initial impressions concerning the issues involved in setting up a construction site, the state of the road network leading to the site, to take photographs and so on. Nothing more than a first general survey. Getting there wasn't easy: from Sharm to Cairo, from Cairo to Alexandria, then from Alexandria a couple of hours in the car with a driver. When he finally got out of the car, he was pleased to feel the mist of atomized water that a gust of wind tore from the spray of a nearby sprinkler in the fields. He sighed long and deep with exhaustion and, in so doing, inhaled the amoeba's microscopic cyst.

29 May 2015, 9.07 a.m.

God doesn't exist. But if He does, then he's definitely down there . . . He doesn't exist, but if He did, He'd live here, behind that stark front of mountains, hidden somewhere in there. Maybe even in a Burning Bush, why not? God doesn't exist . . . But if He does then anything is possible . . . Then it's even possible that He's right there, just a few miles from the hotels and the discotheques on the coast . . . It's even possible that He willed Sharm into existence, that He has it under His governance, like everything else . . .

In the taxi on the way to the airport, Ivo Brandani looks towards the nearest highlands of the Sinai. The sun, already blistering hot, rose hours ago. In his stomach is a cup of coffee and the faint nausea of having got up too early. In his head are different thoughts, which surface in fragments.

In the quasi-nothingness, where it doesn't rain, there is a lack of multiplicity, everything seems simpler . . . And monotheism is a simplification . . . Around these parts a god is needed and you can start a religion with very little . . . In the quasi-nothingness, even the most hardened materialist isn't going to live comfortably, he'll find himself in a state of discomfort, he'll wind up turning to the transcendental. Even the most hardened polytheistic pagan, even the most primitive animist will surrender to the void here, to the maximum level of subtraction. When the world becomes bare and essential the spirit gains the upper hand . . . Where it never rains, you can build airports with a tent, like a circus . . . The terminal next door must be older, in fact, it's certainly older, so it reaches for Western modernism. This one, in contrast, means to express ancestral modernism, that is, Bedouin modernism, like the airport in Jeddah. And so it is, de facto, postmodern . . . But even contextualism is a Western contrivance.

He's out of Egyptian pounds, he pays in Franco-German euros and gets out of the cab, the sun is already pounding down, but the air is still cool, streaked with odorous wakes of burnt jet fuel. He's early, he lingers on the airport pavement, he looks around, the big car park is almost completely empty, there are only a dozen or so waiting motor coaches, a few taxicabs, hotel shuttles. He notices the short-cropped grass that covers the planters between the parking stalls, the sparse young palm trees, all bent over on the same side. The mountains of Sinai rise without advance warning beyond the landing strips, out of the flat expanse of the desert, beautiful and absolute. He likes the smell of the fuel burnt by the jets. He likes the savage, hoarse roar of the engines. He likes it and it scares him. Then he goes in.

There it is, Egyptair to Cairo and then on to the City of God, 11.10 a.m., Gate 24. It's down there, there's still not much of a line, well, that's good. Did I take my Xanax? Yes, I took it.

Waiting in queue at the check-in desk, a young man in front of him is reading a novel by Clifford Simak.

Just think of that: Simak! I used to read him when I was a kid! Science fiction holds no appeal for me now. The Future has become the Present, it would seem that we've consumed everything and there's nothing left . . . My credulity has collapsed, I've lost the poetry of the infinite, I'm not interested in possible worlds and I'm no longer even interested in knowing how this one ends, I don't care about what the future will be like. Franco says that a person can be considered an adult only when he can no longer bring himself to read science fiction. The last piece of science fiction I read was more or less thirty years ago, so I was certainly an adult, and then some . . .

He peers at the cover of the book until he manages to make out the title: *City*. He pulls out his tablet, goes online and googles it.

That's the original English title of the book; in Italian it was called *Anni senza fine*! Wonderful! The generations of sentient species that succeed one another after the extinction of man, no little more than a legend . . . Everything that ever existed, the very memory of the human race, twinkling into oblivion over the course of hundreds of thousands, millions of years . . .

The entire text of *City* is online. He downloads it, and on the display of his smartphone he begins reading the preface.

These are the stories that the Dogs tell when the fires burn high and the wind is from the north. Then each family circle gathers at the hearthstone and the pups sit silently and listen and when the story's done they ask many questions:

'What is Man?' they'll ask.

Or perhaps: 'What is a city?'

Or: 'What is a war?'

There is no positive answer to any of these questions. There are suppositions and there are theories and there are many educated guesses, but there are no answers.

He looks out the windows at the mountains scoured bare by the wind, this land without a blade of grass.

Everything is the colour of dust. Purple dust at dawn, red dust at sunset. All the rest of Sharm is nothing more than a desecration of the emptiness, a gratuitous, artificial obscenity—actually, not gratuitous at all, a paid obscenity. From a plane you see dozens and dozens of hotels, they look like clumps of worms clinging to the coast, eating the dust and making their way inland. In Las Vegas, in Reno, they did the same thing, even though there the delirium has a certain tradition, a sad, demented dignity. Here thirty years ago, it must have been an absolute landscape, like what's found to the north of Nabq, which has been declared a park: nothing but air, mountains, sand, water, no one in sight . . . Where there is nothing, you can invent anything and everything, without anything prior to deal with, without interference save for the inexplicable will of the One God of the Sands and the Void.

The desert has become a theme park and now everyone tells you: 'Here, there was nothing, and now look at it all . . .' But it was precisely the Sacred Nothing that ought to have been preserved, instead of this tossed-together clutter of buildings, swimming pools, mini-waterfalls, neatly manicured lawns, brummagem pyramids and obelisks, streetlamps whose glare cancels out the night sky, which is so pure here . . . In Sharm, just as in all dry places, it becomes once again evident that life is humid . . . The scorpion I crushed yesterday evening on the stairs went *scrrch* . . . It was a shell, a recipient full of some watery substance that splattered across the still-hot stone of the stair tread . . . They, the scorpions, don't have seawater desalination plants: where do they find the water? This morning it was dry as a stockfish, flat, mummified . . . Which is to say, un-alive . . . Here life out of water is counter-intuitive, that is to say, contrary to nature, if you can call something nature that's essentially mineral . . . Let's see if they're willing to give me a window seat . . . I'm hungry . . . And this pain at the base of my neck . . . I have two hours to get another cup of coffee, and to eat something in blessed peace.

It's been years since Brandani last said what he thought, to anyone. He can't. If he let his tongue range free in direct connection with his brain all that would come out would be curses and insults. Directed at people, animals, things, objects, cities. And himself. An incessant gush of unbridled foul language spurts from his brain like a serum, an infected discharge that he's forced to keep in circulation without being able to rid himself of it. That is how he poisons himself every day. A secret and compressed desperation. When he does let it vent, the words emerge in mangled incoherent knots, insults snarled out reluctantly in just a few basic combinations, always the same, stupid and repetitive. Just a short while ago, at the check-in counter, he focused on the airline employee who for no good reason had decided he didn't want to give him a window seat. Brandani gets bored while flying, can't seem to read, likes to look down on the earth below, the sea, the islands, the clouds.

Motherfucking cocksucker filthy piece of shit son of a bitch disgusting snot-rag faggot, why don't you just drop dead this goddamned second right here in this goddamned shitty airport where you drag out your unappetizing life with shitballs hanging off the hairs of your ass that you haven't once washed since the day you were born, you fucking turd . . .

The effort of repressing his inner tirade left him practically breathless, another dose of endogenous venom spurted into his veins, but now the crisis is over, he got his window seat, the quarrel is forgotten and he's gone back to his favourite activity in places like this: observing. He finds a seat in the departure lounge, far away from the gate, where the line is forming for a flight to Stockholm. On his right, just a few yards away, there's a continuous floor-to-ceiling wall of glass overlooking the landing strip and the nearby mountains. The peace of this place, the prospect of an hour and a half waiting in that sort of spatiotemporal hiatus so typical of airports, are restoring his serenity. If the plane is on time, he'll be in the City of God by early afternoon. It's as if he'd already departed, was already in flight.

It's a common occurrence for him to be swept by gusts of contempt. It's weariness; obstacles and hindrances of any sort tend to exasperate him, especially the tiny insignificant difficulties that arise out of the carelessness and incompetence of others: the broken toilet flush handle, the spray of water that comes out too hard, a ramshackle aeroplane seat. He's obsessed by the continual shortfall between the way people ought to be and the way they actually are. But if he manages to keep from getting sucked into it, he's able to express himself in fluent, well-framed language, a fossil relic of years so different from these, long lost to memory. Over the course of time he has gradually persuaded himself that, insults aside, it's almost always a better idea for him not to speak. It's not merely a matter of what's opportune; it's also the uncertainty, the insecurity, the doubt, the lack of solid data. Someone pointed out that he often repeats himself, he's afraid he might appear senile. 'No one ever tells you, so if your noggin stops working right, you never even know,' a friend once said to him. 'While you're certain that you're thinking sensible, even intelligent things, it may be that you actually come off as nothing more than a senile old fool blathering on about nonsense. Not even the most well meaning doctor will ever tell you: "Listen, you're well into your second childhood." So just resign yourself to going senile without realizing it.' 'But I'm not senile, not yet . . .' 'There, you see? You're convinced you're not. But just how can you be so sure?' His name is Rasca, the friend, a little older than him. That's his obsession. 'When we're young, we're a little too ready to be convinced of other people's ideas, and when we're old, we're too quick to be convinced of our own. When everything seems suddenly clear to you, be careful, because what's probably happening is that you're already going senile.' Across from him sits a young couple, two kids talking raptly. Actually, the boy is the one doing all the talking, she listens and every so often answers, looks him in the eyes, smiles, nods her head. They don't transmit a great sense of familiarity, if this is the beginning of a relationship, it's certainly early days, seeing the seriousness, the apparent intensity of the conversation they're absorbed in.

God, what a nightmare . . . They must have met just recently, on the beach or at a dance club . . . he's searching for a way in, anything can back his play, anything but silence.

He's reminded of the days when if you wanted to court a girl what you needed were rivers of words, whole evenings at a time smoking packs of cigarettes, drinking beer or whisky, gin-tonics, Coca-Cola or whatever else you could lay your hands on. Evenings in which if you wanted to make anything happen (and you never knew if or when) you had to talk & talk.

And for all he knew, it might even be a girl he didn't much care for . . . The world was full of these half-pretty girls, half-likeable, half-intelligent, half-virgins, half-everything . . . It was full of girls I didn't really like, but they remained a resource, the most plentiful one . . . Talking to a girl without even being sure you feel like doing anything with her, talking all evening about bullshit, the worst kind of bullshit, saying things just for the sake of it, to be there, to attract attention. Talking about travel, philosophy, work, school, politics. Talking about movies-literature-theatre, trying to say something cool, strange, original . . . They always wound up talking about religion, love and sex . . . 'Listen, the way I see things, etc. . . .' she'd say. These half-pretty girls always had someone . . . Donatella . . . Donatella! The half-virgin from philosophy class . . . Why on earth should she come to mind now?! I hadn't thought of her in years . . . You wound up fooling around with her every time the two of you studied together . . . She was supposed to save herself for marriage, so no pussy, but everything else was accessible . . . Then one day she turns up and tells you: 'Starting tomorrow we're going to have to stop studying together, I'm getting married next week.' She'd been engaged to some guy for who knows how long, they'd already filed all the necessary papers . . . And she kept it up with me, as if that was the most natural thing in the world. As long as there were no attempts on her virginity, which had already been deeded to the other man, you could do anything you wanted, practically . . . She was always very careful to keep from getting the bedcovers dirty. Sometimes it happened, but she knew exactly what measures to take. She had a bottle of hydrogen peroxide in her desk drawer. In that same drawer I glimpsed a packet of Kleenex, and there was also a box of sterile absorbent cotton. Technical details all the girls were tremendously well read up on . . . They had sex, there was no doubt about that, but they always seemed to need a framework to justify that sex, that is, they needed that delirious preliminary verbiage and boilerplate that could last for days of dates, strolls, phone calls, afternoon teas, movies, theatre . . . Theatre . . . *Theatre*! *To the theatre on Sunday afternoon*, with the boilerplate of critical discussion during intermission, then continuing afterwards at the pizzeria . . . That's what words were good for, a continuation of high school by other means and for other ends. But it was still just high school . . . In the end I realized that my problem wasn't really with philosophy, it was really with the humanities concentration I'd chosen in high school . . . Did Donatella actually get her degree later? I never saw her again, never ran into her . . . She just vanished . . . Her father had a sports-equipment store . . .

Ivo Brandani is an old-fashioned silent male, a man who looks and says nothing because he cannot say. He remains silent so he won't have to listen to answers, he remains silent because, if you encourage people with words, they'll pay you back in the same coin. 'I deserve it. Couldn't I just have kept my mouth shut?' is what Ivo often says to himself, every time a comment escapes him, a word of irritation, a phrase that strikes him as witty, a wisecrack whose ironic twist goes wholly misunderstood. These are unexpected ventings of the mental monologue that torments him even at night, in his sleep, when his brain sets out gratuitous spectacles, variously bloodcurdling or embarrassing, mortifying. A continuous brooding is the principal secretion of his solitude, especially when he's travelling, as he is now. 'Did I really have to shoot my mouth off?' Yes, he had to, it's something beyond his control, when it happens, it happens. To the employee manning the check-in desk he had said, in his broken English: 'What does it cost you? Do you think it's fun to fill the plane row by row? Is there a problem of weight distribution, static balance? I hardly think so, since I was one of the first to arrive.' 'It's difficult, sir . . .' 'Oh spare me the *difficulties*,' he'd replied in his native Peninsular, 'just say you don't feel like it, that you don't give a flying fuck.' The employee had understood him perfectly and clearly took offence. In the end, he managed to get a window seat anyway, but losing your temper isn't something that does him any good. Now that he thinks back on it he's sorry, it strikes him as out of keeping with his character to be so discourteous.

To speak is always compromising, risky, better to be more cautious . . . What do I give a damn by this point anyway, soon I'll be leaving . . . The game is over . . . With my age I've been out of it for a while, there's no point in hammering away at it, I'm tired, I can't take the pressure any longer, especially on the deadlines . . . And after all, I want to buy a house somewhere the fuck out of the way, maybe I can find something on the Island . . . Get out, slip away smooth and easy, get lost somewhere, definitely on the water so I always have the horizon in my eyes, maybe on the Island . . . I'd go back there to stay, in spite of the way the tourists have ruined it, I'll buy a boat, a plastic gozzo, an 18-footer, and I'll go out trolling for porgies, up along the cliffs . . . That is, if they don't establish the marine nature reserve . . . If they do, no real problem, I'll just head the opposite way, down the coast to the south . . . It was there, in the shallows outside of the points, that Manolis would catch his oversize monsters . . . Better not speak, because no one listens to me, because the things I'd say are bound to be confused, inadequate, irritating, counter-productive . . . Because the world has changed too much . . . I say nothing through suffocation, annihilation, humiliation . . . I say nothing because at this point I've succumbed and nothing can get me back on my feet. Is it right to say that I'm now succumbent? Molteni always thought it was funny to refer to someone being 'succumbent . . .' I liked being his student, listening to him, even if what I could take from him no longer matched what I needed . . . What was it you needed, Ivo? I needed matter, concreteness, weight, gravity, action . . . I needed to 'connect what is separate', 'separate what is connected', more or less . . . A stupid undertaking, you could see that for yourself, you miserable imbecile, you never achieved fuck-all anyway . . . Imbecile, imbecile . . . I'd have just become a high-school teacher or, the best you could have hoped for, an academic, that is, a product of the Peninsular-school philosophy, the most pinchbeck of its kind in the history of world thought . . . I have a headache . . . And after all, who says that I've never achieved a fucking thing? For instance, what do you have to say about the work I've been doing on the corals? . . . That's enough . . . Here, if you just take a look around, you see a world in sandals, in flip-flops . . . A universe of such badly made feet that you only need to take a careful look at them and you see immediately that these are nothing other than the deformed hands of a quadruman . . . But it took us centuries to realize it and even now there are those who don't see it, those who say: 'It's not true, this is how we were created, *with our feet.*' This whole thing about deformed hands won't let go of me . . .' When everything seems clear and simple to you, that's when you need to be worried, that's when you're starting to go senile.' And yet the Japanese and even the Egyptians and the people at the company, they all listened to what I had to say, they paid attention to my advice, they gave every sign of taking into consideration my recommendations, and so? I have a headache.

'How long will it take?' That's the question that he's heard most often, as long as he's been working here at Sharm. The politicians and the technicians from the Egyptian government always asked that question, it was continually on the lips of the government commissioner for restoration. How long for the *reconstruction*, for the *remaking*? And his bosses from the City in the North constantly on the phone asking: How long? It's not a technical question, that is, not entirely, it's a political question asked by politicians or by para-technicians, that is, technicians who have by this point been denatured, it's a question asked by someone who doesn't really want to know and understand.

If you want something done right, it's going to take the time it takes . . . The time needed to do it properly, without cutting corners, without killing yourself, without killing the workmen . . . Unless they've already accepted the usual prohibitive terms at headquarters, as long as they're not negotiating on costs and timelines without asking me . . . Here, taking into account the conditions on site, I have a hard time putting together an operational plan . . . As I try to beg or borrow a few extra months, they might very well already be changing the terms without letting me know . . . I'll come off looking like a fool and it won't be the first time . . . But it will be one of the *last*, Brandani: before long, you'll leave and so long, it's been good to know you . . . You wanted to be a technician and here you are, you were one . . . But you never took into consideration the existence of politics, its hunger for results, money and power, you never considered the merry-go-round of positions and contracts, the minuet of bribes . . . They want it all and they want it now: they demand results but also money for themselves . . . All the same, whenever *they* have to make a decision, they take all the time they need . . . At the top of the decision-making chain, time can't be compressed, but once the decision's been made, it's all over in a hurry, they won't listen to reason and everything has to be done as quickly as possible . . . From that moment on, the principal question isn't *how much* money, or *how* we should do it, or *who* we should have do it etc. There is just one question: *How long will it take?*

Puddu said to him, with his distinctive Sardinian accent: 'Engineer, I'm a surveyor and I never studied the way you did, but I'm convinced that an engineer doesn't understand a politician, can't understand him, never will. From what I've seen over all these years, *they* don't really believe anything, they don't think anything, everything they do, they do it out of consensus. Vertical consensus and horizontal consensus, I mean to say. You follow what I'm saying, don't you? If there's a consensus, then it's fine, if there isn't, then we're not doing it, even if it's the right thing to do. That's their reality, because consensus is the water they swim in. Take it away from them and they'll drown. That's it, they're done for. So, Engineer, what the fuck are we even talking about? If they say yes in the City in the North, then down here we say yes and we bow nicely while we're at it . . . Forgive me, eh, for speaking frankly.'

I like Puddu, he's straightforward, he's travelled practically everywhere, he knows how to deal with any situation, he's not afraid of anyone or anything, in unfamiliar settings he's absolutely cautious, until he starts to understand something, but once he's figured it out, he acts . . . These are the men who build the world, who've always built the world, who are *in it* up to their necks . . . He is exactly what I would have liked to become, but was never able . . . Someone who's comfortable everywhere he goes, solidly planted on the surface of this planet . . . And instead you, *mon cher*, you've never been fish nor fowl and now it's too late . . . Puddu has just one defect, and it's not a negligible one, and that is that he likes young boys . . . He'd say to me: 'Engineer, I know your views on the matter . . . That is, we don't share the same opinion on this . . . But, look at it this way, the politicians with personal convictions went out of style some time ago, both on the right and on the so-called left. Those were the kind of things you could have in the twentieth century, stuff they don't make any more. Now, let's not even talk about Communists, Fascists, Catholics, liberals, anything else you care to name—in their ranks were people who believed in what they said . . . They had a sense . . . of honour. Even the Communists were people you had to take seriously.' He smiled. 'Would you believe me if I tell you that I like democracy myself, even if I am . . . let's say . . . a little bit of a right-winger? That authoritarian regimes turn my stomach? Still, democracy's day is over, it's in the terminal phase of its illness, on its deathbed, but it's something that hasn't happened before, a completely new way of passing away . . .' He wasn't kidding around . . . In spite of his appearance, and to use the word shabby to describe it would be an understatement, and the frenzied lust for little boys that eats him from within, Puddu knows how to become authoritative . . . He may be a paedophile and he may be a Fascist, but he isn't stupid, he's not uneducated, he's not a son of a bitch, disloyal or dishonest, Puddu . . . He's just a damned soul . . . I didn't pry into his business . . . Let him seduce whoever he wants off the job site but I don't want to see him dare to use the chance of work as a lure or the threat of dismissal as a way to extort young boys . . . He says that here, before getting married, all the men do it . . . I don't give a flying fuck, if I catch him at it again I'll talk to the people at headquarters and fix his wagon once and for all . . .

'I'm talking about the democracy of nothing,' Puddu has told him more than once. 'The democracy of today for tomorrow, you know. The kind that makes promises but never proposals. Certainly, it's not like there's a hell of a lot left to propose these days, but I grew up with a politics that promised better worlds . . . Do you remember that, Engineer? Not all the parties were like that, but behind what they did in the present day, there was always an eye out for tomorrow . . . Because tomorrow is useful today, so that we know what to do with it, with our today . . . We are technicians, so we're accustomed to the idea of planning, of something that doesn't exist today, but that needs to be built, and that has to be done inside x amount of time, with a specific sum of money and with what's available there on site . . . What do politicians know about it? When have they ever given a damn about doing something well? About tomorrow? About something lasting, precise, about building something to professional standards, according to the state of the art, or the mathematics, physics and science of construction? I'm sure you could tell me yourself, Engineer . . . What do those people know about *rules*, any kind of rules? All that matters to them is today, the rest is just the distant future, it doesn't concern them, it has nothing to do with the immediate present, with an instantaneous consensus, the kind that can be measured by polling . . . I'm talking about *our* politicians, not about the kind that once they rise to power, stay there for the rest of their lives . . . Then someone stages a revolution and they put someone else in power to remain there for the rest of their lives . . . We are *technicians*, we'll never understand them . . .'

If Puddu stays here, I can leave without worries. It's Friday, by four, no later, I'm home. I'll turn off my cell phone. A weekend of total laziness, a long walk, an art exhibit, dinner at some friend's house, then Monday morning we can talk it over again . . . Fuck, though, what a headache!

Brandani here is the only one in suit and tie, the only one not in T-shirt and shorts. His snuff-coloured linen suit, wrinkled, his green roller suitcase, with a red border, easy to identify on the conveyor belts in the midst of other luggage, for the most part black, perhaps because dirt doesn't show, but all the same, and therefore necessarily tagged with labels, ribbons, bows, splotches of paint in some cases, indelible signs drawn perhaps by someone who's already suffered the trauma of suitcase mix-ups, who's checked into a hotel to find that his clothing belongs to someone else, with someone else's locked suitcase and no key. Even Engineer Brandani's multicoloured roller suitcase required further markings, because he's happened to spot other ones that were perfectly identical, so he availed himself of red duct tape, the really durable kind, and branded his luggage with an asymmetrically placed longitudinal stripe, like the stripes he remembers seeing long ago on souped-up cars, on Fiat I-wish-I-could-but-can't 600s, with Abarth kits and scorpion decals. In his mind, he calls his rolling suitcase 'the Abarth', he loves it, it belongs to him and it bears his trademark of dishevelled contempt for the chic elegance of travel accessories. Aside from his returns to the Island, he always and only travels for work, because by now he hates travel and everything that goes with it, but he is still comfortable in airports and on aeroplanes. When he's at the airport he goes into a sort of cataleptic trance, a stupefied state of inner peace, all the more profound the longer the delays stretch out, but then there's a point past which he regains consciousness and starts getting pissed off at those delays. Once he's done with the check-in, after going through all the checkpoints and submitting to every type of scanner imaginable, after allowing himself to be rummaged and searched, after removing belt and shoes and finally touching down on the other side, all he needs is to breathe and think. Sometimes to read, eat a sandwich or sip an international-style cappuccino. But most of all, what he likes is to observe. At an airport Ivo Brandani feels himself to be one of the the righteous among the righteous. There all normal human activity is suspended, it's an existential pause, a sort of pacification, a state of nirvana: the airport is the only space of mystical decompression afforded to those who believe in nothing. From a departure lounge you set off into flight, and perhaps that is why the air already seems different. It's nice to be here, in a legitimate and necessary state of waiting, in a sort of suspended middle ground, separate from work, holiday and any other activity save that of waiting for a plane. To him aeroplanes are sacred objects, of a sublime, because necessary, beauty. Soon a technological deity will arrive, capable of lifting us up into powered flight, in a wonderful & superhuman roar.

People who use these places to open their laptop and get straight to work . . . The mid-level manager, young, sharply dressed and churning with career ambitions, as full of work as a stuffed calamari, who sits down next to you and has on his screen all those identical PowerPoint presentations, with pie charts, trend curves, elementary slogans . . . This stuff, economic and financial plans, market research, timeline charts, etc., they may even pay a handsome price for it but it's almost always staggeringly self-evident, when it's not actual bullshit. We do dozens of these feasibility studies every year . . . The customer expects them, even demands them: just a few pages in colour, laid out horizontally on a letter format, with a plastic binder spine, an acetate jacket, thirty to forty copies, and they're happy: the 'foot soldiers' ask for an explanation, then they carry them back to their bosses . . . The 'foot soldiers of finance'—that's what Franco calls them—all of them with crew cuts or heads shaved entirely, bronzed, designer sunglasses ready in their breast pockets, all dressed alike . . . One year the fashion is a navy-blue three-piece suit with three buttons and trousers with two pleats, the next year the two-buttoned charcoal-grey suit, pipe-stem suit trousers, without pleats: a real annual revolution, and woe betide anyone who fails to keep up with it . . . Two hours in the departure lounge gives me the same relief as a year of transcendental meditation . . . Then, of course, there are airports and there are airports, there are waiting rooms and there are waiting rooms, there are trousers and there are trousers, there are passenger seats and there are passenger seats . . . An uncomfortably hard passenger seat, a pair of ball-crushing trousers that can become a form of torture when those balls have already been intensely puréed by hours and hours of travel . . .

Ivo wears just a few items of clothing, all of them carefully considered, selected and made to order by his tailor: roomy jackets that practically slip off him, loose trousers, easy on the crotch, with deep pockets, broad-soled shoes with custom-made orthopaedic insoles, shirts with comfortable collars, short socks without elastic, because he can't stand the death grip of long socks on his calves. All of which makes him look clumsy, exacerbates the advancing years, in defiance of his traditional and legendary beauty, but at least it puts him at his ease; the mere sight of a pair of skin-tight jeans makes him feel unwell: 'How do they manage to wear them so tight? How did I ever manage?'

The perfect departure lounge is never too silent, otherwise a crying child becomes too annoying, if you happen to cut a fart there's a risk of it being noticed, if the air is too muffled and solemn you get sleepy, whereas the ideal state is a vigilant pre-somnolence. Ivo is a connoisseur of boredom in airports and he reflects on it. In the departure area, the air already seems thinner, more rarefied, the people appear dreamy somehow, raptly absorbed in something, everyone spontaneously lowers their voices. Children take advantage of the opportunity to bust balls to greater effect, it seems that there they somehow perceive a certain weakness among the grown-ups, a diminution of their authority. You sit down and wait for someone to honour the undertaking to take charge of his body for a few hours of flight and at the same time ensure the satisfaction of certain primary necessities. You expect to be kept alive at 30,000 feet, to be set back down gently on solid earth, and finally set free. Fine, so long, get your suitcase and get the hell out of here, from here on you're going to have to make your own way: no more flight attendants, hostesses, stewards, to look after your needs. No one with the vacant smile of those young women in uniform and self-massaging compression stockings and the gestures of well-trained counterfeit geishas, no one who'll come if you press the right button, eager to know what it is you desire, no more directional air jets you can turn onto your face if it gets hot in the cabin. Here too at the check-in desk, there you see them, the young women in uniform, with their stewardess expressions, slightly different from those you find on the in-flight staff, but still, air-hostess expressions they remain. Brandani has been pondering the mystery of that meta-smile for years, for decades.

What is it? Boredom? Professional detachment? Is it the effect of having seen too much, travelled too much, the constant process of delocalization? Their gaze never rests on anything, least of all in your eyes, to discourage anyone who might have a mind to launch into the international courtship of stewardess, abetted by the many legends—or are the stories true?—of spectacular standing sex in the restrooms with horny flight attendants. As long as there are people who go on regaling us with these tall tales—or are the stories true?—stewardesses are going to be obliged to avoid looking you in the face with anything but the frostiest of professional smiles, frozen in place, alien. But perhaps it's because if you take away a woman's authentic relational sphere or, worse, if you professionalize it, then she empties out and nothing is left but a shell.

Brandani thinks that stewardesses are nothing but the rinds of women who are no longer there, who have gone elsewhere or perhaps are dead, exoskeletons, like seashells without their mollusc, lovely to look at perhaps but empty. Or else females with a hermit crab inside them, in place of the original soul. This is because, to the best of his knowledge—he knew a couple of stewardesses, years ago, one of whom had large breasts with the consistency of a cream custard—when a flight attendant is on a break or on holiday, a whole woman doesn't reappear, only the semblance of one. There always remains an indelible patina of uncaring stewardessness, like an appalling layer of dead relational cells. The custard-breasted stewardess had a remote, distracted demeanour, during sex she kept her eyes open, she never denied herself but never really offered herself either. Once she said this to him: 'If you've been flying for a few years, you wind up never coming down to earth.'

What about the stewards? Why do they all seem like faggots? Why do they all have the same slim trim physique, at the very most a size-38S jacket, a 32-inch waist, neither tall nor short, all the same age, somewhere between their mid-thirties and their mid-forties? Why are they all so unpleasant, obnoxious, lacking even the ability to form a meta-smile, without ever managing to seem courteous? What is the exact phrase? *Smartly turned out*, that's it. Tanned, with manicured hands, fluid gestures, dull yet chilly gazes, and when they have nothing to do, they indulge continuously in idle chitchat with the female flight assistants, they huddle in the far back, or all the way in the front, and you can hear them chatting away and laughing. The ones that don't seem gay have the general air of professional sex hounds, lewd, expert, you see it from the way they're capable of eyeing up a female passenger. A lightning-fast evaluation but it's impossible to miss. Maybe that's how they want the cabin personnel, they choose them specially with alienating physical and personality traits.

To Brandani the stewardesses seem more differentiated one from another, but perhaps that's just his gaze, the observing eyes of an ageing decommissioned male that rests upon them with greater attention. Every time he goes on a plane, Ivo, who is a professional envier, envies the whole crew, including the pilots, so delocalized that the world seems to be something that has nothing to do with them. He imagines atopian people who live in neighbourhoods close to the airport, who come and go from home to aeroplane, from aeroplane to home, travelling along outlying bypasses, moving across remote locations, industrial districts, residential expanses with trees and lawns. Places that make Brandani think of a hateful novel by J. G. Ballard, *Crash*, that he never managed to finish, but then he never finishes books by Ballard, because of the cold, excessively intelligent writing. He imagines that these pilots, these stewards and stewardesses, live in subdivisions of clean and modern townhouses—the streets spick and span, the can in the garage—and that they stay there, taking showers, going for swims in the pool, spending their days off at the gym and their nights having group sex with the neighbours or in erotic private clubs. It isn't their lives he envies, it's the fact that they seem to belong so wholly to this nothingness.

Belonging to nothing, being nothing. I'm getting closer.

Monsoon

The weather channels were showing a low-pressure vortex hovering stationary over the Country. Something was keeping it anchored there, a sort of conspiracy of the surrounding high-pressure fronts, southern and northern, western and eastern; wedges of depression were trying fruitlessly to break out of the encirclement towards the east—the satellites showed an increasingly dense vortex that instead of contracting was expanding northward, day by day, involving other geographies and other nations, perhaps more accustomed to this intensity of clouds and rains. No, that's not right, since these were practically monsoon-like precipitations—which means when unheard-of quantities of rain gush down and the cars come to a halt because no windshield wipers can keep up with this, or they slow down and put on their emergency blinkers, when the underpasses all flash-flood and anyone who happens to be down there can easily be killed—rains like this create problems even in the Northern Countries of the Continent. Even in places right above the mountain chain that encloses and circumscribes the Peninsula, such heavy rains are rare, because up there it drizzles light and continuous, for days at a time, creating grass and pasturage, keeping the meadows green even in the summer, when down here everything turns yellow and you need a sprinkler system to keep your lawn at an acceptable level of green, instead of the dust it would turn into if abandoned to the summer drought.

But it wasn't summer, this was rather a late autumn pervaded with a muggy heat, and it was growing particularly vicious in those last days of November, turning into weeks and weeks of clouds and increasingly intense rains, until that vortex that, they were saying on TV, was making it rain harder than it ever had in the past two hundred years, even though there were some who objected, pointing out that yes, it was certainly raining a good deal but two hundred years ago they didn't have the proper tools to measure precipitation, and the various levels reached in previous floods of the River, engraved into marble plaques inset everywhere on the ancient walls of the City of God, proved a prehistory of tremendous rains, and in any case those four hundred years of cold weather that they referred to as the 'Little Ice Age' couldn't have been a stroll in the park for anyone.

'A sick autumn,' he said to himself, an autumn that was muggy and wet with rain loaded with red sand, whose provenance was the Great Southern Desert, something that alone proved how many things on this planet can change over time, and not just slightly. The television was showing rain and more rain in every part of the Country, with landslides, masses of mud coming down off liquefied mountains, burying everything before it, floods and bridges with the arches semi-submerged in the waters of rivers so swollen as to be unrecognizable. Rivers that in just a few days had swollen into savage monsters tearing at breakneck speed downstream, that is, towards one of the two or three seas that surround the Peninsula, to empty vast quantities of dissolved silt into them, and you'd say from the colour of the water that it was dark, cold cappuccino.

The River, enclosed between its high retaining walls, poured through the City, its level rising 'hour by hour'. 'The warnings are growing more serious,' the television announced, and then it reported that the River had 'reached the danger level', adding that it was constantly being 'monitored' by the experts at the National Emergency Protection Agency, as if once it began to overflow its banks there were actually anything that could be done. Evacuate the neighbourhoods 'at risk'? And just how?

Large exhausted nutrias had made it up onto the parapets of the stairways that once led down to the gravel riverbed but were now lost in the swirling current; ducks and cormorants had taken refuge who knows where, while the seagulls truly had no problems at all and were merely looking around in bafflement at all the people clustered along the parapets, and on the bridges, people

34

who were watching in fascination the succession of whirlpools moving in deeply etched depressions across that shifting dark surface, itself rising visibly all the while.

Every time a train from the underground rail system rose to cross the River, the passengers fell silent at the sight of the swollen stream, while someone in the crowd inevitably reiterated the well-known facts, that is, that one of those large moored barges had broken free and had floated downstream, getting wedged under an arch of the Ancestral Bridge downstream, with the risk that the water might build up there so massively the River might finally overflow its banks. But no one really believed it—that the River would overflow.

The morning he started his job at the District, Engineer Ivo Brandani had a chance himself to stare out at the rain-swollen River and to mull over the prospects in the near future for the City, as well as to listen to the commentary from the travellers on the underground rail system, as it emerged onto the surface and the Cement Bridge.

'It hasn't happened in a hundred years or more, but still, it could happen. Who says that the embankments *can't be* breached?' he thought to himself.

First day at the Eighth Urban District, Technological Management, Supervision of the Public Patrimony. He needed it, that position. After the fiasco at Ediltekne, he needed a job, he needed a salary, and retirement was far in the future but not so far that he could afford simply not to think about it. He had to go on paying his mortgage and his insurance, he was cutting into the money he'd set aside, but he was tired of travelling. He's heard that at the Governorship they were looking for managers to work on a contract basis, and by contravening his innermost instincts he managed to force himself to hustle his friends who worked there, until a breach opened in the wall and he managed to wangle a temporary position, on a contract that could be renewed from year to year. He'd hoped to secure the directorship of a central office, but that had proved impossible.

'Trust me, they're never going to give you that'—Polano had told him—'go and take a directorship outside of here, in some out-lying district. Life is horrible in the districts, they're a fever nightmare of fuck-ups, you're on the firing line, not much staff, not much money, zero equipment, you have all the local politicians busting your balls every other day, into the mix. That's why no one wants those jobs, you're much more likely to get a full contract as a director there. Trust me, things are set up already so you either have to give up the idea entirely or you go spit blood in a district. You know I love you but that's the way things stand. For a directorship here, my hands are tied, but I know that there are districts that have gone without a director for months now and others that have a director with good inside connections who's looking for another position. In places like that, you'd have an even better chance. I can give you a hand. The salary is good just the same.'

He'd liked Polano's frankly straightforward way ever since they had both worked together at Megatecton, and once again he proved useful. Not even there at the Governorship was there anything that he could claim for clearly established merit, for his years of work, for the quality of his outstanding CV, a quality, for that matter, that he self-attributed: they'd taken him and this, for someone as isolated and out of the game as he was, had been a sort of miracle.

'Never forget that the Governorship is a cold monster and that you, like all the rest of us, will be a matter of complete indifference to it. It will gnaw on you for a lifetime and then, when it no longer needs you, it will spit you out again wherever it chances to be. If you haven't been sufficiently farsighted to procure yourself some cosy niche somewhere, then, my dear Ivo, you would be well advised to grab onto the Eighth District and keep mum . . . There are people doing much worse than you and me . . . By the way, did you hear about De Klerk? You don't know? He's dead. He stayed at Megatecton, rose through the ranks, he'd become the managing director. A few years ago, I had dealings with him again, they were involved in a major real-estate deal . . . Apparently he had a fulminating heart attack right there in the office . . . All that work—you remember how hard he worked?—all that power, and he just dropped dead at his desk . . .'

As the train crossed over the bridge, Ivo Brandani thought back to De Klerk, to the summer all those years ago. There was nothing in him now of the emotions that had so troubled him back then. It was all over, freeze-dried, reduced to dust and carried away by the passage of time.

A few days earlier, in the Eighth District, he had met with the outgoing director for a sort of changing of the guard. The fact that Brandani had managed to land a contract was largely to the director's credit: the technicians working in the Administration would stop at nothing and were exerting political pressure of all kinds to avoid winding up in places like the Eighth, so for this guy to find a presentable replacement, even though Ivo came from the private sector, had made things all that much easier. The guy could scarcely believe his good luck, now that he was actually leaving: you could see he was about to burst with happiness, that he was once again filling his lungs with fresh air and when he said, 'You know, it's not at all bad here,' anyone could have told that he was lying. But Brandani didn't realize how badly.

It was daunting to see the sheer violence with which that brownish mass of foaming water swept downstream, rushing just a few yards beneath the subway car.

'What's become of the cormorants? And the ducks? How do the fish manage to stay in one place with this current? Are they all going to be swept out to sea? Will they find shelters in certain cavities on the riverbed? Along the embankments?'

He thought about the deep, dark caverns of the River, excavated in a bed of millennia-old detritus, where the City's weighty memories were stacked: statues and fragments of statues, pieces of decorated cornices, weapons, sarcophagi, gold sunk in the silt, pistols, muskets, weapons and objects from every era. In the dark, fish chilled by the cold of the water, seeking shelter from the immense power of the stream. The image of the River bed had always made him shudder. The ancient filth, the bacteria and the viruses, the mud, the rubble, the scrap, the water so muddy you couldn't see a foot from your face.

He had recently read that in Amazonia—or perhaps in Asia, he didn't really remember—there are catfish living in the silty slimy rivers that practically cannot see, because of the murk. And so they not only use the sort of vibrissae, or whiskers, that they have under their throats or on either side of their mouths but can also *feel* what's in the water through their skin. 'They sniff the water, or actually they taste the water with their whole body, they have taste-buds all over their body, as if it were tongue tissue. They're completely covered with sensors, what they can't see they feel with their skin, and from the taste of the water they decide whether what they have near them is an enemy or a friend, whether it's something good to eat or whether they had better take to their tails.'

He had always made use of the aquatic image of the filter-feeding mollusc to explain to himself the role of the Politico, otherwise incomprehensible to him. But not the fact that the Politico was a mollusc, the fact that he was a *filter-feeder*. 'Politicians, like bivalves, breathe and feed at the same time, preserving the particles of consensus/dissent in suspension in the environment where they work and live . . .' But now the catfish, capable of *tasting* the water in which it swims, struck him as a more precise and pertinent image.

'How do the cormorants along the River manage to hold their breath when they dive under to fish? When they go under, how do they see with all that mud?'

He'd often see them go flying past, labouring through the air at a low altitude, skimming over bridges that in this stretch of the River dated back more than a hundred years. They reminded him of the cormorants on the Island, but these were from some larger species and their eyes were circled with yellow. They perched on the occasional trunk rising from the water or on the branches of tenacious saplings that had grown in the cracks between the rocks of the embankment; he'd watched them dry their outstretched wings in the sunlight.

'They lack the waterproof substance on their wings that all other marine birds possess. Theirs is a life of tribulations. I can't claim to possess any protective substances either. And in fact here I am on the train from the Eighth District of this horrible city. If they'd told you, you never would have believed it, Brandani. You're a miserable fool, Brandani.'

'The first thing to go under has always been the Pagan Temple. It's the lowest point'—someone nearby was saying in an accent that belonged unmistakably to the City, that sounded like poached, pan-fried chicory—'The water comes gushing up out of the sewers before it rises over the parapets, the Temple goes underwater when everything around it is still dry. Then if the water really does rise, it's a fucked situation. Go take a look at the plaques around there, the ones on the facade of Santa Maria—there are marks at various heights, the tallest one might be 10 feet high, you wouldn't believe it.'

The City of God, which had also become the capital of the entire nation in recognition of an ancient pre-eminence, was said always to have been the favourite of one god, the only god capable of separating the lands from the waters, at least at first, until he broke his promise—after nearly one hundred forty years since the last flood, the City of God was in danger of going underwater once again.

Brandani, who had always loved the Apocalypse as his once chance to witness something truly stirring, deep down actually wished for it. It was the young boy who still rode along with him inside, a reckless half-criminal, who so desired it. He wanted to watch that odious city drown, even though it was a place where he'd been born and would probably die alone, struggling in his death throes at the dark end of a hospital ward, at the mercy of the adepts of the religion, the proponents of the official *pietas* who oversee the passage into the next world. A life, his had been, spent in the vain attempt to mitigate the sensation that he'd long, indeed always, been caught in a trap. Over time he'd developed a razor-edged hatred for all that human and divine stuff that constituted the City, so that now the prospect of watching it sink underwater—

39

under 10 or 12 feet of water, he grimly hoped—would have given him a deranged, self-destructive sense of delight, of ultimate triumph.

'The millenarian city can go fuck itself, at last some genuine destruction. It doesn't matter to me, I'm up high, up in the Adobe Clay Valley, the water won't reach up there . . . There was a time, fifty thousand years ago, when the River apparently ran through there. That's the reason for all the clay, the ruins of the ancient kilns . . .'

On the Cement Bridge, the train had practically crawled to a halt. It often happened, as if the drivers had been instructed to handle the trains with care, as if they might break them. In what couldn't have been any more than half a minute, the cars were deluged with a solid wall of rain, and if the River hadn't been there, just few yards beneath the bridge, with its dense and impetuous swells, they wouldn't have been able to see a thing.

At the next station, the people boarding the train were drenched, their folding umbrellas dripping. As they entered the car, they muttered or grumbled phrases as if in search of solidarity and justification for the state they were in. The sense of a looming apocalypse brought people together with their fellow souls who were usually reciprocally chilly and indifferent.

At last Engineer Brandani got out of the train, onto the slush of the rubber flooring in the Piazza of the Imprint Station, and trooped into line for the long escalator that would carry him, steeped in the smell of wet fabric and wet metal, up to the surface. Once out in the open air, he'd have to face up to that wall of water with his old raincoat and a fragile techno-folding umbrella.

Gradually, as he got closer to the surface, Brandani saw people coming downstairs drenched with rain, women with their hair plastered to their foreheads, carrying dripping umbrellas. At the foot of the ramp leading out to the open air, the rubber flooring had become a puddle where the hesitant, the under-equipped, the protectionless mustered and gathered—there weren't many of them, considering that it had been raining for days—immediately set upon by unlicensed vendors trying to foist off their pinchbeck umbrellas for a relative pittance. From there he could hear and see the water come pelting down in a violent rush, gulped down with difficulty by the grate of the drain under the riser of the first step.

He dodged the street vendors, pulled up his collar and lapels, undid the strap that held his umbrella tightly furled, pushed the button and watched it burst open, spring-loaded, not without a surge of engineer's delight at its automatic efficiency, and then started quickly up the stairs; he didn't want to come in late on his first day at work.

But the water pouring out of the sky was too much, he hurried his pace with the result that, when he reached the top of the stairs, he was out of breath. At that moment, it was impossible to cross the piazza on foot. The rain was creating a sort of solid wall and the cars, though they were moving slowly, kicked up sprays as tall as a man—this was no time to try to get across. He cut to one side and took shelter under the portico, meaning to wait for the downpour to slacken.

The semicircular porticoes housed small settlements of homeless people, customary in that part of town because they were drawn into the gravitational field of the nearby Big Train Station which, as is so often the case in all cities, constituted for them the chief reference point, and always had. The Station was certainly a resource for tramps and hobos, perhaps because of the large enclosed public spaces where they were able to find hoboish company, spend their day, eat, panhandle, maybe steal, while at night they could find places to hole up and sleep in the surrounding neighbourhoods. From that immense, beautiful and structurally daring railroad station there had always emanated out into the surrounding city a sordid aura of physical and moral deterioration that made it unpleasant to cross through those spaces, but on that particular day, everything appeared ravaged and seemingly purified by the tepid deluge that was showering down.

That was one of the areas of the City in which one could most unmistakably perceive—it was there in the very name of the subway stop—the footprint of a past that had left substantial and visible traces there, configuring the City's plan in its semblance. The urban fabric all around there, when it didn't actually simply leave them in plain sight, incorporated the ruins of the Ancient Empire, ruins that in the city were the object of a veritable cult. A cult celebrated in institutions founded for that purpose, staffed by hundreds of functionaries, employed in tens of thousands of square feet of office space, all of them assigned responsibilities for the maintenance, restoration and 'exploitation' of that immense agglomerate of ruins, for the most part still underground, which constituted the glorious and unforgettable Dead City: 'unforgettable my ass,' Brandani would say to himself, because even as a child he had detested the archaeological relics that surfaced everywhere you looked. They were traces of a great power of Antiquity, something that the Living City still boasted about, and which it still considered a source of pride that sank its roots deep in the heart of every single inhabitant, even though all and every cultural link, and possibly the biological ones too, had long since been cut between the living citizenry and those ancient forefathers.

While he was there, waiting for the rain to diminish, Brandani thought back to the words of Enzo Rossetti. Rossetti had some time ago accepted the position of technological director of the Twelfth District and a couple of weeks earlier had told him: 'Here, it's like playing tennis . . . Yeah, let me explain. At first you're just terrified, then when you start to understand a few things, you fool yourself into thinking that you can make and do, manage, control, plan—at that point you tend to relax and think, OK, I can do this. Wrong. *You thought* you understood. Things are much more complex and dangerous than you ever realized. And just as all this starts to dawn on you mentally, you get the first real missile up your ass . . . What missile? Huh. Hold on. I was telling you that it's like playing tennis, except that instead of a tennis ball, anything can hit you and you have to react, you have to smash this *anything* back over the net. It might turn out to actually be a tennis ball, or else a missile, or a hand grenade, a medieval mace-and-chain, a cube of candyfloss. Let me say it again: *Anything*. And it's usually *against* you and it's dangerous. Maybe it's a time bomb that actually looks more like a baby doll. If you don't know what it is, it can blow up in your face when you least expect it. Basically, there are two things you need: unwavering attention plus an assurance against legal risks. Then there's the whole chapter on the delegates, that is, the politicians. I'm not even turning that page, it's a book all its own. You'll see. I'm not trying to frighten you. There are people who wind up even liking it. Look at me, I've been in the job for a few years now and I don't have any intention of quitting—by this point the challenges are something I almost enjoy . . . It's action, you understand? It has an allure all its own. You're accustomed to the private sector, which is a whole different kettle of fish. Here if you need money you won't get it, if you need technicians you won't get them—you're on the front line but you're unarmed. It's one thing to know it and you can brace yourself mentally, but even so, for the job of Technological Director of a district, the only thing is on-the-job training.'

Under the portico, amid all those people waiting to be able to venture across the street on foot—they all kept a safe distance from the tousled rumpled dirty men, bundled up in rags, who had slept there all night and still lay stretched out on their flattened cardboard boxes, or else sat up smoking a cigarette with their dog curled up at their feet—Brandani took a moment to observe the stress being placed on the piazza's rainwater-collection-and-dispersal system.

The water was running clean and impetuous along the paving, made up of small basalt cubes that had been scrubbed for days right down to the tiniest cracks, a pavement that now looked reasonably clean, perhaps even *too* clean, considering the depth of the erosion between one cube and the next. Brandani's mind, though on the one hand he was filled with worries about his new position, was on the other hand engineerishly occupied with the observation of this entirely exceptional weather event and its consequences.

The rain was pounding the ground furiously and then rushing along the various inclines that had been built with the collection of that very rainwater in mind; the rushing flow did its best to drop down drain grates that had been designed for much smaller capacities and were therefore incapable of gulping it all down. As a result, around each drain grate, large puddles and small lakes began to form, and there the car tires kicked up towering jets of water. Brandani knew perfectly well that the people behind the wheels enjoyed making those sprays.

As he watched in fascination that convulsive blast of rain, the people around him spoke and sympathized in the local parlance. It appeared that they were thinking of themselves as a community once again, that they felt they all belonged to one shared fate. Formulations sprang to their lips along the lines of: We're all in God's hands now; sooner or later Mother Nature will have her way. Or, more prosaically: It's that global warm-up.

Brandani, engineer that he was, knew that if the River had overflowed upstream, it was unlikely to overtop its banks here in the city, provided that they manage to keep the arches of the bridges free of flotsam, provided the water level didn't rise above the keystone of the Ancestral Bridge, which was low, with three arches and no drain openings. That was certainly dangerous—it constituted the one real problem, the point to keep in mind.

On television, he had seen that in fact, to the north of the city, vast areas of the ancient river valley dating back to the Pleistocene were several yards deep in slimy river water, while the flood plains closer to the densely populated urban areas remained dry. A sign that the time had come? It all depended on a flood bore expected— and feared—to come downstream later than morning or, at the very latest, in the early afternoon of that day. It all depended on how massive the swell proved to be and how much flotsam capable of blocking the bridges it would sweep with it.

Brandani agreed inwardly with himself: 'Yes, We Are All in God's Hands Now, even though I'm on the seventh floor and, what's more, high on a hill . . . Provided, that is, that the down-spout of the gutter system finally opens up—right now the drip area is spreading a little too wide. Would I mind seeing this city go underwater? I can't say . . . Admit it, Brando, you wouldn't mind a bit. There've always been floods and here comes a nice big fat one. And after all, the City deserves it, we deserve it. So we believe in nothing? We don't give a flying fuck about nothing? Well, then here's a healthy helping of nothing. It's on its way. What other city deserves it more than this one, the Eternal City? Will they evacuate us? My district is far away and, most important of all, it's up high, even though it overlooks the valley of the Little River. That river, sure, it's a beast, but it has a deep bed and it's well banked. Oh, certainly, all those shacks along the banks and the garbage tossed down onto the gravel . . . By now all that's been swept out to sea.'

All the people who had made their homes in the flood plains of the Little River, shacks and shanties thrown together haphazardly with scrap wood, plywood, old doors and new, galvanized sheet metal roofs weighed down with blocks of cement . . . They'd run electric lines down to them, TV sets, all properly installed and organized there, in the midst of the mud, where years ago, while out on a hike, he had seen large red-haired sewer rats perfectly at their ease rummaging through piles of river trash, mountains of stolen roller suitcases discarded down along the gravel banks. The eternal metropolitan rubbish heaps that formed outside his own home, as well. All it took was for the street sweepers and garbage trucks to stop coming, stop cleaning for a couple of nights and anything you care to name started piling up next to the overflowing dumpsters, including clothing to wear and building materials to make a home. He liked seeing the water flow like that—scrubbing the city's pavements, it carried off all the filth that had accumulated.

'By now the purifying flood will have swept everything away, so long, it's been good to know you. Before two months are up, it will all be just as it was along the Little River.'

The automobiles, the buses running the public transportation lines, the taxis had never once stopped going by for an instant, kicking up waves of water as they went. The only difference from the traffic on normal days was the absence of motorcycles and scooters, with the very rare exception of a truly well-equipped motorcyclists, that is, wearing a waterproof jumpsuit covering his feet as well, a full-face helmet, waterproof gloves—motorcycles are motorcycles, they seemed to be saying, they demand dedication, you don't turn your back on them just because of a little rain.

'There are always people who play with water, even when there's too much it, even when there are people left homeless, or drowned, garages and cellars that flood, along with tunnels and underpasses. The city is full of hollows and ravines, the drainage system is clogged up, the sewers are full of leaks, blockages, defects. The shack towns along the Little River, but also the ones to the north of the Rapids on the Big River, have built up over time, ignoring the danger that always looms along the banks of a water-course: What can have become of them?'

The downpour was starting to subside, but the street was still a rushing torrent and the people sheltering under the porticoes were hesitating. Brandani looked at his watch.

'The first day of my new job I don't want to get there too late. But the whole city is in these same conditions. Well then. Years ago, do you remember those people who built themselves that hut on the subway-track escarpment near where you lived, in the midst of the underbrush and saplings that grow up everywhere. There was that insane cloudburst, so powerful that I got my camera out. I was taking pictures of that wall of water that practically cut visibility to zero so you couldn't see what was around you when I started to notice pieces of wood coming down the slope, like matchsticks in a rivulet, the hut was coming apart under the impact of the flooding, a man and a woman with some children were doing their best to get out of there, a bundle of rags, garbage just melting in the flood. Rudimentary, prehistoric living conditions, in the heart of a major Western city, built in cement, up-to-date, organized, with all its impressive roofs and shingles, rain gutters and downspouts. People who were fleeing the downpour. Drenched children, the traffic on the main road at the base of the escarpment moving along placidly, inside the cars were people who were warm and dry, listening to the radio, making calls on their cell phones, while the primitive hut-dwellers were fleeing the cloudburst and taking shelter under the viaduct, standing on the pavement which at that point might at the most be two, two and a half feet wide, clutching their children close . . . Ah, now I can cross the street.'

He reopened his umbrella, once again enjoying the click and the snap, and joined the group of pedestrians on the zebra crossing trying to make their way to the far side of the street. They constituted a critical mass and the traffic came to a halt to let them get across. At this point all he had to do was head up the street that cut through the middle of the Great Ruin. Divarication Street, along which Engineer Brandani was now walking briskly, sidestepping one puddle after the other, trying not to drench his pants legs and his shoes, had been given that name because instead of coming to a respectful halt in the presence of the majesty and complexity of the Ruin, it brashly ran through it from one end to the other, splitting it in two, revealing in cross-section its powerful structure, revealing the dozens and dozens of rooms, by now stripped of roofs and vaults, that constituted it, some of those rooms large enough to contain a modern block of flats, others smaller, but all of them with a primary shape that remained autonomous with respect to the adjoining space. Squares, circles and apsidal semicircles, linear galleries, porticoes and cryptoportici, lengthy lines of rooms, all apparently windowless. It had been years since he last took these pavements on foot, in fact, he might very well have never walked on them at all, and so he observed the walls of bricks and rain-black rubble, interrupted by what seemed to be ancient collapses, or perhaps intentional caesurae carved out by the Living City to make way through the viscera of the Dead City. On the pavements and on the stone parapets overlooking the deep archaeological ditches he saw drenched traces of homelessness, layers of water-soaked cardboard laid out on the ground as a pallet, abandoned tin cans, filth and human shit that the pouring rain had swept away and almost deleted, but only in the areas directly exposed to the downpour. He walked past a couple of niches reduced to genuine and full-fledged latrines, the bricks coated and corroded by the yellow patina of urine, the stone pavement smeared with shit: he clamped his nostrils shut with his free hand and accelerated his pace.

'Tomorrow I'll take the opposite pavement.'

Suddenly it dawned on him that this was already territory under *his jurisdiction*, that is, it belonged to that Eighth Urban

District of which he was accepting the post of techno-director. 'This is a veritable latrine . . . We'll have to find a solution . . .' The idea that he had a say in how to handle such a vast physical stretch of the city gave him a strange sensation of unease ('will I be up to it?'), but also of satisfaction ('at last I can get my hands into something concrete'). In fact, more than a feeling of satisfaction, Brandani felt an urge to do, to intervene and improve. With regard to those places, he no longer had the status of an ordinary citizen who approves/disapproves, who praises/condemns: he could take concrete initiatives for which he would assume complete *responsibility*.

Divarication Street, after carving itself a breach through that massive and massively ancient imperial complex, literally ripping it limb from limb, pushed off into a section of the city that Brandani knew dated back more or less a hundred years.

'Here, no doubt about it, there must already be the jurisdiction of the Superintendency over the Patrimony . . .'

The urban fabric here had a repetitive regularity that had been imposed a century earlier by planners and architects steeped in Masonic geometry and rationality, but over time that clarity and cleanliness had been altered by the proximity of the Big Station, whose gravitational force emanated a certain soupçon of sordidness, like some veil of moral opacity drawn over the entire neighbourhood.

'Ugly. That is, beautiful but ugly.'

Buildings in bad shape, or barely restored, for office use, streets empty of pedestrians, everywhere pedestrian barriers and mass transit lanes down which large buses roar, striped with dirt-streaked rain, no-parking and one-way signs, electronics stores, model and hobby stores, Bangladeshi emporiums, dimly lit ethnic restaurants and everywhere enormous puddles marking clogged sections of the sewer system. Down the enfilades of those streets, running at strictly perpendicular angles, jutted out the numerous signs of hotels and *pensiones* and bed-and-breakfasts, all more-or-less seedy and rundown, two stars or three stars at the most.

As he was walking briskly along those pavements, trying to dodge the torrential rivulets rushing down parallel to the building facades from broken rain gutters, he was struck by the appearance of the bars he was passing: they were all small and dreary, dirty-looking, the furnishings dating back to previous and now obsolete phases of modernity. Compelled by necessity to go into one of these to take a pee, he ordered an espresso and asked to use the bathroom. Someone gave him the keys and pointed him to a narrow and almost vertical flight of stairs. He descended cautiously, but that didn't keep him from slamming his forehead straight into the corner of the intrados of a spine wall, hard and cold and painful. Clamping his hands to his cranium, he continued down the stairs until he reached a dark cubbyhole of a bathroom devoid of toilet paper and hand towels, piled high with cafe equipment and buckets full of floor rags. He rinsed his forehead, cursing all the while, and then dried it with his raincoat sleeve.

Once he returned to street level, he gulped down a bitter espresso, while the pain still throbbed strong, paid at a cash register almost entirely hemmed in by tall display cases crowded with chewing-gum-candy mints-sweets-pastry snack-batteries-razors-etc., to the point that the money had to be thrust through a sort of canyon no wider than a foot or so, at the far end of which sat the supreme indifference of a withered old cashier.

'Decadence . . . There was a time, say, thirty years ago, when this cafe was newly built. It was doing well back then, certainly not now. That is, I doubt it. And anyway, a sign saying Watch Your Head right there wouldn't have hurt. Unless they're doing it on purpose: You're going to bust my balls about how you need to pee? You're going to force me to hand over the keys to the restroom? Then go ahead on down and split your skull open.'

In the meantime, it continued to rain cats and dogs.

There it was, at Number 87, an oversized late-nineteenth-century palazzo, dirty and dark. 'Palpable decadence. Of course, what else would you expect?'

His small collapsible umbrella hadn't done much to protect him, so when he walked through the front door of the Eighth District, it was with his shoes full of water and the hems of his trousers thoroughly drenched. He was in the throes of a sort of perceptual redoubling: he saw himself from within and without at the same time, it happened whenever he was under extreme stress.

Just inside the large ground-floor door, the atrium floor was scattered with wet sawdust, and a little further on there was a twin-panelled glass door, spring-loaded, with push handles, which led to a staircase covered with a thin layer of well-trodden, smeared mud.

'Human feet, humanoid feet, primate feet, dirt-bringing feet, the modified hands of quadrumans that became bipeds, millions of years to get to this atrium . . .'; when Brandani split in two, part of his mind went on spinning, freewheeling.

At the centre of the staircase a large tubular handrail separated the flow of those who were transiting through there, until the lift. The walls were covered with dusty bulletin boards full of notices on legal- and letter-sized paper, but there were other notices attached directly to the wall with pieces of scotch tape. Some were handwritten, others were half torn off, others were old and yellowed, while others still were enormous, with various academic and civil-service competitions announced in large black letters. The lift was as wide as a single person, it reeked of wet wool. A fairly young woman had entered the lift ahead of him, carrying a file box bursting with documents contained in small pink and yellow folders.

The minute Brandani got in, the woman pushed a button. She kept her eyes fixed on the floor and said to him: 'Everything all right? The harvest later. Do you know Mamma? How are the manners?'

She was wearing a very dirty windbreaker. On her feet were a pair of high-heeled sandals, the heel of the foot left bare at the back, and she looked strangely tan. The lift stopped at the fourth floor. The woman pushed him aside with a good hard shove, then opened the doors, exited the car, and left without shutting them behind her.

On the fifth floor, immediately outside the lift, there was a glass booth and inside it was a counter piled high with forms.

From a clear plastic skylight came a loud noise of falling rain. Next to the glass booth, in front of a large dirty, dinged-up air conditioner on wheels, was what he assumed to be an usher. He was an old man in bad shape, in a rumbled baby-blue grisaille tweed suit under a safety yellow emergency vest, and a baseball hat with the emblem of the Rolling Stones. He was sitting in a partially reclining position, his legs sticking out into the hallway, his feet in two silvery rubber shoes that sat in the dampness of a marbled tile floor.

The usher saw him and shouted: 'Ye-e-es, what is i-i-it?' Brandani replied that he was the new Man in Charge.

'Aah!! *Buongiorno, Dottó*. Aah! I'm the usher, here!'

He talked in a blasting loud voice, laughing and displaying a strange choir of teeth, each separated from its neighbour by a wide space. There were deep dark circles under his eyes. As he looked Engineer Brandani up and down, one of his eyes seemed to be going off on some trajectory all its own, in a strange involuntary winking sequence. He went on shrilling: '*Dottó*! I'm done here, I'm retiring at the end of June!'

A woman went past, an office worker with an armful of files and the usher yawped: 'Hey go-o-orgeous . . . I'm done here! I'm retiring at the end of Ju-u-u-une!'

The woman didn't even look in his direction, just went on walking as she said: 'Yes, Carmelo, I know. You're leaving, that's what you've been saying for ten years now. Stop shouting . . . it's early, it's nine in the morning, it's been raining all week, and I've already got a splitting headache . . .'

'Engineer, the situation here is complicated, you'll have a chance to realize that for yourself . . . We don't have much staff, they're relatively unqualified, very few resources, very little cash. I'm giving you a rapid update because this morning I have to leave, I have some personal time off . . . And with these resources we have to do everything. This year in our budget, they've given us practically half of the money we got last year. What's more, we don't have the contract for the maintenance of the school buildings . . . I don't have time now, if you need to know more you should be able to talk to the surveyor Marcotulli . . . Ah, no, he asked me for the day off today . . . Oh well, we'll talk to over tomorrow, if that's all right with you . . . The Man in Charge is you now, you'll need to know the way things are around here . . . But I can't report to you on that myself, like I told you, I have some time off . . .'

Technician First Class Proietti stood up and left, leaving Ivo, baffled, to look out at the rain pelting down outside the window panes, propped up at his executive desk, with a faux-printed wood-veneer finish (quite a good imitation), perched on an executive office chair in fake leather (quite a good imitation), a chair whose only defect was the back rest, which tilted backwards at the slightest pressure, each time making him feel as if he were fainting. The mental doubling continued, Brandani was stunned, he felt suddenly sleepy, he kept yawning. His forehead, after the smack it had taken on the basement steps of that little cafe, was aching.

'Can I come in? What did you do to your forehead, Engineer?'

It was Cinzia, the secretary of the outgoing director. That one time they'd met, his predecessor had spoken highly of her, had recommended he keep her on, and had even left in his office a couple of large cartons sealed with packing tape.

'Oh, right. I banged my head on the ceiling . . . I was going down a staircase . . . It's nothing . . . Does it really show?'

'No, it's just a little red . . . Now then, you're expected at noon in the Ar Bee . . . RB means restricted board . . . The technician Basile is in the waiting room, he says it's urgent . . . There are a great many things I need to bring you up to speed on, Engineer, but we'll have time . . . Now it seems that there's an emergency . . .'

She didn't have time to finish the sentence before three people entered the room, practically at a dead run.

'Ah, here we are, Technician Basile . . . Basile, don't we knock first?'

'Forget about that, Cinzia . . . Forgive me, Engineer, but there are a few problems . . .'

He was a powerfully built stout little man, energetic, ramrod straight, who moved quickly and spoke in a raucous, determined voice, as if he were pissed off at someone. Of the other two men, one was tall and strapping, in his early fifties, while the other was short and skinny, with a salt-and-pepper beard. They introduced themselves: they belonged to the Maintenance Unit. Then Technician Basile went on.

'We're in bad shape, Engineer, the world's going to hell out there, everything's underwater, we're being overwhelmed with phone calls, the streets are turning into ponds at the points where the storm drains are backing up . . . We have three schools that are leaking like sieves. There are problems with the downpipes and the outlet drains. They're either blocked up or they're broken. At the Di Ruscio school there's an even more serious problem—the waterproofing on the roof has failed at several points, there's too much water coming down and it's starting to leak. We've had to take two classrooms out of use . . . Piazza of the Intercession looks like a lake, there's actually water coming up out of the drains, it's mixed with sewer water, somehow, by some miracle, the traffic police have managed to reroute traffic, there are traffic jams miles long. This morning, we even had a death: a young man on a motorcycle who skidded out of control in a puddle over near the Station . . . From downstairs we're starting to get the usual pressure . . . Marcotulli and Proietti aren't in today. We need directives, we need to establish priorities. Engineer, now the man in charge—the one who's *responsible* now—is you, understood?'

'What kind of pressure?'

'Well, when there are problems concerning the larger territory, the Delegates get complaints from the citizens and they dump them on us first thing, as if it was the easiest thing to solve all the different emergencies in one clean sweep . . . The weather's been like this for ten days now. It was obvious we were going to wind up underwater . . . All the other districts are in the same shape as we are, with the difference that we . . .' He broke off and pointed out the window: 'Just look at that, Engineer.'

Brandani looked out and saw a blank wall of water coming down unbroken from a sky that was a uniform lightless dark grey.

'You were saying? What difference?'

'The difference is that this year we haven't subcontracted the maintenance of the buildings and we're running out of money for the maintenance of public spaces . . .'

'Which means?'

'Which means, Engineer . . . that we can't do anything about the schools . . . And out in the streets we can only deal with the very worst cases . . .'

Brandani couldn't seem to concentrate, he kept getting distracted, the strangest things kept popping into his head, more than listening he was studying his interlocutors: 'Technician Basile's breath reeks of soup from 6 feet away,' he thought. Then he said: 'You're telling me that there are schools being flooded and we *can't do anything about it?*'

'Exactly, Engineer. We can't do anything by standard procedure. We'd need to assign projects on a special urgent basis, without any prior spending budget . . . Are you *ready to do that?*'

'Which school is in worst shape?'

'The Di Ruscio school, no doubt about it. But if it goes on like this, the others are going to be in the same shape before long. The alternative is to shut them down. Now *you're* in charge, you're *responsible*, are you ready for this?'

Brandani raised his eyes to the ceiling. He didn't know what to answer. He remembered almost nothing about emergency procedures. He noticed a vast stain of yellowish dampness, and noticed that right at the centre of the stain a few drops were glistening.

Following the engineer's glance, Technician Basile turned around, saw the patch of dampness on the ceiling, and said that there were leaks everywhere in that building too. The other two technicians both nodded their heads yes.

The engineer said nothing, then looked over at Cinzia sitting beside him. He must have had a quizzical expression on his face because she jutted her chin defiantly and said coldly: 'Engineer, you're *responsible*.'

'She isn't pretty and she isn't ugly, neither tall nor short, likable nor unlikable, not a slob and not especially well groomed, her tits aren't big or small . . .' thought Brandani, distracted, still completely bewildered and beside himself, as if he'd just smoked a joint minutes ago. The last one actually dated back a good thirty years, roughly. He yawned and said: 'All right, Basile . . . thanks. But at least in the streets there's something we can do, or not?'

'Fuck, we're doing it,' said the tall strapping man while the skinny one nodded. 'The company is doing what it can, but we only have the resources we have. Fuck, there's only a few workers we can rely on, the situation is what it is: we're doing everything we can . . . The company is complaining about delays in payment. Fuck, Engineer, it's been months since the Accounting Office has issued an authorization . . . It's not our fault but it's got these guys' balls tied in a knot, they're pissed off, they're working on expenses, which is to say, they're not doing much of a job . . . If you could talk to them, that would be better. You're the *Man in Charge*, now, they're surely going to take you more seriously than they do us. You should also talk to those fucking dickheads in Central Accounting, light a fire under their . . .'

At that point, Cinzia put in: 'Forgive him, Engineer, he only knows how to talk like a sailor . . .'

The out-of-body half of Brandani thought: 'If you want to see who knows more curse words, fatso, you've come to the right place.' The half that was still there in the room said nothing.

The only thing that had stuck with him out of that whole conversation was that outdoors there was one huge mess and he was now *responsible*. He said they'd return to the discussion in the early afternoon. As the technicians were leaving, Cinzia reminded him that in a few minutes he was expected downstairs for the RC of the Delegates.

'What does it mean to be responsible?' he wondered. 'Does it mean you have to give a response? No, it means someone who has to respond for his actions concerning something. In fact, he's *answerable*. He's someone who is asked a number of questions, and is *required to respond*. He's the one who takes the blame for everyone else, even if he doesn't know anything about it, has nothing to do with it, just showed up . . . He's the one whose ass they kick because it's the only ass they have to kick. There's someone responsible for everything, Brandani, it's tough shit now, you've entered the chain of public responsibilities. The golden age of private enterprise is over. In private enterprise you talk to other people like you, technicians who can understand you, here you're dealing with politicians . . . They'll skin you alive and hang out your hide, over the front entrance, Brandani . . .'

Outside it was pouring down, the traffic had come to a complete halt, the horns were blaring, the sirens of ambulances caught in the traffic jam were wailing continuously. He got up, looked out of the window, saw two pigeons on the cornice of the building across the street, their feathers puffed up in the cold, huddling close together. 'Lucky them, no one expects anything of them. They're free to live and die as they please . . .'

Just then, Cinzia rushed in and said, breathlessly: 'The River's overflowed, Engineer, down by the Ancestral Bridge . . . That's what I hear . . .'

'So this is it,' thought the out-of-body half of Brandani.

'Is there a television set?'

'Yes, in that cabinet. The keys are in the desk drawer.'

It wasn't true. The local TV news, which had been broadcasting without interruption since that morning, was reporting on overflows into the floodplains of the Little River, areas covered with shanties and shacks: the gypsy camps along the gravel riverbeds had been swept away by the high water. The correspondents were standing on bridges, their backs to a river swollen beyond belief, you could see people clustering along the parapets gazing incredulously down at all that water rushing headlong towards the sea, its surface dense, mud-coloured, shuddering and twisting with ripples and regurgitations and whirlpools, like a mollusc shell. The television correspondents were talking about 'apprehension', 'constant monitoring of the water level', saying that the flood wave, the real one, hadn't even gone past yet, they were saying it was expected around two in the afternoon, they were broadcasting a crane at work to unjam a boat that had got caught under the already normally narrow arches of the Ancestral Bridge, they were also saying that the situation had been 'taken in hand' by the National Emergency Protection Agency, which by this point had claimed jurisdiction over both the municipal authorities and the river-basin authority. They showed maps of flood risk in the city, experts were deciphering the meaning of those graphics for the home audience, doing their best not to spread alarm, but it was abundantly clear that the whole area around the Pagan Temple, if the river did overflow its banks, would wind up under 10 feet of water, if not more.

'Cinzia, are *we* responsible for the overflow areas of the Little River?' Brandani asked, aghast.

'No, Engineer, not *you*—as far as I know the River Basin Authority has always been in charge of that, but if you like I can inquire. Now it's time to head down to the RB. I found you a notepad to write on.' Then she added: 'You should look into getting insurance to take care of potential legal advice and defence. I made an appointment for you tomorrow morning with the company set up for these things, I'll go with you. Probably best to start an insurance policy immediately, don't you think? All the District technical directors do it. Trust me, it's the best thing . . . While you're downstairs, I'll put together a file with all the pieces of paper . . .'

Brandani still needed to fully process all the water that he had drunk that morning the minute he woke up, while still lying flat in his bed, until his belly was full. It was a way to placate the anxiety of the day that awaited him. The restrooms on that floor greeted him with marbled beige porcelain. He set his foot down on a round drain cover meant to catch spillage from the sinks and it skipped across the floor, leveraged out of its collar because it had been poorly seated. Brandani, still using his foot, did his best to put it back in place, but there it remained, off-kilter. The restroom was lit by a dim fluorescent light. Not only was there no toilet paper but there wasn't even a toilet-paper holder. 'Whoever built this restroom doesn't clean their ass,' thought Brandani before noticing the newspaper wedged between the drainpipe and the wall. Black spurts of dried shit embroidered the inner lip of the toilet, while the outer rim was covered with footprints and a little cigarette ash. 'They stand on it and use it as a latrine, one of these days they're going to shatter the porcelain.'

But once he stepped out of the stall to wash his hands, he was forced to admit that the liquid soap dispenser was *full*, even if the paper-towel dispenser was empty. Cigarette ash in the sink: the bathroom was a secret hideaway for people sneaking a smoke, as was the case in any office anywhere.

'At least put an ashtray in here,' the engineer made a mental note to himself, 'these disgusting conditions need to change, I want clean, fully equipped restrooms, by God . . .' He felt once again a strange sensation of strength, he was thrilled by the idea that it was within his power to order the improvement of those places and the material things that occupied them, and therefore both the streets of the District and the restrooms of its offices: physical deterioration had always stirred a state of impotent fury in him. For years, he had been reciting an old axiom of his: 'The only duty we have as men is to combat against chaos with the rationality of form, defy the deterioration and desuetude of time.'

The main stairs were inundated with the water that was leaking in great abundance from above, where there was a roof in transparent Plexiglas, and which resonated like a drum under the raindrops. The intermediate landing between the fifth and fourth floors was drenched. 'We ought to do something about that, too . . . But for now, better take the lift, even if it's only for one floor.'

In the hallway, a skinny young man, wearing glasses, was walking towards them. As he walked, he wobbled strangely, as if he was having difficulties with his motor skills, his neck kept twisting continuously to one side, making him bend his head and lift his chin, forcing him to look at things sideways. 'Here's

Collotorto, a born traitor . . .' Brandani thought to himself, though he'd never seen him or met him before in his life. The name Collotorto meant 'twisted neck', and it was perhaps the Italian equivalent of Uriah Heep, falsehood personified.

The young man went through a glass door with push handles, reached the stairs, looked down and went back to the lift, which they then took together. Collotorto looked to him like any of the many handicapped people—or 'disabled', or 'differently abled', according to the politically correct terminology, or, as Mother would once have called them, 'unfortunates'—who populated the offices of the Governorship. Instead, Collotorto, for the ten seconds of time in which they coexisted in that all-too-confined space, uttered several observations that were perfectly sensible, reasonable and well informed, concerning the massive downpour, and then said goodbye with courtesy and a sort of chilly and treacherous nonchalance, as he was leaving that cubicle of glass and anodized black aluminium, all scratched up with graffiti of tiny cocks and balls, out of which you could see the filthy wet stairs.

The dwarf in charge of the fourth-floor lobby sat sunk deep in an armchair in a room filled with furniture—old armchairs in a diarrhoea-brown Naugahyde. There was also a large black table with carved lion-pawed legs, the kind you used to see in lawyers' and notaries' offices many decades earlier. The dwarf's eyes were strange, shiny and violently blue. His puffy face had a smile plastered onto it.

Ivo inquired about the RB, and the dwarf pointed him to a pebbled glass door, on a spring. He entered, walked down a hallway and reached the RB secretariat, where a young woman with very long, smooth, shiny hair was staring at a television with the sound turned low, which was broadcasting a news report on the flooding river. She looked away from the set for a second, greeted him with a smile and cordially invited him to enter the adjacent room.

Brandani opened the door, stepped across the threshold and immediately shook hands with five people sitting at a round table, though he was unable to actually *see* their faces. Still, before sitting down, he did have time to notice that not far from the window there was a puddle of water mixed with sawdust, a bucket and a rag: the walls of the room were a bright salmon pink.

They introduced themselves: there was the Chairman of the Delegates, the Delegate for Culture and Schools, and the Delegate for Transportation and the Environment—these last two were women—and the Delegate for Public Works and the Territory. There was also a Delegate for Social Welfare.

While the chairman was reading the agenda for that day's meeting, everyone carefully scrutinized the new arrival, like fishermen who'd found a strange fish in their net and were wondering, So what are you exactly? Are you good to eat?

'I'm under a scanner,' thought the half of Brandani that was present in the meeting, while the other half worried about the origin of the water on the floor.

Outside, the splattering noise of that downpour straight out of the Pleistocene continued, constant and intense.

The chairman, who was a large, imposing man, smiled cordially, owning the room, dominating in particular the delegates, male and female, all of average height or less, and a woman who sat to one side, taking minutes on a notepad in her hands.

'The first order of business today is the mismanagement and inefficiencies of the Technical Unit, both in the face of the emergency and in ordinary administration,' the chairman began, 'but in the meantime allow me to greet the new director, Engineer Brandani. On this point, the Delegate for Public Works and the Territory will report to us.'

'Yes, now then. Let me begin by saying that I expected that as soon as the engineer arrived, he would have made a round of introductions, so that the delegates could get to know him. But that's not something he did. Oh, well, better luck next time . . .'

Brandani started to reply but the delegate, a small, smartly dressed man with a piping nasal voice, waved him off with one hand.

'Please, let me continue, afterwards you'll have all the time ... Having said this, I should add that we're very dissatisfied with the work done by the Technical Unit, at least the work done in the past year. Flooded roads, potholes, accidents, defective maintenance, new work poorly done, early deterioration, complaints from the citizenry, storm drains backing up, pedestrian safety railings knocked down, flooded basements ... We're facing various lawsuits that we're bound to lose, we're going to have to indemnify, those are funds we could have used in other ways ... And till now I've only talked about the streets. The problem of the school buildings is even more serious. For days we've been getting reports on flooding in various schools, at the Di Ruscio school there are two classrooms that they've had to stop using for lessons, they just teach those classes in the hallways now. The parents call us up and they're furious. Broken windows, defects in the electric wiring, the heating, even the phone systems, the intercoms ... '

The delegate went on methodically listing shortcomings, in a whiny, punctilious voice. He was doing his job and every now and then would look over at the chairman as if expecting a gesture of appreciation, but it wasn't to be. In fact, before long the chairman's cell phone rang; he answered, stood up and quickly left the room.

Brandani, who had already been having trouble following what the man was saying for the past several minutes, suddenly felt a surge of panic rising inside him; he was flooded with a profound and ancestral sense of guilt. It was like a regurgitation of Original Sin that produced a flush of heat and then a cold sweat that started dripping down into the middle of his chest, into the hollow of his sternum between what had once been his pectorals: 'These people have it in for me, because I'm now the *Man in Charge!*'

As he was reaching into his inner jacket pocket for his wallet, where he kept a blister pack of anti-anxiety pills, he told himself it was time to fight back: 'Keep calm, Brando, don't forget that you've been here for two and a half hours, all this stuff, all these shortcomings, negligence etc., can't be blamed on you, you realize that, right? Not even the flooding, nothing—but *nothing*, I say.'

He continued this thought process aloud, saying: 'Yes, Delegate, we'll try to take care of matters as soon as possible, but for that matter, as you'll surely understand, I can't really be up to speed on the situation yet . . .'

'Engineer, let me finish . . . Excuse me, but haven't your technicians briefed you yet?'

'Yes and no. Proietti, I believe is his name, is on leave. The other one, who's in charge of schools . . . Marcotulli? Right, Marcotulli is on holiday. Technician Basile did tell me a few things, but on the run . . .'

'What? With the mess we have on our hands, you let them go on holiday, on leave? We aren't beginning at all well, Engineer . . .'

'It's not as if I let them go on holiday, Delegate. Let me remind you . . .' His voice quavered slightly, bitterly, betraying the panic that was starting to flood through him. 'I-got-here-today . . . If someone signed holiday requests and days off for today, that someone wasn't and cannot possibly have been me . . .'

'If that makes you happy . . . Let me be crystal clear, Engineer. Starting today you are the *Man in Charge* in this agency, and so you're answerable for it. I don't want to seem brutal to you, but if things aren't going well, you are the one who can expect to be held to account for it. Any member of this organization, inside or outside of the office, reports to you. To be even clearer, if something grave happens, you can expect to be hauled into court . . .'

Brandani was struggling to contain his panic, his armpits dripping with sweat. He was frightened, tense, irritated. The others sat silently and gazed at him with a very effective expression that conveyed many things and all at the same time: 'Who even knows you?', 'Sure, we were laying an ambush for you, and now you've *walked into that ambush*, what the fuck do you want to do about it?', 'What kind of fish are you?', 'We don't trust you, don't deceive yourself, you won't be getting any special treatment', 'You're in our hands now, you'll answer for every act you take.'

But all in all, what Brandani—mute, by now completely overwhelmed by the surge of panic, hoping against hope for the anxiety pills to kick in—saw in all those gazes was something that struck him as unmistakably evident: 'We are mediocre & nasty. To us, you're no better than anyone else. Don't trust anyone in here.'

The summation and diatribe against the Technical Unit—called for on the agenda as intimidation, pure and simple, for the incoming director (since the outgoing director had left several days ago and was now living the high life in some central office equipped with clean bathrooms complete with toilet paper and powerful electric hand dryers)—continued with the various speeches of the individual delegates.

The Delegate for Schools, a woman who was endowed with a blond and savagely curly head of hair, reiterated point by point what had already been said, adding that this was a simply unacceptable state of affairs. Brandani's objection that no one had made a proper request for bids on the school maintenance work at the appropriate time fell on deaf ears: the potshots continued. The Delegate for the Environment and Transportation, a dark-haired woman wearing a grunge sweater, complained about the fact that the streets were literally underwater and that no one had done anything. She also turned a deaf ear to Brandani's objection concerning the entirely exceptional nature of the weather event currently underway, a downpour that was abundantly outstripping the capacity calculated for the existing storm drain system. It served no purpose to offer the example of a faucet left all the way open and a sink that, even with the drain open, would eventually inevitably overflow: the delegates were *politicians*, each of them had to play their role as a politician. There was a certain logic to that. Beside himself and irritated though he might be, Brandani understood that. They were telling him: technical explanations and administrative considerations are of no interest to us, we don't understand them, they don't fall within our jurisdiction, all we care about are results and results are what we want to see *immediately*. The Delegate for Safety was strangely gentler than the others, saying that he didn't want to give the new arrival the impression that they were heaping blame on him for things that hadn't been his responsibility, even though in the end he reiterated the concept:

Brandani was the new *Man in Charge*, and therefore . . . (he needed to get things under control).

At last, the anti-anxiety pill he'd dissolved under his tongue took effect and the two divergent Brandanis, who had each been following separate trajectories since early that morning, began to chemically converge, until they were once again one Brandani.

That one Brandani began to wriggle out of the death grip, defending himself with words and glances, but to no discernible effect because, in the meantime, the thing he had feared was happening, his panic was being replaced by a drop in blood sugar. For that matter, it was already 2.35 in the afternoon and none of those present were giving any sign of wanting anything to eat.

For Brandani the first low-blood-sugar sweats were already beginning but the delegates seemed unfazed, they weren't hungry.

'They must have had a late breakfast, that's why they aren't hungry . . .' the engineer was just thinking when the secretary with the shiny smooth hair threw the door open and cried: 'She's gone!'

'Certainly, the chairman left, he had an appointment,' the Delegate for Interventions said promptly.

The secretary replied in something approaching a scream: 'No, no . . . the River! She came over her banks at Ancestral Bridge!'

In the adjoining room someone had turned up the sound on the television set. Everyone leapt to their feet, hurried out of the salmon-pink room and clustered in front of the set.

Brandani started to get to his feet, but he felt weak, his hands were shaking.

He pulled out a box of liquorice and tossed a handful into his mouth: that would help him to get over his low blood sugar. He sat there listening through the open door to the special edition of the television news broadcast. The throttled voice of the correspondent was betraying great emotion.

'. . . the River overflowed its banks at twelve minutes after two this afternoon on a line with the Ancestral Bridge, spilling over the parapets with a sudden rise in water level that may perhaps have been attributable to the damming effect produced by the bridge itself once the water rose above the tops of the arches . . . Ten or so minutes ago, when the water level began to look threatening, there was a general rush to get away from the banks . . . The people clustering along the parapets began to run, in haste and hurry we moved our broadcasting location to the terrace of a school not far from the Bridge, which is where this footage now reaches you from . . . It is an apocalyptic sight . . . A horrifying mass of water is spilling over into the narrow lanes of the ancient city, devastating and overwhelming everything in its path . . . We now repeat, for anyone who may have just tuned in: the River has overflowed its banks only on the side of the left parapet—looking downstream— and it's flooding the City . . . Such a thing hasn't happened in a hundred and forty years, that is, since the construction of the stone embankments . . . The City of God, which has experienced devastating flooding in the past, felt certain it could never again be hit so brutally, but instead . . . We saw cars literally swept along by the rush of water and slammed one into the other . . . Down there is a heap of cars, forming a sort of dam and worsening the situation in this street, where the water level has risen almost to the second floor . . . The vans with our technical equipment are also about to be submerged, we don't know how much longer we will be able to continue broadcasting . . . We've watched as people were swept away by this murderous mixture of mud and water, the whirlpools are powerful and violent . . . There are people clinging desperately to street lamps, traffic lights, they're shouting in terror . . . You can still hear people crying for help, shouts from the street below, from the ground floor rooms, from the basements . . . Unfortunately, right now no one can do anything . . . We have seen many vanish beneath the surface of the water in just seconds, flailing without being able to find anything to hold onto . . . No one, I repeat no one, can do anything for the . . . *scrr* . . . Our line has been cut off, we now resume broadcasting from our studios located to the north of the City, quite close to the banks of the River . . . There does not appear to be any immediate danger here, but we are moving to our upper floors all of the most important equipment that will allow us to go on broadcasting in case the embankments give way . . .'

Brandani felt his blood sugar starting to regain altitude, but he still stayed sitting where he was, amid those bright salmon-pink walls, as he detected a muffled agitation coming from the room next door.

'The City's going underwater, Brandani. Do you care? Can you say that you really care? No, eh? As for you all, *You'll never take me alive.*'

He decided to pop another 1-millimetre Xanax under his tongue.

Outside the plate-glass windows, there they are, the aeroplanes.
He's moved, getting comfortable on a seat in the first row to be
able to see everything conveniently. If the Egyptair flight is on time,
he has an hour to wait, but his aeroplane hasn't appeared on the
landing field yet, it hasn't been announced on the display yet, the
gate is still deserted.

Why are aeroplanes so beautiful?

It's a question that's been occupying his mind for many
years, ever since his class in aesthetics, when Professor Cremaschi
made the distinction between *form* and *conformation*, between
aesthetic intentionality and dis-intentionality. Faded notions, of
which nothing now remains but some sediment that's settled to
the bottom of his earlier mind, once ancient and philosophical,
by now almost entirely overwritten by the subsequent, not always
victorious, engineering mind. In all this time—the years he's
devoted to becoming at all costs a structural engineer, a maker of
bridges, only to find himself now, at his career's end, working as a
construction-site consultant for a major developer in the North of
the Peninsula—he's toyed incessantly with the concept of technical
form. It doesn't strike him as complicated, it's been clear to him
from the very start, that is from the day he heard it set forth by
Cremaschi: 'Have you ever opened the rear-engine compartment
of a Fiat 500? You have? Good. Well, that's *technical form*. You
may like what you see or you may not, but it wasn't built for you
to like it, that is, with an aesthetic outcome in mind, as is the case
with the bodywork. Under the lid of that rear-engine compartment,
what you're looking at is something designed and built only for
its technical function, which is to give power to the engine, with

no aesthetic intention whatsoever. Or almost none.' Of course, what counted was that *almost*.

Almost, Professor? Why didn't I stick with my studies of philosophy? Why did I think I needed to be an engineer? What were you thinking? Have you forgotten about the Firth of Forth Bridge? Have you forgotten that afternoon? The only clear-minded afternoon in your whole life, Brando . . . Clara asleep in the car, the cold, that gigantic structure, way up high, above your head . . .

'I said "almost" because, if you carefully observe the individual components of the Fiat 500's engine, here and there you'll glimpse intentions of form and not merely technical conformation: the carburettor casing, the Bakelite distributor cap and so forth. Whoever designed these components had a certain margin for manoeuvre—limited, admittedly, but nonetheless—and made certain arbitrary choices, which we can only describe as *aesthetic*. Careful, now, this is important: here, by "arbitrary choices", we mean choices that are of no interest as far as the principal function, which remains technical, is concerned.'

Well, Cremaschi was right. But in that case, how should I think about an aeroplane's beauty? Ours, in fact, has just arrived. It's one of those Boeings made of a composite material, a 787, built in a single piece, or almost. They weigh less, they have better fuel economy, but there were problems with the prototypes . . . Seven-eight-seven stands for 'July 8, 2007', the date set for the first flight, but those poor suckers weren't done in time, as usual the schedule was too tight: the first flight was delayed practically two years, that is, until late 2009 . . . Who can say how many heads rolled in that situation, too? The wings are too long and thin for my liking, actually, but by now that's the way things are being done: it seems to save fuel . . . It's not stopping here, that isn't my plane after all . . . This one isn't heading for the City of God, and in fact it looked too big . . . Blue tail unit, blue engines . . . A handsome blue . . . But the picture of the god Horus, I'm not sure that would have been my first choice . . . Is that Horus? I think it is . . . I've always thought that the Egyptian gods are unlucky, that all of ancient Egypt is bad luck, starting with Him, the Unnameable One.

Depressingly, he touches his balls through the sweat-soaked linen. It's an involuntary gesture, something he does whenever Tutankhamen's name is mentioned, or say the city of Samarkand. Just the thought of such things prompts the act. He claims he doesn't even believe in such things, but he does it, all the same. It's an infection he caught from an old friend, a classmate back in university. He too said he didn't believe in it, he'd grab his balls and laugh: but you can never be too safe. As a little boy, Ivo had listened to a radio drama based on the discovery of the Unnameable One's tomb, and what later happened to the discoverers. He still remembers the archaeologists' whispers of astonishment, and the way they echoed in the grotto of that accursed tomb. And then there was the movie about the mummy, the curse of the mummy that awakens and roams through the night, dragging after it its train of tattered bandages. There's nothing he was more scared of as a child than mummies, and they left him with a deeply impressed phobia when it comes to ancient Egypt.

Grabbing his balls is an idiotic thing to do, but no dumber than lots of other things, including the Restoration of the Coral Seabed of the Red Sea . . . So, that's not my plane after all . . .

What about that Egyptair flight that went down because one of the two pilots was determined to commit suicide? When did that happen? In the '90s? A huge dispute between the American civil-aviation authorities and the Egyptian ministry of transportation. Where had he read that story? Or had he seen a show about it on TV? Step by step, as the truth emerged, the Egyptians that were on the investigating panel curled up like hedgehogs, refusing to admit even to the possibility that things might have gone that way, the national airline would have been too badly damaged by those findings. Then they'd found the black box, they'd reconstructed the entire sequence of events, there were no lingering doubts, but the Egyptians had received orders from the top and they rejected, denied, boycotted, set up stumbling blocks.

Nice story, but only for all the people who weren't on that flight . . . One of the pilots had decided to throw the plane into a nosedive with all the passengers, there'd been a fight with the co-pilot. Beyond belief. Then it had happened another time, but in Morocco, I think, not with the same airlines . . . I wonder if my pilot today is happy with the life he's leading . . . I always think that a pilot needs to do things right, first and foremost to make sure that he isn't killed . . . But what if the pilot doesn't care if he goes on living?

Brandani hums softly under his breath to chase away that sudden fear that always sweeps over him right before he boards a plane. Over the last thirty years, he's taken hundreds of flights, but every time the uncomfortable realization descends upon him that he is about to entrust his life *entirely* to someone else's care, someone about whom he knows nothing. A flush of heat rises to his cheeks. He begins to sweat. He tries to focus on the large flying machines that he sees outside, on the traffic, on the take-offs and landings, he attempts to decipher the technical operations, the personnel busying themselves around the aircraft, he wonders what their responsibilities might be, whether they're doing their job well. He's taken a Hyper-Aleve, it dissolves under his tongue, and twenty minutes later the strange headache is better. He doesn't know how to put up with it, because he gets headaches only very rarely . . . And after all, it's strange, first thing in the morning like this.

I can't take it, and why should I? There's time for suffering. The final suffering is almost certain, so why should I *put up* with a headache if I can avoid it without any real consequences? What the fuck does it mean to say 'medicine is bad for you'? You're saying an analgesic is bad for you?

The burst of sweat and the surge of fear start to fade. Once again, Ivo has returned to watching the aeroplanes raptly. He's spent a lifetime in admiration of all flying machines: aeroplanes, helicopters, missiles. He's even been interested in hot-air balloons, dirigibles and hang gliders. When he was a boy he built plastic model planes, the kind you could buy in clear cellophane bags from the news vendor, complete with decals. At first he'd worked on a P-40 and it had captured his imagination, then one by one he'd made nearly all the model planes of the War, especially the planes flown by the RAF, the Hurricane and the Spitfire leading the pack. He'd also assembled a Stuka, Boeing B-17 and B-29 bombers, the de Havilland Mosquito and the Mustang P-51 fighter. Then came the aircraft that were destined to become his two idols, his guiding lights, one American and the other Russian, destined for places as the Dioscuri flanking the Sacred and Unequalled Spitfire: the F-86 Sabre and the MiG-15.

No one knows their names now, no one knows anything about them. They clashed in the skies over Korea, the Americans had made a couple of movies, one was with Mitchum, I think. Who remembers Mitchum any more? They always won, but later I found out that it wasn't true, not entirely true, anyway. The MiG was a good-looking plane, with that gaping maw, like a manta ray, its towering tailfin, which looked like the dorsal fin of a killer whale. The F-86, on the other hand, had that snout, a less murderous appearance than the MiG, less wicked looking, it was on our side, it protected us from the Communists. The Americans added pictures to the gleaming metal fuselages, women in bikinis, decorations, they gave a name to every plane, and then there were stars and stripes everywhere, red and blue, numbers . . . The Russian fighter jets, much more understated, a sandy beige, a red star, the CCCP logo, the aircraft identification number. The pilots' helmets, at least to judge from the snippets of documentary that they spliced into the movie, were *still* made of leather, while the helmets worn by the Americans were already rigid and colourful. Still, the MiG was a dangerous foe: better armed, easier to handle, tighter turns, faster, higher ceilings . . . Deadly dogfights, they shot to kill, fearlessly . . . Father said that in war you're just scared, everybody experiences it . . . I'm afraid just thinking about it: fights to the death . . . I'm afraid even just to board an Egyptair Boeing 787 for the flight home . . . I've been flying all my life, and always with the same fear . . . Those were magnificent, expensive pieces of machinery . . . They'd explode in the sky, wings sheared off clean by the ammunition from the on-board cannon . . . Grainy black-and-white footage, you could see the trajectories of the tracer bullets, trajectories that slewed off-kilter, sinuous like handfuls of incandescent rocks, instead of running perfectly straight the way you'd expect, they way they looked in the comic books. *Whaam*! The enemy fighter jet would start spewing smoke, losing parts, tilting off to the side, or else it turned belly-up, or the tail might be shot to bits . . . Just a split second before, it had been a glistening thing, intact, and an instant later, it had turned into a swarm of wreckage. Men who died like that . . . Who could say what it must be like to disintegrate in mid-air in a MiG, to die torn to shreds in the chill of the high thin air, before the eyes of a practically black sky . . . All right, but why were they *so beautiful*?

That's the question that he always asks himself again when he's at the airport, the question Brandani toys with whenever he has time to kill. He's jotted down lots of notes on the subject, but never come up with anything solid in reply. A long-standing philo-sophical predisposition that's always there, lurking in ambush, a mind that continually harks back to those two years in the depart-ment of philosophy, studies that remained impressed in his mind, or perhaps he should say, carved, deeply etched: the course in aes-thetics under Cremaschi, the few lessons in theoretical philosophy under Molteni, before the Movement put an end to all teaching. Most of all, his books. Molteni, who had left an indelible imprint on his mind, still lay concealed in the words he used, as a man and as a technician, in the way he organized the materials he needed to think. 'Don't ever be too intelligent, all that's good for is to make matters more complicated . . . If you *are* intelligent in the first place,' he'd muttered once during a seminar. 'The truly intelligent know how to rise or fall to the mental level of the others, they immediately understand whether or not they're going to be under-stood, they don't strut, they hide, they learn how to handle them-selves. It's pointless to deploy great forces if there's only a short distance to go, and especially if it's counterproductive, if it irritates the person you're talking to . . . Intelligence, when shown off, can be intimidating, irritating, in other words, stupid.' Molteni had grown inside him over the years, he'd become flesh in the flesh of his cranium, electric impulses along the networks of his exhausted neurons, which struggled to remember everything, much as might have happened to his teacher more than forty years ago: 'What's

72

the name of the author of that textbo-o-ok . . . Ahem, let me see, the one who wrote that textbo-o-ok . . .' His teaching assistants hastened to offer suggestions but he kept answering 'no-no-no . . .' which sounded like an exhortation, like a 'come on, put some effort into it, let's see who can be the first to guess.' It was a kind of game, Molteni found it amusing to pit them against each other, perhaps he was only pretending not to remember. It seemed as if he felt contempt for them, not one of them was anywhere close to his level, there were those who said that he selected them carefully to make sure that he had teaching assistants who were absolutely mediocre, dull and servile. Franco said that Molteni ensured that no one around him could grow, 'he's a horrible man, an academic power-monger of the very worst kind, and yet he's a maestro . . .' Ivo had only spoken to him once, when he'd dropped by the institute to ask him a question about an issue discussed in his book. Actually, he was there to bask in the spotlight, he wanted to get noticed. Molteni's answer had been very simple, straightforward, disappointing. Ivo had had a retort, arguing with the quick-witted intelligence he possessed at the time. A brief discussion, then Molteni had fallen silent for a short while, looking at him with those blue eyes of his, bright and lively behind the lenses. At last, slowly, and as if he were reflecting aloud, he'd said to him: 'You might be one of those pseudo-intelligent guys . . . what's your name again? Ah, that's right, Brandani. There are people like that, you know? The ones who always lay it out as if it's super-complicated, who seem interesting because they formulate problems in a way that looks original, learned, but that's as far as they go . . .' For Ivo it was a deep cut, and a gratuitous one, which still smarted more than forty years later.

Maybe he was right, I'm pseudo-intelligent. He must have wound up in Hell, together with Schoolteacher Proia . . . Why are aeroplanes so beautiful? Perhaps that's a poorly formulated question, or else it's a pseudo-problem, typical of someone who's pseudo-intelligent. Franco used to say no, that it struck him as a genuine problem, but he also used to say that he didn't know anything about aesthetics. He suggested books to read, things that turned out to have nothing to do with it, or that were too difficult. My head still hurts . . . The double dose of Aleve ought to be working already . . . And I'm going to have to take a dump soon . . .

Ivo Brandani emits one of his deep sighs. The woman sitting next to him turns to look at him for a second, her curiosity piqued. Then she goes back to her tablet.

Why are aeroplanes so beautiful? The narrow cockpit clung to the pilot like a flying jumpsuit . . . It was as if somebody had constructed around a human being a compact silhouette capable of flight . . . Behind the three-bladed propeller, the V-12 Rolls-Royce engine, 500 horsepower . . . Behind the engine, the fuel tanks: if they caught on fire, the pilot would go up in smoke in a single puff . . . Behind the fuel tanks, the cockpit with the teardrop canopy: looking down into it the aeroplane's structure was instantly unveiled to your eye, that naked framework, as bare as the rear of a stage set, aluminium beams, chilly to the touch when they came in contact with the pilot's body. The Spitfire was a piece of flying skin, a costume worn by a superhero. The thing I liked most was the elliptical shape of the wings, the way they joined with the fuselage, with a sort of membrane that tapered back towards the tail, until it disappeared, absorbed into the curvature of the side panels. I liked these fluid forms that were, however, made up of lots of riveted pieces . . . You could clearly see underneath the wings the exit holes of the burst of machine-gun bullets that the Spitfire in the City by the Sea had caught before bellying down onto the water, the shreds of sheet metal splayed open in a corolla due to the force of the impact . . . From the gaping wounds in the fuselage and the wings, but especially from the tail rudder, almost completely stripped bare by the machine-gun bursts, you could make out the aeroplane's structure, the dense framework made up of ribbing and spars serving as an underframe, giving shape to the aircraft's skin . . . I adored the smooth, neatly joined curvature of the flying surface, or perhaps I should say, of the flying *form* . . . Machines, any machines, we always tend to build them in our own image: a structure that holds everything together, the way the bones do, then the internal organs sort of arranged here and there, and on the exterior a thin wrapping, which works more or less like the skin, that is, it summarizes, protects and, like the skin, can break at a given point without the entirety being decisively compromised by that break, in contrast with what happens if you damage a major organ or the structure as a whole gives way . . . If we were crustaceans, we'd build with a crustacean mentality, no internal structure, just organs and muscles and tendons, the protective function would coincide with the tough structure and it would all be entrusted to the outer shell, like a lobster. But if we were crustaceans, it would never occur to us to build aeroplanes, only tanks . . . Then there was the Mustang, and I really loved lots of other fighter planes, but the Spitfire was . . . Well, it was *perfect*. And it was perfect in the most perfect way imaginable. Handsome, noble and fast like a large pelagic fish built for the air. It practically didn't have a top or a bottom, if you leave aside the cockpit, the tail fin . . . The Sacred Spitfire just sits there, guarding the first half of the twentieth century, testifying to the involuntary attainment of beauty and strength, tapered and joined and shapely as a boomerang, an exceedingly modern and ancestral product of the War, a total and unequalled synthesis of the art of attack and flight . . . I know that the Messerschmitt 109 and the Focke-Wulf 190 might have been faster, more heavily armed, more powerful, but they had this basic shortcoming, this unforgivable defect: they-weren't-Spitfires.

That's it right there, all of the Well Made of the twentieth century, the perfect form that sprang from the necessity of overcoming the enemy. I read that the engineers wanted to achieve 'the smallest, simplest fighter plane that could be built around the Rolls-Royce PV-12 engine'. Well, they certainly did it: they created that one-of-a-kind object, right there before me, reassembled on its pedestal, I could go to look at it every single day . . . It was the preterintentional beauty of the Well Made, achieved not in order to stir feelings and awe but to attack and defend, to destroy and get away, using atmospheric gas as the load-bearing structure, high-explosive gunpowder as the offensive weapon and fossil fuel as the energy source. I'm a pacifist, my secret sin is that I worship war machines, I envy those who have experienced combat, I admire those who have lived in the space between the two alternatives of Life/Death . . . To me that old hulk of an aeroplane was sacred, a holy totem looming against the horizon of the Western Sea . . . Certainly that beauty, evident but devoid of *intention*, derived from an evolutionary process that has endured over many generations of aircraft, one attempt after another, the path of adaptation to flight, towards the greatest possible aerodynamic efficiency in relation to the power of the engines . . . Every technical innovation on the enemy's part *had* to be met with an even more daring and advantageous invention: it was a matter of life and death for the pilots, a question of survival for the nation . . . The competition among fighter planes resembles that between gazelles and cheetahs, which wind up resembling one another . . . The Sabre F-86s and the MiG-15s, which to my mind are *still* pursuing each other and fighting in the skies over Korea, have actually been doing it for millions of years: each generation survives if it's a little more efficient than the one that went before it, faster, able to dodge and fishtail suddenly and rapidly, faster and faster . . . The beauty of aeroplanes is a *natural beauty* . . . The lines of the aircraft used in civil aviation are more abrupt, less integrated, less fluid than the lines of the aircraft I loved. As if in the meantime the air had become lighter, easier to penetrate. And perhaps that's the case, considering the altitudes they fly at . . . Yes, that's it, it's because of the cruising altitude, practically stratospheric. They climb rapidly through layers of air that are progressively less and less dense, until the sky turns almost black—nowadays, that is the habitat of passenger planes, bombers, fighter planes. Then there are the spy planes that go even higher, much much higher, where there is no air, where there is nothing left but infrequent molecules of air that must be captured one by one with enormous wings . . . I'd like to build a model Spitfire just one more time . . . They could lower it with me into the grave, resting on my chest, like a cross . . . 'Hey, look at what we have here. It's a tomb with objects from the twentieth century. This must have been a British fighter pilot . . . That was a fighter plane, wasn't it? Maybe he died in combat. When did they use this kind of plane? I'm not really sure. First World War?' Just think how many glaring mistakes of chronology, of dating we make of objects found in graves. That novel I cracked open years ago in a bookstore . . . Right in plain sight on the first page of the book was a tremendous mistake that I was probably the only one to notice: a bombing raid in 1944 was being carried out by B-52s, a historical obscenity, the B-52 was an aircraft from the Cold War, it dates back at the very earliest to 1955 . . . You were furious, as usual, you wanted to write a letter to the publishing house, make a phone call to lodge your objection, demand that the editor be fired . . . By now you know what your disease is called, IMS, Irritable Male Syndrome, it hits men around your age. Your anger is typical, there are books on the subject, the legacy of Father, the Wrathful One, has nothing to do with it. Perhaps he suffered from IMS too, maybe a case of early onset—the way I remember him, he was always like that, always every bit as much of an asshole . . . I told a number of people about this glaring error, B-52s in 1944, but nobody gave a damn . . . It didn't strike them as important . . . 'This aeroplane or that one, what's the difference?' What do you mean, *what's the difference*? People aren't as interested in aeroplanes as they ought to be, if the author had put, say, a kind of car that didn't exist in 1944, everyone would have noticed it, I think . . . The past is being lost, the Spitfire in my grave would completely derail the archaeologists of the early 5000s, that model might be the only surviving evidence of the existence of that fighter plane . . . But you're going to have yourself cremated, it's not going to be a problem, you're going to wind up fertilizing basil plants. In some distance future your atoms might wind up in some girl's tits, right there, at the tip of a nipple: it's the carbon cycle . . . There was a time when the rudder, the wings, were joined to the fuselage, slabs of aluminium with beautiful curvatures . . . Now planes aren't built that way any more. They don't have to fasten things together any more. The wings are inserted into the fuselage in a hard, decisive way. Look at that rudder—what is it, a 777? The rudder is a precise trapezoid, inserted into the back of the fuselage, without invitation . . . The shape of the tail isn't affected, it doesn't accommodate it . . . But it's all beautiful just the same: they make them the way they make

them, I still like them all. *Why?* The MiG-15 had this huge tail rudder, with the horizontal stabilizers situated quite high up, it looked
like the dorsal fin of a shark. It could reach the speed of sound and
at that velocity it could hold its own or nearly against the F-86
. . . No one really knows who won, the Americans and Russians
still fire off numbers picked from a hat, but in the final analysis,
most likely it was the US that won. The Sabre was less interesting
than the MiG, it was a little too American, a little too full of itself,
but maybe I liked the shape of its wings a little more than I
did that of the Russian fighter jet . . . The F-86 had the snout of a
basking shark over the gaping maw of the air intake, the tail rudder was much more traditional than the MiG's. The MiG was simpler, more severe, more spare and essential, newer, better looking.
More dangerous & more Soviet. It had forms dating back to sub-
sonic technologies, rounded wing tips, perhaps the only part of the
MiG I didn't like . . . The tail angle was as pure as could be, I liked
the large air intake and the circular cross-section of the fuselage,
very Soviet, Suprematist . . . Perhaps there really did exist a margin
of stylistic freedom, maybe that aeroplane wasn't pure *technical
form* . . . It gulped in air through two large symmetrical gills, and
the flow was channelled down two conduits split in two to make
room for the cockpit, so that the pilot sat right in the middle of a
ferociously violent torrent of wind, which was compressed behind
him, thrust into the engine, set aflame, and transformed into a controlled delirium of fire: more than two metric tons of thrust, I can
still remember the figures . . . It was an engine disguised as an aeroplane, with just enough extra material to let it fly with the agility
of a bat, pure power with a man serving as its brain . . . Having
one of those things under your ass, sitting there, at the tip of the
snout, in a space with just the bare essentials for survival . . . In
American movies the Asian pilots wore black helmets, had cruel
yellow faces: they always got shot down in the end . . . Often the
footage was authentic, with *real people* inside the cockpits, people
really dying in the skies over Korea . . . You were just small,
Brandani . . . The instant in which those men died was inserted
into the realm of cinematic fiction and remained in there for all

time . . . Like in footage of big-game hunting, the instant in which the bullet strikes the elephant's cranium, the tiny burst of dust that it kicks up as it tears through the flesh, shattering the cranium . . . Now you see combat aircraft that can be very ugly, angular planes that fly badly, built not so much to travel through the air, but to elude radar. The Spitfire is the most beautiful aeroplane ever built, the most elegant and aristocratic. There was a compact, consistent idea behind it . . . I'd ride my bicycle out to it, always in the early afternoon, when the sea turned dazzling and the west wind blew hard . . . It was hot, the wind would chill the sweat under my T-shirt, there was a clearing overlooking the shoals, where someone had planted a few scrawny trees, withered flowerbeds, benches, a small fountain . . . And then there was the Spitfire . . . I'd sit down to look at it, I'd walk around it, there was never anyone there, the sacred Idol of War stood there, angled on its pedestal, they'd installed it in a dynamic pose . . . It had one broken wing, the blades of the propeller curved backwards from the impact, the tail rudder, destroyed by cannon fire, was reduced to an aluminium framework. The cockpit canopy was missing, maybe that was a sign that the pilot had bailed out, but as a whole the aeroplane was intact. Intact but wounded, humiliated, the belated false trophy of a lost war, in a Country that had been unable to build anything like it . . . Then they took it away from there, restored it, and now it's in that museum on the lake . . . With that warplane, the English *couldn't lose* and they didn't lose. *We* were the ones who lost. '*We're* the ones who lost the war, whatever they tell you,' Father used to say. Then, enunciating his words clearly: 'This is how things went—we joined the war as *allies of the Germans against the Anglo-Americans* and we left the war as *allies of the Anglo-Americans against the Germans*. What do you think we should call that? If someone calls it *treason* they're not far wrong . . .' 'My father, when he heard that I was dating one of you Peninsulars, told me that you're all traitors.' That's what Lotte told me: 'He fought in the war, try to understand him . . .' I now believe that she must think the same thing, all these years after I simply disappeared . . . I left her to get an abortion, all alone, in Germany,

I didn't even have the money for the ticket . . . The Sacred Spitfire, I went to the museum just to see it again, it was hyper-new, it looked like a fishing trophy, a taxidermically preserved fish, shiny, stiff as glossy cardboard . . . They'd emptied it of its technological viscera, no engine, nothing at all, exactly the same as a taxidermist does with an animal, leaving nothing but the skin, every trace of the drama of warfare had been deleted, the aircraft was brand new again . . . I wonder if the pilot got out alive? And if so, who knows if he ever found out that his one-time fighter plane is now sitting in a museum on the shores of a lake, buffed and polished so that it looks like a model aeroplane? The Messerschmitt 109 was to the Spitfire as the Sabre F-86 was to the MiG-15: it was a specific adversary, that is, suited to the clash with an exact counterpart, with known velocity, ceiling, manoeuvrability, armament, every-thing . . . The Me-109 was a handsome aeroplane, but so *German* . . . No one outside of Germany would have agreed to let it fly with those *struts* under the tailplanes, the way it was in the first version, *anyone* would have come up with another solution. The Sabre and the MiG were still planes, and then there was the F-104, which in contrast was a stone, even though it was streamlined, powerful. Inside it was the ideology of the rocket, which in those days was pushing to replace the ideology of the aeroplane. Every now and then some machine will become too purposeful and specific, exclu-sively dedicated to a single characteristic, one function, to an exces-sive degree . . . For the F-104 it was velocity—it was a beautiful monster but it was practically without wings. The Americans understood immediately that it was a mistake of an aeroplane, a giant lung that was all-engine, and they foisted it off on us . . . These jets fell out of the sky like pellets of hail, the people who lived in towns near the airbases went everywhere with their heads scrunched down into their shoulders for fear that one of those gad-gets might come crashing down on top of them. And sure enough down they would come. This one outside here is made of carbon fibre, a few big pieces assembled together. They're light & flexible, planes breathe, under stress they deform, they twist, they're elastic, and yet they punched straight into the Towers like knives into hot butter. You could see that Boeing impact with the facade, immersing itself into it, the material of the tower no longer existed as a solid thing, under the blow it behaved as if it had become some sort of foam, instantaneously. At work we discussed it for days and days: Why had the Towers fallen? The jets sailed in from one side nice and smooth and emerged on the opposite side having turned into pyroclastic conglomerates, plasma, except for the engine which in the videos you can see falling into the plaza below like a ball of fire—it penetrated the tower and plummeted like a rock out the other side. The stairway-lift bank core was very solid, if it had just been a matter of steel against aluminium it would have been an uneven match, but the decisive factor was fire . . . I turned on the TV around 3.30 in the afternoon, I'd come home early that day . . .

Brandani hadn't felt well and had left the office about 2.15 p.m. A stomach ache, he doesn't remember now, maybe an attack of colitis. At home, afterwards, he felt a little better, he sat down at his PC and was involved in a chat session, when someone typed in: 'Something's happening in New York. Turn on the TV. Maybe it's a movie, I can't really tell.' It did seem like a movie, in every way, but it was showing on the news broadcasts on every network. At first he was stumped, and then he was breathless. Even the television news reporters on the line from New York were confused, they didn't know exactly what to say, they couldn't believe what had happened, they were talking about a plane crash. No one understood what was happening, but in the instant that followed the impact of the crash into the second Tower, the reality of the terrorist attack became blindingly obvious to everyone.

I thought that the core of the Twin Towers was cement, that it was a very rigid structure, but that's not right, they were too tall, the weight would have been excessive . . . So the core was built of steel, a forest of pillars clustered close together, supestrong; well, many of them were sheared clean in half and the ones that survived melted after not even an hour of exposure to the flames . . . All that dust was the floors disintegrating: a hundred floors pancaking, pulverizing, and all that paper that started flying in all directions, the streets were full of sheets of letter-size paper, for blocks and blocks: words . . . Along with the lives of three thousand people, the first things to be lost were words . . . Written words, contracts, confidential reports, correspondence, financial prospectuses, business plans, memos, bound summaries, carefully drafted, dossiers with pie charts, pages to be laid on the boss's desk that very morning . . . Words already read and filed away, archived. Words still waiting to be read, edited, proofread. Spreadsheets, calculations, the same things that we produce, the mountain of paper that overwhelms us every day, there it flew free in the sky . . . The WTC was full of paper, printer ribbons fluttered in the wind like snakes, ghosts in the sky over Manhattan. They looked so solid, gleaming, Cartesian, the Twin Towers . . . But it was a temporary order: inside, like in all buildings—it took me years to understand it— lay nested a chaos of forces reconciled in spite of themselves, contained under restraint, channelled along precise lines and frameworks . . . Modern collapses are different from those in the ancient world, in those piles of rubble you can recognize the components that made up those buildings . . . The Greek temple is an array of independent elements, you can consider them as parts, but also as wholes, that is, with a dignity and a formal completeness all their own and which persists even after a collapse: plinths, capitals, shafts of columns, architraves . . . Instead, when a modern building collapses, it is the utmost form that plunges into the utmost formlessness, into chaos, into the saddest and most unmitigated of wreckage. Nothing is recognizable, nothing can be recovered. Nothing, or practically nothing, remains of the Towers—just a couple of fragments of the facade in an expressionist pose, immediately hyper-photographed and used as icons . . . As Franco says: 'The Americans are the best at funnelling mass emotion into visual synthesis . . .' I can't bring myself to think about it: twenty thousand . . . Twenty thousand human fragments mixed with steel, shards of glass, tons of paper, pulverized cement, electric cables, scorched plastic . . . They tried to identify them with DNA, the victims' relatives provided clothing, dirty laundry. Months of searching, but in the end they brought it to an abrupt halt, many shreds concealed in the mass of detritus were purchased as scrap along with all the rest, and went into the crucible to be melted down, I imagine. They must have found lots of others later, in the dump, they must have tossed them into the garbage . . . That was the most awe-inspiring event of my life, even though I watched it on TV . . . The fate of the unfortunates caught in that trap, those resigned souls who settled their accounts with the world, people bleeding, in their dying agony. I imagine that for those who jumped, time simply stood still. That's how it was for me in my motorcycle crash and, even before that, during my fall into Bomb Crater . . . Since September 11th, fourteen years have passed for us, but they're still falling . . . They're probably still there, suspended in mid-air, asking themselves: 'Is this *really me*? Is this really my human body falling down off the World Trade Centre?' . . . What can their *death* have been like? I imagine a sudden, crushing sledgehammer blow. Yes, the Boeings penetrated the Towers as if they were butter . . . Fully loaded, these aeroplanes weigh at most 150 metric tons: take a Boeing 767 and hurl it in one piece against something at 500 mph, and it's possible to calculate the kinetic energy that is thus liberated . . . It's, let's see, the half the product of the mass multiplied by the square of the velocity, that's right . . . Now then.

He pulls his tablet out of his bag.

Let's see . . . 150 metric tons equals 150,000 kilos, 500 mph is . . . let's see . . . 730 feet a second . . . which, squared, 532,900 feet squared per second squared . . . OK . . .

He pulls his notebook out of his jacket pocket and jots down a note.

OK . . . 150,000 multiplied by 532,900, divided by 2, gives me something on the order of 3,675,000,000 joules, which is a little less than the energy released by a metric ton of TNT . . . Then you need to take into consideration the thermal energy from the burning fuel . . . According to the reconstructions of the 9/11 Commission, there were many columns sheared at the moment of impact . . . There's an official reconstruction on YouTube . . . What must it have been like for the terrorists to *die* in the cockpit? And for the passengers? A split-second, true, but how long does consciousness endure, for instance, in a brain flying into fire? The heads of people who'd been guillotined still rolled their eyes for a few more seconds . . . Affirmative, it was fire that made it all collapse, it wasn't the impact, terrible though it was, but the fire . . . Flying is counterintuitive, we ought to stop doing it. I ought to stop this idiotic work I'm doing, here in Sharm . . . Stop it all, plop down in front of the TV for all the time left to me . . . Travel only by boat, along the cliffs, and never fly again . . . And after all, what is energy? I mean to say: What is energy *really*? You say 'the quantity of energy . . .' Or you say 'the quantity of motion . . .' And it seems like everything's taken care of, it seems that everything adds up: quantity, motion, energy, these all seem like clear, intuitive concepts, unquestionable, unobjectionable, like force, pressure, molecule, etc. . . . We've let science pull the wool over our eyes, they've given us words that have an exclusively mathematical meaning, concepts that can be expressed only through equations and an equation is a tautology, it's saying that something is commensurate with something else: the mystery remains, at least for me . . . *E equals M times C squared* means only that the energy contained in a body is equal to the mass of that body multiplied by the square of the speed of light . . . the *Speed of Light* . . . *What really is* energy, *what is* mass, *what is* speed, *what is* light? What does it *really* mean to multiply a number by itself? Nothing can be expressed per se, everything, even the simplest things, can only be stated in reference to something else . . . And this is a curse, there is no handle, no nail driven somewhere that serves as an absolute point of reference, that can begin the process of reasoning: the fluidity of knowledge, or rather of non-knowledge, in fact, of science . . . But still the most incredible thing is that it *works*: the planes out there fly thanks to a series of equations. That is, it's not the equations that make them fly, Brandani, the equations only tell us how to build them so that they'll fly, they tell us the necessary conditions for flight, the relationship among the parts, the curvatures, the air foils, the power of the engines, they tell us how to build the engines to keep the heat from melting them. It is from them, from the equations, that we draw the principles, some of which can be stated in words, though most can't . . . Once you've formulated the principle, you rely on it, until another can be formulated, a 'truer' one, but it's just a process of bringing the unknowable back to the perceptual and mental means that we've evolved, over several million years, on the African savannahs . . . The strange thing is that organisms aren't mathematizable, that is, not quite yet: we still don't have an equation that will tell us how to make a cat, there is no theory of a cat, just as there is no theory of a human being . . . Perhaps we really are mathematizable but no one's been able to do it yet . . . They say that the mathematics of life is chemistry, all right, but *why*? That is, why is mathematics stumped by life? Why is it capable of representing only a few, a very few, of the phenomena of non-life? We the living are too chaotic, Brandani, we are configuration, not form, we have a-geometric outlines, as shifting and indeterminate as the outlines of clouds, like the borders of nations on maps, like the leafy sails of trees . . . This is chaos . . . The configuration, that is, the non-form of things derives directly from the Big Bang . . . How can we expect there to be order if we live, or actually, if we *are* what's left over after an *explosion*? Or better yet, no, we're not the *residue* of the Big Bang, *we are* the Big Bang, because the explosion is still going on, the All is still blasting apart, we are exploding matter inhabited by some exceedingly rare episode of aspiration to order, to geometry—an orbit, the imperfect sphericality of a planet, the structure of a crystal, the line of the horizon, an aeroplane—that is, with a few initial fragments of regularity in the overall irregularity, a few seeds of purity of which perhaps Matter, sooner or later, will take notice, from which it could take an example to regulate itself and allow itself to be expressed in simple equations . . . And so we too can aspire to the Reflective Sphere, to absolute cleanliness, the flavourless, odourless, colourless: purity . . . Purity cannot be other than mathematical: the aircraft outside of here are the purest, blindest and most innocent objects we know. They are mathematical objects and are among the most beautiful there are . . . Certainly, inside them is human intent, and in some cases it's an aggressive intent, as was the case with the Spitfire and the Messerschmitt 109, but it is precisely the intent that drew them out of the chaotic post–Big Bang state in which we are immersed, it is intent that reconfigured a portion of disorderly matter into matter with a purpose, crystallized in the beauty of adaptation to flight . . . And it was all done through the grace of the mystery of mathematical measurement, the manipulation of numbers and concepts without there being any *real* need to *understand them* . . . That is, most of us, even those of us who work in the field, have never managed to understand them and those who have succeeded were unable to explain it to us in words, only in equations . . . And equations work, Brandani, they work and how . . . Even if you wouldn't remember how to formulate one by now, any of the equations that long ago you were taught to formulate during your course in the Science of Construction . . . You don't remember anything, you never built a bridge, or maybe I should make that: you never built anything at all . . . You did other things, you've only ever organized construction sites for other people, a builder of *conditio sine qua non*-s, an explorer of possibilities . . . You're a technical hustler, Brandani, and that's not what you wanted . . .

The Sense of the Sea

Thinking back on that song, singing it to myself, in my ears, so that no one can hear me while I do it, brings back to me the Sense of the Sea. But not always. Certain times it doesn't work.

I don't even know how I learnt to perform the 'Valsalva manoeuvre', without meaning to, without realizing I was doing it ... It's perfect for use underwater, to compensate for the pressure. And in an aeroplane, to unplug your ears. But it also works as a way to sing a song to myself, inside-to-inside so that only I can hear it.

The first time that the Sense of the Sea formed inside me, there was *Voce 'e notte*. That was the piece that played most often on the jukebox, the song heard most frequently on the platforms— marble with a light grain, dusted with sand—where at night we danced.

In those nights out there was something ... a promise of water and of the future, a sense of distance, a complete physical faith in what I was and what I was becoming, as if on the sea and in the sea anything could happen, as if destiny were there and nowhere else: not in the City of God, not in the fucked-up construction sites dotting the world, which is in fact what my destiny turned out to be. It was an indescribable sensation, difficult to reproduce now, looking back ... It was an error of judgement, one of the many I committed.

Here it's different. On moonlit nights, there comes a moment when you go all the way to the end of the pier in search of the Sense of the Sea, and every time it's as if you're about to grasp it, but then it refuses to be taken and instead moves away. Tonight I'll do the same thing. There is no doubt that the word *nottata* in

Italian has a meaning very different from the simple word *notte*, which just means night. A *nottata* is a night out, a night without sleep, whether you can't or just don't, a *nottata* is the unspooling of a night, an epic of the time of darkness. A *nottata* is when you don't sleep, or can't sleep, it's when you work all night long, it's a night in which someone leaves this life . . . When Mother died, that was a *nottata*. *Nottata* is a watch at the helm of a boat sailing through these islands, it's a night in a sleeping bag on the deck of a ship. *Nottata* is when you make love one more time and then you go out looking for something to eat, and then the two of you come back to your room, lock yourselves in and do it again, and you think, 'This is something I'll never be able to do without.' Another error of judgement . . . *Nottata* is when the moon in the sky corresponds to the hours that the night affords you, until dawn appears on the water, the strangest, coldest moment, when it's pointless to stay any longer and best just to leave and lock yourself in a room to sleep.

You could only catch a whiff of the Sense of the Sea just after nightfall, *a prima nottata*, when all the city's lights along the bayfront were glowing brightly, when the breeze wafted the smells of cooking to you, grilled shrimp, fried seafood and music, when you could see the outlines of boats with fishing lamps heading out to sea and you heard the chugging of an old diesel boat engine, the shadow of a man sitting at the helm while another man readied the boat. You have no words for the Sense of the Sea, you can't tell anyone else about it, but you know that it coincided with those old lampara fishing boats against the line of the Tyrrhenian horizon. Later, you experienced it when you went out squid fishing with Nereas, when the fishing caique left a wake of luminescent foam behind it.

The Sense of the Sea from many years ago, when the Summer was endless and more closely resembled a geological era than a season of the year. The Summer that shaped you more than winter did, the doing nothing that was so much more important than school. Stocks of vitality being laid in for future years, lean years. Lean years, indeed.

The Sense of the Sea came all at once and unannounced when I was a boy and I leant out for the first time from a balcony on the sixth floor of an apartment building overlooking the harbour of the City on the Sea. This first act of stretching out over the sea was one I committed without thinking in the early days of June of some unspecified summer in the late '50s. It was a sort of perceptual shock that practically left me breathless.

It's late afternoon, smells and colours never before experienced, the sea never before glimpsed. That is, not from this point of view and this height, but only a few times before, from the beach, at the water line, so to speak—waves, green water, grey water, murky with sand. Here there's only the intense azure of a smooth, spherical surface that stops at the sharp border of the horizon. The water has a different surface quality, it seems solid, with striations of wind, areas that—it takes me a little while to understand—are ruffled by the air. The air is blue as the water and smacks intensely of the sea, it carries with it two or three strong strange scents, verging on the disgusting. The stench of rotten fish that rises from the equipment of the fishing trawlers and fills the entire harbour below. The odour of tar, hot iron, sawn wood, grease, welded metal, the shipyard that occupies the wharf area. The complex stink, transported by the wind, of seaweed and salt water, of the wet strand, of cement encrusted with shellfish, of rust in the final stages.

With the passage of time I realized that that wasn't the smell of the open sea, they were only miserable whiffs of the battle between land and water in the domestic port of the City by the Sea. That instant of perceptual stupefaction contained a promise of pleasure, at the time impossible to specify, that the sea (and the sea alone) later fulfilled far beyond all expectations.

Those were the initial instants of the formation of a specific sense, which blended Water and Summer, a single unutterable concept, not actually expressible. It was the paradigm of life in winter that was overturned into its exact opposite: put away all your clothes, four months in a bathing suit, no shoes, no washing, you have the sea for that, nothing will ever be truly dry, everything will reek of damp and brine, impossible to ever really get rid of the sand that sticks to your heels or the sand that works its way into your crotch, between your swimsuit and your thighs . . . The abolition of all schedules: meals at any time of the day or night, stay up as late as you like, sleep in until one in the afternoon when the best breezes for sailing spring up, everything is optional—by the end of September I'd forgotten how to write my name. We ate stuffed rice balls on the beach and ate smoked mozzarella at home, frittatas with zucchini and split tomatoes, cold spaghetti that sat awaiting me in a bowl covered with a plate until four in the afternoon, rice salads, oven-broiled rice-stuffed tomatoes, stuffed zucchini, eggplant parmesan. It was the utter collapse of Being as Duty according to the expectations of Father and the establishment of the reign of Being the Way You Please under the tolerant and companionable reign of Mother. Then the Sense of the Sea took flight from that beach, from that port, from those reefs, to set up housekeeping elsewhere, on another basis, with other materials, in landscapes that were more open, more solitary, more mysterious, more vital. More violent, more imperious, simpler and more mature, like this one . . .

Comfortable plastic chairs that must have cost nearly nothing. You find them everywhere. Some of them broke fairly easily but this one seems to be a fairly solid model . . . It all depends on the material and where you place the ribbings, they have to line up with the points of greatest strain, it's no simple matter, it takes some careful calculation. I'd like to know what weight load they're tested for, the characteristics of the material they're made of and how they test them. Already my weight is a considerable burden, I can feel the chair deforming beneath me, the legs splaying, as it adjusts to my 200 pounds . . . I need to lose weight, even these trousers are starting to be too tight on me. In the '60s, the industrial designers of the North of the Peninsula made some nice chairs, but they were expensive, uncomfortable and a little heavy—these are just the continuation of those by other means.

Everyone buys these Allibert brand chairs, it must be some kind of multinational . . . Who can say whether these chairs are going to last for eternity, like plastic bags. Greece is full of them, the world is full of them, it's the global democracy of the chair, elements of planetary socialism. I find them almost-pretty, they seem to have been made of a single sheet of plastic, hot-pressed and folded as needed, they are an outstanding synthesis of form-function-price. And they're stackable . . . This ought to be modernity, that is, mass quality: affordable objects that last for all eternity and are quasi-beautiful. For all eternity, literally speaking, plastic lasts for ever, it breaks down into microscopic fragments that make their way into living creatures and then enter us with our food—we're full of plastic. In a million years what will remain of that chair? What dump will it have wound up in? When they uncover it, they'll put it in a museum; dumps will be the happy hunting grounds for the archaeologists of the future, full-fledged cultural deposits, complete and carefully stratified, with inside them everything that we are . . . Even now an excavation into a dump from the '50s would tell us what that world was made of . . . I lived and forgot the '50s, just like all the decades that followed. That's the way it is for everyone, it's a mass forgetting, every thing, every person is forgotten, lost, it's just a matter of time . . . I took the second Xanax at six o'clock, so there's still time for the third. I'll take it after dinner, it'll help me sleep. Today I almost forgot it, when I'm feeling all right I forget them and then it hits me hard, and all at once. The blister pack? Here it is, right in my pocket . . . A cigarette.

'Karelias are the poor man's Marlboros, Sara. I finished the carton of Gauloises and I don't feel like smoking. These cigarettes don't give the same fist to the lungs as the French ones do, when you can feel that you're getting hit with that nice fat puff of dense yellow smoke, loaded with nicotine. The marvellous stench of Caporal tobacco, oh how I miss it. In this wind, Gauloises go out easily, but how good is a ciggy smoked halfway down and then relit?'

'Those cigarettes are just disgusting, Ivo. The Karelias don't stink like that. If you don't like them, why don't you try the Papastratos?'

'I used to smoke Papas before you were even born and even then I hated them, Babe, but they do have a wonderful Flavour-of-Greece. I smoked them the first time I came down here on a trip with my school, in 1960, I think it was . . . Ever since then, the odour of Papastratos gives me a sort of flashback, it takes me back to that year, when I was young and a complete jerk.'

'Are you trying to say that you *used to be* a jerk and now you're not any more? Are you sure you don't want to come?'

'Please . . . I was hoping you wouldn't ask again. You go without me.'

'I'll go, I don't want to come off as the usual boor. I don't feel like *always* being rude.'

'I don't care what people think of me. I'm comfortable here. Then I'll go get something to eat somewhere . . . But the tableful of thirty people is more than I can handle. You know that I can't handle it, so why do you even bother asking?'

'OK then, *ciao*, now I'm running late, too.'

Now she's gone too. She's had her fill, as usual. Certain times it seems that Sara doesn't know me. She needs to stop trying to change other people. By now I am what I am, I can only modify a few details, and even then it isn't all that easy.

Alone at last. It's getting dark, Cape Atreides passes from purple to dark blue, later it will become practically invisible, but under the moonlight it will step back on stage. I adore that mountain, I consider myself to be one of its subjects, its contemplator and its servant. I come here every year to see It. To watch it change colour at this time of the evening, to be able to analyse every rocky inch of it, to watch it hurtle sheer down into the sea, to admire it as it builds its cloudy crown out of nothingness, continuously . . . It spins that cloud like a spider, all day long, and the wind shreds it away into fragments that it then dissolves piece by piece at some point over the horizon, right there, where those last tattered bits of pink are disintegrating right now. I like to see them vanish way up there, while they can still catch the light of sunset. I like to sit here, after a shower, with my cigarettes, even if they aren't Gauloises. I like to be inside this old blue two-pocket shirt. Once it's really worn out, I'll have it framed . . . I like the way these trousers accommodate me. I like having my feet in these Tevas, even if the plastic inners tend to burn the soles of my feet a little bit. I like the way the backrest of this Allibert twists and bends when I change position.

Olives, ouzo and cigarettes, this faint burning sensation down my oesophagus after a day on the sea. It's irritated by the salt spray that comes down through the mouthpiece. I don't mind it a bit. The exhaustion, my fingers sliced by the sharp rocks, the hole from today on my left palm—how it hurts. The tremendous quills of the sargo. Never once do I manage to remember that I'm supposed to grab them by the eyes, instead of from under the gills. If I water down the ouzo it smacks too strongly of liquorice, it burns a little less, but I get less of a bang out of it. Better to drink it straight, with maybe a little ice. That sargo didn't deserve to die, it wasn't worth it anyway, it was too young. When you want to catch something at all costs, you wind up shooting at newborns: how can I hold my head up when I walk into a restaurant, or if I go to Nereas, carrying that little baby sargo, and ask, 'Could you cook this for me please?' There was a time when we had eight or nine pounds of fish every night, there was enough for ten of us. A minnow like this one at the end of the day is something you give away, just toss it into the basket of some kid on the beach. You give it to Bruno, he's not picky, he takes anything and has it all cooked up for him. He always buzzes around Ugo at night, he stays within earshot, just in case there turns out to be a fish dinner he can take part in, whatever the company. There are people who go crazy for fish. Personally, I like it less and less with the passage of time, it smacks of alien, the smell is at the outer bounds of the natural, the healthy, as if the minute it died it was on the verge of rotting. If a living fish is too full of life, too full of energy, speed, strength, a dead fish is too dead, as if the world, after creating something so marvellous, perfect, silvery, were in a hurry to reabsorb it. It is life in its smoothest, purest, blindest and most voracious version—it seems that the All has some furious urge to put it away, such a thing, to take it back. You need to take care to keep fish on ice, then eat them in a hurry . . . That dentex years ago . . . When we bought it, it was nine in the morning and it was still alive, in its death throes in Nereas's net, its mouth yawning open and shuddering so powerfully that you couldn't stand to look at it. A mouth like a dog's, 'Look out for the teeth!' Nereas had said, laughing and baring his own, so strikingly similar to those of a sargo. Long story short, that night we had to spit out that wonderful fish—it must have weighed ten or eleven pounds—into our plates because it had gone bad, and Nereas was mortified, saying over and over: 'I can't understand why . . .' Here's another flaming blast of ouzo, like an X-ray of my oesophagus. Hot stomach. Olive. Gulp of water. Treatment complete.

'Aren't you coming to Nereas' place?'

'Hey there, Alfio! I hadn't seen you, *ciao*! You want an ouzo? You going to come keep me company? No, I'm not coming . . . Listen, I just don't feel like it, you know I don't like big tablesful of people. And what is it with these people . . . They travel everywhere in a group . . . I don't know, we've talked about it before . . .'

'OK, Ivo, I know this song of yours. What am I supposed to say about it? Everyone here knows it. No one takes it personally, you are the way you are. I'll take a sip of yours, is that OK? Jesus Christ, this ouzo is shitty! Doesn't Kalliope want to serve even a drop of decent ouzo?'

'I like it the way it is, Alfio. I prefer it to the so-called *good* ouzo. I just like this kind . . . That is, *here* I like this kind. It's part of the place, I sort of grew up on this ouzo, these olives, Kalliope's chickpeas. To me, they're all part of the Island package, they're not things you can split off, I'm not looking for high quality, I'm looking for *this place*, it's what I need. Listen: here, the ouzo *is supposed* to be awful . . . It's a default setting, it's programmed into it and I don't feel like changing things.'

'How many have you had already, eh?'

'Am I talking nonsense?'

'A little bit. But I understand you . . . I'm in agreement on everything.'

'Why do we all feel this constant need to tell ourselves that we like this place? And how much we like it? And why we like it? It's as if we felt obliged to justify to each other the fact that we see each other here every year . . . With the whole big world that's out there, we always wind up here . . .'

'It's because we basically feel like fools, Ivo, so we give each other a little comfort, a little solidarity. Every time I say to myself: Why the fuck do I have to go back there again this year? Who's making me do it? No one's making me do it, Isa wants to come too, but just like me, when the time comes to decide, when it's time to buy the tickets, she casts around for false alternatives, she makes suggestions that can't even be taken into consideration. This year she suggested Dublin . . . *Ireland*, I mean, you realize? Can you picture me spending my summer in Dublin? She does it on purpose, so that at the end we're forced to say, oh well, if that's the way things are then we'll just go to the Island. We even manage to tell each other that it's in our *best interest* to come here. Our best interest? We like it here! There's Isa, here she is now.'

'Aren't you coming, Ivo?'

'No, Isa. I don't feel like it.'

'Oh, Madonna, Ivo, you're so predictable! There's a big catch of fish tonight. And a couple of karavides. Big ones too.' Karavides were small lobsters.

'Yes, they're big, I saw them last night, they were getting them off the dinghy. No, I'm not coming. I really don't feel like it. Kalliope, ouzo, *please*! *Ciao, buon appetito.*'

There now, it's practically dark . . . Sitting here and getting crocked on this nasty concoction, that's fine with me for tonight, the tamarisk tree blocks the light from the street lamp, it casts a shadow and it hides me, anyone walking by won't see me. The sky is this unheard-of transparent colour, indescribable, it's changing instant by instant, it directly hits the layers of sensation I ought to have under my skin, somewhere.

I wish that I could make changes in all this, change the shape of Cape Atreides, dim the colour of the sky, to keep it from grabbing me the way it does, from dragging me somewhere I don't want to go tonight. Ahh . . . too big a gulp, burning my throat—water. Today I got sunburnt right behind my knee; after more than a week, I still get sunburnt, my ass cheeks are bothering me too, I could have put some Nivea cream on it, like Sara says, but I hate that greasy feeling. Still, I like the smell of Nivea, it's a time machine, it takes me back to the City by the Sea, it gives me a sense of Mother and Sisters . . .

The sea does its part too: this pier out front, so spare and unadorned, starts heading east, perpendicular to the beach, and then stops before it gets started. What is it—50 yards long? Not even. The usual three boats tied up, plus a couple of fishing caiques. And down there is the Red Caique: that violent, almost absolute colour. The deck and the mast are light blue . . . That decisive light blue that they use here for wooden chairs, for window frames and door jambs. They use a light blue or green enamel to paint the skirtings in the houses, the cafes. That same light blue is used to paint the hulls. It's the hue of the islands, we all know it well, in this light it gives you a deep and soothing pleasure. The Red Caique is all the more pleasurable to look at sunset, when the sun itself has vanished behind the mountain and all that remains is this rosy luminescence. While the shore is already shrouded in shadow, for a few more minutes the sun still strikes the open water of the roadstead. If the Red Caique is riding at anchor, it visibly seems to burst into flame . . . That's part of the pleasure I've taken ever since I learnt to sit and observe this stretch of water. I've done it for months and years, all the times I've come back here . . . The geographic room of this gulf: to the north is the Cape, a mass of rock that plunges in sheer cliffs down to the water, to the south is the Point, with the lamp, made up of red dirt eaten away by the sea, two completely different landscapes separated by this broad arc of beachfront. When I came here for the first time, here where

I'm sitting now was already beachfront, there were stones, it was shingle. Now it's cement. I don't have anything against cement, but I didn't want it here, just as I didn't want these faux-nineteenth-century street lights—they put out a hellish light, from the ship you can already see them twenty miles out, and from here they blind you, they erase the sea. I also didn't want this two-tier fountain in Renaissance style, I didn't want the reinforced-concrete benches and I don't want all the houses that they've built here since 1978 . . . Ivo, there's no point in pretending: you accept everything here.

I've been in negotiations with this place for many years, but we still aren't anywhere near a breaking point. First we'll take away this thing that you love, then this other, we'll cement over the beach, we'll throw up rows of holiday homes, we'll build a port for the ship, and to do so we'll dredge up out of the seabed mountains of wonderful boulders covered with millennia-old encrustations, riddled with holes bored by molluscs and sea urchins, studded with still-living sea creatures . . . Years ago that huge barge dredged those rocks up one by one and stacked them up beneath the Point, at night it would anchor right off this spot, they'd eat dinner outdoors under the crane, then they'd come to Kalliope's to drink and smoke all night long. The technicians did something incredibly stupid: all winter long they left the cement blocks parked on the beach right where the stream out of the gorge had its outlet to the sea. It was as if they'd put them there intentionally, carefully stacked up to serve as a dam. Incredible that no one here said Careful, here when it rains hard the channel goes into a tremendous spate. Then spring came and with the usual rains the bed of the torrent filled with water that came pouring down, the cement blocks dammed the outlet to the sea and the spate was bottled up . . . The village wound up under 10 feet of water . . . There are people who survived by a miracle.

'Another ouzo please, yes. No, no ice. No ice, please.'

And yet you came back. And you came back even after the Great Fire, when the Island's forests were destroyed. You came back anyway, even now that there are practically no fish in the water. These people are going to age, they're going to die. Men that you met in the prime of their lives, when they were paying out and reeling in miles of fishing nets every day, are going to retire but you'll come back. Maybe not every year but you'll keep coming back.

Twenty years ago, when Clara and I first arrived here, we thought we were dreaming . . . A land covered with forests, ancient people who spoke a Doric dialect of Greek, the women wore the traditional costume, there was no electric power, the beaches were empty, the wind blew hard and was dense with aromas, the sea was teeming with fish, the mountains were inhabited by goats and eagles . . . Here there was still a typological culture, practically everything corresponded to a type. As time passed I guessed what it was like, its dreariness shut off from the world, I understood what a type is and what it's good for, that is, why the houses up in the village are all identical, inside and out, and why the women dressed rigidly in the same way . . . Then, with the end of the isolation came the end of the norm and the typology . . . Everything that until just a few years earlier had been untouchable tradition now became a tourist attraction, antiquities. A sudden entry into the contemporary world, though without becoming modern . . . Way back when, it was the same thing for us Peninsulars, we happened to become contemporary without ever having been modern. It's a condition that comes with a bitter price: there's no longer any model, there is a loss of all aesthetic anchorage, all custom, all uniformity. In places where everything was once done in accordance with ancient norms, suddenly there springs up the freedom to *do everything* . . . Which is how we got to this point well beyond second hand, there are things that are third- or even fourth-hand.

Before, if you wanted to build a house here, or a boat, you already knew what it would look like before starting, without any preliminary design . . . In the uniformity of the objects there was a prior approval, a social consensus, which meant nothing unexpected could be produced in an isolated society, immobile for centuries. Then, twenty years ago, there was a sort of collapse: to their eyes every traditional custom became emblematic of provincialism, old-fashioned, retrograde, poverty-stricken . . . Nowadays the type has returned in the form of a quotation of itself, as something picturesque and folkloristic, for the purposes of tourism, but you can't force them to embrace immobility just because *we* don't like what they're doing now . . . The thing would be for me to succeed in not coming back here . . . It seems quite likely that by now the number of days I've spent here is greater than the number I can hope to spend here in the future. I'm fifty years old, I have a 40-inch waist. There was a time when I wore a 34-inch waist and I was already coming here . . . Every time, Nereas asks me how old I am. When I tell him, he exclaims: 'That's nothing!' This year he told me: 'Fifty-two is nothing!' He says it because he's almost seventy and he feels the burden of every one of those years weighing down on him. For someone who's lived a life like his, always out on the sea, he's remarkably healthy, but he's had to give up smoking and his hearing is shot. Thirty years ago he handled several miles of nets every day—a couple of hours to lay them out at night and the same amount of time to reel them in the morning after, at dawn. They caught lots of fish, they had seasonal labourers on the caiques: Tunisians, Moroccans, Egyptians. There were still boats that went out for sponges, with an air compressor and an air line for the divers. At night the Arabs would sit in the stern, smoke their hookahs and sell enormous triton shells. Even now there are fisherman, but who knows where they go. Off the coast, there's nothing now. These days, Nereas only uses his boat to take tourists to the beaches. He says that he goes out a lot in the spring and autumn, tosses out the trawl line with the small boat and he says he catches some nice fish.

He's a serious man, intelligent, proud, not given to imparting confidences, a hard worker, but now he seems tired, fed up, he wants to rest. He says that it's beautiful here in the winter. He says that they sit and talk and do things slowly: harvest the olives, look after the pig, the nanny goat. They go off to Piraeus to see their children. Or to America to visit other relatives. In Baltimore, in New York, which pronounced in Greek is *neaiorki*. I can imagine how Nereas must feel sometimes. He must think: 'Well? Is that it? Was that a life?' I'm sure that's what he thinks, because it seems to me I can see the question in his eyes: '*Is that all*? THAT'S IT?' And he's certainly seen it all and been through it all. He once owned his own cargo caique, before that he worked on freighters, he's been everywhere in the Mediterranean: a seaman, a skilled mechanic, a skilled carpenter, he built the house and the tavern all by himself, making mistakes in his design, making the beams too big. 'This is earthquake country, I asked an engineer to give me the minimum dimensions and I doubled them, you know . . .' He's a modern man, he reads books, he's attentive to and curious about new things, he never takes part in local religious rites: 'I'm a complete atheist.' He's told me that a number of times, his voice emphasizing that 'complete' and then cursing as evidence of his utter sincerity. He seems proud of his atheism but I don't believe that it's actually possible to be an atheist here, there's too much silence, it's all so bare and essential . . . He's a *faber*, a maker, like me, only I don't know how to fix engines and he does. I'm convinced that, in spite of a full and active life, in spite of the travel and the fish, Nereas still wonders: is this all there is? He knows that I wonder the same thing, which is why he once said to me: 'Don't think that your life is over. *Mine* is over, yours isn't.' He was taught our Italian language to the tune of face-slaps by the Fascists during the occupation, he speaks it well and he chooses his words with a certain care. Years ago, one afternoon when we were alone in the boat together, I asked him if he still enjoyed going to sea. 'More than ever!' he replied, and looked away . . . Those strange eyes of his, with the dark cornea, ancient Turkish eyes, welled over with tears. It was a blistering hot, windless afternoon, the Island's mountains had become remote, lightened by the mist, offshore the water was velvety and still. I could sense the surface tension of that liquid mass, a still, pearly expanse, with small distant ruffles breaking the calm, where some creature from the deep had decided to rise to the surface to graze on schools of small fish, which every so often you'd see leap out of the water, all together. We both fell silent at the same moment, I believe we felt something in unison, but each of us in touch with his own private, incommunicable heartbreak . . . You're drunk. Three ouzos on an empty stomach are more than you're allowed, you idiot. You're going to be sick . . . Do you imagine that you shared a sensation of cosmic loss in unison with Nereas? You must have dreamt it, he was probably thinking about how he was going to cook the octopus that Sara had asked to have for dinner that night. In those conditions of sea and wind, at that time of the day, everything gets tangled up, water and sky become a single thing—if it weren't for the foam that the hull produces, the sound of the engine, you'd feel as if you were sailing along suspended in mid-air, on the border of limbo. For once the wind doesn't roar in your ears and every sound produces nothing in you but a sense of estrangement and distance. The signs of life that appear on the water's surface accentuate the biological mystery of the sea . . . At that point, it doesn't take much, all that's needed is a conversation like the one you were having with Nereas, slightly different from the ones you always have, and for an instant it might seem to that you've been riven through by a consciousness of chaos, as the matrix of everything, yourself included . . .

We've known each other for years. But I don't know really know anything about Nereas, except for that pride, so unmistakable, his cursing. I'm not hungry yet. It must be all these olives and peanuts and chickpeas that they serve you with the ouzo. There it is now, rising, with the colour of a cheddar cheese, it's enormous. When the moon is full, I almost always sleep badly. Especially when I'm sleeping outdoors. That terrible night so many years ago, on the other side of the Island, I could practically feel it burning my skin: it illuminated everything as bright as day, there was no way to come to terms with it . . . But maybe it was actually the stink of mule piss that was keeping me from sleeping. These days, a night like that could probably kill me, they'd find me dead the next morning: *Aegean Sea, Italian engineer dies of full moon.*

Nereas used to lose his temper with his ship's boys all the time, he was also firing them and hiring new ones, and while they worked for him, he treated them like doormats. Except for Khristos, not him. He looked like the Yugoslavian actor Bekim Fehmiu, the same face, skinny and muscular, he wasn't forty yet but he'd already lost all his front teeth. And the other one? Dark-haired Georgios. He was the one who caught more abuse than anyone else. Young, stunningly handsome, he made no distinctions between men and women. He slept in the caique, surrounded by cockroaches the size of heifers, and the stench of fish. Still, every morning there was always one human shape too many emerging from below-decks. The time that those two Nordic girls, slightly rotund, sunburnt, apparently pleased at having chalked up a Greek fisherman, while he complained in English, sober-faced: 'Too much work, this night, eh . . .' The women laughed and revelled in the fresh air. No one but me seemed to think there was anything awkward about the situation. I was there for the fish, I was putting on my wetsuit, looking ahead to the dive into the waves at the foot of the cliffs that would soon start my day underwater. Just think, I envied those young men who worked like dogs on Nereas' caique . . . I'd got it into my head that they were *free* men . . . Salt-encrusted pants and T-shirts, callused feet gripping the deck even in a strong swell, they hopped from island to island working on fishing boats, sleeping on board, drinking at the bar every night, and always finding someone for sex. It wasn't hard, back then the Greek Fisherman was *in*, provided he had the right physique: long hair, a week's stubble, skinny and muscular, dressed unpretentiously, shod in sandals—a primitive, an outcast. These were the '70s, that's the way we were, these were our legends, I was in that culture right up to my neck, the same culture that made me envy them, because the Greek Fisherman was part of a cluster of potential 'alternative' ways of life. It was a sort of mass fantasy world: level-crossing guard in New Zealand, Postman in Ireland, lighthouse keeper who knows where, woodworker, craftsman, member of a farming commune, vagabond, full-time biker and so on. And, of course, Greek Fisherman. This was the series of bullshit fantasies we amused ourselves with, to keep from looking directly at a reality so out of keeping with our confused expectations. We still thought we lived in a time of changes, even though those changes had already been made and locked up in a sealed envelope in a safe that sat who knew where: in your envelope, it was written 'Structural Engineer Who'll Never Design a Thing'. We couldn't even begin to suspect that our work really would be our *whole* future, that we were going to have to play out the whole game there, inside the triangle of work-family-free time. In your future, there was a bar on a beach in Costa Rica, or in Mexico, not being an engineer, even though that was what you were trying to become after changing your major, what you'd spat blood for during the first two years, the Biennio, and the successive three years, the Triennio. That thought was always there: *You'll never take me alive.*

But in fact you took your place in the great Chain of Yes. At Ediltekne you say yes to your direct superior and he says yes to his. Before Ediltekne, you did the same thing at Megatecton, where you'd nourished too many illusions . . . There you committed certain errors in judgment, you were still just a kid, you fell in head over heels . . . By now it doesn't even sting any more, it's twenty years ago now . . . From Sofrano you could just glimpse the Island, there was just that ridge of high mountains over the horizon, the clouds . . . You didn't succeed in worming your way into any of the troikas of professionals who were friends of this or that party. Do you remember that group of careerists? They were my same age but they knew a lot more than I ever did—they were out for themselves, cold, distant, and they quickly learnt to swim in the world as it was then. The first thing to be done was to join a political tendency or movement and then, if you could do it, figure out how it worked. You were never able to figure it out and you took refuge at Megatecton. If things hadn't turned out the way they did, it would have been a good idea—now it's the people at Ediltekne who tell me: Now do this, Now do that, Go here, Go there . . .

Forget about a bar on the beach in South America—*this* is my South America. From a certain moment on, this is where I took up my true residence. It was in 1987, with Clara—we were both enchanted by this place. For me, after years of separation from the City by the Sea, it was a return to Summer and to the Water Mother. The water was denser than it is at home, especially at sunset, when the hollows between the waves grew purple, turquoise: primordial water, dense with life and yet, especially at dawn, so transparent.

Year after year I saw things that I'd never seen before, I got an idea of the sea, perhaps no more precise than the one I already had but certainly more in keeping with the ferocious vitality of what really happens there . . . The moray eel that lunges suddenly upwards, hurling itself into a school of grey mullets to sink its fangs into their bellies, only to fail . . . The groupers when they're hit vomit out half-digested octopuses that, pale and limp as ghosts, are set free into the water, but dead now, and they settle white on the seabed as a silent warning. And again, moray eels come in to shore to vie for the fish as you're cleaning it—you feel a jerk and there just inches from your hand is that mouth, those yellow eyes. Then there's that triton stretching out of its shell, eager to suck down a living spiny spider crab. You see the octopuses do the same thing, and then they decorate their lair with the empty skulls of their victims, just like the savages did in *The Phantom*. This is ferocious water, where day and night there is a never-ending lunge and twitch to kill, sink fangs and flee.

This is the last year, after this I'm done, it's no longer right for me, I lack the necessary cruelty, a harpooned fish fills me with pity, remorse. And then there is the cold, the hard work, the fear of being stuck down there, of not being able to fight my way back to the surface—that makes my breath catch in my throat. The darkness of the lairs where groupers hide, when they're deep, you can see something big moving fast, you glimpse the convex silhouette of a back or just a fleeting shadow of the oversized head of an old Inca fish, when you have at the very most a second to pull the trigger and if you hit it, you're going to have to haul it out of there and if it's big then it turns into a real struggle, a bloodbath for you and the fish. Enough is enough, I never want to do it again. Those goat skulls, those downturned lips with a sneer of indifferent contempt, those large mobile eyes that seem to be hinged on some kind of gimbal: groupers have practically vanished . . . Lately I've run into them only occasionally and I've always hesitated at considerable length, unable to pull the trigger, as if in some hypnotic trance. I spotted the biggest one of them all in the waters off the sheer rock cliff, how much could it have weighed? It was floating under a rock shelf, its face in the sunlight, and when it saw me it had a sort of lurch, and so did I—too big, too beautiful. The water was shallow, I could have done it, but I remained there, motionless, grasping the rock with one hand, entranced; between me and him, and he was certainly a male, there was a bond of some kind. I can't tell anyone about this but there was something, a sort of correspondence of emotions, a brotherhood of creatures sharing the same planet . . . Underwater, you have experiences that are silent, intimate, which last just seconds . . .

Now, when divers go after groupers, if they want to find them they have to keep going deeper and deeper, they dive stubbornly, spending four or five hours in the water, exhausted and chilled to the bone, and they do it to make sense of being here, so that they can *banquet on fish*, like we did tonight. Platters with the day's catch at the centre of Grand Banqueting Tables, the litter of dismembered karavides, the towering heaps of skeletonage stripped bare from teleosts, organic material, gooey and greasy, decorticated craniums of all kinds of fish, lives from some distant planet, totally alien, and all that is left to show for it are the eyes blanched from the oven and the red of the gills . . . Each and every fish-design, whatever the species, no matter how many millions of years it's taken to construct it, no matter how much beauty and wisdom it possessed when it was alive, is profaned, dismounted and deconstructed, ingested, assimilated and then shat out: all that *pure life*, tidily assembled into the fish-creature, is reduced to a single faecal substance and winds up joining the human excrementary flow of every day. Millions of glittering free lives that are turned into shit . . .

The silvery sheen of the schools of grey mullet off Kalamia, large as your arm, fast as U-boat torpedoes. All you need to do is show up when they start to come in to the coast in the early afternoon. The minute they see me they have a thrill of interest, more than fear, and for an instant curiosity wins out . . . What are you? Are you dangerous? Then they always do the same thing: instead of fleeing into the blue depths, as you would expect them to do, they lunge towards any potential safe shelter, they dive into the first cavity they find. They never go very far, you can usually see pretty clearly where they've holed up, so you take a deep breath, you descend, you align yourself just off the seabed, with your arm extended, you introduce the speargun into the lair, then you have a couple of seconds to identify the fish and shoot. To get free of the harpoon, they burst into a sequence of deranged writhing jerks, you have to get your hands around them and hold on, or they're probably going to make good their escape . . . No one ever taught me these things, I learnt them on my own, under the water . . . If you hit it from above, in the centre of the head, you might not even penetrate a grey mullet, and in that case the fish will vanish, leaving you just a few scales from the cranium, floating in mid-water. Their bellies are soft and easily torn open, so if you hit them too low you'll lose them, and watching one flee with its guts trailing behind it isn't nice. You have to chase it, the wounded fish, and track it down somewhere in the vicinity, as it lurks in the shadow of a jutting shelf of rock . . . If you do manage to find it, you see it puffing, leaning against the rock, in the agony of pain, of impending death. Hit a second time, it will still be capable of struggling furiously, and if you failed to target it dead centre this time as well, it will flee again, slower and slower, wearier and wearier—you *have* to chase it and kill it, but how many times, out of tiredness, have you let a fish in that condition get away? Underwater fishing was a ferocious, irresistible passion that you first contracted as a little boy during the summer in the City by the Sea, when you explored the Little Shoals with an old-fashioned speargun in hand—it's a passion that's lasted all this time, but now it's starting to wane . . . What sense is there in killing a 65-pound grouper? Anastasios has done it many times. Once he would hang them from that tamarisk, the tail touched the ground, the whole town stood in a circle around him. After the public display, he sold it off in strips in a separate venue. Anastasios, so kind on land, is a ravening beast in the water, some kind of fish-man. As a little boy he'd come with us on Nereas' caique, he'd be gone all day long with a handheld fishing spear, he'd catch octopuses and tuck them into his swim trunks. At the end of the day he'd climb back into the boat, his face pale from the water, his lips blue, with a quantity of tentacles squirming out over the elastic waist, they'd wriggle and writhe, cling to his thighs, climb up his back, crawl over his belly . . . Then he'd pull open his swim trunks and detach them one by one from his genitals, extract them from his ass crack, where those poor creatures had been agonizing for hours, he'd give them one last sharp bite between the eyes, toss them into a bucket, and so long octopuses.

For these seabeds, Anastasios is the apocalypse, he kills anything, he captures every living thing he spots, he takes up any creature that appears even remotely edible. The time that I saw him land at Papa Minas, when he'd grown big and strong and hairy, wearing a torn and tattered half-wetsuit, he was carrying an old crossbow, and the mesh creel tied to his waist was bulging beyond belief. He was tired, he was on his way from the village, he'd been fishing for at least four hours. He emptied the mesh creel onto the stones on the shingle beach. Inside was every sort of creature imaginable, a vast assortment of the life forms found off these coasts, like in some seventeenth-century still life: dying karavides that were slowly waving their tails, the death throes of parrot-fishes, sargos, grey mullets, honeycomb groupers, wrasses of various kinds, even an umbrine, scorpion fishes, date mussels, octopuses. He collected all the sea creatures he'd scattered across the beach, carefully killed the octopuses, put everything back into the net, then tied the net to a rock, sank it in the shallow water by the shore, and fell asleep in the sun. I imagine that at the time he had the certainty of the unchanging nature of a sea that would never cease to bestow its creatures upon him . . .

This year, Anastasios and I made a deal: at the end of August, before I leave, I'm going to sell him my speargun and everything else he could possibly need; I'm turning over a new leaf, I'm done with fishing . . . From now on, if the sea is going to die it's going to have to do it without any help from me . . . I no longer want to kill a single living creature, with the possible exception of the occasional mosquito, a cockroach or two, if I really must. In fact, starting tomorrow, I'm not going out any more, no one can force me to: whether I stop now or in fifteen days makes no difference; when you can see that everything is getting worse—*because everything is getting worse*, always and everywhere—you can decide to pretend you don't know it, or even if you know it won't do any good, you can stop helping make things worse . . . that's what Ugo does, he pretends that there's still plenty of fish, he knocks himself out, going out every day to catch as many as he is able, at night he weighs his catch on the beach, piles it up in Nereas's freezer, then he has these long drawn-out dinners, where he sits at the centre of the table like Jesus Christ, dispenser of food, surrounded by apostles & apostlesses in short shorts, beachwraps, miniskirts, linen trousers, impalpable chemises over shoulders reddened from the day out on the sea.

Giving up underwater fishing means you're going to have to abandon the watery depths, the prehistoric avalanches of rock on the north of the Island, the vertical plunges going straight down at the foot of the sheer rock cliffs, vanishing into the blue. Abandoning the seabeds to their imminent future as watery deserts, never coming back, knowing nothing more about them, not having to witness their violation and deterioration, which won't stop . . . Forgetting the sight of a yard-long yellowtail emerging without warning from the deep water, passing close to take a look at you and immediately, with a single vibration of its caudal muscles, it accelerates and goes back into the blue before you can so much as lift a finger . . . Forgetting the mid-water encounter with a vast school of *loutsos*, pike fish, as straight and coordinated as a shower of medieval arrows, alive, so vibrantly alive. I'd only ever seen them before dead in the nets of the fishing caiques in the morning, with those huge staring eyes, the strange mouth, the aeronautic chin, prominent & oval, to fend its way through the water as efficiently as possible, the sharp, dangerous teeth . . .

It's not worth the trouble to come back here next year. I no longer have the light heart of a tourist who knows nothing about the places he fetches up; by now, I know everything about everyone here, and in particular I know the way things were *before*, I met the old people when they were young and they met me when I still had a 32-inch waistline . . . There's no need to stay here and watch things as they come to an end, or else change until they render themselves no longer recognizable. There's no need to watch people until they die, I can make do with the explosion of my own family, the death of Mother & Father. I can settle for the loss of several of my friends, though not before they had time to became assholes, or Fascists. I can settle for my city as it lets itself go, all pleased with itself, as it allows itself to be corrupted and enlarged without thought or consideration . . . Already it's enough for me no longer to be able to find the objects I care for in the shops, such as water-buffalo sandals, the trousers that don't constrict your balls, the trousers with double pleats or, even better, triple pleats . . . I need to cut myself loose from here and go find another island . . . Hours and hours of solitude in the water, as the sun vanished behind the mountains and everything, as you pulled your head up from underwater, had turned dark blue and the meltemi was gusting straight down from the mountain tops, hitting the water like a sledgehammer and kicking up vaporized whirlwinds . . . That's when I'd go, following the wind, plenty warm in my 5-millimetre wetsuit, hearing the air as it hissed through my mouthpiece and kicking back with my fins as I slid underwater, where everything was warmth and calm and silence, to the point that there were times when I could hear my heartbeat echoing in my ears . . . Your heart, when your excitement made it go off on its own, could take your breath away, you found yourself on the sea floor looking up towards a terribly faraway surface and you felt as if there wasn't a molecule of oxygen left in your lungs and you'd set off back up, taking care to deliver one kick of your fins after another, slowly . . . Suddenly the joy of turning into a fish was gone, the watery world around you became alien, hostile . . . On the surface your vision grew blurry from anoxia: there was no one around, if anything had gone wrong you would have died there, all alone . . . Every once in a while the sea devours someone; occasionally it will spit them back out dead onto the shore, but usually it doesn't even take the trouble. The ferocity and ambiguity of water, of the same sublime water that welcomes me naked every year . . . Don't ever let water fool you, even it it looks as if it's always been there waiting for you to come back, even if it looks as if it wants nothing so much as to have you for company, even if you're certain that it's from the sea that you originally come, even if it's to the sea that sooner or later you would like to return, to swim away ever southwards . . . You must not trust water, not even when it seems so pure and loyal, because in fact it's dripping with life and packed with filthy unholy creatures . . . It's neither on your side or against you, it's just there and that's all . . . It seems to have come from the sky, from the Oort cloud, if that even exists . . . That it is actually an alien thing is something you realize only on the day of your first swim of the season, when it strikes you as an extraneous substance and you have to get used to it again, you have a hard time swimming, you get an odd headache . . . Water, which is responsible for life and will take it back, coldly, when it pleases . . . Intelligent oceans, like in *Solaris* . . .

In those days you thought there couldn't be anything finer, the substances that were still circulating in your bloodstream pushed you to do things that now have no meaning: tamper, modify, capture, kill, penetrate, build & destroy. It was *doing*, always and inevitably. No relationship with this landscape and especially with the sea and the creatures that lived in the water, could make any sense without intrusion & tampering, without leaving *marks* of some kind . . . There's a strange violence that inhabits us, first as little children and later as young men, so strange that it later becomes incomprehensible, as it is today for me: the thirst for predation has been slaked, Brandani, today there are only two things you can do. The first, unthinkable, is to retire from the sea. The second is to remove yourself entirely from dry land—where life out of the water and the force of gravity are chopping you to pieces—and become a tuna fish and flee at top speed, away for ever . . . Away, heading for southern riptides, your mind full of fishy thoughts, with no thought other than that of finding food . . . All right, admittedly that's more or less the same hellish condition as life on dry land, with the difference that there's nothing personal between one fish and another, there's no bullying between one fish and another, no dominance, no humiliation, these are things that mammals do—in the water the massacre is never-ending, but it's chilly and pure . . .

Becoming a tuna would mean removing myself from terrestrial ethics and, especially, from gravity; after a few hours spent in the sea, when you set foot back on the beach you feel the oppression of your weight . . . It's daunting in a way, for a couple of seconds your vision is blurred, you feel weak, you can't seem to struggle up onto the shore, your body refuses to return to a vertical orientation, it seems reluctant to participate once again in universal gravitation, of which fishes know nothing . . . The Collapse on Saria was no laughing matter, maybe it was just due to low blood sugar, as I was emerging from the water it became clear to me that I'd be lucky if I actually made it past where the waves were breaking . . . I lay there for hours, stretched out on the rocks, waiting for someone to come get me, I was convinced I was going to die, but I didn't really mind, it was a final and all-encompassing exhaustion, as if the Earth's gravitational field had suddenly tripled its power . . . I concentrated on the sun that was setting behind the mountain and I gently bade the world farewell . . . Then Nereas showed up, I managed to stagger to my feet and climb into the caique, I threw myself into the bunk belowdecks and I slept the whole way back; that year I was here all alone. The terror that I might die there hadn't entirely cancelled out the solitary beauty of that place, the cries of the hawks, the poetry of the setting sun, as I gradually recovered . . . At first I had thought to myself, 'I'm dying, I have to get completely clear of the water, before the bearded fireworms can get to me and eat me alive, if they realize that I'm dying they'll stampede me . . .' The grouper on Opsi beach wasn't even dead yet, and those little monsters were already devouring its eyes . . . They'd find me without eyes, like so many of the sea creatures that fetch up in the morning in Nereas' nets . . . When the caiques anchor offshore to clean their nets, under the hulls you can see the carcasses of the fish they've discarded and tossed overboard with dozens of bearded fireworms, motionless, clustered in filthy weltering bunches, intently sucking dissolving stripping away flesh . . .

That afternoon in the bay of Saria, more or less on the site of the Collapse of so many years before, the young couple from Athens with their supply of water, only six bottles, their sleeping bags, a grill to cook fish on, were calm and unworried, without a thought in their heads, she was beautiful and so young she hardly seemed human to me. They wanted to stay there for a few days. 'That water isn't going to be enough,' I told Sara, 'they think of everything except what they need . . .'

'Because they already have it, Ivo,' she replied. Then she said, 'If we were in their shoes, we'd bring a hundred pounds of luggage, including nose drops . . .'

We were both very taken by their bodies, by their absolute buffed and polished youth. In my disgraceful English I said that their water supply seemed skimpy and the girl shook her head, as if to say they'd be able to make it last. Then I asked, What will you eat? She replied, *Don't care*, Vassili will take care of that, and Vassili showed us his net. He was a city boy, probably incapable of catching anything bigger than a mystery blenny, and yet it was as if she were saying to me: 'You see, flaccid old tourist, you don't understand that for the next two or three days, I have decided to *be his*. It's ever since we got into the boat this morning that he's been undressing me with his eyes and you still haven't noticed the fact? I'm *his* and *he* is going to take care of me, he'll catch fish for me and I'll cook them on this grill.' I didn't understand? Of course I understood! I savagely envied Vassili and I was sure that at that very same instant, Sara was envying her. The girl from Athens had a kitten with her that immediately started playing around the rocks, chasing after a crab. After a few hours, Vassili had caught two or three greenish wrasses, the size of my forefinger, then the sun went behind the mountain, the water under the cement mooring dock lost all its reflections and turned absolutely transparent . . . There, less than a yard deep, among the rocks on the seabed we could see masses of bearded fireworms intently gnawing away at the carcasses of other sea creatures that just a few hours earlier had been tossed overboard by a fishing caique. The indifferent horror of the sea was right there, lapping at our feet, threatening to devour us, the beauty of those two children wouldn't be enough to stave it off. As our boat pulled away we called out to them in English, *Be careful*! But they were there, relaxed, he was still fishing for those tiny fish which she was cleaning on the beach. I thought: 'Soon it will be dark, the glittering stars will overwhelm them.' And yet the beauty of those young people and the bay and the sea was fictitious, I mean to say that *in and of itself* it didn't exist; we were immersed in the purest, most savage and unmistakable barbarity, the brutal and chaotic reality of creation was all around us, but we couldn't see it—our gazes were lost on those faces and those bodies, they wandered up among the rocks and along the mountain crestline, they followed the wheeling flight of the hawks out hunting while the bearded fireworms proceeded with their blind and revolting labour and at that time of the evening the entire sea was one boundless incessant mysterious pitiless bloodbath, enveloped in the eternal lugubrious silence of the water.

But still, you see, Brandani, in spite of the fact that you know all this, you'd still happily become a fish, you'd sign up without a second thought, right here and right now, to become a tuna fish, a handsome 250-pound tuna fish, gleaming, lightning fast . . . Or else you'd incarnate as a big carangoid on the Australian reef, a pelagic fish, one of those fish that swim in the perennial blue of free waters, that have no lair, no home, that—like all fishes—have no experience of the feeling of weight, nor could they tell you the difference between up and down . . . Only fish truly experience a three-dimensional existence and to them, the acts of descending or ascending are equivalent . . . But still, there's always the pearly film on the water's surface, where the air begins, a barrier through which they can propel themselves at high speed, remaining *on the other side* only for seconds, in the thrill of the full light, of the drastic diminution of the world's frothiness, followed by the fall back into the water. For a fish, I would imagine that Dryness and Air are equivalent to what the void is to us. There it lies, gasping on the boat's floor gratings, or else on the scalding stones on the shore, as it experiences for the first time the sensation, for it horrendous & terminal, of possessing *weight* in the *non-water*, as it starts to die of asphyxiation ... This whole silvery fish, in other words, that begins to return, kneading itself back into everything else, a temporary state of vital order, extracted directly from chaos and composed in a wonderful fish-form, now corrupting and dismembering itself in an irreversible entropic process, no long re-assemblable: end of the fish, annihilation, return to the All, after a brief period of existence in what may well be the most perfect and ancient configuration that there is ... The evolutionary time that went into it, the reproductive effort, the vital energy, the emotion spent on its being-inasmuch-as-a-fish, all this, to make a *fritto misto*, a platter of grilled fish, and then flop into a dish to set before *Homo sapiens*, a recent species, imperfect and poorly tested, absolutely incapable of perceiving the *technical* perfection of what they are eating ...

'The sea is big, we'll never run out of fish,' we thought. But we were wrong, *they're all gone* ... Or anyway, nearly all, but we all keep on pretending that that's not the way things stand ... Even Nereas, who when he catches nothing just says, 'Not much fish this year!' pretends that there are still fish out there, but he knows as well as we do that it's game over: life has practically died out in this sea and what's left is being hauled into shore in larger and larger volumes ... I would never have believed that it would have fallen to my generation to witness the Death of the Sea.

God, that morning, up towards Palatia, there were enormous sargos in just a few inches of water ... A grouper on the outer reef, it weighed almost 20 pounds and we caught it in shallow water ... Moray eels bigger than any you'd ever seen, stingrays, tortoises, schools of yellowtail, porgies in little groups of two or three making their escape into the blue, gilt-head bream, grey mullets in vast numbers. Karavides lurking, motionless as rocks, in the dark of their lairs, and you'd never be able to spot them if it weren't they who were the first to startle and flee. Then there are small groups of parrotfish, the usual scorpion fishes, and a great quantity of groupers everywhere ... None of this can be seen now, it's gone ... That water, crystal clear at sunrise, the silence, the solitude of the sea and all those creatures were there just for you. But those were different times for the World, different times for the

Island. It was before the enormous forest of Aleppo pines that marched all the way down to the beaches caught fire and burnt, it was before they built the road, before they brought in electricity. Before they started throwing up four-storey-tall hotels on the hillside and along the gorge, leaving the metal bars on the roof in view of who knows what future new floors. Before the green slime formed that now you can see scattered everywhere on the rocks. Before you could drive to the shoreline of beaches that had always been held sacred until then, before you could see tin cans and yoghurt cartons lying on the seabed. Before the Grotto of Opsi— where you'd caught your biggest-ever grouper—filled up with brushwood, before the Man Without an Arm died. It was before Nereas' wonderful old caique caught fire and was burnt, before Nereas himself turned old and taciturn and almost entirely stopped going out to sea. Before they built the port, before the village flooded. It was before the Island started entering into the contemporary world, at first timidly, and then faster and faster, that is, when Manolis was still alive and chain-smoked and went back and forth to Thelos on the old mail caique. It was before I turned forty and we dined every night among friends, laughing. And then, Lotte, that was the time of Lotte, her white flesh in this tremendous blast of sunlight. The time when after sunset the lights that flickered on were the stars instead of these blinding street lamps . . . The time when you could still see eagles flying high above the beaches. It was before I understood that everything moves and deteriorates, inexorably . . . My oesophagus is burning now, naturally . . . Water.

We, having been born in a second-rate country, have already travelled our path towards the less good; so why should we insist that *they* remain at the starting gate? Just so we can preserve places like this as a theme park where we can holiday? It's the end of the Nineties, they want the same things we have and they're getting them. We expect the Island to remain anchored in time, that everything be kept 'intact' (what does it mean for something to be 'kept intact'?), we want it to be like one of those dioramas at the Museum of Natural History in New York. But it is we who are responsible for contributing to the accelerating change and therefore the destruction of all the reasons we like to come back here . . . We come back here every year and by so doing we progressively destroy the very reasons that bring us back, which in the end are nothing more than earth, air, water. Silence, wind, fried potatoes . . .

'Ah, so this is where you are?'

'That's right.'

'Hiding in the dark. Why aren't you at the banquet?'

'Too many people, I didn't feel like it. Where did you guys eat?'

'At Grigoria's. Tonight they had lentils, *bifteki*, the usual fried potatoes. Fantastic . . . This is still the only place in the world where you can eat potatoes like that. Real potatoes, yellow, cooked in olive oil . . .'

'The only place in the world—you exaggerate! Ivo, don't pay any attention to him.'

'I'm going to go take a walk.'

'Sure, that's good, go take a walk, *ciao* . . . Basically that's what he comes here to do, to walk, this is the only place he can come for a holiday with the family, but *alone*. You've seen him, haven't you, setting out every morning, he does his six to eight hours of hiking, he comes home, he takes a shower, he has dinner, he takes an ibuprofen because his feet are aching—he's a nimesulide addict, I don't know why his liver isn't totally shot, why his stomach isn't ripped to shreds—then he goes to bed and the next morning sets out again . . .'

'I can also say that I come here almost exclusively for the fried potatoes . . . I say "almost", though . . . Your husband is right to walk as much as he does.'

'He's crazy, take it from me. Look, Ivo, I'm serious about this, I'm worried, because I can see that he can't keep it up much longer, he can't stand his profession any more. It's as if all the pain and grief of his patients were piling up inside him and he can no longer find a way to process it. At this point, he's stopped talking, even to me. He just absorbs poison all year long, unless he gets out and walks, he can't purge it, so he heads up into the mountains all day long, he sweats, he wears himself out . . . You know how far he went yesterday? All the way to the Strait!'

'Yes, I heard that, someone told me . . .'

'It's kind of like a chain letter . . . His patients unload all their problems on him, they vent, they tell him about every unimaginable kind of pain, all sorts of things . . . That's why they pay him . . . Every so often, he looks like a wreck, he comes home with his eyes as red as if he's been crying . . . He used to be enthusiastic about being an analyst, now I don't think his heart is really in it any more . . . He has patients who've been coming to see him for ten, fifteen years now—sorry if I tell you this kind of thing . . . please, keep it to yourself, can I rely on you?—people who have problems they're never going to solve, because their real problem is that they don't have a fucking thing to do all day, Ivo . . . The point is that they've never had a *real problem* in their lives, like how to earn a basic living, get enough to eat, for instance. Where I come from the expression is that they don't know how to darken their day . . . Oh well, forgive me . . . you were just sitting here without a care in the world and I . . .'

'No, not at all . . .'

'. . . but those ones, actually, he doesn't really even mind them all that much, it's the ones with serious problems that he struggles with. Because, among other things, aside from pharmaceuticals—because pharmaceuticals, if you take them, they work, and how—people who are really sick can't really be cured with sessions of analysis: he knows that, but he doesn't say it . . . I stopped going years and years ago, when I realized it didn't really suit me, and I'm fine with it. He's almost fifty years old now and at this point he's in up to his neck . . . So he walks and he walks . . . All alone, because he doesn't want company, at night he comes back wrecked, with circles under his eyes, his hair all wind-tossed, his face looking exhausted, in a grim mood, black as coal . . . Sorry, Ivo, sorry I've been bending your ear like this. The two of you hardly even know each other . . . Have you eaten?'

'Not yet. Tonight I've had a little too much to drink before dinner. Four ouzos. I'm drunk. I'm drinking water and trying to get over it. Then I'll go to Grigoria's too, and I just hope that there'll be something left to eat.'

'Well, I'm going to say goodbye now . . . *Ciao*, maybe I'll run into you later.'

Paola had never confided in me like this . . . Maybe she's right: that guy really is walking to sweat clean his filthy psychoanalyst's soul, if there really is such a thing as Hell, psychoanalysts are going there, for sure, every last one of them. In fact, in all likelihood, Hell exists only for them, that is, to take in and punish no one else but psychoanalysts and psychiatrists—all the various circles of Hell, descending, with Sigmund Freud enjoying pride of place at the centre of the bottommost circle, immersed in ice up to his chest, his gaping maw open to devour his adepts . . . I'd like to go on long hikes myself, if it weren't for the sheer effort of my 200 pounds . . . There was a time, when the planet was colder, that it was colder here too, and the wind was stronger, drier, and everything beneath a certain weight sooner or later was carried off. The hair would fly off your head, your pubic hair off your crotch, they'd wind up falling into the sea or beyond, setting down on the highlands of Asia Minor, in Anatolia, in Syria. The misty drops of your respiration, mixing with the drops of spray torn by the wind off the waves, only to wind up in Egypt and Mesopotamia. Your stream of pee would fly away, horizontally, you had to look out. The pages of books left open would be torn out, towels wound up in the sea, as would any other article of clothing left lying around loose, even your sandals and flip-flops. I lost a pair of eyeglasses once, a tremendous gust of wind simply tore them off of my face at the mouth of the Strait . . . One of my dive flippers flew away, and so did an inflatable mattress, a football, a dive boot from my wetsuit, and lots of other things . . . But you never get overheated from walking in the wind, all the sweat dries off you immediately, it freezes on your skin . . . In fact, one of the reasons I always came here was for the wind. And I come back here for the wind, for those clouds that form high in the sky and plunge down towards the sea only to dissolve: I would say that it's a case of adiabatic compression, natural air conditioning. I come back here for the Swiss crystal clarity of the air, for the strong colour of the sky, something you'd never expect in summer at this latitude ... I come here for the quality of the light, so strong and precise, scrupulous in the way it goes to pick out objects one by one, describes them with such exactitude down to every last detail. I come here to sit naked in the busy air, to observe the horizon, to build tiny sailboats out of pine bark and then launch them in the sea, hoping they might wind up in Lebanon, in Egypt ... I come here to walk naked up the gorges that run down to the beaches, when all of a sudden a flock of partridges bursts out of the bushes and you practically have a heart attack from the surprise. I come back so I can walk again through the undergrowth of juniper and sage, through the oleander bushes, the wild fig trees, the thyme and all those spherical thorn bushes you'd be well advised not to fall into. Every year I come back here for the feeling of when the air gets compacted into the gorges, when the wind accelerates because of the Venturi effect and it violently tosses every bush and the whole valley murmurs and heaves a deep, ancient sigh ... I come back so I can lie stretched out, eyes shut, in the shadow of the rocks, trying to sleep but unable to, because there's always a fly that bites until it draws blood, an ant that walks over you, that stings you. I come here for the shoals of Saria, for the whole island of Saria, to watch the moray eels as they slither out of their dens, mouth splayed open, when they catch a whiff of the fish that you have hooked to your belt ... I come back to the Island for the solitary huts that you find in the olive groves, where you walk in and you find everything you need to start a fire, a flask of oil, a jar of salt, a pallet of pine needles, a blanket, a few utensils and tools. I imagine these men in the winter, in the silence of a calm day, the sea that you glimpse at the mouths of these valleys, the boat tied up, the work, the meal, the sleep, the classical landscape on all sides: olive trees, dry-laid stone walls, sweet-smelling bushes, nanny goats, donkeys—a day in April like the one when Hektor lost his arm. He was crying like a veal calf over his lost arm ...

But why on earth would a man who had seen his seventieth birthday come and go still even think of going bomb fishing? He had no need of it, he wasn't poor, he had his pension. And what's more he went alone. Hand and forearm blown clean off. They transported him to Athens and gave him that pair of stainless steel pincers: I don't know how he managed to open and close it, he looked like Terminator. He'd give you a price to take you somewhere in his boat and then when it came time to pay he'd name another price and refuse to honour the price negotiated at the start. He died this last winter. He'd told me about his bewilderment on that day, the motor he couldn't get to turn over, he said that he passed out more than once in the bottom of the boat, on the burden boards. Then he came to, but he was weak as a kitten: he lay there on his back in the bottom of the boat, who knows for how long, looking at the little church high above, a white spot atop Mount Profitis Ilias. He consigned his soul repeatedly to the saint . . . 'There was no one there. Only Hektor. But Prophet Elijah was watching me, from mountaintop . . .' If I were in his situation, I'd have died of the sheer horror: to set off from that beach, leaving a part of your body there behind you. Who knows what he thought he was going to catch, with that dynamite . . . Probably some fine fish, maybe the schools of yellowtail that come in to the coast in April to spawn. It was a tough lesson, by now he limited himself to fishing for whitebait, by night under the pier, with a lamp and a small fine-mesh net.

You can see the mountainside clearly now, the moon has grown brighter, more luminous, down below years ago some of the forest burnt in a fire, it was before we discovered the Island, Clara and I. Once I took Lotte there, the first time we had sex . . . Lotte . . . I wonder what became of her? Sweet compliant willing intelligent funny, fair-skinned, blond, Nordic blue eyes. Those three days of wind and storm, we spent them shut up in a room, screwing, at Nereas' place, with the windows shaking from the tremendous blasts of air. It was after the Great Fire, a significant portion of the woods was charred, billions of bits of burnt wood and cinders were hurtling rapidly through space, lodging in the eyes of anyone still outdoors. We'd pushed the beds together in my room, we only came out for meals . . . Her flesh was raw and white, it stood out against the enamelled green wainscoting along the walls, we were free, adult and single, we'd both just got out of similar relationships. The minute I saw her, up at the pass, I understood that she needed to be embraced and held tight. I limited myself to asking her what language she spoke. Do you remember, Brandani? You suggested French, because you speak English so badly, then we went down together to the village, taking the ridge trail, the one that's gone now, because there's a road. On the way down, step by step, we recognized each other, our experiences had been so similar, the same political activities, a similar sequence of alienations, hesitations, betrayals . . . There was only the slenderest of partitions between us to demolish: you did it the following day in the most anxious, the clumsiest manner imaginable, way up there, at the end of the trail that ran across the middle of the slope, where the forest first thins out and then gives way entirely to bare rock. We'd laid down on the bed of pine needles, I lifted her skirt, I slipped off her panties—that tuft of tawny pubic hair had aroused your curiosity . . . Maybe the pine needles were prickly against her arse cheeks, you asked her if she was taking anything. *N'est pas un problème*, she said. It wasn't true that it wasn't a problem but there was no time to inquire further. You were tense. Why at that exact moment was it *obligatory* for both of you to have sex? What made it necessary? Certainly not lust. For my part the desire was weak, and she didn't seem especially enthusiastic either, but we needed to determine the nature of that friendship, we needed for it to be a matter of sex from the outset, neither one of us needed anything more than to lie naked in someone else's arms. That initial act so poorly conducted could easily have been the end of it all, but then it turned into genuine passion . . . I wonder where she is now, she was the same age as me, now she's probably a wasted-looking woman in her early fifties . . . *Je ne suis pas un homme particulièrment propre*, you had told her, it was just a matter of this Peninsular habit of washing your genitals frequently . . . You suggested going out without anything on under her skirt and she immediately complied, the idea amused her and excited her. With the passing days, reference was made to her political past. She'd skirted dangerously close to German terrorism, which had been something apocalyptic and terrible from the very start—she'd managed to avoid getting tangled up in it practically by chance, no details, I saw that the mere thought of it was giving her a sort of tremor . . . *Embrasse moi, baise moi.* Then things went the way they went, back then you didn't have a penny to your name, you couldn't afford to travel to be there with her when she had the abortion; she was weeping over the phone. Having a child with her was the last thing you wanted. You were furious at her recklessness. Everything broke off, total communications blackout, the end of it all. Our meeting, that morning up at the pass, remains something out of a dream, it might never have happened: a girl sitting on a boulder in all that wind, no one around for miles, just nanny goats on the mountainside, she wore a scarf to manage her hair, she had high cheekbones. There's nothing left now that can constitute proof, except for a headshot taken in a photo booth in the City of God. I could never identify the stone she'd been sitting on, someone ought to have put a plaque on it:

Here Lotte and Ivo first met,
in the year of the Great Fire.

Or, down in the village, a plaque next to the door of Room Number 2 in Nereas' inn:

Here a pair of lovers
lived many hours of happiness
in the year of the Great Fire.

She liked to wear wraps that nowadays we might call ethnic. Many of the things between us never needed to be spoken, we already knew what was involved. In Cologne she was a little taken aback by the sight of my loden coat but she liked the fact that I wore a wool cap. She drove an old Mercedes and I needed a continuous supply of Xanax. The unexpected gentleness of Germany, the forests, the rain, the Rhine, too wide and slow, full of barges, a vast and different world . . . Now she and I are the only ones who know what those days were really like, but I don't know any more where the only person with whom I share these memories even is . . .

They're unloading a few crates of fish and they're still cleaning their nets—at this time of night! It's hard work and I've never been able to figure out how much they earn, here, as fishermen, what the rules are, when the fishing bans go into effect. They're pretty small caiques, nothing comparable to a deep-sea fishing boat. From the beaches, about five in the afternoon, you can see them pass: they stand in the stern, helm clamped between their legs, the caique solidly planted in the water, the aft sunk low in the stern wave, they come up along the cliff front after Cape Atreides, the engine pounding out its regular beat, one detonation clearly distinct from another, the gurgle of the exhaust in the water, there they are with their perennial cigarettes in their mouths, the perennial woollen cap on their heads, their ripped T-shirts . . . They aren't cold, they wave, they raise their arms, they seem formal, harsh, or perhaps just resigned to another night of hard work: toss out the nets, haul in the nets, come back to port, unload the fish, load it onto the ship, and once again clean the nets . . . The high prow of the fishing caiques, so ancient, is good when the short sharp swell of the Aegean kicks up, the traditional shape of the stern, which is less well suited to the engine . . . The time comes when its necessary to abandon the past, especially when it conflicts with the present, when it nullifies the advantages of the present. Nereas knows it all too well, his old and beautiful caique burnt to the waterline ten years ago and now he has a fast boat, made of plastic, that'll do faster than twenty knots . . . Fifty years isn't nothing? I'm not sure . . . Certainly, that's a long time in terms of the technology of seafaring, among other things: someone my age might as well have been born in another geological era. Fifty years ago, around here, we were using oars, Hektor used to say. Sixty years ago Nereas lost his father and a brother in the waters off Agios Minas, I don't know exactly what happened, it seems to have been because of a sudden and very violent squall, the boat was sail-powered and it capsized. Nereas never talked to me about it, maybe it was Hektor who told me.

Nereas, who's lived his whole life here, has also transformed these places over time though he's never been able to seriously undercut their classical quality, neither he nor others . . . This is the point, this is something that you can tell yourself without a second thought, Brandani: I come here to be *inside* this classical landscape, I come here because this is the place in the world where so far I have encountered the least conflict between what I am and what I see . . . *What I am?* And just what am I? You've been an engineer for a quarter century and you still haven't purged yourself of this bullshit? The study and the practice of engineering after all these years ought to have scrubbed your cranium clean . . . The idea was to do what Heracles did with the stables of . . . What was the name? In any case, mountains of manure so huge that he was forced to alter the course of two rivers, the Alpheus and the Peneus—who knows why you remember these names and not the other—so that they'd run through there . . . You fell in love with that Scottish bridge, since then and for all this time you've let yourself be filled and by the practice of *Homo faber*, but the philosophical manure has left its slag, you can't help but think in terms of cultural categories: *classical landscape*, for instance. Could you actually tell me just what a classical landscape is?

Another ouzo? Yes? No? Are you trying to get yourself sick tonight? Sure, another ouzo . . .

All right, let's see. To compose a classical landscape, first you need the right elements: for starters a great many bushes typical of the Mediterranean maquis, olive trees, pines, rocks, mountains rising sheer over the sea, also fig trees, tamarisk trees, oleanders and junipers. You need thyme and sages, you need well-shaped arcs of beach line, you need relatively well-sheltered, cosy bays, you need gorges full of shade. You'll need goats—also wild goats, perched high on inaccessible rocks—and donkeys, hawks high in the cliffs and cormorants, not necessarily seagulls, because they live everywhere and aren't necessarily a marker of classicity. You'll need sequences of promontories and you'll need shoals as solitary as a medieval mystic, you'll need ancient ruins that stand untouched by an archaeologist's hand, you'll also need a bit of cement and some high-prowed boats. You'll need the odour of the water's edge and especially the smell of the wind, you'll need lots of sunlight and, if possible, blue sky . . . Ah, you'll also need distant islands, landmasses looming on the horizon: the classical landscape lives on water and earth, in the same amounts. Perhaps you might need bucrania & garlands, and then horses, dolphins, sirens, tritons and harpies, but this is nothing but iconography, Ivo . . .

With all these ingredients you can construct a classical land-scape, it's not all that challenging, you just need to be judicious . . . The classical landscape is solitary and sun-kissed, it has a great deal to do with the horizon line, and so constantly with the sea . . . In the future they'll need to fence off a few particularly exemplary portions of this landscape, or else even uproot it physically . . . That is, slice off a nice substantial chunk so it can be installed in a special Museum of Nature the Way It Was, the MNWIW, where one might be able to view an entire tourable repertory of themed landscapes of earth: Amazonian Rainforest, Alpine, Andean, Patagonian and Polar landscapes, and also a few nice sections of classical Mediterranean landscape, with genuine water and a very well-constructed virtual horizon: Item Number 246, *Mediterranean Bay* . . . Kandri would be perfect for it, all you'd need to do is saw it off with all its roots, working on a criterion of *ad abundantiam*, which means you'd want to start the cut a good 200 metres from the centre of the bay and extract it all, with all its underwater shoals and reefs, the stones along the beach, the trees and bushes. Then you pick it clean of the occasional plastic bottle and you place it in a display case at the MNWIW. What do we need the natural world for any more, when there's nothing nat-ural about it, and that's the way it ought to be? Wouldn't we prefer a planet completely covered with buildings but dotted with neatly cut patches of nature, perfectly intact and museologically curated? What other destiny awaits us if not this? Item Number 38, *Tyrrhenian Island* with ancient settlements: Palmarola would do just fine. Palmarola deserves a display case all its own. If I think of that pergola, the yellow wine of Ponza, the silhouette of Palmarola turning purple on the horizon, to the west. Maybe that's it, perhaps I came to these seas in search of another Ponza, another Palmarola, something to take their place, something that would fill the void of no longer being able to go there. Sofrano was only a foreshadowing of what awaited me further south . . .

Ponza: the initial shock, the revelation of what the sea *could be*, Ponza on that incredible day and Ponza in the years that followed . . . How could the water be so transparent? How was it possible to detect every tiniest detail of the seabeds at that depth? And the schools of fishes? How could the earth have shapes and colours of that sort? What did the World conceal beyond the horizon, if a simple three-hour boat trip could unveil such wonders? During the trip here what struck you was the colour of a sea that you'd never seen before, so blue, so open, so windy . . . The dolphins that swam along beside the bow, the man who said, in a formal tone: 'I believe they're porpoises . . .' Then the boat that Father hired, the tour of the island, the stops to dive in with a swim mask, the strange geometric cavities carved high up in the grey rocks. Gradually, as we went around the island, the rock turned dark, then white, then it became red and then yellow. I couldn't wait to come back to Ponza, when I was older I was sure I would do it. And I did. But meanwhile, during those long, slow endings of the summer that extended out until the beginning of October and the water turned cold and on the beach there was hardly anyone any more, the days of the north wind that swept clear the horizon while I began waiting to see the Islands appear down there, in the distance, with their promise of an endless Summer.

Then it was here that I found something much more powerful and decisive and grandiose, with respect to my initial aquatic imprinting and the dream of the Islands on the horizon . . . It was aboard the magnificent *Falesá* that I discovered the Aegean, it was on Sofrano that I rediscovered the sea and the age-old promise of Summer . . . I've always needed the Summer as a utopia, rather than as a season. Perfect definition, Brandani, even getting drunk on ouzo helps to expand your consciousness—the summer as utopia because what were mere *holidays* for other people, for me became segments of an alternative existence, the only true and just life, the only one worth living . . . Because I never acknowledged that life in Winter deserved to be called life . . . Because I've never taken into consideration land without Water and without Summer . . . Only here, on the Island, or there, on Ponza—and on Palmarola, as an implementation of Ponza all the way to the Aquatic Sublime, Absolute Island of the Mediterranean paradise—was life worth living . . . In Winter, as far as I'm concerned, I'd even be happy to hibernate, I could just vanish from circulation, go to sleep for eight months. Still today, I think of things the way I did when I was fifteen: Winter is duty, cataleptic trance; Summer is pleasure, life. Maybe I really should have made that my life, but how?

For your Museum of Nature the Way It Was, perhaps you should carve out and remove Caprera, the way you discovered it at dawn on the *Three Clouds*, dead ahead, because who knows how, we'd lucked into the perfect course: Item no. TBD, *Granite Tyrrhenian Island*. Or even better, you might carve out Lavezzi, even though the ticket-buying public, the visitors to the Grand Museum of Nature the Way It Was might not believe that there was once a place of such beauty. I think of Piero Gilardi. He was the first to understand that we ought to have diced up the world like a watermelon, so we could save a few particularly significant pieces and preserve them for our children's children's children. We were walking barefoot on one of his *Nature Carpets* in 1967, perhaps the least visited show on earth. And also the least guarded. Who would let you walk on one of Gilardi's carpets these days? They were made of foam rubber, that is, expanded polyurethane foam, and hand-painted to make them look fake and real at the same time. Palmarola as a reference to itself. Technically the most feasible approach would be to redo it in foam rubber, all you'd need to do is take a cast of it, or really a well-planned series of casts, until you could perfectly reconstruct its shape. You'd also need to take a cast of the surrounding seabed out to 100 yards from the coast, at least, because the setting is very important. Once you'd done this, I'd *demand* that the whole thing be hand-painted, faithfully reproducing every detail, even the bushes which had been rigorously relocated. The water ought to be depicted realistically but we shouldn't make use of real water, rather I'd use that transparent plastic that the Japanese use to make fake soup . . . And inside it, reproductions of sea creatures, like in the dioramas by Akeley in New York, magnificent, if it weren't for the real–fake ambiguity of the stuffed animals. Fake–fake is honestly the only way . . . The fake-real, on the other hand, is what is kept artificially alive in spite of the fact that it is already virtually dead to all meaning, as is starting to be the case with these places . . . Oh what a pain in the ass, Ivo . . . It must be close to eleven by now, you're drunk, you need to eat something . . . Get up . . . Let's take a piss here at Kalliope's and then let's go . . .

The usual stench in here, you can't breathe, no toilet paper, no paper hand towels, I got a lot of sun again today, I ought to buy myself some suncream for my nose, it's turning red, it's burning . . . I wonder why my dick never gets sunburnt, the glans always tans nicely, never burnt once . . . That's me . . . Is that me? For a second there . . . I wasn't able to recognize myself . . . My face looked like someone else's . . . Is that death on its way? Here if you have a heart attack, or a stroke, what are you going to do? They got Nereas to the hospital in time, by helicopter . . . The world rocks, but death is nothing to us, since when we exist there is no death, and when there is death we do not exist . . . Got to get out of here, air . . . Death . . . Calm down, here or somewhere else, it's all the same . . . I'm lurching, I'm sweating like a pig, but I'm still on my feet, I just need another Xanax . . . It's nothing but a panic attack . . . Another Xanax . . . Here it is: the three for Wednesday are gone, I have two extra. Water. Done . . . Death is nothing to us. It'll take half an hour, the wind is freezing the sweat on my skin, the air makes me feel better, that's enough ouzo: with all I've had to drink plus the Xanax, I can go to sleep . . . And then, if I'm going to die, let it be . . . How many Xanax does it take to die in peace?

'Are you still here? Have you had anything to eat, at least? What is it, what's that look on your face?'

'It's nothing, Sara, just a stab of anxiety, I think . . . Something terrifying happened to me: I went into the restroom, I took a look in the mirror, and *I was unable to recognize myself* . . . Maybe I've had too much to drink, it was on an empty stomach . . . A tremendous moment of alienation, it hardly lasted a second but it scared me . . . I felt as if I was floating, it was if I was on the verge of falling . . . I thought I was having a stroke, you know . . .'

'You took a Xanax, didn't you? How many Xanax a day are you taking at this point?'

'Sara . . . leaving aside the fact that it's none of your fucking business . . . You're not here inside my head. You don't know what a panic attack is like . . . In any case . . . I usually take three . . . Tonight, I took four, OK?'

'That's fine, Ivo, but you know that you need to go easy with them . . . Do you feel better now? The alienation is because you've had too much to drink, that's the same sensation I've had when I was drunk . . . The others are going for a walk. I'm stuffed, I'd like to stretch my legs. You coming?'

'I wouldn't even think of it . . . After all, I still need to eat. You go ahead. How was the banquet?'

'But are you OK? Do you want me to stay here with you? The dinner was good, fantastic. Nereas had fried up a delicious octopus. Then lots of fish. Grouper filets. Some karavides. There were twenty of us, at the table. Are you sure you don't want to come with us?'

'No, thanks, you go on alone. I've had a couple more ouzos than usual. Now I'm chugging water . . . I'm feeling better, I don't need anything . . . Having *twenty people* at the dinner table is just a horrible thing . . . It's like going to a protest march . . .'

'Oh what a pain in the ass you are, Ivo, I've heard this routine. Every once in a while you could make an exception, don't you think?'

'Tonight was no time for exceptions, sweetheart . . . I'm going to go get a *bifteki* with fried potatoes at Grigoria's. I'll catch up with you later, or else I'll see you at home . . . Sure, I'm fine now: a Xanax under your tongue is like a saint's healing hand . . . You look beautiful, as usual. Lucky boy who lands you.'

'*Ciao*, dummy. See you at home.'

Who knows why she's turned so damned sociable . . . Usually she's more of a bear than I am but in the past few days she keeps asking me to come to these more or less *mass* dinners. Maybe it's because having dinner with me and no one else bores her; if I'm the first one to be bored by myself, why shouldn't she be just as bored with me? Come on. Get up out of this Allibert chair and go over to Grigoria's before she's completely out of food: you can do it . . . You can stand up, you see? It could be that you survive the evening just fine, it could be that you don't die, it could be that you live to see tomorrow. Sara can't understand, she's not fifty, she's thirty-seven, in fact, *she doesn't have to* understand, I don't want her to understand . . . If only I could figure out *why* she's with me! What does she get out of it? Bald, overweight, massive but deteriorating physique, glasses, constantly complaining, depressed, anxious, in rapid decline as a lover, short on money, hypochondriac. What the fuck does she see in me? There was a time when I could figure out the reasons a girl would like me, but now? If I only knew why Sara wants to be with me, I'd feel more confident, I could relax . . . What kind of thrill can she get out of being with an engineer who's not professionally particularly successful, out of shape and getting along in years? What's more, there seems to be a decline in hormones: it might not be pronounced, it might be physiological, but it makes its effects felt. She's young, she has her job at the law office, and she likes it, she's building a career, she was just recently made partner, she's moving along at full speed . . . I feel like I'm not in anybody's target market, unless you count unattached women in their fifties. I'm already amazed to see myself ageing, but it had never occurred to me that it would mean becoming *invisible* in the eyes of women . . . You fuck with more or less anyone you like for a lifetime, and then, just when you're starting to think it's not all that difficult after all, you realize that you're over the species' biological horizon: your body is no longer business, much less pleasure . . . Soon, if you let your gaze linger a little too long on a young woman's body, people will be able to say that you're a *dirty old man* . . . And that will mean the party's over . . . None of the young women you meet will preserve you in their memory as *a man* but, at the very best, *some guy they know* . . . There was a time when it was fun to look at women, especially to lock eyes, for that instant of contact, something that could prove—only rarely, but it's happened to you, Ivo—intense, on occasion such a bolt from the blue that you've never since forgotten it . . . The power of the fortuitous contact, an instant of sheer celebration for the imagination, an instant in which possible worlds open up for you . . .

Usually nothing happened, but the exchange of glances would give me a sense of fulfilment, it signalled the erotic density of the world, the possibility of seduction, it confirmed in me the aware-ness that I still had a *biological* value . . . These days none of the chicks I see in here would be willing to give me a kiss, much less go to bed with me . . . Are you sure of that, Brandani? Don't forget that when it comes to these things, you have never, ever been able to figure out how it works . . . Just the other day, that girl—do you think she was even twenty?—that you were helping out of the caique—what was she? French?—when you lifted her by the waist, your hands encountered a firm silky dry flesh and they *remem-bered*, faster than your mind could, that they'd had dealings with flesh of that kind, with youth . . . You brushed together and the scent of that girl suddenly activated the memory of summers years and years ago, when they expected you to touch them, or at least to try . . . But you were almost ashamed to have touched that young French girl, full and womanly as she was . . . While the boat was pulling away, you were still embarrassed . . .

You've become more attentive to beauty, Ivo. When you were a young man, or even just ten years ago, you didn't understand any-thing about it. Now you've become more demanding, also more sensitive to details. It happens to those who pass from practice to theory, you become an aesthete because you look much more than you touch, caress, brush your fingers over . . . More than you grope or penetrate . . . More than you get a chance to part, to suck, to unfold . . . All right, all right, calm down, it's just a passing moment of horniness, a mental erection, calm down . . . The other day, when you were siting in the cafe, you stared and stared at that girl's feet, so absolutely perfect in their pinstriped sandals, you were enchanted and she noticed it, she was young and brunette . . . She looked you right in the eyes, smiling, and once again you were ashamed . . . She liked being examined with such close attention and she wanted to let you know that . . . She was looking for complicity but you didn't smile back, you said nothing to her, you turned away pretending nothing had happened, then you got up and you went inside to pay; Yannis had just put on the piece by Miles that you'd requested, 'Time After Time', and he was hurt that you were leaving . . . Practically speaking, you took to your heels, the *contact* with that young woman, her direct gaze, these things threw you into a state of panic, you didn't know to handle yourself . . . But what could I have *said to her*? And in what language?

But then Sara is precious to you, Ivo, this is your last chance to have anything to do with youth, *her* youth. She's always told you that she loves you, she says that four years ago she liked you immediately, the minute she laid eyes on you, she says that she doesn't care about age, in fact, she'd like it if you grew a beard, 'But mine would be white,' you told her. 'I know that and it doesn't matter—in fact, it makes you even more intriguing,' she replied. Maybe she's a gerontophile. It's possible that she's projecting onto me images and fantasies that are entirely hers, that have nothing to do with me: she even says that she likes my 'big old bod', that's what she calls it . . . The true, absolute novelty, with Sara, is that when I'm with her I can say anything that comes to mind, I can be myself . . . Even though being yourself doesn't really mean anything, let's say . . . It had never happened to you before with a woman, Brandani. Certainly, even she wishes you were different in certain ways, that's only to be expected, it's just that she doesn't do everything within her power to change you, that's the thing . . . You should be happy about it, come on! There's nothing about her that you'd change, except perhaps for the relative length of her toes—you wish those were more graduated . . . Maybe you'd change the way she walks . . . Another thing that gets on your nerves is her unwillingness to wear heels of any kind . . . Otherwise, Sara is pretty, reliable, intelligent, perfect . . . Do you love her? If that word meant anything, then you'd have to say yes . . . And then, admit it, even if you don't understand anything about her, even if you don't understand why she's with you, *you trust* Sara and and being able to trust someone is important . . . You like her intelligence, even the fact that she's a little bit lesbian. Sara *brings out the best in you*, Ivo, be satisfied and resign yourself to it: you may very well be out of the Great Game of Sex, but you have her. *You have her*!

'*Kalispera, can I seat here? Is free?* Bring me a beer in the meanwhile. *Nè, mia mbira. I go in the kitchen just for looking.* To see what you have . . . Is there a *bifteki*? Ahh, there it is in its reddish lard. *Ena bifteki* and *patatakia. Polì patatakia.*'

The Xanax is doing its job, everything goes back to normal, now things seem really real, I've gone back to feeling like one person, instead of two or three . . . Why do you eat this stuff if you know it's bad for you? For three reasons. The first is that everything that isn't bad for me is something that I'd rather not eat. The second is that what I do want is a *bifteki*. The third is that back in the room I have a healthy supply of Maalox . . . But you don't like *bifteki*—why order it? That's not quite right, Lieutenant Brandani, it's not that I don't like it, it's that it always disappoints me a little—more than anything else I'm seduced by the *idea of bifteki*, ground meat mixed up with spices and minced garlic, a concept that became clear to me for the first time in Port Axenion, where they were cooking it over a wood fire and it took three days to digest it. Here they cook it *sto furni*—in the oven—in those big aluminium baking pans, swimming in a tomato sauce and in a mysterious and abundant lard that unfailingly drips onto your shirt. T-shirt, trousers, etc., staining them *for life* . . . *Bifteki* and fried potatoes—now let me tell you the whole story—is an intensely pop dish, both in terms of its nature and its appearance:

the red of the tomato scattered over the meat, the intense yellow of the *patates*. Like all dishes with fried potatoes it's just an excuse to eat the potatoes . . . Wonderful, unrivalled, the best in the world: piping hot from the frying pan, practically impossible to touch . . . The first one you pop in your mouth will scald your palate, etc. . . . Tonight again the place is full of French people . . . I really shouldn't have anything more to drink, especially with the Xanax, but this Mythos beer is welcoming, vaguely sweet . . . In short, what is it that's so French about the French that you can spot them instantly? They belong to the French Universe, Ivo . . . It's a closed and complete cultural system, sufficient unto itself, that endures through time and, when necessary, knows how to change. The French are self-sufficient and that's the point that always baffles us . . . More than others, they wear the marks of the culture to which they belong—they dress as French people, they cut their hair in a certain way, they adore scraps of cloth wherever they find them, especially if they're ethnic. They don't travel in Europe, the French, because they consider *themselves* to be Europe and think that they have everything worth seeing in Europe . . . They travel to distant, ethnic countries, where they collect scraps of cloth to wrap around their necks in Paris in the winter: *Ça, cet hiver à Paris, sera le number one!* There they are, predictable as ever: I'm crazy about them. I envy them the Frenchness of their women, their *oui* breathed in like a sob, a sudden jerk of fright, an unexpected surge of pleasure . . . They eat the big dish of goat meat, untroubled, by no means worried about the fact that they're going to have to digest it later . . . It takes me a week . . . To me, goat meat cooked that way is pure antimatter . . . No one understands me when I say that there's a French version of everything . . . The French irritate the shit out of us Peninsulars, because we're not even capable of conceiving what it means to belong to a *complete* culture . . . Over there, on the other hand, those two are a lesbian couple, probably German; faggots don't like this place but lesbians do—they always have that stern, intransigent, Jansenist appearance, the rejection of all feminine signals, short hair, no make-up, hairy legs, neglected skin, sloppiness, the inevitable Birkenstocks on their feet. Who knows why they want to be that way? Here, for gay males, things aren't quite right, there's no night life, there's not a sufficient biomass to ensure a high likelihood of chance encounters. While lesbian couples want quiet, out-of-the-way places . . . But why do they uglify themselves in that way? Why this urgent need to defeminize themselves, in fact, this hatred for cosmetics, make-up, embellishment, care of self? This total lack of feminine exhibitionism, which is the salt of the earth . . . They look like defrocked nuns, but unhappy ones . . .

Ahh, here it is, the *bifteki*. Look at what a fine piece of meat, oily, red, 3,000 degrees. Potatoes that, just from the look of them, you'd say were slightly undercooked, a few seconds more, you would have left them in. But you never really know: one dish of fried potatoes here is never the same as another. We aren't at McDonald's, these are *real* potatoes, they were peeled two hours ago, set to soak in a basinful of water. For years and years now they've been using these aluminium basins, by now they're all dented, they put their bread dough in them to rise, they hand-wash their clothes in them, they toss their catch into them, they soak their fine-sliced potatoes in them, I saw a woman walking around with one under her arm and in it was the decapitated head of a blessed, innocent nanny goat . . . The nanny goats know when they're about to wind up just like John the Baptist . . . I don't know how but a nanny goat knows when she's being taken somewhere to end her life, and so she bleats, she tugs on the rope but she never *really* rebels. Nanny goats are strong, bony, their heads are hard as basalt, they could escape with a sufficiently hard yank, they could start horn-butting their executioner; but they don't do it, they seem intimidated by human beings right up till the end. When I first came here, in the silence of the early morning you would often hear the laments of a condemned nanny goat. Goat and fish were the only kinds of flesh eaten here—no cows, very few pigs, just goats, donkeys and sheep. Chicken, but only frozen . . . Lots of cockroaches and flies and wasps. There are fewer flies than there used to be, an indication that people don't live as closely with animals as they used to, but there are still plenty of wasps—they tumble into your honey bowl at breakfast, you have to pull them out with your spoon and set them down somewhere, they sit there, imprisoned in the honey, they struggle until they exhaust their strength and die.

Always the same basins: some things change more slowly, they become almost obvious, in time you become used to them, you forget what there used to be instead of them, but things change even here. The only possible defence is *to forget the way things used to be*: it works everywhere and for anyone who has lived in this accelerating century, this century that sweeps you away except towards worlds that are different and much worse, worlds that you'd glad do without experiencing . . . Modernity can go fuck itself . . . If nothing is fated to remain intact, if everything that exists is destroyed or reduced to little more than a staging of itself or else deteriorates into garbage and waste, then why not just back to prehistory . . . If the world rejects a person old enough to have attained wisdom, if this is the world where the older you get the less sense it makes to you, well, then that world can fuck itself, let it self-destruct . . . To figure anything out would require a decade's truce, a little social, political, economic and technical stability, but it's impossible with this pace of change; old people at this point are useless, stupid people capable of going bomb-fishing at age seventy, flaccid flesh full of aches and pains and impediments and bruises, stinking of rancid sweat—old people are ridiculous figures who don't understand a fucking thing about the world around them, a world that by now belongs to someone else. You're not like that yet, Ivo, however much you want to get depressed, you have to admit it . . . But it won't be long, you have to admit that, too . . .

Ouch, those potatoes are burning hot! Tonight the bread is fresh, it's still steaming: loaves made to last three, or four days, after baking they're perfect for just twenty-four hours, after which they lose their freshness, they become increasingly *'nzallunute*. The Mediterranean idea of bread is different from the French idea, urban and Parisian, certainly priceless in its way but with nothing *classical* about it. The immense round loaves from here must weigh

10 or 12 pounds, if not more, the crust is hard, greyish, the crumb is dense, I love to dip it in the sauce that drips to the bottom of a Greek salad: let it fully soak in the fresh tomato juice mixed with the olive oil, the chunks of feta, carefully gather it all . . . This pergola was perfect once, now less so. The structure is still the old one, made up of water pipes—there it is, the joints are completely normal, threaded, no welding—it used to have a simple bare cement floor though, but then they must have decided that something so simple, so well made, so cheap, and so durable, somehow wasn't *dignified* . . . That's what happens when objects, and the way objects are made, transition into a subsequent system, which seems more fitting to the new economic status attained: it's what happens everywhere: pipes and raw cement floors were a single unit: ingenious, poor, but consistent . . . Now they've decided to change the floor to a rustic-style thing. Here it is, these sections of flagstone, stuccoed and painted with something you'd say was *copal* . . . To them it looks more elegant, they spent money on it, it's something you have to respect, because they have to, at all costs, *they must*, reduplicate the path we've followed, right down to the last detail, destroy everything that was one way and make it all over again, new and improved, only to figure out, a long time later, that they'd got it all wrong . . . But we Peninsulars are devastators and we surely can't give anyone lessons about anything . . .

It's been a while since I had a single thought about work . . . What line of work are you in, Ivo? No, actually, make that what line of work *were* you in? A consultant on major engineering projects? Oh, really? And just what the fuck line of work would that be? Ah, you don't know? Better that way, don't you think? Yes, we'll remember that at the end of the month, if it's absolutely necessary, that is, if we don't decide to just stay here for ever . . . But for right now, no work, *nisba*, *tipota*, *nada*, *nothing*, *rien*: just sea, a clear horizon and fried potatoes.

'*Ena cafetaki, parakalò, in the glass.*'

The party of French people are done, they even drank Grigoria's wine by the carafe and they're still alive . . . Grigoria makes a pretty bad cup of coffee, it tastes of iron filings, but it's not as harsh as Kalliope's coffee . . . If I'm going to drink Greek coffee, I want it to be bad, on the Island coffee *should be* bad, that's the way I like it, I've grown accustomed to it that way, that's how I want it, I enjoy the whiplash that it delivers down my spinal cord . . .

'*Parakalò*, Grigoria, *logariasmò*. Yes, the check, please.'

Again, tonight, the check wasn't even 6,000 lire, about five bucks, Sara has vanished on me, tonight. Oh look, here's Paola again.

'Have you seen my husband?'

'Huh? What are you doing here? No, the last time I saw him he was with you.'

'I don't know, I'm dead tired. We were drinking together at Kalliope's, then he said he was going to go for another walk. He just vanished. Strange, in theory he ought to be exhausted, he hiked his heart out again today, he says that he almost got to the foot of the Profitis Ilias, he always tells me that one of these days he's going to climb right up to the summit. If you see him, will you say that I decided to go to bed? Did you have a good dinner? Do you mind if I sit down here for a minute?'

'Not at all, take a seat. Do you want me to order you something?'

'No, let me just take a sip of your beer, can I? Yes, thanks. Ahh . . . Why didn't you go to the dinner?'

'Paola . . . didn't we talk about this earlier? Too many people. I didn't like huge tablesful of people. I know it's my fault, but I hate them. Every so often, you're allowed to hate something. Every once in a while it's nice to be able to choose—this yes, that no. Eating by myself, *yes*, tablesful of twenty people, *no*. Sara chose to go anyway, the little bitch. She's suddenly turned sociable.'

'Don't talk that way, you ought to hold on tight to that woman . . . Kiss the ground she walks on. To think she puts up with you . . . I mean, do you realize?'

'What are you saying, Paola? What do I lack?'

'Forget about it, Ivo . . . You don't lack a thing . . . How old are you? Fifty or so, am I right? You're not a kid and you're not an easy man to deal with. She's a tender young girl and it's obvious that she loves you . . . Hold her close, where are you going to find another one like her?'

'You women have this bad habit of looking out for each other . . . And it's only a game, an appearance that you like to put on, because usually underneath the sisterhood—do you remember *sisterhood*?—under the affectations of friendship and female solidarity, things aren't what they seem: you cultivate rivalries that are incomprehensible to us . . . You and Sara hardly even know each other—if you don't really know who she is, how can you tell me to 'hold on tight to her'? You do it out of conceit . . . When I was a boy, I'd see you go into the bathroom together, two or three at a time, holding hands: 'Will you accompany me to the bathroom?' What the fuck was the point of *accompanying each other to the bathroom*? How is to so *obvious to you* that Sara loves me? She might very well love me, I don't doubt it . . . But what do you know about it? What need do you have, you women, to show off all this *friendship* among yourselves?'

'Sweet Jesus, being alone has turned you vinegary tonight, Ivo . . .'

'What vinegary, I'm feeling fine, nothing's bothering me . . .'

'It's obvious, Ivo, you can see that she's in love with you . . . A woman sees it . . . It's clear from the way she looks at you, the way she stays at your side . . .'

'She stays "at my side"?'

'Yes. And after all, it isn't true that Sara and I don't know each other. We've had long conversations this year, we told each other a bunch of things. We talked about her job, she told me about her ten years in analysis . . . She told me that she really cares for you, that you taught her a great many things. She's a girl who's got it together, she's lovely, intelligent, young . . . When are you going to luck out like this again, Ivo? I mean, you, have you taken a look at yourself in the mirror anytime lately?'

'There, I knew we were going to circle around to that point eventually . . .'

'No, that's not it, you're still a good-looking man, certainly, you've developed a bit of a gut, since last winter you've definitely put on quite a bit of weight . . . But there are lots of women who like their men corpulent . . .'

'You say it with such disgust in your voice, Paola . . . Not all of us can be as skinny as your husband . . .'

'Come on, Ivo, you see that you're out of sorts tonight? The Analyst is like that because of his metabolism, he couldn't gain an ounce if he scarfed down a side of beef. It makes me furious. Plus he's a little younger than me, he hikes, he stays in shape, he doesn't smoke . . . You can't pretend you're not the age you are. She's thirty-seven, she told me, and she's childless. You don't have kids and you don't want them. For her, being with someone like you, with your personality, it isn't easy, you get it?'

'Again with my *personality* . . . I can see the two of you have done a lot of talking, eh? And what kind of *personality* are you saying I have? Did she tell you that "it isn't easy"?'

'No, no . . . She didn't say a thing to me about the two of you. We talked in vague terms, only in general . . . But I'm just saying, certain things are clear, we understand each other among women, even if you don't say it in so many words . . .'

They understand each other *among women* . . . On the fly, certainly: they're immediately fast friends, sisters on the spot, because they're *women*, not men, not the sort of brutal rough-hewn mess that we are . . . Right away, a cascade of saccharine compliments, even if they never met once in their lives. The first time they lay eyes on each other they perform a mind-blistering once-over with their internal high-res scanners: 'Who are you? How are you dressed? Is that real gold, the chain that you have around your neck? Do you belong to my same social class? Are you prettier than me? Is your husband richer / poorer / as rich as mine? Do your tits stand up higher than mine? Is your ass firmer, less firm, just as firm as mine? Do you have cellulite? I'll bet you do, don't you?' Then they move on to the relationship phase, where they take it for granted that they share all and every possible friendship and sisterhood and mutual comprehension, full willingness to listen sympathetically, give advice, offer help—they simulate good feelings, more good feelings & more good feelings still, squandering pat phrases, then curiosities to be gratified, just because, for the fun of it, for the sheer delight of finding and maybe later telling others . . . Little masterpieces of social micro-engineering . . . Everything is balanced exquisitely on the nothingness of conventional interactions, everything runs on those particular tracks and never once do they veer from them: What pleasure can they take from it? I can't even begin to guess . . . But not all women are like that, Sara isn't like that . . . What can she have told her? Paola is trying to make it clear to me that she knows a great many more things about Sara than I do . . . She can't imagine that I couldn't give less of a damn about what she knows or doesn't know . . . I'd like to tell her to go to hell . . . Why doesn't she stop busting my balls, get the hell out from underfoot and go get some sleep? *We women–each other–among women* . . . She doesn't understand that I don't know anything about Sara and I don't want to know anything about her, not because that's the way I want it but because it frightens me just to think of knowing things about her without her knowledge . . . It is *up to her* to decide, what I ought or ought not to know: for myself, I know nothing, I think nothing, *I'm just afraid of losing her.* Paola, why don't you go fuck yourself, or go to bed, whichever you prefer?

'Has it ever occurred to you that she might want to have a child with you? You've been together for four years now, she told me. Before long, she'll be too old . . . Don't get mad, I know it's none of my business. I'm just saying this because it seemed to me . . .'

'Oh, really? It seemed to you? *We women* understand one another—*we* listen to one another —*we* help one another, etc.? Paola, I'm asking you, let's just drop this line of conversation, do you mind? Don't be offended, I just don't want to discuss it, that's all . . . Not now, anyway, maybe some other time, or else, better still, never . . . This is how I feel about it, if you want to know . . . And really, I hope you don't take this the wrong way . . . But it seems to me that it's none of your fucking business . . . So if you're good with it, here's what let's do: let's just never talk about it again, whatever it is that Sara might or might not have told you, OK? . . . Listen, the last thing I wanted to do was hurt your feelings! Paola! Come on, Paola! Wait up for a second, hold on! Listen, I beg your pardon, I really didn't want to be such a jerk . . . It's just that you put your finger on a sensitive point . . . Listen, maybe I've had too much to drink tonight . . .'

'It's OK, Ivo, don't worry about it, my fault. I shouldn't have said anything. It's never a good idea to stick your nose into other people's business . . . If anything, I beg *your* pardon. I crossed a line . . . I thought we were close enough friends that we could talk about things like this, too. It's really no problem . . . But now I think I'm ready to turn in, good night.'

And she left . . . You're always the same, you never change, you could have let her talk, what difference did it make to you? Sara is definitely going to hear about this latest outburst . . . After all, what was she really saying to you . . . ? Nothing. Nothing? What do you mean, Ivo? Paola was telling me that Sara wants to have a child with me . . . She was telling me that instead of talking to me about it, Sara told *her* . . . How dare she? What the hell goes on in people's heads? She should be thankful I didn't tell her to go fuck herself, right then and there . . . I was rude, unpleasant, a complete oaf, she thought she could talk to me, we're been friends for so many years . . . And there you go, in the end you're the one apologizing, as if she wasn't the one sticking her nose into things that were none of her business . . . I need to swing back by Grigoria's and pay the check, then let's take a walk, because this damned woman has got me so I won't be able to digest my dinner . . . Then let's go talk to Sara . . . She must be at Longaris . . . So Sara wants to have a child with me and the first thing she does is go tell Paola? Certainly, anything's possible, but if I know her as well as I think

I do, it doesn't add up. Forget about it, Ivo: you, do you want to have a baby with her? If she did talk to you about it, what would you say? Yes or no? Would you be willing to become a father for the first time at age fifty? Why did tonight have to go this way? What does all this have to do with my solitary evening out? Here we are, more or less 7,000–7,500.

'*Efharisto, kalinihta*, Grigoria.'

Maybe the reason Sara still hasn't spoken to you about it is because she sees you the way you are, so . . . so, so wrapped up in your own business, that is, so selfish. A word that means nothing: she never accused you of being selfish . . . And what are you saying, that not wanting kids is selfish? This is your last chance to become a father—it's not like time is running out for Sara, it's running out for you. Sara is the last chance you have to give even a scrap of meaning to your life . . . What does that even mean? Life doesn't have meaning in any case, whether you have one child or ten . . . It's just that it might be a nice thing . . . Nice, that's the right word for it, selfishly nice . . . Father didn't seem particularly happy about having you, maybe about having your sisters, but you he just shredded to ribbons: it didn't seem as if it was particularly nice for him, if anything it seemed like a burden, a responsibility, a pain in the ass, something he made sure weighed on you every day. As if I asked to be brought into the world, that fucking asshole . . . You're just like him, Father is lurking inside you, hiding in ambush until you fuck up and have children of your own and then, *sproing*! the old marionette lunges out, ready to massacre the poor little creature . . . Christ on a crutch, does everybody really have to have a family? Do we all absolutely have to perform our duty? Still, it must be nice, Ivo, to have a child with Sara . . . So we could set up our own personal domestic meat-grinder? Whatever a family really is, this is your last chance to have one, to build one for yourself . . . Your son would be an SOF, Son of an Old Father . . . Maybe that's better, an Old Father gets the hell out of your way before a young father does . . . He's around busting your balls, if you're really unlucky, for twenty years, then it's so long dad. An old father who stinks and drools, a sick father you have to take care of, a

143

father who can't walk on his own. How many times have you seen that, Brandani? The horror . . . You want to have a son now, so that when you're eighty, he'll be . . . What? Thirty? Well, OK, thirty's not that young. That might make sense, I guess . . . I'm staggering, I've had too much to drink . . . I'm sleepy. My stomach's in turmoil, I must have smoked a dozen Karelias, I think I bought the pack at seven. You have to quit-quit-quit but meanwhile, that is, until then, that is, in this brief span of time remaining before I give up this bad habit, let's just smoke one more . . . At the far end of the beach it's dark, there's finally shelter from the blinding yellow light bulbs of these fucked-up streetlights. I'll get that far . . . It's ten to one in the morning, look out for the tamarisk leaves, they're full of *kazzaridos*, flying cockroaches on my shirt . . . Brrr! Nereas laughs at my terror of the *kazzaridos*. He just crushes them and ignores them. They crunch. *Scrtch*! The hunt under the bed, the other night. He must have thought to himself: 'The things I have to do to make a living, I even have to crush cockroaches at the engineer's command . . .' There's nothing wrong with hating cockroaches, he feels the same repulsion for moray eels . . . The shameless *kazzarido* that strolls along the bed's headboard, 2 inches in length, is more than I can take, I can't sleep with it there . . . It fled in a flash under the bed, he moved the bed and caught it all the same, it went *scrtch*! Brother *kazzarido*, it's your life against my sleep. I'm a higher mammal, a primate, but you aren't, proud little *kazzarido*, you're just a tawny bug—I can summon Nereas, who'll crush you with his plastic sandal the colour of old leather with fake stitching; but you, mysterious ancestral beetle, who will you call? If you had a son, for a couple of years you couldn't come here any more, forget about the Sense of the Sea, your useless life as an overgrown selfish baby-man would be over: for the first time you'd have to do something for someone else. You'd have to live for him, support him for decades. And for her, for Sara . . . And what if it turned out to be a girl? A daughter! How wonderful that would be! She'd make an alliance with her mother, they'd put you in the minority, you'd turn into one of those silent retirees, subject to the whims of wife and daughter . . . A daughter would be pure, unadulterated joy! The only thing missing tonight were fantasies of paternity, the last ones before being unrigged and scrapped . . . But you really are still in time, it's still possible, you really could have a baby, Sara and you . . .

At last, darkness.

Large cold round stones that jut into my ass cheeks . . . I need only remove the most impudent ones . . . There . . . It's just a matter of technique: carve out a small hollow that will accommodate my butt . . . My eyes are getting used to the darkness . . . I'm a little cold, tuck my shirt into my trousers, pull out my woollen watch-cap, another cigarette, light gusts of wind . . . Down there, at the end of the beach, is someone . . . No stars, the moonlight is too strong tonight, but you can clearly glimpse the horizon, the clean line that cuts across the reflection on the water's surface, down there where the sky begins . . . The horizon, which every time imparts to me this yearning to *go away*: that's how it's been ever since I was a boy in the City by the Sea, during the sacred summer, before Father could inexorably drag me back to the City of God . . . How he loved being able to finally drag me out of there and restore me to his daily supervision, in the suffering of winter and school . . . So, first and foremost: never be like him! Don't devour your children, keep that in mind, Brandani . . . To observe the horizon and think of going away was a single thing: you'd set off aboard the *Mandrake* straight out to sea and you'd never turn back until the land had vanished, or almost. Sea and silence . . . Even now, if I had a boat, I'd set out straight to sea, perpendicular to the horizon, following the wake of the moon, heading who knows where, out into the open sea, to Syria, Egypt, the ports of Turkey. After a while, someone might ask: 'I haven't seen Ivo for the past few days, Sara, is he all right?' 'I couldn't say, he just disappeared into the horizon the other night.' You read *Lighea* recently: there, Tomasi di Lampedusa tells of a moonlit night just like this one, when the Professor performs his Act of Reunification and plunges into the sea . . . Concentrate on the atmosphere of that short story, Brandani, and you'll see that tonight you'll grasp the Sense of the Sea. When there's wind, it's harder to do, it's better when the sea is calm, like on those Tyrrhenian nights on brightly lit cement rotundas, with the jukebox going full blast. *Si 'sta voce te sceta 'int'a nuttata.* Nothing is going to come back, no promise has been kept: God didn't exist, the world wasn't waiting for you, no one was searching for you, across the sea there's nothing but restaurants serving fried mixed seafood and your work, which promised so much but in the end rejected you. Or maybe you just didn't have what it takes to succeed at it, Ivo . . . Wait: Sense of the Sea. Think of the transparency of the depths, the free-ranging ferocious creatures that are swimming right now through the darkness, that come to the surface, attracted by the moon. Flocks of phosphorescent squids, lightning fast. The massive heads of groupers appear among the rocks. The bluefish that the kids talked about, excitedly, on the wharfs of the City by the Sea. The noise of the waves under the side of the boat, the incessant lapping and splashing of the nights anchored offshore. The whistling of the sirocco wind in the shrouds. Sofrano. A procession of distant islands along the horizon, one after the other, each of them a world to itself, with its land and its waters. The white beaches where Odysseus' comrades slept, the sweet-smelling woods behind them. The ship hauled up on shore. Stars, mosquitoes, moths. The rapid silence of tuna fish heading for Gibraltar and from there down along the west coast of Africa, towards other undertows. No one knows anything about them, except that it's possible to catch and kill them. There are 15,000 species still unknown in the Mediterranean alone, that supreme & sublime sea. The big sea stack in the port of Ponza. The basalt cliff wall on Palmarola. The deserted beach of the City by the Sea, at night, the naked body of Stefania who let herself be kissed all over and you didn't have the nerve to take her, you poor jerk. She smelt of air. Now, for all you know, she could *be* air. There's nothing to be done about it, tonight you're not going to grasp the Sense of the Sea. There's too much wind here, let me move back and get some shelter, behind this rock wall. Who could that be down there? You can't see a thing, I hope there's no dogshit here . . . There, right here it's practically warm. The rock has been drinking in hot sunlight all day long and now it's spewing forth the heat it digested. The wharf in the City by the Sea too, if you walked on it at night, would let you feel the heat of the daytime trapped in the limestone . . . They're coming this way but they can't see me. They stop, they embrace, they kiss. They can't see me. He's caressing her ass. Look at them. He's the Hiking Analyst, Paola's husband. Is that her? No. Paola is much taller and skinnier, she's not blond, and her hair is straight. This one is blond, wavy hair, loose trousers that flap in the wind, they look like those viscose pants that Sara wears . . . Sara! *That's Sara*!

I need to pee . . . Did I sleep here? . . . It's 5.30, the sun is about to come up . . . My neck hurts . . . It's getting light, the night is over, I'm cold, my mouth is dry, I'm thirsty . . . Sara must be out looking for me, alcohol and Xanax knocked me out all at once . . . I need to get to my feet, go find a cup of coffee . . . It's too early . . . I have to go back to my room, otherwise where would I go? I'm cold, where should I go? Go up to your room, take another Xanax, and get some sleep. Sleep: there's nothing else to do . . . Everything's still closed . . . You shouldn't come back here again . . . This is no longer a place for you, there's nothing here for you now, by now not even Sara . . . This time she's going to leave you, she's going to hook up with the Analyst, your best bet is to move fast and dump her first . . . They don't know that you saw them, they'd just had sex . . . But really this place belongs to you, you'll come back anyway, probably on your own . . . You know perfectly well why you come here . . . You come here to watch the shadows lengthen across the beaches, you come to breathe in the scent of the underbrush dusted off by the gusts of wind, the overwhelming aroma of sage. You come here for the water off Kandri at sunset, when it turns purple and when you dive in it's warmer and denser and it seems not to want to let you go. You come here for the exhaustion of this wind that roars in your ears all day long, for the solitude of the beaches, for the naps in the grotto of Opsi on Karpathos, or else in the shadow of the rocks of Nati, with your backpack under your head, a rag wrapped around your face. You come here for that moment of hesitation in which you pass from the land to the water, from heat to cold, for the icy veins of fresh water that trickle out of the rocks by the shore . . . All I need is another Xanax, a bottle of water, my bed . . . You come here for the walks up the dry beds of the mountain streams, when you venture up into the high valleys and your push inland until you come to a halt when faced by the unscaleable obstacle, a sheer rock cliff. You come here for the wild fig tree in the valley of Kandri, for the fig trees of Papa Minas, for the huge sweet-smelling fig tree of the Fork in the Road in Avlonas, for the little fig tree clinging to that retaining wall in Olympos, which had turned black until you thought it was about to die, but when you returned you found it thriving. You come here for the endless dry-laid stone walls of the prehistoric terracings of Saria, for the nanny goats' hard heads, for their cephalopod eyes. You come here for the scent of what remains of the Aleppo pine forest, after the Fire, for the purple shadow that condenses on the mountain sides around sunset, for the clouds like immense red rags stretching out over the sea at dawn, for everything that the Island is no longer, which you experienced and saw and sampled but which is gone now. You come here for the concrete pavement, the plastic chairs, the white lead brushed onto the trunks of the tamarisk trees, for the surge of disgust you feel for the cockroaches, to sit in the morning at the base of the Stele of Saint Nicholas and drink a cup of coffee made by Kalliope. You come here for the gulps of bad ouzo and because every gesture you make cuts the horizon. You come here because you don't know how to let go of this place and because of the dawn that's coming up now . . . I need a bottle of water . . . The tap on the wharf: Is that water potable?

11.05 a.m.

Clearly, the flight is going to be late. By now, engineer Ivo Brandani reeks of sweat and he knows it. It's not yet obvious to those sitting near him, but still he reeks. Wafting up to his nostrils from under his jacket comes proof that he is overheated and still alive, evidence that he's been sitting on this chair in this airport for two hours now, waiting to board his plane and finally fly back to the City of God. He stands up and goes to get some more information. At the check-in desk there's a line of northern Europeans. He looks up at the departures screen and sees there's a flight for Düsseldorf scheduled to depart at 11.15. Outside on the tarmac, a brightly coloured Airbus stands waiting, its tail cluttered with the giant icon of a flying duck, as Brandani realizes to his annoyance: it's the desecration of the divine aeronautical form, it's one more instance of the mass infantilization that blights the Western mind, especially when that mind goes on holiday; it's something inappropriate and blasphemous, something he can't seem to adjust to. The young fair-haired woman behind the desk speaks briefly into the phone, then hangs up and tells him that the flight is in fact running late, that that's all the information she has now, and as soon as they find out anything new they'll make an announcement. This time of year the airport in Sharm isn't particularly crowded, they're just moving the last flights of the season through. Summer's almost here, soon the heat will become unbearable, the tourist trade is declining but there's still plenty of traffic. There are groups deplaning or embarking all together, all arriving together by motor coach, all lining up together, forming impenetrable walls with their bodies, their bundles, their shopping bags full of purchases, ethnic gifts to take home, duffle bags emblazoned with various trademarks, containing diving and snorkelling gear. Everyone tricked out in shorts, short skirts, jeans, many of them shod in impressive, highly technical river sandals or unpretentious flip-flops, but most wearing elaborate rubber sneakers, enclosed, semi-enclosed, breathable, spring-loaded, shock-absorbing, metallized, brightly coloured or with heels that flash brightly at every step.

Interesting. How do you think that works? Batteries activated by heel pressure? Motion-activated piezoelectric devices?

Every article of clothing, with only the rarest of exceptions, every shoe, every accessory, hat, backpack, fanny pack, every pair of dark eyeglasses bore its nice trademark, logo or designer name, enjoying pride of place: T-shirts emblazoned with bizarre effigies or texts, others that are more neutral, like D&Gs, which say only, 'This T-shirt, otherwise completely nondescript, stands out from the others because it was designed and manufactured by D&G, respected designers' (or it's a counterfeit, which is easy to imagine here, where everything seems to be staged, the second- or third-hand reproduction of an original located elsewhere), others that are comical or provocative, allusive, with soft-porn double entendres, or with a drawing, not badly done at all, of a tropical fish, usually an angelfish, white and red, or yellow.

Observing people's feet, their shoes: I've been doing it all my life, since the day I was born . . . These guys at Ecocare are crazy to even think of taking on jobs like this . . . The Japanese are the best, they invented the field in the first place, starting with the imitation plates of sushi you put in the front window . . . From fake food, to fake landscape, and fake world . . . If you know how to make a perfect fake fish soup, a plastic tuna filet, perennially fresh, that makes you want to eat it, then you're ready for the next step . . . And in fact they expanded into new sectors, they started making life-sized imitations of whole slices of the world . . . At first they were a little clumsy, they were only good at imitating certain elements, but they were good enough to make those enormous glassed-in warehouses that contained beach, shoals, (real) sand, (real, salt) water, artificial waves, that is, fake/real, and (real) palm trees. They filled up with beach-goers, huge investments, real business. At first, it was a real challenge to imitate the sun, but then, working on it, they managed to produce the entire arc of a day, a fake day, complete with clouds and sunset . . . No matter the weather outside of the terrarium, the fake sun starts shining at nine in the morning: outdoors it might be snowing but all the customers inside are in their bathing suits, having more fun than they ought to, they're paddle boarding, swimming . . . Crystal-clear, clean water, where are you going to find that nowadays? It must be twenty years now since that movie . . . *The Truman Show* . . . It seemed like science fiction but actually . . . Still, it's one thing to make fakes inside of what is clearly & unabashedly make-believe, quite another matter to reconstruct what's real with fakes, as if it were real, in an authentic context. These guys in Sharm are seriously worried . . .

Ankles toes heels, chapped skin, chipped nails, or dirty, long, badly cut nails. Veins and varicose thread veins, purplish swollen toes of women trying to walk in shoes with too-high heels, yellowish calluses. Or perfect feminine feet, tapered toes sorted by size, splendid calves edgy in stark, hard-working relief, the rarest kind. Feet with toes that feel the terrain beneath them and curl up at every step, or they spread out in the flip-flops like the ribbing in a duck's foot, or they remain admirably composed, politely assorted. Stout toes, fat ones, long white nervous toes, weary, exhausted, overworked, inflamed. Feet that emerge from their clogs at every long stop of the line, fleeing the pressure squeezing the toes together, resting on top of the other foot. Sandals that have collapsed, allowing the toes to protrude beyond the raised edge of the sole, extending out until they practically touch the floor. Then there are feet shod in Nikes and Pumas, sheathed in Adidas and Reeboks, occasionally neatly laced up. Ivo can imagine what it's like in there, insane temperatures, sweating and bacterial fermentation rapidly and reciprocally proliferating, feet like cultures in agar. He can barely even tolerate his old leather loafers—made that is entirely of *animal* skin, made with the living exterior of a creature that once breathed and lowed—and he has to turn his gaze away from those *stuffed* feet, crammed uncomfortably into plastic and rubber, enclosed in shoes with symbolic shapes and designs that are senseless to the appearance, expressionistic shoes with springs and visible shock-absorbing air chambers, or else covered with multicoloured ribbings in relief, connected at the laces' traction points, staging a completely non-existent system of channelled forces. On the legs and especially on the ankles of many, as well as on their forearms and backs, we see tattoos small, medium and large, shown off to a greater or lesser extent, almost all of them ugly, always meaningless, because randomly done, not premeditated, done out of a collective spirit, for fashion. Para-ethnic mini-symbols, faded outlines of geckos that were popular a few years ago. Then there are tiny butterflies, little spirals, dolphins, diminutive snakes, palm trees, Maori motifs, everything.

Why had the gecko caught on the way it did? Is it a special symbol? What does it mean? Where does it come from?

Ivo knows that he belongs to prior, twentieth-century cultures in which the tattoo was considered something self-destructive and abusive, a badge indicating a predisposition for crime, outsider status and waterfront, back-alley culture, which someone with a petty-bourgeois background like him would never dream of adopting. You need to aim high, not in the opposite direction, Father used to say. But for many years now he's realized that this is bullshit: aiming high means having more money, no question about that, but it doesn't mean anything else. The heights he was supposed to aim for involved a state of 'inner nobility', as Father liked to say; in a moment of lucidity he'd even added: 'I've never succeeded at it myself, but that doesn't mean it can't be done . . .' Thinking back on it now, he realized that nothing had ever harmed him so badly as those words.

It took him dozens of years to understand that living a life according to the principle of pride is senseless, that pride is a devastating form of stupidity, capable of steering you straight into ruin . . . It induces types of behaviour based on nobility and honour, that is, on principles that are abstract, outmoded, unattainable, relative & Fascistic, completely imbecilic, extraneous to the world you've always lived in and still do. The only thing that matters isn't style, it's what you've actually done and the way you did it, that is, either well or badly . . . All that counts are *results*, Brandani, just results: Where are yours?

His buttocks are tingling and numb, his right leg has gone to sleep, he changes position continually, he'd like to slip off his shoes, he loosens his belt, takes off his jacket, folds it and places it with his bag on the seat next to his, he rolls up his shirtsleeves, from his armpits an aromatic blast of sweat wafts up to his nostrils.

All these people bring money. They come here because they believe in the fairy tale of unspoilt nature. They believe in it, in the unspoilt part, for real . . . They don't realize that the spoilers are them, all of us . . . Here just the sheer quantity of shit that gets flushed out into the sea every day in the high season is monstrous . . . Certainly, it's been purified, the treatment plants are underground, or on the other side of the first line of dunes, concealed in some manner . . . But it's still contamination . . . Nonetheless, it's not this, or it's not just this. It's something else, something that's been going on for decades: the coral is dying here, too. It began suddenly a few years ago, no one knows exactly why . . . They didn't know what to do, the only measure they took was to prohibit diving along certain stretches of coastline where the phenomenon was most unmistakable. No remedy . . . Then they realized that there was a remedy after all: rebuild it all, fake, and issue an absolute prohibition to touch it. Without a coral environment, it's not clear how the fish can survive, even though not everything that encrusts on the seabed is dead. They say that they're going to try to feed the fish in secret . . . Fish food dumped in the water by night? Here their livings are dependent on the myth of unspoilt nature, if the ecosystem dies on them, they're screwed . . . Fake coral, come on! What do we care? Who'll even notice? The contract we signed is a substantial one . . . That's exactly why, the absolute seal of silence must endure as long as we live . . . Think what a scoop it would be:

THE CORAL REEF OF SHARM IS FAKE!
The revelations of a Peninsular technician.
At Sharm el-Sheik vast portions of the seabed
perfectly reproduced in synthetic materials

I'm not going to be the one to tell the whole story, the penalty would be crushingly expensive, but one thing is certain—sooner or later someone is going to do it . . . I'll play by the rules of the game, I like the Apocalypse, I'm comfortable in it, I enjoy it . . . The Japanese have been studying the seabed where it's still healthy for years . . . Thousands of photographs, electronic scans of the current state of the seabed, latex casts, living samples passed through the scanner underwater in the aquariums, experiments on how long the pigments to be used will last, the structural problems, the encrustations, the tides . . . We're in charge of the hydraulic installations and systems . . . We're going to have to camouflage it, we're going to have to establish a fake temporary marine park, officially for purposes of research, completely inaccessible, dimensions still to be determined . . . The Largo Project: a fairly large fake support ship, practically hollow on the inside, with a crane and everything necessary . . . It was an idea of Ezio Croce's, he's a free spirit, it came to him watching an old James Bond movie, the one with Adolfo Celi playing an evil millionaire who wants to rule the world . . . His name is Largo . . . They gave him an eyepatch, to make him seem more wicked . . . Then they cast Brandauer as the same character in a remake with Kim Basinger, La Suprema . . . At first, we had our doubts, but Ezio insisted: 'The only reason I'm mentioning that movie is to give you a rough idea of the solution, obviously we're going to have to work on it . . .' They finally came around at Ecocare, they looked around, they checked into the maritime registries, they visited shipyards, looking for something that would work, a ship that could be converted, with certain technical specifications. It had to look like a research vessel, so reasonably small but not too small . . . Aside from cordoning off the area, from the keel of the ship we'll lower to the seabed a kind of ballasted curtain to hide everything. For now, we'll just work on a couple of acres of seabed, on an experimental basis, to test the results and the working methods. Then we'll see . . . The scuba divers will do the hard work, they'll have to install everything practically by hand, concretion by concretion . . . They're still undecided on the adhesives to use, they're testing various kinds . . .

Things are pretty well advanced, in Japan they're ready to get started but the Egyptians are hesitating, even though they've already coughed up a fair amount of money . . . It's a political decision . . . If the projects goes badly, and it can't help but go badly, someone's head will roll . . . It's nice to be a technician, after all: all you have to do as a technician is tell someone whether something can be done—and everything can be done—and how much time and money it will take. Then, if you say go ahead, I'll do it for you . . . You decide, and I do it . . . It's fascinating and totally Asian, the painstaking art of reproduction . . . We've discovered that in Hong Kong too there are some excellent companies working in the same sector . . . Maybe we should contact them for the bulk of the work, that is, for the subsequent lots: we'll ask them for an estimate . . . If the thing actually comes off, it will be like a grand, immense underwater pop installation . . . One thing's for sure, if I'm planning a holiday, I won't come here, even though elsewhere, that is, everywhere, it's not as if we're destroying and modifying any less than here, but every species produces modifications in the environment it lives in, I was reading . . . Feet adapt to shoes but shoes adapt to feet as well: we, *necessarily*—that is, whether or not we want to—modify the planet . . . In fact, we're rebuilding the planet to suit our preferences and, most importantly, our convenience . . . When it's all finished, no one will know what's real, and everything will once again look as if it were real . . . Franco tells me that we're slowly transitioning from the natural to the post-natural: right then and there I didn't put too much stock in what he was saying, he often says things that are slightly involuted, but instead as usual he had hit the bullseye . . . I haven't talked to him in months, I miss him . . . He had added that once the transformation is complete and the entire planet has become post-natural, we'd consider it nature all the same, because we'll have forgotten its previous state: 'Ergo *nature doesn't exist.*' As he uttered the word 'nature', he'd made scare-quotes in the air with his fingers, something quite un-Italian that he'd learnt at Columbia . . . He's picked up these Americans mannerisms that get on my nerves, but every time that I talk to him he teaches me something new—he's my *horizontal mentor*, that is, someone my age I can still learn from, who still has something to teach me . . . It's the acidification of the seawater, apparently, that's killing the coral. First it's bleached, then it dies . . . The excess carbon dioxide in the atmosphere dissolves into the water and, apparently, makes it harder for the coral polyps to extract the calcium carbonate that they need to build their structures . . . But they're not certain that this is the way it works . . . There are those who claim that, in no more than thirty years, the coral reefs all around the world will have become gigantic boneyards . . .

Ivo Brandani adores water, the idea of water, everything to do with water. As a child, during the endless Postwar summers at the beach, he fooled himself into believing that that was his true world. It got to the point that he yearned to change into a fish and escape towards the South Seas, where no would ever be able to track him down and tell him what he should or shouldn't do. He went diving every day with a spring-loaded speargun that he'd found underwater, and over the years he'd come to realize that fish don't think about the future, they're all-present, in fact, all-instant, without a plan, nothing more than impulses, emotions, voracity, velocity, energy, pleasure. But then those images started to fade, for some time now he's resigned himself to the idea of living on dry land as a biped: all that lazing around in the water, allowing himself to be caressed by it for hours, had failed to produce any physical mutation in him, he didn't grow fins, the water just marinated his fingers, turned his lips purple, and nothing more.

Is the barrier reef dying? Are the seabeds of Sharm going to wrack and ruin? Oh well, so be it . . . Let's just rebuild it, fake, the planet . . . We have the means and we have the opportunity, since no one's coming down from outer space to keep us from doing it, seeing that God doesn't exist, or if He does exist, He seems mighty determined to mind His own business . . . That means the Planet is all ours, we can do whatever the fuck we like with it . . . Just don't say another word to me about *nature*, please, never again: let's relegate usage of this term to advertising spots, let's just let those people juggle with it like some kind of mental plaything. Do you want multicolour coral reefs? Fine, we're getting equipped for that exact thing, soon they'll be ready . . . Behold, the World's Middle Class exercising its right to Leisure Time . . . Behold, they arrive, behold, they depart after allowing themselves to be sucked dry of vast quantities of cash, for a carefully planned week in unspoilt nature—beach—coral & colourful fish—sex—good food—music—relaxation, all stuff that's going to be converted into a lovely slideshow on Flickr . . . They have fun, they've had fun, they'll have more fun next time: Sharm is nothing more than a diverticulum in the intestinal twists and turns of their lives . . . Nothing wrong with it, if only they didn't emanate such an over-powering whiff of *absence* . . . The Great Uniform Middle Class of Western Democracy, the class that has devoured and incorporated within itself all the other classes, including the working class . . . No, not all of them: there are the outsiders, the losers, the unincorporable, they're being expelled with ever greater determination outside the boundaries of the social agglomerate, increasingly cast aside from its uniformity . . . In short, this Middle Class, with every day that passes, gives me an ever stronger impression of having turned its back on active reason . . . It seems to have embraced wholeheartedly some kind of passive reason . . . It seems to be wallowing in what is ultimately a sort of global surreality, where everything is an image of some vanished original, or else has become unattainable, or too expensive . . . The World by now has become a theme park . . . Think of Marx: culture as a superstructure, as a misleading decoration of the relations of production . . . But that was *before* the advent of the media-driven democracies, it was *before* power managed to reach the minds of men, directly, one by one. These people standing in line, these Germans, the Russians down there, the Swedes that departed an hour ago, those squawking Peninsulars, in short, all of them, all of us, we're *all culture* . . . 'In this sense, ours is a hyper-baroque era,' says Franco, 'just as in baroque the ornament becomes structure, likewise today culture, from the superstructure it once was, assumes a central role and succeeds in bringing about consensus in defiance of reality. You don't earn a fucking penny? You don't have a job? That doesn't matter, those aren't thing that form part of the media truth, and so they're of no concern to you, in fact, they don't exist . . .' Et cetera . . . Each of us normally inhabits our own niche in the imaginary world but what really counts is the mass imaginary world—whoever has the means to build it these days wins . . .

Ivo always stops at this point. It's his usual analysis, it's his old Marxist education, its his old professors, like Molteni and the others, the documents of the Movement, it's his fossil history that's at work again. Only with Franco can he speak freely, otherwise he sees that they're giving him strange looks, people don't understand or they get irritated. Nowadays, nearly everyone's different from him, they all have more recent roots. The native of a media capitalism no longer possess the notions of opposition, alternative, and in the contemporary they're as comfortable as mice in cheese. It was Franco, with the readings that he recommended to him, who helped him to assemble his picture of the post-natural. Ivo always pays very close attention to it—the philosophical discourse has always been instinctive with him, something he developed over one long summer many years ago—but in particular, over the course of a lifetime as a builder and a traveller, he has had a chance to verify for himself the reliability of his theses in the vile bodies of the world.

It was Cremaschi who had adopted that old definition of Baroque aesthetics . . . In Baroque it is the ornament 'that becomes structure . . .' If the imaginary, that is, ornament, draws a veil over our perception of reality and 'all our actions hinge on it', as Franco says, then the 'Baroque' overturning is complete and 'nothing structural can be perceived any longer . . .' 'But sooner or later we will have to take reality into account again and when that happens, then there will be a revolution once again, but this time on a planetary basis . . .' Franco apparently still believes that . . .

Under the thighs and buttocks of a sweaty man who is sitting for hours on a chair made of perforated sheet metal, even the creases in the softest linen can become as sharp as knife blades. A young woman sitting across from him, her legs bare/bronzed/crossed, dangles her simple flip-flop from an arched foot, shapely toes perfectly manicured, her flesh a homogeneous golden hue, nothing reddened, nothing callused. Ivo focuses, first on the foot, and then on the girl.

Too bad about the push-up bra . . . And what need is there for one, at her age? The problem is similar to that of the dying reef: nature can't compete with its own imitation, with the exaggeration and relentless implementation of its aesthetic characteristics . . . The natural shape of a tit . . .

Do you remember, Brando? When you were a little boy you'd sit in rapt admiration, hypnotized by the sight of a completely nude breast in a baby's mouth, suckling on the dark, turgid nipple, leaking milk. A breast subjected to the normal force of gravity can't compete with these prosthetic devices and has to do what it can: If a fifty-year-old woman can flash the tits of a thirty-year-old, what is the thirty-year-old supposed to do to win the battle? Hence the birth of the hyper-tit & the hyper-ass, bound and determined to kill the market for any spontaneous curvature of the flesh, as well as the very idea of a natural woman . . . And this in itself is post-natural . . .

He's already slightly aroused, as he focuses on the girl's foot. To the point that perhaps she notices, perhaps she smiles ever so faintly, a vague, passing, disinterested thing. She's used to being looked at, that's obvious. But then the process of alienation of the foot begins for Ivo, something that's habitual with him: he does it, when the opportunity presents itself, with the feet of both females and males, if he happens to be able to observe them, bare, for a long-enough period to succeed in glimpsing them as hands deformed by ambulation. Airports like this one at Sharm, packed with tourists, are ideal places in which to perform the mental ritual that he calls the 'loss of the sense of the foot inasmuch as a foot'. The ritual constitutes a recovery of the fleeting awareness of what a foot actually is: the hand of a quadruman that has been deformed by standing erect. It's a challenging task, it's a little like when you continually repeat the same word aloud until, if only for a few moments, it loses all meaning. Brandani is a very careful observer of shoes and 'inferior extremities' (this description alone makes the task easier) but he doesn't feel any special sexual attraction to women's feet. That is, he's not a fetishist, but the feet of his women have always been important, if for no reason other than the fact that his glance seemed to land on them constantly, obsessively, all the time. Now this lovely foot of a girl, a girl who might be English-Danish-Dutch, or maybe German, it's hard to start *un*-seeing it, that is, to observe it without bringing into play the aesthetic, anatomical, sexual notion of foot-of-a-human-female, to remove the concept of foot, which belongs to it by right, and replace it with the concept of hand-of-female-primate-that-has-been-deformed-by-standing-erect. But this is precisely the kind of exercise that can only be performed here, in an airport waiting area, by taking full advantage of the para-meditative state induced by an airport, a mental experiment involving the Darwinian veri-fication of the human shape as a form in transition from a previous version to a successive one . . . The neo-Darwinian readings that Franco pointed him towards ultimately brought about a profound modification of the way he viewed life on Earth, human beings, and himself, and brought him around to a vision of the world of the living as a huge, repulsive, sloppy soup of life, a soup to which this girl sitting across from him, in all her glowing golden Nordic loveliness, actually belonged. In that instant, Ivo is so completely focused upon her that she came dangerously close to levitating.

Fuck, I am determined to see her as a monkey . . . The headache suddenly returned . . . I need to take another Advil tablet . . . Who knows what a girl is going to look like, in another million years . . .

With all the science fiction he read as a young man, Brandani has become an imaginer of futures, a theorizer of possible worlds that differ from the present one. All the future he's been able to experience has disappointed him—nothing has taken place that justified the optimism in which he felt himself immersed in the '50s, true, but neither has the pessimism of the apocalyptic extremes. The year 1984 was as bad/good as any of the others. In 1997, New York City was very liveable, as distant as could be from the place dreamt up by John Carpenter. In 2001, no one set out on a space odyssey towards Jupiter in search of a monolith, but in just two hours someone managed to knock down the entire World Trade Centre with almost all the people in it.

An entirely artificial world had been prefigured but not in keeping with the trends we can glimpse today . . . Someone (but who was it?) had fantasized about something I liked very much, that is, an *entirely built* world, a single immense multi-level spherical city which extended over the whole surface of the planet, oceans included . . . Instead (for now) something different is happening: the substitution of nature with an almost perfect copy . . . Let's see now, what will happen once we've falsified everything? When we've obtained a *fake planet*?

There's no sign of his flight, the check-in desk is once again deserted. There's time. Brandani bought a newspaper that he doesn't much feel like reading. He sits there, distractedly gazing out of the plate-glass windows, where it must already be hotter than 90 degrees.

For thousands of years we suffered through a state of transition from the natural to the post-natural . . . As the modification of the Planet gradually grew more marked, our sense of nostalgic yearning for a mythical initial state, natural & uncontaminated, grew and grew, a state of which we found the residual traces here and there . . . There were corners where Mother Nature could still be recognized in all her beauty and power . . . We reached the point where we chose to enclose and protect these ever-shrinking authentic areas, museifying everything that exists within the perimeter: plants animals land and water, even human beings . . . But the process of total modification is still very far from completion: it will take many hundreds of years, perhaps more than a thousand, to successfully construct a *completely* artificial nature, one that is so well made that it appears more real than the real thing, beyond real, a hyper-nature that is turgid and fecund and vital like a state-of-the-art rebuilt tit . . . And we'll be inside it, super old, regenerated and reconfigured countless times, forgetful of what the body was even like at the outset, the body we were born into, centuries ago, that is, long before we had the option of reshaping at will our own soma . . . A few fake–real human beings, in a fake–real world, pursuing activities that are inconceivable to us now and, in all likelihood, completely useless, perhaps erotic (but what can become of Eros in the absence of Thanatos?), possibly aesthetic, and therefore artistic . . . At the very moment in which everyone is an artist, well, in that same instant art itself also becomes fake-real, like the bionic lobsters, the GMO deer in man-made forests, the electric eels (with remotely controlled voltage) in the rivers of Amazonia, like the bionic birds, the bacteria (all benign, all of them genetically rendered useless or at any rate harmless) that will no doubt work for us . . . Artificial life capable of reproducing like real life, synthesized life that believes it's real . . . The solution won't be to entrust all work to machines, but rather to bacteria, even though I have a hard time imagining a table produced unconsciously by a colony of microbes . . . These are just idiotic examples, the future can be imagined, but what we imagine has nothing to do with what will actually come to pass . . . No one had foreseen that we would all be using computers to write, communicate, phone, play, produce and reproduce images, draw . . . Back then we thought of them as immense, like Asimov's Multivac, and assumed they could speak, that they could be questioned like oracles, computers as big as planets, etc. . . . Where is all the science fiction I read when I was a kid? Whatever happened to *that* future? Where are the flying cars, the roads suspended between skyscrapers towering miles in the sky? Where are the girls from the early issues of *Urania* sci-fi magazine, the ones in silver miniskirts? Where are the wrist television sets? The space ships, the colonies on other planets . . . None of it, nothing at all . . . But still, there are personal computers, cell phones, sailboats with rigid carbon-fibre wing sails that can go 45 miles per hour, an orbiting space station, not ring-shaped though, not like the one described by Arthur C. Clarke . . . It seemed like such a simple idea, like the artificial satellite hooked up to a cable . . . Until I understood that the cable would have to be 22,000 miles long . . . The future has deteriorated, it seems that nothing good awaits us, everyone is in agreement on that point, but when I was little that's not the way it was: the future might have had some problems but, all in all, it was radiant, glistening, interplanetary, interstellar, intergalactic, trans-spatiotemporal ... Now they make science-fiction films in abandoned factories, it's all a mass of wreckage, post-atomic & feral, as it awaits the first green shoots of a rebirth that can unfailingly be *just* glimpsed by movie's end ... We all know that the present doesn't actually lead anywhere but day by day it continues unchanged, as if in a trance ... There is no shortage of signals: the coral reefs that are being bleached and dying everywhere you look, the drastically diminishing presence of marine microorganisms, millions of dead molluscs littering the beaches, suddenly, cyclically, and no one can say what the causes might be, and the same is happening to the fish in certain rivers in Asia ... The water is no more contaminated, no more polluted than usual, there is no particular event, aside from the progressive rise in temperature, fractions of a degree, nothing catastrophic, and yet I have seen them, those foul-smelling seashells, heaped up along the Thai coastline ... Hundreds of whales rotting on the sandy southern beaches of New Zealand ... Perhaps they were the few still left alive, the ones who had survived the ferocity of the Japanese who slaughter them in a sea red with dense, oxygen-rich blood—when I look at those photographs in the newspapers I imagine a strong smell of rust billowing across the water ... Dying as a whale, with a metal harpoon driving into your back, then down, deep into your lungs ... That long-ago documentary, I've never forgotten it: there was an iron-hulled Norwegian whaler, its yellow sides all crusted with rust, a harpoon cannon in the prow, which fired short, stout, terrible harpoons, with four flanged tips that opened out inside the flesh of the beast ... There too the blood was dense, the sea water around the ship filled up with that opaque creamy red substance that the cetacean used to store the oxygen it needed on its dives ... The fair-haired whaler, with a turtleneck sweater like the lead fisherman, the *rais*, of the *tonnara*, or tuna traps of Favignana, which has turned into a tuna slaughter for tourists, with ever-smaller tuna and, there too, a lake of blood ... The world will die only after the sea is dead, and not until then. So there's time: Twenty? Thirty years? A hundred years? I'll have time to die myself before then . . . I'll miss the Apocalypse, even though it will probably be a nuanced event, not traumatic, a slow dying of the light, with anaesthesia . . . Just as there was never a clearly defined Beginning, likewise the End will probably drag out endlessly . . . With the possible exception of a catastrophic asteroid strike, of course, which all things considered is the likeliest outcome . . . We'll construct life artificially, starting with nice fat GMO tuna weighing 450 pounds, full of parasynthetic blood that's still good to drink . . . I don't have anything against GMO, quite the opposite . . . Once again the words of Franco Sala, the only one who seemed to me to understand anything at all: 'The tension of politics, art, philosophy, and even religion, towards the reformation of the world is over, Ivo. The world's not going to be reformed. No one, even if they wanted to, has the power to do it. The world can only be destroyed or else, though I don't see how and by whom, revolutionized. Capital still has to finish its work, we don't know how long it will take, but once it's done, nothing will remain of the planet as we know it.' I won't live long enough to see the world emerge from this stage of inauthentic truth, only to regenerate itself in the form of complete fiction, total artifice: my fate was to live in the intermediate era of deterioration, when you can watch things dying out one by one, and not even all that slowly, only to be replaced, when it's possible, by a more or less successful copy . . . What species will replace us once we're extinct? Dogs? Monkeys? Ants? There's time, millions and millions of years . . . And after all, what does it matter to me? . . .

Sofrano

From the very beginning, he'd been struck by the way De Klerk matched up with the perfect persona of the successful manager. Assuming that such a thing existed somewhere, and there were certainly dozens of them, a manager's manual, complete with illustrations and graphs, diagrams on how to dress, hairstyles, etc., suggestions and prescriptions on the gestures and words to use, the kind of language, on how to lead meetings, on how to treat staff and coworkers, would surely have cited De Klerk as a paradigm and model.

Perfectly bronzed in summer and winter—not just his face but also his well-tended hands—he wore a thin wedding ring made of gold neither too yellow nor too faded. Hair always freshly shampooed, still thick even though he was pushing fifty, that is, appeared to be close to that age, because at the low level of technicians responsible for limited sectors to which the young Ivo belonged in that era, not much was known about De Klerk and what little was known was hearsay more than anything else. His hair was just barely grey, smooth, swept back, neatly cut but worn in a slightly unkempt manner, just long enough at the neck to graze the collar of his shirt, rigorously French in style, very sober, not too wide and three fingersbreadth in height. Shirts custom-made, with tiny pinstripes, maybe red and blue, or blue and green, careful calibrated in thickness to ensure that it was possible to see, even from a certain distance, that these weren't coloured shirts, but white shirts with coloured stripes. On the chest, low and to the left, the monogram NDK discreetly enjoyed pride of place. His general appearance was always that of someone who had just taken a revivifying shower, he always looked as if he'd just stepped out of one, dewy with droplets and aromatic freshness.

'He makes us all look as if we'd just stayed up all night, as if we'd just washed our faces in an enamelled iron basin, with a few chips here and there. As if we'd crapped in a filthy latrine and had emerged buttoning our trousers, before coming in to Megatecton.'

But De Klerk didn't give off scents of any kind and if you got close enough to him—something that could only happen when you were sitting around a conference table, because he generally kept a safe distance from everyone else—you could detect, especially in the morning, a faint whiff of laundry, absolutely clean clothing, carefully washed and pressed. Knotted around his neck, slightly loose and absolutely standard in terms of size of the knot and breadth and length, a dark tie, usually navy blue, with tiny polka dots, usually in one of the colours of the pinstripes of his shirt. Ivo recalled Father's Maxim No. 3: 'A necktie is a piece of drapery, the knot should never be too tight.' During those meetings, which no one ever left until it was absolutely clear just what De Klerk wanted, Brandani had reflected at length and had come to the conclusion that in all likelihood the ties too were made to order, out of a fabric that went with the shirts. He wore three-piece suits, charcoal grey or navy blue, and sometimes, very rarely, a blazer with light-coloured trousers, English or American shoes, wingtips, or else black loafers, invariably Saxone of Scotland brand, never new but always a little worn. But when he wore a blazer and a pair of chino trousers (one time, when he took his jacket off, we noted a label, Abercrombie & Fitch, which some time later began to appear on the trousers of some mid-level technicians), the loafers looked like they were natural brown leather. He wore absolutely opaque dark socks, but when he wore a blazer one time, Ivo caught him in a pair of fire-engine red socks. On his wrist, an old Baume & Mercier chronometer, wrist strap in cloth, which he usually took off and placed before him on the table, so that he could always keep an eye on the timing of his next engagement.

'So much for all those people who think that if you're successful you necessarily have to wear a gold Rolex—that's an old family watch, and it might be gold, but you wind it up by hand, the strap is red cloth, Ivo.'

Everything about De Klerk's appearance was class and nonchalance, nothing smacked of ostentation, imbalance or uncertainty. Ivo noticed the bright white handkerchief that always peeked out of the breast pocket of his jackets, and decided that perhaps that detail might seem a bit frivolous, show-offy, and really the only weakness in a general picture where there was nothing to be criticized, only things to be learnt. If anything, in all likelihood what might have appeared to him as a slight slippage in taste, a minor misstep, a somewhat conventional and over-dressed contrivance, was in fact a studied reference, an imperfection intentionally inserted into the overall image, which might otherwise have seemed excessively poised and restrained. In all this, Ivo noticed at least two things: that he wore suspenders with leather tips and that he had the habit of undoing the top button of his trousers whenever he sat down, something that was more than understandable in a man of a robust constitution and his age, when it is difficult to fight against that inevitable bit of gut. It was a flaw in the image but Ivo liked it, he saw in it a hint of disregard, of neglect and therefore, he thought, of genuine class. De Klerk spoke in a mellow and comfortable way, with a faint northern Italian accent but without the twangy northern singsong that was so objectionable to those who were born and raised in the City of God. He chose his words carefully and used them well but unaffectedly, every so often he'd toss out a curse word but never emphatically or in an overstated manner. He never raised his voice, but he never spoke in a confidential or seductive tone: instead he always seemed alert and attentive, never distracted or superficial. The time of every one of his days was strictly measured out in commitments, he was impatient with people who took too much of his time, he was continually demanding that people get to the point, he required that all reports be no longer than a page, because, he liked to say, there is no matter, however complex, that can't be summarized in less than 500 words. When he was irritated, his words could become quite stinging but his tone of voice always remained composed, as did his face and his persona. To Engineer Brandani, who considered himself to be genetically quite an emotional person, these were superhuman qualities.

Advertising in newspapers and on TV constantly touted the figure of the 'up-and-coming manager', often referred to in Italian as an 'executive'. The successful man—who used a certain cologne, say Dunhill, and wore a certain watch, say Bulova, and smoked certain very chic cigarettes, say Benson & Hedges or Dunhill, and dressed in different and highly codified ways according to whether he was at work, say on Wall Strett or in the City in London, or employed his leisure time, say playing golf, or polo, or sailing boats in regattas—this successful man happened to coincide with the up-and-coming manager and all managers did their best to adhere to this image, even the ones who weren't particularly successful. Brandani couldn't have named the exact moment when the successful manager made his appearance in the registry of myths of which the iconosphere of the time was comprised, but he was certain of two things. First: that the successful man, calm and unruffled, had survived the recent political tempests, slithering unharmed under the egalitarianism of the years that followed. Second: that he wasn't very fond of that image. What he didn't know was that the successful manager, underneath this dislike he felt towards him, had also become for him, as he had for everyone, a secret model to measure oneself against: a sort of tacit I'd-like-to-but-I-can't, I-mustn't. De Klerk adhered to that image, practically to perfection, and what didn't match it in him was a sign of a priceless and bizarre and unexpected and unpredictable personalization, even if after all it was just about shirts and ties and watches and suspenders and the hue & degree of tan. Moreover, De Klerk had another characteristic capable of fascinating him: he seemed to adhere to the *world as it is*, adapting to it perfectly, in a critical abstention that struck Ivo as total. Not like him, tormented by an infinity of objections based on an idea, and not an especially precise one, of the *world as it ought to be*. It was this unruffled existence of De Klerk in his own image, in his own role, that he most envied and admired. But without telling himself, without admitting it to himself.

Nico De Klerk had recently taken over as director of inter-national business for Megatecton, one of the leading construction companies in Europe, with offices in Asia and Africa. When it came to major contracts—especially in that portion of the planet Earth that was then known as the Third World—Megatecton was quite competitive, showing no fear of its British or French or German rivals. Created out of the mergers of a number of different mid-sized companies, with the decisive contribution of Italian state industry, Megatecton was willing to operate in even the most challenging environmental situations, making the most of the Peninsulars' proverbial flexibility and adaptability, qualities that were especially appreciated in the world's eastern and southern regions. Megatecton, a company that traded on the national stock exchange, with head offices in the North of the Peninsula, where the chief executive staff worked, and in the City of God, where the operating staff was based, regularly won international contracts in part, or actually primarily because of its lack of rigidity in terms of internal procedures, an approach that afforded it a notable degree of adaptability to local conditions: the company did not hesitate to operate in countries under Communist regimes as readily as under democratic governments, it showed complete indifference whether Fascist dictators were in power or bloodthirsty tribal satraps, whether guerrilla warfare was underway, or feuds, or ethnic conflict —if conditions were tolerable and it appeared there was a chance at profit, then Megatecton tried to get into the country and, if that effort proved successful, then it not only attempted to maximize returns but also to leave a good impression with the various func-tionaries when it left, with a view to new prospects in the future. Politics & public works: an inseparable pairing that always needed to be taken into account, along with the level of corruption of the local administrations. Megatecton always did its best to make sure everyone was happy. That was why the general director for inter-national business was such an important position and enjoyed extensive freedom and discretion but was also under a significant burden of responsibility. De Klerk, who reported only to the mem-bers of the board in the City in the North, didn't seem particularly troubled by the complexity and delicacy of his role. As far as could be detected, he didn't sense the burden of his job's responsibilities.

'I wonder how he does it,' Ivo asked himself. 'I'm someone who freaks out the second my deadline is moved forwards, I could never man his desk . . . Brandani, you're not a combatant, you're not a competitor . . . Maybe you were when you were a kid, in the primeval dawn of the Postwar years, but you aren't any more, that's something you've known for some time, and specifically since March 1st in 1968 . . . People say that De Klerk is good at his job and also that he's a tremendous son of a bitch, those are the rumours that circulate about him. He comes out of the School of Management, he's worked for various companies, until he became a middle-level manager for De Kooning & Fast, in Belgium . . . He seems to be half-Belgian . . . He worked hard there and he climbed the ladder by a number of rungs at a time . . . Finetti has a friend there and he says that De Klerk is spectacular at his job, he says that he outclassed the competition, devouring his rivals one by one, he says that by the end he was so widely detested that the managing director didn't trust him any more and got rid of him, he says it was just in time, he says that De Klerk has special talents, that he's very intelligent, that he knows how to get the best out of people until they start feeling ambitious or try to turn on him . . . He says that if they do, it's trouble, he's not someone who limits his actions to self defence, no, he actually destroys his rivals . . . Apparently he trusts no one, he tends to centralize power . . . But isn't that a portrait of the typical manager, I ask? Aren't they all like this?'

In the nearly two years that he'd been working at Megatecton, how many times had Brandani heard accounts of similar biographies? As far as he was concerned, these were special life forms, with particular aptitudes, self-selecting, self-relegated to a closed world that celebrates the secret rites of power, where everyone is busy bullying one another, cutting one another's throats, until one individual rises to the top and seizes the reins of leadership. 'A technician is always, by definition, an underling, Ivo,' Franco Sala used to say. And he reminded him of the distinctions made by Hannah

Arendt, in *Vita Activa*: '"Labour, Work, Action." You're in charge of the Work, you know the goals of your action, you know the final form that will be taken at the conclusion of a productive effort, but beneath you are those who just work and nothing more, and above you are those who simply decide the When, the How Much, the What, and the Where. And nothing more. You are nothing but a transformer of money into Work and therefore into more money. You're just one of those assigned to transform the energy produced by money into something solid, useful, concrete, occasionally beautiful, from which Capital can take its profit, the politicians their benefits, the managers their careers, the workers their daily bread, and all of us a certain *utilitas*, which might be, in the case of a bridge, the ability to cross over the bed of bridge where it had previously been impossible to do so . . .'

'Good point that Sala makes, even if it doesn't take a philosopher to figure it out . . . Maybe I should have stuck with it, Philosophy . . .'

Ivo had struggled mightily to get his degree but in the end he'd succeeded in getting top marks. During his university years he'd been with Clara and now he'd married her. But marrying someone had never been part of his plans, just for that matter as studying engineering hadn't, any more than taking a job in a major corporation, where he would not have been put in charge of organizing construction sites but, rather, of structural design and planning, if possible, of bridges.

'In physics it's called the Coriolis effect, Brando: every trajectory undergoes a curvature, in some cases to the point of spiraling in on itself . . . You've never been where you wished you were, you never reach the point towards which you set your prow but always somewhere else, and you consider yourself lucky if you manage to wind up anywhere near your original objective . . . If I ever did have an objective, not only did I miss it entirely but from here I can't even see it any more . . .'

He had already turned thirty and was entering the years that for a good-looking man like him are the peak of physical splendour and force of attraction for the opposite sex. He was dark-haired, dark-skinned, with light blue eyes, a full head of hair, a slight sprinkling of grey in his sideburns, and a few streaks of white on his chin if he stopped shaving for a day or two, a well-built body, just slightly deteriorating from the absence of athletic activity. He had a general, if unintentional, air of perennial discontentment, in his usually furrowed brow, the seriousness of his expression, the infrequency of his laughter, the rareness of his speech, words usually carefully chosen, because Ivo hated bullshit and people who spoke without thinking, and he kept himself constantly under control. But he especially had to keep an eye on himself to snuff out before they burst into existence the flashes of anger to which he was subject. He was convinced it was a genetic disease, a bequest of Father, the Wrathful One. When he lost his temper he couldn't think straight and he was capable of saying and doing things that could be irreparable at times, things that he regularly regretted. He hated himself for it and, to an even greater extent, he hated his father, because he believed that he had bequeathed that illness to him.

After taking his degree, he'd worked in a few private technical offices, he'd done engineering calculations for office buildings, industrial sheds, warehouses and small structures; the last professional he'd worked for had offered to take him on but he was looking for something more, he wanted to work on major projects, build bridges, and, after an interview with HR and a six-month probationary period, they'd given him a job at Megatecton. At first, they'd put him in the Africa Division, Southeastern Africa Subdivision, Site Preparation Sector. He was, as the name suggests, responsible for the preliminary work on construction sites, all the logistics necessary before building could get underway, siting of the structures, construction of the temporary housing, offices and workshops, building materials, technical logistics and so on. In other words, everything that was needed to set up a major construction site in a godforsaken and underdeveloped corner of the world. He wasn't satisfied with these responsibilities, it was a field where he had to learn everything from scratch: during his initial interviews he'd told them loud and clear that he would rather have been part of a team of structural engineers. As his second choice, he had opted for the technical direction team which, as he imagined it, consisted of supermen present on a daily basis in the battlefield that was the construction site, which he, in the exaltation of the neophyte that he was, saw as a place of bloody & mystical conflict, between matter and form, between chaos and blueprint, between the planned and the unexpected. 'Planning and design later,' they'd told him, 'right now you need to get some experience working in the field. That's our policy: no technician who works here can afford to lack direct knowledge of how construction sites operate. For now, you're going to be in charge of organization, later, if we're both happy with how things work out, you'll have to spend a few years on job sites, and then you can graduate to planning and design. Here, for our technicians,' the guy in personnel pronounced the word *tennicians*, 'we have a mandatory principle: only people who have thorough and direct experience of construction sites can join the design and planning team.'

Africa was the area where Megatecton was doing the greatest number of projects and was earning the biggest profits, which is why Brandani immediately found himself in the thick of the action and the problem. They'd started by sending him for short stints in Mozambique, working and travelling with the director for East Africa, then he'd moved over to Finetti, in the West Africa Subdivision, which was responsible for overseeing contracts for bridges, roads, railroads and most importantly, dams. What constituted work and profit for Megatecton, constituted life for the Africans: Brandani's old yearning for social usefulness thus found a substantial and satisfying fulfilment, if not the actual gratification of being on the side of the angels . . . And yet over the course of the first few traumatic months of his apprenticeship, he found himself thrust face to face with the truth of the prophecy that Franco Sala had uttered years before, when Ivo had informed him of his decision to leave philosophy for engineering: 'You're going to deliver yourself into the hands of Capital, you're going to become a cog in the machinery of profit. What they're going to want is for you to be good enough, but not spectacularly good. What they're going to want is for you always to be ready to say, "Yes, that's something that can be done." What they're going to want is for you to understand that there's no such thing as the neutrality of things technical. What they're going to expect from you is full and complete respect for the idea of profit lurking in every job, every contraption, device, installation, in every piece of technology, system of production, motor or engine, sector of production/ distribution. The engineer should not ask questions outside of the realm of knowledge and pursuit that are commonly described as *technical . . .*'

Ivo earned a good salary, worked hard, travelled frequently. In those first two years at Megatecton, his struggle to learn, to understand, to do was anxious and spasmodic. He went from less than a pack to a pack and a half of Gauloises, cigarettes that he had started smoking at the end of the '60s, when they were particularly fashionable in the circles of the militant left because they were so French: the stench of Caporal tobacco filled the offices of the West Africa Subdivision: 'Can't you just smoke Marlboros like everyone else?'

Clara had graduated a few years before him and had been working for some time now at the Actuarial Office at the Assicurazioni Generali insurance company ('Did you know that Kafka worked for Assicurazioni Generali?'). A very solid, pragmatic choice, decidedly at variance with her chosen field of endeavor and interest, which was political economy, but even though it was so radically distant from her initial ambitions to do research at a university, she seemed to be perfectly at peace with it. Her professor, who had advised her as she worked on her thesis on Third World economies, had made it clear to her that her career prospects were limited, that there was a long line of people ahead of her waiting for a position, that he could guarantee nothing except, perhaps, at some indeterminate future point, a scholarship. An honest and straightforward talk, or at least that's how Clara had taken it: 'He didn't outright tell me no but, on the other hand, if he'd really wanted me he wouldn't have discouraged me in such a decisive manner, don't you think?' And yet those two years at Assicurazioni Generali had changed her, she had hardened somehow, there was a precocious disenchantment. The welcoming softness in which Ivo was accustomed to seeking refuge was disappearing: as if it were evaporating in the baking aridity of the everyday battle with the world, which couldn't be any easier for her than it was for him. Clara kept things in, she told him practically nothing about her daily experiences but it was clear that for her too there were harsh realities to be confronted every day. Now that the protection of their families was gone, and now that their original plans had shifted in directions that weren't expected, or particularly pleasant, neither sought after nor pursued and yet so concrete and remunerative, Ivo and Clara now were having to work things out between the two of them, for what they had been and what they were now becoming. When he wasn't travelling, they ate together in the kitchen, in the flat they'd rented the month before their wedding, the window panes frosted by the steam from the stove, trying to come up with things to talk about, things they had in common, things that the other partner could listen to without being bored by the distance from his or her own experience, own interests: work, their respective jobs, at this point, meant everything, or almost. What was left to them was the cinema on weekends and a few friends, a few married couples they could invite over for dinner, people their age who were living through comparable periods of their lives. This was a time when it was necessary to come to some reckoning with what they had once been; the cost demanded for the beginning of a trajectory into the world of work and life in general was a high one, and it meant giving up, to the point that it entailed negation and even betrayal, a certain impetus and drive to change the world, something they'd so completely envisioned for themselves until just a few years ago. This fracture lurked deep within them all and, even if no one ever or hardly ever spoke about it openly, still it split couples, to the point of blowing them up entirely, or more simply laying bare what had become, for certain of them—more than a period of growth and maturity—an early failure. Who are we, what the fuck have we become? What is left for us in life? What adventures are there? What kind of life is conceivable without the idea of revolution?

Without at least pretending to really want to change something? The obliteration of what they believed they'd once been, and what perhaps they really had been, was something that Ivo and Clara had never been able to establish as a shared possession. In fact, if anything, it pushed them in different diverging directions: Clara accepting pragmatically the transformation they were undergoing, Ivo experiencing it as a defeat that required some acceptable reparation, whatever its nature, from wherever it might come. Still, it would be best—and this was not an idea he dared to say or admit to himself—if that reparation consisted of success: social, professional and financial success.

'Otherwise you're truly done for, otherwise you're shot, you're dead, kaput . . . Otherwise what is left for you to do except what Father and Mother did, that is, bust your ass all your life, have children, and then either drop dead or retire?'

And in an instant there flashed into his memory the exact moment that Mother died, a few years earlier, at little more than age fifty. His chest had split open when he was faced with the inconceivable, a red rent that still ran through his sternum and refused to heal.

Clara in contrast didn't seem to suffer much, really, or if she did, she gave no sign of it. Ivo's expectation that the world would open up to him, instead of his having to adapt to it, just got on her nerves. To her mind, things were simpler than that, she came from a family that had worked for the railroads, Socialists and Communists as far back as anyone could remember, she expected nothing, neither from her studies nor from having belonged to the Movement, not from her friends, not from anybody. She counted on her strength to live and to work, with no frenzied need for self-affirmation, without any of the mental reservations Ivo had as he faced each day, without that stupid afterthought, along the lines of *I'm not like you are, you'll never take me alive*, that she sensed both in him and in many others like him. What Clara detected in this attitude was an underlying pretext, a lie, a piece of self-deception. Actually, more than self-deception, a self-consolation for the fact that they felt they were prisoners, or even worse, that they had allowed themselves to be recruited into the enemy ranks, something more or less like: 'If I maintain a certain mental reservation then I'm not the same as *they are*.' *They* who? 'Don't they see that *they* means us? That there's no difference? That we want the same things? That we have no basis for feeling that we're so special? I mean to say, that we're inside already and it couldn't be any other way, at the cost of being marginalized and, more importantly, the failure to be emancipated from the condition of our parents? Of *my* father and *my* mother?' Clara understood that her husband, and practically everyone else like him, had never had the slightest intention of renouncing their privileges, all she needed to see was the humble fascination with which they talked about their bosses. For Clara, those had been hard-won victories, the opportunities that Ivo had enjoyed since birth. And now what was most important was making sure they didn't lose them, those opportunities. So now shut up and pedal hard.

But almost every night the distance that was opening between them (perhaps it had always been there, but it just hadn't been visible before) was bridged by the sexual intimacy of their bodies which, whatever their minds might think, knew each other well and yearned for each other more than they ever had before. Ivo couldn't manage to conceive of himself deprived for so much as an instant of free access to Clara's body, which he'd always experienced as a supreme concession. Each and every time, inexplicably, the same apparent miracle unfolded: her body would arch towards him, helping him into her, as he held her and breathed in the perfume of her saliva, driving into her as deeply as he could, searching for her moans, until she'd suddenly turn to take him in her mouth. Or when he'd stroke her thighs in the lift on their way home from a party and she, completely tipsy, would rub up against him, caressing his cock. And then, once they were inside, they'd put on some music in celebration of the ritual of undressing and then she'd move in front of his inevitably astonished eyes. Every night the bridge of carnal friendship formed again, never losing any of its original solidity, if anything growing stronger, amid the irremediable expansion of the space separating their minds and their lives.

It had been a month since De Klerk's arrival and already in the International Section everyone was noticing changes from the way the previous management had run things. De Klerk made decisions rapidly, he was a centralizer, but he didn't ignore his coworkers, in fact, if anything, he encouraged them to make their opinions known, he'd assign them to do reports and updates, though he insisted they be very concise, and he never failed to read them. He demanded summaries: 'I wanted material that has already been processed,' he would say, 'it's not up to me to digest the issues at hand, that's your job, I need to show up last of all to make a decision, because I'm being held responsible for the whole operation, so it should be clear to you all how important is that you always provide me with a precise, up-to-date, brief, point-by-point picture of the situation. Anyone who's unwilling to work to these requirements can start looking around for another job immediately'—apparently those were his exact words at the meeting of the subdivision chiefs.

'Likeable, well, he's not likeable,' Ivo said to himself, 'but at least he's alive. Whether he's good too is something we'll find out in time. With Stortini things just weren't working any more.' 'This guy is vicious,' he'd tell himself. At the lower levels, the list of descriptions grew longer by the day. He's an organizer. He's a decision-maker. He's an efficiency expert. He's a technocrat. He's a son of a bitch. He's just good at what he does. He's just an asshole. Give him time and we'll see if he's any good. Megatecton has chewed up and spat out lots of other guys just like him. I wouldn't want to be in his shoes. He'll be cracking the bullwhip on all of us soon enough. And so on. Only a few people had left with Stortini, most had stayed. Those who had champed at the bit under Stortini were now hoping to find some breathing room and were doing everything they could to get noticed. Those who had consolidated their positions turned cautious out of fear they might now lose it. Those who had burrowed into a niche were afraid they'd be smoked out and did all they could to remain invisible. Those who felt they were precariously balanced feared temblors. Some of them even thought they were in danger of being fired. 'They've brought him in to restructure, to downsize, I'm not feeling good about things . . .' Uncertainty, fear, curiosity, mistrust. The atmosphere wasn't good in the International Business Section. But this was standard practice, the kind of thing that happened every time there was a change at the top: the directors were always brought in from outside, no one at Megatecton had ever climbed to the level of general director of a division, it was a sort of unwritten rule on management's part: those who are put in charge can't have had any previous interactions with their underlings.

That morning Engineer Finetti, chief of the West Africa Subdivision, who had a fairly early meeting with De Klerk, had decided to bring a couple of sector technicians with him. Brandani had been invited too; he'd put together a report on the construction site preparations now being planned, and to complete it he'd travelled to three equatorial sites that would soon be underway: two dams and a long railroad viaduct. Finetti hadn't had time to talk it through in depth, possibly not even to read it, so to be safe he brought Brandani along with him. As is customary in the West, where hierarchical scales are bound up with an up–down symbolism (as opposed to centre–periphery, as is generally the case in the Far East), the executive offices were on the top floor of a twenty-five-storey building; Megatecton occupied the top five floors. It was a glass-and-steel building, dating back to the early '60s, when the Country wanted to prove at all costs to the world, but especially to itself, that it was modern; the only idea of modernity in those years came from the United States of America and it had as its paradigm the glass-and-steel skyscraper. Access to the executive conference rooms ran through De Klerk's secretariat: it was a large room and it overlooked, through a floor-to-ceiling plate-glass window, the manmade lake of what had once been the Fascist Universal Exposition. Ivo was intimidated and anxious to make a good impression but he was also gratified, flattered to be there. He wanted to attract notice, his usual mental reservation, *I'm not the same as you are*, had almost entirely given way in the face of the eagerness for acknowledgment that his ego demanded. De Klerk was waiting for them; seated at the short end of the table, he was making a phone call. He gestured for them all to sit down and after a few minutes the meeting began. The first thing he said, glancing at his watch, was: 'I like punctuality. We have forty-five minutes, and not a minute more. So I urge you, be concise.' He was chilly and polite. At first he didn't seem to notice him, but when Ivo's time came he listened thoughtfully to his presentation, then he said that they'd talk it over again once he'd read the file, even though it was too long for his tastes.

'Engineer, I want you to summarize this report for me in a single page and let me have it no later than the day after tomorrow, understood?' He also gave instructions, while everyone took notes, on the spacing and number of copies for the reports. He had a mellow voice, a smoker's voice. During the meeting he smoked at least three Craven 'A's, the unfiltered kind with a cork mouthpiece. When Ivo lit a Gauloise, De Klerk shot him a vaguely curious glance. He seemed to be very quick to grasp the core of any problem, he conducted the meeting with an iron-fisted control and timing. At the end of the meeting, he gave instructions concerning certain matters and asked further information about others. He looked at his watch and abruptly left the room, asking his secretary, who had been present for the meeting, to schedule another one for the following week. In the lift, there were a number of comments on the meeting. What made a special impression on his colleagues and irritated them too, first and foremost Finetti, was his demand that they deliver reports only one page long. Ivo chimed in with the chorus of complaints, nonetheless for the rest of the day and all of the the day that followed he worked furiously to give the report the form and extent that his boss had requested. He'd never been particularly good with words, compressing what he'd written proved to be impossible and he was forced to rewrite it, in fact, rethink it. While he was doing so, he understood De Klerk's real reasons: to force his subordinates to be extremely concise, so that they'd come to meetings with the topics already precompressed in their heads. In the end, he succeeded in delivering a report written and typed in the required format. In the afternoon, his boss called him personally and said only: 'First-rate work,

Brandani, we'll talk it over soon.' In the weeks that followed the meetings in the director's conference room intensified and Ivo had a chance to watch De Klerk at work at considerable length.

'There, that's what a *real* manager *is like* . . . He may still be an asshole, a foot soldier serving capital, but he's good at what he does, he knows his job, he makes decisions quickly and correctly. He has to delegate and centralize, cyclically . . . He works with an alternation of systole-diastole-systole, etc.—he takes in the data in compressed form, then he processes them, he issues directives, then he takes in more data, processes them again and issues directives for the next step . . .'

De Klerk worked ten, twelve hours a day. 'Capitalism doesn't afford anyone a break,' Franco had told him, 'you'll find yourself locked into the hellish machinery of profit, where you either compete or you're done for before you get started . . .' But Ivo confusedly understood that, if that was the game, then that was the game that he'd have to play. In fact, more than understanding it, he *sensed it*, that is, he perceived an overpowering anxiety to be there, to make himself visible and, at the same time, to serve his boss as a samurai would, with efficiency and loyalty. He immersed himself up to his neck in the problems, he thought about them continuously, he suggested alternatives, he worked tirelessly, he travelled frequently, he constantly took notes, took photographs, gathered materials, investigated each question in depth, to ensure that he could always suggest an adequate array of solutions. He wanted to be appreciated and respected, he wanted to be held in high esteem, given recognition, promoted, paid well. His initial aspiration to be a structural engineer faded in the face of the fascination that De Klerk and his decision-making method exerted on him. More than construction, he was now interested in decision-making and through it, he wanted to advance his career at Megatecton. The more he absorbed the company's climate and culture, the more he began to believe that he *deserved* a career as an executive and he did everything within his power to put himself in the spotlight. Even if he had not entirely abandoned his desire to Invent and Implement in concrete terms, it was the moderate recognition that his abilities seemed to be garnering that now led him, though he wasn't capable of admitting it to himself, to *want it all*, and that was why his colleagues by this point considered him to be an ambitious and arrogant careerist. In other words, what would have been unthinkable for him just a few years earlier had happened: he'd acquired a competitive corporate mindset, he'd become exactly what the Capitalist system wanted him to become.

Clara, aside from her husband's usual official statements of detachment, along the lines of *You'll never take me alive*, had watched the unmistakable process of this transformation: they'd taken him alive, and how they'd taken him alive. She understood it from the intensity with which he always talked about work, from the implicit admiration with which he referred to De Klerk, and from the sense of belonging towards the corporation that she could detect in the things he said. This boss of his, to hear what he had to say about him, sounded like the usual asshole, arrogant & a right-winger, someone to hold at arm's length, the classic type who, if you absolutely have to deal with him, you should treat with the frostiest formality, or at least that was the rule she abided by when she ran into *someone different from her* on the job, and there were plenty like that around. She understood that Megatecton was different from Assicurazioni Generali, that at Megatecton, decision making and work in general took place in very different conditions from at an insurance company, she understood how these figures of men of action, simplifiers, decision makers, were captivating Ivo, whose education still remained that of an intellectual, even though he was one who had decided to take his vows to enter the world of technology, for whatever reason. She'd never understood that surprisingly drastic decision, just as she'd never understood the ridiculous state of exaltation that had seized him, one summer day many years before, at the sight of the old Scottish bridge.

'This is nothing but the fascination that the concrete nature of action exercises on people like him, on reflective men,' she told herself, 'it's nothing more . . . He's deceiving himself, it's an infatuation bound to vanish, eventually . . . It will happen when he comes face to face with his first and inevitable real shitstorm . . . And he'll find himself once again with his feet planted solidly on the ground. For now, he likes all this very much, he's earning money . . . And it's fine, it wouldn't be a problem . . . The fact is that he too is turning into one of those "social-climbing, careerist assholes", about whom he still thinks that they'll never take him alive.'

In other words, Ivo was starting to *fit in*. That didn't entirely displease Clara, but what did annoy her was the way he pretended he wasn't, that he insisted on waving a banner of nonexistent difference. The situation had been turned on its head: to her, the job she did was nothing more than a paycheck, she didn't need a sense of identity and loyalty to the Assicurazioni Generali. The more Ivo got an exaggerated sense of importance, the more he struck her as a fish caught on a hook and line, leaping high out of the water as he's being reeled in to the boat. This grated on her nerves, his constant talk about work bored her, the respect that she'd always felt for him was becoming tattered, and the desire that she felt for his body was becoming a separate path, isolated to itself, increasingly intense and shameless and animalesque.

Ivo and Clara loved the movies. As students they went to the movies almost every night. Ivo would swing by to pick her up around 10.30 in Father's Fiat 600, and after a brief discussion to decide what movie to see, they'd head straight for one of the many repertory movie houses that existed back then in the City of God, or in a second- or third-run cinema. They almost always got there when the last show had just started a few minutes before: they loved to savour a movie, maybe on a Monday night when the rest of the city was staying in, sprawled out in a half-empty cinema, smoking freely. In this way they'd watched a great number of Peninsular films, but also Japanese or Polish or French ones, and especially American movies. Films by young directors, the cinematography grainy and mellow, the plots steeped in violence, with a distinctively anarcho-American spirit, but also many classics certified by the critics with the official seal of approval. There, in

American filmmaking, they found their *real* myths: it was the para-
dox of a generation with egalitarian beliefs that remained, however,
enamoured of the culture of a country whose imperialist politics
and competitive ideology they deeply despised. America was the
non-Europe, it was the non-Peninsula and it remained a powerful
symbol of space and freedom. In spite of their Marxism, they felt
like Americans, but implicit and imperfect Americans, and therefore incomplete ones. That contradiction, like all contradictions,
could be resolved in words, at least, with a certain sophistry. And
so in the Peninsular culture of those years the commonplace had
sprung up that you could—in fact, that you *must*—hate the pres-
ident of the USA but not the American people and their culture, as
if those presidents had materialized out of thin air and hadn't been
elected by that very same people that instead it was all right to
love.

In other words, they went to the movies, and one Saturday in
February when it was cold out and it was raining cats and dogs,
they decided they couldn't miss Wim Wenders' *The American
Friend*, which had just come out. They were showing it in a big
first-run cinema in the city centre, which had recently been reno-
vated with criteria of considerable elegance, that is to say,
damasked, wall-to-wall carpeted and velvet-upholstered. Going to
the movies on Saturday night was still a social ritual, in a city
sunken in a provincial slumber that had remained unbroken for
more than two centuries. With some difficulty, Clara had managed
to find a parking place nearby for the Fiat 500, they had an
umbrella but all it took was a few hundred yards outdoors, and
when they entered the lobby of the cinema, they were practically
drenched. There was a smell of wet people and a long line at the
indoor box office. As they were getting in line and Ivo was thinking,
'It's a good thing we got here a little early,' he saw De Klerk, right
there in front of them. At his side was a tall, well-dressed woman
who emanated an intense scent of perfume; all he could see of her
was her hairdo, fresh from the beauty parlour, her hair had lighter
streaks. He had no desire to say hello to him, if anything, in fact,
his first impulse was to leave or at least move away from them,

but it was raining hard outside, it was late and the line behind was getting longer. 'Maybe he won't notice me, and even if he does, what of it, we'll say hello, it won't be the end of the world.' But as he was formulating these thoughts, he realized he was already bathed in sweat. He took off his raincoat and whispered in Clara's ear: 'This guy in front of us *is my boss*.' 'Ah,' she said, as if to say 'what the fuck', immediately irritated at Ivo's obsequious tone of voice.

De Klerk didn't notice Ivo Brandani was there until by chance he happened to turn around. He then smiled politely and said: '*Buonasera*, Engineer.' Under his white raincoat he wore a dark blue crewneck sweater, and under that one of his usual striped shirts. At that point the woman who was with him also turned around, revealing herself to be an elegant, defiant, very beautiful woman in her early forties. De Klerk said: 'Let me introduce Sabina.' 'A pleasure,' said Ivo, 'this is my wife Clara. Clara, Engineer De Klerk.' He felt his face turn hot and the sweat drip down his neck, and he understood that his discomfort was quite visible but there was nothing he could do about it. De Klerk asked if they knew anything about the film, if they were familiar with the director. Ivo was astonished that De Klerk didn't know anything about Wim Wenders and, under Clara's clinical gaze, he launched into a somewhat excessively complete and detailed exposition of the director's personality and work. De Klerk listened to a certain extent ('*Kings of the Road . . . The Wrong Move . . .* the titles don't exactly reach out and grab you . . .' he tossed in), then he seemed to grow distracted, but Sabina was very focused on what Ivo was saying, she was watching him with close attention and, at the end, she said in a gentle, calm voice: 'Well, now, I didn't know all those things. You seem to know quite a bit about this director. How come? Do you like him?' 'Yes,' Ivo replied, feeling like an idiot for having droned on, boring his boss. 'Well, that's a good thing,' she said, 'tonight we came here just to go out to the movies. We live nearby . . .' Then she turned to De Klerk and said: 'Nico, apparently we're about to see an important film . . .' 'Well,' said Ivo, 'I can't guarantee anything. It might turn out to be horrible . . .' They went on chatting for a while, then they bought their tickets and went their separate ways without anybody making any moves to sit together. Ivo and Clara sat in the fourth row, as they usually did, and De Klerk and Sabina disappeared into the audience somewhere behind them. As soon as they were seated Clara said to him, wryly: 'I see you've made quite an impression on somebody.' Ivo, still red-faced and sweaty, replied distractedly: 'Eh?' 'The first lady couldn't keep her eyes off you. For that matter, you're still a good-looking boy. I even like you, just think of that . . .'

As was a habit with them, when the film ended they remained sprawled comfortably, watching the end credits as the audience cleared out of the cinema. Ivo had liked it. So had Clara, who asked: 'If you have leukaemia, can you just die like that, while you're driving a car?' Ivo had likewise been struck by that last scene: a sudden death at the wheel of a red Volkswagen. As they were leaving, Ivo calculated that De Klerk would already be long gone, but instead there they both were—De Klerk and Sabina— waiting for them beneath the flood of fluorescent light under the marquee. 'We wanted to say goodbye,' said Sabina, smiling at him—Ivo felt instantly flattered—'what did you think of the film? I enjoyed it . . .' She was speaking to him alone, roundly ignoring Clara, to such an extent that De Klerk seemed to feel obliged to patch together a separate conversation with her. Ivo overheard that he hadn't liked the film, that it had seemed a little 'over-intellectu- alized', in short, 'an imitation of a good American movie'. And so, while Sabina was still expressing her opinion to him, he turned to his boss and interjected: 'But it *is* an imitation of an American movie! That's exactly what it's meant to be . . .' Then, in an apology for having interrupted her, he smiled at Sabina, whose gaze had turned instantly chilly. It was no longer raining and the lights of the cinema were blinking off. Sabina said: 'Shall we go get some- thing to drink?' Clara, before Ivo had a chance to say yes, as he actually was about to do, said: 'Thanks, but I'm not feeling very well, I'd better head home. But if you all want to . . . Ivo, you can certainly go, it's not a problem for me.' 'I don't think your husband would leave you all alone,' said De Klerk. Once they were in the car, Clara turned on the ignition and said: 'You really did make quite an impression, didn't you?'

The following week at Megatecton there was a great deal of work to be done. There was a preliminary plan to be drafted for a major construction site in Sierra Leone, an earth dam to be built in the heart of a tropical rain forest, a complex project that would take years to complete, the kind of thing for which Megatecton was famous. The meeting with De Klerk was scheduled for the Friday afternoon and the days leading up to it were filled with the necessary preparations. It was necessary to decide a number of things immediately, principal among them: where and how to procure the material to build the dam, namely, 7 million cubic yards of crushed rock of the proper gauge. There were a number of different hypotheses to be explored in that connection and the meeting was principally about that specific matter. Sitting around the table, besides De Klerk and Finetti, were a number of different technicians, and Brandani was there too. Finetti laid out the issues in broad outlines, then he gave the floor to the specialized technicians so they could treat the various problems in their sector. Brandani summarized his chief concerns, laying out all the critical points. In the end, the best solution seemed to be to gradually blow up an entire hill a few miles from the dam location and transfer it, truckload by truckload, to the construction site. Finetti listed the specialized companies capable of doing the job with the appropriate explosives. Right now, there were a number of offers on the table, but the only company that offered complete reliability was an English one, with whom there had been some major disagreements concerning payment for a previous job, and so, before contacting them, they were waiting for the all-clear from the executive offices.

De Klerk, who already at the beginning of the meeting hadn't acted particularly courteous or accommodating, gave him a chilly look and then told him that for something of the sort, if a company is a good one and the prices are attractive, then you don't wait to receive an all-clear, you just get in touch and you ask for a bid. He added that he didn't give a damn about history, that this was something that had to do with the previous management, and then he added that, since they lacked a crucial piece of information, that fucking meeting was pointless, that they were just wasting their time. When he was done, Finetti remained silent and everyone else sat with their eyes on their notepads, some writing, others doodling and sketching. De Klerk asked his secretary to make a call to the company in question, in London. Finetti ventured that it was Friday and that there probably wouldn't be anyone in the offices. De Klerk silenced him with a glare as he picked up the receiver and began speaking in good English with someone at the other end of the line. Then he murmured under his breath: 'There's someone in the offices, and how . . .'

The scene had captivated Ivo heart and soul: that was a real manager, someone without hesitations, someone who cut straight to the chase and acted, someone who asked permission of no one. Eventually, De Klerk spoke to the managing director of the English company and, after hanging up, announced that London expected a fax on Monday morning with a technical report and a draft list of tender specifications. This meant, for everyone in the West Africa Subdivision, that they'd be back in the office on Saturday.

'Now let's all get to work,' said De Klerk, and as everyone was standing up, he added: 'Brandani, could you stay?'

Everyone present exchanged curious glances. It was late, Ivo should be heading home, they were having friends over for dinner. De Klerk's invitation was courteous but also peremptory. He immediately said: 'Of course, Engineer.'

His office was only slightly bigger than Finetti's. Outside the floor-to-ceiling plate-glass windows extended the lights of the outskirts of the City of God. De Klerk asked him to make himself comfortable, removed his jacket, took a seat at his desk, shoved back his backrest and propped his feet on a corner of the desktop. Behind him was a large framed photograph of a sloop under sail, on a beam reach, listing slightly, the bow carving through the waves and forming a lip of foam. 'It's planing,' thought Ivo, who knew something about sailing.

'You like her? Do you know much about boats?'

'Is she yours, sir?'

'*She was* mine . . . This year I bought a slightly longer one, much nicer. Do you know how to sail? Do you know your way around a boat?'

'I'm reasonably knowledgeable, Engineer, I sailed in a number of regattas when I was a boy . . .'

'Let's be on a first name basis, please, don't call me sir . . . Well, good. Look here, let me show her to you, I have a brochure.'

He pulled a file out of the desk. On it was written NEW BOAT. It was a 42-footer from a pretty well-known French boatyard.

'They're getting it ready for me right now. I chose this solution, you see? Two cabins in the bow, plus the master bedroom in the stern. A single bathroom will be enough, but that means the *dinette* will be bigger. Did you see what a great cockpit?'

He pulled out a box of cigars and offered him one. Ivo accepted. The aroma of the Cuban tobacco filled his nostrils, long since accustomed to the stench of the unfiltered Gauloises he usually smoked, he took a couple of drags but almost immediately his head started spinning and his fingertips went chilly. De Klerk warned him against inhaling the cigar smoke: he was affable, relaxed, cordial, the very opposite of how he'd behaved in the meeting just a few minutes ago. Brandani was expecting to talk about work, but that's not the way it went. De Klerk went back to their conversation about the Wenders movie, he wanted Ivo to go back over his arguments in favour of it. Ivo was very uncomfortable, he was sweating, he couldn't seem to bring himself to call him by his first name, he limited himself to muttering a couple of sentences, he said that it was based on a novel by Patricia Highsmith ('never heard of her,' said De Klerk), then added something about the director's intention of paying homage to American filmmaking. De Klerk listened to him with what struck him as an ironic expression, sort of a my-God-you're-spouting-a-load-of-bullshit-though! look, and when he was done said that he didn't go to the movies much but he did like the films of Sergio Leone and Dario Argento. Then he told Brandani that he didn't strike him as your run-of-the-mill engineer, that there was something unusual about him. He asked him how he'd wound up at Megatecton. Ivo—by this point all he wanted was to get out of there but he was flattered by the attention his boss seemed to be lavishing on him—told him briefly about his philosophical studies and his decision to break them off in order to fulfil his father's wishes. It wasn't true, that wasn't why he'd done it, but he hardly felt like laying out all his private considerations in front of some stranger. They went on talking for a while longer about boats and regattas. Then, hesitantly, Ivo meekly told him that he ought to get going, that he was going out to dinner with some friends that evening. Whereupon De Klerk invited him to dinner the following Friday night, he was going to be away all of next week, his secretary would let him know the name of the restaurant. 'I won't take no for an answer. You and your lovely wife, of course. What was her name again?' 'Clara.' 'Ah, that's right, Clara . . .' Ivo thanked him, awkwardly, the invitation had caught him off guard. He struggled to come up with some answer and in the end he said confusedly: 'Why sure, of course . . . That is, very glad to come, only I . . . Let me talk to Clara first . . . If she . . . Unless she's already planned something else . . . You know how it is . . .' He exited that unexpected meeting with emotions churning, his sweat-drenched shirt clinging to his back, but also confused, annoyed, perplexed and, at the same time, sordidly pleased with himself. An hour, more or less, had gone by and his picture of De Klerk had changed, with the addition of a perception of strangeness and ambiguity. In that explicit proffering of friendship there was something contrived, unusual and unjustified: What did that man want from him?

His satisfaction increased the next day, when Finetti called him into his office and told him: 'Well? What was that after-*briefing* tête-à-tête all about . . . if I may ask?'

Finetti was suspicious, mistrustful, slightly resentful—he'd been upbraided in front of everyone, then De Klerk had closeted himself with that smug kid: What did it mean? Ivo sensed that Finetti was worried and very quickly considered whether it was in his interest to keep him on tenterhooks and act reserved or else reassure him. He liked Finetti, the man was a little obtuse, but he was energetic, pragmatic and efficient, and he treated all his direct reports with great respect, delegating freely to them: even Finetti, though, especially when he was under pressure, was liable to explode into furious tantrums. Ivo decided to reassure him, but not entirely, he hated to spoil the mystery that the separate meeting must have posed for everyone else in the subdivision. 'Not at all, Roberto, it had nothing to do with work. You know that De Klerk is a bit of an oddball . . . Last Friday we ran into him at the movies and afterwards we talked about the picture . . . He didn't like it, I did. Since there hadn't really been time for a thorough discussion, De Klerk had wanted to talk it over with me last night . . . Still, I didn't bring him around . . .' That's how he explained it all but the aura that that after-meeting had conferred upon him among his colleagues of similar rank stuck to him. He noticed it and enjoyed it and was proud of it, even though the nature of his relationship with De Klerk, which remained an enigma, did worry him a bit. He said nothing to anyone about the subsequent invitation to dinner: De Klerk's secretary informed him that she'd made reservations for the following Saturday at the Tenda Bianca, which was considered quite a swank restaurant in the City of God.

He and Clara had argued about it, she was irritated by that invitation and even more by the unmistakable gratification she could see that her husband was taking from it. 'I couldn't say no,' he'd said, as if to excuse himself.

'All right, but what does it mean? Are you asking yourself that question? From the stories you've told me, and after meeting him in person, I don't like him much, he strikes me as the usual self-confident hard-on, sun-lamped, with a carefully modulated voice, impeccable salt-and-pepper hair, the vintage Baume & Mercier wristwatch, the silk scarf, the thousand-dollar cashmere sweater, the rumpled Aquascutum trench coat . . . I wonder what we would ever have in common with these people . . .'

'Vintage? How do you know that it's *vintage*? You didn't miss a detail, you even took a peek to see what make of wristwatch he wore! Listen, Clara, *they invited us to dinner*, and that's all . . . Please try to remember that he is *my boss*, so what can I tell you?

I don't think I have a lot of choice in the matter, and you can't make me go alone . . . Now, if you want me to tell you that he disgusts me because he's an up-and-coming manager, well, I'm not going to say that. He doesn't disgust me, in fact, I respect him, I don't consider him anything more than what he actually is, which is to say, a man who knows his job but also nothing less. In other words, not only do we *have to* but I'm also *happy to* go . . . One more thing, that suntan isn't from a lamp, he has a sailboat, he sails, he likes fresh air. Not like us, the way we never get out into the great outdoors . . .'

I'm not the same as you are, you'll never take me alive. But instead all it had taken was the first ambiguous extended hand and already the world, the real world, had bought itself the thirty-year-old Ivo Brandani, veteran militant of 1968, precocious philosophical turncoat, anomalous technician, lost creature, handsome young man. It had been enough for him to meet a real-world specimen of everything he thought he had ever fought against, the diametric opposite of everything he thought he was, and he had been captivated by him. Like when you encounter a rare animal, one you've never seen in flesh and blood but only in photographs, an animal you've long hunted and tracked, when suddenly there it is before you, wild, full of life, totally justified in its existence and in its environment, exactly as you are in yours—the finger is unable to pull the trigger of judgment and that moment's hesitation is fatal, because that rare creature wouldn't take two seconds to pull you over to its side. For the first time in years, Ivo Brandani admitted that something different from him had a right to exist. In fact, there he stood, rooted to the spot, watching in fascination the movements & actions of that stranger-with-power, listening with interest to the words he spoke, evaluating his tastes, his appearance, his odour. De Klerk appeared to him as something intact, a man who seemed to have crossed untouched through the '60s and the early '70s, without allowing anything to undermine his non-convictions, or hinder his career, or modify his tastes in clothing which, while remaining conventionally Old England in derivation, still struck Ivo as just, appropriate, elegant, in comparison with his own way of dressing, every bit as conventional, his casual style, blazer & jeans, shirt with the collar button left undone, a pair of Clarks desert boots on his feet, even though he was still required to wear a tie in the office.

Perhaps it was an incipient, unconfessable annoyance towards that insistence at all costs on being identified as the die-hard defenders of Marxist truth, in which he and all those like him were deeply steeped, that made De Klerk so fascinating to him, or it was the awareness that there existed a world much vaster and more complex than what he had ever imagined, a world inhabited by very different life forms, by creatures with strange mental horizons, very different from his own but not necessarily illegitimate for that reason.

'OK, he likes movies by Dario Argento and Sergio Leone. So what? He's sure to be fond of Morricone's soundtracks—so the fuck what?'

The restaurant dining room was carpeted with a verdigris moquette, the tables were covered with tablecloths, each with its own hanging lamp, chairs upholstered in a light pink fabric, hanging on the walls were lithographs by contemporary artists, in the air was the subdued sound of piped-in music. De Klerk and Sabina still hadn't arrived, the maître d' showed them to the table and served them a couple of aperitifs. It had been a problem getting dressed for that dinner, they'd argued about what to wear, whether they should go dressed to the nines or just nicely dressed, or even slightly casual, to put a sharper emphasis on the unstated idea that *We aren't like you are*, which Clara found ridiculous but which was a point that Ivo really wanted to make. And so she had chosen to wear an elegant and understated dress, while he wore the usual jeans with a blazer over a white shirt, unbuttoned at the neck, and on his feet, instead of his Clarks desert boots, he had put on a pair of old wingtips, burgundy and well made, tenaciously resuscitated and polished to a gleam just a couple of hours ago. Getting to the Tenda Bianca, in the centre of town, had been no simple matter, they'd had to get a cab, which was something they almost never did, accustomed as they were to the Fiat 500, the moped, public transportation. They'd arrived at their evening's destination with their nerves on edge and the fact that their hosts hadn't yet got there gave them a few minutes to decompress, which was a welcome development. After a while the alcohol from their Negronis had soothed them and now they felt close and united again. Ivo smoked, drank and after a while felt fully satisfied that he was there with Clara, cute, nicely turned out, witty, a perfect attribute to the way he now saw himself, a handsome, young & intelligent technician, capable of dazzling his supreme leader to such an extent that he'd invited him out to a restaurant like this one. All around them were middle-aged people with all the markers of comfort, well dressed, necklaces around the necks of beautiful, elegant women, Rolexes on the wrists of very well-tended men, in jackets, a world that Ivo thought had vanished but instead, in the years of political firestorms and ideological violence, had always still been there, like a subterranean river running under the foundations of the City of God to undermine them, still pulling the economic and political strings, shaping the larger, territorial decisions in accordance with their vested interests. Generations of dominant figures with understated power, invisible to the majority but solidly linked among themselves, were piloting the city, squeezing out of it the most nutritious juices, exactly the way it had been prior to the great period of political revolt, the way it was during it and the way it would still be afterwards. It constituted a local but not negligible portion of what Ivo imagined power to be. And for him, young and gregarious animal that he was, it emanated the same fascination that glowed in De Klerk.

Sabina and De Klerk arrived a short while later, apologizing for their lateness. She was beautiful, dressed in a style that struck Ivo as restrained and elegant, while Nico was in a sporty jacket, corduroys and loafers, he too without a tie. Sabina had brought a present for Clara: 'It's just a silly little something, a piece of Moroccan cloth, you can use it as a scarf, a foulard. Cute, don't you think?' Clara accepted, surprised and embarrassed. That kindness and courtesy only increased her distrust, which became unmistakable even as she thanked her effusively. De Klerk chose the wines and piloted the ordering process. A waiter behind them made sure that their glasses were always full. Clara was asked what kind of work she did and De Klerk stated that he knew the director of the Actuarial Office at Assicurazioni Generali *very well*. Sabina said that she worked for a public relations agency. Ivo, his tongue loosened by the alcohol, asked her what one did in a public relations agency. Sabina explained it to him briefly, looking him in the eye as she did so: 'We put people in touch with other people, so what we do is *networking*, you understand?' Ivo wanted to reply with something subtly ironic but nothing came to mind, that woman's beauty inhibited him and rendered plausible anything that had anything to do with that woman. The food, served in portions that struck Ivo and Clara as skimpy, was very good, with unexpected juxtapositions, the bread was warm, the wine was delicious, biting, aromatic. They went on talking for a good while about *The American Friend*. Ivo, his inhibitions by this point thoroughly lowered by the alcohol, talked about it freely, reiterating and articulating his position, the words flowing out fluid, precise, well chosen. De Klerk listened to his performance with an increasingly ironic expression, until Ivo noticed it, blushed and suddenly stopped talking. De Klerk reiterated calmly that it was a movie that had zero credibility, irritating, wooden, absurd and pretentious. Then he added with a smile: 'I wonder why it is that you Communists always fall for those things, what do you see in them?' Ivo replied, in a wavering voice, that he wasn't a Communist. 'I'm beyond that,' he said, and as he said it he was ashamed of saying it, especially in front of Clara, who knew perfectly well that he was a dues-paying Party member. They dropped the subject at that point, but in spite of De Klerk's good manners and affability, his unmistakable psychological dominance over Ivo irritated Clara. For the first time she was watching her husband struggling to deal with the power of that two-bit corporate chieftain, she saw him set aside all his reservations, retire his classic *I'm not the same as you are and become something approaching* submissive, swept away by his eagerness to please, to be approved and respected.

Certainly, the wine was dulling his senses, that setting was intimidating him, that woman, so beautiful and distant, who was dedicating her unflagging attention to him, was disorienting him. Clara could see he was embarrassed, confused, half-drunk. At the end of the meal, Ivo clumsily insisted on paying the bill himself but De Klerk cut him short, saying that it was out of the question, that they were his guests. Then he added that they should get together again. They took the same taxi. Downstairs, at the apartment-building door, as they were fumbling for their keys, Clara felt a sudden surge of tenderness for her man, she kissed him and as she wrapped her arms around him she told him: 'You really made a conquest, eh? That woman was eating you up with her eyes . . . You're a good-looking boy, and I get that, but De Klerk isn't bad himself . . . What do they want with us, Ivo? Or maybe I should say, what does *he* want with you?'

'I don't know, Clara, maybe they don't want anything at all . . . Maybe they just want to be friends . . . Couldn't that be?'

A few days later, Finetti took Brandani and a number of other technicians with him to West Africa. They were there to survey on site a number of the leading issues in connection with the bid for the contract on the new dam in Sierra Leone. After a few days, Finetti went back to headquarters, leaving behind a couple of his men and Brandani to commute back and forth between Freetown and the dam site, in the heart of the rainforest where they were busy gathering information and materials for the general planning of the installations that would be necessary for the various phases of the project. Ivo was gone for almost a month. The situation in Africa worked once again to revivify his anti-imperialism, his belief in the possibility of emancipating humanity from hunger, from slavery to primary needs, from exploitation. He seemed to regain access to that side of his mind that seemed to be on the side of the right, that is, in favour of the weak and the exploited all over the world. That is the way he had always thought and, although he had almost always been forced to keep those views to himself, that is what he still thought.

Upon his return he hastily and determinedly wrote two reports, one for Finetti and one, in coordination with Finetti, for De Klerk. This second report contained all the issues at play but condensed into an extremely concise form. To fit them, as required, onto a single sheet of A4 paper, Ivo had to work furiously, but in the end, after having the various versions typed and retyped, he was successful. Before the end of the week, it was all on the boss's desk. De Klerk discussed it with Finetti alone, but then, once he was done with him, he sent for Brandani. He was courteous, friendly. He pulled a sheet of extra-strong paper from a pile on his desk and asked if this was his work. Ivo said that it was and De Klerk complimented him on it, saying that it was very well done, that at last someone had understood the right way to draft a report. Then they talked about work and Africa and the equatorial forest and black women; Ivo said that he had no experience with them. 'Too bad,' said De Klerk, 'that is some unforgettable sex.' De Klerk who, aside from the occasional curse word tossed in to spice up the conversation, was so careful and polished in his language, now talked to him about sex in a vulgar, racist way. He told the story of several of his erotic escapades in Africa, many years ago. Ivo listened with a smile, surprised that he was confiding such things to him and annoyed, practically to the verge of indignation, at the tone in which he recounted them. And yet, nonetheless, once again, flattered that his boss would open up to him like that.

'That's what this man is like, take him or leave him, he has his good points and his defects.'

Then De Klerk told him that work on his sailboat was done, that the boatyard would be delivering her to him in a matter of days, and then he invited Ivo and Clara to spend two weeks sailing around the Greek islands. Sabina would be there, and so would another married couple, friends of theirs. 'I've found a skipper who'll rig and stock the boat and sail her to me in Piraeus by mid-July. I named the boat *Falesá*, do you like it? Will you come?' Ivo said that Clara wasn't crazy about sailing, that she suffered from seasickness. De Klerk insisted, telling Ivo that it meant a lot to him. Ivo said that he would see what he could do, but he didn't think it was likely. De Klerk seemed very put out as he retorted, pointing out that there were pills, anti-nausea bracelets, that after a while a person gets used to it, etc. Ivo became increasingly open to it, he wouldn't rule anything out, he didn't want to say no, but then there was Clara. 'Well, sure, you'll see, Brandani . . . that is, *you'll see, Ivo*, we'll bring her around.' Right then and there, he didn't feel in the slightest like taking a sailing trip with De Klerk, but how could he turn him down?

A few days later, Brandani received another invitation to have dinner with his boss. De Klerk asked whether Ivo would be willing to dine at Tenda Bianca, he told him he'd made reservations for next week, on Saturday night. Ivo thanked him and said that would be fine with him, but he'd have to ask Clara. Clara wasn't enthusiastic about the idea, in fact, she really didn't want to go. They argued about it. She didn't understand the reason for all the attention his boss was lavishing on them, she didn't find De Klerk very likeable, she distrusted him: 'He's ambiguous, there's an air about him, I don't know . . . Maybe I'm wrong . . . I have an instinctive dislike for the man. As for her . . . Here's what I say, the beauty queen wants to take you to bed, Ivo.'

'Oh, come on!'

'It's so obvious! I'm surprised that her man, who seems so clever, shouldn't have noticed . . . Or else he's perfectly well aware of it and he's just pretending not to notice . . . Maybe he thinks it's amusing. Maybe they're swingers, Ivo . . .'

Clara had read Updike's *Couples*, she thought she knew every-thing about the corrupt mores of the wealthy: 'They're *swingers*! You wait and see, sooner or later they'll proposition us . . . There's no other explanation . . . If they proposition us, what are we going to say to them, Ivo? Will we tell them yes or no? After all, that's your supreme leader we're talking about, if we tell them no, it might ruin your career . . . And I have to say, I don't mind his looks one little bit . . .'

Ivo took umbrage at her irony, Clara's mistrust irritated him. While she might be satisfied with her position in the Actuarial Office at Assicurazioni Generali, he wanted more from life: 'I want to become a builder of bridges,' he told himself, but what he wouldn't admit to himself was that in the meantime he wouldn't have turned his nose up at a management career, at Megatecton or elsewhere. In short, he felt that he deserved money & power: he saw himself as the head of a large projects division, where he could surely rise due to his talents. And De Klerk's friendship would help him.

'Swingers or not, after dinner, we need to invite them over to our place. I'll get a couple of good bottles and we'll ask them.'

'Good God, Ivo, is it really necessary? We'll have to clean this rattrap and tidy up. They'll be disgusted to come here, who knows what kind of a place they live in . . .'

'We're a *young married couple*, Clara, it's normal that we live in a one bedroom.'

At the restaurant, things went better than they had the last time: they knew what to expect, they drank in moderation, they were more relaxed. De Klerk did most of the talking, interrupted every now and then by comments from Sabina, while Ivo and Clara for the most part just listened. He told them about his travels, the absurd customs of the Japanese, the atrocities of Africa, he told them about New York, which in the last few years had become the cultural capital of the planet. A man who's been around, thought Ivo, a man who knew the world, a freethinker who was surprised at nothing. Someone who seemed to face up to the challenges in every situation, a true executive, a man who made it clear that he believed in nothing and enjoyed his privileges. 'If I were an American I'd vote Republican,' he said. 'Here in Italy politics is just laughable. The only party worth considering are the Liberals,' he said, mentioning a centre-right Italian party. Ivo had no objections but remained silent, and Clara was privately astonished. After they left the restaurant, they invited their hosts to come get something to drink at their place. De Klerk and Sabina accepted. As they were drinking a glass of the peated malt whisky purchased for the occasion, they talked about the summer holidays and De Klerk came out again with his invitation to spend the last two weeks of July with them in their sailboat. 'Did Ivo talk to you about it? What have you decided, Clara?' She still didn't know anything about it, but she kept it from showing.

She said that it was a wonderful invitation but that she had a real issue with being on a boat, she suffered from seasickness, she didn't swim well and she was afraid of the open sea. 'What's more,' she said, 'I've already put in my request for a holiday in August and now it's too late to change that.' De Klerk said that that was the least of the problems, he reminded her that he was close friends with her boss and that he'd be glad to give him a call and arrange to reschedule her holiday. Clara blushed bright red in alarm. It was clear that she was quite annoyed as she said rather brusquely that there was no need for that. De Klerk insisted. Reining in her anger, Clara said that she would really rather he didn't, thanked him, but when it came to her own holiday schedule she'd take care of that herself, and that moreover it would be a counterproductive intrusion into her relationship with her boss. De Klerk's gaze grew suddenly chilly for a brief instant, but immediately afterwards he smiled and replied: 'Fine, as you prefer, I'm sorry, I was only trying to help.' From that time on, the four of them would never meet again as a group. Clara began to detest De Klerk.

It was towards the end of June and Brandani had just returned from yet another stay in Africa, where he had been captivated by the challenges of working in the jungle, such as the fact that really, there was nothing there, not even drinking water, and that everything or almost would have to be transported from the Peninsula. He liked the idea that, in order to build the dam in question, they would have to use dynamite to blow up entire hills, transport the rubble downhill with dozens of trucks, every day, for months and years. They would build a large village of prefabricated, air-conditioned huts, and it would be completely self-sufficient. They would have to provide complete sanitary plumbing installations and even procure turkeys to rid the area of the snakes that infested it. In short, if Megatecton won the contract, he thought that he'd like to be part of the team, take part in person in the start-up work on the construction site. He intended to ask De Klerk to let him do it, but not right away, only when the time was right, after the summer.

He saw De Klerk again at the West Africa meeting. In mid-October, Megatecton was going to submit its bid. The watchword handed down by De Klerk was that they had to win that contract, no matter the cost. The contract would be for several hundred million dollars: too big to risk losing it. Everything had to be done properly and with precision, there was no room for any errors of economic judgement any greater than 5, or at the very most 8 per cent on the more complicated undertakings. Ivo sat silent the whole time, then when he thought his turn had come, he expressed his doubts concerning certain decisions. He said that there were some issues that simply couldn't be determined in advance, some costs, especially those bound up with local conditions and situations, might well turn out to vary widely from the initial estimate. De Klerk asked him for more detail. Ivo expressed his concern about the political situation, for the tribal feuds that were continuously breaking out in some areas of the country and which could easily cut the supply lines between the coast and the construction site. De Klerk looked at him they way you would a child who's blurted out something naïve, then he taught him a little lesson, which came as quite a surprise from someone like him, about what Megatecton's goals were in this phase.

'The essential thing is *to win this contract*. Everything that comes after that point can be managed, recalibrated, wheels greased, we can negotiate and renegotiate: this is Africa, not Sweden, Brandani. A construction project like this one is nothing other than constant *management of the unforeseen*. Nothing ever goes the way it's planned, but still, you need to plan . . . There will be very few things that we're not going to have to re-plan entirely, but for now we need a plan in any case . . . Some things will cost us less than we expect, many things will cost us more . . . Nonetheless, right now it's indispensable to have an estimate . . . In situations like this, respecting the projected deadlines is practically impossible, but a timing roadmap with deadlines is still necessary. If we win the contract—and winning this contract is a *categorical* imperative—it's not as if we're going to go down, there, build the dam, and leave ... That's not the way these things work. If we win, then Megatecton will open a *situation* in Africa that's going to last, if things go well, for at least a decade, during which time there will be changes of government, the political situation might become very unfavourable or, contrariwise, improve and become advantageous, there are going to be uprisings and tribal feuds, if not outright guerrilla warfare. Many of those who are currently running the majority government, and likewise others who are in the minority opposition, are going to want to get a piece of the pie. We're going to have to thread our way around the various contenders, pay something to this one and something else to that one and, when all is said and done, and this is the most important point, make money ourselves ... But when I say *when all is said and done*, I'm not necessarily talking about the completion of work on the dam, because other opportunities might crop up in Sierra Leone for us: what I'm trying to explain to you is that for the next ten or fifteen years, Megatecton is going to take part, as one of many players in the field, in the *history* of Sierra Leone ... It's not as if we like it, but we do need to know from the outset that that's the way it's going to be. The purity, the beauty of the project, issues of technical neutrality, are of no interest to us, we can't afford them ... Everything is going to be different, derailed with respect to the way we imagine plan predict programme, everything is going to be dirty, difficult, compromised and modified ... In these cases, it works for us the way it does for political parties: it's one thing to be elected on a platform, but actually putting it into effect is quite another matter ... There are times when it might actually be preferable to just break off entirely and leave, until the situation changes, maybe even paying a penalty long after the dust has settled. Megatecton builds things, but its goal isn't to build things, it's to *make profits* ... So now have I made myself clear? Very good, gentlemen, we'll meet again in eight days, at the same time ... Brandani, could you stay here, please.'

'Again! Fuck, couldn't he just have his secretary call me back afterwards? This is getting awkward with everyone else ... They already hate me ... And Finetti doesn't trust me any more ...'

Brandani, who had been deeply impressed by his boss's speech, tried to conceal his embarrassment as De Klerk was already holding the door of his office open for him. He didn't have much time, he wanted to know if he and Clara would be coming with them on the sailboat. He said that if they went on holiday in the second half of July, then they'd have all of August to work on the bid for the dam project. Finetti already knew about it, he was in agreement, and he was adjusting the holiday schedules accordingly. In September his calendar was going to be jam-packed, but he wanted to be closely involved in this thing, so most of the work would have to be drafted in August. Ivo, who had discussed it again with Clara, who was increasingly opposed to it, impulsively said yes, that they would come. 'Oh good,' said De Klerk, 'now get out of here, I have work to do.'

That night Clara and Ivo got caught up in another argument. He told her in no uncertain terms that the holiday in question meant a lot to him and that was something she ought to understand, that if she took the right pills she shouldn't have any problems with seasickness, that she'd get used to the boat, that it could be a wonderful thing, that she wasn't familiar with the Greek islands, that now that the dictatorship of the colonels was over, they could go there without any problems. 'Thousands of islands, can you just imagine?' She was angry at him for having said yes without checking with her. She didn't like De Klerk and Sabina, the idea of the sailboat filled her with horror, as for swimming, she could barely swim: Why should she feel obliged to take a trip like that? He might have issues with his career but she didn't. But the next morning she'd already changed her mind and she told him that it was all right, that she'd have to reschedule her request for holiday, but she couldn't imagine that would be a problem: there would be someone to substitute for her, because most of her colleagues took their holidays in August.

But a few days later, her request for a change in holiday schedule was rejected. The reason given: there would be no one to take her place. Clara was stunned: what are you talking about, her colleagues had reassured her, she had no reason to worry, someone would certainly cover for her, at least officially . . . It did no good to argue, the director of her office was adamant. One of her colleagues made it clear that she'd better not press her luck, that she was a new arrival and already that request for a variation on the usual holiday schedule might have made her look bad . . .

'Listen, I don't know, I'm almost happy that it turned out like this, I won't have to spend two nightmarish weeks . . . I really didn't want to go, and you know it . . . You'll go anyway, right? Separate holidays this year? You're going to leave me all alone so you can go with the two of them? Are you certain? Why have you got it into your head that this thing is so important for you? If that guy respects you now, he's certainly going to respect you even if you don't go on his sailboat with him . . . Or am I wrong? If you ask me, you *want* to go, and how . . . To my mind, *you like* the idea of going on a sailboat with your boss . . . Nothing wrong with that, as long as you don't come to me later telling me how different you are from *them* . . . Unless what it is is that you've decided you want to take *her* to bed . . . But, come to think of it, even if you wanted to, I don't think you could pull it off . . . And after all, think of the consequences for your career: going to bed with your boss' girlfriend aboard your boss' sailboat has never been a particularly clever move for anyone . . . Go ahead and reserve your flight right away, otherwise you might not be able to get one. Go on, go on, go on . . . If things turn out differently and they let me take my holidays when I requested, I can catch up with you later . . . There must be a flight I can take . . .' Then she added: 'You talk a good game, but you can't wait to fit in.'

Ivo was rolling the crumb of his bread into little balls and he said nothing for a while, and then: 'If you don't want me to go, I won't go. It's not as if I necessarily have to accept, I can always come up with some excuse. He invited us to come because he needs help and he knows that I used to sail . . .' The technical argument, the idea of helping his boss, struck him as powerful and plausible. 'I should have thought about it before opening my mouth,' he told himself, as he said again: 'And anyway, if you don't want me to go, I won't go.'

'Oh, do whatever the fuck you like,' she said, getting to her feet and slamming the bathroom door behind her. He heard the click of the key in the lock. That night, in bed, they turned their backs to each other, each curled up in their own jurisdiction. The next day, Ivo called Megatecton's trusted travel agency and reserved a flight to Athens. This would be their first separate holiday in all their time together.

'Fit in, my ass, she's the one that fits in. Maybe it'll do us some good to spend a little time apart . . . That's bullshit, Ivo, you know that's not right, it's never been that way for any of the couples you've known, "separate holidays" are just an unofficial way of saying that you're going to go look for someone else to fuck, a way of declaring that it would just be too much of a pain in the ass to go on holiday with your partner, that the two of you no longer have fun together, that the sex is no good, that you're constantly fighting, that you just can't take being stuck together any more, that you have nothing to say to each other, that you're starting to look around for something else . . . It means that *you're happy* to be going without her . . . It means that by this point you're experiencing this marriage as a cage, as a constriction, while out there is the vast world having fun . . . Separate holidays might seem like a liberated thing, but really they're just the waiting room for a divorce . . . So what if there was a divorce in the offing? Clara has changed, she's grown hard. Maybe it's because of the work that she does, but to me it seems like she's falling into line . . . No, she's always been in line. In line with her family, with the Party, the petty bourgeoisie of the Left, the dreariest ones of all, mistrustful of everything, and everything they do is with a mental reservation . . . That's not the way I am . . . She's dragging me onto her terrain, and then she tells me that I'm trying to fit in . . . But this isn't the life that I want, this isn't the world that I want, all this is provisional, my real life is about to start and then I'll show you all . . . Sooner or later they'll carry me in triumph, like the time my composition was voted first in elementary school . . . But no, she's right . . . She understands me perfectly, she understands that this invitation flattered me, that this desire to go is a mix of flattery &

ambition . . . And there's also a fair share of servility . . . OK—so what? The division chief, someone who rides high in the empyrean of this corporation, has asked you to come for a trip on his yacht and you leave your wife behind in the city and you go: What could be so bad about it? They're good-looking-rich-elegant, you're young, smart and well put together: for you it's the basic minimum . . . But what if Clara really does leave you and *winds up with some other guy?*'

Until the day of his departure, Clara did her best not to show her resentment. She pretended that those separate holidays were just a normal thing, typical of the kind of open-minded couple they thought of themselves as. They joked about it, they laughed, but deep down the thought of it was upsetting to them, but it also kindled a flame, because an unstated freedom for sexual manoeuvres was implicit for each of them. And even though they were both doing their best to think of that summer's holidays as something normal, it was still a bellwether of something, perhaps a signal of an impending end, the approach of the unthinkable, of an opening crevice, a breaking point, something that appeared as the tacit but logical outcome of the slow drifting apart of the past two years. The night before Ivo's departure, their love-making was something very intense for each of them. 'You'll see, I'll be able to catch up with you,' she told him. 'Oh yes, please, try to make that happen . . .' was his reply. It was a heartfelt response, but only for the part of Ivo that was terrified of the unknown. In reality, he *wanted* to go alone and Clara knew that better than he did.

De Klerk had hired a skipper who was already sailing the boat to Greece. Ivo had told him about Clara, that they hadn't let her make a change in her holiday schedule. De Klerk said something like: 'Too bad, it would have been nice if she could have come.' Then he added that it could have been taken care of, if only she'd let him make that phone call, 'but far be it from me to meddle where it's not wanted . . .'

'We'll leave from Milos, Cyclades . . . Then we head south-east, with a following wind . . . Down there the meltemi is strong, sailing on a bowline is out of the question . . .'

'How many of us will be in the boat?'

'There should be six of us: another couple, a friend of theirs, a girl, then me, you and Sabina. You might have to sleep in the dinette.'

'It's better if there are some other people: a 42-foot sloop is a chore to run with two guys and a woman . . . Especially if it's windy . . . Are these people experienced?'

'Sure, they're all seafarers . . . Nice folks . . . And anyway the *Falesá* is a technological boat, with an automatic helm, all the most important rigging has controls in the cockpit. You could sail it solo, if you wanted . . .'

If it had just been the three of them from the start, perhaps Ivo would have changed his mind: travelling alone with De Klerk and his girlfriend, frankly . . . But if there were going to be other people, two other friends plus a *single girl*, that was quite a different matter. 'There's a girl for me,' he thought excitedly, but having decided to act upset about Clara's absence, he made sure that excitement couldn't be detected by anyone else, or at least so he believed.

Clara would be going to the beach, to a girlfriend's place. 'I'll leave at the end of the last week in July,' he'd said, 'unless there are changes in plan.'

De Klerk and Sabina left a week before him. At the travel agency they told him that, if he wanted to take a ship the morning after his arrival, the best thing would be to get a hotel in Piraeus. That was fine with him, as long as it wasn't too expensive. That evening, he took a cab straight from the airport. Athens was hot and white, the blistering air that poured in through the car's windows smacked of the city night and calcined cement, the streets were full of people out walking, crowding around the kiosks. The hotel in Piraeus was filthy but that was not a problem as far as Brandani was concerned: he didn't like pretentious hotels and that kind of squalor was perfectly suited to his attitude of *I'm not the same as you are*, which, even though he was about to set off on a cruise with a successful manager, or perhaps precisely because of that fact, was a stance that remained in effect. It was as if that circumstance, precisely because of its inherent contradictions, forced him to keep himself *politically pure*, at least in his mind.

He'd only be spending the one night in that hotel and the wharf where the ship tied up was only a few hundred yards away. He dropped his backpack off in the room, and no sooner had he done so than he felt his blood sugars plunge, so he went back out without even bothering to take a shower. He walked into the first open restaurant he found, right around the corner from the hotel. He ate the usual Greek fare, bad food, gulped down in haste, but still he was happy he hadn't had to go in search of a restaurant where you could eat-well-&-pay-very-little, which is what he'd have had to do if he was with Clara. She scolded him for this culinary laziness of his, but it wasn't that he had no interest in good food, it was really his fear of the uncontrollable hunger that would come over him without warning, throwing him into a state of panic. That night, of course, the meal left him with a case of indigestion. It was his latent anxiety about that holiday without Clara, and with De Klerk. The frozen *kalamarakia*, or fried calamari, caught fire when they came into contact with the ouzo he drank at the end of the meal and started to scorch his oesophagus. He took a stroll along the piers. He liked harbours. The air was still hot and dry, but a light breeze was blowing and it quickly dried the cold sweat on his forehead and down his back. He was starting to feel a little better, he pulled a couple of Maalox tablets out of the old leather bag he wore on a strap over his shoulder and which he'd had since he was a kid, and chewed on them. The faint night wind buffeted him as he turned the corner at various intersections, and he enjoyed it. Every so often his field of view opened out over the water where, in the reflected light of the ships riding at anchor, he could glimpse the water, its surface ruffled by the gusting wind. Yellow navigation lights. Cranes. Shipyards. The corrupt smell of bilge water. The aromas of tar, kerosene, grease, diesel engines, marine paint, the mixture of iron and salt brine, the tang of rust. His mind was flooded with the memory of long-ago beachfront holidays, in the City by the Sea where he went as a boy. It only lasted for a brief instant, but it was enough to alter his state of mind. His anxiety over all the unknowns of that journey began to subside, his mental reservations, his *I'm not the same as you are*, began to relax. He was free, alone, still young, women liked him, he was making decent money, his future lay before him, he was making good friendships. Nothing could exist outside of capitalism, so what was the point of continuing to oppose it? And what did Clara have to do with his future? Now there was this holiday in a sailboat travelling the islands. People with money and power and beautiful women. What did Clara want? Let her go to the beach with Franca.

He'd been to Athens once years before, on a cruise with his school. Many of his classmates had gone off to whores in Piraeus, only to come back to the ship all excited and snickering, as they traded opinions and considerations on their respective experiences. He hadn't, he'd been too afraid of the blonds, ravaged and unnatural, who walked the streets down by the wharves. In spite of the tawdriness of his friends' accounts, then and there he regretted not having seized the opportunity to put a halt to an endless litany of jacking off and finally have sex with a woman. That sordid filth repelled him and attracted him at the same time. Before his departure Father had taken him aside and warned him about the danger of diseases: 'For a moment's pleasure you can ruin yourself for the rest of your life—if you really have to do it, wear a rubber . . . And after all, what's the fun if you have to pay for a woman?' Ivo had been scared out of his wits, and when push came to shove, he chose not to join that expedition of beardless and snickering whoremongers.

He went into a bar to buy a pack of cigarettes. He was thirsty. Inside, the lights were dimmed, the music was pumping at full volume, there were a few people drinking at the bar and there might have been a couple of whores. In his rudimentary English he asked if they could make him a half shot of Fernet Branca in a glass of soda water. It took him a while to convey his request but in the end he was able to relish that sense of gastric pacification that comes from the warmth of the bitter herbal liqueur. He was feeling better and better, freer and further away from Clara. A young woman came over to him, bleached blond hair, dark, dark eyes and eyebrows, a dark fuzz on her upper lip. They exchanged a few words, still in English, she told him that her name was Irini, she came up with a few phrases in Peninsular language. He bought her a drink, then they left. She was very young. When they were out of there, he pulled her close to him, put his hand on her hips and found them strangely flabby. He took the girl up to his room, the night porter had no objections. The room was blistering hot, the walls dotted with the stains of smacked mosquitoes. She stripped naked immediately, led him into the bathroom, undid his trousers and washed his cock thoroughly. She was small, her body heavy, her breasts already tired, she called him *honey*. She took him by the hand and sat him down on the bed, took off his trousers, removed his underpants and took him in her mouth. After a few minutes the phone on the nightstand rang. Irini stopped, lifted her head and gave him a quizzical look. 'Clara! Why did I give her the number of the hotel?' He thought about just not answering, but then, as he gestured to the girl to go on with her work, he picked up the receiver and said: 'Hello?'

Clara wanted to know how the trip had gone, how he was, whether he'd had dinner, what the hotel was like. She'd just been informed that her request for a change in holiday schedule had been turned down definitively: she'd have to keep going to work for another ten days or so. He didn't know what to say to her, so he just gave a series of brief answers: 'Strange . . . I'm sorry to hear that . . . What assholes they are, though . . . Is it hot there?' Talking to his wife while a Greek whore was sucking his dick excited him to the verge of the spasmodic.

'Strange, I'm not sure it's strange,' said Clara, 'but whatever, that's the way it went this year. It's broiling hot here . . .'

'Same here . . .'

'Are you all right? You sound different . . . What's wrong?'

'Nothing . . . I'm just tired.'

The conversation went on like that for less than a minute while Irini went on working on his cock with professional expertise.

Clara didn't ask him about De Klerk. He told her that he would board the ship tomorrow morning. He hung up and came immediately. He abandoned himself to his orgasm with no thought for anything but his pleasure. He could feel the sperm jerk out in spurts with every spasm of his loins, he was flooded by a sense of freedom and domination. 'The first time . . . The first time in my life that I've been with a whore!' He'd taken pleasure in a different and uninhibited way, without worrying about anything but his own enjoyment. The girl's work was done, she was cleaning him off with a wet Kleenex. Brandani understood how distant he was from Clara, with her family's Communist culture, her moralizing, her mistrust of everything that failed to jibe with her convictions. He felt as if just a few minutes ago he had leapt into another universe, different from the one his wife occupied. 'I'm not the same as she is.'

The ship for Milos was scheduled to sail at 8.30 in the morning, but by nine it was still loading. It was packed with young people searching for a good place to unroll their sleeping bags. Towards the stern Brandani found a plastic chair unoccupied and sat down to smoke, in the shade, next to the deckhouse wall.

'They all have these very technical backpacks, narrow and tall, with aluminium frames, very nice. Mine drags my shoulders down, it's trying to flip me over onto my back . . . Miserable heat already this early in the day. I reek of sweat. Who knows where downtown Piraeus is. Lots of ships off-shore . . . Out on the water there's wind, it must be cool, if only they could just go ahead and get underway. I'm not really all that different from them . . . They stretch out on the deck, relaxed, on rubber mats. *Jaws*: everyone's reading that book. The coffee was shitty, it burnt my tongue, the *tiropita* is already burning my stomach . . . Immediate effect . . . White and green paint, coat upon coat, bubbles of rust, by now you could never undo one of these screws . . . This ship is just one single chunk of rust underneath the paint . . . Lifeboats welded to the hull with the paint . . . It's all paint, and underneath the paint it's falling apart . . .'

He watched the young people who'd boarded and felt uneasy, a secret pang of envy. What got on his nerves was their state of suspended confusion, the fact that they didn't actually need to decide anything of any real importance, the latent arrogance that could be detected in the way they sprawled easily in space and time, smoking laughing chatting reading sleeping. That wasn't the way it was for him: despite the fact that he was only thirty, he already felt cut off from youth. Those young people would be spending the nights to come on the solitary beaches of the Aegean Sea. He'd be on board a boat with his boss, a corporate executive, and his boss' friends. The summer of '69 had been like that, for him and for Clara, just like the summer those kids were going to have. The South of the Peninsula was alien and baking hot. He'd joined her on the island of Vulcano on the night that the *Apollo 11 mission had landed on the Moon*. Everyone was in the bars and hotels watching the Moon landing on live TV, but he'd fallen asleep and hadn't seen a thing. Maybe there was something going on between Clara and the piece of beefcake who was giving her scuba lessons. Maybe it was the volcano that sent up plumes of smoke in the night that gave him that tragic sense of apocalypse. They spent the rest of the summer tent-camping around the islands, without a cent to their name, eating practically nothing. He remembered that night on the deck of the ship that was taking them back to the mainland, the stars, the incandescent gusts of smoke from Stromboli, rising a thousand metres out of the sea, life as it spread out before him, looking like a road that would never end . . .

'They have blond hair, they're all fair-haired, their eyes are light-coloured, empty . . . The people working on the ship, seamen with endless cigarettes in their mouths and a general air of indifference. For real, they don't even see us passengers, look at how they're hauling that armoire on board . . . Boom! Nice work, boys, I wonder where the crane operator got his certificate . . . Water greasy with diesel fuel, filthy stuff bobbing, grey mullets . . .'

The odour of the port seized him again, taking him back to that long-ago cruise with his class. They all went ashore in boats, because in those days genuine harbours were few and far between. A seaman with no front teeth laughed . . . 'Nice pictures, very interesting, only for men, poco lire.' 'What the fuck is it? Let me see!' Black bushes of pubic hair. Cocks and pussies in black and white, none of them had ever seen anything like it. They looked like shellfish out of the depths, mysterious, incomprehensible, repellent organisms. Pedrini on the top bunk was capable of giving himself a blowjob: he just jammed his feet against the cabin ceiling, bent over like that he could get his dick into his own mouth, he wasn't ashamed, everyone was laughing. Pornographic photos. Everyone but Ivo bought one or two of them. Then there was a jerk-off competition to see who could squirt the farthest. He left the cabin before he could find out who was the winner.

'It was an Easter trip, with a tempest off Crete . . . People vomiting and people jerking off . . . The *Kriti* was white, just like this ship . . . When we were in the waters off the port of Alexandria, the ship was covered with flies . . . God, it's over! It's over—I'm never going back to school, I'm never going to study again! I have these two weeks ahead of me and already this ship is a bellwether . . . Something that goes far and loses itself, something to enjoy . . . The captain's sweat on that khaki shirt, saline, off-white stains, plastic fake-leather sandals, here everyone wears them . . . He shouts and he smokes, he's yelling himself hoarse . . .'

The ship was packed, on the third-class deck there wasn't even a square inch of space, he had a second-class ticket, the second-class deck was half-empty.

'There's no one here, except for those two . . . He's French, look at those chilly green eyes, he's got the face of a Frenchman . . . She . . . yes, she. They're necking, kissing each other . . . Is she Peninsular? Greek? She's definitely not French . . . She's Greek . . . Pageboy haircut, short skirt, tanned legs, long and muscular, unusual around these parts . . . The sleeping bag spread out on the deck and now it's time to get some shut-eye, money and ID are right here, in my bag . . . The bag is under my head, my handkerchief over my eyes . . . We're pulling out, we're on our way . . . This ship vibrates like a drum . . . The ones who were heading out to find a whore in Piraeus, with their money and their Marlboros in their pockets, came back and told the tale of a fairly sterile experience: "They wash your thing, did you know? Before and after." "How disgusting," I thought, but I didn't know anything about it, I didn't know the way things were, what a whore was like, much less a woman, I knew nothing . . . Yesterday evening I checked it out for myself—it's true that they wash your thing before, they scrub it off afterwards. Here's some shade, all you have to do is roll over facing this wall painted white, shut your eyes, and bingo, I just need to relax and get some sleep, I still have a few cigarettes . . . When you get out into the open water the wind will break the heat . . . Everyone's reading *Jaws*. Fried calamari . . . I could stay here for ever, not doing a damned thing . . . The smell of harbours in summer . . . Leave for ever, no one would ever be able to track me down . . . Vanished, me too, reading *Jaws* for the rest of an endless summer . . . Later I'll go belowdecks and buy a pack of Karelias.'

It was early afternoon, Nico and Sabina were waiting for him on the dock in the port of Milos. It was strange to see De Klerk again in that place, so far from the company and from his position. He was already pretty tan, in a T-shirt and shorts, with skinny legs. He was welcoming, but not effusive. Courteous, but in a way that struck Ivo as distracted. They'd come to get him from the ship with the tender of the *Falesá*, which was anchored offshore a good distance away, on the far side of the bay. Sabina was wearing a white camisole over her swimsuit: when she gave him a kiss on the cheek, Ivo breathed in the scent of her hair and her usual strange and perverse perfume. She struck him as very pretty, with that faint golden sheen on her skin. She barely smiled.

'She can probably smell the stench of sweat on me, the smell of a dirty ship.'

Brandani was very tired. He took off his shoes, climbed down into the inflatable rubber dinghy, and put his backpack under the bow. Then he sat on the wet side, his bare feet shivering in the shallow water sloshing around on the bottom of the dinghy. Perhaps it was the water that once again triggered in his mind the sense of bewilderment that he'd already experienced briefly in Piraeus.

'What on earth was I thinking? Why am I here? Who are these people? Unknown landscapes, unfamiliar people and places, this boat, De Klerk and his girlfriend, and their guests, never met them before in my life . . .'

But he instantly corrected himself: 'Adapt, adapt rapidly, it's only a holiday . . . Only a holiday . . .'

The *Falesá* was a beautiful sloop, with a nice cockpit, dual helm, a nicely designed deckhouse that barely rose, like a slight swell, from the teakwood deck. They boarded from the stern, where a platform descended towards the water and from there, via a ladder, they climbed up to the boat itself. He looked up at Sabina from below, as she saw clambering up the ladder, and he saw a shapely derriere, but a nasty red birthmark winked out from beneath her swimsuit, on the back of her left thigh, right under her ass cheek.

'What about the others? Are they on shore?' he asked once he was aboard.

'Eh?' asked De Klerk, distractedly. 'The others?'

'You'd said there were some other friends who were coming, that is, there were supposed to be three other people . . .'

'Ah, right, sorry . . . It's true, I'd forgotten about it . . . No, they're not coming, they cancelled at the last minute. The couple was having family problems . . . I think it was because her mother wasn't well. At that point, the girl decided not to come either . . . Well, she's a friend of theirs. I've never even met her, you know. She didn't feel up to it. I didn't insist. So it's just the three of us . . . Do you mind?'

'Why no, of course not,' Brandani said in a faint voice.

He was lying, though, because a wave of furious irritation was actually surging inside him. He felt he'd been betrayed. 'That's something to look forward to, fifteen days alone with these two!' But what could he do at this point? Leave? It was absolutely not a good idea, just the two of them alone wouldn't be able to handle the boat, ditching them now was out of the question, it would have meant breaking all ties with De Klerk, with obvious negative repercussions for his future at the company, just now when things were starting to hum. He was trapped, and he was pissed off. He was reminded of the young people on the ship, free to roam unimpeded around the islands with their sleeping bags. He suddenly felt he was being held hostage.

'On this fucked-up boat, on a fucked-up island, anchored off fucking shore, in a fucked-up situation! Clara was right: "Don't put too much trust in them, Ivo" . . . Oh, fuck Clara too . . .'

De Klerk seemed to understand his state of mind perfectly. He stared at him, interrogating him with his chilly, courteous eyes. He seemed to be saying: 'And now what are you going to do? As for leaving, it's not as if you can leave.'

'Nice boat,' said Ivo, and turned his gaze away, to the rigging, the equipment, the helm, the large black boom with a rectangular cross-section. Everywhere was solidity, first-class technology, quality, money. Brandani was an engineer, he sailed, he had an eye for these things, he found them interesting, he took pleasure in them. De Klerk started explaining a few things about the *Falesá to him*.

'What's this name? What does it mean?' asked Ivo.

'Stevenson,' he replied. 'Have you ever read his books? It's from a short story by Stevenson. It's called "The Beach of Falesá". I read it many years ago, I don't even remember what it's about . . . Just the name, *Falesá*. I have it here, on board, if you want you can read it. You'll find it on the shelves in the *dinette*. Ah, there's something I need to tell you, Ivo—here there's only one rule, but it's ironbound: never-talk-about-work.'

Some of the controls were electric, such as the halyard of the mainsail, the jib sheets, the roller reefing systems on the jib and mainsail. It had an automatic helm, very nice instrumentation and even radar: if you had to, you could pilot that boat all by yourself. 'What a nice sailboat, the money he must have spent on it,' Ivo thought. Belowdecks were three cabins, a comfortable bathroom, wood trim, a very clean, unpretentious design. He chose one of the two guest cabins. Belowdecks was a strong smell of wood and suntan lotion, mixed with Sabina's perfume. A bikini was tossed on the little sofa. Magazines, books, nautical charts, he couldn't help noticing everything. The beauty and the comfort of that boat attenuated his rage and uneasiness. He got unpacked, took a shower, went up on deck. As soon as he set foot on the deck he was swept by a hot, sustained wind, charged with the smells of the Mediterranean maquis: the Aegean Sea, which he had never seen, and the Goddess Summer, which he had worshipped all his life, caressed him benevolently.

De Klerk said they could even leave right away: 'If you want, we can set sail now, we've got plenty of water, our supplies are topped off, everything's shipshape. Towards southeast, that's right. The Cyclades and points south.' At the end of the trip they'd leave the *Falesá* on Rhodes. Someone would come to get her and sail her back home. He showed him the route he'd charted and told him that along the way they could decide on any eventual alternatives, depending on the weather and the seas. Ivo was stunned. The wind had died down a little, but it was still quite strong and the deck was heaving a little. A slight sense of nausea, a headache. He didn't know what else to say, except for Yes, that was fine with him, he just needed to get a little rest. Sabina was sitting in the cockpit with them, she'd put on a sweatshirt and was sitting silently, bare-legged, goosebumpy. Nico said that there was an island a short distance south, right then he couldn't remember the name, that he knew a deserted bay that was sheltered from the weather to the northwest, he said that with that wind it wouldn't take more than three hours, three and a half hours, he said that they could anchor there and spend the night. Again, Ivo agreed.

'Just give us a hand with the anchor and the sails, then you can go get some rest. We'll take care of things here.'

They left the anchorage under power, hoisted jib and mainsail, and pointed the prow southeast. There was wind and a sizable swell. The boat danced over the waves, increasing his sense of nausea. He took a Xamamine and lay down in his bunk. He was happy to be at sea, in *that* sea. But it annoyed him no end that there was no one on the boat but Nico and Sabina. He barely had time to think these things before he fell asleep.

The bay that De Klerk had mentioned was tucked away and well sheltered from the western winds. They sailed into it towards evening, as a handsome fishing caique came sailing out, with a high prow, white and sky blue, nicely riding on its own bow wave. The man at the helm with the cigarette in his mouth shot them a glance and then waved in their direction. The sun had set behind the interior mountains of the island. Brandani had awakened after nearly three hours of sleep, covered with sweat, his mouth parched. The meltemi had pushed them scudding along at a fine speed. The *Falesá* was wonderful under sail. When they came level with the inlet, they turned the bow into the wind and dropped the mainsail and jib, and went in under engine power. He still had to get used to it, but it was easy to handle. In the inlet, the wind dropped and the water was smooth as oil. The hollow of the swells slowed green and purple. They dropped anchor. De Klerk and Sabina went below decks to wash up and get changed. Ivo was feeling a little dopey from the Xamamine, but he was better now, the nausea had passed, he was hungry. He fooled around in the little galley and made pasta with tuna. Sabina prepared a Greek salad, with olives and feta cheese. There was white wine in the storeroom. They ate in the open air, under the stern awning. They talked some more about the itinerary of the next two weeks.

'Down as far as Rhodes, all with the wind amidships or astern. The ones who bring the boat back can worry about sailing close to the wind,' said De Klerk, slurring his words, 'we can just take our time and be comfortable.'

His complexion was already dark but slightly reddish, his nose was smeared white with suncream, his face was greasy. Ivo noticed his usual remote detachment behind the friendly words. Ever since he'd come on deck, Ivo had noticed in him a certain decisiveness, an authoritarian impatience in the orders he gave him concerning the handling of the boat.

'He's the commander and the owner of the *Falesá* . . . Aboard ship people change and I would have expected an attitude of the kind from him, it's only normal. Moreover, he's someone who's used to giving orders . . . And anyway I'm his subordinate . . . Come on, Ivo, he thinks of you as a friend, otherwise why would he have invited you onto his sailboat? What the fuck, he's my boss in the office and he's still my boss even when we're on holiday, more the fool me for having accepted the invitation . . . And after all, it's the most normal thing in the world, he's responsible for the safety of the boat . . .'

These perceptions, so tangled and confused, were filling him with anxiety, a tension that perhaps De Klerk was already starting to detect. 'We'll see in the next few days,' he was thinking, 'Clara was right, I shouldn't have come.'

Sabina didn't talk much, she smoked and looked out to sea. Ivo went to lie down in the prow, that was his first real Aegean Night, though many others would follow. The almost-perfect silence was marked by the lapping of water against the hull, by the halyards smacking against the mast every now and then, by the occasional sharpening gust of wind that made the shrouds hum. Against the starry sky you could clearly make out the black, sweet-smelling silhouette of the island. It was easy to see the Milky Way, he recognized a few constellations. He'd noticed an astronomer's handbook belowdecks, with a star chart and guides to identifying stellar objects. He'd dip into it tomorrow. Right now he was feeling good, even though he couldn't shake the sensation, subtle & para-noid, that he was being held hostage.

After an hour De Klerk said: 'I'm going to sleep, try to be good,' and went belowdecks. In the almost absolute calm the sound of the water running in the bathroom could be heard, fol-lowed by an indistinct noise under the prow in the double cabin, and then silence. Sabina came over to sit next to Ivo.

'You see how nice?' she asked.

Ivo replied that yes, it was beautiful, that he'd got out of the habit, that he was reminded of the boating holidays he'd enjoyed as a boy in the archipelago in the waters off the City by the Sea. The wine had loosened his tongue. He spoke fluently, telling stories in a low voice, his eyes half-closed, without any of the intimidation he usually felt with Sabina. At a certain point she reached a hand out towards him, slipped it under his sweatshirt and caressed his belly.

'How young you are,' she said to him, as she ran her fingers over his skin, making him shiver.

Ivo was stumped, confused. 'That's the last thing we needed,' he thought immediately. After a few instants he grabbed her hand and pushed it away, as gently as possible.

'Don't take it the wrong way . . .' he said to her softly, to keep from being overheard by De Klerk, who was in a cabin directly beneath them, 'excuse me . . . but it really doesn't strike me as a very good idea . . .'

In the shadow of her hair he couldn't manage to make out her face, but she said something, very softly, very harshly. Then she stood up and left.

What the fuck kind of situation had he got himself into? What fresh hell was this?

'If a woman likes me, I notice it, so how come I've never noticed that this one likes me? Still, Clara tried to tell you . . . What does she want? What is she looking for? She can't be thinking of starting an affair here, on the boat, right under her boyfriend's nose, with the added detail that he's my boss! Or are they looking for a three-some? Christ! This could mean the end of my career . . .'

Then he was seized with a retroactive yen for Sabina and he lay there, chain-smoking in the dark until his erection subsided, his eyes started to sag shut and the cold seeped into his bones. Only then did he go down to his cabin.

Early the next morning it was already hot. Everyone was still asleep. The minute he woke up, the first thing Ivo did was to go up on deck and dive into the water off the stern of the boat. The water was crystal clear and chilly, and it supported him in a friendly fashion. The water of the world was still there, immense and treacherous, apparently pure and welcoming, beautiful. It was the water of his childhood and his youth. Molecules that had already passed through him who knew how many times before returning to the sea. He climbed aboard the *Falesá*, the cold lash of that dive had put him into a good mood, he went towards the prow where there was a hand-pumped shower spray.

'Take it easy with that water, we won't be able to get any fresh supplies until tomorrow night!'

It was De Klerk, in an unpleasant voice, from the stern. Ivo was already turning the handle. He stopped, then said: 'All right, I'll be careful, I'll just take a quick rinse,' and then asked him if he'd slept well. 'Fine, sure. Make coffee. There's a large moka pot in the kitchen cabinet. I want a lot.' Then he dived in. Not long after that, they were making their way out of the bay, hoisting mainsail and jib, and setting a course to the east.

Before setting sail, while they were drinking a cup of coffee no one had thanked him for, Ivo listened to the course De Klerk had charted.

'We can set course east to Sikinos, pass to the north of Ios, double around it, then head south towards Anafi and beyond, towards a group of desert islets that I know. Then east again towards Rhodes. Or if you want we can sail under Folegandros, towards Santorini.'

'I've never been to Santorini, I'd love to see it,' said Ivo.

But De Klerk cut him off tersely: 'The place is overrun with people in this time of the summer. Let's head for Ios. Go to the anchor winch, make sure the chain comes in without snags.'

This last phrase had been uttered in a peremptory tone, as he turned the ignition switch to the engine.

As he was hoisting the anchor Ivo thought: 'So I've never been to Santorini? I'd like to see it? Well, De Klerk couldn't give less of a damn. First he says: "If you want, we can go via Santorini." Then he says: "No, no Santorini for you, that's how it is, period."'

The *Falesá* was already under sail when Sabina emerged sleepily from the companionway. She said nothing. She didn't smile. She didn't look at them. As she was heading towards the prow of the boat, Ivo once again noticed that red birthmark that winked out from under her swimsuit, on her left buttock.

It was a fine day, beautiful sea and nice wind. The *Falesá* was a first-rate boat. 'I wonder who rigged it so nicely for him,' Ivo said to himself. In a gusting wind there was no windward pressure on the helm and sailing on a broad reach it came close to ten knots. De Klerk asked him to take the helm a couple of times for a few hours. For the rest of the time Brandani lazed around, or looked after the rigging and handling, getting accustomed to the boat.

Just above Folegandros they veered slightly northwards: suddenly De Klerk ordered, without warning: 'Ready to come about!' Then, immediately afterwards, he said: 'Come abou-ou-out!' and started turning the boat. Caught off guard, Ivo started to release the jib sheet but he couldn't seem to get it free of the cam cleat. De Klerk could see he was having difficulties but went on yelling all the same: 'Come on, come on, come on, faster!' and he continued decisively in his tack. What happened was that the jib was taken aback before Ivo entirely managed to release the upwind sheet, slowing the boat and forcing it to veer. In the end, though, he managed to complete the manoeuvre and as he was busying himself with the winch on the downwind sheet he heard De Klerk shouting at him: 'You let my jib be taken aback, you might have ripped it to shreds. You told me you'd sailed before but it doesn't look that way to me. Where on earth did you learn to come about like that?'

Ivo headed for the helm, doing his best to keep his balance on the sharply tilted deck and, most important of all, to keep his temper.

'Sorry, Nico,' he replied, 'you didn't give me time . . . What need was there to come about so suddenly, without letting me know? It's not like we're in a regatta . . . Who's chasing us? I still need to get accustomed to the boat, don't you see?'

'*I'm* chasing *you*. If I say "come about", it meant "C-O-M-E A-B-O-U-T". Understood?'

'But why did you come about?'

'Just because. I'm in charge of making the decisions around here. Is that clear to you?'

Brandani noticed that De Klerk's face was tired and bewildered, as if what he was doing annoyed him, as if he were sorry now that he'd invited him to come on the *Falesá*, as if he no longer considered him to be up to it.

'Or maybe not,' he thought, 'maybe he's just depressed on his own account, maybe he's having problems with Sabina. She wouldn't have acted like that last night, if everything were going smoothly between them. But who is Sabina? What is she to him?'

In the meantime, Sabina was in their cabin. Maybe she was asleep, because before going down she had asked them not to do any unnecessarily rough manoeuvres.

Nico was every bit as unpleasant with her: 'You just worry about sleeping while I take care of sailing the boat.'

He said 'I', not 'we'.

That's how the rest of the day went, under sail. In the afternoon they tied up at the port of Sikinos. They moored at the wharf around evening. In spite of De Klerk's unpleasantness and the way that he'd treated him or less like a hired swab, in spite of Sabina's relentless silence, sailing that boat downwind, under a stiff, steady breeze, had been something magnificent. Ivo fell in love, immediately and intensely, with the *Falesá*. It happened to him in a way that someone who's never sailed before has a hard time understanding. It's a mixture of gratitude, admiration, dedication and affection, it's the feeling that you belong to that boat, that it's your duty to see to its care and maintenance, a dedication to handling it, concentrating instant after instant on its safety: and this is because the vessel on which we are sailing in turn saves us from the waters beneath.

The days that followed were pretty much the same as the first. Always some island or other on the horizon, mountains, clouds. They'd cross wakes with large ferries packed with people. At night they'd anchor in some solitary inlet, or else in a port where they could stock up on supplies. They'd get groceries, fill the tanks with fresh water, go to a restaurant on dry land. At the restaurants Nico refused ever to let him pay, and likewise Brandani was *never* allowed to make a contribution to the costs of food, supplies, or docking. It made him feel uncomfortable, it put him in a condition of inequality, as if he were just a kid. At first he'd protested loudly, but De Klerk refused to listen, in fact he had lost his temper the few times Ivo had purchased something on his own initiative, and so from then on he had stopped objecting: Did De Klerk insist on paying for everything? Let him pay. Their conversations at dinner, whether in the cockpit or elsewhere, had dwindled to the bare minimum. They talked about the boat, the watches they stood, the courses they were charting and the food they were eating. There was the occasional comment on the places they were seeing, but otherwise it was as if De Klerk couldn't care less about what Ivo might have to say, while Sabina usually remained silent and just smoked and looked around. She took very good care of herself, she was always impeccably made up, her tan was perfect, not too dark, honey gold. Everything she wore was clearly carefully chosen.

Aside from feeling that he was no longer held in much consideration by his boss, even though in the past he had displayed great respect for & interest in him, Brandani was starting to see himself as a hostage caught between a rock and a hard place. On the one hand, there was De Klerk, who was increasingly treating him as an underling—interrupting him and contradicting him every time he opened his mouth—and he was becoming increasingly irritable, unpleasant, authoritarian and at times a downright oaf. On the other hand, there was Sabina, who said nothing but was continually making advances, increasingly aggressively, stroking his ass when no one could see and, when they crossed paths in the cramped spaces on the boat, intentionally rubbing up against him. She did all this in silence, without uttering a single word. When he could manage it, Ivo avoided passing close to her, but that wasn't easy to accomplish on the boat. She was beautiful, but she always kept her swimsuit on, she never even took off her bikini top. She didn't talk much and when she did talk, she had only distracted things to say, full of indifference, as if saying them and not-saying them were all the same to her. Nothing really seemed to interest her. The sea, the islands, sailing, diving: in her rare utterances, everything seemed to be made up of the same uniform substance, devoid of meaning. She liked to sunbathe and swim, and she liked cats, which she sought out on the piers of the various marinas and in the lanes and alleys of the villages. The stray cats on the islands are feral. One time she came back to the boat with scratches on her hands and a lovely orange tabby kitten in her arms; she said it had a 'wicked Egyptian face'. When De Klerk told her to take the cat immediately back onto dry land, she said nothing but simply obeyed with great docility, tossing the kitten directly from the cockpit onto the wharf, where it landed as only cats know how to land. She'd spend hours and hours at the prow, stretched out in the sun on the mats outside the deckhouse where Ivo liked to lie at night, looking up at the stars. Every so often she'd help sail the ship, though it was taken for granted that that was Ivo's work, as was making coffee in the morning and pasta at night. At the very most, she'd make a salad, because it was an unstated fact that the cook was Brandani, who felt obligated to run the galley if for no reason other than his sense of gratitude for that all-encompassing hospitality.

With De Klerk, Sabina displayed a certain respect; she was never genuinely affectionate. There was never a gesture of tenderness, never a caress, a kiss, a sweet word—and yet they slept in the same cabin. Ivo couldn't seem to imagine what sort of relationship they had, but whatever it might be, he was determined to steer clear of it. In fact, if he hoped to salvage what was left of the friendship with Nico (with everything that it might still mean for him), *he had* to steer clear of it, which naturally meant that *he had* to reject her advances.

The boat was anchored in a cove, sheltered from the meltemi wind, it was early afternoon and it was hot out, and they were preparing to cross a short stretch of sea—perhaps a couple of hours' sailing towards Amorgos, an island on the horizon, some ten miles away or so—when Ivo went belowdecks into the *dinette* to get a quick glass of water. Sabina, slipping up from behind, thrust her hand down the front of his bathing suit. The pleasure he experienced was immediate but he pulled away *almost* instantly. Still, he'd let her touch him a second too long and now he had an erection, spontaneous and pagan, he could feel his cock throbbing unremittingly hard, a thing with a mind of its own, entirely autonomous. De Klerk, who had already been busy in the cockpit for a while getting the engine started, was calling him—'Ivo, to the anchor winch!' he was ordering him, calm and arrogant.

'Just one second, I have to go to the bathroom!' he answered from a distance, shoving Sabina towards the ladder.

He stepped into the head, pulled his dick out of his swimsuit, and ran it under the cold water from the sink. It didn't do any good. De Klerk kept calling him, increasingly impatient.

'Ivo, for Christ's sake, you can go later,' he was saying.

And he added: 'You'll have all the time you need later to go to the bathroom! Do you have a weak bladder? Get moving, I don't want to get there in the dark!'

Brandani went on deck and just outside the companionway he noticed Sabina's ironic gaze resting on his swimsuit. He looked down and realized that it was soaked with the water he'd just drenched his dick with. And the erection was refusing to subside. De Klerk noticed it too, gave him a chilly glance and said: 'Go to the winch.'

Then, in a loud voice: 'He's a rough, touch macho man . . . We could take him to get his pipe drained on Mykonos. That's a veritable island of porn.'

Then, addressing Brandani, who was returning from the bow: 'Ivo, we need to get you some sex or your balls are going to explode.'

He laughed and turned away, looking out to sea.

He kept saying that kind of thing, addressing Sabina, without ever looking at him. He would say 'we need to', 'we'll take him', ostentatiously, as if he were talking about the ship's dog. He kept on saying the same thing over and over, obsessively. Then he started verbally attacking Sabina, asking her if she'd seen 'the nice hard woody' under the swimsuit and whether she liked it. She objected feebly and Nico went on, undeterred: 'Admit it, you're tempted, eh? Eh? This time I picked you a nice one, what do you say?'

He was talking loudly, snickering into the wind—dark glasses, baseball cap, his nose covered with white sun cream, tall and skinny, in Bermuda shorts—while he started the engine and gave the order to hoist mainsail and jib.

During those days, a new and vulgar side of De Klerk emerged aboard the *Falesá*, and it increasingly yawned open into the downright filthy. Ivo was baffled and disappointed: What had become of the elegance and quiet class of the successful executive? Still, Sabina never admonished him, nor did she question him on any other point. She seemed like an independent woman who had voluntarily allowed herself to be subjugated, tied to him like a fish to its reef—she never allowed herself to be apart from De Klerk for long, nor did she ever venture very far from his side. She was always there, apparently indifferent, but it seemed that her vital functions could only carry on in that man's orbit, in the physical territory of his dominance. And that was the same territory—by now there could be no doubt, he no longer nurtured illusions—in which Ivo too had wound up.

That afternoon, as he hoisted the anchor and raised the mainsail and the jib, and while Nico heaped lewd jests and double entendres upon him, Ivo understood that *he belonged to* De Klerk, that by now he was property and chattel, along with Sabina and the *Falesá*. He realized that Sabina herself saw him as such, that she considered him to be *her peer*, that is, an *attribute* of De Klerk. It seemed to him that she moved as if around her neck were a collar attached to a chain that was securely gripped in Nico's hand, and it was clear to him that Sabina saw that same collar wrapped tightly around his neck, hooked to the very same chain. 'She's wrong,' he thought as the erection suddenly disappeared and he was covered with a clammy sweat, 'she's wrong!' But he wasn't so sure, what else had he been doing for nearly a week, if not following every one of De Klerk's commands and instructions? Where was he if not on his boat? What else was Nico saying, if not that he considered Ivo to be his dog in heat, a dog he needed to take to get serviced? Why was he passively submitting to his lewd mockery? What was happening to him?

Then came the doubt that this might all somehow be his fault: 'Why is he treating me like this? Maybe he can see me for what I am, an incompetent little engineer, ridiculous and dreary. And yet in the office he seemed to hold me in high consideration, he included me, he wanted to go on this holiday with me . . . Why is he behaving like this? Does he hold me in contempt? Does he think I'm stupid and servile? Am I servile with him? Then it was all fake, when he acted like a friend . . . Did he just need someone to crew his boat? He could have got anyone else, he could have hired a seaman, or a skipper—there are plenty to be had and they don't cost much . . . What are his intentions? Who is De Klerk? Maybe this is just what rich people are like, they enjoy being brutal . . . Maybe they *are* brutal. And what about Sabina? Who is Sabina, where does she come from, why is she with him?'

'I have to find some way to get out of here, and fast,' he thought to himself as he unfurled the jib and hauled the sheet taut. But he needed an excuse, a pretext: De Klerk was the absolute chief of the division, he'd made it clear that he had power, contacts, know-how and influence. Making a false step would mean losing his job or being catapulted who knows where, in what godforsaken corner of Africa.

'That guy wouldn't think twice about leaving you in a patch of scorched earth, just on a whim. You were a real asshole to let yourself get trapped like this . . .'

While the *Falesá* got under sail with her usual grace, tacking slightly and picking up speed, he went back to the cockpit, sat down and raptly kept his eye on the jib, easing up slightly on the sheet, as Nico had told him to do.

Anyone who's spent time sailing knows the pleasure of being on a boat under sail with a fair wind, not too stiff. Ivo knew the beauty of the curvature that a jib takes on with the wind coming across the beam, when you ease the prow into the hollow of the wave and then gently ride up the face of it, only to settle again into the next trough as you feel the boat follow you, comply with your will. He was filled with such a sense of servitude and humiliation that he'd lost all power to react—all he wanted was to get away but it was as if he'd lost the will to step over the gunwales of that hull, which he now perceived as a trap, a prison. And yet he took pleasure, meekly but with a growing delight, in sailing that boat, he found that he cared for the vessel, so lovely and so innocent, which, if only De Klerk and his woman were gone, would have been entirely his friend. He liked the new sails, the well-tautened shrouds, the way the mast seemed capable of taking on the most appropriate curve for any point of sail, the *Falesá*'s sleek stability under sail, he liked the water and all that air, he liked the line of the horizon, always dotted with the islands that are never far out of sight in the Aegean, some of them perhaps so far off that nothing could be seen of them but the condensation cloud overhead.

All of a sudden he felt exhausted, he wanted nothing but to go get some sleep. He'd think about the sailing capacity of that boat some other time. After taking care of his chores on deck, he announced that he was going to go belowdecks.

'Coil that line a little better,' said De Klerk from the helm. Then, shouting loud enough for Sabina to hear, he added: 'You going below to spank the monkey, are you? Sabina, you want to go below with him? Do you want to give him a hand?'

As he was heading belowdecks, Brandani heard what struck him as an uncertain giggle from Sabina. De Klerk continued to bray nonsense in a mocking voice, but the wind erased his words.

'At this point he's completely out of control, he's daring to say things . . . Mabye he's crazy . . . I shouldn't let him do it, I shouldn't submit the way I'm doing . . . And what if he does fire me? If he fires you, you'll get another job . . . It's not as if Megatecton is the only company around . . . I'm going to punch his face in, is what I'll do . . . I'm not the way he is, I'm not the way they are,' he thought as he flopped down in his bunk and instantly fell asleep.

He reawakened bathed in sweat, as usual, with a sensation of muggy heat in his ear. As he was opening his eyes he heard Sabina's voice whispering something along the lines of: 'Wake up, macho man, there's work to be done on deck, the captain is calling you.' Immediately afterwards he felt her tongue slip into his ear and he felt a profound shiver run through him, making him twist in his bunk. He whipped away from her hastily but once again he found himself with a full-blown erection, with his cock protruding from his swimsuit. She laughed and said: 'Looks like someone's wider awake and far more reasonable than you . . . Come on, sailor, get your ass in gear, *along with everything else . . .*'

He shoved her out of the cabin and put on a pair of Bermuda shorts to conceal his erection, but there was no need because, once he came to a full realization of his position aboard that sailboat, all excitement rapidly subsided. Sabina's continual advances were never friendly, never fond, there was always an ironic and imperious flavour to them, as if he were a toy she'd long possessed, which she could use without bothering to seduce him. Ivo understood that there was nothing playful about this, that it was something else, something serious and vaguely threatening, spasmodically exciting, and which he needed to flee at all costs.

The *Falesá* was entering a well-sheltered bay on the south side of the island, where De Klerk had decided to spend the night. They dropped anchor, the coming night promised to be clear and hot as usual. And, without those two, it would have been just beautiful.

While De Klerk sat smoking in the cockpit, Ivo cooked a pot of pasta, Sabina made her usual salad with olives tomatoes and feta. They opened an ice-cold bottle of retsina. They ate in silence. Ivo wasn't particularly hungry, he was confused, pissed off, and he didn't feel well, nonetheless he drank heavily and the retsina didn't sit well with his stomach. The idea of running away was becoming an obsession, he mulled it over for the rest of the evening, trying to think how best to approach the topic. He was afraid of De Klerk, both because of his immediate reaction, and the subsequent backlash that might ensue, and which he expected would be inevitable and devastating. Dopey from the wine, he tried to come up with something. It had to be a plausible excuse, but since he had no way of communicating with the Peninsula from there, he couldn't rely on some sickness to be attributed to his mother, some other relative or even Clara.

'It has to be something believable . . . Like an attack of haem-
orrhoids . . . That's it, a rectal haemorrhage! I can tell him I've
blood coming out of my ass, that I'm scared, that I want him to
take me back to Amorgos where there's an airport . . . It's believable, because it's such an embarrassing thing to say . . . Plus it's
not easy for him to check it out.'

So he said to him: 'Nico, I have a problem, we need to talk . . .'

De Klerk interrupted him instantly with a loud 'No!'

He'd had more to drink than Brandani, he was slurring his
words but he seemed reasonably lucid. He went on, raising his
voice: 'You aren't leaving, Ivo, don't even think of asking . . . I
mean to say . . . If you want to keep your job at the company,
you're not leaving here, you took a commitment and now you're
not going to dump me in the middle of the Aegean Sea . . . Where
am I going to find someone willing to crew this sailboat? And after
all, what's bothering you? Aren't you having a good time? You
thought you were coming on a Greek cruise? Well, that's exactly
what this is: a Greek cruise . . . There's some work to do but not
that much after all . . . Make coffee, cook some meals, wash the
dishes, help handle the boat, take a watch at the helm . . . Did you
take offence earlier today? Can't a person even joke? You came on
deck with a hard-on, do you remember that or not? The two of
you had been fooling around down below, eh? . . .'

He'd leant back with his elbows propped against the padded
side of the cockpit and smiled as he stared at him, his eyes glazed.
Ivo neither denied nor confirmed his intention of leaving. Quite
simply, he said nothing, surprised at De Klerk's sharp intuition. He
could feel his own mind scraping against the walls of his cranium
as it attempted to grasp this new twist. 'How the fuck did he figure
out what I was going to tell him? Does he know that Sabina's been
coming on to me? Of course he does! He certainly knows, he
knows everything, he understands everything . . .'

In the meantime, De Klerk was still talking: 'I wonder why
you'd want to leave. Don't you like the boat? Are you uncomfortable? Is there something about us you don't like? Am I annoying
you? What do you lack, Ivo? The *Falesá* is a magnificent sailboat,

it's comfortable, you can't complain. These islands are beautiful, and you'll see when we get further south, when we get to where I want to go. I'm paying for everything for you, lunch, dinner, supplies, fuel . . .'

Then he snickered, looked over at Sabina, and added: 'You even have someone to fuck, what the hell else can you ask for?' Sabina said nothing and looked at Ivo.

De Klerk paused, thought it over, and hissed: 'You know what I say? If you want to leave, go ahead . . . Just leave . . . But don't bother *coming back to the office*! . . . Don't imagine that you're indispensable. Don't imagine that you've done who knows what kind of work . . .'

He talked, he drank, he slurred and stumbled over his words. Ivo listened, paralysed, but it was as if he wasn't hearing him, he understood everything he was saying ('don't bother coming back to the office') and at the same time, he focused on that 'you even have someone to fuck' and on Sabina's gaze.

'Then it's true! De Klerk knows that she's been coming on to me! Maybe they were even in cahoots before we left. Maybe it was all a trick, maybe there never were any other guests! What the fuck do they want with me? Are they looking for a threesome? Does he like to watch? What a fucked-up situation . . .'

'. . . if *I* make up my mind, no one will hire you, not in our sector . . . if *I* make up my mind, you won't be able to earn a penny! You'll have to find a new line of work and if you're lucky you can open a shitty little bar on the seashore . . . You'd better rethink your approach, don't be so pernickety and let's enjoy the rest of this holiday!'

He seemed almost completely drunk, the word 'seashore' had come out 'seashwore' and he'd pronounced 'pernickety' as 'perschnickety', but he'd continued his little speech with great consistency and brutality, without hesitation. Then suddenly he fell silent and finished his cigar in silence. In the end he stood up and patted him on the cheek, then he descended the ladder of the companionway staggering. Once belowdecks he shouted: 'Goodnight to the swabs and crew!'

Ivo wasn't much better off than him, he felt sick, his stomach was burning, his head was spinning, he almost felt like crying because he'd been unable to say anything, to retort, to tell him to go fuck himself. Once again, he needed to lie down, but out in the open air. De Klerk's brutality was becoming increasingly explicit, all semblances of kindness, friendship, interest seemed to have disappeared.

'He's just a vulgar piece of shit.' Exactly the vulgar piece of shit that a few of his coworkers had tried to warn him about: 'Apparently De Klerk isn't what he seems, Ivo.' Then, when they'd said to him: 'Certainly, he's no cherub, Ivo, but I've noticed that he's very friendly, very nice to you. Everyone's noticed it around here. Stay on your toes, though. Don't trust him,' he'd replied: 'I don't trust anyone.' But it wasn't true. He actually was flattered that his friendship with De Klerk had attracted notice, he was happy to be, or even just to seem, like a member of his inner circle. Now all those warnings were flooding back into his mind, along with Clara's. But immediately he objected to himself: 'If he actually holds me in such contempt, then why did he pick me of all people for this holiday? Why me, why did he decide Engineer Brandani, from the West Africa Construction Site Prep Sector, should crew for him? Why pick me, with all the young men eager to crew on sailboats in the summer?'

He stretched out on the thin little mattresses forward of the deckhouse, with the intention of lying there as usual until the middle of the night, gazing up at the sky, and then he shut his eyes. Everything started spinning. He remained motionless for a long time, in a sort of waking dream. When he opened his eyes again, he was unsure whether to get up, lean overboard and throw up, or remain there on his back, hoping that the nausea would pass.

Where was Sabina? His watch said three o'clock. Maybe by that time of night she was asleep.

'Better that way . . . better, better and better . . .'

He was still fast asleep on his back when he woke up with a start, unable to breathe. A sort of suffocation, a sense of pressure on his face, a strange odour, as if of seaweed drying in the sun.

Panic, he tried to get up, but he couldn't move his head. He was fully awake by the time he realized that Sabina was squatting nude on his face and swinging her pelvis back and forth. Ivo snorted, trying to get a breath, he swung his head to one side and managed to gasp a mouthful of air, but she just jammed her pussy down harder onto his mouth. She was whispering: 'Come on, lick my pussy, what would it hurt, slip your tongue in, aw . . .' He grabbed her by the thighs, turned her over on her side and got to his feet. She was completely naked. She lay on the little mattress on her side, while he leant over the pulpit and vomited his dinner into the sea. His head was spinning but throwing up made him feel progressively better, the masthead light faintly illuminated the scene, as his retching echoed throughout the silence of the anchorage. The moon was dropping behind the promontory to the south of the inlet. He turned to look back at Sabina and noticed that the red mark that he'd often noticed poking out from under her swimsuit bottom extended over almost the entirety of her left ass cheek. It was a broad dark thing, it seemed to have some hairs, but he couldn't be sure.

She turned to look at him and said: 'Do you find me so disgusting that you actually had to throw up? Don't you like pussy? Are you a faggot? I'd had that suspicion. So you're a faggot, eh? Strange . . . Not even Nico had you figured for a faggot. Or is it me that you find so disgusting? Are you in love with your little clam back home? What's your little redneck girlfriend called? Clara? Wow, what a sweet name . . .'

She'd stood up. She was very pretty, with high, firm breasts, long legs. Ivo just wanted to go astern and get out of that situation. He felt nauseous and he couldn't think of anything to say. His mouth tasted of vomit. She stepped to one side, as if blocking his way, and at that point he impulsively dived into the water.

It was cool and calm. As soon as he surfaced, he rinsed his mouth several times. He took a few strokes and swam away from the hull, and then stopped, just letting himself float. He felt better. The absence of weight, the breeze in his nostrils, the cool water and the sight of the bay in the light of the setting moon were good for him. He noticed the phosphorescence in the foam of every smallest ripple. The silence was absolute and the stars were shining more intensely.

'I've got to get out of here,' he said softly, as he swam a slow breaststroke, 'away, away, away. *I'm not the same as they are.* They'll never take me alive, I'm getting out of here. Whatever happens, happens.'

Sabina had vanished from the deck. He floated there for a long time, on his back, looking up at the sky. All he could hear was his own breathing: 'How nice, soon it will be dawn . . . Soon I'll leave . . . I'll go home, to Clara . . . I'll go back to Clara . . .' He kept saying it to himself and it comforted him, but he was starting to feel cold: How long had he been in the water? He couldn't say, maybe while floating on his back he'd actually fallen asleep. He swam over to the stern of the *Falesá* to climb back on board, but there in the water, holding on to the ladder, was Sabina waiting for him. He was tired, so he swam closer to grab the handrail. He brushed against her and said: 'Come on, let me get aboard.'

'Wait,' she replied.

She swam closer to him and touched him until she'd succeeded in obtaining an erection, then she turned around, grabbing onto the ladder with both hands, placed her feet on the bottom rung, underwater and proffered her ass to him, rubbing it up against him. Her birthmark was under the surface of the water and couldn't be seen. He took her from behind because he couldn't resist her for another split second. The memory of her odour from just a short time before was still vivid in his mind and had changed the way he imagined her, and so had the sight of that dark birthmark that defaced her left ass cheek, and yet he lusted for her all the same. He was brutal, unceremonious. All he wanted was to come inside her, as quickly as possible, and completely. It took no more than a few seconds, and that's what happened. As he abandoned himself to the orgasm, he shut his eyes, moaned softly and instinctively lifted his head to the sky. When he opened his eyes again, he saw De Klerk standing in the cockpit and looking down at him with a mocking expression, shaking his head disapprovingly. He broke away suddenly from Sabina, looked up at the cockpit again, but no longer saw him, only heard the patter of his feet descending the companionway ladder.

Sabina had remained in silence the whole time, but at that point she turned around and with a completely different tone of voice, almost sweetly, she said to him: 'You've finally made up your mind. Why did you make me wait all this time? What do you care what he thinks?'

From Amorgos towards Anafi and from Anafi straight down to the southeast, at a broad reach. The moderate swell driven by the meltemi almost hit them from the stern and there were times that the *Falesá* fishtailed violently. They reefed their sails and De Klerk left him at the helm for long periods: 'Be careful not to do anything stupid, focus, don't let her heel over.' Their destination was a cluster of desert islands that rise at the centre of the vast expanse of water to the southeast of Crete. They have strange names, the largest one is called Sofrano and it has a lighthouse which De Klerk had selected as their destination, keeping it to starboard.

'I want to go back,' De Klerk had said, 'I saw those little dots of land years ago, and I want to go back there.'

'But . . . is there any shelter?' Ivo had asked, without looking him in the face, because looking him in the eye after that night was unthinkable, at least for him.

'Yes, there's a roadstead where we can ride at anchor off Stakidha and a nice inlet on Sofrano. We'll set a course to the west of Sofrano, see? Then tomorrow morning we'll come about to the east downwind. It's going to take all night . . .'

He didn't like De Klerk's plan. Too far away, too deserted, those islands. Too difficult of a situation aboard. He would have preferred Anafi. There was a port there, a village. There he could make an attempt to take to his heels, he could board a boat for Athens and be gone. He'd gathered his strength and told him that it was best to go to Anafi and, in so doing, he'd been forced to look him in the eyes. Strangely, the other man's eyes hadn't been flinty; for the first time since he'd boarded that boat, Nico seemed to *see him*, even though his answer had been as brusque and disagreeable as usual. But in that *absurd* situation, there was something that acted on

De Klerk as a sedative: it was his unmistakable love for those seas and those islands.

'No, Ivo, what would we go to Anafi for? I know the place. It's not an especially pretty place, there's a little village at the summit, a small marina, a few sand beaches . . . No, I don't feel like it, that wasn't the plan . . . We'd better keep going . . . You see, here, further south there's a large stretch of open sea and look, four or five islets, these are isolated shoals, completely deserted, only a few fishing boats ever go there . . . These are the last inner patches of land before the great southern belt of the Aegean . . . Here you can see it, Crete-Kasos-Karpathos-Rhodes—beyond that chain of islands there's a watery desert until you reach Alexandria in Egypt. In less than ten hours we can make it to Sofrano, the closest one. Then we'll see. Come on, let's get busy, Sabina, you make us a few sandwiches, for now. Then, for tonight, we'll need a thermos of coffee . . .'

On the chart, to the south of Sofrano were Karavonisia, Avgonisi, Kamilionisi, Ounianisia and, a little further east, Stakidha. Tiny islands, fairly distant from one another, possibly the remains of an ancient archipelago almost completely devoured by wind and water. De Klerk pointed to them with his finger and seemed to sweeten, captured by the prospect of launching himself with the *Falesá* in the midst of all that blue, swept by an unbridled wind.

The wind was picking up, they'd further reefed the sails. They'd left Anafi in their wake to starboard in the late afternoon, without halting—it rose out of the water, dark and dry against the setting sun, and with it, for Ivo, the last chance of putting an end to that nightmare was disappearing behind them. He'd mentioned how low their fresh water supplies had been getting, that the sea was looking rough, that the wind was stiffening, that they'd be sailing by night in search of a single godforsaken lighthouse in the wide Aegean Sea, but his words fell on deaf ears: De Klerk had made up his mind. Had the man figured out his intentions? Most likely he had, and perhaps that's why he had decided not to lay over in Anafi and instead sail through the night—'We'll stand two four-hour watches each'—or it might have just been his impatience to turn *Falesá*'s prow in the direction of that isolated group of craggy hermitages lost in a watery desert, islets whose magnetic attraction were surely more powerful for him than any other rational consideration.

Then the meltemi wind dropped a little, as it always did towards evening. To the starboard the sun had vanished behind distant clouds. It was starting to get chilly, they put on their oilskin jackets and woollen watch caps. Ivo, at the helm, focused on the set of the sails and the swell: bearing up slightly to settle the prow of the *Falesá* in the hollow of the swell, gently, and then luffing gently to bring it up to the crest of the swell until dipping into the next hollow. He could feel that it was a finely tuned vessel, when sailing slack it sat in the water as if it had four legs, and it sailed fine and fast, accelerating in a gusting wind. 'It feels like a Flying Dutchman,' Ivo said to himself, as he became increasingly comfortable with the boat.

He'd always been a good sailor, he'd learnt many years ago during the long summers spent in the City by the Sea, sailing regattas on Flying Dutchman racing dinghies. Now that almost forgotten set of skills had fully reawakened and, in spite of the absurdity of his situation, he once again felt the old joy, as he drove the *Falesá* through the open seas, a boat he had by now fallen head over heels in love with. He had always fallen in love with the boats he'd sailed on, but this time the emotion was even stronger: in those hours the docile *Falesá* was not just the only thing on the face of the earth that seemed to be his friend, but she was also performing her duty admirably, keeping him safe from that inhospitable watery desert, a desert he might be somewhat afraid of, though never as much as he was of De Klerk. Once they reached their destination, he certainly wouldn't be able to take off, the way he'd planned to do if they'd tied up at Anafi: so he might as well enjoy the sailing.

Before sunset, a large oil tanker heading southeast had remained visible on the horizon for a long time; now, in the darkness, it was possible to make out the running lights of a few faraway caiques, but that stretch of sea seemed to be largely empty of vessels. De Klerk had gone belowdecks some time ago but Sabina remained, smoking wordlessly, sitting across from him, her back resting against the deckhouse as shelter from the wind. She'd put on a pair of jeans and was wearing a woollen watch cap pulled low over her eyes. After a few hours she stretched out on the cockpit cushions wearing an oilskin jacket and with a blanket wrapped around her legs, and dropped off to sleep. She had been near him all afternoon, practically without speaking. After the night before, she'd changed her attitude to him. She was no longer the dominatrix demanding performance & submission; now she seemed to want to communicate to him a sort of affection, a solidarity between the oppressed, as if there were only one oppressor—De Klerk. Brandani, standing at the helm of that watercraft under sail, experienced pure joy as the fossil semblance of the age-old feeling surfaced in him that had once seized him during the long afternoons of mistral wind, spent scudding over the waves off the City by the Sea, when the surface of the water broke into a crazy chaos of golden flakes. He was tired, but when the appointed hour came he didn't go down to awaken De Klerk, he just drank more coffee from the thermos and stayed up the entire night, only abandoning the wheel at dawn, with the lighthouse of Sofrano in sight for some time. Further off, straight ahead, he could see the flashes of the lighthouse of Kamilionisi: they were exactly where they ought to be. At that point, satisfied with himself, he shook Sabina awake where she lay curled up in the cockpit and sent her to call Nico.

He was asleep when, at one in the afternoon, De Klerk was about to drop anchor just off the island of Sofrano. He came down to wake him up and told him to come on deck. Ivo made a pot of espresso, then went up to the cockpit. They were just a few dozen yards from what looked like a small sheltered beach at the far end of a narrow inlet. The island was very small, a hump of low hills jutting out of the water, but high enough to shelter them from the meltemi. De Klerk had already gone to shore in the dinghy to tie a long rope around a large rock.

'There's an iron ring cemented into the rocks . . . This must be a place where fishing boats come. Do you see how beautiful it is? The silence? There's nothing here but birds, fish and seals. Just wind, space and water. You see where I've brought you? A paradise . . . Where are you going to run away to now, Ivo?'

'Right,' he asked himself, 'where am I going to run away to now?'

Ivo spent much of the morning in the water, with fins and mask. The bottom was beautiful and teeming with life. The sand in the middle of the bay, beneath them, was scattered with marine relics: fragments of coral rock, crab skeletons, lots of seashells, the carapaces of two or three tortoises, picked completely clean, but also tins of meat, large tangles of fishing line, torn sections of net. All things that the caiques toss overboard at the end of a day's fishing. The water was stunningly clear.

'Where are you going to run away to now?' he'd asked him, practically hissing. In spite of the joy that he must have felt at returning to those places, De Klerk had still found a way to remind him of his condition as a hostage. Ivo steered clear of him all morning and only returned aboard when he saw him in the dinghy with Sabina, heading off on some excursion. He wasn't to see them again until late in the afternoon, he'd almost forgotten about them in the solitude of that place—those rocks, that silence, the desolation, the cries of the hawks as they hurtled down off the cliffs and glided on the wind, almost without ever flapping their wings, prompted in him a state of rapt and introspective stupefaction, a sort of hypnotic ecstasy. And so, in the noonday quiet, in the shelter of a far-flung shoal in the Aegean Sea, he had thought of Clara again and, for the first time since he'd left, he really missed her, to the point that tears came to his eyes.

If a few days ago he had gone so far as to think that Clara already formed part of another life, that she was for him nothing but the residue of another time, now he was overwhelmed by how much he missed her, and particularly those aspects of her that he had started to detest. Clara and her concrete pragmatism, devoid of snobbery, Clara and her realism, her capacity for careful observation, her sensibility towards a broad array of different environments, her aptitude for fitting in without being touched. This was intelligence, not narrow-mindedness. And then there was the sweetness, the intensity of their sexual bond, a solid friendship of the flesh that rendered mechanical, and devoid of any real pleasure, sex with other women. In the confusion of the last week he'd thought that he was on the verge of breaking up with her, but now the thought of her brought him comfort. Everything had changed again in just a few days and those places, which might have no real meaning for her, induced in him a state of continual brooding about the years he'd spent with Clara, from the times of the City by the Sea, where they'd met, to the university years, right up to the most recent changes and transitions.

'We aren't the same as they are. They'll never take us alive.'

The meltemi was faint and towards evening the water off the coast turned smooth and transparent. Under the hull they could distinctly make out grey mullets the size of a man's forearm swimming in formation, their heads and backs convex, lead grey. 'This is their feeding hour . . .' He grabbed some bread and started breaking it into crumbs and dropping it into the sea while the fish below went into a frenzy, practically shooting out of the water to seize it out of one another's mouths. You could hear the sound of their thrashing on the surface, the sucking sound of their gaping maws. The wind carried the island's hot breath to the boat, the scent of the arid sparse underbrush. All this pleased him in an *all-encompassing manner*, in the sense that there, in a place like that, he felt, for the first time in many years, a complete harmony between himself and the things that surrounded him. But *they* were there, ruining everything.

He got out some packaged Dutch cheese, put it in a plastic bowl and mixed it with bread crumb and olive oil, then worked it into a compact paste that he used to bait the hooks of a bolentino fishing line.

Later De Klerk climbed aboard without a word while Sabina just smiled and said: 'It was nice, we went all the way around the island.' Ivo was sitting in the stern and he had a couple of fine grey mullets in the bucket, the kind with golden cheeks. He picked them up by the gills and hoisted them, showing them off to Sabina, who clapped her hands and cried: 'Nice! Good work!' He got a knife and crouched on the transom in the stern. He was getting ready to scale and gut the fish when he heard Nico behind him saying, in a fairly loud, irritated voice: 'No! Not here. They stink. Fish shit! If you want to clean them, you can go to shore! Shit-eating grey mullets!'

'No, Nico, you're wrong . . . They don't stink. These are reef fish, there aren't any sewers here. They're fresh, delicious, you'll taste how good . . . And I'll wash it all off, I throw the guts into the water . . .'

'Listen, asshole, you're not cleaning your fish here! This is my boat and you're not going to get it all covered with shit, period! Take it to shore!'

Ivo remained motionless for a second with his knife blade resting flat against the side of a fish. Then he suddenly shot to his feet, threw fish and knife into the bucket, reached the cockpit in a single leap and hit De Klerk with his fist right in the face.

It was a strange sensation: the face of the Director of International Business for Megatecton, Nico De Klerk, seemed soft and flat, pasty, yielding. It hadn't been much of a punch, more a closed-hand smack, but the man fell backwards, hitting the wall of the deckhouse with his shoulder, possibly with the back of his neck. Then he sat there, motionless, on the floor grating in the cockpit.

Brandani too seemed to be paralysed by the enormity of what he had done. 'God, what have I done! I've killed him!' His legs were trembling, he seemed unable to speak, his heart felt as if it had leapt above his clavicle and now it was pounding directly in his throat. He hadn't hit anybody since he'd been in middle school. But beneath that wave of stupefaction there was a strange sensation, a kind of *criminal joy*.

When the tension had become intolerable, the fist had shot out automatically, like the whiplash from a rope that breaks when it's stretched too tight. Sabina had shouted: 'Ivo!' and she had rushed to De Klerk's side, but the other man got to his feet almost immediately, blood streaming from his nose, his eyes fixed on his attacker. Ivo, who was out of breath and trembling, had expected that sort of reaction and had taken a step backwards and slipped into a defensive crouch. But all De Klerk did was to press his hand against his nose, smearing it with blood; as soon as he noticed that, he sat down on the chair in the cockpit, took his face in his hands and suddenly burst into tears. The impassive elegant detached demanding chilly Director of International Business for Megatecton was crying because he'd been smacked and as he wept, the drops of blood slipped through his fingers and fell onto the teak grating. Then in a low, teary voice, as a pink streamer of drool hung from his lip, he said: 'You broke my nose . . . You see? You broke it! I'm going to die of blood loss . . .'

He thus launched into a disjointed monologue, that rang out over the silence of the bay, while Sabina and Ivo listened in silence. Far away, behind De Klerk, the silhouettes of other islets like this one loomed against the sky. This islet was turning purple in the last light of sunset, while to the southeast, far above the horizon, the high mountains of Karpathos emerged from the mist. Ivo tore his gaze away from the scene that was unfolding aboard the *Falesá* and looked around for a few seconds, perhaps for a few minutes, at that theatre of solitude.

'. . . All I said was for you to go clean them on shore, those fish . . . And you punched me IN THE NOSE! I hit my head, I could have been killed . . . Have I stopped bleeding?'

Sabina had hurried belowdecks and had quickly returned to the deck with the first-aid kit. Now De Klerk was sitting with his head tipped back and two cotton balls sticking out of his nostrils. He was still crying, his face twisted with his sobs.

'What's with him? Why is he acting like this? It wasn't even a punch . . . In the face, though . . . Maybe I did hurt him some . . . But not much . . . And now he's wailing like a little boy!'

De Klerk was swallowing his words between his sobs. He seemed overwhelmed: 'I came here twenty years ago . . . I chose to come back here with you two . . . with you . . . You could say I didn't even know you . . . I did it because I liked you and this is how you repay me . . . You could have killed me . . . I gave you my trust, I invited you aboard my boat, and you, instead of showing gratitude . . . You act all snotty . . .'

Ivo was astonished, he'd never heard De Klerk talk like that. He was always harsh, proud, sharp-edged, scrutinizing, never relaxed, never entirely friendly. What the hell was happening? He hadn't hit him hard enough to make him lose his senses. He looked quizzically at Sabina and she calmly looked back, as if to say: Let him vent, we'll talk about it later. She'd delicately felt his nasal septum and she'd said: 'Nothing broken, you're fine, Nico.' She said that she needed a plastic bag full of ice. Ivo went belowdecks and got it. When he got back up on deck, Sabina told De Klerk to tilt his head back and hold the ice against his nose. She stroked his hair.

The shadow of Sofrano stretched out over the water as sunset proceeded. Ivo looked up and saw that only the top of the mast was still lit by the sun. All the rest of the *Falesá*, the deck, the cockpit, the nautical equipment, the tender moored to the stern, was by now steeped in the light-blue shadow: the water was devoid of glints, and if he looked overboard he could distinctly make out the bottom of the bay.

De Klerk was shaking his head and he went on feeling sorry for himself. His voice had become nasal on account of the cotton balls, it rang through the air, thudding against the emptiness and silence. He was now no longer crying. His eyes were going back to the way they usually were, chilly and yet weary. He got up, tipping his head back, with the ice held to his nose and, without another word, went slowly belowdecks to the cabin.

Sabina and Brandani sat there for a long time, in silence, with no idea of what to say. Later they opened the table in the cockpit and laid out paper plates, a bottle of chilled white wine, a bag of frisella biscuits, a can of tuna. Sabina went belowdecks and came back saying that De Klerk had fallen asleep and seemed to be all right.

'Except for his nose being a little swollen, there's nothing broken. I have a certificate as an emergency-room nurse, you know that? Let's eat something.'

Ivo was exhausted from the tension, he wasn't hungry, but the wine was delicious, the frisella biscuits with tuna were tasty, he was slowly feeling more relaxed. Sabina was picking at a cold salad in a steel bowl. They spoke in low voices to keep from waking Nico up, but especially so that he wouldn't overhear them. From the open companionway towards the bow they could hear him snore.

'I need to take the cotton balls out of his nose,' said Sabina. 'You kind of lost your head, there, didn't you? You could have really hurt him, did that occur to you? You screwed up big time—he isn't hurt, but you can rest assured you're not going to get off easy . . . They'll fire you at Megatecton . . .'

'I know . . . I was being pushed to the limit, it was automatic . . . He'd been going on for days—you can't invite a friend on your boat and then treat him like that . . .'

'Yes, I understood that . . .'

'He had such a strange reaction, I thought he was going to hit me back but he didn't do anything of the sort. He was crying like a milk calf . . . He's always so cold, controlled, remote . . . Such a strange thing . . .'

'Ivo . . . Do you or don't you understand that De Klerk hates you? That is, I don't know if he hates you, but he doesn't like you enough to invite you come on a fifteen-day sail with him . . . Forgive me for telling you this, but he's always said that you're a bit of an asshole, that you were always kissing his ass . . . That you practically wagged your tail when he showed you a little friendship . . . I'm reporting his words, verbatim.'

The wine he'd drunk on an almost empty stomach had got him half-drunk and Ivo was sort of split in two: he was listening to Sabina and at the same time he was trying to think how he could get out of there immediately.

'That is, maybe Nico doesn't hate you, but he definitely doesn't respect you either, that's for sure. You want to know why he asked you to come on the boat? I don't know . . . To have some fun with you, to intimidate you, because he needed a crewman . . . Ivo, how can you be so naive? Haven't you realized yet that De Klerk is a son of a bitch, but I mean a *real one*?'

All around them was darkness and silence. Sabina had finished eating and was smoking a cigarette. They were sitting in the cockpit and they were continuing to drink wine from Crete, white, ice-cold, deliciously bitter. The lamp hanging from the boom reflected off the jute of the awning and illuminated the table. Sabina stood up and turned it off. Suddenly everything was dark, but soon the landscape reappeared in the starlight, the luminescence of the sea. The silhouette of the highlands of Sofrano stood out black against a lighter sky, covered end to end by the Milky Way. Ivo felt as if he was paralysed by the things that Sabina was telling him. He was trying to organize them in his mind, but he couldn't do it. He almost felt like crying and he continued to speak harshly of De Klerk: 'He treated me like a puppet . . . Son of a bitch is what he is. And why? For what purpose?'

'Come on, cut it out, that's enough,' said Sabina, unruffled, 'you hit him, you came close to killing him for all I know, aren't you satisfied? In any case, the answer is yes: for a whim, just because. For instance, you don't know that he phoned that guy . . . What's the name of the guy he knows at Assicurazioni Generali, your wife's boss? Well, he called him and told him *not* to let her change her holiday plans . . . He wanted him to keep her there a few extra days, so she couldn't go with us. That's who De Klerk is, you understand? He wanted you here alone, without Clara . . . The guy at Assicurazioni Generali, to keep him happy, did what he asked and prevented your wife from being able to change her holiday schedule . . .'

'What are you saying? Clara was forced to stay at work! . . . Then it was him! . . . That bastard son of a bitch! . . . And who the fuck are you, Sabina? Are you his wife? A girlfriend? A paid whore? Who are you? What do you want? What did you want from me? What do you want now? What is De Klerk, a faggot? A pervert? Does he like to watch his employees fucking his wife?'

'I'm not his wife, Ivo. What did he tell you? That I'm his wife? I'm a hostess, a paid escort . . . Or I guess I should say I used to be, before De Klerk hired me full time. Now I'm a full-time hostess. At first he used to hire me on a regular basis as arm candy for when he had evenings out with important clients . . . But I'm not a whore. It was just a job. Sex wasn't part of the deal. At least, it wasn't for me . . . Later, he started calling me to go out to dinner or go to the movies with him. Then he took me on holiday for a month in the Caribbean. Maybe he fell in love with me, I couldn't say . . . He offered me a full-time contract, a very advantageous one for me. Since then, I've lived with him . . .'

It was dark but, all the same, he could detect something resembling a smile on her face. She was drinking wine and talking, more and more uninhibited: 'He usually introduced me as his girlfriend, but sometimes if he feels like it he says that I'm an escort. Other times he'll even say that I'm his wife . . . Nico is unpredictable . . . I've always taken my pleasures where I please and I've always kept him separate from that . . . Then he started to want to know more, he can't stand to be excluded. In short . . . I don't love him and I'm not sure I even like him . . . For me, he's a *job*.'

Ivo felt stunned, confused. In the darkness, the cigarettes lit up intermittently. Then Sabina reached out a hand towards him, leant forwards and started stroking his thigh. Ivo moved his leg.

'Oh cut it out . . . Stop playing hard to get . . . What is it about me you don't like?'

Ivo said nothing. She went on talking, increasingly loose, slurring her words, completely drunk. She let herself go to an ever greater extent, she offered him every part of her body. Ivo wouldn't let her touch him. In the end Sabina mumbled: 'You really a filthy piece of shit' and dragged herself belowdecks. After a few minutes, in the absolute silence, Ivo heard her throwing up. He stayed there in the dark alone for a while, smoking. He didn't feel up to sleeping in the cabin, he was thinking about going to get his sleeping bag to stretch out on the deck. Then he got hungry. He turned the light back on, picked up the bag of frisella biscuits that was on the table, dipped one in sea water, rubbed a tomato on it, sprinkled it with salt, and drizzled it with olive oil. He remained seated on the transom, his legs in the water, eating the frisella biscuits, with the oil dripping through his fingers. Every time he moved his feet, the ripples lit up with a tenuous, diaphanous luminescence.

Around midnight, he descended the ladder at the stern and slowly immersed himself in the water. He swam towards the little white beach a few dozen yards away from the *Falesá*, the same beach where De Klerk had tied up the stern line. He laid down on the shingle, the wind had ceased entirely, he could feel the heat radiating out of the rocks that had been beaten all day by the rays of the sun, the water dried off in a hurry and he fell asleep. He was awakened by the high tide that lapped up against his feet. He felt cold. He walked into the sea and it seemed warm and welcoming to him. All around him, the night was as bright as if there were a moon, the silence had a profound and distant echo. He started swimming slowly towards the boat, the water caressed him and held him up—after the *Falesá*, it was the only friendly thing he had left in the world. He did a breaststroke for a few more yards and then heard some subdued voices coming from the deck. He couldn't understand what they were saying but he saw the silhouettes of Sabina and De Klerk in the cockpit. It seemed to him that they hadn't seen him or heard him. Ivo didn't want anything more to do with them, or at least not at that moment, so he took a roundabout, arch-shaped course and headed under the rocks where it was darker, and then, from there, he swam towards the bow and grabbed onto the anchor cable.

'. . . No, come on, Nico, that's enough . . .' she was saying to him.

He couldn't see them, but in the silence he could clearly make out every word they said. Sabina, in a low voice, went on: '. . . What's the point, you tell me . . . It's completely pointless, you're only going to hurt yourself . . . You have a nice fat nose, have you seen yourself? Come on! Cut it out . . . I don't feel like getting excited for no good reason . . . Now stop it! It's useless!'

'You'll see if he doesn't come down off his high horse . . . All I need to do is tell him that I'll throw him out of the company on his ear . . . Why do you think he agreed to come on this boat trip with us? For your beautiful eyes? He came so he could be with his boss, he feels all flattered by the idea of holidaying with the boss . . . Did you notice that until just yesterday he was kissing my ass here, too? Come on, sweetheart . . . Tomorrow you'll get to do him . . . But if he won't go for it . . . In other words . . . He's an asshole . . . I mean it's not my fault that you have a weakness for assholes.'

'What are you talking about? He came this close to killing you . . . What need was there to treat him like that?'

'Maybe I overdid it a little . . . But I can't stand him and the way he has that attitude, that "I'm not the same as you are," like some two-bit left-wing intellectual, I just have to treat him badly . . . Hold still, let me do this . . .'

'Have you forgotten that you can't get it up? I want a *man* . . . You understand? M-A-N . . . A man.'

'You think he's a *man*, don't you? He's an asshole, I twisted him around the way I wanted, but to judge from the bulge in his pants, he must have a nice cock . . . He has a nice cock, doesn't he?'

'Certainly, he has a nice cock . . . And what's most important is that he has a cock that *gets hard*, Nicola.'

'Don't call me Nicola, bitch. Come on, let me touch your pussy, and then I'll lick it . . .'

Holding on to the anchor cable, Brandani could hear Sabina laugh and from the muffled sounds he guessed that she was trying to wriggle free.

'Cut it out, stupid,' she was saying to him, 'but listen, tomorrow you have to apologize to him and then make sure you start treating him right, at least until the end of this holiday. Do you promise? Then you can do whatever you want—fire him, I don't give a damn—but now *I want him.* You promised I could have him . . . And a deal is a deal . . . Get your hands off me . . . No! No . . . Until you promise me . . .'

'All right, I promise . . . You haven't been able to get him out of your head since that time at the movies.'

'Listen, Nico, I didn't ask you for anything, you're the one who started spouting promises: "You want him? I'll give him to you. If you like him, he's yours." It sounded as if you were talking about something you owned, a head of livestock. What were you trying to prove? And get your hands off of me . . .'

He heard the muffled sound of a slap, but Sabina went on laughing under her breath, then started emitting muffled moans. Ivo remained under the bow of the boat, hanging onto the anchor cable, until they were were done. Then he heard them go down into the cabin. He waited a little while longer, now the water had become ice-cold. He climbed silently aboard and dried off with a towel that had lain on the deck all day long and was caked with salt. He lay down on the little mattress in the prow, he curled up the towel, and closed his eyes, exhausted.

Around six in the morning, he was awakened by the noise of a diesel engine. It was getting light and a handsome red caique was anchoring about a hundred feet away from them. He went down into the cabin and hastily threw all his things into his backpack. He came back up on deck and cautiously opened the door to the cabinet under the cockpit seat. There was a 50-yard-long rope there. He climbed into the dinghy, fastened one end of the rope to a stanchion on the *Falesá* and the other end to the bow ring of the tender, then he pushed away from the boat, fitted the oars into the oarlocks and rowed towards the caique. The men on board looked at him, motionless, as he rowed towards them. He was helped aboard. They saw his backpack and after a while they were made to understand what he wanted from them. '*Now*,' he said. '*Absolutely now, it is an emergency.*' They haggled for a few minutes, and in the end they agreed on a price of 50,000 drachmas: for a little more than 200,000 lire, a couple of hundred bucks, they would take him immediately to the closest island with an airport.

'*To Karpathos*,' they said, '*is OK?*' He replied that Karpathos would do fine. By the evening of that same day, he was sitting in the waiting room of Karpathos Airport, which was little more than a hut, waiting to board the last flight to Rhodes.

2.32 p.m.

Just six months ago, another terrorist attack, horrifying and inexplicable: it was further south, along the coast . . . Here they are, it's them, or, rather, it's us . . . We are the pink-cheeked hale and healthy sunburnt fair-haired pudgy besandalled be-T-shirted Westerners, with the vacant blue-eyed apparently mild-mannered gaze, open to amusement and slightly bewildered, of someone on holiday . . . We are the target, the cannon fodder of terror . . . We are the ones who are unexpectedly mown down by machine-gun fire as we get off a tour bus, baseball caps on our heads, reflex camera around our necks, to go see the pyramid . . . And after all there's nothing worth seeing in a pyramid, devoid as it is of details . . . Or else kidnapped while, with our wallets full of Western currency but without any real reason other than simple enjoyment or the desire to *help out*, we venture into savage territories only to have our throats cut in the end, in front of a video camera . . . At the sound of shots, we turn in surprise while we're in queue at the airport check-in counter, just a split second before our apparently innocent craniums, the craniums of business travellers, tourists, sweet & democratic Westerners, progressives who wouldn't hurt a fly, evening strollers who clean up their dog's poops, citizens who separate their garbage and recycling with eight different plastic bags, health nuts who don't smoke and go running every morning and have a physical check-up once a year . . . Who at age fifty have no doubt already passed their first routine colonoscopy . . . Before our cranium explodes into a certain number of fragments, scattering in all directions our apparently innocuous brain matter . . . Here we are, in potentially hostile territory, enclosed in this box that runs on air conditioning, waiting to be able to think 'OK,

I've been down there . . .', waiting to be able to debark from our plane in Stuttgart, in Copenhagen, in any place whatsoever in Northern Europe and then to be able to say to our friends at dinner: 'They're nice people, they're just like us, they want peace, the extremists are just a minority . . .' And there was no need to spend a week here snorkelling to be able to say such a thing, which is actually not true, because *they* aren't the same as we are . . . We are the red-skinned yellow-haired whites whose women go everywhere with plunging necklines and short shorts, we are the ones who live to advanced ages and believe in nothing . . . And for that we might be killed in the middle of the night by a hand grenade while we sleep comfortably in a four-star hotel in Mumbai, Sana'a or any other place . . . While we lie in the hollow we've burrowed for ourselves in the bed, while we fuck some whore that the desk clerk procured for us . . . We are the ones, tall & bemuscled, who one tender evening full of promise are blown sky high along with an entire pizzeria on the island of Bali, mixing the shreds of our body with the wreckage of the gridwork steel roof beams and the canvas awning, along with the shrapnel fragments of the plastic laminate that covered the tables before everything was blown to smithereens . . . Here too these things have happened before, and more than once—it seemed that it was all over, but that seems not to be the case . . . Bombs in the streets and in cafes and pubs in multiple locations over the course of a single night, planned so as to cause the greatest possible number of deaths, explosive devices filled with bits of iron to do as much harm as can be . . . And yet we come back all the same, trustful that, mixed in with the great mass of tourists, it's unlikely that anything is going to happen to us *of all people* . . . It's the thought process of the gnu who crosses the crocodile-infested river with his herd and heads straight for the opposite bank, while the beast struggling along beside him, a gnu like him, has its throat ripped out by a 20-foot-long monster, dragged down into the water and drowned there, in the midst of all that mud, only to be eaten in due time . . . 'The difference between you and us,' they said after Atocha, 'the difference is that we aren't afraid to die and you are . . .' That's what they said after

Atocha and I was reminded of those Fascist phrases carved into the wall in certain places in the City of God, certain posters of youth groups dedicated to the cult of death and dying for some fucking cause or other, because no one told them: Look, there doesn't exist, there has never existed a cause for which it's worth giving up your life . . . Or at least, nothing that has to do with politics . . . Maybe it's worthy dying to protect the lives of your nearest and dearest, your children, your woman . . . But you, Brando, you don't even have any experience of this, you've never been a father and you were a husband for too short a time . . . We are the apparently mild-mannered and civil and democratic ones, struggling to deal with an intolerable *taedium vitae* that drives us out beyond the borders of our countries in search of that nothing that is known as amusement, fun . . . We are the ones who don't shoot and fight in the first person, but only through a third party, a powerful and well-organized military, we are the ones who would suck the last marrow from the bones of this planet all by ourselves if we weren't forced to share at this point with the Chinese and the Indians and the Indonesians and the Brazilians, who until twenty years ago didn't have a pot to piss in but who now want to join the party . . . Which is an annihilation party, a party to the death . . . And once we've devoured the earth and the sea and the mountains, we'll have to rebuild everything in a fake version, and that will be a nice piece of business for someone, too . . . But in the meanwhile the jihad will continue as before, as it's done for thirty years, five hundred, a thousand years, in fact, for thirteen hundred years . . . Shreds of human flesh and rivers of blood as well in the market-places of Pakistan, Afghanistan, Yemen . . . In Egypt, in Morocco . . . And trains in the subway systems of the West will continue to explode while according to the law of the gnu, on the preceding train all that's felt is a distant blast, a sudden rush of air . . . The gnus stampede and then reassemble, resume their daily march, the usual boundless quotidian mobilization towards their distant sources of income, the same income that allows them to come here, to this place that is inhabitable only in the fictional world of resorts, to absorb a massive and harmful dose of ultraviolet rays . . . Here they are, the gnus, the Westerners, who seem to have been hollowed out by peace . . . They want peace and more peace for ever . . . It's not that they're opposed to war, quite the opposite: they're fine with war, as long as it's far away and not too burdensome, as long as it guarantees peace at home and the security of our sources of energy and safety in the places where we holiday . . . When it comes to peace you can't lodge any objections, Brandani, you're a perfect product of it.

The headache continues. The Xanax, by now fully in circulation, let him sleep for a few minutes, his head thrown back. He woke up because someone touched him, maybe he'd started to snore. His mouth is gummy, he looks straight ahead, he takes a number of small gulps from the mini-bottle of water he purchased a short while ago.

What had it meant to live seventy years in peacetime? In what way were we different from our fathers and from our fathers' fathers? Fathers, grandfathers, great-grandfathers, tracking way way back in time, each of them had lived in their own world, and those worlds weren't comparable to the one we lived in: there had never been such a long period of peace, never such a rapid acceleration of things, never before had this set of objects been so rapidly transformed into other objects, never such an accentuated state of instability . . .

He feels completely stoned, the Xanax, the reawakening, the headache, his belly full of air, and he abandons himself to a slow, distracted reflection, which strikes him as strangely lucid.

When you feel lucid, don't trust it . . . And all this in peacetime. There's never been such a long period of peace. Yes, certainly, in my lifetime there have been countless wars, but all of them outside of the borders, with an involvement that was political, and therefore symbolic, more than anything else, or military, but limited. The Cold War: Korea, Vietnam, participation in invasions of Islamic countries, apparently distant, where we Peninsulars were always protected and safely in echelon behind the American superpower . . . We fought those wars speaking their language, the language of the Americans: *My name is Cocciolone* . . . The voice of that captured Italian aviator in Iraq. All this took place, but it wasn't war-war, with draft levies, mobilization orders, fanfares, armies marching off, bombing raids. No one ever bombed our cities again, no one ever destroyed a Mantegna chapel of ours again . . . Already the destruction of a Mantegna chapel is a sufficient argument in favour of the universal abolition of warfare, forever . . . War had no effect on us except in terms of opinion, as a topic for political action, it never affected us directly and personally, forcing us to make life-or-death decisions, no one forced us to depart for the front, to fight against our wishes, to obey irrevocable orders: let the enemy kill you, or we'll do it for him. People like me are creatures of peacetime, specific organisms, with special adaptations, like those insects you find in caves, blind but with no idea that they are blind, white due to the lack of light, and yet convinced that the world is all right there. We have no idea what it means to fight for the fatherland, in fact, we have no idea what the fatherland even is, we feel nothing towards the fatherland, if it weren't for a vague sense of pride that surges up inside us when someone says pizza-mandolin-mafia-devil-horns . . . The Germans until not long ago referred to us as traitors: Lotte's father, for instance . . . There's never been a *true* external enemy, it was of no interest to us, it didn't affect us, as long as we were left in peace, as long as they didn't drop the Bomb, like they were about to do in 1962, I was sixteen years old, I was a virgin, I would have been burnt to death even before I began to live, before I had a chance to make love with Clara, they would have deprived me of one of the few moments in my life worthy of having lived . . . In these seventy years of peace the enemy, when there was one, has almost always been personal, never national. Can you say that you've had enemies, Ivo? I don't think so: you have enemies if you count for something, if you act, if you try to carve out a space for yourself, but me? In my inertia, I never managed to make any . . . Could I consider De Klerk to have been an enemy? No, not even him: to him, I didn't even exist, I was just a toy, he wanted to have fun with me and then, perhaps, crush me . . . He did crush me but it was no fun for him. I'd hate him, if I had it in me . . . Peacetime is nothing but a silent war of all against all. Nothing apparently ferocious and in any case, not at my level: war among people at my level is never a serious matter, it almost never entails genuine annihilation, even though in corporations there are people who kill themselves out of stress and humiliation, or else they submit until they can't take it any more and one fine day they go into work with a handgun and unleash a bloodbath . . . Now that capitalism no longer has anything or anyone capable of standing up to it, you find metal detectors everywhere, they're no longer needed to prevent terrorism, instead they're to stop workplace murders . . . Peace is a war of all against all: there isn't much physical violence but the struggle is malevolent and cruel, in the need to clear a space for oneself, in the fight to obtain even a tiny sliver of the available resources, or a smidgeon of power, for those who desire it . . . A war without heroes, waged with weapons like lines of cocaine, glasses of alcohol, antidepressants, anxiety medications, chain-smoked cigarettes . . . There are few official heroes, few monuments, all of them intentionally anti-rhetorical and therefore nearly all of them stunningly ugly . . . In Italy the heroes are all anti-mafia, anti-Camorra, anti-crime, anti-racket, and therefore cops, carabinieri, magistrates, here and there witnesses without fear, someone who might have stood up against the shakedown, who invoked an imagined state monopoly on violence in contrast with the territorial control of the mafia, and they have therefore of course been rubbed out . . . Plus a few mercenaries who went to Iraq, Afghanistan, Lebanon, for money, a few professional soldiers, volunteers and overpaid, who believed in the fairy tale of Everyone-Just-Loves-Us and Peninsulars-Are-Good-People, while someone was parking a 2,000-kilo bomb right under their ass. I, the cowardly Ivo Brandani, if I faced a shakedown from some protection racket, I'd have paid and said nothing, if I were a witness to a mafia murder I'd have kept my mouth zipped, if I was a judge in the South I'd have requested a transfer, if I was a soldier I would never ever have gone into combat . . . If I'd been on that subway car in *The Incident*, I wouldn't have done anything to stop Tony Musante . . . We, the organisms adapted to Peacetime, in fact, produced by Peacetime, don't give our lives for the fatherland, we don't sacrifice our existence for a civic battle, for a political ideal:

those few, those very few who still do it are, in the final analysis, misfits . . . But there were years in Peacetime when the struggle was harsh and political. There was sharp conflict between different ideological affiliations, 'between opposing extremisms', at the outset, then it was between opposing parties, and then between opposing interest groups, and finally between opposing financial groups. There was a great deal of violence, but it wasn't war, no one was forcing you into it, even though you might wind up as a victim by pure chance: I never got into scuffles with right-wingers, never with the police, for me the violence was only private, trading punches between individuals for contingent and trivial motives, issues of supremacy, of self-defence . . . Only the thrust of fear, those few times that I found myself backed into a corner, ever drove me to violence, or the force of anger, when you'd gladly kill the man you have before you with your bare hands, for the sheer hatred that you're experiencing . . . Even *our* political struggle, the one I took part in, as it later became clear, was actually pretty much unfounded. There were apparent differences, but all it took was a single decade and what prevailed over it all was the unifying blanket of what high school you attended, which university you went to, the Desire-to-Be-Part-of-the-Ruling-Class, the battle for ideas became the battle for power, for money, for positions . . . Over time the various political projects proved to be nothing more than bickering over principles, because in time it became clear what the common destiny was going to be: grab yourself a slice, large, small or minuscule, of power & revenue, whatever the initial ideological capsule you set out in . . . Those who failed to understand were killed, or they wound up in jail or lived the life of a veteran, an outsider, in a world that was progressively alien to them . . . Let's see, in the early '70s, describing the full 360 degrees, working anticlockwise, we encountered: right-wing terrorists, ultra-right-wing extra-parliamentary terrorists, Fascists, monarchists, Liberals, Christian Democrats, Republicans, Social Democrats, Socialists, Communists, ultra-Communists, extra-parliamentary Communists, Communist terrorists: a crowding and a clutter that would later lose all reason for existence because already by the early '90s no one knew anything about them any more: what the fuck had the PSIUP (Italian Socialist Party of Proletarian Unity) ever been?

And yet Ivo Brandani could easily describe, one by one, with considerable exactitude, all of those subtle nuances, because he is a native of the Postwar years who has lived in Peacetime, when political Multiplicity reigned over all, that is, something that seems inconceivable today.

To think about it more carefully, Peacetime was most of all the polio vaccine, the availability of electric power, water that came out of a tap without giving you typhus, dairy products free of brucellosis, increasingly curable diseases, the sexual revolution, medical clinics, family physicians, divorce, abortion, the Pill, lots of colour movies . . . It was also bikinis & sand, beach umbrellas, lounge chairs, beach buckets, sandals—such friendly, tame objects, dedicated to the pleasure of Being by the Water. The girls . . . at first they used to wear those pastel-coloured capri pants with the narrow ankles and the slit, do you remember? Pedal pushers with a side slit. Capri sandals, shoulderless white lace tops. Brigitte Bardot . . . just thinking about her still hurts . . . Then miniskirts and later *bell-bottom* pants . . . Peace was making love at night on the beach . . . Peace was youth, holidays, Father stuck in the city working and for a little while relaxing his grip on me . . . It was school, American-style pants, girls going out at night, trips without a penny in your pocket, pergolas in the summer, parties on Saturday afternoons . . . Peacetime was work, then the Renault 4, paved roads everywhere, trains & planes, ships. Nursery schools were Peacetime, as was the family doctor, mopeds when they first came out and then the ones that no longer spewed oil all over you . . . Peace had been the Alfa Romeo GT Veloce, the Volkswagen, the Flying Dutchman . . . Peacetime was the university and everything that happened there. And everything that happened afterwards and after that . . . Peacetime has been my whole life. We, natives of peace, don't realize the way that non-war has shaped us and made us different from everyone who's lived before us . . . Peace, peace, peace, for us filter feeders, who will never know anything about ourselves, because that is exactly what peace turns you into, it doesn't test you, except in the very worst part of you, it cooks you for the rest of your life, slowly, and when you get to the end—and it won't be long now—you're still asking yourself the same questions you were at the beginning, when you wondered whether you too would be capable of piloting a Sacred Spitfire in combat, of keeping yourself from turning and running for your life when an Me-109 came barrelling straight at you . . . Still, I learnt a few things about myself all the same: I'm a non-hero, a non-courageous person, a non-dominant, someone who doesn't believe in things, who doesn't believe in anything, who has never believed in anything, not even when it seemed to me that the opposite was true . . . I'm someone-who-gives-up, someone for whom nothing really matters, if not staying alive in the most comfortable conditions imaginable . . . That's what I've discovered about myself, as a specific organism produced by Peacetime. Others, a very few, weren't like me: they fought. Some died and killed others, but *they believed* and even if nowadays they're held in contempt by everyone, I respect them. They weren't acting out of personal self-interest, they were acting out of their own convictions and many of them served decades in prison, in some cases without having killed anyone. Incapable of accepting Peacetime, they acted as professional revolutionaries once did, killing and getting themselves killed, filled with faith in the advent of the Era of Justice . . . The Era of Justice will never come and no one ever really yearned for it . . . Here, capitalism was always fine with everyone: for the bosses, because they were the bosses; for the workers, because in the second half of the twentieth century prosperity had washed over them too; while in the East the societies that emerged from the Revolution slowly imploded . . . Being terrorists was useful to the ego, it compensated for their desperation, it kept them from sliding into the nothingness of a lack of purpose, it indemnified them for the impending failure, of youth . . . Deep down you've always admired them, Brandani . . . *They* had put themselves to the test, *they* had learnt what they were really made of and they'd paid a very high price for that privilege . . . The struggle for/against a Communism that no one wanted was useful to everyone as a by-product of the war . . . Long before the years of blood there had been a watershed phase, which served to mark the distinction between *our* culture of little kids, children of the War, and *their* culture as fathers who came from a remote historical elsewhere and who had fought in that War. Between the two worlds, right at the very summit of the crest that marked the watershed, was where we were, poor assholes who believed . . . It was the transition from a hierarchical authoritarian democracy, along the lines of 'you'll be what we want you to be and shut up about it,' to a democracy based on civil liberties and money, just like in America . . . It took us forty years and now here we are, we live in a present that is the achievement of *that* project: the democracy of money, the full and unreserved acceptance of the *state of things* . . . Here we are in the full culmination of capitalism, all ideological models, all affiliations, all discordant hopes are dead . . . Everything that was based on a different promise has fucked off . . . The idea of a just world— no one knows what that might turn out to be—has gone bad, rotted, dissolved once and for all . . . It took decades but in the end the process came to completion and here we are in the super-Westernized West . . . All of us, the comrades from back then, swept away or drifted over to the other side—but is there really *another side?*—even the ones who wanted to burn everything down, in fact, especially them . . . And yet, in the phase that came after 1968, during that horrible *Afterwards* that stretched on for ten years or so, or maybe fifteen, during the bloodbath of the clash with the State, something changed all the same, the country tried to improve: certain elements of that initial political promise did filter into society, that is, into all of us, and they remained . . . Something changed, and all the *Afterwards* after that was nothing but an effort to dismantle, piece by piece, that *something new*, because the only thing that mattered was to widen the gap towards *this* modernity, towards this stuff that can no longer be defined any differently than *money in its pure state* . . . A more just world, my ass . . . A richer world, no doubt about it, just look at these people: every one of them, compared to what we were sixty years ago, possesses unimaginable wealth and for all I know, feels poorer than we did . . . Even 1968 was nothing but one last demonstration . . . The political outcome of a cultural revolution that started up in the '50s and lasted ten years or so, the amount of time it took for the petty-bourgeois *Baby Boomers* like me to grow up and look one another in the face . . . Look one another in the face, and say to themselves: What the fuck do we have in common with *these people*? Were we different from our parents? Sure, of course we were . . . Everything they told us at school, in church, everything that was officially important, everything that was imposed upon us as not-open-to-discussion, meant nothing to us . . . That was the *real* revolution . . . It was in the air as a lifestyle issue for the whole decade from 1958 to 1968 . . . That was the birth—something absolutely new in the history of the West—of the Youth Movement . . . We were different, and we knew it . . .

Franco and I had discussed it at length. He had no doubts, as usual: 'In the *free* western hemisphere nothing takes place without the consent of the powerful. In fact, many of the things that apparently take place in opposition to capitalism are actually created by capitalism. And so it's quite likely that the Youth Movement of those years was actually the product of the invention of a Market Movement, that is, a generation for which specially designed products were now available. The young petty bourgeois who was responsible for 1968 is merely a consumer, though a new and different one, created by the Market. What happened in 1968, Ivo, is nothing other than a product of what was called at the time "neo-capitalism". At the time, that was what is was being called, do you remember that? In other words, it was neo-capitalism that was intolerant of the old hierarchic and authoritarian societies. It was more useful to have a more fluid and open world. What was needed was an egalitarian society, they needed freer individuals, both in terms of behaviours and consumptions. All this originated long before, in America, during the transition from a hierarchic and authoritarian society to a fully consumer society. Here that transition is taking place well behind the United States, where the youth revolt is anti-Communist and explodes several years earlier: when the European Revolt of 1968 bursts into flames, the American revolt is already over, it's already been transformed into something else. For us, at the beginning it was anti-authoritarianism,

then there was an adherence to or, rather . . . a fundamentalist
appropriation of Marx: we took what we found, there was nothing
else on offer that possessed such a powerful concept of justice, such
a robust revolutionary praxis. Those of us who knew anything
about politics were either Fascists or Communists, they came out
of the youth federations of those parties. The Fascists were dis-
qualified from the start . . . The ones who were capable of taking
on leadership positions in those early years, that is, in '66 and '67,
came out of Communist education and militancy, and that was the
direction in which the Movement was steered. There were no other
outlets outside of the twin contexts of Communist revolution /
hippie revolution: Lenin & Mao, or Spinello & Pink Floyd. Who
even gives a damn about these things now? Our political platform
was a historical *objet trouvé*. We overlooked the horrendous contradictions between Marxist liberation theory and the Communist
practice of oppression. We chose to do without a radical critique
of actually existing Communism, we turned our backs on the Soviet
tanks in Prague, no one got unduly fussed. A decade of struggles,
transformations, innovations came into the world already infected,
it was a disease that later showed all the virulence of which it was
capable . . . It was a historical *loop* in which capitalism produced
a powerful opposition force to itself. That opposition was needed
in order to transform and rejuvenate society. A great number of
youthful individuals, *us*, were raised in the enjoyment of capitalism's opulence without believing in its values . . . With the help of
the market, we constructed an apparently alternative culture that
seemed new and dense to us, even though it was actually riddled
with holes. No one sat down at a drawing board to plan all this,
even though, in the referential interplay between the world and its
representation, a number of minds did apply themselves actively
to the verbal and visual narrative of "our" youthful imaginary universe. The Revolution of '68 was fabricated by a capitalism in
search of new structures and new outlets: we were juvenilized by
this continuous dribbling between reality and market . . . The classical thesis is that at the end of the '60s a redistribution of income
became necessary. Here in this country there was the immediate

admonition of 12 December 1969, when someone blew up that bank in the City in the North—that was when it became clear that this was no laughing matter, that the game was turning ugly. We wanted to belong to a different country, a country that bore our imprint as well. But that's not the way it went. It was just the usual take-it-up-the-ass-and-keep-pedalling, or pick up a gun and shoot, nothing that had anything to do with the old trinity of Civilization, Progress and Socialism.'

Bridge and Door

Molteni is over sixty, corpulent, not particularly tall, with lively blue eyes, his voice is always low, mellow, the words he uses are surprising and recherché, they seem to flow easily to his lips without hindrance or pauses, as if they'd always been there, just waiting to be chosen and uttered.

No one ever interrupts Molteni. He always has all the time he needs to say what he wants to, and then some. He often takes advantage of the fact to indulge in digressions, ironies, tangents. He seems perfectly well aware of his powers of seduction which he uses without restraint every chance he has. Much the same uninhibited way that he uses his academic power. Molteni is a *barone*, an academic power-monger. Molteni doesn't believe in anything. Molteni is intelligence in its purest state, he's neither benevolent nor accommodating. He's very cunning, he misses nothing that happens in the rooms that he frequents, he understands instantly which way the wind is blowing at a meeting, whether matters are going favourably for him or if instead they're being derailed, if there's someone who's pushing things in another direction. He speaks slowly, he utters his words with the rhythm of an old diesel motor. He sounds to Ivo like the engine of an old fishing boat that turns over slowly but steadily, one bursting combustion after the other, clear and distinct from the one before. Words free of all accent, perfect pronunciation. Behind his old-man eyeglasses, Molteni eyes the female students with particular attention, often, during the exams, he lowers his lenses to observe them all the better as they turn to go. Ivo heard someone say that once Molteni murmured to one of his teaching assistants: The true *difference* is right there. During the exams, he's exquisitely courteous, especially to the girls, he's not stingy with his grades, he's unlikely to flunk you, but then he's unlikely to give you the impression that he's impressed with you.

'How many among you are going to be able to make a serious contribution to philosophical thought? One out of five thousand? One out of ten thousand? But is that a problem? Certainly not. As a teacher I think it would already be a great achievement if the school were able to shape you into "carriers of method", active containers of knowledge, transmitters of thought. What we are building and training here are not so much new philosophers, something we care little or nothing about, but the very neurons of society. I was about to say, of all mankind . . .'

As he talks he sprawls half-reclining in his chair, with his right hand he tugs and twists his white beard while with his left hand he toys with a pen. One leg has been bouncing rhythmically for at least half an hour, incessantly. Molteni betrays disquiet and uneasiness. Perhaps he's getting bored. He's chilly and yet his gaze remains quite piercing. His teaching assistants sitting in the front row listen more attentively than do the students: that's how it always is with power-mongers. They don't exert their power on their students, over whom they have no sway other than their task of teaching, grading or flunking. The students know it and, unless they've already made up their minds to pursue a career in academia, they consider them as nothing more than shoals, momentary hindrances and, however intimidated they may be, they basically don't give a damn about them. The *barone*, the academic power-monger, is chiefly important to the faculty, which is to say, to those like him and those who aspire one day to reach his position and his level of power and influence.

But there are times when the *barone* can be important to an entire culture, can be a crucial mainstay in the measurement of the state of a discipline. A *barone*, in other words, can be a great teacher, a master. Molteni has been a master and remains one, despite the fact that he has almost entirely stopped producing. Perhaps his writings have not withstood the test of time particularly well, because they sink their roots into a somewhat obsolete school of thought, both as viewed from the right and from the left, especially from the left. They situate him in the ranks of the reformists, the much-reviled Social Democrats, they've dubbed him a *barone*, they attribute to him, and it's impossible to say that they're wrong in this, a minimalist approach, a call for tactical retrenching, a *gattopardesco* attitude (evocative of Tomasi di Lampedusa's *The Leopard*) towards what might seem to be an uprising underway. These are things that might be tossed around in a student political meeting but no one has the nerve to proclaim them in his presence. His prestige still serves its purpose, then, even among the most extremist student leaders. The ones who shout themselves hoarse, until they're red-faced, at political meetings and demonstrations, howling slogans into a microphone, simply smile nervously when they're in Molteni's presence, displaying dignified deference: they know that they won't be able to go on being student leaders for ever, they know that they're being watched, they know that the time will come to spend judiciously the social capital of renown and student power that they've accumulated. A scholarship, a grant, a position as teaching assistant or researcher. Their contact with Molteni, Molteni's esteem and consideration are still extremely important things, essential. But he doesn't respect anyone openly, he supports those who are useful to him, he helps some when it is convenient to him to do so, more out of a necessary exercise of power than out of any actual scholastic need. Molteni doesn't believe in anything, everyone in academia knows this. He has attained the highest possible position, a summit from atop which he can look down with irony upon everything and everyone. And that is what he does regularly but never upon himself. Rumour has it that he's arranged to assign a chair in German studies to his mistress. It's the very least we can expect from a *barone*. The deference shown to Signorina Boccacci by Molteni's teaching assistants would be enough to confirm the hushed allegations, but Ivo Brandani is just a student and no one tells students about this kind of thing. To them, these remain, and must remain, nothing more than vague rumours. Academia never washes its dirty laundry in public. Molteni was one of the most highly respected scholars of Marx, and therefore, also of Hegel, but in the last decade he's blazed a path all his own, he's discovered Popper, he's broken away from the Marxist *mainstream* which meanwhile has become increasingly abstract, extreme and revolutionary. Ivo likes him as a public figure but is also enormously intimidated by him.

'Our goal, here, in this school . . .'

'Why doesn't he call it a university? Or department? Why does he insist on calling it a *school*? We're already done with school, this is *university*, which means that if you have to go to the bathroom, you don't have to raise your hand and ask . . .'

'. . . is precisely this: to scatter into the human environment a diffuse intelligence. In brief, not so much bodies of knowledge, as much as the ability to think. Many of you will wind up working for corporations, newspapers, many will teach school. You'll work for publishing houses, in the public administration. Some of you will go into politics, many of you are already involved in it. All of you will need to *know how to think*. All of us, Peninsulars in the second half of the twentieth century, need for you to be able to think. It will be indispensable for us to be able to rely on people capable of thinking . . .

'Then again,' he adds suddenly, without anyone expecting it— to judge from the attitudes of his teaching assistants, this is the first time they've heard him say anything of the sort—'we must admit that systematic philosophy is dead, done with, we haven't needed it for the past hundred years or more. It was the mother of all bodies of knowledge, all the sciences. Now that each branch of scientific pursuit has been able for some time now to walk on its own two feet, the mother no longer needs to instruct or nurse her children. She is no longer needed and it's just stupid to keep her alive merely because we have a building here with Department of Philosophy written on it, just because we have some endowed chairs and we're paid to remain sitting in them. If we were serious people we'd just go ahead and padlock the front doors for the next hundred years. But we all need to make a living and you're going to need the scrap of paper we issue. So we continue the way we

268

always have done. But the substance is no longer there. Someone may object: "But what of the eternal questions of philosophy?" What questions of this sort are there that aren't already arrant bullshit in their very formulation? "What exists outside of us?" In your opinion, is that a question that still has meaning when you cross the street, or do you take it for granted that the trolley arriving from the opposite direction has an existence of its own? Does it strike you as serious that we still ask questions such as: "What is the ultimate nature of reality?" And what can we see about that other one that rings more or less like this: "Is it possible to know this ultimate nature?"' Laughter. 'There's nothing to laugh about. Our questions will speak to this issue and many others. But know that this year we shall not limit ourselves to establishing the principal problems of theoretical philosophy and expecting you to know how they have been treated by modern philosophy, that is, from Descartes to the present day. This year we shall also give our own answers, not so much *to* the questions, but *about* the questions. We'll express a judgement on these. We'll demonstrate that some of them are nowadays pointless and unsubstantial.'

The teaching assistants exchange glances, clearly agitated, they whisper in one another's ears while Molteni continues, unwavering. From the seats a female voice can be heard, asking loudly: 'What about Marx?'

Molteni breaks off. He's not irritated, if anything he seems grateful to that voice because it gives him a chance to turn to the topic right away, without having to work his way up to it gradually by opening a whole series of doors. He knows that everyone calls him the Red Baron, or actually, he's just one of the many red academic barons. His membership in the Party's Central Committee is no secret. Ivo barely possesses a notion of what a 'central committee' might even be. His teaching assistants are agitated: Where is this class heading, today?

'Are you asking about Marx, Signorina? Or perhaps, Signora, I wouldn't know . . .' Molteni has always been quite gallant and old-school with his female students. Officially gallant in their presence, but with his teaching assistants he sometimes chances to make lewd, vulgar observations. Which are then gossiped about, circulated. Everything that Molteni says is conveyed to others and so on. He knows it, he is indifferent, it forms part of his power, part of his status as a maestro.

'. . . Ah, sure, Marx . . . Well, you see . . . Marx gave us the tools to understand what kind of world we live in, he told us which and of what nature the *true* laws are that govern our so-called societies, and therefore our lives. He revealed to us fundamental things about the *true* nature of our social consciousness. About History. Etc. But he's still a systematic philosopher, his thought tends towards the interpretation of reality in all of its parts. And that would actually be the least of his shortcomings. The greatest of Marx's shortcomings is that he pointed us to the wrong path by which to change the world. His mistake was to deceive us and, when all is said and done, to have paved the way for Capital. Some of you might know that I studied him for many years, and I have never regretted doing so. A substantial portion of this course will focus on Marx. Nonetheless, I should warn you this is not a Marxist course, nor is it a course in Marxism.'

The lecture hall is full of sweaters and fatigue jackets, scarves worn very long, jeans and suede desert boots, especially Clarks. Many, a great many are wearing suit and tie. Ivo has on a navy-blue blazer with shiny steel buttons, a white shirt, a tartan tie, over a pair of beige fine-wale Levi's corduroys. The room smells of wet overcoats. The sky has been overcast and rainy for days. It seems like an ordinary rainy November, the usual punishment for a summer that was too beautiful, for the crystalline water in the inlets of the South, but nothing in comparison with the Novembers of despair he experienced until two years ago, when he was still gazing out of the oversized windows in a classroom of a parochial school run by priests, and all he saw was a dreary world with no future, exactly like the world on this side of those windows, a world made up of idiotic, priestly lessons, of which nothing now remains in his head, without so much as a glimmer of interest, for four or five hours every blessed day, all year long, for ever and ever. Even then there was the same odour of wet overcoats and, like here, it was possible to perceive a stench of young specimens of humanity with unwashed hair, foul breath, bacteria. Many of them have colds, they're constantly sniffing and blowing their noses. This is a November for taking notes on the first lessons of theoretical philosophy, even though he knows that soon he'll stop taking notes entirely, and then he'll stop coming to lessons at all, except when he, Molteni, is there. A November to buy a raincoat at the used clothing store, to buy single cigarettes or at most in packs of ten. A November for going every night to the repertory movie house to watch, depending on the programme of the month, mostly Japanese films, such as *Harakiri* or even worse, like *The Naked Island*, beautiful and dispiriting. A November for seeing Clara, phoning Clara, having furtive sex with her, hiding somewhere, at her place when her folks are out, or in the car, when and if Father lends it to him. A November that brings with it, even now, after almost two years, a sense of liberation from school, but also the stunned bafflement of fall. A November in which the year actually begins, during which the usual pressure is brought to bear on him, more intense than the year before and progressively growing over the days and months and years to come. The important thing is for Ivo to feel unfailingly confused, wrong, inadequate, mistaken; the important thing is that he perceive himself as a piece of shit. That's the way everyone wants him. In particular, that's the way Father wants him, he works at it every day at lunch and dinner, without a break, like one of those jackhammers they use on his construction sites, as if that were his life's one true mission, as if Big Sister and Little Sister didn't exist and also need to be *forged*. Father is uninterested in them, Ivo has always been his objective, he is the element to be shaped, the one who constantly needs to be reminded of what a mistake it is to major in philosophy, especially if his father has a contracting business, if his father is a builder. A *padre palazzinaro—an apartment-house-building father—*he wishes he could tell him but he's scared to.

It's a pressure that arrives from all directions, and no kidding around. Once again, no kidding, there's never been any kidding around, anywhere and with anyone. The Peninsula is narrow, poor in resources, Catholic, mountainous, full of people without a penny to their name—you can't seriously believe that just because you've come along, the others are going to step aside and let you pass, right? You can't think that they're going to welcome you with open arms, that they'll extend handclasps of friendship, that they tell you that you're welcome, make yourself comfortable, as if you were at home, as if we were your fellow citizens, as if we were your brothers, your fathers, your teachers. As if we cared about you, about the quality of your life. Don't harbour any illusions, you're going to be whatever we want you to be. Already in elementary school, Schoolteacher Proia (may he burn in Hell) should already have made a fair number of things clear to you: Do you remember when he pressed the palms of both hands against your temples, in a vise-grip, and picked you up off the floor? Do you remember how you felt? It was as if your head were about to be crushed, a sort of electric shock. Do you remember the way he made fun of the kids who started crying? He'd pull up their smocks in the back and mock them, saying: 'Aprons, aprons.' What do you think Schoolteacher Proia was trying to *tell you*?

Ivo is going to take a while yet before he understands what Schoolteacher Proia meant and just what the content of that ancient and primary message really was (*We will crush you*), he experiences this November of cold feet in wet Clarks desert boots, trying to handle the pressure and stay afloat at the university, trying to keep something for himself, something he cannot tell anyone else, because he doesn't know what it is.

'To be like them, quite simply, isn't possible. I live in a different world, a parallel universe, indeed decidedly off-kilter in comparison with the world in which they live. They don't know anything about Elvis, nothing about Pink Floyd, the Stones (they don't know how wonderful "(I Can't Get No) Satisfaction" is) nothing about Clifford Simak, Arthur C. Clarke, Philip K. Dick. A piece by Coltrane, Davis, Coleman Hawkins, Roland Kirk means nothing to them (it just sounds like a symphony orchestra tuning up, Mother told him once). They don't know how to go underwater, they know nothing about Kerouac, they haven't read Ginsberg's "Howl", they don't know anything about Ernesto Guevara ("What's the name of that Communist they killed in Bolivia?"), nothing about anything.'

This is the first time in History that such a profound cultural gap has existed between generations. They, the fathers and mothers, fought the War, suffered hunger, ate black bread, lived as refugees and evacuees, rebuilt their Country. When the fathers were young men, they went to brothels. That was the only known way to get sex at the time, aside from getting married.

'It seems to me that Big Sister has fallen on the far side of the watershed, on the opposite side of where I am . . . Under the Bernina Glacier there are two lakes, one is white, and the other one is darker, they call them the White Lake and the Black Lake, one beside the other, they're separated by a morainic strip, the waters of the White Lake (or maybe of the Black Lake, I'm not sure . . .) wind up in the Adriatic Sea, but the waters of the adjoining lake go much farther away, they run downhill to the Inn River and, with the Inn, they flow into the Danube, and on from there into the Black Sea. Big Sister is only two years older than me but she's flowing in a different direction from me . . . With every passing year we move further apart, we've reached a level of alien estrangement, but different and far more serious than what separated me from Father and Mother, because it makes me lonelier . . .'

They had all been Fascists. Father says: 'We were all Fascists, even the ones who deny it now, the ones who drape themselves in the robes of the Resistance to anyone who will listen.' Father says that many of those who were actually in the Resistance later made use of the fact to advance their careers in the political parties, in the cooperatives, in the labour unions, in the state-owned industries, in the newsrooms. Now everyone's making money—after the poverty of the War Years and then that of the Postwar Years, they're now obsessed with money. Even Mother, in her wonderful welcoming laziness, is a little tense, because the husbands of her sisters seem to be making more money than Father, they have new cars, big homes, flats in gleaming new buildings that were built in the past few years, beach houses, they go skiing in the winter, they travel.

Father always says: 'If it hadn't been for all of you.'

He says: 'If it hadn't been for all of you, I wouldn't have had to break my back the way I do every day. If it hadn't been for all of you by now I'd be a bush pilot in Africa.'

Well, fuck, why don't you go? Go be a bush pilot in Africa, who's keeping you? Go and bust your face in half, if you care so much. Don't you understand that around this table that's what me and the Sisters, that is Big Sister and Little Sister, think? It would be better to die of hunger, better to have to live on the street than to have you always here, pontificating, threatening, dealing blows. Get the hell to Africa, go on! Father always says that everyone, even people who live in shanty town, have TV sets, he says that they all watch *Rin Tin Tin*, he says that everyone has a car, every-one, even the ones who were born and grew up in rags, who deserved no better, even the ignorant cattle who talk about nothing but football, Father says that even they want a car and a television set and a refrigerator and a vacuum cleaner. That is, everyone wants what he already has or would like to have: 'I don't know how they do it. The only explanation is the two-bit fraud, overdue instalment payments, debts.' So why did he bother going to school in the first place, if every turnip head, every illiterate, every moron can make the same amount as him, can aspire to have the same things?

'What he doesn't understand is that, even if I'd become an engineer, a surveyor, an architect, I'd have killed myself before I'd have gone to work for his company, for him, and wind up like Ortolani . . . Ortolani, a surveyor, sat all day long at his desk in the corporation offices, with his French magazines of "artistic nudes", his *Playmen* in his desk drawer . . . What did all these adults who now expect us to become like them ever teach us? What did Father teach you? You can say that he taught you three things . . . The first thing, the most useful one, is that the knot in your tie shouldn't be thought of as a knot but, rather, as a piece of "drapery" . . . The second is that when you drive a car, it's best to assume that the other drivers are all lunatics and drive accordingly . . . The third is that if you have to deal with someone you're afraid of, you need to remember that "he's afraid of you, too". This last item is the one I find least persuasive, even though it derives from having been Father at War, from having fought as an aircraft engineer on trimotor SM.82 bombers, from having been a boxer, from having taken on the dangerous local delinquents, in the bad old Fascist times of his youth in the outlying neighbourhoods he grew up in . . .'

A November for understanding once and for all how to behave inside this confused and echoing hellhole of students, hallways, bulletin boards and dust. He's in his second year—the first year was a full-blown shock, a virtual catastrophe: flunked at his first exam, a D when he took it again in June, then a subsidiary subject, nothing much—but still, it's complicated. You need to understand what courses to take and which ones to skip, what exams to work towards for June. The Bulletin Board is the most powerful symbol of the university, of the passage from a state of passive pupil—who is told things, who is instructed to write those things down in his notebook, the pupil who has to ask permission if he wants to go to the bathroom—to an active student who doesn't have to ask, who is required to read the notices, who must gather information every day, either directly or through word of mouth, about new developments, lessons, bureaucratic procedures to be taken care of in the administrative office after hours spent standing in line, about exams and how difficult this or that course is, the books, the study notes and where to procure them—everything. Nothing is said explicitly and in such a way that it is sure to reach you, nothing is *provided clearly*, no one is obliged to inform you, for example, that the scheduled date for an exam has been moved: that's something you'll learn the same day of the exam, in the hallway, along with a mass of other candidates for that exam, each of whom has the problem of figuring out what day they're going to have to show up. Every piece of information has to be torn loose with clenched teeth, you might say, like a piece of meat off a large body, shapeless and unknowable. Listening to Molteni's opening lecture forms part of this work of orientation. And that's not all: in the department it was quite an event, because Molteni counts, and how.

There is a buzz of perplexed confusion, verging on open disapproval, though expressed under their breath, a sort of muttering. It's the late autumn of 1967, mimeographed documents from the universities in the North are circulating in the department, but what will later become the Movement does not yet exist. Ivo managed to lay his hands on a copy of one of these documents, but he has a hard time understanding this language to which he is unaccustomed, a language that is political but which has nothing to do with his idea of politics: the proletarianization of the technician, the right to study . . . Marx applied to the 'process of formation of the intellectual labour force'.

. . . the university is a productive institution as well, in the sense that within it there takes place a process of exploitation of goods.

The *input* (a student, a graduate of one of various high schools) enters the transformation process with a value of x (which can be set by the market) and emerges (output: college graduate) with a value of $x+y$. The added value y is greater or lesser depending on whether or not the process is finished.

If the process is finished (*output*-graduate) the value of y is maximum. Both the range of opportunities and the level of pay the output will fetch on the market are broader and higher than at the beginning of the process . . .

In it, the university is denounced as a place of authoritarianism, paternalism, as part of the industrial process of standardization, a factory of consensus, as an initiation into subordination. Ivo's generation hasn't yet constructed anything that would allow it to openly dispute Molteni's words, to insult him, to berate him as a *barone* and a Fascist. But that generation is maturing, and very quickly: every day they talk about things they weren't talking about the day before. Molteni is no Fascist, but he's certainly a *barone* and apparently to his own full satisfaction: as he goes on with his opening lecture he remains certain of the unassailability of his position, he's unruffled, seems unconcerned, because the university is still an institution based upon an unquestioned, obvious, tacit Principle of Authority.

The professors are our class enemies.

For a teacher the university is a feudal landholding, for a student it is merely a part of the apparatus of repression . . . a form of violence . . . concealed beneath the semblance of the requirements of learning . . .

Molteni isn't a courageous man, it would never occur to him to stand up against an auditorium in open revolt, but today he feels that he has nothing to fear. Today his power is still intact, and so he goes on speaking into the microphone with that soft and slightly hoarse voice that is so typical of him. He has read the political documents circulating among the students. His teaching assistants procured copies for him and he's discussed them with them: he's said that he's generally in agreement with what he's read. 'Very well written, especially those from the northwest,' he said. He added that there is no form of education that is not also a repression and standardization. 'But our job is to ensure that it is not *only* that . . .'

. . . the students at the university must learn first and foremost to command and obey, they must unlearn any inclinations they might have to argue, they must understand that Science and Culture are the private property of the teachers and that in order to claim ownership of them they must submit to their oppression . . .

These words have already been uttered, already written, already mimeographed, they're circulating, but they haven't emerged yet, they still haven't penetrated, it will take time before that happens, before they are transformed into slogans, into political practice. Smug and authoritative, Molteni goes on unruffled, always at the same pace, like a chugging diesel fishing boat engine. He's accustomed to charming everyone who listens to him. Unlike many of his colleagues, he uses absolutely plain language, almost elementary, and he expects his students and teaching assistants to do the same. Of the many stories that are told about him there's the one about him telling a student who was using complicated language during an exam: 'Either start speaking in clear, simple Italian or you can leave immediately. I don't teach in philosophese and I expect that when exam time comes, my students don't speak philosophese.' It is also said that, of all phrases, the one that annoys him most is 'pregnant with meaning' ('Be careful not to say pregnant with meaning' is the wisecrack everyone exchanges at exam time). There's a story about a student who uttered that phrase and saw his grade book go flying out the window. Until the end of November of this year, it will be conceivable for a student's grade book to be thrown out a window. Just two months later, such a thing will become unthinkable.

'It's too early right now for you to see it coming, but soon we will be in a time when many of you will renounce what they feel themselves to be today and everything they think, or believe they think. I know that it seems inconceivable to you, that it seems absurd. But history has a nasty habit of overturning conditions that seemed immutable. You'll be left as naked as worms, defenceless, and with you the social classes whose interests it is your intention to defend—unless you succeed in renewing a body of thought that you see now as utterly perfect, but which is in fact riddled with holes, unless you succeed in breaking it away from its practical application which is proving to be the most glaring failure in all of modern history . . . Strive to become the intelligence of your world. If you are defeated, with nothing and no one to oppose it, capitalism will transform itself into an invincible monster, eager to destroy everything before it, including itself, including the planet on which we rest our feet. The World will burn, it will collapse, it will self-annihilate for an extra penny of profit. It will become necessary to build a new opposition, based on a renewed, flexible, astute body of thought . . . Just as it is no longer conceivable to have a philosophy that sets itself up as a system, that is, as a body of non-scientific thought that claims to offer a complete analysis of the world, likewise we cannot conceive of a political utopia that posits a radical refoundation of human relations, the construction of a new man, a society based on perfect equality. Positions like this one generate the governmental and political monsters that we know all too well, they engender the concentration camps, the gulags, the secret police, Stalin. Setting out to cure all of human society's ills on the basis of a philosophical and political theory, however excellent it may be, admittedly useful though it is as a way to understand the world, means failing to cure any of them, means renouncing the chance to alleviate and reduce the effects of capitalistic greed in the very name of its abolition . . . Would you allow yourselves to be treated at a hospital that had a slogan engraved on its facade reading something along the lines of: 'In this building we cure all diseases and recovery is guaranteed'? You won't be able to change the world but you may be able to improve it, and more likely you can consider yourselves lucky if you just manage not to make it worse. All the same, allow me to express my very strong doubts: you *will* make it worse. Not now, not in the next few years, but later on, when your initial drive will have lost its impetus, when many of you will have gone over to the other side, then you'll realize that the point of arrival will be much worse than the point of departure . . . As long as we're on the subject, let me add, apropos of nothing in particular, that it wasn't that way for our generation . . . We were Fascists and later, luckily, anti-Fascists, we even went to war, we took up arms to show our opposition, we did it too late but we did it, to those who were dragging our country into the abyss and so forth . . . Today I can say that the point of arrival of our trajectory is better than the point of departure . . . Close parenthesis. In any case, over the course of these lessons this year we'll have an opportunity to re-examine in greater depth a number of these topics. This is only a first presentation, a series of summary points . . . I want to warn you not to expect a course *of* theoretical philosophy but instead a series of lectures *on* theoretical philosophy and its future, or perhaps I should say, its *fate*. Those among you who were expecting confident answers are still in time to switch to a different course . . .'

The teaching assistants exchange questioning glances, they understand and they don't understand. He ought to be more cautious, more conciliatory, given the situation. None of the students today understands a word of what Molteni is saying, or why. But that's the way he is, he's tossing out lightweight provocations, he's sniffing the air to see which way the wind is blowing, he likes taking a contrary stance, he likes putting people on their guard, in the final analysis, he likes teaching. Even today, that's what he's doing, even though the atmosphere in the lecture hall is anything but serene, even though no one dares to raise any substantive objections. The questions that follow are by and large practical in nature, and they're answered by the teaching assistants.

Franco Sala is sitting next to Ivo and he says: 'I can't figure out what game Molteni is playing . . . He's surely read everything that's circulating, he must have thought it over, he can tell which way the wind is blowing . . . This is tantamount to a warning shot, it's as if he were trying to tell us that in no case is he going to be on our side. He's saying: "I'm a *barone*, an academic powermonger, but I'm also a teacher, and if you want me as a teacher, here I am, but you're also going to have to accept me as a *barone*—and in any case, for now, this is the beginning of the course, because that's what they pay me to do." He's a sly old devil, he gets on my nerves, but I respect him, I can't bring myself to hate him . . . I don't see the point of hating him . . . what do you say?'

Ivo knows that Molteni is important, but he doesn't know much more than that, he doesn't want to spout bullshit, he's unsure of himself. Sala is cultured, well informed, 'politicized', but he's also ironic, he wants to be friends with him, and Ivo is flattered by the fact that he's already spoken to him on other occasions. Sala is well known, esteemed, respected. Ivo ventures to chime in: 'I don't know

'... It strikes me that he's saying: "Don't expect that this state of student unrest is going to change the curriculum of this course" ... But it strikes me that his teaching assistants are surprised, too ...'

'He's a provocateur, he's enjoying himself, he's just flexing his muscles in here. He thinks he's untouchable ... But he'll learn his lesson. I would have expected him to be shrewder, more intelligent ...'

'Couldn't it be that he's just informing us about what's going to be taught in this course?'

'Sure, of course, that too. But still he'll learn his lesson.'

'Do you think he's a Fascist, too?'

Sala gives him a look and replies, decisively: 'Let's get one thing clear, Ivo ... He is a caryatid of the Resistance, he's no Fascist. It would be a mistake to think that he is one. If he ever was one, he isn't any more and never will be again. If you want to know what I think, I think he's an invaluable teacher. But he's the typical kind of figure that is so crucial to academic power, as a subalternate extension of capitalist power. And so, right here and now, *to me* he's an enemy ... The university needs to be turned inside out like a sock.' Franco Sala always knows exactly what to say. He knows what's happening.

But what really *is* happening?

... the university is a feudal structure controlled by the professors: Research is their heraldic crest.

 ... a continual process of indoctrination in which the student is forced to play an increasingly and purely passive and receptive role. A set of academic rituals ... a continuous waste of time to which the student is forced to submit, because he is being asked to believe that this is the one true way to gain possession of Science and Culture, the same academic science and culture that exist only because there are people paid by the state to celebrate their academic rituals at the university ...

More than two months have passed since Molteni's opening lecture. From the end of Christmas holidays until the occupation, the course in theoretical philosophy might have involved four or, at the most, five lessons, all of them conducted by teaching assistants. Then the occupation interrupted everything. In the South of the Peninsula there was a major earthquake, in Vietnam the Tet offensive, the universities in the North have been occupied for some time now, even the students in middle school have been heard from. The odour of dust is everywhere. But it's not the same odour of dust you can smell, say, in the countryside, on a dirt road, this is the stench of filth, that is, the odour of human sweat and foulness: there's filth everywhere, on the floors and on the furniture, on tables and chairs, because here when you say furniture, you're basically talking about tables and desks and chairs and stools. There are a few filing cabinets and a few blackboards. There are glass lamp globes hanging from the ceilings. There's not much else in the department, Peninsular universities are squalid, barren, dirty, echoing, even when they're not being occupied. Inasmuch as they are part of the public administration, they've always been like that. It's just that now, with the occupation, the echoing is almost intolerable, the dirt and the waste paper are ankle deep. In the executive commission the decision is made that cleaning shifts should be organized, but then no one does, no one knows where the find the brooms, the rags. Many of these pieces of furniture are made of beechwood, and have metal inventory plates, or else they're made of metal and plywood. Some of them have been stacked in piles, heaped in barricades, against the glass front doors. To get out, you have to follow a figure-S between the first and the second barricade. To get in you have to be identified by the sentries standing guard or someone that they know has to vouch for you. The idea would be to keep 'Fascists and provocateurs' from getting in, rumours are circulating that the Movement has been infiltrated by cops and agents: often at night people come rushing up breathless to announce that the Fascists are on their way, but so far the Fascists haven't tried doing anything. They're staying cooped up in the School of Law, which is like a protected nature reserve for a species that seems to be on the verge of extinction, but that's not how it is. In there, the comrades are oppressed and in the minority, practically clandestine. No one seems to know why the School of Law is traditionally majority Fascist.

... the students enrolled in the departments of literature, philosophy, educations, law, and political science meet in a general assembly; the general assembly in turn is made up of various subassemblies articulated on the basis of shared cultural and professional interests, independent of the department in which the students are enrolled ...

... the academic year is subdivided into two semesters. At the beginning of each semester, the teaching curriculum for the semester that is about to begin is done. With this end in mind, the assemblies are convened and, during the course of each, the students propose topics of study for potential groups ...

... the study groups select the people with the technical expertise necessary for their work ...

... the actual participation in the work of the group is a necessary and sufficient condition for receiving a passing grade on the student's gradebook ...

... the actual plan of studies, devised on the basis of seminars selected by the student, replaces the plan of studies currently obligatory for the individual degree courses, though leaving them formally in effect ...

... the working students will be offered three options:

—actual and ongoing participation in the study groups that have been formed in the assemblies ...

—the formation of independent study groups with full rights to choose their topic of study ...

—individual preparation on the same topics that the study groups are working on, in coordination with the study groups themselves ...

Continuous assemblies in the auditorium. Then there are seminars, committees, working groups. All of it begins with the assembly and all of it comes back to the assembly. The assemblies are run by those who already have political experience of some kind or other, who know the basics of democratic procedures, who know what a motion is, how and on what votes are taken and so on and so forth. In other words, the ones who take their places at the head of the Movement are those who already have some familiarity and contacts with politics and political parties: that is, the ones who were going to their Communist Party chapter up until just a few months ago.

But the Movement appropriates these leaders (and it continually creates new ones), leading them, in some cases *by the scruff of the neck*, in the direction it is *naturally* heading already. The power game inside the Movement, among the peers who lead it, possesses one fundamental rule that you have to follow adroitly if you want to stay afloat: whoever manages to *outflank* all the others *on the left*, and to do it at the exact right moment, *wins* the assembly of that day, gains that particular advantageous position, in that particular department, and that gives him the right to represent it in the central committees of the Movement, which already exist somewhere, if only in embryonic form.

Ivo is there, he's present, he participates, he wants to understand, but he remains silent, he expresses no opinion, he's cautious. He, like many others, has no experience with what is happening, knows nothing about it. Till now he always believed that politics was something that involved the parties, the parliament, and he's always steered clear of it. In politics he's always thought according to the things that he's heard Father say, a former 'not-particularly-fervent' Fascist, and now a member of the centre-right Italian Liberal Party: the government should do as little as possible, personal initiative, business is the highest form of human labour, it creates wealth for the workers as well. Father hates the Christian Democrats, the Socialists, and the Communists, he doesn't care for priests; Ivo feels the same way, but only out of imitation. But here, now, he's glimpsing a way of thought that is different and new to him, reasonings whose meaning he often fails to grasp, new languages, new terminology. Are they Communists? Yes, no doubt about it. Are they right? Yes, I think they are.

The assemblies are interesting, Ivo takes part in them on a regular basis, but he almost always wonders: 'What are they really talking about? Why can't I understand practically a thing of what they're saying? Why does it seem to me that I'm the only one who isn't getting it? Why does everyone talk about democracy and then when it comes down to it the only ones who can say anything are those who are in agreement with the majority? How can the others be for or against something they don't understand? Why does it seem to me so absurd and wrong, but at the same time so exciting and right? What am I doing here? Do I belong to this movement, or am I nothing but an observer?'

ALL POWER TO THE ASSEMBLY.

Every day in the auditorium the speeches come one after the other, numerous, in accordance with the new ritual of direct democracy, of the *rejection of delegatory governance*, meaning that there is apparently no intermediary between the Movement's base and its top leadership. But everyone knows that the only words that matter are those of a special few, while most of the talking is strictly filler. It is never stated openly, but the assembly consists of waiting for the two or three speeches by the most important leaders. Ivo thinks that some of the ancillary speeches, apparently secondary and strictly delivered to distract the audience, are very interesting, indubitably more interesting and reasonable than the speeches they hear from the leaders, which are often verbose, larded with curse words and jargon, words used to make those listening feel ignorant and in order to dominate the assembly: if you don't understand me you don't understand shit. The things that Oreste says are almost always like that. And so when Ivo dares to ask him for a few clarifications, Franco Sala, who is also considered a leader, gives Ivo an ironic glance then replies: 'Forget that. The meaning is always something different from what is being stated, they're talking to each other, in code. These are nothing but overgrown, over-politicized high school students, they've read a book or two, and now they are engaged in "analysis", but they have a high-school culture, something straight out of De Amicis. All this is a power struggle, Ivo. We're petty bourgeois, like all, or nearly all revolutionaries. It's a game, but one played in deadly serious. Or at least it's serious to me . . .'

It is also tacitly well known that anyone who wants to represent a conciliatory, or, worse, party-based, political position cannot, de facto, speak: they will be drowned out by shrill whistles and catcalls, they'll have the microphone yanked out of their hands, they'll be threatened, intimidated, ignored. There are those who might complain that this isn't democratic. Ivo is in agreement, in a democracy everyone has the right to speak, but he doesn't dare to say a thing . . . To anyone who raises this objection they answer that the democracy being practised at the assembly is a 'revolutionary democracy', which necessarily can't offer room for *all* the ideological positions, only those allowed by the revolutionary nature of the Movement . . . He manages to talk it over with Franco. Franco says: 'What the hell do you care, we aren't here to defend and reaffirm the rules of a bourgeois democracy . . . We don't give a flying fuck about that . . . We're doing something different, we're *B-L-O-W-I-N-G U-P* the university, that is, one of the fulcrums of the system . . .'

The standard language of the Movement changes rapidly, neologisms coined just the day before spread like wildfire through all the assemblies and the committees in the various departments. These are regularly recurring words, used by everyone, often referring to vague concepts, and frequently possessing referents that transition from one meaning to another: an exam is a 'taxable moment'. It takes Ivo a little while to figure out that taxes have nothing to do with it, but that they're referring to the 'accounting audit of the conventional cultural absorption, necessary for the grading and selection of students'. In the assembly and in the seminars, curse words and obscenities are also useful in stalling for the time needed to formulate the successive proposition: it is the liberation of language from all respectable bourgeois polish. There's irony but not really all that much. Often their mockery of this or that academic celebrity becomes open, defamatory, and very aggressive, sometimes obsessively repeated. Molteni is one of their favourite targets, but in the words used to attack him it is possible to detect a residue of respect, of intellectual subordination.

Trying to be noticed in the assembly meant succeeding in over-turning the paradigms of the day, instilling in all those listening the sensation that 'they hadn't understood a fucking thing', saying that 'the problem lies elsewhere', that they were 'clinging to retro-grade positions', that it was 'necessary to raise the level of the clash', etc.—it's an arms race. The meaning, consistency, and *truth-fulness* of what is said counts a great deal less than the tone and charisma of the person speaking. What counts are the kind of words and the way they are used, the linguistic stylemes. What counts are the physical appearance, the timbre and sonic level of the voice, the style of dress, the brand of cigarettes that are smoked. Trying to be noticed also means dressing in such a way as to be perfectly recognizable as comrades-in-the-Movement. The basic reference is the look used in the Cuban revolution ten years earlier, but there are also those who choose not to comply with that stan-dard, those who insist on wearing their leather jackets, their cash-mere sweaters. There are those who don't give a damn and go on dressing the way they always have.

Ivo realizes that what counts most is one's sense of timing in speaking up, the capacity to surprise and overwhelm, to outdo, to go beyond, to bring the assembly gradually along until it comes to these further convictions, with new watchwords. The one thing you can't do is stop, you can't say the same thing tonight that you were saying this morning, it will be obsolete. Being there means perceiving this incessant transformation, being inside it, sharing it, submitting to it but also contributing to it. The assembly and the Movement itself have a constant need for new tasks and objectives to attain and it is on these that they reconstruct themselves day after day. 'But the mobilization cannot go on indefinitely,' says Franco Sala, 'sooner or later the journey will run out of energy and start to slow, therefore what's needed are results, because in the end it will be the results that really matter.'

Stupidity & intelligence, conformism & originality, novelty & staleness—they all coexist in a continuous incredible miraculous daily contradiction. When he talks to the comrades, when he discusses the fate of the Movement, when, very rarely, he takes the floor in the committees, in the seminars (never in the assembly, he's never had the nerve and he never will . . .), Ivo uses the language of the Movement, he makes a show of having internalized the decisions and he complies entirely with the lexicon in use that day; only with Franco does he know that he can freely express his doubts. Ivo senses that revolution is not going to take place and deep down he doesn't think he wants it to, but he too speaks of its as a desirable and possible event. He senses that all this will come to an end, but he also knows that the university will never be able to go back to being what it was before. It hardly strikes him as a minor achievement.

In the Movement everything seems to be the fruit of convictions and free individual choices, there is no apparent constraint, but Ivo quickly comes to understand that what really matters is the collective spirit, that is, the instinctive desire everyone feels not to be left behind, a yearning to belong, to be part of something, to share in the final analysis in the struggle against poverty and malaise and against a system of power that is both internal and external to the university. The motivations for being there and acting within the Movement, for running the risk of a fractured skull or even worse, need to be reconfirmed, implemented, bettered and bested on a daily basis—that's something that the leaders know full well. And therefore, never a step back: 'Always forward, always *beyond* until the point of dissolution is attained, until self-annihilation is finally reached, things that will happen soon . . .' Franco Sala tells him at one point. For that matter, there's the deadline of the June examinations; the February session was skipped and it's clear that in June the exams are going to have to be held at all costs, at the cost of simply cancelling the academic year. 'This will be a crucial moment,' says Franco, 'but this is just the end of February, it's early to worry about that. First let's see how things shake out, how the system reacts. Because they're going to react, and how . . .'

One fine morning, Ivo goes with Franco to the Department of Architecture, which has been occupied since 2nd of February, the site of historic student-protest activities dating back five years. Today an assembly is going to be held with representatives from various departments, including the Movement from the Departments of Literature and Philosophy. Far from the deterioration and chaos of the university campus, the Department of Architecture strikes him as an Eden of privileged students very conscious of their attire, some of them wearing parkas, others in jacket and tie, loden overcoats, cashmere sweaters. For years the myth has been circulating throughout the university that the Department of Architecture is a place of emancipated women and loose morals. Ivo looks around, the young women in the Department of Architecture are every bit as pretty as those in Literature, but they look *different*: they don't give the impression that they're there to get a degree before getting married and starting a family, maybe with an idea of teaching, to round out their husband's salary. These young women seem to be here because they're interested in architecture. They look confident, many of them went to artistic high schools, they're wearing miniskirts, their eyes are mascaraed, they really do seem to want to be professional architects. They intimidate him, he likes them a lot.

There are people stretched out on the lawn under the pine tree in front of the entrance, smoking and talking in the sunshine. Higher up, above the canopy, standing on ladders, there are students chiselling at the facade. They're working according to an outline traced in chalk directly on the plaster by a major artist, the *pictor maximus* who sits on the Central Committee of the Communist Party. Nude figures and bunches of grapes, an unfinished arcadia, strange in this context. But those who are working on that stuff belong to a different group, there are those who describe them as 'situationists', but very few people know what that means: they call themselves Birds. Over the past few days, they've occupied the lantern in the cupola of a Baroque church in the City of God. They climbed all the way up there, they perched on the spiralling architecture at a vertiginous height, they stayed there for more than twenty-four hours, like roosting pigeons, until they were forced down. Ivo doesn't know who the situationists are either and doesn't dare to ask anyone, not even Franco, but he liked their exploit, it seemed to him to have some meaning—there they were up there, in the chilly night, from the piazza below they were dark silhouettes smoking cigarettes, or maybe joints, clinging to Borromini's capriccios. The Birds perform symbolic acts, totally off the beaten path, abstract. They get on many people's nerves, but Ivo likes what they do. Franco disagrees: 'Breaking into other people's homes, making them choke on their dinner, strikes me as personal violence, or camouflaged frat-boy prankery.' The Birds graze sheep in the rooms of the Institute of Architectural History, they've transplanted a fig tree into the patio outside the auditorium, they break into the homes of leading left-wing intellectuals who have openly endorsed the Movement and lay them waste. Ivo thinks that what they're trying to show is that publicly endorsing costs nothing, if one risks nothing.

'Violence, but not against people, against things, instead . . .'

'It's still violence,' says Franco, 'and violence is allowed only when it's public and *political*, Ivo . . . They ruin dinner parties, evenings with friends, they terrorize families . . .' Franco continues, talking to himself, but Ivo listens to him eagerly, because he teaches, points the way, understands things, and explains them without showing off: '. . . on the other hand, violence is there, it's a necessary option, always present, it's an integral part of everything we do and everything *we make happen* . . . You can't eliminate it, because being nonviolent means being nonexistent in the terms by which we choose to exist . . . And these terms, even if they are by no means entirely clear, certainly don't allow for mediation with the existing situation, at least so it seems . . . Violence is *necessary*, some of us don't understand that but factory workers and farmers have always known it—necessary because the opposition cannot truly take shape without *physical action*, without manifesting themselves concretely in the space-time continuum . . . Likewise, no repression can exist without the concrete threat of coercion and physical violence . . . No one, at the Movement's assemblies, openly states this . . . In fact, they say the opposite, we constantly emphasize that we're the ones being attacked, brutalized and arrested, and in fact that's the truth, by and large . . . But everyone knows that without a physical confrontation, the Movement wouldn't exist in the same way, the things it states wouldn't have the same political force . . . What we need is for there to be a dialectic of violence between the Movement and the system, a sequence of call and response that will lead to a genuine culmination . . .'

Then in a lower voice, speaking to himself: 'Everything that has to do with humanity, even the most abstract thing, involves the body, Ivo . . . Politics is political only if it entails the potential transition from word to direct action *on the body* . . . Without the option of violence there is no politics . . .' Ivo isn't sure he understands. They're sitting on the steps, in front of the Japanese Cultural Institute. It's a horizontal building, modern, with faint Asian references. It is here that Ivo discovered Utamaro, Hiroshige and Hokusai: a show that Clara dragged him to see the year before and that bewitched him. Before then he thought he hated everything Asian. Chinese or Japanese, it was all the same to him. On the department facade were streamers and dazibaos that proclaimed a die-hard occupation. Before them were the green treetops of the pines and holm oaks standing on the prehistoric ridges of the River Valley, to the left was the Neoclassical building of the British Academy, further down was the Museum of Modern Art. A department for the privileged, if compared to the Literature and Philosophy Building, to say nothing of the Teaching College.

'. . . words matter, and how . . . But I believe that the most important battleground is physical, spatial: on the one hand, the university space of the occupied departments and, on the other, the space of the city, the streets, the squares. Notice this: years later, the things we remember aren't moments in the assemblies, political resolutions, but events of territorial conflict, contests for the conquest of symbolic extensions of space, which remain bound up with the names of the places where they occurred, where *they were made to occur* . . .'

'Are you saying that the time has come to create opportunities for physical clashes?'

'It's what we're doing, Ivo . . . This situation can't go on for much longer . . . Sooner or later they'll clear us out of the departments—we'll fight back and they'll step up the repression, we'll react to that and so on . . . The comrades who have political experience know that it is only in violence that the true intentions of the state can be seen . . . In the leadership meetings, at this point, they're openly saying that it's going to be necessary to move on to a repressive phase, in order to assure that the Movement makes the hoped-for qualitative leaps . . .'

'What qualitative leaps, Franco?'

'The way I see it, these are the qualitative leaps . . . From an anti-authoritarian movement, generically opposed to the idea of the system, to a political movement with a revolutionary bent . . . From the struggle against the exploitation of intellectual labour and in favour of the liberation of knowledge, to the struggle for the proletarian revolution . . . In other words, we need to break out of the university and shift the field of battle onto a broader territory, principally in the factories . . . It means that it is necessary to seek connections with other subalternate subjects in society . . . The university, the condition of students, is a ghetto that will ultimately strangle us, if we can't figure out how to emerge from it: that's as much as I can tell you here, today . . . We'll see how it turns out . . .'

'Franco, can I ask you a question?'

'Well of course.'

'When you say "proletarian revolution", are you talking about a proletarian revolution like, say . . . like, say, the storming of the Winter Palace? In other words, are you talking about something *like that*?'

'Are you pulling my fucking leg? It's obvious that the historical conditions of *that kind* no longer exist and will never exist again. However, you see . . . Beings Communists without aiming at a revolution makes no sense . . . So there's no way to have a revolution?

292

All right, but still, *that* is the objective of any Communist party, any Communist movement . . . We can't say when the favourable conditions finally will exist, but it is *there* that we must arrive. Not today and not even tomorrow. But *this* is what it means to be a Communist . . . If we say it openly, we force the Party to come out into the open, to reveal its true nature . . . Et cetera, it's not a simple matter . . . But this is the policy: prefigure a future that might give some meaning to the struggles of today, and I'm not talking about *our* struggles but the struggles of factory workers and the subproletariat. We don't know what the future holds, in part because we still have to construct it, you see? . . . Let's get going, or they'll get started without us.'

Inside the building the setting is similar to that of the other occupied departments. The walls are covered with posters and streamers, slogans in shiny red paint or in spray paint. Everywhere is the reek of filth that Ivo knows all too well by now, here too crumpled paper litters the floor. There's an intent to defile, to desecrate, in all this. He likes it. In the assembly, Franco has been shouting himself hoarse for fifteen minutes, the way he always does, and his voice is practically shot. His raucous voice, along with a number of other peculiarities of his in terms of language, have become the target of imitation and sarcasm, but at the same time they're an unmistakable trademark. The meaning of what he's saying is reasonably clear but, more than by his meaning, the assembly seems to be fascinated and, perhaps, captivated, intimidated, by the *way* Franco speaks. He seems to be aware of it, perhaps it's something conscious, he tested it out in the first few days and then he carefully fine-tuned it. Everyone else constantly uses curse words, obscenities, meaningless phonemes: their purpose is to stall for time before adding some other formulation whose purpose is to intellectually intimidate the assembly, to *grab it*. Not Franco, his words are prepared, but simple. They come out of his mouth in a carefully reasoned sequence, punctual, moving: '. . . if we allow ourselves to be corralled inside this enclosure, where you could cut the paternalism with a knife . . . If we let them keep life and society and the ferocious contradictions of the world out of the things that they teach us and the things we talk about . . . If we accept that the reality in which we actually live is kept separate from the academic aura of the authoritarian bodies of knowledge, pre-packaged and dominant . . . Listen to me, comrades, if we allow the university to shape us in accordance with the standards that Capital requires in its current phase of restructuring . . . If we let them cage us in the industrial sector that produces the predictable proletarianized technicians who serve the system . . . In other words, if we allow all this, then we can call ourselves—not only *already finished as a movement*—but already dead as human beings!'

There is a lengthy burst of applause.

Ivo wonders whether he believes in what he says. Or whether for him the game of being a revolutionary leader is merely that, a game, conscious and temporary, before he goes on to dedicate himself to something completely different. Franco is pale, skinny, tall, always dressed the same way, in a black crew-neck sweater, a hand-knit red wool scarf, a rumpled jacket and, if it's cold out, a heavy blue double-breasted peacoat over it. He wears wire-rim glasses and has his hair cut short, at a time when everyone else has long hair.

'That question makes no sense, Ivo. Why, do you believe it? Do you believe in all the things you say? Surely Franco believes in it more than you do. And after all, what does it mean to "believe in it"? To be convinced of it, that's what it means. But in this case, convinced of what? Of the possibility of revolution? Oh come on . . . He explained to you earlier, what that means . . .'

'All around us, the society of the dead wants us, calls out to us, has no intention of giving us room. It needs us, we are the new recruits it yearns for . . . Fathers, professors, schoolteachers, priests and *all* the politicians, including the Communist Party!' A pause, more applause. 'Including the industrialists, including the police, the carabinieri, and the various institutions . . . In short, all these subjects, in practical terms, society as a whole, have no intention of kidding around, they're not going to give up even an inch of their hold on us, their power over our generation . . . They already know how many of us are going to be fed into the machinery of the capitalist system as factory workers, how many as technicians, how many as executives and how many others will be left, *physiologically*, out on the street . . . The university is a sorting machine for the new non-proletarian recruits to the capitalist process of production . . . No one is going to give us any free gifts, everything we obtain we're going to have to rip it out of their hands piece by piece!' More applause, an extended wave; Ivo feels a shiver run down his back. Then Franco's speech becomes more technically political: 'With all their disagreements, the leadership of the Movement do have a shared Leninist vision, according to which there can be no revolutionary movement without a social class with a vital interest in building it, a class that will take hegemonic control and guide it to a successful outcome through the appropriate alliances . . . To manage the qualitative leap in our struggle we have already witnessed the growth of political formations unwilling to put up with the limitations of the traditional parliamentary left or the confines within which the Movement has thus far manifested itself but which remain solidly bound up with the university as a place for the shaping of consciences and, therefore, as a site for the production of extra-parliamentary political recruits in the embryonic state . . . What is needed are closer ties with those forces . . .' And so on and so forth. Franco is reporting to the assembly the generic conclusions of the National Liaison Office. The speech ends in a burst of shouts and cheers. What had seemed like a routine assembly has taken a 'qualitative leap', even though no one seems to know in what direction. The objectives of the leaders who from this point on take turns at the microphone is to guide the assembly to take a vote on a unified motion which, however, remains to be drafted. A small group of leaders, deputy leaders and intellectuals of the Movement has already secluded itself in some lecture hall to draft the text of that motion, while another group is focusing on a less hasty counter-motion, one that calls for biding time for the moment. In any case, the assembly will vote for the motion advocated by Franco, but the group behind the counter-motion will make its presence felt all the same.

At this point, it would seem that no political approach aiming solely to obtain results within the context of the university can be allowed to gain a position. Such an approach must be opposed at all costs. The more ambitious leaders have sensed that in the Movement even the most delirious proposals will encounter neither obstacle nor opposition, provided it rings revolutionary. The race towards the most extreme formulation ensures the loyalty of the masses, the silencing of all dissent. Curse words are fundamental, no speech can do without them: they express the revolution's bold contempt for any and all gods and any and all clergy or spiritual power other than that springing from the revolution itself. Foul language too expresses contempt, it's practically a linguistic manifesto, but with the goal of erasing all differences between high and low language, between the burnished eloquence of the press, the TV, the bourgeoisie and academia on the one hand, and the actual spoken language of young people, the proletariat and ordinary people on the other. 'It is obligatory to violate with determination the Catholic-televisual language of the bourgeoisie, shine a harsh light on its obscurantist hypocrisy.' The things that remain beyond the pale are the sexist insult, the lewd double entendre and, above all, vulgar frat humour, which was abolished instantaneously from the very outset. In the Movement, irony, sarcasm and satire all manifest themselves in accordance with sophisticated, extreme protocols, in some cases invasive and destructive: on the wall-to-wall carpeting of the Department of Architecture sheep are allowed to shit, the offices of the 'baronial' potentates are smeared with balls of shit, scattered with bales of hay. The offices are ransacked, ravaged, the books have vanished from the shelves, the furniture has been dragged off to add to the bulk of the barricades at the department's front entrance, that is, if they haven't simply been carted off, looted. The barons themselves have simply vanished from circulation some time ago. The last time that Molteni set foot in the department he was greeted by a wall of jeers and catcalls, shrill whistles. As he hurried, lurching, down the stairs, everyone had been able to see that he was frightened—even he, sharp as he was, couldn't really say what was happening, what was really in the air. At that moment, Ivo felt deeply uneasy and stepped away from the railing. 'Fuck, though, that's Molteni!' Only a few young teaching assistants ever showed up in the department, took part in the work of the collectives or proclaimed their own personal solidarity with the Movement, their faith in the revolution, their always having been 'on the other side' when it came to power in the university. 'These loyal revolutionary souls don't understand two very basic things,' says Franco, 'the first is the self-image that they project when they participate in assemblies and seminars: dreary, opportunistic, capable of engendering only mistrust and dislike. The second thing they can't understand is that baronial authoritarianism is strictly a secondary target and we don't give a flying fuck about their solidarity . . .'

The declared objective is, 'fucking hell, comrades', the unification of student struggles and worker struggles, the shift of the epicentre of the revolt from the university to the factory. 'Anyone who tends in this historical moment to ride the tiger, in the hopes that once the party is over he'll be an unmarked striker and enjoy a personally advantageous position as a mediator between the student masses and the academic baronry, has reckoned poorly . . . And another thing, the party won't come to an end all that soon, Ivo.' Ivo can only nod his head, Franco's lucidity and intellectual determination are stunning, he doesn't feel up to it, but he's flattered by the attention Franco is willing to pay to him and the second-hand prestige that this friendship confers upon him.

The questions that Ivo asks himself aren't the same as those that Franco does; rather, they resemble the topics of Molteni's opening lecture, when he was talking about the wrong path to changing the world. Ivo doesn't know much about politics, about Marx he knows more or less what he studied in high school, lately he's read Lenin's *The State and Revolution*, he bought all of *Das Kapital* on the instalment plan, he's read here and there, in a disorderly manner, like Che's *Bolivian Diary*, Adorno, Lukács, he's reading Marcuse, like everyone, he buys Communist journals, magazines and zines, *Quaderni piacentini*, *Quaderni rossi*, he forces himself to read the *Monthly Review*, periodically he even inflicts upon himself *Marcatré*—all according to regulation. He chose to major in Philosophy because he's liked it ever since he first studied it in school, or actually since he had to study it for the whole summer of 1962 with Giorgio, the college student who was tutoring him and who was good at talking and explaining and smoking a cigarette all the way down to the filter without letting the ash drop. It was Giorgio who made him fall in love, for real and for the first time, with the history of thought. Ivo remembers very well, it was a summer dominated by St Thomas Aquinas's Immovable Motor, and even now that's how he still imagines it: an immense diesel engine, black, covered with grease, lost in the vast emptiness of space. Ivo hates non-understanding: 'If there are men like me who have written important texts, I, inasmuch as I'm a man like them, must be capable of understanding them, just as they were capable of writing them.' This is the impulse that drove him towards the Department of Philosophy and in the past few months, while Franco has been reasoning in terms of political practice, Ivo, consistent with the premise of his decision, asks himself questions that strike him as philosophical. Till now he has participated by saying nothing, observing, learning new things. He has seen (or anyway, he thinks he has seen) that in the Movement there has formed, spontaneously and in just a few days, a centralized group holding power. Around this small core various concentric and subordinate circles have stabilized, with different hierarchical positions, all the way to the outermost circle, that of the revolutionary unskilled labour, menial workers who are given orders and execute them with considerable docility. The leaders are with their subordinates, they show themselves where the various sentinels stand guard, they go to sleep in the occupied departments. But few among those who stand sentinel take part in the narrower meetings of the leaders. Officially these hierarchies don't exist but they're clearly visible and in fact everyone sees them, just as they see the sexual favours that the leaders receive from the female comrades. Power, the Eros of dominance, subordination, the struggle to be on top, all these things exist in the Movement exactly as they exist outside it, anywhere else, without exception.

'It's not cold today, I can go out wearing just a light jacket, the usual navy blue blazer, red knit tie, Levi cords, Clarks desert boots: I'm looking good, admit it . . . Marshalling point in the Oblong Piazza—there aren't that many of us, but still a good number . . . We march off northward, keeping a healthy distance each from the other. We're on the side of justice, there's no doubt about that . . . The police entered the Department of Architecture and cleared everyone out, they beat the comrades who were inside with billy clubs, they hauled them into the police station . . . There were only a few of them, they didn't put up a fight, and they were right . . . It's the right thing to do, to demonstrate against everything that's happening—Franco said it, they're going to kick us out of the university, we need to show a reaction . . . He's up ahead, in the front line right behind the protest streamers, arms locked with the other comrades in leadership . . . In the front line are the security crew and the Movement leaders, in the second line are the deputy leaders and so on, in order of prominence attained . . . The security crew has put together a cordon along the sides of the protest march— situation normal: all the shops up and down the street pull down their metal shutters . . . This is my first genuine demonstration, in the street, on the piazza . . . I came because it's the right thing to do. In the procession I saw people you rarely run into at the department, these days, including students who usually don't take part, but today they're here . . . The sun is out, it seems as if spring has arrived, I feel good, a light breeze manages to worm its way between my jacket and shirt—it's still a little chilly—button up the front . . . Clara isn't here . . . She's come into the department a few times with us but that's it . . . She's in her first year, newly enrolled. In the Department of Economics almost nothing's happening, she's bewildered, she hardly knows which way to turn . . . I try to explain things to her but I'm not comfortable indoctrinating, I'm not an indoctrinator—and especially because I don't really know the doctrine . . . We've talked about the fact that the university is baronial, authoritarian, selective, the universal right to study, the rejection of delegatory political process, the idea of pure politics, without intermediaries, the power of the assembly, in other words, everything I've learnt in the past few months . . . She's in agreement . . . We've talked about the Movement: being part of it is important, it makes you feel good, it makes you feel like you're part of things, together with the others, the comrades . . . Maybe I'm turning into a Communist—and if so Father can go fuck himself . . . If he knew I was here, if he could only see me now . . . He knows all about the occupied departments, he reads the news in *his* newspaper . . . That newspaper is a piece of shit: the articles talk about bivouacs in the university departments, sex, orgies, they even went so far as to suggest we hold 'black masses' . . . What the fuck is a 'black mass'? A nice headline on the front page . . . I'd never really considered the issue of truth in newspapers—that is, I assumed they told the truth . . . Or at least that's what I thought about *Il Messaggero*. Mother reads it . . . Mother is Justice, Truth and Love, and so it can't be anything other than a *sincere* newspaper, a *good* newspaper . . . Instead it turns out that's not the case, things aren't that way . . . Nossir: concerning everything that's happened, things I've seen happen before my own eyes, completely different versions can be presented . . . I hardly ever used to read the newspaper and only the one I found at home and almost only local news, especially *Avventure in città*, "Adventures in the City", in dialect, it made me laugh . . . Now I buy the newspaper, I read it. I started buying *L'Espresso*, *L'Europeo* too . . . I know that we have *friendly* newspapers and *hostile* newspapers . . . The friendly ones are few in number, *Paese Sera* in particular, two editions a day, occasionally three, just a few pages and the minute you touch one your fingers are smeared with black ink, the movie pages are good . . . I buy it every night . . . Piazza del Popolo, full of cars like always . . .'

POLICE OUT OF THE UNIVERSITY!

'This piazza ought to be empty . . . This ought to be the piazza of the void and the nothingness, instead it's a parking lot . . . Traffic blocked solid . . . Just think how they're cursing us, the angry oaths . . . A complete traffic jam, it must be having ripple effects throughout half the city . . .'

'Do you know who was in the department when they arrived?'

'I don't know, not many—who?'

'I don't know . . . Apparently some people hid in there . . .'

'No, really?'

'So they say, apparently they managed to phone out, last night . . . They don't know how to get out, the Department of Architecture is cordoned off by lines of cops. If they catch them, they'll beat them bloody . . . So they're waiting for us . . .'

'But what can we do? It's not like we came here to beat other people up . . .'

'Stop talking bullshit, Brandani, we're going up to take back the Department of Architecture . . .'

THIS IS A PEACEFUL DEMONSTRATION!

'Stay together in rows of eight, at regular intervals, don't fall for any provocations! We're not here to pick fights, we're here to lodge a democratic protest against the police brutality at the university! The university belongs to the students! Today we must recognize that the struggle students have undertaken for a just, anti-authoritarian and anti-classist university is the target of a concerted, concentric attack from all of society's institutions, including the press and the media, including the political parties, an attack that yesterday took concrete form in the violent police intervention and the clearing of the Department of Architecture! The university belongs to us and we are going to take it back!'

'I haven't walked down this street in years: there's practically nothing here, just walls, the Ministry of the Navy, private homes . . . The Cinema Arlecchino, that old cinema with the strange, multi-colour marquee . . . I like the Cinema Arlecchino, as a cinema . . . I like all cinemas as cinemas, for that matter . . . Every day, a cinema, a movie, a promise of enjoyment . . . The sun rises, the air grows steadily hotter . . . There's this nice mild breeze . . . They stopped the Red Ring Route, the finest trolley line in the city, to let us through. There's a line of articulated trolleys waiting . . . Everyone is watching us, a few people applaud, but not many, all the others have mistrustful, pissed-off expressions on their faces: they have their lives to lead, they're not occupying anything, they're not engaged in the struggle, quite simply, they're minding their own fucking business . . . They're carrying on business as usual, moving from one point in the city to another for work, they're out doing their grocery shopping: they're plumbers professionals housewives couriers lawyers—proletarianized, exploited or else exploiters . . . As Franco likes to say: "What adventures await us, if we don't procure them for ourselves?" And what about me? What kind of life awaits me? What do I want to do? What am I? Who am I? Will I become like them? No, this is simply *not possible*, because before that happens, I'll hang myself, I'd rather jump in the river and drown . . . That is, unless Father, the Forger of All Things, doesn't kill me first . . . The factory workers won't do anything, their fate is to become members of the petty bourgeoisie. Marcuse wrote that. The affluent society redistributes income, you're being exploited but you feel rich and you aim at rising into another class . . . That's how they fuck you . . .'

'So they really stayed in there all night long? In hiding?'

'That's right. Or so they say. Roberto's in there, I heard . . . And a few others.'

'How many of them are there?'

'I don't know how many, just a few . . .'

'The tufa-stone ridge, beautiful, prehistoric, indifferent to everything: it's been here for hundreds of thousands of years . . . It's the erosion of the River that ate away at the hill, millennium after millennium, and that created these plateaus . . . Today at the base of the hill we can put petrol stations and it's fine all the same . . . "Environmental aesthetics is something reactionary, bourgeois. When the proletariat takes power it will take from nature everything it needs." Levelling archaic tufa-stone ridges, if necessary . . . It will bulldoze mountains, build gigantic hydroelectric power stations in futurist style . . . That's what will happen at first, then the futurists will be considered degenerate art, they'll all be purged, they'll die of hardships and starvation in the gulags, or they'll kill themselves, the new power stations will go up in neo-Gothic style . . . It will mean liberation from slavery to nature . . . "We need science to fight *against* nature," says Franco . . . The German Academy, with a Doric colonnade, very tough, in the style of the

Me-109, if you see what I mean . . . The British Academy, also neo-classical, but gentler, more graceful with Corinthian capitals, in the style of the Spitfire . . .'

'Fuck, those are carabinieri cars!'

'Where?'

'There, at the corner!'

'We're standing still, packed too tight . . . The people in the back are pushing forwards . . . There are armed men on that truck . . . Fuck, that's a *machine gun*. *A machine gun*! They showed up with *machine guns*!'

POLICE OUT OF THE UNIVERSITY!

POLICE OUT OF THE UNIVERSITY!

'The carabinieri remain behind us, at the intersection, above the escarpment of the department, on the plaza, all I see is pigs . . . I can recognize them by their heavy blue-grey overcoats, they look as if they'd just returned from the retreat out of Russia . . . I'm too close. I'm too jammed in with the others, the march is getting squeezed together . . . Not much air, there's no space. Everyone here is very aggressive, determined . . . The policemen up there are few in number, stumped, intimidated . . . Maybe they didn't expect such a big march . . . Steel helmets, white bandoliers, billy clubs, pistols on their belts. Here among us there's no one with a steel helmet . . . The comrades on the roof! Then it's true, they hid in the department, they spent the night, flying a red flag . . . There's Roberto, blond, tall and skinny, a second-rank leader, this is his moment . . .'

COMRADE POLICEMEN!

THIS STUDENT PROTEST MARCH HAS COME TO TAKE BACK THE DEPARTMENT OF ARCHITECTURE!

WE HAVE NOTHING AGAINST YOU!

LET ME REPEAT, WE HAVE NOTHING AGAINST YOU!

'They're starting! Up front they're starting to throw. They're throwing eggs at the policemen . . . They're pulling back, most of all they don't seem to want to get their overcoats dirty . . . They've run out of eggs, now those are . . . Those are cobblestones flying

303

through the air! A rain of cobblestones towards the plaza in front of the department . . . The policemen pull back again! Very young. They're just a few, frightened, the usual faces of peasants . . . They weren't expecting. They weren't expecting to be attacked . . . Everyone's shouting something, everyone seems very excited, the girls are shouting too . . . The pale-faced pigs reacted, urged on by their non-commissioned officers, the cobblestones fly back where they came from . . . God! They're falling on this compact crowd . . . Every cobblestone hits a head . . . Sharp-edged cubes of basalt, 6 inches on a side, super-heavy! They crack. They crack every head they hit, they sail down in search of human skulls to crack. They find them, they're killing people! Blood on the ground, oozing out of foreheads, from the backs of cracked skulls, like so many open taps . . . There's so much blood in a head . . .'

MURDERERS! MURDERERS! THE POLICE ARE MUR-DERERS!

'The demonstration starts off, half of them surge ahead . . . They go towards the British Academy . . . This half is holding back . . . Avoid. Avoid the cobblestones, defend yourself . . . Comrades running up the escarpment, comrades who rip the boards off the benches in the gardens, they used them as clubs, policemen backing away . . .'

'We've won! We're taking back the department!'

'That is, *they're* taking back the department . . . Not me, *they* . . . I'm way back here because I'm wetting my pants . . . The cobblestones . . . I can't do what they're doing . . . I'm not here for this, I don't know how to do this, I don't want to do this. That is, Brandani, *you'd like to do it*, but you're afraid . . . How do they manage to do it? My heart practically leaps up my throat, my legs go slack . . . Comrades, male and female, stretched out white as sheets on the ground, their heads shattered, their faces covered with blood that drips onto the ground, black dense dark drops . . . The Japanese Academy . . . Let's get this girl inside . . . She's bleeding like a fountain . . . I'm inside.'

'Puh-rease leave.'

'But can't you see she's badly hurt?'

'Puh-rease leave. Puh-rease leave.'

'Fuck you, are you deaf? Call an ambulance. Am-bu-lan-ce! Where is the telephone?'

'Here are more of them . . . Girls especially, they're being carried in in people's arms, their clothing in disarray, their skirts hiked up, pale, blood on their thighs, on their stockings, on their garter belts . . . You lack. You lack the courage to fight alongside your comrades, your legs are shaking, you're getting horny at the sight of the bare thighs of these poor wounded girls . . . You really are a piece of shit—do something . . . But what?'

'Puh-rease leave.'

'From the window you can see what a mess it is outside—there aren't many policemen . . . That's Franco . . . They're ripping slabs of travertine off the top of that low wall . . . They're throwing them. They're throwing them down, onto the roof of the paddy wagons . . . Crashes. Shouts. Gunshots. Smoke. Sirens. How can he do it? How does he manage?'

'Puh-rease leave.'

'How do they do it? How do they keep from running away? Where do they get the courage to do what they're doing? Why can they and I can't? If Father could see me . . . The first blood to trickle down my forehead since the Accident with the Bicycle . . . I was full to the brim with blood, all that was needed was a tiny puncture and the blood spurted out like a fountain . . .'

'I've got a handkerchief . . . It's clean, here, hold it tight.'

'It isn't a deep cut, don't cry, Beautiful Thighs, you aren't badly hurt, Thighs of Splendour . . . I'm leaving, I have to leave . . .'

'Puh-rease leave.'

'Sure. Sure, I'm leaving . . . If I turn right that will take me to where the fighting is going on, where my comrades are . . . Instead I turn left towards the main avenue, I take to my heels . . . The carabinieri paddy wagons . . . They're still parked here, they didn't wade into the fray . . . Now I'm going to get shot, I can smell the reek of burnt rubber . . . Running away down the hill, breathless, it's a miracle I can stay on my feet . . . Run away, run away, run away. Away from here . . . Away from this stuff I don't know how to do, away from the battle, away from courage, away from my comrades, away from my female comrades' bleeding thighs . . . There, I head uphill towards the Bridge . . . Lines of stopped trolley cars, traffic blocked solid . . . To walk along at a brisk pace, beyond the parapet the water of the River coming slowly, indifferently downstream . . . It was this same indifference that it cut through the plate of Pleistocenic tufa stone upon which the City rests . . . That was before all this happened, before I was put to the test, the way I was today . . . I ran away. Ran away. *I did.* Not the others, *me alone. I* ran away . . . The test was a failure . . . I can't stop myself, I just want to go home. Home. That's where my bedroom is, the Swedish furniture, there's my bed, the bedspread dotted with flowers, I'll shut myself in, I'll lower the blinds, I'll lie down, I'll go to sleep . . . I'll walk home . . . There's the Drinking Fountain Where I Beat Up Nasini—the water in this city is ice cold . . . It's dripping down my shirt, onto my tie . . . I want to shut myself up in my room, lock the door behind me, stretch out on my bed, put on a record . . . Street fighting's not for me . . . I wasn't really certain that I was a coward. I was almost convinced I wasn't one, but until today I never really knew for sure . . .

'The Moto Guzzi Trotter is hard on your ass, no rear suspension, you have to look out for potholes, the seat vibrates directly against your prostate: I have a prostate, after all, just like the one they removed on Grampa Paolo . . . The usual cops out here, paddy wagons, tour buses full of officers . . . This tall, horrible, intimidating, Fascist colonnade . . . Franco says that the idea of culture that the university still transmits has remained unchanged since they first built this crap . . . "It's something empty, bourgeois, for privileged morons—but high school's even worse," he says . . . "Classical high school pumps you full of an idealistic and obscurantist vision of culture, of the world and of relations between human beings and social classes. And that's the hard core of our formation—you see all these people who are here? Me, even you,

we're all impregnated with this humanistic & metaphysical crap—
just so much bullshit . . . We grew up in the cult of emotions, we
chose to major in Philosophy in compliance with the culture that
inculcated us, stuff that was perfect for building the false consciousness that we're going to use for the rest of our lives, in the
management of that thin slice of power of which we are share-
holders inasmuch as privileged members of the bourgeoisie, or in
as much as we are petty bourgeois busy climbing the social ladder
even now . . . To the children of the proletariat, and I'm talking
about the few who even attend, high school teaches them to forget
the only thing that a factory worker really needs, class consciousness . . .' The other day, these were Franco's deductions, out front
of the university campus . . . It's late . . . This pergola-covered gal-
leria has always given me a strange impression, from the very first
day I set foot in here . . . The Bronze Statue, the Fountain . . . A
nightmare of lines leading up to the teller windows of the various
secretaries—in order to enrol I had to come back two or three different times and each time I was missing something: a form hadn't
been filled out, the processing fees . . . A hellish stack of bills to
pay, the people from the agencies that simply step up to the front
of the line and shove a packet ahead of everyone else . . . The floor
is filthy, but so are the floors in public offices everywhere . . . There
they all are, the piazza is full of them . . . The steps in front of the
department, black with people, dotted with patches of red . . . The
crowd is black, it's always black, but here there are little flags . . .
They're all males, or nearly all, they have beards, long hair. The
long hair of our Italian males—curly, kinky . . . My hair seems like
lint, the kind of fine hairs you find under the bed when no one
cleans . . . Dark heavy jackets, here and there green parkas . . .
Black attracts, it relieves you of all individual chromatic responsibility . . . And yet if I asked each of these guys what was his
favourite colour, not many of them would tell me "black" . . . Here
there's also red, a lot of red: black and red and olive drab—these
are the colours of the Movement . . . There's a hell of a lot of people
inside the university, today . . . And a hell of a lot of police outside
. . . A national assembly of the Movement, even middle school

students came, kids from Bertazzi especially, which would have been the natural school for me to go to, if Father & Mother hadn't decided to send me to that fucked-up religious boarding school. Who knows why they sent me there? Maybe because Big Sister had a bad time at Bertazzi? She always said that it was *too diffi-cult*: 'The principal is a Communist, he goes everywhere with *L'Unità* in his pocket, folded specially so you can read the name, the teachers are too demanding and what's more, they're all Communists,' Big Sister used to say . . . Just imagine what kind of an opinion my folks must have gathered about Bertazzi: that wasn't the kind of school to send any son of theirs, especially now that Father had made money and we were all so utterly respectable . . . I had to put up with that shitty school for five years . . . A bunch of people on the department steps . . . Italian tricolour flags outside of Law! Are they Fascists? Are the Fascists here too? The police at the front gate must have let them in . . . They've always been in cahoots, the Fascists and police—no daylight between them. The tricolour flag at this point is strictly a Fascist thing . . . Better. Better to climb up on the steps, if I can do it. Here on the right, a con-struction site . . . There's a bit of room . . . Long greasy hair, every-where, and they're all standing here: Why? There's no one that I know . . .'

'What's happening?'

'The Fascists! They want to get in here. There's Almirante and even Caradonna. They've holed up at the School of Law, but now you'll see they're coming . . .'

WE URGE THE COMRADES TO REMAIN TOGETHER! COMRADES, DON'T GIVE IN TO PROVOCATIONS!

'It's true, Almirante is there, supervising operations . . . Distinguished . . . Elegant, in his overcoat, a member of the parlia-ment of the Italian Republic, hat on his head, it seems that he finds being here vaguely distasteful . . . Caradonna, there he is now! If he's here it means they're planning to beat us up . . . Slovenly, he gesticulates . . . Those flagpoles, all identical, long and thick as shovel handles . . . Those are just clubs for hitting people. Nasty. These Fascists here are nasty, scary too . . . These aren't Fascists from the nice part of town, these are lower-class thugs, ex-cons, older men . . . These aren't students, they've never been students in their lives—they're here because they're paid to be here, they're professionals . . . My legs start trembling. What. What should I do? Should. Should I move? But where? There's not much room . . . For some time now, everywhere I go blood seems to flow . . . I hate blood.'

FASCISTS OUT OF THE UNIVERSITY!

'Here they are, they've ripped the banners off the poles . . . They're pale, their faces are cold and old. They're afraid & they're brave, there are a lot more of us than there are of them. It's all organized . . . Here they come. Here they come at a run . . . The blows to the head that the comrades up front are taking! The blood, here we go again, with blood oozing down faces. Comrades passing out, female comrades screaming . . . They're beating up women—Communists, and therefore whores . . . Blows with flag-poles, insults, they're shouting at them. They're shouting "Whore!" at them. But I. I'm not beating anyone up, I don't want to beat anyone up, I don't want anyone to beat me up. Too afraid . . . Once again breathless and once again this terror of seeing blood ooze down my forehead—I need to keep it far away, my head, far away from hard objects, metal, rock, sharp edges . . . Because it can get fractured, you can feel the hard bone against other hard things, hard objects . . . But *they're* not afraid, the Fascists and the comrades aren't afraid . . . *I'm* afraid, they aren't . . . Here. Here there's a space, I can get away from this mess . . . The comrades are fighting back, they're converging in this direction . . . Here they come, marching fully armed out of the department, clubs, army helmets, motorcycle helmets, hard hats . . . Look, there's Franco!'

'Stay together! Don't let yourselves get isolated! Be careful, don't become a straggler, or these guys will kill you!'

'He's in charge, like always. He commits himself in person, like always. Cool, like always. Courageous, like always. He reasons, like always . . . Out in front . . . It's a horrible mess with clubs and dust . . . A few seconds of fury, crashes, shouts . . .'

FASCISTS OUT OF THE UNIVERSITY! FASCISTS OUT OF
THE UNIVERSITY!

'These guys are common criminals, who-knows-who hired
them, thugs paid to hurt us, and I mean hurt us badly . . . It's the
whole front steps of the Literature Building, crowded with students, lunging forwards . . . The Fascists can't take the weight,
they're retreating . . . They're taking to their heels! They're running
away!'

FASCISTS-WRONGDOERS-BACK-INTO-THE-SEWERS!

'They're giving ground, but they're not leaving, they're
retreating towards the School of Law. Fascists . . . This is going to
turn ugly! Almirante unruffled, off to one side . . . With his overcoat, hat on his head . . . Caradonna will take of directing his men
. . . Down off the steps, Ivo, head for the holm oaks . . . A bunch
of kids, roaming around here, come from high schools all over the
city, look how young they are . . . Is that what I looked like just
three years ago? Was I that little? They're scared but they're not
as scared as I am . . . I'm here without being here, I'm taking part
without doing anything, saying anything, helping in any way—I'm
always there and I'm never there. "You're not the only one, there
are lots of other comrades who show up regularly but don't get
involved. It's because you're gaining consciousness," says Franco,
"until yesterday you were just another apathetic student, today
you're building a political position all your own, you're taking part
in your fashion . . . But don't turn into a fanatic on me, that's not
who you are . . ." What does he think he knows about my real
nature? He doesn't know that I'm crazy like Father, but you can
only see the craziness when it's very hot, or when I'm feeling humiliated, when I have no escape route—at times like that I could even
kill . . . I'm a rude beast, I've always got into fistfights, on the street,
when I was a boy, when I used to go the parish afterschool. Even
then I was afraid but I knew how to fight back . . . "That's right,
exactly. It's because you're only capable of private, ancestral,
biblical violence, an eye for an eye . . . You only know to conceive
of violent action as a way of settling your personal rage, violence
as a vendetta, instead of as a civil, political act." The fact that I

don't lunge into the fray, that is, I don't have the slightest intention of doing so, it's not because I'm wetting my pants in fear, it's that I'm not pissed off enough . . . And do you believe it? I've seen many comrades who enjoy themselves in the clashes, have no problems, don't seem to be either pissed off or anything at all—as if were a chore to be got out of the way, to be done carefully, maybe, to avoid getting hurt too badly . . . Father is capable of cold, silent, murderous rage, but also hot, fanatical, out-of-control fury, which is what he saves just for me . . . Franco doesn't seem pissed off, or even emotional, ever . . . And yet there he is, with a hard hat on his head, a lead pipe in his hands . . . Almirante has vanished: he unleashed his men and now he can leave, unseemly to let himself be seen together with his thugs . . . From here, from beneath the holm oaks, you can see the entrance to the School of Law, the Fascists have entered the building and they've barricaded themselves inside . . . A group of comrades with helmets and clubs who want to break down the front door . . . It's a medieval siege . . . The besiegers lunge towards the doors, trying to break them down with the lumber from the construction site . . . The people inside, under siege, looking down from windows and terraces, toss objects over to keep them from breaking in . . . They throw things down. They throw things down that are heavy enough to kill you: chairs, desks, beechwood cabinets all fall to the ground . . . Even filing cabinets. Metal filing cabinets! How can it have come to this point? What is the basis, what are the reasons for all this hatred? The people under siege are grey-faced, pallid, bewildered by fear . . . They didn't expect their adversaries to fight back so fiercely . . . These are professional hitters, head-crackers accustomed to brawls, but now they're shitting their pants—they figured they were dealing with a bunch of mama's boys with no fight in them, incapable of lashing back, maybe they just didn't realize how many of us there were . . . The comrades are trying anyway, to knock down the doors . . . They're under a hail of furniture! They're going to get themselves killed! They have. They've hit him square on! Oreste! A bench! Right on the back! It plunged straight into his back, falling vertically. Slicing like a blade. He's on the ground! He's dead! A shout . . . A shout goes up from all of us . . . He can't have survived that, it's impossible! They grab him by his legs and arms, rapidly, four or five guys drag him away from there . . . He's white in the face, like a dead man . . . Shouts explosions screams sirens . . . Cheers, someone shouts that the police are arriving . . . Here they are, they've entered the university campus . . . They're not charging, they're not swinging their billy clubs . . . They head straight towards the School of Law, and there are a lot of them . . . The siege has been interrupted, the besiegers are regrouping, they collect tables to hold over their heads, for protection. The pigs are arriving . . . They've come to save the Fascists' asses! They're here to rescue the Fascists, to help them get away scot-free . . . The applause continues, hard to say whether ironically or not . . . Just as well, the clash was too ferocious primitive unbearable . . . Oreste is dead, he can't be anything but dead, as hard as he was hit. It's like he snapped in two . . . The clashes with the Fascists—the age-old hatred has once again risen, we're taking on old feuds our fathers failed to settle.'

'Have we lost our minds? We're applauding the police now?'

'Get out of here, Ivo, leave . . . The comrades are organizing who-knows-what protest march . . . They never seem to get enough . . . The entrance is still being guarded by about a million cops . . . Get your Moto Guzzi Trotter—there it is, right there, the ass-busting Trotter.'

'This huge rectangular piazza, today . . . The comrades arrested, the ones who are still behind bars, the other ones who've been released but are still looking at a trial and maybe jail time. Let's have a demonstration of solidarity. What they did, we all did, we could say . . . Yes, but I didn't do it . . . We're all guilty—only I'm not . . . All the same, I stand with them, united against repression . . . "We need repression, it serves our purpose," says Franco. Anyway, they're putting us in the thick of things, and then some, the national elections are going to be in less than a month . . . "That's not anything that concerns us," many say, "we're *beyond that*." Or perhaps, "*elsewhere*". Some of them talk about "voting tactically" for the

Communist Party . . . If you ask me, the Communists don't want our votes, that is, *officially* they don't want them. I'm going to be voting for the very first time . . . Pothole! The Trotter isn't made for vertebrates . . . The demonstration starts out from the university campus and runs all the way through the centre of the city . . . They'll break some plate-glass windows before they get here: the central office of some bank or other, a few shops . . . No thanks, been there, done that . . . But Franco is one of the comrades who might be looking at jail time: on 1st March they arrested him, charged him, and released him. So now here I am . . . Down there is a pretty sizeable group of cops . . . And it's a sunny day, spring has sprung, I'll chain my two-wheeled beast here, among the other bikes . . . Hmmm, is this a little too close to the piazza? Oh well, what the worst that could happen? It's a demonstration outside the Hall of Justice, against the attorney general, there are no physical targets . . . Still, there's just a little too much of a police presence . . . The gardens are full of comrades: streamers-megaphone-slogans, the whole contraption is already operating . . . I wonder where the Movement finds the money—it's not a lot of stuff, but still someone has to pay for it, just passing the hat isn't going to do it . . . Or is it?'

FREE THE ARRESTED COMRADES!

'There's a row of campaign posters standing perpendicular: modular structural tubing, galvanized sheet metal wired in place . . . From here you can't see a thing, you'd have to venture further in, but at the centre of the gardens there is this huge monument to the founder of the fatherland . . . So I move further over, onto the pavement in front of the Hall of Justice . . . There we are in the front line, there's a relaxed atmosphere, if it hadn't been for those guys down there, in rank and file behind the hedges below the Hall of Justice, they're in camouflage jumpsuits, armed . . . Who the fuck are they? What do they want? Better get out of here, Brandani . . . A few of the ones who were arrested still have bandaged heads, they're off to one side, they're uneasy, worried, solidarity is a fine thing, but they don't want to be painted as recidivists . . . Several of them have been gone for weeks—word is that in the past few days on the ski slopes there were a lot of bandaged heads. That they weren't proletarian was a well-known fact but, for the love of Christ, going to recuperate in a ski resort . . . Franco, on the other hand, is here, in the front line . . . He looks serious, concerned, in a jacket and tie, he knows there's a chance he'll wind up behind bars . . . They're using the megaphone to harangue the crowd with a sort of summation against the prosecuting attorney who's been assigned to the investigation . . . He gives me a hug.'

'*Ciao*, Ivo.'

'The piazza is full of comrades, no one is acting aggressive, there are only a few streamers, flags, banners, many of them have friends who've been caught up in the investigation, no one wants a clash . . . Except for maybe a few assholes among the ones who came down through the whole centre of town throwing rocks through plate glass windows . . . No one is moving, everything's cool . . . Don't be tense, Ivo, today nobody here is tense . . . In a little while we'll leave.'

'. . . this is no laughing matter, Ivo, these guys are playing for keeps . . . Even though they say they're being pressured to drop the case. On 1st March we kicked up such a ruckus that they're going to remember it for a long time. But the wounded officers, the burnt paddy wagons . . . Did you know that they caught me on the trolley?'

'I know. They stopped all the trolleys on the Ring Route and rounded up everyone under age thirty that was riding on them, something that not even the Gestapo in 1943 . . .' Franco goes on: 'They have a bunch of photos, they charged me on the basis of the photos. You know the slabs of travertine we threw onto the paddy wagons? They also got me while I was helping to overturn a car. Then we set it on fire too, but I had already moved on. Property damage, I don't remember exactly what the legal terminology is . . . This is the moment of repression, the Movement is weakened, fragmented, the elections are coming up—that's the crucial point. Whether they want to present themselves as a law and order government or as appeasers and mediators. You know that Oreste came out alive. He's in a cast from head to foot, everything but his

314

legs, actually, but he can walk. He was so lucky . . . There's too many cops here, I don't like the smell. I'm slipping out of here, Ivo, if they pick me up again, I'm fucked, *ciao*.'

'*Ciao*, Franco, I'll give you a call . . .'

'The plain-clothes cop out front is putting on an armband, he must be an officer detective . . . He's saying something, the bugler is lifting his horn . . . I'd better get to one side, these guys are about to charge . . . There they are! Get out of here! Out of here! Out of here!!!'

REJECT ALL PROVOCATIONS! THIS IS A PEACEFUL DEMONSTRA . . .

'They're charging . . . Sons of bitches . . . Here they come. They're coming straight at us, heading for the bulk of the comrades, grouped in the centre of the gardens . . . Get out of here, Brandani, run, run . . . A premeditated attack, this time they're planning to do some damage . . . Christ, enough's enough, I don't want anything to do with this mess any more . . . The campaign billboards! They're blocking the way for everyone trying to run . . . People are getting jammed up against them! Someone's going to get hurt on that sheet metal . . . They're breaking through, girls tripping and falling on the fine gravel, dust . . . This way. Towards this side of the piazza, it's quiet here, people are standing outside the cafes, enjoying the show . . . None of the comrades is able to fight back, but now they're ripping the legs off the metal chairs at the Bar del Teatro, two guys at a time, they're ripping them off at the base, now they're swinging them like clubs . . . But they can't take the impact . . . A running retreat down the street . . . The pigs are stopping to club the comrades in the gardens, they're taking their time about it, the others are running in all directions . . . There we go again, faces covered with blood . . . Again . . . I'm getting out of here, my moped is parked at the corner . . . If they decide to make a barricade they might burn it . . . I have to get it out of here . . . I don't have anything to do with all this craziness, it's not for me, I'm scared of it . . . Again. Again I'm breathless, my legs turn to jelly, my heart is pounding against my clavicle . . . There it is, the Trotter, right in the middle of a herd of policemen all suited up. Back in the piazza the beatings are continuing . . . The comrades are forming a defensive line further up . . . Here come the cops in camouflage jumpsuits! The street is clear, shop doors locked, shutters rolled down, I'll get out of here this way . . . I stop, now I can stop, no one's after me. Better head back there, act like I don't have anything to do with this, get my moped and get out of here . . . I'm wearing a jacket, jeans and a beard, they might let me through . . . These guys are heading towards me . . . The first one is kind of old, he must be an officer of some kind, they're not wearing helmets, nothing . . . He looks like a reasonable sort . . . Walk normally, Ivo, you're an ordinary citizen . . . What the fuck is this guy doing? Christ, a handgun! He's waving a gun! He's aiming it at me!'

'I'll kill you all, you sons of bitches . . . I'll kill you . . . Hey, who are you? Come here, you bastard, come here . . .'

'He's moving slowly, he's fat, he's wheezing, white as a sheet, his lips are blue . . . If I run he can't catch me, but he's waving a gun! This guy's going to. This guy's going to kill me . . . There's another one right behind him . . . He's putting a hand on his shoulder, he's restraining him . . . Better not. Better not run . . . You remember Rex, if you ran he'd chase you, he'd jump up and put his paws on your shoulders, from behind, he'd knock you down . . . Never run . . . An open apartment-building door, that's what I need . . . Way down there the comrades are putting cars sideways, they're throwing cobblestones in this direction . . . An apartment-building door left ajar . . . I dart in, I close it behind me . . . I have to get out of here, those guys could come in, the officer with the handgun, he'll kill me! Lift, top floor, then I'll come down the stairs and see what I find . . . Sixth, down I go, fifth fourth third, a notary's office . . . Pebbled glass door, open . . . The waiting room is full of comrades, male and female, terrorized by this unprompted, criminal police charge . . . There are people who just happened to be in the street too, some aren't even students. No one here has any problem with us being here. A notary who's a comrade? There's a window overlooking the street, let's take a look . . . They've gone past, now it's the barricade at the end of the street that they're interested in . . . If I stay here, they'll catch me when they go door to door . . . It was a planned assault, they want to make us pay for 1st March! Franco was right, as usual: "They're going to make us pay for this, sooner or later. They can't let us just get away with it. We won. They're going to ask the minister to give them a free hand and they'll pay us back every cent, with compound interest." There's no one around the parking area—I'm leaving, going down the stairs . . . No problem. Walk nice and slow, look around curiously . . . There, that's right, mind your own fucking business . . . Those guys. Those guys at the end of the street are setting fires . . . Unlock the chain, get on the Trotter, pull the choke, pedal, depress the choke, there it's started . . . Away, wind on your face . . . Away away. Today they could have. Today they could have killed me. No one would have done anything to that guy, they wouldn't even have put him on trial . . . He would have retired, a beach house somewhere. He'd be on the water's edge catching clams, I'd be in my grave. These guys can do whatever they want to you, no one'll touch them . . . Wind . . . They can legally murder you . . . Wind on my face! I, Ivo Brandani, officially declare that I'm scared, that I want to live, that I need time to become a fish, according to plan . . . This is the last time anyone's going to see me at a demonstration . . . Never again . . .'

That day, what Ivo had foreseen did in fact happen. After the clashes, all the students who had taken refuge in apartment buildings, in lobbies, in courtyards, on apartment-building terraces, in the garbage rooms, in the basements, in the spaces under the staircases, in a circumference of 500 yards from the piazza were swept up for hours and the students beaten bloody, one by one, methodically, to make sure no head remained uncracked. Two hundred of them were taken into custody and conveyed to the police station, their details noted down, and not released until quite late at night. A few of them were actually charged.

In the weeks that follow, things relax. But what's happening in Paris is important, in fact, unprecedented. Impossible to imagine that such things might happen here, in Paris they know something about barricades. Here everything grows smaller and eventually dwindles and extinguishes itself, the Movement still exists, but so do final exams. Negotiations with the faculty to agree on the political passing grade. Ivo disagrees with it.

'If you do one thing, you can't do the other . . . If you're going to start a revolution, you can't expect the powers that be are going to stamp it APPROVED.'

'Wrong, Ivo, in part because, and you know this perfectly well, we *haven't started and we're not about to start any revolution* . . . The Movement declared it from the very start, it's already there in the November platform: the political work in the in-depth groups, in the committees, in the seminars would be considered *study* to all intents and purposes, for the purposes of the final exam as well. If you want to take the traditional exam, go right ahead. We certainly wouldn't try to stop you . . . That is, actually, I couldn't say about that: if you show up all alone to take your exam, you're sure to find someone who will call you a scab, they might even beat you up . . .'

Franco maintains that this issue of the political grade on the exam is a key point, that it's an official recognition on the part of the university as an institution of the cultural, 'that is, legal', value of the struggle and that it sanctions the principle of student self-determination on the topics and the subjects to be studied. The faculty has different views, but on the whole it is willing to negotiate.

'Basically, the political struggles have blocked all teaching, we can't make the working students lose the year . . . That's not all: their grades can't endanger their grade point average, which is important for their scholarships—so high grades . . .'

The state of tension is still high, there are few people in the department. In early June the police clear the building once again. Bob Kennedy is assassinated, shot, just like Martin Luther King, in April.

'American imperialism and capitalism—which are the same thing—won't tolerate backpedalling. They've physically eliminated anyone who constituted a threat, real or perceived. Let it be a lesson to us all,' says Franco in the assembly, 'we should never forget that capitalism will stop at nothing in order to defend its own interests. That's not a slogan, comrades: things that have happened in and around America have once again demonstrated that that's exactly the way things stand. It is necessary for the Movement to conduct an in-depth analysis of the situation of the Peninsula within the American sphere of influence. In any case it's always a good idea to understand that there will be no tolerance on the part of the Americans for any shift in the political configuration of the country. In other words, for Christ's sake, *this is Yalta*, comrades! Anyone who forgets that is making a serious error . . . It's important to understand that, if in Vietnam the anti-imperialist forces succeed in opposing the American aggression, it's not only because are they relegated to an outlying area of the Western Empire but also because they are being massively supported by the two largest social-imperialist powers: Russia and China. Here in Italy, the situation is completely different, any modification of the existing equilibrium will be met with an unrestrained reaction . . .'

And so on. Ivo had never really given it any serious thought, but ever since he's read the movement's holy scriptures, this seems to be an uncontestable truth to him: *we are an American colony*. Negotiations with the faculty arrive at an agreement over the protocols for the political grade, even though not all the professors accept the terms. Ivo sees Summer drawing closer and Real Life opening out before him, as it does every year. He's sick of politics. In Paris they've evacuated the Sorbonne. De Gaulle called in the tanks, then he won the early elections. People in France don't want to even hear about revolution. In the return to normality, Ivo senses a subtle and unconfessable sweetness, even though the situation at the university really is changing.

'In a certain sense, we've won,' says Franco.

Yes, it's true. In a certain sense, they've won.

In the end he manages to wheedle a politically negotiated B+ out of Molteni. He showed up for the exam saying: 'I studied, and I want to take the exam. But I won't take a different grade from the rest of my comrades.' Molteni replied flatly: 'No, if you want to take a *real* exam, then you have to be willing to take a *real* grade.' Ivo was struck dumb. Making this preliminary statement seemed to him to be a good idea: he'd make a good impression on Molteni without having to give up being thought a member of the Movement. Molteni's determined answer confused him, he stammered something incoherent and blushed violently. In short, he gave up the idea and got in line for his politically negotiated B+. All he had to do was hand his grade book to a teaching assistant, who gave it back to him at the end of the morning with a grade and a signature. There was a wave of euphoria and embarrassment among the students: getting a grade on a university exam without having had to study. Ivo decides that it was an inevitable but slightly depressing outcome. Like many others, he missed the opportunity to attend Molteni's lessons, to absorb his teachings. He buys a few books to fill that void but it's not the same thing— Molteni writes differently from how he talks, more complicated, a little woolly: 'He's a talking genius,' someone told him.

The Movement has demonstrated unexpected strength, it's changing the face of the university, wrote the political analysts in the newspapers. The majority of the commentators add 'for the worse', naturally. Ivo Brandani knows that it isn't true, but all the same, he's confused, bewildered: so far the access to knowledge that he'd naively expected from his university studies has eluded him. It's been denied him, pilfered, and postponed to some date yet to be determined. All the same, it's been an important year, but not in the sense that he was expecting at the beginning, something much bigger than him dragged him with it in a very different direction, he saw and learnt many things, all together, about himself and about the others. He needs to digest them, he needs some time off. He saw the mechanisms of dominance and submission at work, even among his comrades. He saw the force of the collective spirit in action, he watched the establishment of power groups, he saw the struggle to dominate within the Movement, he saw the duplicity, he saw the cynicism of a few exploiting the naivety of others. He saw a few work very hard but with an eye to their future academic careers. The university system immediately expressed interest in the most brilliant and dangerous leaders. They understood it immediately. He knows comrades who are preparing to head north: they're going to where there are factories 'to keep from being ghettoized inside the university'. It's called 'political work'—this is the first time that Ivo has heard this expression—and there are some who seem determined to devote themselves to it body and soul from now on. The Birds set out on foot in the opposite direction, they're heading south, towards the territories devastated by the earthquake. Two different ways of going in search of so-called reality. For Ivo it has been a year of massive initiation, a sort of school from which he has the sensation he has learnt nothing, because at the end of June he's more confused than he was before. He doesn't feel the impulse to devote himself to politics, that's a temptation that never so much as grazes him, but his intentions are no longer very clear to him. 'Can I go back to studying philosophy as if nothing had happened?' Events have overwhelmed him and crushed him underfoot, but he's secretly still convinced that the world is waiting to carry him in triumph, it's just a matter of time now.

The Movement turned him inside out like a glove, it shocked him, it filled him with doubts. For the first time in his life, he's taken part in something, he's entered a network of interpersonal relations, he heard speeches and conversations that covered a broad spectrum of views, he read new books and essays, but he lost Molteni. In July, last session of exams. After the political B+ in Theoretical Philosophy, Ivo takes a supplementary exam and gets another B+. He's increasingly perplexed: 'What am I doing here, amid all these philosophers? What do I really care about philosophy?'

Clara, on the other hand, has no doubts, in spite of the Movement, and she's been charging straight ahead. She takes two exams, gets an A and an A+, she's planning to take a third. They see each other practically every day, in the car, in the early afternoon, when Father usually takes a nap and Ivo takes the Fiat 600, or occasionally the 1800, and parks it not far from where she lives. Clara arrives punctually and they talk, they kiss, they feel each other up. It's hot out. For sex, things are a little different, more challenging, the opportunities are more infrequent: at her place when her folks aren't home, in the car at night parked somewhere, in Clara's little beach house, secretly. Every time it's like starting over from scratch, there's a thrill of discovery that twists his gut with anxiety. Clara doesn't have problems of any kind, if anything, Ivo has them. She's confident, he's much less so, but Clara drives him literally crazy—there's only her body her smell her hair her breath her mouth, there's only her. If they can't manage to see each other, then there are long evening phone calls that piss his Father off, when he finds him on the phone in the hallway, sitting on the floor for hours. 'Go on, go on, after all it's me that's paying. What the heck do you care?' This coming summer Ivo wants to go camping in the south. Clara makes an improbable, strange suggestion: a trip to Scotland, alone, just the two of them. Why Scotland? She doesn't know what to say: 'Because Scotland is Scotland. I don't know, to travel, instead of sitting parked in one place, baking in the sun, to have a destination, to get out of the heat of this year, to be alone just the two of us, because getting there in a Fiat 500 will be fun . . . Did you know that this year everyone's going where you want to go? The whole Movement is going to the Archipelago, Ivo. A nightmare. I don't want to talk about politics all summer . . .' 'Get away from the sea, the water, the Summer, the Sacred aquatic Summer? Lose a whole Mediterranean Summer? All right . . . If that's what Clara wants, it's fine with me . . .' It's the thrill of having her all to himself. 'OK, let's go.' Ivo doesn't have much money, Clara is going to have more money than him, during the year she's helped out in a legal firm, doing some typing. They'll leave around July 20th or 25th, one week after the exams. They'll take the car as far as Calais, then ferryboat, then London, then Edinburgh, Glasgow, then up north, who knows where.

Meanwhile Ivo, with great effort, is reading Georg Simmel in German, his essays on aesthetics. He forces himself to do it because Molteni has always urged them to read the authors in their original language and because he wants to take advantage of the five years he spent studying German in school while all the others his age were learning English. Simmel, like all German culture from the years between the World Wars, is fashionable. Franco recommended him, though not this book, which hasn't been translated yet. He ordered a copy from the German bookstore, the volume includes a very brief essay, *Brücke und Tür* (*Bridge and Door*), four or five very dense pages that sweep him away. Simmel is no walk in the park, but he's not as challenging as many German philosophical authors, he thinks he can understand it, he applies himself, he studies it, he is struck by it, fascinated. In *Bridge and Door* he finds something unexpected, something that leads him to think, it's a very simple formulation, which strikes him as the basic conjunction of the human activity of *thinking* and that of *doing*, practically a definition of what it means to be human beings in the world:

In an immediate sense just as in a symbolic sense, in a physical as well as a spiritual sense we are, at each moment, the ones who separate what is connected and connect what is separate.

The activity of connecting/separating coincides with thinking, *it is* thought, Ivo says to himself and he continues with his speculation: 'When we think, all we are doing is continuously disassembling and reassembling data until we find some meaning, some sense— philosophy is incessantly that . . . It is in an argumentative way, sometimes even only intuitive, approximate, poetic . . . It is almost always gratuitous, because it can't actually be falsified. Science too is a continual dismantling/reassembling/acquisition of data, but in the sense of exactitude, reproducibility, making something a common heritage . . . Between science and making there is technology and prior to this is the will to make. Now then . . . Only in technology, in a concrete creation, does the activity of philosophical thought materially find completion—connect what is separate and vice versa: "Only for us the are banks of the river not merely in different places but 'divided'." And the activity of scientific thought is to define the physical conditions in which what is thinkable is also possible . . .'

Perhaps it's Father's incessant pressure, his own secret need to do as Father wishes, that makes him read Simmel's words as a revelation. He convinces himself that the highest, most abstract form of thought, and at the same time the most concrete and visible, accessible, useful one, is that of the *pontifex*, that is, the builder, the maker of bridges, the overcomer of dis-continuities, real & undeniable. He had read somewhere that the *pontifex* was an authority who was at once spiritual, administrative and technical . . . The very existence of the City of God is based on the human capacity to see the two banks of the River as *divided* and therefore the determination to *re-unite them* with a passageway, a contrivance, a technical invention capable of giving concrete form to the unifying philosophical intuition. The Ancestral Bridge was a territorial singularity so powerful that it was capable of transforming itself into a city and subsequently into the capital of a great empire . . . Ivo Brandani isn't giving the slightest thought to the possibility of becoming an engineer, of changing his major: 'It would be a nightmare to work with Father. He wants me to work for his company, he does everything he can think of to get his paws on me so he can continue his process of demolition . . . But I'll never be there for him.' For his part, Father doesn't know that he's already demolished his son. The wounds that he has inflicted on him are critical, but they're still hidden, they can't be seen. They'll emerge later, it won't take much to reveal them. Perhaps even now—in that secret malaise, in the feelings he has of being inadequate and cowardly, in the slight but constant weakness of his spirit—it is possible to read the first signs of them.

They leave Edinburgh, they take the A90 and head for the Highlands. They want to continue north, arrive where the land ends and the Ocean begins, but right now they don't really know where they're going, it's early afternoon, they've slept late, they never seem able to get up a little earlier, they always seem to get up at the very last minute, when most of the morning is already gone. It's a long, uncomfortable, youthful trip, and it's a lot of fun. The Fiat 500 runs like a clock, Ivo soon learns to drive on the left side of the road, Clara has a harder time with it, for now she lets him do the driving. They passed through London. They found a bed-and-breakfast on Marylebone Road, the owner was a skinny man with yellow teeth, the toenails on his sandal-shod yellow feet, a yellow face. Tours of the conventional sights: British Museum, Tate Gallery, National Gallery, Piccadilly Circus, Oxford Street, Tower of London, etc. Once they're done with this, they didn't know where to go, nothing else occurred to them. After a couple of days they left for Cambridge, which they really liked. Clara noticed that the parks were full of chicory. 'Doesn't anyone pick it?' It was cold and rainy. 'What the fuck are we doing here? Do you know?' she said. All they have to keep warm is a sweater and a jeans jacket each. Then the weather improved and they got on the highway heading north. Edinburgh made no particular impression on them.

Last night they ate at a *steak house* (they mentally italicized the new, all-too-English terms). The pork chop was stringy, the *chips* had been fried more than once. Cheap, and not worth it. The beer churned the food into a clump in their stomachs. When they went back to the *bed-and-breakfast* they put a coin into the radio in the room, lay down in the bed to smoke a cigarette and drink a mini bottle of whisky specially purchased to neutralize the after-effects of the *steak house*. On the radio they heard a piece of music Ivo had never listened to before; he found it breathtakingly beautiful. It's Rodrigo's *Concierto de Aranjuez*, Clara says. Ivo was a little drunk, in a strange state of mind, a sort of expectation, of ultimate tenderness about something, about the two of them being there, beneath the Northern rain. A sense of farewell, or of departure, something he couldn't really say. He felt like crying, the music helped him. Clara said: 'My brother has a jazz version by Miles Davis. Do you know it?' 'No,' Ivo replied and, from the way he said it, Clara realized that right then and there he was about to start crying, she asked him, 'What is it?' and he said, 'Nothing, I don't know, I had whisky, it's this music . . .' She threw her arms around him, they made love until very late.

They woke up in time for breakfast, then back to bed and then they rushed out just before noon, to keep from having to pay for another night's stay. Now they're on the A90 heading north, a little bit fucking-randomly, distractedly, as they've been doing till now.

Clara is at the wheel, she'd asked him if she could drive.

'Let's say you get tired or something happen, maybe at night, I have to be capable of driving,' she told him. It makes Ivo nervous, but Clara does pretty well, the real problems are going to be turns at intersections.

'In a little while we're going to come to a bridge. There's a bridge over the Firth of Forth,' says Ivo, bent over the roadmap. The road curves to the right, climbs imperceptibly, narrows, and then before them loom the spidery, towering piers of a huge suspension bridge. Now the road is already rising high over the houses, over the water, the deck runs a couple of miles in length. Two huge suspension cables rise towards the top of the piers, the whole thing is extremely light, the immense stays are almost invisible against the perennially threatening clouds of this part of the world. The sun illuminates the landscape with dappled patches of gold. Clara starts across the bridge at low speed, she's cautious, uncertain, she too wants to see the Forth. Ivo looks to the right and not far off he sees another bridge, also made of metal, with a strange, antiquated appearance. It seems to be made of three enormous latticed cantilevers made of light steel. It's a red, extremely long, enigmatic bridge, with high rail lines, also in latticed steel, supported by immense stone or brick piers. He is captivated by it. A bolt from the grey.

By this point, the road bridge they're crossing rises to a higher elevation than the other one, which practically vanishes behind the guardrail of the opposite lane. On the map, it's marked as the Rail Bridge, while the one they're crossing is marked as the Road Bridge.

'Let's go take a look at that bridge from close up, come on.'

Clara is hungry, she doesn't object: 'Maybe we could get something to eat, too. Tell me which way to go.'

'Turn off here, right away, the first left we come too. There's a roundabout. Then we need to go towards the bridge. I'll tell you the way to go, just turn.'

They turn off the A90, take a couple of roundabouts the wrong way round, head into a small town, with the bridge looming over

326

all, incredibly tall, in the background. Along the downhill road everything is so very British: stone houses, one or two stories tall, clean, closed in on themselves, kept as if life were going to go on for ever. On the map it says that the village is called North Queensferry.

'We need to find Main Street, which takes us straight down to the water, that is, to the root of the bridge.'

It's like going in search of that place where you supposed a distant iron rainbow touches down to earth, find out what's there, in that exact spot. At the end of the road you can see the railroad bridge lifted high into the air, red latticework girders set atop gigantic pylons made of yellow brick—a gap in the clouds allows the sun to illuminate the scene like a spotlight in a theatre. Seen from this angle it's all much more massive, the bridge appears as a tangle of trusses and trellises and enormous riveted pipes, painted red with black patches of rust.

'It looks like a dinosaur,' says Clara.

Yes, the backs of three dinosaurs in single file, holding each other by the tail as they cautiously cross the water. Ivo says nothing. He feels an inexplicable swell of emotion, very much like what he felt the night before. They walk the length of Main Street, until they find themselves in a small circular plaza that overlooks the water of the Firth of Forth, where piers and stone structures adjoin the muck of the seabed, left uncovered by the low tide. A long slip-way to haul vessels into and out of the water, a stone wall behind which they see implements for catching some kind of mollusc, or crustacean, who can say. Maybe traps for crabs. On the left the structure of the bridge looms over everything else, crushing it, there's a small stone lighthouse, right under the shoulder of the Rail Bridge, completely overwhelmed by its size. There the bridge already soars high overhead, the railroad tracks must be 150 feet high, the fog gradually swallows up the rest of the bridge as it marches courageously out into the Firth of Forth. Immense strides through the dank air redolent of the scents of water, mud and seawood uncovered by the low tide, an air that grows chillier, the piers low over the water, it's as if the monster were dipping its frozen steel paws directly into the mouth of the river.

'Come on, let's park ...' says Ivo. Clara puts the car in reverse and finds a spot along the road, there's no one around, the bridge looms over the village, intimidating the people so that they tend to say indoors. They get out of the Fiat 500, they head towards the shore, the water hasn't gone out with the low tide, they see only seaweed and puddles and repellent silty muck, they can smell the reek of the wet, the slime, a northern thing that runs like a chill down their spines, like a blade of ice.

'It's cold,' Clara says, in fact, and goes back to the car to get a jacket for herself and one for Ivo. 'We came dressed too light for these fucking places ... Still, look how pretty it is here ...'

Ivo sits down on a bench, opens his guidebook, leafs through it and finds a substantial, well-thought-out deck about it. This is a major, famous bridge. Clara sits next to him, lights a cigarette while he reads aloud.

The gigantic railroad bridge over the River Forth, inaugurated in 1890, is considered one of the wonders of nineteenth-century technology. The first railroad bridge built entirely of

The structural conception behind the Firth of Forth Bridge in a renowned picture from the time.

steel, it was begun in 1883, after a storm had caused the collapse of the bridge over the mouth of the River Tay, in Dundee, while a railroad train was going over (seventy-five people died).

The disaster had called into question the use of iron in the construction of bridges. In order to counter the thrust of the wind, the designers of the new bridge, the engineers Fowler and Baker, conceived of an enormous steel structure with latticework elliptical girders. Steel had been banned by the British Board of Trade from use in bridge construction until 1877. The chief source of concerns about the use of steel in place of iron had to do with problems of corrosion that had been noted in railroad bridges in Holland, but the problem wasn't really with the steel itself, so much as an inability to use it properly and to protect effectively against corrosion. Still today, the girders of the Rail Bridge are repainted on an ongoing basis by a community of technicians who have been working on this bridge alone for over seventy years.

The Firth of Forth Bridge.

To solve the problem of wind pressure, the engineers conducted a series of experiments: three wind speed gauges were set on the bridge of the castle of Inch Garvie which stands on a neighbouring island. For two years the instruments recorded data, and in the end the wind pressure was found to be much greater than that predicted for the design of the Tay Bridge. A different structural conception was therefore required. Fowler and Baker designed three large latticework piers that supported parabolic girders with spans of more than 650 feet, joined by latticework sections extending over 325 feet, resulting in overall spans of 1,700 feet (at the time the longest in the world), for a total length of 8,296 feet. To build the Forth Bridge, 54,000 tons of steel were used. The sections that were subject to the greatest strain were formed of circular tubes with average diameters of approximately 12 feet, made of inch-and-a-quarter-thick steel. The sheet steel, bent and perforated, was first assembled for testing in the workshop, then disassembled and transported to the construction site. The on-site assembly had to proceed symmetrically to avoid any imbalances during construction. Each span is formed of two cantilevered sections 680 feet in length and, between them, a 350-foot girder. The measurements were so precise that there was only a miscalculation of a little over 2 inches, due to the slight contraction of the steel due to the fact that the actual temperature on the construction site was 55°F instead of the expected 59°F. They were obliged to light fires to lengthen the structure so that they could fasten the last bolts connecting the main spans. Up to 200 trains still run each day over the Firth of Forth Bridge.

He shows her the photo of the structural demonstration of the bridge. She laughs. He concentrates on what he sees, he's bewitched by it. He seems to realize that the conceptual grandeur of that object, the simplicity of the underlying conception, the grandiose sweep of its construction, were clear indications of the unheard-of determination to transcend that was so intrinsic to the bridge. It seems to him that this conception goes beyond all and any 'possible metaphysics', that it thumbs its nose at such things and that *Homo faber* is the highest form of existence. He is impressed by the photograph of the demonstration of the structural principles on which the bridge is based, so simple that they strike him as sublime: a titanic problem solved by a simple act of conceptual transference from the small to the gigantic. Those gentlemen with beards, hats and three- and four-button jackets, the clothing with the rumpled, dirty appearance that all humans seem to wear in the photographs of that time. He observes the photo closely: starting from the ropes that run under the two piles of bricks at the far ends of the tableau vivant, he follows the forces in the bifurcation and realizes that the arms of the two load-bearers are under traction, while the wooden staffs braced against the chairs are under compression. He understands that the spinal cords of those two gentlemen must also be under compression. It is all so clear, the third gentleman sitting in the middle is obviously doing nothing, he's simply sitting there, a few feet off the ground, on his little plank settee. Behind the backs of this tableau vivant is a schematic diagram of the bridge. But more than in the design, the Rail Bridge appears beautiful to him in reality, where it exists in an unexpected yet natural fashion: nothing looks superfluous in the solid and reciprocal interbolting of the parts to support the light railway roadbed and *nothing else*. It's a railway bridge after all. Ivo reaches into his bag for a pencil and a piece of paper, sets the guidebook on his knees with the piece of paper on top of it and draws a horizontal line interrupted by two vertical segments: the water surface of the Firth of Forth. Above this line he draws a second parallel line, which is where the train will run. 'Here is the first conceptual step: conceiving the two banks of the Forth as two separate entities, but not "in different places", conceiving them, that is, as something that can be re-unified, as the interruption of a *continuum* whose completion can be conceived.'

Clara smokes in silence and looks in the other direction, at the Road Bridge, the suspension bridge they just drove over: 'It's nice too, though . . .' Then Ivo sketches a simple trilithic construction made of vertical elements supporting a horizontal girder. It looks like a sort of millipede. This, according to the illustration in the guidebook, was how the Firth of Tay Bridge was built, further north, over the Tay Estuary, ten or so years earlier. 'It collapsed almost immediately, it plunged into the water with all the passengers. Just imagine the disaster . . . But it did help to show that the force of the wind can be much more destructive than anyone could believe at the time . . . They built this bridge on the strength of that hard lesson.' He writes on the piece of paper: 'The Promethean faith of *Homo faber* knows no obstacles.' Then he corrects the word 'faith' to 'energy' and adds: 'What can the philosopher do compared with all this?' Upon the trilithic sketch of the Tay Bridge he overlays, working with care and relying on the funny photograph of the structural demonstration, several lines that summarize the shape of the bridge he has before his eyes: 'Not everything that might seem to bring to synthesis two opposites really does so, and, above all, it's not always sufficiently solid to successfully withstand all forms of attack. This bridge is a construction that defines the solution to an age-old tension.' And underneath he reiterates: 'The Rail Bridge resolves in its way the age-old tension between two banks. The same is done, in a completely different way, by the Road Bridge: the solution is technical, the problem is philosophical.' This is followed by another hastily jotted note: 'What the fuck am I doing with my life? How can I relegate myself to the sidelines from the very start? How can I return to the world? How on earth could I have failed to understand anything about the reality of humanity we endlessly chatter about?'

He sits there for a long time gazing at the Bridge, then he starts pacing back and forth on the stone wharf, every so often glancing at the structure which from that point appeared to him in a vertiginous perspectival foreshortening against the first hint of a smoky, faded sunset, which at these latitudes might last hours. It's a sensation that he's never felt before, it's as if the sight of that thing is somehow unbearable to him, as if it had made up its mind to reveal to him, like it or not, something that he'd never learnt before, something simple and decisive. Then he sits back down on the bench of the overlook and murmurs: 'The year 1882, you get that? A mile and a half long . . . You understand?'

Clara is no longer listening to him. He leafs through the guide-book in search of indications for a place to eat, a restaurant, a pub, a bar, anything. The wind has picked up and it's chilly. Ivo slips on his cotton jacket, zips it up to his neck, raises the lapels, and puts on his wool cap. Clara is out of patience, on edge, chilled to the bone and with low blood sugar. She says: 'What are we going to do?' 'Just wait a second,' he replies to her, 'just a couple more min-utes.' 'I'm cold, I'm going to go wait in the car. No, better yet, I'm going to go find a place to eat.' 'Sure. I'll be there soon.'

He sits there for another half hour. He gazes upon an object that declares in an absolutely clear and powerful fashion the rea-sons for its existence, that asserts the indisputable fact of its being, in that singular point in the world, engaged in the incessant effort to hold together the shores of that stretch of water. Simmel wrote that it is man's task to connect what is separated and separate what is connected, because only human beings are capable of seeing the two banks of a river as two discontinuous things that can be rejoined. That act of essential rationality is there, before him, in all its structural power, in all its geometric clarity. He observes the distinct internally converging torsion of the great arches in tubular steel, he understands in a wholly natural way, because the bridge tells him so, which part of the structure is load-bearing and which part is borne as a load. 'No one wonders why the Rail Bridge exists, no one wonders what it is and what it's for, because it jus-tifies itself in virtue of the self evidence of its function.' He is reminded of Simmel's words. He doesn't remember them exactly, but here they are now.

> The bridge takes on an aesthetic value when it accomplishes union of the separate not just in reality and for the satisfac-tion of practical aims, but renders it immediately visible . . .
>
> The simple dynamics of the movement, in the reality of which the 'purpose' of the bridge is exhausted from time to time, have become something visibly enduring . . .

Now he too can feel that his blood sugar is low, he feels weak. Or perhaps it's the emotion, but he's sweating and the chill freezes the sweat to his skin. He goes on jotting down notes, his hands are trembling. 'Clara must be starting to lose her temper. We'd better find a place to get something to eat, maybe we can stay here overnight, I don't feel like driving any further today. I'd better get going . . .' He heads back to the car, he gets behind the wheel, seeking shelter from the wind. He doesn't see Clara, who knows where she's gone. The idea of driving now, on the wrong side of the road, to who knows where, bothers him, it exhausts him. It would be better to go, before it gets dark. The sight of the bridge has upset him and his agitation, alongside the difficulty of driving on the left, has been transformed into anxiety. His hands are still trembling, even if the tremor has lessened. His body must have found sugars somewhere: he's hungry, he's tired, but he feels better. In just a short while his mental landscape has changed and it has transformed the actual scenery around him. No longer the stern and tranquil austerity of Scotland, no longer the comfortable silence, the absence of traffic, the wisdom of heavily used objects, preserved over time exactly as they were in their miserly and slightly pinchbeck austerity. All this changes into hostility, menace, dreariness, and squalor. Ivo starts to reckon with the harsh lesson that the bridge has taught him, the emotional effort leverages the drop in blood sugars and suddenly he's sleepy. He leans his head against the door frame, heaves a deep sigh and falls asleep instantly.

'Someone once said that life is a "disease of matter". I disagree. If there is such a thing as a disease of matter it's what we call the force of gravity . . .' With these words, Leandri starts his lesson. He captivates him instantly.

Young, probably forty, tall and powerfully built, resolute, with the face of a man apparently without doubts other than technical ones, a man apparently without any nagging thoughts of the political or existential sort, the bronzed skin of someone who does sports, of someone who's probably a member of an athletic club on the River, someone who probably boats, someone who often goes to construction sites, someone who cares about maintaining the healthy & efficient appearance of the manager of a technical studio that operates on an international level, supplying everything that's needed to undertake and complete major projects around the world.

'The owner of the studio is his father-in-law,' his fellow students immediately told him.

'Who's his father-in-law?'

'Bottini,' they replied.

'Ah . . . and who's Bottini?'

'What do you mean "who's Bottini"?'

'. . . this applies to everything that exists on the surface of this planet. In fact, everything that is affected by the presence of this planet, the curvature of space generated by its mass. Immediately clear your minds of the phrase "curvature of space". Since you've all taken physics already, otherwise you wouldn't be here, you also know who Einstein is and what his theories state. But we don't need Einstein. The universe we're going to be examining belongs to Newton. It's *simpler* than Einstein's universe, or Bohr's and so on, but it's not *simple*. In fact, if you'll bear with me as I take a brief tangent, nothing, at least in the profession you have chosen, will be *simple*, because every problem demands thought, method, expertise, mind, brain, cunning, exactitude and approximation. No problem can be solved without thinking, unless it forms part of the fundamental actions that our body performs without relying upon the mind, like walking, swallowing, speaking . . . Careful: the mind, not the brain. Get someone to explain the difference to you. We're not engaging in psychology here, we're building *things*. Things that serve a purpose, that need to stand up, often for a very long time, things that might be gigantic, massively heady, enormously expensive . . . All right then . . . Now, we were saying that this disease of matter exists: it's called *weight* and it can be determined with Newton's fundamental equation of physics. Universal gravitation. It depends on the mass, the square of the distance from the planet Earth, but in an inversely proportional manner, and so on and so forth. I expect that you know these things to perfection. I don't intend to go back over them . . . Therefore, I will not be answering questions that have to do with the discipline of physics, only those concerning the science of construction . . .'

Curt, authoritarian, a simplifier. 'A *Fascist*,' Ivo thinks automatically. But he knows he's wrong: Leandri is *only* a Christian Democrat. It's a rumour that's going around in the Department, it's taken for certain. Among other things, he's a consultant for the Ministry of Transportation as well as the Ministry of Public Works. An accomplished structural engineer, Leandri is obnoxious, off-putting, but he's a very precise storyteller, he knows how to capture his audience. But when he writes down a formula, when he begins a demonstration, when he sets out a mathematical procedure, everyone frantically takes notes, because he moves very quickly, too quickly, it's hard to follow all the various steps. Maybe mathematics bores him, it's as if he's trying to get through it in a hurry. It seems as if the only part of the discipline that he likes is the intuitive side, upon which he can construct a lecture made up of imagery, analogies, metaphors. For that matter, in the past two years, Ivo has learnt that here, anyone who teaches a course involving maths— *all* the courses in the two-year cycle of engineering either *are* mathematical or strongly entail mathematics—goes very fast: if you're with it, you're with it, if you're not, there's the door. They're not interested in explaining, transmitting knowledge, they're interested in *weeding out*. But by now we're in the third year, the bulk has been completed, anyone who's sitting in this lecture hall has already been through a harsh selection process and has passed. That means Leandri can afford to teach a genuine lesson, to abandon himself to his showmanship and flair.

'If philosophy needs to avail itself continuously of metaphors taken from the physical world,' thinks Ivo Brandani, 'to explain the physical world, images of some other kind are needed . . . Of whatever kind, but only provisionally, only in the brief intervals between one mathematization and the next . . . Philosophical images, but, far more often, biological ones . . .'

'In other words, it is inside this force field generated by the planet that we spend our entire lives and everything that exists is subjected to it from its very first instant of existence. In short, that is, everything is a slave to gravity. We should make a distinction here . . . I mean to say that what I just said *isn't true*. That is, it isn't true that everything is a slave to gravity. For example, most insects, bacteria and viruses aren't: their mass is so tiny that they practically don't possess weight. Beneath a certain size, molecular cohesion is stronger than gravity . . . There is a boundless world of creatures that have no notion of gravity. All that matters to them is molecular cohesion: think of the surface tension of water and the insects that walk on it, as if it were a mattress. To them, that's the dominant force, the one that allows spiders to walk on walls. If you don't know these things, go and read about them. This isn't a biology class . . .'

Arrogant, authoritarian, but a good teacher. A clear-minded Fascist, or actually a clear-minded Christian Democrat.

'It is necessary to understand that everything that exists, let's say above a certain size, is a response to gravity. Or perhaps we should say, it's *also* a response to gravity. The shape and size of our bones are responses to gravity, for instance. The shape of hills and mountains are, too. So are women's breasts.'

The students are all males, a universal burst of laughter. 'Fascist and sexist,' thinks Ivo.

'Walking is an expedient that allows us to make use of gravity for our own ends. A succession of forward falls. A table, a chair, these are anti-gravity devices. Chairs allow us to remain suspended at a certain elevation off the ground in a position that does not place inordinate strain on our internal structure, in such a way that it transfers a part of our weight to a substitute structure, the seat and the legs of the chair. A table is nothing other than a system for keeping objects within reach. Gravity has an ordering effect, it gives us a way of keeping objects still in a given place. The force of gravity is a powerful antidote against chaos. It produces planetary orbits, it holds together the solar system. The idea of an orderly universe, and I couldn't say whether or not such an idea is exact, though I suspect it's mistaken, is something we derive from the phenomenon of the curvature of space, something that occurs in the presence of a mass. Look, these are challenging concepts, and luckily they are of no particular concern to us, that is, not entirely. Without gravity, as even children know, we'd float in the air like astronauts. Water wouldn't stay in its glasses, the sea would fly away. Our faeces would wander freely at nose-height (more laughter). So this is its ordering effect. Without gravity, the very idea of the world as we know it would no longer make sense and our entire way of thinking would vanish. Everything is determined by gravity. The science of construction is the discipline that allows us to fight against gravity effectively. I mean to say: certainly not to annihilate it but to turn it to our advantage—that, yes. To study the way in which gravity attacks a physical being, the way in which it strains and stresses it, depending on the shape it possesses . . .'

He stops, turns to the blackboard, picks up a piece of chalk and does a three-dimensional sketch of a table, a crude axonometric projection. A rectangle with its four legs, drawn with a single chalk line. The audience is captivated, enthralled, drawn in, attentive, intimidated.

'How simple these kids are, compared to the philosophy students . . . They were already engineers before they started studying engineering, maybe when they were little, from birth . . . Is it an inborn aptitude? I think so . . . I used to play with my Erector Set, I had a toy truck and an electric train, I'd build bridges, I made the Bridge Over the River Kwai, with toothpicks . . . Approximately, it was the one from the movie, which had a stunning resemblance to the Firth of Forth Bridge . . . I was *Homo faber* myself, but then I turned my back on it all, I derailed, I imposed a different, strange, useless trajectory upon myself . . . A man, *Homo sapiens*, is something other than a philosopher, than a professor of philosophy . . .'

'. . . now then, we started by speaking generically about a body subject to its own weight, and now we have introduced the concept of *structure*. Pay close attention, because it's fundamental. What is a structure? You all know the answer, that is, you can guess at it, you quasi-know it, that is, you think you know. Actually, this too is a very complex concept and it can be applied to an infinite array of disciplines. There is the structure of matter, of cells, the structure of a discourse, physical structure, economic structure, social structure, the geological structure of a given place. For each of these examples, the term actually has a different meaning. Here too we won't venture any further, we won't expatiate on the profound meaning of the word, which might be stated as a *form endowed with meaning*. But here I'm speaking in approximations . . . Let's stay with the table: a table is a structure for supporting any object whatsoever provided it does not exceed a given weight and a certain size. If it weighs more than the limit, the table will break. If the table is too small with respect to the object, the object will fall. Let us imagine that this table is made of only five elements: four legs and a wooden top. The whole of these elements, connected to each other *in a certain way*—not *in just any old way* —is a *structure*, it's the table-structure. A set of elements assembled for a purpose that each of the elements, alone, would be unable to fulfil. Each of the elements is indispensable to the whole, and therefore we are in the presence of an *isostatic* structure. But erase that word, just pretend I never said it. We'll explore it later. Right now, let's imagine placing at the centre of this table a weight of, let us say, ten pounds. Or let's make it twenty. Now, pay close attention: the science of construction allows me to determine how this structure is strained under a given load, how the strains are distributed, in what directions, with what effects, and how it all is unloaded onto the floor. Moreover, it tells us what amount of sinking we should expect and at what points in the structure. And it tells us what kind of deformations it will suffer. And so on. Last of all, it will tell us the load limit above which the table will break. Therefore it gives us indications and methods for structural design. There, these are more or less the contents of the science of construction.'

'They dress differently, many of them are slobs, with dirty hair, and a slight reek. The scratchy wool jacket. Under the jacket they wear the grey crew-neck sweater. Clarks desert boots, certainly, but more often loafers with the curled-up toe. All the same. They come to class with a briefcase, they look like so many office clerks. Here's the well-dressed student, the son of a builder, upper class from head to foot: navy-blue blazer, beige trousers, light-blue shirt, Saxone loafers. He has a car, he doesn't take the bus. The others—there are plenty who live here, away from home, and others who are commuters—take public transport. They get up every morning at five, many of them also have jobs: already we work ourselves silly, they do that, plus come and go. They don't care about politics, no one here cares about politics, it's not for them, they don't understand it, they'll never understand it. They'll vote according to their own self-interest, or else in line with faint laissez-faire convictions, in any case, centrist or right wing. They'll do other things, we'll all do other things, we'll build things, that is, concrete things, houses, bridges, dams, engines, automobiles, aeroplanes, electric power stations. I'm for bridges, I want to make bridges. I know that there are companies already keeping an eye on those with a good average in the first two years, some of the students actually get a contract for a sort of pre-hire: they'll pay for the last three years, they gobble them up early. Franco is merciless, and I can't say he's wrong: he says that engineers are fundamental to the process of production, innovation, and accumulation of capital.'

'The engineer is responsible for the design, the conception, the worker is responsible for the work, while all that remains to Capital is to decide what to do. Capital needs invention, but it tolerates the capacity to invent only in the field of technology. It needs proletarianized technicians willing to do anything and capable of thinking only in engineering terms . . . Therefore what an engineer needs first and foremost, more than specialization, which remains admittedly important, is a *forma mentis, a mindset* . . . They must be *domesticated*, tamed from the very beginning. They must feel the bit and the master's hand patting them on the head. They must learn from this point on to say yes . . . How the fuck did it occur to you to become an engineer, Ivo? You're as necessary as bread, so they stay on you . . . No politics, for you the world is only a set of technical problems, one after the other, for the rest of your lives . . . You're oil in the gearings of Capital. Have you ever wondered why you're the only ones who've never had a Student Movement?'

'Have you ever looked at a bridge, Franco?'

'Oh come on now, give me a break with these damned bridges. All right, you'll build bridges. What can I tell you? What are we supposed to tell each other? You have a philosophical mind, you know that. You chose to become an engineer. I don't understand it, it's a move I don't follow.'

'It may also be a sequence of technical problems, but at the base of any technical problem, there's a philosophical question. But a question that demands a concrete answer . . . This is a *calling*, Franco. A *true* calling . . . It's *being among things*, among people who talk to each other in order to communicate, not to prevail, not to show off, to prove how good, how clever they are . . . Let me say it again: *it's a calling*, not a job, an intellectual activity, etc. It's a CALLING, I want to follow this calling. The other day I went to my first science of construction class . . .'

Franco experiences the typical distaste that intellectuals feel towards technicians. It's an age-old thing, it goes back to the classical concentration in high school, it's the basis of the whole humanistic mystification, the prevalence of the emotional values—because that's what's going on here, Ivo tells himself—over all others.

'It was Franco who talked to me about high-school imprinting . . . And now he clearly shows that he's in it up to the neck.'

'Ah how wonderful! I can just imagine the pleasure you felt! I'll bet you jacked off under your desk . . .'

Vulgar mockery, not something he'd expected from him. Ivo ignores it: 'There's a guy people say is good who teaches it. His name is Leandri, a lively Neapolitan.'

'Lively?'

'Yes. When he worked his way up to the concept of structure he said: Look, there are dozens of meanings corresponding to this term. He listed a few, then he turned around, sketched a table on the blackboard, and said: "We're interested in *this* type of structure."'

'So what?'

'Don't you find that *fantastic*? Isn't this conceptual closure wonderful, so sharp and clear, so devoid of sophistries: we are engineers, therefore the structure that interests us is of this type, that is, phy-si-cal. We don't give a crap about all the rest. Exactly the opposite of philosophers, to whom the only interesting thing is the concept itself of structure, the innate idea, it's function in the process of gaining knowledge etc., etc. . . . Engineers don't give a damn about that . . . There are worlds different from yours, and they're not necessarily worse, Franco.'

'They're going to bend your spine, Ivo . . . And you won't be so happy then . . .'

At the end of September 1968, after a brief personal struggle during which he stopped studying for his philosophy exams, Ivo changed his major to Engineering. He'd convinced himself that technical action is a form of a philosophical action but without magnificent robes, without the systematic pretence, the metaphysical aspirations. He decides that technical thinking is a continual verification of the capacity of thought to transform the world and that it will allow us, in the long run, to triumph over the dictates of nature. To him, the human race is essentially a species of builders: *Homo sapiens* is such only if he is *Homo faber*, that is, only inasmuch as he is a fabricator of what we need to live contrary to nature. He talked it over at length with Franco, with Clara, even with Mother. But not with Father. Father, for his part, thought that he finally had him clutched in his fist.

The first two years of the course of engineering, full of mathematical analysis, physics, mechanical engineering, chemistry and so on, is terrible ordeal. Ivo realizes that he has a mental limit beyond which there is no way out for him. He feels he is the only one who can't understand, he can't grasp and he can't retain more than a certain amount, his capacity to intuit the concepts visually no longer works; beyond that limit, which more or less coincides with the differential equations, and not even them, he is unable to construct any usable image. He manages, he has no idea how, to cram into his brain mathematical procedures that he intimately fails to understand, he struggles tremendously, he accepts shameful grades and, in the end, he barely clears the two-year requirements.

Ivo looks back, he'd really worked incredibly hard. Mathematical analysis 1 and 2, physics, mechanics, graphical statics, science of construction, technical physics. During his first two years of engineering, it seemed to him that he'd come from a distant and mist-shrouded planet where the art of disputation still thrived, where they still sought after truth as if there was such a thing outside of the logical and mathematical verities. His betrayal of his origins had been total and extreme, a lunatic negation. Here those who teach take no interest whatsoever in those who learn, no one cares *who* you are, all that matters is what you prove that you can do. Do you or don't you know how to solve a differential equation? Do you know how to calculate a system's nodal stresses? Do you know how to state a problem mathematically? If you do, good. If you don't, so long. If you can't keep up, it's been good to know you. This is the famous first two years of engineering: it's designed to weed out those who are going to go *on* (that is, to being hired for a position in a Corporation) and, at the same time, to shape the mind and personality, to encourage their eventual anxiety for social climbing, with appropriate rewards and punishments. The professor of engineering is well aware of his duties and he performs them using the authority of his position rather than any charisma, which for that matter is almost always non-existent. Ivo sees their cultural mediocrity, in some cases, their paltry humanity, yet he acknowledges their function, their strength.

'Let the Movement go ahead and occupy the other departments. There's no point in doing it here, these aren't genuine professors, to protest against them, to defy them would do no good, they are mere functionaries, colonels, they're sorters, they're just like those military physicians who approve or deny admission to the pilot's academy on the basis of physical fitness . . . Most of them aren't inventing anything new, they're just transmitting things that are generally known, they provide you with a technical & ethical foundation for your future role . . . In other departments, they say that they're trying to shape you, to educate you, here they just want to *cut you to size*. You'll be a member of a team, of a group of technicians, often international groups, you'll use technology to exploit other people's money, transforming that money into works of engineering, and you might be doing the same thing with political decisions . . . You'll provide support for all this, for every step of the way, you yourself will be a part of the substrate of the world, in the sense of a substrate of life . . . You'll help to ensure that philosophers can fly in the aeroplanes that will take them to the conferences where they can discuss matters concerning the existence of a world outside of ourselves, or free will, or whatever the fuck they feel like discussing . . . In order to do so, you'll take as a given the existence of reality, you will decide what is the best solution, you'll make use of the partial truths that underlie every technical solution. You will make it possible for priests and nuns, bishops and popes, missionary friars and Orthodox fathers, Muslim imams and Buddhist holy men, for every other adept of revealed truths, every worshipper of the notions of spirit, guilt and sin, to make their way over all the rivers, to travel down all the roads, to cross over all the oceans necessary for the propagation of their faiths, you'll build their temples, and in those same temples they will reliably rail against technology and science . . . But that's fine the way it is . . . The world needs men like Captain MacWhirr, who is in command of the *Nan-Shan* and takes on the titular storm in Conrad's *Typhoon*: stubborn, "without imagination", but good at their jobs, competent at the things they do . . . The ridiculous "creativity" of those who consider themselves artists—those who insist on "feeling themselves free", "unwilling to accept outside impositions", who see their work as the product of free will, instead of binding constraints—that's not for the engineer . . . The last thing he needs is freedom, he wouldn't know what to do with it . . . An engineer *needs* constraints, he asks you for them—if you gave him total freedom, the engineer couldn't even begin to think, he'd just go on holiday. His bond with reality is foundational and indestructible, at the cost of the destruction of the engineer himself . . .'

Ivo thinks at some considerable length about this, but his gaze is substantially elsewhere: deep down, it doesn't really matter to him what it means to be an engineer; right now all that interests him is to reach the point of being able to *understand* the Firth of Forth Bridge, he cares about gaining the ability to design a bridge so that it will stay up, that makes it possible to 'connect what is separate'. Even so, it isn't easy, many of his fellow students seem only to have lived thus far with the goal of facing the challenge of this department and defeating it. Now he envies all the grinds back at school who always got good grades in the scientific subjects and who here shower sparks of brilliance. He can't stand them but he tries to befriend them; he wants to study with them, but none of them wants to waste time with a guy who has a hard time absorbing even the simplest notions, who is constantly asking for clarifications, who digs his heels in on a mathematical formula unless every step of it is explained to him. The problem of mathematics arose immediately, and dramatically: he was forced to take private tutoring from a professor who helped him to reinforce the fundamentals that he was lacking. During regular lessons, Ivo made notes on the passages that were still unclear to him and submitted them to his tutor, going over the procedure with him step by step, until he reached the final result. The *result*! This word became practically mythical for him. 'There are fields in which you can arrive at an unequivocal, transmittable, shared result!'

'*Objective*,' he ventures to think.

At the first exams they flunk him, or he gets very low grades. At engineering they write 'Rejected' on his grade book. One time, the professor of Analysis 2 actually boomerangs the grade book across the room, with contempt. 'Don't worry,' a student tells him, 'it's not like he has it in for you. He does this a lot, and he'll keep doing it until the day that someone seriously loses it, gives him a nice hard head-butt and smashes in his nasal septum, then he'll finally stop . . .' 'Political consciousness in the nascent state,' thinks Ivo, 'an impulse of authentic anti-authoritarian rebellion.' '*Tovarich*,' he replies to him.

3.48 p.m.

What evidence can I produce to show that I lived?

Every so often, out of nowhere, in the midst of a moment of peace and quiet, usually at an airport, in a waiting room, or in a hotel room at night after dinner, with the TV tuned to a programme in some foreign language, whether it's an evening news broadcast in Arabic, English or Japanese, dreaming of a cigarette he doesn't have, Ivo asks himself a question, always the same one.

What attests to my time here on the planet Earth? Mine is not one of the heads on Mount Rushmore, which are certain to be the human traces that will last the longest in absolute terms, much longer than the pyramids . . . Too bad, Brandani, you won't be placed on Mount Rushmore, there's no more room . . . Sure, I worked on that dam in China, and that other one in Africa, I lent a hand on roads and bridges, etc., but where is my name? And what if instead of being a secret falsifier of coral reefs, I had been the builder of Cheops' great pyramid, would anyone still remember my name? And what would it mean to remember it, since I'd already be dead four thousand years beyond the horizon of space-time? The erasure of Father & Mother's lifelong stories, their clothing, their objects . . . What will have become of the horrendous oval brooch encrusted with semi-precious stones that I brought her—she was embarrassed at being unable to force out so much as a 'Thank you, how lovely!' she hated it so much—from my reward trip to Florence? The sale of the House, the end of everything, the transfer into other hands, indifferent, unaware . . . How much of their lives, of our life, is already in a dump somewhere? How much of it has already been mixed with the unholy infinity of other people's garbage, the traces of alien, extraneous, sordid, enemy lives? What could I save of them? And why should I have? What objects have survived? Why don't I have almost any of them? What became of them? What will become of my things, my clothing, my few engravings, my even fewer books?

He hasn't gone back to Mother & Father's graves, where they buried Big Sister too, after she was sick more or less for a week, a few years ago.

When did Big Sister die?

He can't remember exactly. He can't remember the year, or the month, or the day. It was hellishly hot, that much he remembers. One day—well before Big Sister left the world in such haste, with no children on the face of the earth, nothing but an asshole husband—Ivo, finding himself with time on his hands in the City of God between one business trip and another, had decided on an impulse to pull the car out of the garage and zoom off down the consular road that led to the large Second Cemetery. The Second Cemetery had been built in accordance with the criteria of the more recent city of the living, an enfilade of red buildings, arranged with a certain flair, not aligned according to any principle of perspective or geometric figures of any kind, but quite decidedly at fucking random.

The dead are forced to exist just like the living, in a piece-of-shit city of their own, designed by some unknown piece-of-shit architect, inside their countless columbarium niches, and at night, from the consular road, you can see them all lit up with flickering votive candles, one after the other, like a cheerful little train of red cut-glass candle holders, here and there a cypress tree.

Ever since the day of Father's funeral, Ivo hadn't gone back there once, until one day, in the cardiologist's waiting room where he'd gone to enquire about certain pains in his chest that had been frightening him—'I can't find anything, certainly the thing to do is to have an electrocardiogram done under stress, but for that you'd want to go to a public facility, you need to have an intensive-care specialist present—more likely, it's a hiatal hernia . . . Do you know how many patients come to see me for their heart and it turns out to be a hiatal hernia? Do you know how many come to the emergency room every day for that same reason?' Fuck that shit, he'd thought to himself, do you know how many people shuffle off this mortal coil convinced they have a hiatal hernia and instead it turns out to be a heart attack?—in that waiting room, which was as nondescript and generic as could be, with the pains in his chest, Ivo had suddenly thought to himself, as he leafed through a greasy newspaper: Who will remember Them? Tears had welled up in his eyes, because clearly the pain in his chest hadn't been enough. Tomorrow, if I'm still alive, I'll go. The next day, as he was driving through the immense no-man's land of the car park in front of the cemetery, it had started to rain hard, with sleet. He'd parked in a spot close to the front gate, where the chrysanthemum vendors, devoid of any shelter, were hastily packing up. The icy pellets were slamming violently onto the roof of the car, he'd put a CD on, an old record of Bill Evans live, punctuated at the end of each piece by the applause of what must have been no more than five or six people. He was dead, Bill Evans, and he'd died many, a great many years ago, and yet his fingers on the keyboard of that piano that night in 1961 at the Village Vanguard would live on over time, *still* capable of resonating in his ears, *still* capable of saying: Challenging music, closed up in itself, perhaps not especially welcoming to many but it is to me. And he'd tilted the driver's seat back and sprawled out, waiting for the downpour to pass. But what had at first just looked like a cloudburst had turned into a hard, steady rain. While waiting, Ivo had dozed off. He could have driven into the cemetery, it was allowed, he just didn't feel like it. He wanted to walk the whole way but he'd fallen asleep. Once his nap was over, but not the rain, the last notes of Bill Evans echoed in Brandani's ears without his feeling the slightest desire now to weep over his parents' graves: Why the fuck would I even go? The CD had started over again from the beginning, he'd driven away, and he'd never again set foot there. Father & Mother, one beside the other in the same loculus, like a couple of Etruscan spouses, but without a sarcophagus, would spend that rainy night there— and the night that followed and the night after that, for all the nights that the City of God would concede them to stay in that place—she stretched out in her coffin, and he incinerated in his plastic urn, while the recycling process of the carbon that had once constituted their flesh, a process that was just beginning, would require centuries before it was compete.

Before, long before the deaths of Father and Big Sister, something unheard of had happened, something inconceivable, the intolerable had taken place. An event that Ivo Brandani, for all the years that he had lived until then, had never ever, not even once, been able to imagine: the death of Mother. The word 'death' meant that Mother had vanished for ever from the face of the earth, had become no longer visible, embraceable, no longer sniffable. No more kisses and comforting words, no more of her gentle protection, no caress on the forehead, like when I was little and had a fever, never again would he hear her talking in her classical style of detachment & disenchantment towards something that to him appeared important, absolutely indispensable. Never again the Mother-shield against the aggressions of Father. Being his shield had got her a smack in the face or two, and she'd taken them as the logical consequence of both her submission and of her necessary defiance of her husband, every time that she felt he had overstepped his bounds. Ivo knew that she wouldn't allow Father to go beyond the exercise—however tyrannical and violent—of what was considered in those day the biological *potestas* that accrued to him, a sort of inalienable right of vexation, held by fathers over their sons. It had only taken a few months, everything started with something apparently curable, a gallstone, a simple operation, strictly routine. Father chose a private clinic to the south of the City of God. They specialized in abdominal surgeries there, the usual Professor With a University Chair operated there on a private basis, the chief physician of some surgical ward in a major general hospital somewhere. The operation was successful, or so they said, but after a month she still wasn't feeling well, she was weak, pale, listless. She'd become silent, absent, as if raptly listening to whatever it was her body was telling her: 'It's not right, we're not well, there's something, a malaise, a pain, something producing tractions and spasms in the redness of my viscera . . .' Then a nightly fever began, insistent, and not even all that low. It was a dull and sustained source of fear, the beginning for her of a state of solitude that she was going to have to experience right through to the finish, because no one was going to be *genuinely* close to her, because no one could have believed in her imminent death, because no one actually walks up with you right to the brink of death. And so Mother, despite everything, despite assiduous visits from Father, Ivo and the Sisters, and various relatives, would die alone, like everyone . . . A few weeks later the Professor had operated on her a second time (Why? What was the problem? And had it been resolved? No one on the medical staff ever, to the very end, said a single clear or understandable thing . . .), then they received that unbelievable phone call: Come, Signora Brandani is in a coma. *Your mother is in a coma.* In a *coma* . . . The only creature on earth to whom Ivo had felt he fully belonged was there, her face turned unrecognizable by the colour of the jaundice, rendered withered by a suffering that none of them knew how to alleviate. By now, Mother was on the far side of a pane of bulletproof glass. She couldn't hear, she didn't respond, she seemed completely taken up with that long process of death. She was sliding down an inexorable inclined plane at the end of which she would be gone. It wasn't possible to stop her, to restrain her, you could only stand there and watch her die. A few hours later there was one last gurgle, followed a few seconds later by a sudden gush of black blood and Mother died. The instant of her death, that deep last sigh, that rivulet of blood, would resurface for years in Ivo Brandani's mind. Two more decades would have to go by before that vision began to fade, before the very image of Mother began gradually to be concealed in the curves and crannies of memory. Until she too, the Only One, was lost.

Of all of us who were there in that room, the gates of death swung open for her alone . . . And they slammed shut behind her, and we would never see Mother alive again. Never again . . . We emerged from that room on our own two legs . . . We would go on living but she wouldn't. She remained behind, waiting to be taken away, alone and motionless in the night. Then they took her down-stairs, into the chill of the rooms designated for the dead. From there, she would never again be able to protect me . . . I had been left alone . . .

What had led her to that man? What did she like about him? What had persuaded her that he could become her lifelong companion? The answer is in that picture; Ivo rummages for his wallet in his inside jacket pocket. It's the only picture he carries with him everywhere. As he extracts it from the compartment where he keeps it, he feels a stab of pain in the back of his head. He sits motionless, waiting for it to pass, while the photograph remains, held between the forefinger and thumb of his right hand, as he waits unsure whether to slip it back into his wallet or pull it fully out.

Neck pain . . . Such a sharp stabbing bout of it though, he hadn't felt it like this in years . . . Here they are . . .

He probably hasn't looked at this picture for a couple of years now. In the meantime it's got creased and worn. It's a sunny day in the City of God, the two of them are strolling in some garden in the central area of the city, you can see only the base of a distinctive street lamp, a tree, a few details of the facade of a nineteenth-century palazzo. It's cold out, she's wearing a soft winter coat, possibly brown or grey, that's not clear, and he's wearing a military overcoat. Her hair is pretty long, she has on a hat that blends into the background, he's wearing an officer's cap, a pair of black shoes, a pair of impeccably pressed cuffed trousers. They're walking, they seem to be ignoring the camera, she's looking down and smiling, he's holding her left arm and speaking to her. He's smiling too. Both of them are putting out an evident, pulsing, pure vital energy.

It's carnal urgency, unmistakable, in spite of everything, in spite of the War, the imminent tragedies, life waiting in ambush.

Their gait is light, elastic, seemingly coordinated, both of them are swinging their left legs forwards, Mother's shoes are classical, high-heeled pumps, not too high-heeled, they look like the shoes that Minnie Mouse, Mickey Mouse's girlfriend, wore. Mother is beautiful, relaxed, pensive, she's holding him close to her, she seems eager to welcome him inside her. Father is a good-looking man, even if he already has that nose, tall, apparently relaxed, happy to possess her, to hold her in his grip. It is clear that she is already his, it's the sweetness with which she clutches him to her, it's the accommodating bend of her neck in his direction, it's the fact that she's looking down with a smile, while Father's gaze is focused straight ahead, guiding them both as they walk. It is clear from the hand with which he's holding her arm and which she presses against her breast, Mother's left breast, which Father can surely feel against the back of his hand, beneath the soft material of the overcoat, a firm, generous breast, as it must have been before her three children: the unconscious posture of a carnal closeness, Mother is his, she's already delivered herself up to him, she lets him lead her, Mother is happy in the sweet and primordial fullness of the flesh, which demands, imposes, requires. The happiness that stuns them in winter light of the City of God, the shadows lengthening over what seems to be the fine gravel of a park, is nothing other than gratification, nothing more nor less than a surrender to the heated thrust of youth, the same blind, animal, vital, postwar impulse that engendered him . . . Mother's fine nose, with its delicate nostrils, marks the geometric axis of her face and casts a faint shadow on the other half.

They existed, at the time . . . They were both real, living bodies, warm in the sunlight of the early '40s, they breathed & they thought, they loved, they felt pleasure . . . They were there . . . And now there was nothing left of them . . . Absolutely nothing, but nothing, remains of them. Oh sure, she liked him, she desired him, she loved him, she didn't know him well, or maybe she did . . . After all, she kept him at bay right up to the end . . . When she died, I'd already made my escape, I'd left . . . *They* are my parents, it's *these two right here*, I never chose them, I can't exchange them, I ought to love them both but she's the only one I love.

Another, longer stab of pain in the back of his neck, longer this time, erases all thoughts from his mind and leaves him there, stunned and suspended between pain and non-pain, as he tries to put the photograph of Father & Mother away in the compartment in his wallet.

All the same, because in his cranium everything is still preserved, there are nights when, before falling asleep, that trace re-emerges in Brandani's consciousness, and he sees before his eyes that gush of black blood flooding in a death rattle from the adored lips of Mother, lips that were already green in death. Just as one night in a dream he received a threatening phone call from Father ('But where are you calling from?' Ivo had asked him, 'Don't ask,' was Father's reply), and more than once he'd seen Big Sister sitting on her grave, weeping over that poor sparrow of hers, which had drowned in a chamber pot full of nocturnal urine, so many years before. Then one extremely hot summer night Mother too had come back to visit him in a dream, young, a pink Postwar slip hiked up over her bare thighs, she was fluttering in the air, smiling at him, calling to him. He'd woken up with his mouth parched, with a raging erection. Jesus, that was Mother!

In the end, after almost seventy years of living, what is left? What remains on the ground? What has withstood the devaluation, the erasure of time? What still has worth, of everything that was once useful, of all that mattered? What can I hold as still good, still solid, still present in my day-to-day life? The only thing that occurs to me is *La Settimana enigmistica* . . . the *Weekly Puzzler*. It remains apparently unchanged, but only in its graphic presentation . . . Certain features, certain puzzles have vanished or are radically changed, such as the 'Investigation with Susi': never did understand what that one was about . . . There was a warning at the start that told you: Look out, this is strictly for first rate puzzle-solvers . . . A big cartoon full of things and people and, if I'm not mistaken, in the middle of it all was Susi, in a tight-fitting T-shirt, with pointy breasts, pedal pushers with a side slit at the calf, and those were tight-fitting too, a prominent butt, high heels, and a pony tail . . . She was sexy, Susi was, she looked like Brigitte Bardot . . . There aren't many other things . . . Coccoina white paste, which you can still buy exactly as it was, with that distinctive aroma . . . People said that they made it by mincing dog carcasses . . . When it comes to glues and pastes, there's still Artiglio, I have a tube of it and I also have a tube of Balena anchovy paste, another pillar of my life, or like Assa thumbtacks, long since vanished however . . . I still have two Zenith staplers that belonged to Father, dirty and flaking, but they work perfectly, a rare miracle of solid construction . . . When I was small I played with them, I always thought that particular variety of stapler resembled a sperm whale . . . What else? Could it be that almost nothing remains of what once was? The Moka Express espresso pot, sure . . . and then? What ever became of most of the objects I possessed? The scissors? And the pencils? All my pencils, where are they now? For real, Ivo, where are they? Why have they vanished, since I never used them down to the stub nor did I throw them away? Could there be a pencil cemetery hidden away somewhere? Could there be secret paths down which all the objects tired of living trudge, ashamed of their obsolescence? Do the scissors that feel they've become outmoded leave our world by way of these paths? What becomes of the hammers that have been part of my life? Since I've never lost a hammer, a screwdriver, or a file, why should I have had to buy new ones at a certain point? What became of their predecessors? At what depth and in what dump, of those that have been established over time around the City of God, are the things to be found that belonged to the Brandani family before everything exploded, before Mother and Father so unexpectedly left this world, when death let us know with stunning suddenness, leaving us flabbergasted, breathless, that it would be dealing with us *too*, before the Brandani home stopped being an impregnable redoubt? What has become of our stories, of our lives? Who transcribed them? Where do we appear? Who will take care of handing down our life stories? No one, absolutely no one . . . At the very most, but strictly as a remote possibility, in some distant future when the archaeologists excavate those immense deposits of testimony, our city dumps, something might come to light, a pair of scissors, a fragment of some object that once belonged to us, a piece of the plastic laminate that once covered the American kitchen that Father purchased in the '60s, as a tangible sign of prosperity. Or else a document with our name engraved on it, the way it was on the little chain, long-since lost, that was given to you on the day of your First

Communion . . . Just as it was on the wedding rings that you exchanged, you and Clara, on your wedding day, those too lost, who knows when and where . . . It was made of gold . . . Most of the gold that exists in the world comes from objects made previously, it has been melted down and recycled and reblended and reshaped over and over and over again . . . That's the way it was for the gold in that wedding ring, and who knows now in what other piece of jewellery it has been recast, it too coming from who knows when and who knows where, perhaps from a piece of Sumerian jewellery, or Inca jewellery, maybe from a torque found by chance in a prehistoric tomb in Central Asia . . . Whatever became of the old Fiat 600? And the Fiat 1100? And my Lambretta? Ah, and the Moto Guzzi Sparviero? And Father's Moto Guzzi Falcone? And before that, the Ancestral Norton? And my Bike? And the Swedish Furniture in my bedroom? And Big Sister's flowered bedcover, what can have become of it? What was its fate? In what way can it have returned to the chaos of everything, if that even happened? Who possesses these objects now? And how did they come into possession of them? I can't seem to remember, to reconstruct the way in which every trace of my family dissolved, a family that was once so solid, so firm, gathered in the House during the winter nights of the '50s, when Mother said and repeated: 'Tonight, may anyone without a home find one . . .' There was the constant danger of Father, it is true . . . But outside it was cold & dark, and that was worse . . . Little Sister and Big Sister kept a few things, when Father sold the House, because we discovered that he didn't care about keeping furniture and furnishings and gewgaws, leftovers from the meat grinder that was our life in common for as long as it lasted, insignificant things, so important . . . That light-blue Murano vase . . . I never really liked it and yet it was so much *ours*, such an antique, dating back to the archaic age of Mother & Father, when they were full of youth and love, carnal curiosity . . . There's that picture of when Father had just come back from the War and Big Sister might have been two years old at the very most . . . How long had it been since they'd seen each other kissed each other touched each other fucked? I don't know

. . . But it was there, in the days of Father's Return that they conceived me . . . It disgusts me to think that I was born of his loins, but not to think I was born of Mother's womb . . . If only he'd just left me alone to live my life . . . He's been a-borning inside me over and over again for years now, just like the monster in *Alien* inside John Hurt's belly . . . Though Mother died too soon, he's still with me, under my skin, he never dies . . . He has no intention of setting me free . . .

Instinctively he touches his face, he presses his cheekbones, the bone in his nose, his chin. He touches the frontal zone of his cranium, now almost completely bald. Baldness too is a gift from *him*—he thinks it often. He feels that his skin is oily, he needs to wash his face, freshen up. He can't stand it any more. He wants to go home, even though there's no one waiting for him, even though the City of God has lost all its appeal for him (though it can still deceive him with its beauty). Even though he no longer has a single friend in that city worthy of the name . . .

Or anywhere else, for that matter: steer clear of friendship . . . It only works at the dinner table, and on holiday . . . Then, no doubt about it, everyone's friends . . . But no friendship can withstand the test of love affairs, work, conflicts among the respective interests . . . Not even your closest friend can refrain from canoodling with your woman, if he likes her and he sees even the slimmest chance of success . . . No one ever hesitated to sacrifice a friend in trade for some advantage, say a career advancement, there's no friendship that will triumph over interests of love, work or the future, never . . . But in that case, Brandani, what are you going to do with your home, with that city? What is left for you to do there? Father is in here, underneath my face . . . I'm only a Mask of Father . . .

Time passes, it's almost four. The headache comes and goes, the occasional stabbing pain in the back of the neck. He's enquired a couple of times, no trace of his flight. 'Technical problems in Cairo,' the young women at the gate desk keep telling him, they still know nothing about the new scheduled departure. Time drags increasingly slowly. He can't manage to stay seated, he gets up and wanders around, here and there, he sits back down, constantly shifting position. His trousers are binding in his crotch, his underpants are cramping his balls and his dick, he's continuously trying to adjust them, but each attempt only worsens the irritation. In the end, shamelessly, he jams his hands directly into his trousers and crudely grabs and manoeuvres the entire apparatus. The manoeuvre doesn't escape the notice of the young woman sitting across from him.

Whothefuckcares . . . OK, I adjusted my junk, and so what? It's not like I specifically asked for it, to have a dick and balls . . . I'd have been just as happy to have a pussy, at least it doesn't get jammed up in your underpants, you don't have to find it a comfortable position . . . But then you'd have had problems with your tits, Ivo, with the way your bra binds and strains . . .

'How do you wear it?' 'Huh?' 'How do you wear it, to the left or the right?' that's what the tailor who had made his suit for Big Sister's wedding had asked him. He'd never thought about it before. 'How do I wear it? I don't know. Maybe on the left . . . Is it important?' 'Well, you tell me . . .' the tailor had replied with some irritation. 'All right, then, I wear it on the left.' Since then he'd had a new self-awareness as a wearer of his dick-to-the-left. After the shameful rummaging of his balls, he tries to assume a certain demeanour, a level of nonchalance. He could try to do a little work, in spite of his confusion, his headache. He opens his bag and pulls out a couple of sheets of paper stapled together. They contain the technical report he's going to present in Ecocare in the middle of next week.

The whole thing still needs to be written . . . But the content is there, I have it, the bulk of the work is done . . . Puddu is going to send me the financials and the up-to-date timing tomorrow, in an e-mail . . . He already has the information from the Japanese, he was working on it this week . . . It's a good thing he has Puddu, it's a good thing there are people like him in the world . . . The technical and financial report on the work on the ship will be drafted by the people at Ecocare . . . Wednesday in the City in the North we'll put together the dossier and we'll construct a

PowerPoint, which is definitely something they're going to want
... We're going to have to have it translated into English too, but
they'll take care of that in the company. All right, then, let's see: a
brief introduction on the pre-contractual details, the various under-
standings with the Egyptians and the Japanese, the overall environmental and technical conditions, on all the preliminary steps that
have been taken concerning the biological, morphological, method-
ological, technological and economic analyses, etc.—OK ... Then
a summary analysis of the technical steps as the Japanese have laid
them out, with approximate timing and costs, not including preparation, transfer and positioning of the construction-ship:

1) Identification of area for first experimental intervention, necessary for the final calibration of working methods. There are
   a couple of potential locations to the north of Dahab: on this
   decision the Egyptians have the last word. Surface area of the
   first parcel, roughly two and a half acres. Fine. Installation of
   the underwater grid in order to subdivide the area into quad-
   rants of one yard by one yard. This is an optimal size dictated
   by the technical specifications of the scanner. Preliminary pho-
   tographic survey (already undertaken) with high-resolution
   cameras, calibration of the colour palette for the final selection
   of the appropriate pigments. The colours will need to be evaluated in dry conditions. Also fine.

2) Underwater positioning of the 3-D scanner (three hours of
   work for each repositioning). The Japanese will work with six
   machines simultaneously. They promise they'll increase the
   number once they've completely fine-tuned the procedure. OK.

3) Scanning and data-acquisition phase concerning the current
   state of subject area. Tolerances of one and a half millimetres .
   . . Fuck, only the Japanese can guarantee you tolerances of this
   order of precision. Data transmission to Japan where each scanning module will be reproduced in 3-D with a three-dimensional
   plotter. All the details are in the report from the Japs, which
   could bisect the asshole of a passing sparrow, *as usual* . . .

4) Morphological reconstruction of the substrate upon which the
   fake coral is to be installed, along with all the other species

already identified by the team of Japanese marine biologists (see scientific report, attached). In fact: this is the most complicated problem, because there is no actual geo-morphological substrate, the living coral grows and develops on the skeleton of the dead coral and separation is difficult . . . OK. Now, let's see . . .

5) Construction of an industrial shed in Japan, or adaptation of an existing structure, with a surface area of half an acre, a structure devoid of intermediate supports, the preliminary design has already been drawn up by a mixed working group from Fakenature and Ecocare, where the plottered modules will be laid down one by one. Crucial to comply with norms concerning secrecy: word must not leak, all the installations must be masked by other activities, all personnel will be contractually bound to absolute confidentiality (dossier from the Japanese, attached).

6) Once the first modules have been positioned, the next step is to proceed to full production of the fake organisms, adapting them to the substrate after demolishing the skeleton of the recently dead coral. They've already done a number of test runs. The procedure is comparable to that followed with dental prostheses: detachment of the dead coral, cast of the substrate, construction of the prosthesis with adaptive testing on the cast, final installation of the prosthesis with specific fastening techniques . . . This ought to be placed in the introduction, as an explanatory summary.

7) Every section of seabed, exactly one square yard, will have its own prosthetic coral. Each piece that is reproduced will be catalogued with a serial number for reference, and set aside. There is a minimum range of morphological variations beneath which it will become clear what is going on, so for each species it will be necessary to come up with at least two or three hundred models (details to be determined in the final contract). Materials, techniques, and pigments have already been more or less developed and tested for every species, but of course the full and final test will be carried out on site, and no less

than five years after the installation of the Falsification. Etc. Fine.

8) Then on site demolition of the dead coral, section by section, and its replacement with a copy, not necessarily identical. The organisms that are still alive will be left in their current location, but we cannot say whether they will survive. Only subsequent monitoring will be able to say. A vast stretch of the sea around the experimental area will be placed off-limits to fishermen and all other kinds of activity, both underwater and on the surface, for an appropriate period of time. On this point, the Egyptians insist there will be no problem.

9) There is no point in concealing the fact that the counterfeit seabed will require maintenance and cleaning. An immense undertaking, which the Egyptians will have to take on entirely. And for that matter, they already do so, with the genuine coral.

10) We will provide:
   a) fully equipped ship;
   b) equipment not directly specified by Fakenature, in accordance with appropriately negotiated terms;
   c) all materials and installations that prove necessary;
   d) the specialized workforce to set up construction sites;
   e) the underwater and surface technical substrate;
   f) connections and logistics;
   g) the management of whatever subcontracting and specialty contributions may prove necessary;
   h) healthcare, housing, catering, and management of all the inevitable pains in the neck that might arise with the Egyptians.

The Japanese and the Egyptians don't get along particularly well . . . Ecocare's mediation will be fundamental . . . On this point I'm going to have to be as precise and accurate as I can, even though any attempt to assign numbers and costs to the labour force that will be required would still be wholly premature. But I do already have an idea of the *type* of people that will be required . . .

11) If everything goes according to plan, the Egyptian government guarantees us five more parcels of two and a half acres each. For now it's only a tentative agreement. But they know that, with the prices we're offering, we can only make a profit if we manage to get going at full efficiency with subsequent work. My idea is that this guarantee should be included in the contract, with specified compensation in the case they should change their minds . . . In short, there's work here through at least 2030. But after all, it's the people at Ecocare who are going to make those decisions . . . If they want to run risks in order to keep the Egyptians happy, they can be my guests . . . In fact, on this point it might be advisable for me to keep my lips zipped. It's not part of the expert advice they're paying me for. Amen.

The whole thing will need to be spiced up and seasoned with the facts and figures on timing, costs, and technical issues that they have at Ecocare. In three days I can write the whole thing. Meeting on Thursday afternoon: I have less than a week . . . To me, the thing that kills me is the time . . . I want my time back, I want time to turn back into something that belongs to me, the way it did during the Great Summers by the Sea in the late Postwar Years . . . Back then, yes, that was life. In the water of the Postwar Years, there was all of life's truth, everything that you needed to know . . .

The Unmoved Mover

Though he'd lived in captivity from the day of his birth, Ivo couldn't imagine that this would be the day of his further capture.

The spacious corral within which he was allowed to move at will included a Bay with its Reefs, the City on the Sea with its harbour, and of course, the Beach: this was the place—anything but contemptible in terms of form, size and content—where, year after year, he was allowed four long months of Summer. They were analogue days in an analogue world but consumed as if they were real. Because Ivo was sixteen years old and to him, not only were those days real but, as far as he was concerned, life outside of there wasn't worth living.

From the first seaside holiday of the Brandani family, in the late '50s, he suddenly saw life in Winter—which is to say, any existence outside of that corral of land and water—as an intolerable constraint.

At the very instant he first set foot on a beach, it became clear to him that he had found something special and practically perfect; this in other words was the sole setting that clearly existed for one purpose only, the happiness of its inhabitants. Happiness in air & water, happiness of sand, smells, skin. Happiness of shade and light, happiness of fishes, of sails.

With the passage of time and the succession of Summers, the beach added other, more complicated and hidden forms of possible ecstasy to these basic happinesses. Ivo Brandani's youth and inexperience were capable of transforming them into authentic and specific forms of suffering that he had never before encountered. Four months of analogue existence spent in the enclosed and apparently artificial universe of the beach, which included the arm of the sea contained in the Bay. A perfect niche, if only that year it hadn't been contaminated by a subject he was going to be tested on come September: philosophy. He'd always thought he was good at philosophy, he liked it and believed he had a natural gift for it— that's why he hadn't bothered to study, except in spurts, and that's why Bottazzi had assigned him the test right after summer holidays. Bottazzi. Young, slight of stature, with his tiny feet invariably shod in a pair of worn-out black loafers. When he talked he displayed a pile of crooked teeth that looked as though they'd been tossed at random into his chicken-butt mouth. His lips glistened, he drooled slightly and gesticulated, joining his fingers into cones and windmilling his hands through the air, one whirling around the other, or else he'd place them on the lectern as if he were moving pieces on a chessboard. He was obnoxious, off-putting and gloomy; his teaching style was boring and complicated, and yet every time Ivo found himself hypnotized by those strange movements of hands and lips. Bottazzi was a Catholic and appeared to be profoundly bored: by himself first and foremost, by the profession he'd chosen, by the thoughts of others that he was obliged to set forth in his lessons, thoughts to which he seemed to be utterly indifferent. For Bottazzi it was Curriculum and nothing else. And whatever the cost, the Curriculum had to be finished. In the last dwindling days of that school year he'd managed to complete the Curriculum, but only by stuffing in medieval philosophy at the end, so hastily that Ivo practically hadn't noticed, maybe he'd been absent that day, he couldn't recall. And so it was that during an oral exam based on a 'random sampling' of the topics covered he proved to be completely ignorant of St Thomas and all the rest of them and was therefore flunked and scheduled for retesting in September. A test to take in September was an intolerable insult to the glistening prospect of his Summer, at the precise moment it was about to begin—that was the life that was owed to him, that was his real life and it belonged to him alone.

'At the sea they can't reach you, they don't know how to go underwater, there they'll never lay hands on you, they can't tell you what you can do or can't do . . . Father is far away, usually he shows up Friday night, or Saturday. He gets there tired, on edge, pale, and reeking of sour sweat, aggressive, disappointed, the back of his shirt soaked from the car's upholstery . . . Go ahead, work yourself to death, I wish you'd just die, then you'd finally leave me in peace. What are you even coming out here for? Don't you see how pale and white you are? Don't you smell yourself? What do you have in common with all this? With the Bay, with the Sea, with the *Mandrake*? Do you want the *Mandrake* tomorrow morning? Fine. But why do you insist on taking it out if you don't know how to sail it?'

'No, Papà, tomorrow I can't go, I have something planned with Giacomo, we're going fishing. No, please, tomorrow we have a motorboat, we're going to Ponente. We're getting up early, at six. Tomorrow of all days, no, please, I'm begging you . . .'

Father's pale, embittered face, with his perennial grimace of disgust, his mouth twisted into a crease of disappointment, which only deepens as he says—it's what he always says—that he's 'working himself to death' for them: 'Yes, and for you too, to give you all this and then, when I do come down, not once that we can spend some time together, not even for an outing in a boat.'

Ivo could perfectly well say to him: 'Why do you want to spend time with me, if everything we ever talk turns into a sermon, an endless, infinite busting of my balls? I always wind up saying: Yes, certainly, Papà. I always have to agree that you're right, otherwise you lose your temper and sometimes you even hit me. Why do you want to spend time with your son if you can't tolerate anything different from what *you* think? I already know what you think about everything, and I've known for some time now. All you do is repeat it to me. You agree with the professors, with the priests. You're all just one thing, a single huge alliance of ball-busters.'

Of course, in theory that's what Ivo could tell him, but it would constitute a catastrophic violation of protocol; instead he listens patiently, head bowed, and then slips away as soon as possible, leaves, tries to make himself invisible, impossible to find. You can't joke around with Father, who's already furious about the test to be taken in September: 'I don't care if it's just one subject,' he says, 'the fact remains that you shirked your duty.'

The day of his further capture is more or less like all the others, simple & bright. He sleeps in until mid-afternoon, except when he plans to go sailing, in which case he asks Giuseppa to wake him up around eleven, but there's usually no wind before one o'clock, or if there is, it's not much. Otherwise, he sleeps as long as he likes.

Breakfast very late, with a cafe latte, alone, because Ivo lives offbeat from Mother and his sisters, who are already on the beach, or in town. So when he returns home, driven by hunger, he lunches at three or four in the afternoon. He stays out late at night. First he goes to the arena for a movie, then out for a gelato, after which a drive somewhere, or else he hangs out with his friends, each stupider than the next, strolling aimlessly down the dark avenues of the city on the sea, laughing joking smoking almost until break of day. In Summer, you feel feverish and tense, nothing is really a holiday, nothing is done with ease, everything is challenging, enig-matic, mysterious, dream-like, exciting, effortful, until you crash into sleep.

His body is being transformed, it grows lean. Skinniness & agility, the increase in stature, shoulders already broadening since last winter, at judo class in the gym. In the months to come, swimming, rowing, sailing will all make Ivo's muscles a little more voluminous, toned, tough, articulated and edgy. But leisure is fundamental, reading comic books in the afternoon, stretched out on the flowered bedcover along with the sand that clings to his heels . . .

The *Mandrake* is fast, but winning is entirely another matter. In order to win, you have to be able to sense when the boat is slip-ping through the water the absolute best that she can, so you need to centre her to perfection. In a regatta you have to understand exactly where the wind is coming from at all times, know when to come around and why, learn how to manage the start, avoid being caught in the lee of anyone else's sails, refuse to let anyone else crush you. You have to know how to skip out of the way. You have to know how to depart at the right time. All of these are things he doesn't really know how to do well, and they can be added to the rising tide of other things he doesn't do well, that he does just OK, with no real commitment, concentration or discipline.

This is his first walk on the beach, today—it's hot and, for now, there's no wind.

The asphalt on the beachfront promenade is scorching hot. Villas to one side, changing cabins on the other, a long row of cars parked in the sun, young skinny plane-tree saplings that offer very little shade and are used by dogs to pee on. Ivo has already had the tragic experience of stepping on a fresh dogshit in his Hong Kong flip-flops. You can hear music, muffled by the hot air, coming up from the loudspeakers on the beach, beyond the gaps between the cabins you can see flags barely fluttering in the sea breeze, no more than a breath of air. Brushing past the red-hot line of parked cars, the long seasonal migration of weary people flip-flopping home, still in their swimsuits. People loaded down with bags, women pushing baby carriages, with toddlers holding their hands, the dogshits by now well plastered down onto the marble-chip floor tiles of the walkway. Girls in bikinis, under a beachwrap knotted at the back of their neck, boys holding packs of cigarettes, various brands—Stop Marlboro Kent Rothmans Peer Muratti Winston—or else tucked away in the rolled-up T-shirt sleeve, the Ronson or the Zippo in the pockets of their Bermuda shorts—everyone smokes, they insist on smoking, they show off packs of American cigarettes, they show off lighters that emit powerful jets of flame.

Carriages hauled by horses steaming in the heat have left pestilential trails of manure behind them on the asphalt, manure that ferments in the hot sunshine and assaults every sense. A few people go sailing by full throttle on their mopeds, shirts swollen with air, crushing that manure repeatedly, intentionally, under their wheels: *flap, flap, flap.*

A long line of wooden booths in which to change, cabins for rent for the day or even for the whole summer, a little beat up and chipped from the many seasonal assemblies, disassemblies and stackings.

Inside cabin 348, a wooden shelf, a line of coat hooks, a standard folding chair; light comes in through the gaps between the boards and the shutter slats, set up high, above the door. The wooden plank floor is covered with slightly damp sand—someone's gone swimming, someone's changed out of their suit. A woman's swimsuit lies on the floor, wet and coated with sand. It looks like a mollusc, a beached jellyfish. Ivo has entered a world of specific objects, here everything is very solid, very simple.

The Brandani-Salvetti family's cabin is large, there are also a woman's dress in light cotton with shoulder pads, a striped T-shirt, a pair of men's swimming trunks hanging on a nail, navy blue, with internal netting to contain penis and scrotum. Ivo turns his gaze away as if it were something obscene: Father leaves it here during the week, it's there to remind them that he's still there, that he exists, they they owe all this to him and his work and that it's provisional, undeserved, illegitimate. There's a straw beach bag, another bag made of coloured canvas, robes, cotton hats and straw hats, spare two-piece swimsuits, the bra cups lined in white fabric, women's swimsuit bottoms, the crotch lined with white cloth. The mystery of Big Sister's and the Salvetti cousin's pubic areas, signals of something not clearly imaginable, dark, sordid. Mother's swimsuit, a black one-piece, which she almost never wears. Then there are sundresses, combs in colourful plastic, with oversized teeth.

He only needs the cabin as a place to leave his Hong Kong flip-flops on the floor and toss his T-shirt over a chair. But he loves this ambiguous space immersed in penumbra, the sounds of the beach reaching it muffled, as if from measureless, dazzling distances. There is a strong smell here of creams in small jars and tubes, sun creams and after-sun moisturizers piled up on the shelf: two families make use of this cabin, parents, sisters, uncles and aunts, cousins of both genders. Pure chaos.

In the corners, fishing gear, a net, a fishing spear, the speargun that Ivo found last year in the water, abandoned on the seabed, a Cressi Cernia Velox spring gun, too long and too hard to load, full of sand, practically shot, then a bamboo fishing pole, assemblable, obsolete, with tarnished brass joints; he no longer knows who it belongs to. A toy beach bucket, shovel and moulds, a plastic toy boat that belongs to his cousins, still kids (the battery-powered electric motor broke the very first day), cheap beach games, heavy ceramic beach discuses, sand marbles, a wooden sailboat with red sails, diving fins, masks, and snorkels, a deflated swim ring, a deflated rubber boat folded up in a corner, a child's beach ball, another one for grown-ups. Rolled-up straw beach mats, wooden clogs scattered on the floor, a heap of magazines on the chair: *Oggi, Gente, Stop, Epoca*; a few comic books rumpled from the damp: *Topolino, Tiramolla, L'Intrepido, Il Monello*. All this stuff manages to fit into a small cabin—of course it does, this is the beach. It's late, mothers and children have gone back. No aunts or uncles around. Big Sister is certainly down at the cafe with all her friends, by this time of the afternoon there shouldn't be anyone under the umbrella. From here on, for the next 100 or 150 feet, the sand is scorching hot. Ivo leaps from one cement slab to the next to avoid burning his feet. He veers close to the public bathrooms, likewise made of cement (sand-covered porcelain, the smell of bleach, wet with fresh water, with urine), at a run he reaches the navy blue shade of the Brandani-Salvetti canopy.

Three rows of devices to block light. Large, stout beach umbrellas planted in the sand, a few tiny holes in the canvas that produce an intensely luminous dot of light on the bodies of those sitting in the shade. The wooden pole is thick, professional, the joint is made of bright metal with glints of oil, no rust, well-made equipment, built to last, the umbrella ribs are made of bamboo, flexible, the tip of each rib is covered with brass and a ring grommet to hold the canvas. That wooden pole is a benchmark of Summer. Hanging from one of the ribs is a little pink card marked with the number 348 and, in pencil, the name of the person who rented that umbrella.

Names of families that have been coming here for years and who always plump down in the same place in accordance with a map that we might call inviolable, institutional, universally respected. Beach umbrellas like homes: the way it was last summer and the summer before that, this year too number 348 is assigned to the Brandani-Salvetti family, for four months.

The folding chairs are essential, comfortable, heavy, stout. The kind of thing you only see here at the beach, with the name of the beach club impressed on the outside of the backrest. All in very durable sailcloth. Recliners with adjustable awnings and backs. Simple but ingenious mechanisms, reliable, even though every so often someone does manage to pinch their fingers. There is no such thing as an absolutely and definitively comfortable position on the beach: you have to move, get up, adjust, change, sit back down, in the shade in the sun, stretch out on the sand, on the beach towel, get back up again, take a swim, take a walk. The beach is work, it doesn't take care of itself. Every morning there are the people-with-the-neighbouring-beach-umbrella to greet, and that's a rule; Ivo does his part distractedly but cordially. All around are people he's known for years, Signora Rodoni, skinny, lipstick on her lips, in the shade, reading Mario Tobino, *The Underground*, with the bellyband still on it announcing 'Strega Prizewinner.' People read newspapers, do crossword puzzles, skilfully solve rebuses in the *Settimana Enigmistica*—the *Weekly Puzzler*.

The beach has a sort of virtual affinity and correspondence in the *Settimana Enigmistica*. The beach too is white and useless, dotted with episodes, covered with slight puzzles, rebuses. The entire Eastern Beach is one vast *Investigation with Susi*—it's like a huge double page of *Sharpen Your Eyesight*, full of details to discover, correspondences to find. Ivo couldn't really say why he so adores the *Weekly Puzzler*, which Mother never fails to buy when they're here, as if it were an integral part of the summer package. Idle chatter, riddles, horoscopes.

At this time of day the beach is tired, it's hungry, it's rapidly emptying out, soon the changing of the guard will be complete. Ivo is here out of inertia, because he doesn't know where else to go, and most of all because there's not much wind offshore. But also because he likes the beach at this time of day. He likes the long slanting rays of light and the general feeling of indolence, the relaxation of adult control, the torrid atmosphere that settles over people and things. It feels as if anything could happen, but nothing ever does. This is the moment of the babysitters, the suntan obsessives who lie there in silence roasting themselves to a turn, the serving girls who come down to get some sun in the early afternoon, the off-hours; they have no lounge chairs, no beach umbrella, they sit down on the shore, they lay out their colourful beach towels where the sand is perennially damp and hard, amid the paddle boats hauled up out of the water, the holes excavated by little kids and then left unfilled. They even go swimming. And they take a look around. A few local males, muscular and wearing extremely skimpy swimsuits, pace back and forth, measuring the beach in that very zone and evaluating the resources it has to offer. Groups of dark silhouettes plays volleyball with the sun behind them, just beyond the tideline, where moving is still easy, but the water softens the falls, the dives.

Under the umbrellas or wandering the beach, or else out in the water, or playing ball along the beachfront, Ivo sees friends of his, boys and girls, people from his circle of reference, a group he doesn't really feel he belongs to, but which still possesses sufficient critical mass to draw him into its gravitational pull. He considers them landlubbers, kids who have no sense of the sea, who fail to feel any primary commitment to the water, the fish, the seabeds in the gulf, who don't sail and who don't take part in regattas. Beach people, in other words, like all those who spend their whole days sitting on paddle boats shooting the breeze, fooling around, and trying to make time with girls, who organize every afternoon, in regular rotation, a party at someone's place. Records and Coca-Cola, potato chips, single-portion pizzas, orangeade, Peroni beer, Chinotto soft drinks, even Tamarindo, the tamarind-pulp beverage. There was dancing. Ivo always goes to them, but on the beach he spends little time with the Group. He doesn't feel like getting sucked into all that coming and going with petty crushes, petty quarrels, petty rages, continuously gossiping and backbiting. Ivo doesn't know and can't understand that the true purpose of the Group is to teach a fruitful and convenient social mode of behaviour, to learn the cunning and wiles of living with other people, training in the manoeuvres of courtship, how to leave and how to take, how to know women, the way they think and, finally, their body. He hates the successions of leaders and leaderesses, the formation of royal couples, the spectacular beauties surrounded by their handmaidens, the prestige of the boys with the most money, the biggest and best terrace or garden, the moped, the Vespa, the motorcycle, some of them even have a *car*.

To him it's not even conceivable, the way that Father is by nature, that, once he turns eighteen, he might be given, I don't know, a black, or red, Alfa Romeo GT Veloce, and enough money to buy petrol, cigarettes and all the rest. And yet there are those among the ones who *know each other* here that have exactly that: someone who might even have flunked the year at school, some relaxed smug son-of-a-bitch in gleaming Ray-Bans and tight-fitting Lacoste.

The beach is bristling with platforms set high on cement pilings, cylindrical columns that conceal insidious shadows, full of things that belong to the various establishments, under the jurisdiction of the lifeguards and attendants. The wooden canopies covered with reeds, the awnings in rough blue or green canvas, which protect from the blazing sunshine bars and kiosks that sell mini-pizzas and Coca-Colas, orangeades, calzones and hot pockets, sugar-dusted custard buns and fried doughnuts, but especially packaged ice cream. They sell Toseroni ice-cream bars—Ivo's never tried one, because the trusted family trademark is Algida, if he's feeling adventuresome, Alemagna—then there is Eskibon, Mottarello, Fortunello, Coppa del Nonno, lemon orange mint, sour black cherry popsicles, violently coloured green red yellow magenta, rainbow-hued. Ivo leaves the popsicles whole and sucks away the syrup from the ice until they turn transparent. Round tables, stackable chairs in aluminium tubing and plaited plastic, that leave a bright red imprint on your ass, or wooden folding chairs. Music plays continuously from the jukebox, boys sitting smoking, leaning against the wooden railings. Girls in bikinis and long smooth hair, cigarettes burning, crushed-out stubs on the floor, sand and dampness everywhere. Everywhere what prevails is the unsaid, the lewd eye, the rapid or the carefully considered evaluation, repeated and impudent, or awkward, embarrassed. The silent gaze of everyone rests on the bodies of everyone, withdraws, returns, persists. Barely defined pectorals and abdominals. Hairs on chests, bellies. Breasts, red zits, shaved hair growing back on the insides of thighs, here and there pubic hairs poking out from under swimsuits. Toenails, flaking nail polish. The quality of the human material changes from bar to bar, kiosk to kiosk. As you move from west to east, the beach becomes more well to do, fancier, more obnoxious, unwelcoming. The platforms of the bars and cafes all the way down there, where the sand ends and the rocky shoals begin, are for the wealthier beach-goers. There the girls are prettier and more confident, they appear unattainable, out of reach. Ivo is intimidated, he almost never goes there. The territory where his family can afford an umbrella, a ring of shade that Father's Work can procure them for four months' time, is in an intermediate zone between the rich families that frequent the bar and the hicks and losers of the stretch before the Rotunda, the people at the Bagni Tritone: the beach never lies about your social standing.

When he leaves the circle of shade, which the slanting early-afternoon sunlight has pushed away from the family beach umbrella, Ivo turns westward where, a few hundred yards away, the Rotunda can be seen. Suddenly to go there strikes him as better than sprawling lazily in a lounge chair, nursing his incipient hunger. He estimates that he'll be in time to scarf down one of the last remaining minipizzas. He picks up his pace.

Walking along the landscape of the water's edge he encounters the shower stalls, arranged at regular intervals; on the slippery wooden boards, slightly rotten, velvety moss takes root while tiny torrents of fresh water carve out little canyons through the sand down to the sea. Where children have worked all day to divert the streams with dams and other works of hydraulic engineering, now there lie only ruins made of foul-smelling sand, abandoned to be trodden under by grown-ups. Ivo is very familiar with these minimal, precise geographies, stagnant pools of foam even though the use of shampoo is forbidden: there's a sign but it's ignored. There are people waiting to take a shower, people rinsing off, scrubbing themselves, men holding their swimsuits open to let streams of fresh water pour in, first in the front, then in the rear. It's an obscene gesture and they know it; when they're done they look around, brashly. The water is cold, in fact it's freezing, sickly sweet, slippery, unholy, odourless. There are very few girls, this time of day, beneath the spray; Ivo has always observed the mystery of their bodies and their actions with feverish attention: gleaming, fit, with their skin icy and shivering, drenched hair that they'll brush at length, sitting meditatively in the sun, or chatting with a girlfriend, or a group of friends, or in their boyfriend's company. It's almost three, there's no longer a sign of blue-lipped children wrapped in bathrobes, their fingers pruned by the water, noses dripping—the beach is now fully adult.

Here's the Rotunda, huge, modern, sprawling on the water like a gigantic crab on cement piers all encrusted with mussels. You climb the steps and inside you find a cafe, still crowded with people in swimsuits. They cluster around the cash register, here too ordering the usual things: espressos and Coca-Colas and *supplì* croquettes and doughnuts. There are still a couple of small pizzas, Ivo gets in line, then he goes over to the counter, made of filled and polished travertine and glass, and before long he has a small pizza in one hand, nice and fresh and warm, knowing that if he folds it awkwardly it will spill oil onto his hand and then down to his elbow.

The restaurant dining room, large, half-deserted, echoing behind the glass doors. The guests dine in shorts and T-shirts, in compliance with the posted regulations:

OUR GUESTS ARE HEREBY INFORMED
THAT ADMITTANCE TO THIS FACILITY
IS NOT ALLOWED IN SWIMSUITS

Ivo is attracted by seaside restaurants. As he bites into his minipizza—he can already perceive the oil as it starts to drip down his forearm—he steps close to the plate-glass window and looks in. White tablecloths, napkins, waiters, carafes of wine from a large flask, yellowish. From the kitchen comes wafting strong smells of fried squid and shrimp, seafood risottos, spaghetti with clam sauce, carpet-shell or cherrystone clams as the diner prefers, spaghetti with mixed seafood, linguine with prawns, sautéed mussels, fish soups, octopus Luciana-style, mixed seafood antipastos, tellin bruschetta, grilled sole, sole meunière, stewed sea bass with mayonnaise, sliced houndshark with tomato sauce, sargo, gilthead bream, grilled swordfish filets, stewed angler fish, even lobster—at least that's what the menu claims, printed and framed by the entrance.

'But, if you wish, sir, we can have the chef whip up a nice little grilled steak, a lovely veal chop with sautéed potatoes, or we can offer a bowl of spaghetti with meat sauce, a saltimbocca, that is sautéed slices of veal with ham and sage, or a breaded Milanese cutlet, some stewed or poached chicory, as you wish. Caprese salad, poached string beans or blanched string beans with olive oil and lemon juice . . .' that is, what the waiter had added once, the only time that he had eaten lunch there with Father.

Outside, on the large ring-shaped terrace, there are more tables and chairs and people sitting around listening to a juke box playing at full volume. Men are smoking and watching the women in swim-suits. Groups of boys joke around, shouting and laughing with their dicks hard in their elasticized Speedos, so horny that it takes prac-tically nothing and they have to go hide, to the snickering of the others. Ivo imagines that many of these young men are going to be taking exams in two or three subjects in October, and yet here they are wasting their time, carefree, as if they had nothing in the world to worry about.

'Some of them have surely flunked their year, but it's nothing serious for them, it's just a pain in the ass to have to be left back a year . . . But how can they do it? If it happened to me, Father would kill me, he'd throw me out of the house, he'd send me to work. I can't even stand to think about what he'd do to me . . .'

The girls are wearing bikinis with pastel-hued bra cups: pista-chio, straw yellow, salmon pink. But also black, and white. Their hair has streaks of sun-bleaching, smooth. They laugh, bronzed and made-up; all is calm, thoughts of elsewhere are far away. Ivo bites into his 50-lire minipizza. It's delicious.

Going back to the Brandani-Salvetti precinct of shade, he sees Sandro sitting and reading under an umbrella in the second row. He waves hello to him. Sandro is a member of Big Sister's social circle. He's at the university, a freshman majoring in Political Science, if Ivo's not remembering wrong. Ivo respects him because he looks like someone who thinks, who reads and who stays informed. He's tall, fat, flaccid, homely, with thick-lensed glasses and bulging myopic eyes, a headful of straight black hair, bristly as a rosemary bush. He has large teeth, thick wet lips, a wide mobile mouth, with undefined outlines, and Ivo can't keep himself from staring at it. He laughs, heaving, continuously, practically squeaking like a giant mouse, but he knows how to speak about almost anything, with precision and authority, especially about politics. He almost always has a newspaper, a magazine and a book in his hands, he speaks continuously and explains earnestly, as if he were engaged in a perennial debate. He argues his point of view and never seems to lose his temper. He never goes in the water, he never lies in the sun, his flesh is pasty white, covered with tufts of hair and large moles, he wears a pair of dark, very loose Bermuda shorts made out of some synthetic material. Ivo perceives him to be a kind and open person, slightly patronizing, and he likes talking with him. He walks over and asks: 'What are you reading?' even though he can see perfectly well for himself. Sandro looks up from his copy of *L'Espresso*, a bedsheet of a newsmagazine covered with banner headlines and large black-and-white photos. On the back page, Ivo rapidly reads an advertisement, spare, primitive:

Tell me *bon voyage*, but sell me
SUPERCORTEMAGGIORE
the powerful Peninsular petrol.

On the front page, there is an enigmatic banner headline:

After our electric power supply

WHAT ELSE CAN BE NATIONALIZED?

And then, below that, a headline above a photo of Marilyn Monroe states:

THE WORLD THAT DESTROYED MARILYN

On the bottom right there is a smaller photograph of a smiling Stefania Sandrelli. She's wearing a light blouse, unbuttoned, the hems knotted over her wet swimsuit. The blouse is wet, where her breasts are. 'Her too, her especially.'

At home, that newsmagazine was never allowed, because Father refuses to read it. Father buys only *Il Tempo* and sometimes *Il Borghese*, which is a political publication but which always features very daring photographs of half-nude women, in stockings and garter belts which Ivo uses for his daily masturbation.

Sandro immediately snickers, and says nothing but: 'Late empire.'

Then he says it again: 'We're in the middle of the late empire. Late empire.' He likes the formulation. Right away he emits another one of his electric-discharge giggles. Ivo has heard from his sister that Sandro is 'radical'. But he has no idea of what that means.

'The price, you understand? The consolation prize required to form part of the coalition government, that is, without actually forming part, but abstaining, supporting it from the outside, that is, throwing the stone but hiding the hand that threw it, is the nationalization of the electric system. You get it? They were going to start a revolution and now they're willing to settle for *nationalizing* the electric system. Late empire.' Nervous little giggle.

Ivo hardly understands a word of what he's saying, but he's immediately reminded of Father, who inveighs at the dinner table against the 'little comrades' who want to nationalize the electric power grid, and then adds: 'This is just the beginning: I don't have a lira to my name, but if I did, I'd take it and put it in a Swiss bank, the way the ones who have money do, that is, everyone else but me . . .'

376

Ivo thinks about declaring his opposition to nationalization right then and there, even though he doesn't actually know what it is. And so, just to have something to say, he blurts out a: 'So this is only the beginning, eh?'

'In what sense? If you think that this is the first step on the road to the Soviets . . .'—'What the fuck are Soviets?' Ivo wonders—'. . . you're badly mistaken. This is just a consolation prize and it's never going to be anything more than a consolation prize. The Christian Democrats could eat the Socialists for breakfast . . . That's exactly how Moro split the Socialist–Communist front, he pitted them one against the other, you see that? I'm a liberal, but the establishment of a national agencies for electric power is fine with me. It's necessary. We're a country poor in resources. No coal. Electricity is strategic, you understand? Late empire.'

'But, weren't you . . . *radical*?'

'Certainly (giggle). And what do you think the radicals really are? Huh?'

'Liberals?'

'Sure, good work. *Liberals* and *secular*, there's even another definition, "liberal-socialists", which is of course absurd. We are the only political force that is authentically, *radically* anti-clerical . . . The priests say that the radicals are all Freemasons . . . In other words, your choice.'

Suddenly Ivo is reminded that he too, not just the pinchbeck losers of the Rotunda, has an exam to redo. And today Giorgio is tutoring him! At three! He has just ten minutes. Enough time to run straight home, grab a pen, his book, and his notebook, and head back down. Everything he needs is right there, in a few yards' space. The building where they rent an flat every year overlooks the beach, on the far side of the beachfront promenade. Next to it is the great big villa owned by Giorgio's family, and the tutoring takes place in a small guest house behind it.

He says: 'Are you staying here? See you later, then! *Ciao*!'

And he runs off.

The one-storey building is small and low, under eucalyptus trees covered with cicadas. A din of insect noise in the afternoon heat of a Tyrrhenian August comes in through the open window, under the half-lowered wooden roller blind. Giorgio goes on, imperturbably, holding his cigarette clamped between forefinger and thumb of his right hand, burning vertically, almost never taking a puff. The ashes form a small, ever-taller pillar, which inevitably begins to lean to one side, so that after a while Ivo's undivided attention is there, to capture the moment that it spills onto the table. But Giorgio's pillar of ash remains erect, until the cigarette is almost entirely consumed, until the ember grazes the long fingers, yellow with nicotine, that is, until the moment in which he crushes it out in the ashtray.

Giorgio is very clear, much clearer than Signor Bottazzi. With him, Ivo has the sensation that he understands everything, he waxes enthusiastic, even: the Immovable Motor, the Unmoved Mover, infinitely powerful, is St Thomas's God, at the very start of the chain of causation, engendering everything there is.

'The proofs of St Thomas are five in number, *ex Motu*—you know, when it's time for the exam you're going to be expected to know them by heart—*ex Causa, ex Contingentia, ex Gradu*—don't worry about the ashes, just write down the list—and *ex Fine. Ex Fine*, that is, things in the universe appear orderly to us, they seem to have a purpose, and therefore there must be an Orderer . . . St Thomas proceeds both inductively and deductively . . .'

The Scholastics: Duns Scotus, Robert Grosseteste, William of Ockham, Roger Bacon, Jean Buridan . . . abstruse, he's going to have to know them all. The school where his family has sent him without so much as a by-your-leave is run by priests, it's for rich kids—'You'll see, they'll set you straight there,' says Father ('. . . Father isn't Catholic, he's not especially religious, and he has nothing but bad things to say about priests: so why did he want to send me to that school? What needs to be set straight about me . . .?')—and the priests have a special interest in Scholasticism. That's what Giorgio told him at the beginning of their month of tutoring.

'Which means you need to know them well. Don't try to skimp on this—they can flunk you even if you're only taking a single test. It's happened before.'

'. . . things can exist or not exist, if they exist, someone has acted to ensure they exist . . .'

Giorgio also belongs to Ivo's older sister's Group, but he's older than Sandro, he's taking his degree in Philosophy. Unfailingly serious, reflective, completely chilly, indifferent to any attempts to establish a slightly more confidential tone. Giorgio's mouth resembles Bottazzi's to a certain extent, and like it, is perennially pursed in a chicken-butt pout. Like Bottazzi, Giorgio also moves his hands when he explains, but only his right hand, because his left hand is in use, holding his cigarette poised vertically, with the ash perfectly balanced. Ivo gets the idea that all philosophers are in a vast coalition, explaining one single thing—abstruse, uniform, asexual, detached and fuming: millions of cigarettes—domestic, unfiltered—lit and smoking away.

The lesson continues amid the incessant whirring of the cicadas.

Giorgio lights additional cigarettes and adroitly lets them consume themselves, as he argues points and explains each issue with great precision. It's not as if Ivo understands everything but he does seem to be getting a fairly clear general picture. Suddenly, without really thinking about it, he breaks into Giorgio's stream of words and says: 'But if the Church asks you to take it on faith then what need is there for a proof of God's existence? Isn't there a contradiction there? If you need proof, then what kind of faith is that? What's more: How does St Thomas know that everything in the universe is ordered towards a certain end?'

'Why can't I just shut up? Why do I need to talk? Why don't I just zip my lips, now that the hour is even up?'

Instead Giorgio answers him immediately: 'A Christian has to understand what he believes in. And a non-Christian should be convinced of the goodness and the superiority, philosophical as well as theological, of faith in Christ. *Fides quaerens intellectum.*

Reason serves faith and vice versa. A believer's intellect also requires gratification.'

Ivo dares to say it: 'But isn't it a sort of . . . consolation prize?'

'If you like, you can call it that, but don't even think of uttering any definitions of that nature during the exam. And after all, frankly, to call Scholasticism a consolation prize . . .'

'. . . the consolation prize of the little comrades . . .'

Giorgio looks at him quizzically, as if he had suddenly been startled awake from his philosophical dream. With a complicated manoeuvre of his head and arm, he manages to take a drag on his cigarette, leaving it poised vertically and safeguarding the integrity of the pillar of ash (Ivo adores this move); then, after exhaling a long plume of smoke from his mouth and nostrils: 'Who are the *little comrades*?'

'The ones in favour of the nationalization of the electric power company?' Ivo replies, uncertainly, but at this point freewheeling out of control.

'The Socialists . . .' says Giorgio. 'The nationalization of the power company would be a consolation prize for the little comrades? To get them to join in the coalition government? What would make you think such a thing? And what does it have to do with St Thomas?'

'Well, I was talking about it on the beach, with Sandro . . .'

'In any case, yes. You can call it a consolation prize . . . They broke the unity on the left to jump into a coalition government with the Christian Democrats, with the Social Democrats . . .' Then, pensively, he adds: 'We behave in such a schizophrenic manner . . . In Berlin, they build a wall and seal themselves in . . . Here we give it all away and stroll arm-in-arm with the Christian Democrats, we split the formation, we let our class enemy insinuate himself in the fissures of division and gain leverage, separating us more and more . . . In any case. Let's drop that topic. It's time for you to get going, I have another lesson. I'll see you the day after tomorrow.'

Ivo says: 'Yes, Friday, at three . . . But what does "class enemy" mean? Who's that?'

'That's no simple matter to explain. We can talk about it some other time. On Friday, by the way, we'll come back to St Thomas . . .'

The beach is right down below, Ivo has to go back to see if she's there. She always gets there about 2.30 or 3 in the afternoon, she lies under a beach umbrella in the second row on a line with the showers. She has a distinctive pose all her own, thanks to which Ivo has learnt to spot her from afar. She uses the technique of the lounger with the back stop reversed, a technique that makes it lie lower, almost like a beach bed, and there she lounges, one leg bent, her foot braced against the crosspiece of the chair. She has dark hair that's always wet, and she never stops running an oversized yellow large-toothed beach comb through it. It's the pose of a woman, indolent and fantastic. She seems exhausted, she barely moves, she rarely goes in the water. From a distance she looks beautiful. Little by little, day after day, Ivo has noticed all this from his spot in the Brandani-Savetti circle of shade. The curvature of the foot, sharply arched. The graceful fingers, turned slightly upwards, while the foot points downwards, the heel resting on the canvas-covered wooden frame.

If Ivo had an experienced man close at hand, someone who knew all about life and women, that man would have said to him: 'Ivo, always steer clear of indolent women, beware of lazy, indifferent women, keep your distance from the ones who pretend not to see you, the ones you can't get to notice you, but who watch you sidelong, the ones who are busy minding their own business, lying there without a man at their side, or the ones who might have a cluster of men around them, because they're the sorceresses you can't defend yourself against, they're the ones who'll cast a spell on you just for the fun of the thing, like Circe, for the pleasure of watching you grunt like a pig at their feet. Steer clear of them. It's not their fault, that's just how they are. It's in their nature, trust me on this.' But just now this sage adviser isn't available, and Ivo watches this girl, he can't stop watching her as the days go by and she, steady as clockwork, comes to the beach at the same time of day. She's beautiful, she resembles neither Brigitte nor Audrey, but she reminds him of them both . . .

Brigitte & Audrey are two absolute opposites, two paradigms that battle in his mind and torment his loins. Without giving quarter, without offering conciliation: there is no possible synthesis between Brigitte and Audrey, and all other women are nothing in comparison.

Both of them give him a strange ache in the belly, both of them make him uneasy in a way that can't be described as anything other than heat, down under, between penis and pelvis, in a zone of the body that is directly connected to the eyes, to the mind. These aren't erections, or they're not just erections. He has erections all day long, at the drop of a hat, often for no good reason, sometimes without so much as a thought to justify them. This is something different, a sort of painful yet pleasurable emotion, of the body, as if the flesh concealed within had suddenly turned incandescent and red, flushed with desperately pulsating blood. Brigitte & Audrey, each in her way, stir in him the discomfort of an impossible desire, put him face-to-face with the simple and unbearable truth of the fact that, however much he may be swept away with desire, he'll never possess them. Never, ever.

Both of them are made of velvet, but of two different kinds.

Audrey asks you for protection, for kindness. You have to rescue her from that South American guy, or maybe he's Spanish, take her away from that guy with salt-and-pepper hair and all that money, his name is José Luis de Vilallonga, take her away with you, for ever. Make her yours, her and the cat, in one single toasty embrace of whispers and softness and perfume, while outside it's been raining for weeks and there's a fire crackling in your fireplace and in front of the hearth there's a thick carpet where she crouches in a black leotard, with the cat purring in her arms. All you have to do is love her for ever. Outside it'll go on raining for all time, the fire in the fireplace will never go out . . . Audrey is the goddess of staying indoors in the Winter.

Brigitte promises you nothing, and asks you for nothing. With her you can't even dream of making it, unless you're handsome and rich, unless you have a villa at Saint-Tropez and a chalet in St Moritz and another one in Gstaad, a yacht so you can take her far offshore to go swimming and watch her swim naked and silent in the crystal clear water off the Côte d'Azur and look at her as she climbs up the boat ladder secured aft, as she pushes her hips forwards and seeks the bottom rung with her petite, arched foot, as that lovely fold of flesh between thigh and belly forms for an instant, the fold of flesh you see in pictures. She's something free and dangerous, you can't protect her. She tells you that if you want her all for yourself you'll have to tame her, keep her on a chain, subdue her: something unthinkable, completely *non*-possible . . . Brigitte is the goddess of throwing yourself open to Summer.

Ivo watches her from afar and thinks of the impossible combination of Audrey and B.B., something non-human and non-conceivable, a creature in which Brigitte's sexual power finds reconciliation with Audrey's doe-like sweetness. A woman to love. He ventures so far as to consider uttering the word 'love', a word that's not used by them. They, that is, the boys and girls of the Group, tell each other *I'm crazy about you*, they never say *I love you*: loving each other is for grown-ups, it's a commitment. Can Audrey be loved? Can Brigitte be loved? Ivo doesn't know the meaning of this word—who ever does?—but he uses it when he thinks of them.

It's four in the afternoon, he's hungry, the minipizza he gulped down at the Rotunda has long since been burnt up. He leaves book and notebook in his changing booth and heads off down the beach. The shadows are lengthening, many beach umbrellas are already folded for the night, the loungers and beach chairs neatly stacked against the pole fixed in the sand. He looks around. At first, Sandro is nowhere to be seen. He searches for *her*. She ought to be down there, a little further off, towards the east. There she is, surrounded by people. He spots Sandro sitting next to her on a wooden folding chair with a copy of *L'Espresso* folded on his knees: they know each other! Here's his chance! He heads over and calls hello. Aside from Sandro, there are two other guys he knows by sight, sprawled in two beach loungers, two assholes from the Baretto, the expensive little cafe in town, two guys from somewhere else, not here, a couple of guys from the world of arrogant-assholes-with-money from the Little Shoals. Sandro says hello back, snickering, and since silence has fallen among the others, introduces him. Marcella, do you know ... (and here he seems to make an effort as if trying to remember his name) ... Ivo? And then, turning to the others: Do you know each other? Everyone says *ciao*, but Ivo doesn't even hear the *ciao*s of the two assholes from the Baretto—if he bothered to listen closely, he'd be able to detect mistrust and irritation, like: And-who-the-fuck-is-this-supposed-to-be?—because Ivo is focusing on her, on her *ciao*, on her gaze, which strikes him as particularly attentive, interested, curious. He's taken off his sunglasses to show off his blue eyes. A basic technique that backfires this time: Marcella's gaze is level and confident, Ivo's naked eyes are intimidated, he dodges her glance, his gaze slides elsewhere. 'This is Fabrizio and this is Massimiliano,' she says as she looks him up and down. She's wearing a wet bikini with red pinstripes, with a wireframe balcony bikini top, and the bottom with elastic waistband, slightly poofy. She's totally charming and totally sexy. She's sitting in her usual pose, half-reclining, one leg bent, her thighs slightly open, an undetectable tuft of pubic hair protruding from the swimsuit bottom . . . . There is always that zone of a girl's swimsuit-clad body, between the legs, where Ivo's eyes continually wander; it seems to be slightly protruding, that is, it seems to contain something substantial, fleshy, to judge from the shape that the fabric takes on at that point: Does the pussy possess a certain volume? Is it more than just a void, a negative space? Does it occupy its own portion of convex, hairy space ...?

Marcella stretches, throwing her arms back and twisting in Fabrizio's direction to encourage him to resume the interrupted conversation—she makes this motion in a natural, padded, fluid manner, like a cat, and as she does she reveals an armpit shave that dates from a few days earlier. It's the Regrowth, which Ivo is used to because all girls have it.

'Get yourself a chair,' she says, addressing Ivo, who's put his sunglasses back on and is scrutinizing her from behind the dark lenses. She's slightly cross-eyed, she resembles Lea Massari, brown-skinned, dark-eyed, slightly nearsighted, a perfect voice with a hint of the drawling accent of those who live in the City of God. Her body is ripe, sleepy, buttery, quite another matter from the firm springiness of the girls Ivo's age, though he still adores them. The first and unmistakable message emanating from her is I am a woman grown and aware, even though Ivo, who receives it full in the face like a blast of hot wind, wouldn't know how to decipher it in anything like such a clear and concise form. To him, Marcella is pure emotion, she's one further event in the rushing chaos of the world, an enigma in the larger enigma of the Universe, a mystery among the mysteries of the Chain of Causation. She might be eighteen, nineteen years old, no older, but the gap between her and Ivo might as well be a generation. 'She's out of your league,' the sage adviser would tell him, if he was standing behind him, 'go on home, read yourself a comic book, take a nice nap, and go to the party this afternoon, probably you'll see Carla there, you remember Carla? You used to like her, until yesterday anyway . . .'

Fabrizio is talking about who knows what (calling yourself *Fabrizio*, instead of *Ivo*, is already an advantage to start with . . .), but whatever it is, it certainly has something to do with tennis, the night sessions of this year's tournament. He seems detached, his head cocked to one side, his mop of dark hair hanging lank—Ivo envies him all that smooth hair, Ivo has hair that's not-curly-not-smooth-not-wavy but sickly looking, shambling, with small pretentious waves, unjustifiable, that unfailingly appear whenever he lets his hair get past a certain length. And to think that long hair is in, while his hairline already seems to be receding, and when he tries to grow his out what he finds on his head is a sort of brownish clump of tow, like a plumber. The portion of Fabrizio's face that his Ray-Bans (with the horizontal mother-of-pearl bridge) leave uncovered shows that he has regular features (his nose is somewhat hooked, to tell the truth): a tanned, bored face. He's announcing that he's only going to compete in the doubles, with a guy who's a friend of his, he says they've been training. He has a completely deep, adult voice. He reels off the names of the good players, drawling his words, the names of the ones that he knows are probably seeded, he says that they ought to have two tournaments, one for the seeded players and the other for everyone else: where's the fun in getting crushed by the usual aces? Under a green Lacoste shirt he wears a pair of red flowered Bermuda shorts, tight-fitting, made to order. In one hand he holds a bunch of car keys. 'He has a car,' and he continually points out the fact. He too must be eighteen or twenty years old—a gulf in age and status separates him from Ivo, a gulf of virility, attitude, and hair: Fabrizio is an adult and belongs to the clan of rich patrons of the Baretto.

Sandro snickers, clearly tennis isn't his topic, but he's not entirely ignorant either, so every now and then he throws in a comment or two. The subject of the Pancho Gonzales signature rackets comes up, rackets that feature a photo of the player, it also comes up that Laver and Rosewall are winning everything these days. Gonzales has practically retired. 'It's a posthumous signature,' says Sandro, who seems to be comfortable now, as he tries to win back the spotlight. Marcella concedes him the centre of attention, while she basically remains silent. 'What need is there to pretend that we're having a conversation among ourselves, if everything that's said in this gathering is said to *You*, for *You*, to make *You* laugh, to impress *You*, to interest *You*, to charm *You*?' Marcella is the mass at the centre of a gravitational system so powerful that it holds four young lives clinging to it that would otherwise be elsewhere, each of them busy sizzling and burning energy and emotions in other more enjoyable, more relaxed summer activities, instead of striving to make an impression on her.

Massimiliano only speaks up rarely. He's renowned as an athlete but he doesn't play tennis. His interests include swimming, football, basketball, track and field (he's regional champion of the Eighty Obstacles and he plays centrefield in some Serie C team) and, especially, spearfishing. Ivo has heard it said of him that he free-dives to depths of 20 yards on the Shoal, that he comes back up with 25-pound groupers. Ivo hears that Massimiliano is part of a group of fishermen with real grown-up equipment, professionals, people who own wetsuits, who don't go fishing in T-shirts the way he does . . .

Massimiliano—Max—is wearing only a black Port Cros swimsuit, the kind that hooks on the hip, and has a clearly articulated musculature, you might say scientifically engineered, with a V-shaped chest. He can't seem to stop caressing his pecs. Maybe he's cold right now, but he won't put on something warm. Max too, everything he does and says, he does and says for Marcella's eyes and ears. That skimpy swimsuit instead of a pair of Bermuda shorts, his naked chest—you can tell it's all for her.

These three aren't friends. They know one another distantly, they meet at afternoon parties, in the normal course of affairs they don't even talk to one another, but here, now, it's an intense exchange of views and ideas; they compete to impress her the way superheroes might do, each of them unsheathing their own specific superpowers: money & car (Fabrizio), physique & prowess (Max), culture & words (Sandro). The situation would be clear-cut—Ivo feels useless, tired, would gladly go home, the stakes at this table are too high for him, the other players are too good, the cards in his hand too insignificant, he has no ultrapowers, he's sixteen years old, he even flunked philosophy, sure he's tall, but you can see that he's still growing, just a kid, he's out of his league—except that she's *looking at him*.

With her head thrown back, against the taut canvas of the lounge chair, her chin lifted, her strangely shaped eyes and her long—extremely long—half-lidded black lashes, Marcella doesn't appear to be listening to the exchange of chatter, she seems to be looking at him, Ivo! He can't be absolutely positive but that's what it looks like to him. She's constantly combing her hair, cocking her head to one side, raising her elbow behind the face that some perverse pagan god constructed so that it would trigger pleasure and desire at a single glance: above her full lips, the slight hollow that twists them and keeps them just open, her faintly flattened nose, arching gently out from her brow, her high cheekbones . . . Certainly, in the Group there are girls who are prettier than her but that's not what this is about . . . This is about that way she has, impossible to define, elusive, detached and yet open . . . 'Be careful, what attracts you is just her ambiguity,' an expert and discreet adviser might whisper in his ear, if Ivo had one right now, but he doesn't.

And so when she suddenly stands up and says: 'I'm going for a swim,' and strides through the circle of onlookers and walks straight over to him and takes him by the hand, for an instant he remains seated, turned to stone, and then she pulls him by the arm to make him stand up and says to him: 'Are you coming?' (*Are you coming? ARE YOU COMING? A-R-E Y-O-U?*), when all this *actually* happens, he doesn't shirk, he doesn't invent an excuse, he doesn't turn and run, he stands up, places his sunglasses on the chair and silently follows her . . . We don't know why he doesn't fall to the ground, overwrought, since his heart is pounding so violently in his throat that he can't utter a single word, even if he could think of something to say . . .

And this, without a doubt, is the moment of his *capture*.

You could say he was being dragged along by her, but he finds himself walking into the water, at first easily and then with increasing effort, while she tugs on his arm and says in a voice with the precise and perfect timbre: 'The water is beautiful today, don't you agree?'—she says: 'Don't you agree?'; no one he knows would use such a clear, adult expression—and immediately she lets go of his hand and dives forwards and starts swimming quickly out to sea, then she stops, turns around to look at him, then says, unhurriedly, without anxiety, as if she were fastening a collar around a dog's neck: 'Come on, why don't you?'

Yes, the water . . . It's beautiful today, much clearer than usual here, where it's always murky because of the sand, the currents, the gusting southwest winds. It takes days and days of dead calm, a moderate northwest mistral, before you'll see clear water, when you can go underwater fishing even off the smaller shoals, when you can see the seabed and the bath attendant goes octopus hunting with a bucket and a long fishing spear: these are the things Ivo ought to be doing, not standing here with the water up to his thighs, his head muddled, his heart pounding in his temples, and the hunger you get when you skip lunch. The clear waters call out to him but Ivo Brandani turns a deaf ear, he's been captured and there's nothing to be done about it.

He dives forwards, he's immediately cold, she's far away, swimming on her own, she seems to be ignoring him now. 'I have to catch up with her . . . get closer to her . . . Here I come, I'm on my way.' He starts swimming. Three strokes and a breath, then three more and another breath, in all maybe ten strokes, then he lifts his head and she's nowhere to be seen. He turns around, she's heading back to shore. She's far away now. He floats alone for a while, watching Marcella as she leaves the water. He might feel like a complete jerk now if she hadn't asked him, 'Are you coming?' But she *did*. She stood up and asked him. She asked him and no one else. She didn't ask Sandro. Or for that matter either of the two assholes from the Baretto. She asked him. 'Me,' he says over and over to himself, 'she asked *me* . . . And she took me by the hand . . . And she practically dragged me into the water, with her.' A few drops of salt water sting in his empty stomach.

When he gets back he finds that the circle around Marcella, which at first was a little slacker and looser, seems to have tightened around her. Her worshippers, like Penelope's suitors, have instinctively closed ranks, filling the space that Ivo occupied until ten minutes ago. Ten minutes ago Ivo was no one, they weren't afraid of him. Just some kid, some friend of Sandro's, nothing more. But now things are different: ever since he was *Chosen* to go Swimming, once he'd been made the object of her attention, the situation in the Circle of the Captured has changed: there's a new worshipper at the altar. A new pawn on the chess board, no one can say how powerful, because the mystery of her capriciousness is absolute. So far, Marcella hasn't made a choice, but sooner or later she will. 'Sooner or later she'll make it clear to me that she likes me'—it's taken for granted that each and every one of her worshippers is saying this to himself—'Otherwise why would she keep me here? Why would she give me this sensation, so clear and unmistakable, that she's not indifferent to me?' It's a tough game, and it's been like that for days now. But no one thinks of withdrawing, no one's about to leave, because what's at stake is too valuable, because each in their own way, they're head over heels in love with her.

When Ivo gets closer he sees Marcella standing at the centre of the circle, with a sea-green bathrobe thrown around her shoulders. She's already taken a brief shower. She's chatting and laughing. She shoots him a reassuring glance, another tacit, fatal, murderous, 'Are you coming?' He sits down on a wooden folding chair. He's a little outside the circle but that doesn't matter, she's the one who wants him there . . . In the chain of causation of events, the capture of Ivo and his entry into the circle of worshippers determines everything else that happens. Everything. What had seemed like a happy summer, spread uniformly over an immense four-month time span, suddenly presents a peak in the curve, or perhaps we should say a fracture, a fault: the two space-time planes of the Before Marcella and the After Marcella are no longer aligned, there is no longer a continuity. The fracture runs straight through his mind and splits it in two: What things from the Before still have any importance? What could be worth more than a Kiss from Marcella? The make-up exam? Tutoring with Giorgio? Sailing? Fishing? Water? The west wind? The Spitfire? The gusting winds of two in the afternoon? The shards of light that cover the sea, when you sail out into open water on your own? The Group? The parties? *Carla*? 'CARLA? Does she still matter to you? Did she matter to you before? Do you still like her? Do Mother & Father still count? And the friends you went fishing with? Do you still care anything about them? Is there anything that could be more important than her now?' Ivo doesn't know, but when he isn't sitting rapt in the Circle of Marcella, he goes on studying philosophy with Giorgio.

By now the Circle forms punctually every day when—and only if—she comes down to the beach, that is, around 3 or 3.30 in the afternoon, and it dissolves around 5.30 or 6, when she leaves; no one knows where she lives or what she does when she's not at the beach, she says she studies but it's not clear what, she says she goes to the university but not what she's majoring in: Where does she go at night? Does she go out? Who with?

Outside of the Circle, Ivo continues to take the sailing club's Finn out, but the Time of Wind clashes with the Time of Her, so now he only goes sailing in the late morning, and only when there's a breeze. He also continues to attend the parties of the Group, dances with the girls in the Group, goes out for gelato with the Group, goes to the movies with the Group. Sometimes, early in the morning, he goes out fishing with Giacomo, especially for octopus, they go to the Little Shoals, but also to Ponente, Grottoes and the Mute Arch. In spite of the increasingly impenetrable enigma of Marcella and his piercing desire for her—as she refuses to release him and keeps him chained at her side, and each time all it takes is a glance to inflame his hope of who knows what—Ivo still tries to manage the Sacred Summer, the True Life to which he has a right four months of every year.

But when he tries to break loose, when he tries to say: 'Well, I'm leaving,' to say: 'Tomorrow I'm not coming down to the beach,' whenever she senses any lessening of his faith, a weakening in his hope, then with just a couple of words, or a few—'Oh, you're going? Too bad' / 'You're leaving already?' / 'Aren't you going in the water today?' / 'Will you be here tomorrow?'—or else with a glance, or by touching his shoulder, a knee, or else by employing all three of these weapons simultaneously, she hurls him violently back into the Circle: 'Just where do you think *you're* going, eh?'

Most of all, in comparison with the three other worshippers, Ivo possesses no superpowers. He's a kid, he's penniless, Mother gives him a laughably small allowance, which he rounds out every day with secret pilferings from her pocketbook: 50, at the most 100 lire.

What's more, Ivo knows nothing, except for the things that at school they force him to glue into his mind. He doesn't read the papers, only comic books—before falling into Marcella's gravitational field, he used to like to spend his afternoons lying on his bed with a comic book or the *Settimana Enigmistica*—he knows nothing about politics, except for Father's invectives about the young Communists and the Christian Democrats, which he'd just

391

as happily do without entirely because he, like Mother and the Sisters, just wants to be left to eat in peace, dine in tranquillity, distractedly—'Pass me the salt' / 'Are you going to eat your mozzarella?'—even being able to enunciate the proposition 'I don't like this,' a forbidden statement with Father there . . .

Then there are the books. Ivo hasn't been reading long and he practically only reads the books that Big Sister gives him, books that in her turn she is given by a guy she's dating, a guy who's cultured-even-though-he's-an-engineer. They're all titles published by BUR, the Biblioteca Universale Rizzoli, off-grey covers, tiny type: the complete short stories of Poe, then Chesterton, Chekhov. That guy's tastes—even though Ivo scarcely even knows him—are transmitted indirectly to him through Big Sister, secretly orienting him, partially shaping him, like everything else that touches him in those years . . . There is also a different kind of literature, the books that he uses for masturbating, books that belong to Mother and are considered 'not suitable': Moravia's *Boredom* is perfect for the purpose—by now the volume opens automatically to the most interesting pages, like the scene where he covers her with money before having sex with her—while other titles, such as Pamela Moore's *Chocolates for Breakfast* or Erskine Caldwell's *God's Little Acre*, contain sex scenes described in an indirect and metaphorical manner, as ridiculous as it is irritating. Still, sometimes Ivo takes these books into the bathroom, just for a change of pace. Then there's the insurmountable cliff of Faulkner's *Sanctuary*: an incomprehensible mass of words wherein, as Giacomo assures him, lies hidden the Rape with a Corncob, though Ivo never manages to find it, not even after reading practically the *whole* book without even understanding what it's about. So unless the conversation veers over to Poe, Chesterton and Chekhov, he won't have much to offer—competing is out of the question—in the conversation with Sandro; but for that matter, neither of the two assholes from the Baretto can hope to compete either.

At tennis Ivo is a disaster, he goes spearfishing with a rented pedal-boat and a spring-loaded speargun he found underwater, enormous and rusty, that he can only load by pushing the spear into dirt. So once he's fired it, he has to fall back on using the spear as a hand-held harpoon. He's pathetic at football, as a fullback, like everyone who can't really play, he's assigned to a defensive position, knocking down all the opposing strikers. He's an adequate sailor but not a great one—he's mediocre, he never wins.

The community of worshippers, as it waits for Marcella to make her selection, does its best to ignore him and would long since have called him out of the game entirely, were it not for the fact that Marcella, enigmatically, chooses to keep him as one of the rivals. Every time that the Circle assembles, it's as if everyone were wondering: 'What is this little kid still doing here?' Marcella hasn't invited him to go swimming with her again, she hasn't said to him again in that way she has, so natural, tranquil, irresistible: 'Are you coming?' . . . Once Fabrizio was chosen to go swimming and a couple of times Max, who took advantage of the opportunity to get a running start practically from her umbrella—does this umbrella belong to Marcella, come to think of it?—and plunge into the shallow water like a galloping horse and finally perform an excellent, and, to Ivo, astonishing, dive with a front-flip in midair, making Fabrizio—bored and impassive behind his Ray-Bans— hiss the word 'asshole' loud enough for even Marcella to hear it, though she had just taken off at a dead run too, though no one could say whether or not she actually *did* hear.

Sandro—you have to admire the stamina that he shows in opposing the two assholes from the Baretto—has never been summoned to swim with her alone, but he's been able to participate in the collective invitations, though clearly never happy about it. 'Shall we all go swimming?' is the formulation of the collective invitation. Once or twice, Sandro remained behind to read the newspaper, keeping an eye on the others to check out the situation, just in case there was some new development, some clue that needed studying, something that might finally help him solve the riddle . . . But if Sandro is perplexed, Ivo understands practically nothing; the only thing he grasps clearly is the power of attraction Marcella exerts when she says to him chidingly: 'Are you leaving?' or, even more diabolically: 'Am I going to see you tomorrow?'

'Why why why . . . oh God . . . Why do you want to see me tomorrow? Is there something you want to tell me? Are you trying to send me some kind of signal that I ought to understand but I don't because I'm an asshole too?'

An experienced connoisseur of women, someone unlike Ivo who's just a boy with a few muddled notions about girls, would have promptly decreed: 'I'll tell you here and now, and you can do whatever the fuck you like: at this point either you forget about her, you pull out and you go graze in greener pastures—which would be the smart thing to do: remember Carla?—or else you go and see this bitch's cards, call her bluff. Now if you want another opinion, here it is: if you ask me, she's veering vaguely towards the asshole in the Ray-Bans, because he's more of a grown-up than all the rest of you, he has more money and he has a car. Everything *comme il faut*, get it? What the hell do you think *you're* up to?' This wise man might not understand that it's precisely the fact that Marcella is a *woman*, instead of a little girl, that has dazzled him and is paralysing him and keeps him from breaking out of her clutches. By now he's a swine among swine and he's grunting and rooting at her feet, just like the others. 'But Fabrizio isn't grunting and rooting at her feet,' the wise man behind him would point out, 'so watch and learn, kid . . .'

At 4.30 or 5 in the afternoon Marcella closes up shop and leaves. Where does she live? No one knows. All they know is that she never shows up at the parties of the Groups that Ivo knows. They know that at night she doesn't go out for gelato. They know that she doesn't go watch movies at the arena, alone or accompanied. Perhaps the only one who knows where she lives is Fabrizio, because Ivo has the impression that one time he drove her somewhere in his car, maybe home. But if Fabrizio does know, he's keeping it to himself.

While Ivo stagnates in the Circle of Worshippers, the Group isn't sitting there idly, it's seething and scalding in the flames of Summer: nothing stands still, everything churns and recombines in continuation. There's a constant coming and going, a back and forth of arrivals and departures, couples exploding and reforming in different configurations. And then there are the sub-groups that amalgamate around a leader, male or female as it happens. The quarrels, the gossip, the alliances, the skirmishes. The morning theatre for all this drama is the beach where, however, everything manifests itself as if muffled by the open air, by the sunshine. In the afternoons, the Group shows itself at its best in the parties that it unfailingly organizes—by one o'clock or so, the decision where to go has been set and word gets around—without skipping a single day. At the parties, if you have something in mind, you take concrete steps. If you like a girl, the party gives you a chance to give it a shot. And giving it a shot with a girl at a party is a simple, well-established practice: no talking is involved, nothing needs to get said, there's no complicated itinerary of seduction, you need only comply with the current rules of engagement. Words, if words are needed, will come *later*, when you can say that the situation has been clarified to some extent. At the parties there is *dancing*, and dancing is the crucial medium of communication. Do you like a girl? Then ask her to dance over and over, so she knows you're interested and, after a while, try putting your arms around her: if she goes along with it, it means she's willing; if she doesn't like you, she'll stiffen up; if you get pushy, she'll jab her elbow into your chest; if you keep trying she'll tell you she has a headache and doesn't feel like dancing any more; and that's the end of it. Everyone meanwhile has been watching the whole thing, everyone in the Group will know what's happened, whether the two of you are *an item* now or not. Every move pulled at the afternoon party will then be tested out in final form that night, at the movies. If new couples have formed there will be an unspoken rejuggling of seating assignments to take into account the new amorous assortment attained earlier that day. Once you're sitting side by side, you're supposed to hold hands with her, it's what she expects. Then comes kissing and touching; if you manage to get your hands on her breasts—maybe not right away, it stands to reason—then new horizons open before you, a world to be explored—it's up to you to figure out where the boundaries lie. And the thought that you *might* be about to set out on this journey of research takes your breath away, ties your guts in knots, makes your palms sweaty.

Every Group is an ecosystem unto itself, an inhabitable planet in the universe of summer, it's a corral within the larger corral of the Bay, a cultural capsule: the door is open only to the like-minded, the social selection is strict. The Group knows its own ranking in the seaside hierarchy of status, the kids know perfectly well where they stand, they know who their peers are, who they can consider their inferiors and who occupies a higher level. The Group has a history all its own, its own customs, it's a niche where everyone feels the effects of their own existence among others, where your actions are observed, evaluated and judged, welcomed or rejected. The Afternoon Party is the place where the Group performs its particular rituals, the place where, if you learn how to move, you can find a girlfriend, a boyfriend, where everything you do, you do under the eyes of the others, where everything is reported and everyone knows everything about you, where everything that happens is a collective, participatory product.

A broad terrace on the second floor, covering an expanse of garage stalls, large black holm oaks that provide shade and shelter from the road, their trunks covered with ants and oozing some dark-brown liquid, large earthenware vases full of oleanders and small espaliered trees, smaller planters with geraniums. A pergola covered with blooming bougainvillea. On the white wall, Vietri ceramic inserts. On the table, family-size bottles of Coca-Cola, Fanta, very bubbly mineral water, Peroni beer, minipizzas, tea sandwiches, finger pastries. The quantity is limited, this is the third time that Francesca has shouldered the burden of the Afternoon Party, her mother must be fed up. It's probably six o'clock, Ivo just came up from the beach, he went by the flat to get changed—he threw on a Lacoste polo shirt and a skin-tight pair of white Lee jeans, no belt, on his feet a pair of Positano sandals custom-made for him, just like for everyone else (everybody wears them here), by a shoemaker over by the train station (the shoemaker runs a ballpoint pen all around your foot, slipping between the big toe and your other toes and then tells you, done, they'll be ready the day after tomorrow), thrown around his shoulders is a light fisherman's sweater with horizontal stripes, just in case, scratchy, in navy-blue wool—you can buy them on Thursdays in town, at the market. All the kids are dressed more or less like him. On the table is a portable record player, but someone else bought a spare portable record player, just in case that one broke.

When Ivo sets foot on Francesca's terrace he feels almost at ease, this at least is familiar territory; the party is coming close to the tipping point, that is, the moment when all the boys who have manoeuvred in some direction or other start to see results, if there are going to be any. Giacomo comes over to him immediately and says: 'Hey you'd better look out because Paolo's making a serious run . . .' At first Ivo doesn't understand and then, after Giacomo adds, '. . . at Carla,' he turns around and sees her in the middle of the terrace: she's dancing with Paolo. It's still light out but under the branches of the holm oaks it's already getting dark. The air is still, heavy and hot. Ivo's Lacoste is already damp with sweat down his spine. The music is going, the Group (who brings the records? who chooses them? who buys them? Ivo doesn't really know, he just knows that they're there, that someone always seems to have a record player, he knows that there's never a lack of music) puts on a series of slow dances. No one wants to dance anything else at this time of day.

Paolo is tall, with very dark skin, Ivo's not really on speaking terms with him, they aren't friends. Giacomo says it to him again: 'Look out, he's making a serious run at her . . . And if you ask me, she's up for it.' Ivo waits for the record to end, then he goes over to Carla and says to her: '*Ciao.*' Then he asks: 'Dance?' The question, stated like that, struck him as kind of brutal—*Dance?*—harsh, rudimentary, but Carla promptly replies: 'Sure.'

When the music starts up, Ivo wraps his right hand around her waist while with his left hand he takes hers and, bending his forearm back, lays it on his chest: that's the standard starting position. All the work that follows is going to have to be done with his right hand. Carla's left hand notices that his polo shirt is damp down the spine and it shifts to one side. 'Fuck,' thinks Ivo, 'I disgust her, I'm all sweaty . . .' But then there's her scent, which seizes hold of him almost instantly and wins him over, it's a smell of air and flesh, clean clothing, shampoo, after-sun lotion. Carla gives off a sweet-smelling warmth that makes its way to him and hits him head on. He perceives in her a sort of yielding quality, like a timid, restrained lunge towards him. It's not that she's encouraging, but neither is she defensive: they're simultaneous sensations that trigger a stab of excitement in him. In an instant, and there's nothing that he can do about it, he finds himself virtually stripped naked in the middle of that terrace, with that pair of Lee's, too light and too tight, revealing on the front an unmistakable bulge. It's nothing new, it happens to him every time, or so it seems. It happens to everyone, but today, for whatever reason, it's too visible: Ivo is embarrassed, he hopes that no one notices. He runs his fingers down the groove of her spine, all the way down the accentuated arch of her back, with the narrowing around her kidneys, the delicious jut of her ass out into space. The wise and expert adviser would say to him: 'Yes, exactly, the real *difference* is right there.'

Ivo starts trying things, he does it explicitly, almost brutally. He thinks about Marcella: 'Her, by God, her . . . her-her-her . . . now *her*, yes.' He tells himself that he doesn't give a damn about Carla, that he's trying with her just for the hell of it. 'She makes me horny and *that's it*,' he told Giacomo. Whereupon Giacomo gave him a glare, as if to say: 'Don't you think you're putting on a little too much of a show?'

Without saying anything to her, without using any of the tricks that he's learnt—breathing on her neck, sighing some well chosen words into her ear, like, 'Do you know that I like you?'—he starts to pull her decisively close to him. At first she seems puzzled but not surprised. She gently resists him for a few seconds, then rises to her tiptoes and whispers to him: 'What are you looking for?' He says, and in the very instant that he says it he feels like an asshole for saying it, but still he says it: 'Would you like it if we went steady?' Suddenly he glues himself even tighter to her, pulling her waist to him, adhering to her with his pelvis, blatantly pushing to make her *feel his cock* ('But you did at least let her *feel your cock*, didn't you? Once they *feel your cock* they don't know what they're doing any more ...,' these are the kind of things he and his friends say to one another—miserable overheated young males). Carla pulls her pelvis away from him but her cheek is still pressed against his and she says, hesitantly, breathing hard: 'Have you made up your mind you want to have some fun?' Her hot breath in his ear gives him a shiver of desperation; suddenly, unmistakably, he senses the unbridgeable distance that separates him from Marcella, from her mind, from her life, from her body; everything that has to do with her is completely unattainable—she doesn't know and she doesn't want to know what he could give her, what he could do for her ... 'What could you do for her? ... If she'd only let me go, if she just wouldn't go on giving me hope every time ...' But Carla is here, she's ready *for him*, within his grasp, ready to deliver herself up. She's not saying no to him, she's just trying to understand—women, God only knows why, always have to clarify *in advance* what your *intentions* are, they want to know how much you love them or, even worse, how much you 'care for them'. 'They need to be able to gauge how to handle the situation,' Ivo's secret adviser might tell him. 'It's different for them than it is for us. Being female is very different.' That's right: for instance, if a girl says 'no' it doesn't always mean that they really want to say 'no', Ivo knows that, he's learnt it, though he doesn't really understand it.

In the name of Marcella, Ivo could burn down the whole coast and empty the gulf in a sign of devotion and sacrifice, he could immolate on a stone altar the unsuspecting creature who in this very moment is breathing sweetly into his ear: 'What are your intentions?'

'I just want to *do things with her* ...' he'd confided to Giacomo only a few minutes ago.

She's the lamb whose throat he plans to cut in honour of Marcella, the warm object upon which he'll take revenge for Marcella's uncaring ferocity. If at first he'd had some lingering doubts, now he has none: 'Carla likes me! She means nothing to me but she likes me.' And so he wants to possess her, *use her*, take his revenge on her. His excitement at Carla's closeness and availability goads him into an uncontrolled and confused delirium of possession: *to have* Carla, that's the plan, bastardly and vicious, that Ivo formulates for her, while down inside his Lee's he can feel his cock about to burst.

'I care for you,' he replies to her, very close to her earlobe, and then he presses himself against her. 'There, now she's happier,' Ivo tells himself, 'that's all she wanted.'

Beyond the railing and under the holm oaks it's getting dark, while the sky is still luminous and he's in a secluded corner, dancing with his arms around Carla. Every so often he kisses her on the lips, on the neck. She clings peacefully to his body, thighs against thighs, she presses her breasts against his chest, her sex against his sex.

Giacomo is watching them from afar.

On the record player, *Cuando calienta el sol* is spinning continuously, the Group is pretending not to notice, but the phenomenon now under way, that is, the formation of a New Couple, escapes nobody and is sure to become the subject of extensive commentary, tonight at the ice cream shop and tomorrow on the beach. Paolo, who just two hours ago enjoyed a normal degree of status, is now the one who *shot a blank*. He pretends he doesn't care, but it's obvious that he's unhappy about it. He's over there talking seriously to a couple of girls who are basically window dressing, the kind of girls who become your friends. Maybe they're trying to make him feel better.

Then Ivo and Carla break away and go over to sit on the glider sofa. Ivo's erection is visible, but the worst part is that right at what cannot be anything other than the tip of his penis, a wet smear has formed, a slather that is not only dampening his underwear but the white denim of his jeans too, which has turned translucent at that spot, giving a glimpse, through the thin material, of the blood-charged pink of his glans. He, giddy and confused by the fullness of his new conquest, pays it no mind, perhaps he doesn't even notice it. He plans to have her all to himself tonight, to make a full-court press at the movies and then to take her to the beach.

'Can you come to the movies with me tonight?'

'I can't, I have to be with my folks. My dad is going to be there.'

'So you really can't?'

'No. Not tonight. But tomorrow I can. That is, I think I can, if my folks will let me go . . .'

Just then Francesca's mother is going by, carrying a tray full of empty Coca-Cola and orangeade bottles, crumpled paper napkins, used paper cups. She wears trousers, she's tall, blond, pretty, severe, impassive, with short hair and practically no make-up but with fuchsia gloss on her lips. Clenched in her teeth is a mother-of-pearl cigarette holder with a lit cigarette. A mother who's been around the block, the kind you see a lot of, here. A mother with her eyes wide open and her brain clicking. One of those mothers who doesn't miss a trick. She's been keeping her eye on the two of them for a while now, and even now her level gaze is appraising the situation.

A few minutes after the mother has gone inside, Francesca's older brother walks over to Ivo and says to him, clearly embarrassed: 'Can I talk to you for a second?'

The words he adds, after taking him aside, run exactly like this: 'Listen, it's not my fault . . . So don't hold it against me, OK? But there's something I have to tell you . . . So, it's this . . . My mother told me to tell you to go take a walk and come back when you've calmed down a little . . .'

'Calmed down from what?' Ivo asks him, weirded out and a little frantic. Then he looks down at the crotch of his pants and he sees the state he's in and he feels a flush of heat and sweat surge up into his face. Without replying, he heads for the door and leaves, he practically runs away. It's only one flight of stairs to the ground floor and when he's already in the street he hears Carla behind him, calling down from the terrace. He looks up and calls to her: 'I'll explain tomorrow . . . No, I'm not mad at you . . . Like I told you, I'll explain tomorrow, enough already!'

Giacomo appears at Carla's side, gazing down at him with a quizzical look on his face and, with a gesture of his hands, asks wordlessly: 'What's the matter?' Ivo gestures up to him to come down and when he gets out in the street, curious, corpulent, out of breath, he tells him to come over, out of sight, under the shade of a holm oak, and says to him: 'Francesca's mother . . . She kicked me out . . . That bitch. Because I had a hard-on and it was making a bulge in my pants, can you believe it? I'm so ashamed of myself . . . She could have just overlooked it, but no, she had to shame me . . . You'll see, in a couple of seconds everyone else is going to know about it . . .'

Giacomo figures out what's happened but only after further explanations. At that point he laughs. Then he turns serious and says: 'I saw that Carletta was *willing to be with you* . . .'

'What are you laughing about, Como?' asks Ivo, using Giacomo's nickname. Then he continues: 'Yeah, that's what it looks like, only I had to tell her "I love you", you know how it is . . .'

Giacomo doesn't know how it is, because he still hasn't had a girl willing to be with him, but he nods silently. If Ivo had eyes in his head, if he wasn't so excited confused desperate, if he wasn't so completely absorbed in himself and his own business, if at his side he'd had the expert adviser to suggest he be a little more careful, he'd see the embarrassment and perhaps even the pain and jealousy that flicker in Giacomo's gaze. But his mind is elsewhere and he rattles on, foppishly, about his conquest: '. . . I was horny as a dog, if you only knew how willing she is, she scrubbed my tonsils with her tongue, the minute I get a chance to take her somewhere private, wait and see how I rough her up . . .' As he says these things he feels like a vulgar asshole and a son of a bitch, but he goes on saying them because that's how he wants to think of himself. He goes on along these lines for some time while his friend says nothing, a forced smile on his face.

Then Giacomo asks him: 'Did you tell her that you love her?'
'Yes.'
'But do you give *even the slightest* damn for her?'
'No, Como . . . I like another girl, I can't tell you who she is . . .'
'I'm pretty sure I know who it is.'
'You don't know a fucking thing, Como . . . And if by some unlikely chance you do, keep it to yourself . . .'

'Do you have a chance with this other girl?'

'I don't know, I don't know anything, I'm crushing on her so bad . . . There are times when I get the feeling she likes me, but most of the time she doesn't even know I exist . . . It's been going on like this for a while, with me tagging along after her like a complete asshole . . . She's someone who likes to have her little entourage, you know, guys trailing after her . . . They're all older than me, there's one who has a car of his own, a black Alfa Giulietta Spider . . . Do you understand the one I mean? One of the assholes from the Baretto . . . Giacomo, I just happened into this situation, I don't even know how it happened . . . She got her claws into me and now she won't let go . . . She's a girl who fires you up and cools you down, continuously, she works me however she wants . . . And I just stay there, kneeling at her feet in adoration like a jerk . . . She sends me to get minipizzas for her from the Rotunda and I go, too. It makes me sick to think about it . . . I wind up crying, you get it? And I need to study, too . . .'

'What about Carla?'

'I gotta have something to fall back on . . .'

As Ivo answers him in these terms, Como notices that his face is taking on the vulgar expression of a shitbag son of a bitch: eyes narrowed, gaze averted, a lewd grin in search of complicity.

The Circle has been in session for some time already. Sandro folds *L'Espresso* back to the page that he's reading and hands it over to him: 'Take a look at that.'

ANGOLAN VILLAGE DESTROYED BY NAPALM

At first, Ivo doesn't understand. The photograph is slightly blurry, a little confusing. Then he realizes to his disbelief that it is a picture of heads stuck on stakes that are jammed into the ground. The tip of the stakes are inside the mouths, thrusting up through their throats. Underneath it, another photograph shows white soldiers in camouflage jumpsuits, smiling, gripping in their hands clusters of black heads.

'Africa . . .' Sandro snickers. 'Those are Portuguese soldiers, there's a civil war going on in Angola, and the Portuguese are coming down hard. But they're going to have to withdraw at a certain point, just like the French in Algeria . . . You can see that history teaches them nothing . . .' he continues, still chuckling. '. . . if they had just given them independence first thing, they would have spared themselves fighting and saved themselves money and the lives of plenty of soldiers . . . Instead they're not going to leave until they're forced out . . . Eh . . . But you'll see, sooner or later . . .' Then he suddenly falls silent because she has arrived.

There she is, Marcella. She's just emerged from the passageway between the changing cabins, a beachwrap knotted around her neck to cover her bikini, beach bag bulging with things. She walks towards the circle, she seems pleased to find them already there, waiting, and she smiles in her way, that is, staring at them individually, one by one, with a gaze that seems to state: 'Don't pay any attention to the others, they're just bit players, I'm here *for you*.'

'I'm leaving tomorrow, end of my holiday,' she says immediately. Then she looks around, unruffled, to see what effect her statement has had.

'She's leaving! Tomorrow! She's going away! She's about to vanish, swallowed by the Winter in the City, by another universe, she's escaping into another space-time dimension . . . Like something out of an issue of *Urania* . . . Into a world that is certainly better than the one I live in . . .'

Marcella is leaving the Summer with nonchalance and turning serenely to face the horrors of Winter. For Ivo there's still all of September, still a good solid month or so, with the not inconsiderable interval of the make-up exam. Summer in the enclosure of the Gulf is the only knowable universe, the only place where he can still move with agility and dexterity. Summer is his, it belongs to him by now through well established tradition, it's his right. When, on the 30th of September, he will be obliged to board the train— the rest of the family will make the trip by car—he'll perform his secret ritual of bidding farewell to the sea, he'll climb onto the lowermost branch of the big plane tree in the apartment-building gardens, which towers over the Gulf, overlooking all its geographic institutions, the Islands and the Mountain sitting perched in the distance, just beneath the horizon line, and he'll stay there for a while, looking at the sea and trying to cry. Marcella will be lost, unless he can manage it today, by tonight, or right now, to speak to her to clarify to ask her to make his declaration—to do something, in other words, that can resolve this intolerable doubt . . . He's stunned by the blow he's received, he tries for the umpteenth time to think clearly, to get a grasp on things: 'Max, obviously, is fed up . . . There's just the three of us left . . . Sandro is fat, he's bug-eyed, the lenses of his glasses are too thick . . . He's not going anywhere . . . That leaves Fabrizio, the little asshole from the Baretto, or else I guess . . . Who? M-me? Naaah. And then it'll turn out after all that she was never dreaming of anything serious with any of us . . . All we did was keep her company, like a bunch of lap dogs . . . And anyway, she's leaving . . . But still. Still. Even just a little while ago, when she touched my shoulder . . . Was she or was she not sort of caressing me? Certainly, she was caressing me: if she doesn't care about me, then why would she caress me? Why would she bother giving me the impression I mean something to her? Could I really just be imagining it all?'

The mere thought of meeting her in the city, in the clothing of Winter—he imagines her in a woollen kilt, fastened to one side with a golden pin and a cashmere sweater, white socks and Collegian loafers with the fringe in front, but only because the girls he knows all dress that way in the winter, when they go out in the afternoon, when he goes to meet them outside of the school—stirs him almost to tears and shakes him deeply, triggering flashes of deranged fantasies.

'Maybe she actually likes me . . . In the city we could go steady, we could go to the movies on Saturday afternoons . . . She'd be wearing an overcoat . . . A fur coat made of nutria, otterskin . . . Boots . . . Stockings, garterbelt . . . That stretch of naked thigh that you can reach in the dark with your hand . . .'

As always his gaze rests at some length on Marcella's delicately arched foot, resting as usual on the crossbar of the lounge chair, her heel pushing into the canvas and the toes splayed slightly upwards: he adores her feet, the only feet on the beach that don't make him think of the hands of apes deformed by too much walking. He imagines them in a pair of high-heeled shoes, at a party in Winter, dressed in a fancy outfit, dancing the twist, or the Madison.

The wise man we referred to above, if he could read his mind right now, would tell him in his usual calm voice that smacks of tobacco smoke: 'You're trying to drag her into your world, kid. Marcella isn't a girl your age, she doesn't wear Collegian loafers, she's two or three years older than you, which is quite enough to place her on the opposite side of the mountain that you're climbing —forget about her, trust me on this one.'

Suddenly, if he thinks about Marcella, his natural revulsion for Winter flips into its opposite: now it appears to him as a warm and woolly expanse of grey skies and rain, but filled with love and tenderness and enjoyment and making out at the movies, caressing Marcella's breasts, which seem so generous, so mysterious. But that's not enough, Ivo ventures so far as to imagine her stretched out *nude*, on a bed. A shameful erection which bursts upon him instantaneously, so urgently that his elasticized swimsuit is power-less to conceal it, and he's forced to run to the cabin until he can calm down. But once he's there, in the dark, with the door locked and his cock on the verge of exploding and pulsating like an inner tube with every beat of his heart, he can't resist and he starts mas-turbating. All it takes is a few jerks of his hand and he comes sud-denly and an uncontrolled, sacrilegious spurt of sperm winds up on his little sister's tank top, draped over a chair. He uses the same sacred tank top to wipe off his cock, then he leaves the cabin, goes to wash off the shirt in the bathrooms nearby, comes back, hangs it out to dry on the backrest of the chair—he just hopes it's dry in the morning.

When he gets back to the Circle, Sandro has started talking about the war in Angola again, the Portuguese regime. Marcella asks him questions and that encourages him to go on talking, Ivo can see him swelling with pride. For the past few days,

Massimiliano has been absent from the company of the Adepts of Marcella, but Ivo knows he hasn't left yet, because he saw him the night before at the arena watching *Distant Drums* and smoking sprawled out in his metal chair, his legs stretched over the back of the seat in front of him.

Fabrizio says nothing and plays with his car keys, behind his usual Ray-Bans, wearing the usual Lacoste polo shirt and the usual Positano Bermuda shorts. Whenever Sandro turns to political topics or talks about books, Fabrizio remains impassive, silently nodding, as if he already knew it all, as if he'd already figured it all it and didn't give a damn about any of it, but today he suddenly interrupts and with absolute nonchalance mentions to Marcella that tonight there's an after-dinner party at 'some guy's, I can't even remember his name.' She replies that yes, she already knew about that, it's at Attilio's place and just this once she's planning to go, she'd like to say goodbye before going. Fabrizio seems to regret having shared this information with Ivo and Sandro too, but only to a certain extent; now that Massimiliano has thrown in the towel, he seems pretty confident that he no longer has rivals.

Then that's the other piece of news: tonight, that's where she'll be! Ivo needs to study, the exams are coming up soon and tomorrow afternoon, at 6.30, Giorgio wants to drill him on the whole programme, but he absolutely has to go to that party. He knows Attilio, he's in Big Sister's group of friends; she'll probably be there too; he doesn't have to wangle an invitation, he can just show up at the front door.

'Ivo, don't tell me you can't come. It's the last night . . .'

He looks up at her and sees that she's staring at him in a way that strikes him as intense, exclusive. It seems as if she really does care; his heart leaps in his throat, as it always does, when she looks him like that.

'I have some studying to do but I'll definitely come,' he stammers.

After-dinner parties start around ten, when the Gulf has been shrouded in darkness for hours.

After the doldrums of the late afternoon, a land breeze has sprung up which, in conditions of western weather, that is, pleasant and cool, will sweep the ocean all night long. The lights of the port and the lights of the beachfront promenade dot the coastline, redesigning it. There's no moon. A distant sound of music emanates from the Rotunda which is all lit up, its reflection doubled in the water. The rest of the beach is immersed in complete darkness and the shoreline can be guessed at from the reflections of the lights on the sea, where they come to a sudden end.

Attilio's terrace overlooks all this. It's a spacious platform, with a parapet in Vietri majolica, decorated with fish and crabs and octopuses and seahorses and starfish. Two big white umbrellas, metal chairs upholstered in navy blue canvas cushions, a glider, tables with tablecloths and good things to eat, various alcoholic beverages and a bottle of whisky, even, no wine, lots of beer.

Here Peppino Di Capri is playing. When Ivo sets foot, the terrace is already crowded with people and 'Voce 'e notte' is on the record player, which immediately brings a lump to his throat. All the kids are older than him: they have different manners, different voices, different bodies—university students, already clued in to the idea that in just a few years they're already going to be fulfilling a different role, fully aware, you'd think, of their future responsibilities and money and professional salaries, sports clubs, marriages & children, weddings that for some of them are impending, to be held strictly in early-Christian basilicas outside the Walls of the City of God. For most of them, their career will consist of following in their father's footsteps, they'll be engineers in the company, or else notaries, lawyers, doctors or architects. They'll get some undergraduate degree or other before joining the family business, running well-known shops in the centre of town, or else they'll gradually take over the reins of import–export businesses, a coffee roastery, a construction supplies company. Better yet, car dealerships, which have been making money hand over fist for the past few years. The three or four years of extra age means that they live in other worlds from Ivo, where everything is different.

In this moment in the History of the World, being eighteen or nineteen and belonging to a bourgeois family means taking part in a different and prior culture, in comparison with someone who is only two or three years younger, it means confidently preparing for a future that appears unquestionable, safe, guaranteed, like a road already laid out, with exact boundaries—you only need to take that road. Ivo doesn't know all these things, exactly, but he senses them from the differences in the ways that, here, males and females treat one another: they talk a lot, and in low voices, they don't curse, they rarely laugh loudly, they dance standing straight instead of coiling around one another like octopuses, without tongues in one another's mouths and hickeys on one another's necks, even the steady couples limit themselves to a dignified cheek to cheek. They do lots of slow dances, the occasional twist and the Madison, even a cha-cha. The men wear buttoned shirts or, more frequently, Lacostes, sweater thrown over their shoulders or tied around their waist, long pants only, in white or light-coloured cotton, Capri sandals, but more often moccasins without socks. A few of the better-dressed girls are wearing sheath dresses, with a straight neckline and narrow shoulders, pointy-toe flats or with low heels, but nearly all the rest of them wearing tight-fitting pedal pushers with a split at the calf, sleeveless or long-sleeved blouses, boat-neck sweaters, all of them colourful, their shoes are ballet slippers or low-heeled sandals. Some of them have headbands in their hair. They all carry cheap straw handbags, with a sweater tied around the handles.

Here too the girls are an absolute enigma, none of the boys really knows *what* they are, what they want, but theories circulate. Nearly all of the girls are studying, certainly. The ones who aren't still in high school are enrolled at the university in Literature, or Languages, or else they're going to the School for Interpreters, or the Department of Psychology. Some of them, not many though, are going to the Medical School. The others are all girl departments, departments for girls. These girls, to hear what Mother has to say about it when she talks with Big Sister—but Ivo struggles to believe it—are thinking about, or 'should be thinking about, if they had a grain of sense in their heads, and not all these goofy ideas, landing a *good* husband, setting up housekeeping and having children'. The few of them that actually do work will be teaching school: they'll have their afternoons free to stay home with the children and more or less three months of paid holidays—low salaries, certainly, but you can easily afford to hire a housekeeper, health insurance and social security included. Their husbands will take care of everything else. Some of these girls think they've already found a husband and, for many of them, in the final analysis, that's what the beach is for. Some of the boys see things the same way. The atmosphere is still a little confused—a lot of balls will have to go into a lot of pockets before everything, apparently, can consolidate and crystallize—but these young men and women are already at an age of serious pursuits, clear-eyed planning. The young women especially: no more fucking around and French-kissing the first guy to come along, obviously. But also with your boyfriend (you don't use the Italian slang term 'fiancé', even if he actually is or is about to become one) you don't give up much, because you wouldn't want him to get the wrong idea about you and see you as an 'easy' girl, one who's a little too willing—a loose girl, one he can have 'some fun' with.

This is the air that you breathe, undeclared, unenunciated, unstated, on Attilio's platform, a terrace suspended above the sea on this night in late August of 1962. The problem is that certain specimens of the alien species Older Girls aren't behaving at all as if the only thing they had in mind was the husband–family project, in fact, they seem to be interested in continuing to have fun, to seduce, to play with the boys. They have a way of acting that attracts them, catches them off guard, excites them, reels them in, disorients them, makes them fall in love. They're rare and, above all, they're dangerous and Ivo would immediately count Marcella among their number.

Instead of being on this terrace and among these people, he ought to be somewhere else, say at home, studying William of Ockham in the Lamanna textbook, or at the cinema giving it his all with Carla; instead he's here, looking around in search of *her* while everyone dances chats and drinks, leaning on the blue majolica parapet or sitting on the recliners, the canvas folding chairs, the glider. But he doesn't see her. Instead he sees Big Sister dancing with Attilio and he sees the silhouette of Sandro leaning against the parapet, chatting with a couple of friends. He pours himself a glass full of beer—he hates beer but he needs to buck himself up—goes over to him and says *Ciao*, expecting to get enough of his attention to be able at least to ask him about Marcella. But Sandro continues spouting a river of words and laughing, Ivo stands there staring at that large wet mouth that keeps moving incessantly, the lips forming syllables with great precision, without accent, and which stretch into laughter, baring large serrated incisors. When the two others finally move away, Ivo asks him: 'Have you seen Marcella?'

'No.' Sandro is a little brusque, almost rude.

'Do you know if she's coming?'

'Attilio says she's supposed to come . . . But aren't you a little . . . out of your depth?'

Ivo reddens, he doesn't answer.

'The fuck do you care, you overweight piece of shit, where I might or might not be? Exactly what depth do you think I belong in? Are you trying to tell me that I'm too much of a kid to be here? Have you taken a look at yourself in the mirror anytime lately? What are you laughing about? What do you have to be laughing about, continuously, like that?'

That's how he'd like to answer him, because he's furious. But deep down, he's ashamed: it's true that he shouldn't be here, because there's nothing here for him; even Attilio, when he saw him at the door, got a look of surprise on his face, but then he probably didn't say anything to him because he's a friend of Big Sister's. Ivo could leave, but he stays and goes to get himself another beer. Then he tucks himself away into a dark corner of the terrace, he leans against the Vietri majolica parapet and looks out at the sea.

Sistavoccadesider'evase, nun è peccate . . .

The music pours into him, encountering no obstacles or lines of defence. He looks out at the distant sea and almost bursts into tears. The song by Peppino Di Capri arrives from the Rotunda, it's muffled by the distance but it's clear. Ivo contemplates the Great Room of earth and water where he is allowed to live out his Summer in partial freedom: the City, the Beach, the Wave-Tossed Rocks, the sea, more or less stretching out to the Horizon, and the Faraway Mountain—they're all *his*. Behind him there is only land and, an hour and a half away by car, the unparalleled ferment of the City of God, where he will spend the Winter, where everything always seems to be under construction, building sites as far as the eye can see, an expanse covering the hills and spreading out into the plain and then up other hills, endlessly. In this muddy waste-land of building sites is Father's Work, there are his Machines, his Trucks, his Cranes, on the scaffoldings are his men, labouring, with paper hats on their heads. It is from there—Father never forgets to remind him—that the money comes which affords him those four months of oblivion . . . So to flee in the opposite direction from the land, far from Father, towards the Horizon, towards the Islands that every so often you can glimpse there in the distance. And then, like a fish, to plunge into the open sea, towards the far ends of the Mediterranean, towards the Ocean water and more water, nothing but water.

'There they could never find me, they'd never take me alive.'

He even tried once, to escape over the sea: one afternoon he sailed the *Mandrake* straight for the horizon and decided to go *really* far. He got out so far you almost couldn't even see the land any more, as far out as the time of day allowed, then towards evening the wind drops and you might get caught having to row for hours. There, if you look westward, you see the water all covered with luminous scales. Before turning back, he put the prow into the wind and lay there for a while, drifting, in the silence of the water lapping against the side of the hull, until his fear of the sea, of distance, and of being becalmed all pushed him to come away . . .

'I need to take Carla there,' he thinks, as he wards off the tears from the music, 'I need to take her far away and *undress her*.'

He turns around and sees Marcella come in. And that's Fabrizio, with her!

At first, he struggles to place her, he's always seen her in her bathing suit, with wet hair, and now she's made up, her hair gathered in a bun, a Saint-Tropez blouse in white lace that leaves her belly button and hips uncovered, tight black pants, red dance slippers, a necklace of small chunks of amber around her neck, her glasses low on her nose. No one here is dressed like her. She reminds him of another French actress . . . Anouk Aimée. Ivo has three glasses of beer in his bloodstream, he's sweating, and he can't believe his eyes: she's beautiful and different from all the other girls. Tonight on this terrace, no other female human being is exuding the same degree of power and confidence. Fabrizio is right behind her, relaxed as always. He smiles and looks around, says hello to the few people he knows, he doesn't belong to this social circle.

Leaning against the parapet, Ivo watches her from a distance and realizes that she too knows almost no one there.

Sandro is already clustering around her, Marcella says hello to him, smiles and looks elsewhere.

Ivo doesn't feel good, he's sweaty and his head is spinning slightly, he doesn't know if Marcella has already seen him. And so he turns the corner of the terrace because the situation has suddenly seemed intolerable to him. He finds a canvas folding chair, sits down and stares out for a long time at the facade of the house across the way, which emerges from a dark mass of magnolias and cheesewood. He observes the light-blue majolica tiles of the parapet, the octopus, the crab, the lobster, the seahorse, the conch shell, he carefully compares two tiles with the same subject and from the differences he notices that they really are hand-painted. Here it's possible to hear the distant music from the Rotunda more clearly: they're old songs, worn and tattered now, he can't make out the words but he knows them, they're about summer love, beaches, holidays at the sea—it's the Summer working on the nascent myth of itself.

'I need to tell her . . . It's why I came here tonight . . . She's leaving tomorrow and I'm going to be stuck here, like an asshole

. . . For another whole month . . . Like the kids who have to "stay at the beach" . . . Maybe she really does like me . . . She said: "Make sure you come, it matters to me, don't miss it." If she said it, she must have had a reason. Otherwise why would she have said it? What reason would she have to say it? She said, "It matters to me" . . .'

Ivo begins working up a plan for his Declaration.

'I'll ask her to dance a couple of times and then I'll tell her that I have a crush on her . . . But how can I tell her? I have to find an unusual, funny, non-obvious way of doing it . . . I need to tell her something that will surprise her, that will make her laugh, that will interest her . . . In the mystery of her mind, maybe she's already chosen me . . . Yeah, right, and what about Fabrizio?'

Someone has left a mini-Peroni beer—a *Peroncino*—on the parapet. It's half-full. He grabs it and drains it in a single gulp. How can he tell her that he loves here—not that he 'has feelings for her' but that he loves her—if he can't keep himself from crying?

An original and imaginative way of telling her.

A light, unconcerned way.

An intense, dramatic way, that smacks of ultimatum.

Some way that's original with him, that is entirely unlike anybody else's, that lets him overcome all his disadvantages, his lack of superpowers, the fact that he's still in school and all the rest.

He steps away from the parapet and heads over towards the centre of the terrace, where people are dancing.

Right now they're doing the twist, and as he walks Ivo has the sensation that's he's weaving slightly. He feels as if he's been split in two, it always happens to him when he's had too much to drink.

Marcella is dancing with some guy he's never seen before.

She waves at him from a distance.

She's cute, cordial, relaxed, magnificent—everyone on the terrace has noticed.

The twist comes to an end, a slow dance starts up, Ivo goes over to her and asks: 'Care to dance?'

'*Ciao*! Of course, I'm happy you could come . . . I was looking for you before, where were you?'

'She was looking for me!'

Fabrizio isn't far away, he's leaning on the parapet, drinking, watching them.

As soon as Ivo wraps his arm around her waist, Marcella relaxes against him, chatting easily. She clings gently to him, she touches her cheek to his. Ivo is so excited he can scarcely breathe, he feels completely beside himself, a part of him observes the scene as if it had nothing to do with him. He's sweating, but she doesn't seem to notice.

'She likes me! She's encouraging me!'

'When they're interested in you, they let you know, always . . .' Giacomo told him once, during one of their conversations about the ways of women. The only come-on technique that Ivo knows is the one accepted and practised by the Group: dance and hug close. The only variants are the timing and the intensity of the manoeuvre. This is a situation that demands caution.

'I can't just start hugging her close like that . . . But I can give it a try, little by little, I can try to see what happens if I start to put my arms around her . . . I have to start saying sweet nothings to her, breathe close to her earlobe, see if I can give her the shivers . . . I have to work up to it slowly, tell her that I'm head over heels about her! She's trying to make me realize that by now there's no more time to waste, that I need to make my move now . . . If I don't do it now, when am I going to do it? Don't try to grab her, don't be obvious, don't trot out the usual bullshit that little kids come up with, this isn't Carla, this is something very different . . . I can't tell her just like that, directly, I have to get there by degrees . . . Otherwise she'll laugh right in my face, that's what she'll do . . .'

A secret adviser would have told him some crucial facts.

But he doesn't have one, so Ivo, after much hemming and hawing, turns of phrase and hesitations, makes his declaration.

'Well, your teacher is Catholic and your school is run by priests
... That's why the curriculum is skewed towards patristics: usually
St Augustine, St Thomas Aquinas, Ockham, and the others are
studied only if there's time. Instead, you've studied them in depth.
Therefore, first and foremost, we can expect one or more questions
on patristics, while at the other end of the scale you're less likely
to get any questions on the pre-Socratics, though maybe you
should expect one question ... In fact, expect it for sure. Socrates,
Plato, Aristotle are all names you're bound to hear about. So study
them carefully, those are the ones you're going to have to study
exhaustively, but study up on St Augustine and St Thomas Aquinas
too ... Concerning those two, don't come up with any ideas of
your own ... Remember they're at the basis of Catholic doctrine
... Stoics, Sceptics, Epicureans, they're all less likely, but still, they
might ask you a question on them ... The Hellenists are the ones
I like best, if I could write the school curriculum, I'd give them
much greater importance ... They didn't give a damn about metaphysics and all that other bullshit—they were interested in man,
they're the only ones who bothered to help us live well ... We were
supposed to talk about Communism, remember? About the "little
comrades", as your father likes to call them ...'

Ivo pays him no mind, Giorgio is wandering strangely off-
topic, maybe because this is the last time they're going to see each
other before the exam. He's drilled him on spot questions to determine his degree of preparation, he gave him one last round of
advice, and now he's addressing the matter of the little comrades—
Ivo had forgotten about it completely. 'Oh God what a pain in the
ass, what the fuck do I care about Communism? Oh, who knows
when we'll get out of here now ...'—Giorgio talks as if he's pre-
occupied, he goes on and on, it's evident that this is a subject that
he cares about. Ivo isn't thinking about anything, now that the
questioning is over he's gone back to the mental state of the past
few hours, which is that of a boxer still dazed from the bout, who
is moreover ashamed of how short a time he lasted in the ring, of
how easily he let himself be knocked out. The make-up exam is
next week, he knows that he's going to have to study, but that

doesn't really worry him. After the body blows he took last night on Attilio's terrace—when he got home he wept and he vomited—he's still stunned, he took an aspirin. He's just pleased that he managed to answer nearly all of Giorgio's questions. It's almost night-time, the days are getting shorter and today, in the afternoon, there was the usual party at the home of one of the girls in the Group; but now he's sitting here drinking in Giorgio's unscheduled speechmaking, which is going on and on and now it's not really all that clear what he's even talking about.

'. . . they'll talk to you about the abolition of private property, but also about theories and philosophies of the opposite persuasion . . . They'll sing the praises of the free market, of the self-adjusting economy, and so on . . . They'll tell you all about free love, or its opposite, the value of virginity as a supreme good before marriage . . . They'll talk about liberty, fraternity and equality. They'll tell you about the soul & the spirit, about the afterlife, paranormal phenomena, different and better realities. All right, some of these things are wonderful and even I, I'm not going to say that I believe in them but I hope they're true. Which ones? Well, for instance, equality and the end of all subjugation and exploitation . . . But unlike other comrades of mine—after all, I'm a "little comrade" myself—I don't have any illusions: humanity is what it is. So Ivo, look out . . .'

But Ivo isn't paying attention in the slightest, he just wants to leave.

'. . . there's nothing left but *science*. When all is said and done, after you've gone through all the metaphysics and all the religions and all the proofs of the existence of a God . . . When you're done with all abstract reasoning, with all possible and adoptable spirituality, when you're done with all materialism, *there's science and nothing but science*. Science is humanity's one true hope, Ivo . . .'

He suddenly falls silent, as if he'd just awakened from a hypnotic trance, and that is the end of his philippic. Giorgio, usually so distant, so reserved, seems sorry that he's always kept him at arm's length. It's as if, aside from the study plan for the exam, he suddenly wants to make up for lost time as a teacher.

Ivo is already elsewhere, he mumbles something, as he hands him the envelope with the money that Mother gave him: 'I'll call you after the exam . . . Maybe if there's something that isn't clear to me, I could come see you for an explanation?'

'Certainly, come whenever you like. Most of all, don't worry about the exam—you know everything, so . . .'

Giorgio remains seated, the usual cigarette held vertically, clamped between forefinger and thumb, the ashes poised, and says to him: 'Break a leg!' while Ivo is already going through the door.

Ivo manages to reach the ice-cream shop in time to find people from the Group still there, hanging out before dinner. They're almost all males, he asks them about the party.

Tall skinny blond and hunched over with an already grown-up voice—his voice is already disenchanted, already drawling— Ernesto, who has always irritated him, replies. He replies with his head tilted to one side, the back of his hand turned towards him beneath his mouth, and speaks to him in an unfriendly tone: 'Are you trying to find out if Carla was there?'

'Why no, I was just asking . . .'

Ernesto snickers and says: 'If you only knew who she was making out with . . .'

'With whom?'

'Ah, you see that you're interested?'

'Fine, I'm interested. Who was she making out with?'

'Aahhh . . . go on, calm down, she wasn't making out with anybody and wasn't dancing with anybody. She was talking the whole time with Giacomo. I'd be worried if I was you.'

Ivo changes the subject: 'Where's everyone going tonight?'

'And where do you want to go? To a nightclub? To race up the coastline in a fast car with a bottle of champagne in a cooler in the trunk? Do you want to speed out into the night in your motorboat? Do you want to set sail for the South Seas? We're going to the *movies*. To the arena. Whatever's on is on. Where do you think you are? Saint-Tropez? Who do you think you are? Gunter Sachs? Jean-Noël Grinda? Do you have a car? Do you have money? No. So where are you going to go? Here, at ten o'clock, obviously.'

Heading home at a brisk pace, just ten minutes on foot, alone up the hill—the coast stretches out progressively wider as the gulf opens out into the east—with tears in his eyes and no appetite at all. But he's going to have to go inside, he'll have to eat something, he's going to have to get his hands on 500 lire for the night out, two hundred to get into the arena and three hundred spending money. September starts tomorrow. Normally he doesn't even notice, normally Summer flows uninterruptedly well beyond the beginning of September and beyond, right up to the 2nd or 3rd of October, with the scattered few who stay at the beach, the last plunge that you're almost embarrassed still to be there, but, rather than facing up to Winter you'd stop time, you'd halt the sun in its tracks. This year you have a make-up test, a subject to brush up on, and it acts as a barrier, a wall to be scaled before you can enjoy the declining delights of September, when the City by the Sea emp-ties out, when on the beach they remove a line of umbrellas, and at the beach club it's no longer necessary to reserve the Finn sail-boat, staying out late at the Bar Caravella becomes something approaching a mystical experience, because of the fact that there's no one around, the silence, the engines of the fishing boats coming and going in the darkness. But the make-up exam is nothing, it's the departure of Marcella that suddenly emptied the Summer and turned it into a plaything for children, something involving pad-dling in the water, shovel and pail and boredom, parties that turn into birthday parties for tweens, scratchy records, family-size bot-tles of Coca-Cola, ritual ice creams and hot slices of pizza, kissing in public at the arena, driving around at night, four of you packed into a Fiat 500, annoying the faggots who are hooking it at the wharf or in the pine grove . . . Everything that before Marcella seemed funny, nice, intoxicating, including Carla, now just seems like greasy kid stuff. Even the *Mandrake* is now just a little wooden toy boat. Going fishing with Giacomo early in the morning, riding your bike down to Ponente, all the way to the Mute Arch, diving into the cold calm water in your T-shirt: it's no longer a serious, grown-up thing, the way it used to seem, now it's just fishing for minnows, strictly for poorly equipped incompetents. Even the afternoon contemplation of the remains of the Sacred Spitfire, imprisoned on a pedestal in the plaza at the edge of the wave-tossed rocks, no long has the same powerful meaning. All this, the entire Summer with the Gulf and the Islands, everything, everything, has been rendered meaningless by Marcella at a single fell swoop. By her, when she went away into her mysterious Winter in the City, vanished into the warm unattainable intimacy of her life and her things. Ivo doesn't know where she lives, but he imagines her in a big house, with lots of carpets, furs on the beds, etchings of hunting scenes on the walls. He even imagines a fireplace with a crackling fire, her sitting on the deep, soft carpet, in a black leotard, barefoot, her feet arching, the cat, she's on the phone, she's laughing, on the other end of the line the guy who's going to come by and pick her up around nine, tonight . . .

'You're completely out of the running at this point, but there's still a month before Summer is completely over . . . And there's still Carla . . . She likes you, she's cute, you could start trying with her tonight, if she comes to the arena . . .'

At home, Mother is out for a game of canasta, his sisters are home. Big Sister is about to go out, Little Sister is with the nanny who's getting her to sleep, on the table there's a zucchini frittata, covered by a dish, a smoked mozzarella, some leftover eggplant parmesan, a little bread, peaches, plums. The Idrolitina fizzy water, made with a tablet, has almost gone flat. He eats with growing, ravenous hunger, he stuffs himself with bread and mozzarella, the eggplant parmesan from last night is delicious. The 500 lire he was counting on isn't there. He pesters Big Sister until he can manage to pry 250 lire out of her, 200 for the movies and 50 for the ice cream after the movies. In the dresser in his parents' bedroom is Mother's carton of cigarettes, from which he steals one whole pack of Murattis. Mother knows that he smokes. Mother sees, monitors and benevolently tolerates. Mother who lets him live his life, who understands the Summer and its power.

At 10 p.m. he's back in town. The members of the group are all standing around, clustered in a very specific section of the ice-cream shop. The wind has shifted, it's turning into a southwest wind. The air is hot and damp and sticky. Carla is there with the others, silent, with her regulation light sweater over her shoulders, her hair in the wind, whipping at her face, suntanned to berry darkness. She's pretty, but she never had the court of a young queen, like the other two or three stars of the Group had, she doesn't surround herself with girlfriends to laugh and whisper with all the time, to take with her when she goes to the restroom. Carla isn't the kind of girl who likes to stand out and she doesn't seem to give a damn about it either. Tonight she's keeping Ivo at arm's length, she talks with the others, she turns her back on him, while the Group heads towards the Arena Excelsior—Giacomo still hasn't shown up. He manages to work his way to her side in the ticket line. The Group has acknowledged that they've now *become a couple* at Francesca's party and it facilitates his manoeuvre: it's logical that tonight Ivo and Carla should watch the movie sitting next to each other. The way it is for all the other couples, that's the way it should be for them. They're showing a French cloak-and-sword movie. Ivo hates cloak-and-sword movies. He hates the swords that look like skewers and they way they laugh as they fight, conversing and ribbing each other. He hates the way the duelists leap and hang from chandeliers. He hates the little moustaches and the king's guards who always come off looking like fools. He hates this stuff and he loves Westerns and the very rare ones, science-fiction flicks. But tonight he's not here for the movie. He's here to try to go all the way with Carla and the thought alone takes his breath away, makes his knees weak. She barely even notices his presence, she doesn't object to him sitting next to her but she doesn't facilitate it either.

'She's ignoring me, but that's nothing to worry about . . . It's when they act like that they're willing . . . The more they ignore you in public, the more willing they are . . .'

Giacomo's not there, in the end Ivo manages to get a seat next to Carla, in the back row. The metal seats take a while to warm up and at first you feel them through the cloth of your T-shirt. Scattered all around them are the other couples of the Group. That's how it always is, at the movies, no one wants to be up close to whoever's making out, nobody wants to just standing there holding their coats, so a couple zone forms spontaneously, where everyone gets busy and those who aren't making out watch the film happily clinging to their girl, smoking one cigarette after the other in blessed peace. In other words, for the entire duration of the show, from the precinct of the Arena, a great billowing cloud of smoke rises skyward, visible from outside as if something were burning inside. But when those who are inside look up they see the starry sky: around the Night of St Lawrence, or Night of the Falling Stars, more than once some large falling star has shot past and behind the screen, and the whole audience burst out with a collective 'Oohh!' and then everyone has turned around to say 'Did you see that?'

Ivo begins his manoeuvring, he puts his arm around her shoulders, he stretches out in his seat, he lights a cigarette. Carla is wearing a skirt. Is that a sign? Did she put it on especially for him? He sneaks a peek down at her bronzed legs, the gleaming taut skin of her bent knee, the half-visible thighs, the skin-tight T-shirt with the low neckline, the breasts on view, her bra straps. He sees her body as a job to be done, he tries to evaluate the challenges of gaining access. And he grows excited at the mere thought of touching it, while Carla, who isn't even looking at him, talks and laughs with the girl next to her, who also has her boyfriend next to her, she too yoked to her boyfriend's arm, so that the hands of the two males are almost touching. Everything is ready and on track, as the movie starts up and sure enough it is a meatball of a cloak-and-sword flick. Once he's finished with his cigarette Ivo takes her hand and starts kissing her on the neck working up the back, he starts kissing her on the back of the neck, brushes his lips over her ear and drinks in the fresh smell of her skin, the odour of wind in her hair.

With her face turned towards the screen, she lets him do as he wishes but doesn't reciprocate, she doesn't turn to kiss him. At that point, Ivo leans forwards towards her mouth but he finds closed lips. He tries to turn her head towards him but he encounters resistance, she remains stiff, she refuses to turn.

'What the fuck's happening? What's come over her? Until yesterday she was all in, and now?'

'What's wrong?' he asks her.

'Nothing.'

'What do you mean "nothing"?'

'Nothing.'

Once again confronted with the mystery of female behaviour: Ivo must have done something wrong, but what?

'Yesterday I couldn't come, I had to study, you know that . . . And today I had my last lesson. Do you think that I've been enjoying myself for the past few days?' he whispers in her ear, making sure that his warm breath wafts over the lobe of her ear. Carla tilts her head towards him and moves away, just slightly, with a smile. Then she says: 'Watch the movie.'

'What the fuck do I care about the movie?'

Ivo is wounded, so she must be despised in revenge, like a sacrificial lamb to be immolated in the name of Marcella, superhuman entity, unattainable, who left for the city, where she'll be surrounded by adults, leaving him here to finish his summer, a kid among kids.

Carla seems to be enjoying the movie, Ivo lights another cigarette, he props his feet up on the back of the empty seat in front of him, for a little while he feels exhausted, he gives up his manoeuvring, he loses interest. It's a French movie, not even all that much of a cloak-and-sword flick, a meatball with actors he's never heard of, a real piece of shit. He even thinks he recognizes an actor he's seen before on some television series or other: What's he doing here, an actor contaminated by TV? The guarantee you get from American movies is that there are hardly any Peninsular faces in the cast and the ones that you do see are super-famous and only in certain movies and they always play Peninsulars. You'll never find them in Westerns, where they're unthinkable, and where everyone, except for the Indians and the Mexicans, have blue eyes. After a while Ivo returns to the attack, but Carla, closed tighter than a tortoise, thighs locked and arms clasped across her chest, is impenetrable and there's no budging her. Ivo feels like an idiot, he chain-smokes and keeps whispering into her ear: 'What's the matter? What did I do to you?'

She replies: 'Nothing, nothing's the matter, just let me watch the movie.'

But then, during intermission, since he won't give up asking, she tells him calmly: 'We'll talk about it afterwards.'

'Ah, there, you see that something really is bothering you?'

For the whole second half, Ivo puzzles over what can have gone wrong, he formulates plans of action, he realizes that he's willing to stoop to any sort of lie, to tell her that he loves her, even, just so he can get his hands on her breasts, between her legs, as long as he can get her to touch his cock. *But then the movie ends.* Out in the street she says that she has to go home early, he says, 'I'll walk you,' he takes her hand, they head towards the beachfront promenade. The gusts of wind hit them directly the minute they turn the corner, the north wind has got stronger. Ivo returns to the attack: 'Now are you going to tell me what's bothering you?'

She remains silent, he persists.

At last, Carla replies without looking at him: 'Someone told me some things . . . They told me that . . . you just want to have your fun . . .'

'What are you talking about? Who told you that?'

'Forget about who it was . . . I'm not going to tell you, anyway . . . Is it true that you're just planning to be an asshole with me? That you're just looking to have some fun? Who do you take me for?'

The question is so simple and direct that Ivo says nothing. When confronted with the truth, he doesn't know what to say. He ought to lie but suddenly he no longer has it in him. Maybe it's the muggy wind that's made him change his mind, or else the light of the street lamps, the mist, the damp, chilly air coming off a choppy sea, this road with the buildings on one side and the cabins on the other, so familiar with its young plane trees and the dogshits crushed underfoot on the cement slabs of the pavements. Tonight, here and now, he won't be able to lie. So he says nothing.

He feels like nothing more than some poor jerk on this beach-front promenade, after he came away empty-handed from his encounter with Her, after he ran the risk at Attilio's party of doing and saying all those idiotic things, after having watched Her smile at him, politely, *politely*, as She told him that he must have misunderstood and that in any case She wasn't thinking and had never thought about him that way, not then and not ever . . . After getting drunk and leaving in tears, because he felt as if his chest had been split open, after vomiting all night long, so that Mother had heard the sound of him retching—Mother, he knows, is a light sleeper—and she'd got out of bed and held his forehead as he was voiding his gut and sobbing and she'd asked him gently: 'What's wrong, why are you crying? What's happened? Why did you drink like that?' And then she'd walked him back to bed and stayed there with him and stroked his forehead, while he went on crying, and she finally stopped asking questions, as if her son were sick. After all this, walking down to the beachfront promenade swept by the north wind, he suddenly feels like a complete jerk for having tried to have his way with a young girl, in a young boy's summer as it comes to an end, in a beach resort for families, and he remains silent when she repeats the same question that he's still unwilling to answer, because he doesn't feel like lying, but he does feel like weeping.

'Is it true that you're just looking for some fun?'

He says 'No' to her again but without much conviction. And then: 'Who told you? Will you tell me that?'

Suddenly, without Ivo having to ask again, she answers him: 'Giacomo told me.'

He feels exhausted tonight. He feels like staying home. He's cold. But he went back, he walked the whole distance of the waterfront esplanade to the ice-cream shop. He waited for him and now here he is.

'Hey Como, where were you?'

'Having dinner at my aunt's . . . It ran late. How was the movie?'

'Don't ask, it was a piece of shit . . . You know that you're a jerk?'

'Ah . . . *She told you*, did she?'

'What need was there to go and repeat everything to her? You're a nice gossip . . . To think that I trusted you . . . Instead, there you have it, you couldn't wait to run your mouth, just like everyone else . . .'

'You're the jerk . . . And don't use that tone of voice with me . . . It wouldn't take me long to smash your face in, Ivo.'

'Why don't you go fuck yourself . . . You just try, and I'll beat you bloody.'

Giacomo is determined, resolute.

'No, you're the one who needs to go fuck yourself . . . Yeah, sure I told her . . . I told her, I didn't skip a detail . . . You think you can just do whatever you want? That you can use a girl like Carla for your foul purposes and then, when you're done with her . . . Just give her a shot and dump her, is that it? Well, with Carla you can't do that . . . She's *my friend* . . . She doesn't deserve to be treated like that . . . I don't even know what the fuck she sees in you . . . We spent the whole afternoon talking . . . I don't know where the fuck you were . . .'

'I was at tutoring, Giacomo. At tu-to-ring! Next week I have my make-up exam, or did you forget?'

'OK, well, we talked . . . She's head over heels about you . . . She was all happy, all charged up . . . She was convinced that you care for her: she was like that the whole time, she refused to dance with anybody else, she was waiting for you . . . She only wanted to be with you . . . In the end I couldn't take it any more and I told her: "How do you think he cares for you? Ivo is just looking to have some fun . . ." For the rest of the evening she just cried. Then she came to the movies and gave you the back of her hand . . . Or not?'

'Yes, Como, she gave me the back of her hand. She seemed like the tortoise you have in your backyard . . . You know when it gets scared and pulls into its shell? But what the hell do you care about Carla?'

'I care for Carla . . . Hadn't you noticed? She doesn't even know I exist, but I'm not going to let you play the asshole with her, understood? She's not just some object you can use to take out your frustration from the smacks in the face you get from other girls . . . So that other girl won't give you the time of day? That's your fucking problem, wrap your head around it . . . And leave Carla alone.'

'What, do you have a crush on her? Fuck, I never noticed a thing . . . Couldn't you have told me first, at least?'

'What, am I supposed to tell you everything? It's my own fucking business . . . I have mine and you have yours.'

'But I tell you everything, Giacomo . . .'

They remain sitting in the back, against the wall, talking until two in the morning. It's cold, the southwest wind has picked up some more, but it's not raining. The air is dense with droplets of brine. Ivo is wearing his light sailor's sweater with horizontal stripes. The ice-cream shop is closed, but the small knots of boys are still hanging out in front of the place, determined to shoot the shit until dawn, the way they do every night. The girls have all gone home, the more emancipated among them are somewhere with their boyfriend.

'You want to come to the wharf to see the waves?'

It's Ernesto and Lorenzo, calling to them from the open window of a sand-coloured Fiat 500. Ivo and Como stand up. Ernesto say: 'Do you guys have any cigarettes?'

'I've got half a pack, but don't smoke them all, eh?' says Ivo.

The wharf is large and it curves back around towards dry land. It's sheltered from the north winds by a high stone wall. On the opposite side there's a narrow walkway and then a breakwater made of huge cement blocks to ward off the storm surge. In the wall there are two or three apertures to connect the inside with the outside. The Fiat 500 has slipped in there, in one of these apertures, with the high beams pointing into the raging sea, the windows rolled up and the windshield wipers going full.

The incoming waves smash against that chaos of cement. The spray flies high, so high that it occasionally overtops the great stone wall, the waves splash through the aperture and slap violently against the windshield.

'Look at this one coming in!'

'Madonna, tonight the sea is so rough it makes you shit in your pants just to look at it.'

'Can you imagine being out in that . . . Can you imagine being *out right now on an FD*? You wouldn't have time to say amen and you'd already be in the water . . .'

'Sure, you wouldn't even be able to hoist the mainsail before it would be ripped to shreds. But just think how you'd cut through the water . . .'

'Just think about the men out fishing . . .'

'None of the fishing boats went out, the wharf is full, didn't you notice?'

'There's always someone out . . . Madonna, look at that!'

This wave was really a big one, it's scary. When it hits the base of the breakwater it disintegrates into a wall of spray that hits the windshield like a sledge hammer. The interior of the Fiat 500 is saturated with smoke, they can't breathe and their eyes are stinging. Ernesto is sitting behind the wheel because the car is his, he's eighteen years old already, he's a year behind at school, but his folks bought him a car all the same. He lowers his window a little to let in some air, but instead a burst of spray comes in and hits Giacomo in the face, in the back seat, where he's sitting next to Ivo.

'Fuck, roll it up!'

'Then stop smoking, you can't breathe in here! Ivo, what did you wind up doing with that girl? What was her name? Carla?

Nice little piece of ass. She giving you any? Did you let her feel it, eh? Did you put it in her hand?'

Ivo says nothing, Ernesto intimidates him. But the older boy continues, calmly, mockingly. He finally replies (but his voice quavers slightly and everyone in that car notices): 'Cut it out, it's my own fucking business . . .' Giacomo says nothing.

'What are you, acting all indignant? What's got into you? Do you see yourself as a *gentleman*? Do you think of yourself as some Porfirio Rubirosa?'

Ernesto knows everything about playboys, they're a fixation of his. That's his dream life. Instead of living in the old unhurried and familiar City by the Sea, right now he'd like to be in Saint-Tropez. Instead of being parked on the wharf, training his headlights on the crashing views whipped by the southwest wind, right now he'd be drinking and dancing the night away in the nightclubs of the Côte d'Azur.

'. . . do you see yourself as Baby Pignatari? Ah, you don't talk about pussy, eh? You don't kiss and tell. Do you think that when they give you their pussy it becomes *yours*? Don't you know that pussy belongs to everyone, at the most you can hope to take a ride or two?'

Everyone laughs. Ivo laughs along with them, in half-hearted embarrassment. He hopes that Ernesto cuts it out soon. Giacomo is laughing too, and he puts on an amused tone, as if they hadn't just talked about it all night long, as if he hadn't just said to him: 'I'm crazy about Carla.' Now, in here, the conditions are different, it's necessary to put on a certain demeanour, act as if they're up to Ernesto's level, so now Como too plays the mocking gang member: 'Come on now, tell us that you've done it. Don't be an asshole, that stuff doesn't belong to you, after all . . .'

The summer is no longer the immense, glowing, perfect thing that it seemed to be just a month ago. It's starting to display the first sores, like this gusting southwest wind, too violent and cold to mean anything other than the arrival of something very different, something still distant but inevitable. The night goes on, the sand-coloured Fiat 500 withstands the assault of the spray off the stormy sea. Inside the car, in the air supersaturated with smoke, everyone's laughing and gazing distractedly into the future. Far far away, nestled in the depths of the universe, the primary cause, the giant black unmoved mover or motor, covered with grease, emits a subdued roar, as it has from time out of mind.

'You want to go bust the Faggots' balls?' someone calls out.

4.42 p.m.

It's afternoon and he's already very tired, he'd like to stretch out on this seat, with his bag under his head, and go to sleep. He'd give anything for an hour's nap, even better, two hours. Take off his shoes, his pants, the socks that are tight around his ankles, change his underwear, take a shower.

That's how that year ended, no home, no bed, at the very most, a sofa in some friend's flat, but only for a few days. Staying longer was an imposition. They never said so, but it was obvious that the quicker he got out of there, the better.

Comrades or non-comrades, all the people that he knew would have preferred to lend him money rather than have him underfoot in their home for longer than a week. And so Christmas had come and he still didn't know where to turn. After being fired from Megatecton he struggled to make a living with freelance work for the various technical studios, already he wasn't making much money and the breakup with Clara, moving out, had destroyed his monthly accounts, already he was spending more than he was earning, and the bank would call him from time to time to ask when he was going to bring things back in line. He lived here and there, eating tea sandwiches in cafes, a lemon chicken piccata with fried potatoes in a trattoria, a banana smoothie around eleven at night so he could make it to the next morning without having to go out in search of pizza or a bowl of spaghetti. With exceptions, like that night in someone else's flat—a flat they'd lent him for a few days, completely empty, but with a kitchen, a refrigerator turned off, a sofa, a bed, a Schifano Coca-Cola hanging on the wall—where he'd tried to sleep, without success because of his hunger. He'd tried to fill his belly by drinking litre after litre of water, but in the end he'd just slipped out of there, to find a place where he could cram something down his throat before going back to bed. In those days the places where you could eat all night long were certain cafes or delicatessens or tea sandwich shops or luncheonettes or very simply hot-table cafeterias—now that the term *friggitoria*, or fry shop, had long since been abolished as too downmarket, evocative of a postwar past of greasy hot foods, *supplì al telefono* or rice croquettes, potato croquettes, calzoni, panzerotti, etc.—situated strategically close to the main train station or the general markets, at the terminuses of the main night buses and trolleys. Or certain 'spaghetterias', or wine shops and clubs, though they were more expensive, where they'd cook you anything you wanted at any time of the night or day. These were frequented by uninteresting people, the residue of previous seasons of nightowling, powerfully political times, little knots of kids, sometimes even with girls, who didn't know where else to go, people who looked like lowlife thugs, penniless homeless losers, misfits and sociopaths, itinerant whores, factory workers getting off or starting their shifts, bus and trolley and taxi drivers, all-night security guards or just people who, like him, couldn't resign themselves to the fact that another day had gone by without anything at all really happening.

He'd learnt one more thing that year: the social milieu in which he happened to live was as harsh as any other and it worked more or less like the game of musical chairs—there wasn't enough room for everyone to sit and anyone who wasn't fast enough to nab a place was destined to remain standing for who knows how long, possibly for good. The friend who had agreed to let him stay in his place during the week of Christmas had left for the mountains and wouldn't be back until the 5th or 6th of January. He had a place to stay for a few days, he didn't know what to do with it, nor did he feel like getting busy in the kitchen to make anything more demanding than a cup of coffee. He decided that he wasn't going to touch anything, he'd just stay on the wicker sofa in the living room; it had a fairly comfortable assortment of cushions, though he had to sleep slightly curled up because the seat was short for him. Still, he had no problem with it. There were days, months, of dazed confusion and short rations, living on scraps, constantly shuttling between the various places where he was working, days and days of evenings at the movies, often alone, days of sporadic couplings with women he didn't like, whose very smell repulsed him, to whom he didn't know what to say, about whom he didn't know what to think, except that he was very unlikely ever to see them again, to start a real relationship with them. It would be years before he found himself in a time in which he could feel love again. Meanwhile there was this feverish life in the invincible health and energy of almost-youth. All the seats were taken and he was standing, desolate, clinging to his profession like a lifesaver, searching for a crack in the compact wall formed by all the others, friends and enemies, arms locked solidly together. This was the time of 'backlash', when all those who held party membership cards were starting to use them to gain advantages in terms of work and money. It was a colourless, closed society, in which the dawn of a genuine *civitas*, which had first seemed to rise more than ten years earlier, had in fact never arrived. Everywhere he saw the age-old propensity for temporary alliances of convenience, for fleeting personal objectives, some of which were camouflaged in order to cover up the one thing that was inevitably at stake—but which he, punk kid that he still was, would not understand for a good long while yet to come—that is, Power & Money. The game of musical chairs penalized those who moved slowly and cumbrously, as he did, he who was at risk of spending the many years to come standing up, while so many others had already sat down some time ago. The same thing was true of his place of residence: he lacked one. His wife was living in the old flat, because the wife is always the one who keeps the flat, and also because his wife, in this specific case, was also the legal owner. What had become of the comrades of ten years ago? What had become of what had seemed to him to be an ineluctable pressure and mass movement towards change? Nothing, or almost nothing. An enormous majority had fallen this side of the watershed and had adjusted to living in conditions very similar to those they had once fought against. While a minority—just a few but capable of setting the tone for an entire decade—had fallen onto the other side, plunging into a familiarity with violence, on behalf of a revolution that could never actually come about, because no one wanted it, because no one was willing to undertake it, because the Western Bloc would never tolerate such a thing, and for a thousand other reasons. Now the closeness, the solidarity he'd once felt for the comrades of the Movement had vanished. What had taken its place was the all-against-all of life in Peacetime. No one gave you anything, no one acknowledged anything, the way we'd once felt different and special was nothing but an illusion, a lie.

And yet there was a strange and subtle pleasure in that first genuine solitude, in that feeling that he was the master of every instant of his own non-working space and time. Because of the economic collapse that followed on the heels of the divorce, he'd had to accept working conditions that would have been inconceivable before, impossible to reconcile with the idea he'd always had of his future: work as a necessity & a constriction, instead of as a choice, instead of as a passion, a pleasure . . . It was the first genuine collapse of his plans and intentions in his life: there was now no mistaking the fact that his trajectory had gone badly off course, he could clearly see the distance between where he was and where he would have liked to be. But he observed his own failure as if from some point outside of himself, with a strange indifference, he told himself that after all he was an *artifex*, he told himself that he wasn't a combatant and, not knowing how to fight or not wishing to fight, he had been overwhelmed by circumstances . . . And yet . . . What else had they been, these 'circumstances', if not *other people*?

Yes, it's true, that was Hell, Brandani, other people . . . And so, make sure you never wind up in the trajectory of someone stronger and more powerful than you . . . Never believe in friendship and mutual esteem . . . Never believe that the world is there waiting to bear you up in triumph . . . Never try to make use of others while those others are making use of you . . . Never entrust your own fate to circumstances that don't depend on you, your skills and your will, but instead depend on the skills and will of someone else, someone *you trust* . . . Et cetera . . . And, most important of all, Ivo, never think for one second that in a world at peace, someone who feels that he is a non-combatant won't be called into combat nonetheless . . .

And that was exactly what was happening to him in those years: he was discovering the hard, rough, dolorous core concealed beneath the initial bourgeois upholstery of his life. Then, but only after long years and many different jobs, he happened to find something that was still soft and warm, the memory of which still stirs him. He stares at the aeroplanes outside the plate glass, the great tails rising with the emblems of the various airlines, he feels the past surge back up, as if in his oesophagus, while his vision is blurred with tears: Elena. He took her that same morning, after breakfast . . . He'd awakened her, calling her early from the airport, and he'd asked her if he could come over for some coffee. He was returning to the city from Algiers, he ought by rights to have gone home, got something to eat, taken a shower and then gone to work, but suddenly he was assailed by a yearning for her, by a brand-new sense of closeness, which he hadn't felt in years for any woman, and making that request of her had suddenly seemed completely normal to him, even though they'd only gone out once. In a way that was every bit as natural, she had replied: 'Come on over.' They'd thrown themselves fully dressed onto the bed, she wearing a heavy, loose woollen house sweater.

While I kiss her I slip my hand under the sweater, in search of her breasts . . . There they are, encapsulated in a bra . . . I try to figure out how the fastener of this gadget works . . . No luck. She stops me, lifts herself up slightly, arching her back, gets both hands behind her back, then falls back onto the bed. 'Done,' she says. Now all I need to do is push the bra cups up and the bra is annulled, completely deconstructed. I feel the warmth and roundness of her flesh, I start to lift the sweater, she helps me again . . . There they are, her breasts: they're heavy, buttery, the nipples brown and hard . . . I liked her so much it was driving me crazy . . . I'd been after her for months, in the end I wrote her . . . She didn't answer her phone, but when I saw her for work, she'd stop to talk with me, she paid attention to me . . . I've never met a creature like her . . . A totally unassuming intelligence, silent, strange and welcoming . . . She spoke in a low voice, understood everything instantly, was mistrustful of me, but in the end she wanted me . . . I'd suspended contact with any other women so I could focus on her, on how much I wanted to take shelter in her, on how badly I needed her as safe haven in the storm . . . I turned monastic for her, I deprived myself of all other women—just when every female seemed to have become easy for me—to consecrate all my desires to some future encounter with her . . .

Enough is enough, he'd said to himself, I want her to understand how much I desire her, I want her to feel it. Contacting her outside of the occasions offered by his work was practically impossible, because she never answered her phone. She was an art restorer, and she was working on certain frescoes in a church where Ivo's company was undertaking a structural consolidation. They ran into each other there, he'd climb up onto the scaffoldings and watch her work, ask questions. Once when she was up there alone, they talked for almost an hour, sitting on the work benches. Those visits went on for months, he asked her for her phone number, she replied: 'I'll give it to you, but I never answer.' 'Why not?' 'Sometime I'll explain it to you . . . it's complicated.' 'Well then?' 'Well then what?' 'Well then . . . how can I arrange to see you off the job?' 'Why?' 'What do you mean, "why"?' 'Why do you want to see me?' Ivo didn't know how to answer that, and he said, 'Just because . . .' So she wrote down an address on a piece of paper and said, 'Write to me.' He immediately wrote her a letter that she must have liked, because she wrote back, giving him an appointment and adding, at the foot of the page: 'I'm not interested in parlour games.' 'No parlour games, agreed. But you're going to have to explain to me just what you mean . . .' he said to her the minute he saw her.

Now that it's happening I'm going crazy with excitement . . . She's only a woman, I tell myself . . . You need to *use her* for your pleasure, that's what I tell myself to diminish her, to minimize her in my mind and allow my sex to remain unafraid, to fill itself with blood under pressure . . . She's a woman just like any other, there, those are her breasts . . . Nothing special, that's for sure . . . But they're *her* breasts! *Hers*! This woman beneath me, whose sweater I took off, with her consent, with her help, is *her*! Her! This is her mouth, wide open beneath mine, her tongue, her entire oral cavity wide open to my every exploration . . . This is her respiration, this is the sound that our saliva makes while I suck her tongue, her upper lip . . . She keeps her eyes closed, she abandons herself, she entrusts herself to me practically without knowing me . . . Don't take off her skirt, there's no time, just got off these panties . . . Lift the skirt over her hips . . . The brown flesh, the dark hair of her sex. Its *hers*. Nothing special, that's for sure, but it's *her* pussy! Hurry, get off your trousers, get your underwear off . . . There's no time. She opens her eyes, looks down, tries to scrutinize my cock, but I don't think she's able to: it's already between her thighs, the unheard of happens again . . . There's no time, I have to do it in a hurry, immediately . . . I don't care what she'll think of me, I don't care whether she comes or not . . . Now it's her who's said it: 'Put it in me.' Do it, slowly . . . I encounter no obstacles, no contractions, nothing I have to force, she's wet, she welcomes me slippery with her inner heat . . . As I enter her she emits a suffocated 'Oh,' a deep sigh, she opens her eyes, she looks at me . . . She remains silent, she studies me, as my pelvis moves the way she expects it to, according to custom and nature, in the banality, primary and supreme, of the act. Keep me from thinking I'm *inside* her or I'll come . . . And I don't want to come, I need to mount her . . . Don't think the phrase *mount her* or you'll certainly come immediately . . . You're on the verge of coming, think about something else . . . Everything's warm and odorous, everything's wool and pussy . . . She goes on sucking my lips, after a few more seconds she half-closes her eyes again, she moans softly . . . I'm about to have an orgasm that's going to be hard to put off . . . Don't come inside her! Pull it out, now . . . While I'm jerking myself off, I think again, 'I need to use her without fear,' so I get up on my knees until the tip of my cock is on a level with her face . . . I have to move quick. She's not expecting it, she seems frightened, but she opens her mouth. Now I have to think, 'You can come in her mouth, after all, she opened it.' Abandon yourself to the spasmodic contractions of a place hidden deep in your guts, there's nothing else you can do, nothing to be ashamed of, she expects it . . . The sperm squirting, almost a vibration . . . It's all the semen of a lifetime that's accumulated there, on the threshold of that love, as if trying to prove it to her: here, this is everything I am, an ordinary man . . . I'm just a man, I'm all here, I'm simple, *I'm yours*. At first she holds it on her tongue, then she swallows it . . . She's swallowing carefully, as if this were the first time, her eyes wide. She looks like a frightened doe . . . This seems to be the first blowjob in her life . . . She looks like Bambi's mother at the moment the hunter shoots her . . . Before tonight, I'll take her again. And then again. Until the end of time.

This violent regurgitation of memory excited and stirred him. The young woman sitting across from him, attractive and suntanned, is reading a book in German, with the typical cover of a bestseller, and she has earpods connected to some device—from her long blond hair, freshly shampooed, two wires run down into her bag. She's wearing a pastel T-shirt, the colour is a pale, domesticated red, a pair of loose black trousers, maybe silk, and over her shoulders a light-grey jacket in slightly rumpled linen, on her feet she's wearing a pair of untanned leather sandals, very elaborate, which rise to cover her ankles. She's extremely elegant, almost without make-up, entirely at her ease and, in every sense of the term, light years away from him. And yet just a second ago, when their gazes met—sooner or later it was bound to happen because Brandani has been staring at her for a good long while—she smiled at him. 'What are you doing here, sublime creature, in the midst of this pack of tattooed mental defectives?' Ivo is asking himself at the exact moment that she looks up, looks at him and immediately smiles. His smile of response is all wrong, he can feel it tug at the skin of his face like an embarrassed smirk. A humble, submissive smile, a smile as if from behind a plate of bulletproof glass, off-blue.

My smile was the grimace of an old man fortuitously blessed by the indulgence of youth, the smile of a concealed lusting yearner, it probably struck her as lewd, slobbery . . . She can't possibly find

me attractive, hairless as I am, unmistakably long out of play . . .
Not necessarily, Brandani . . . Naaah, too old, *much* too old . . .
She smiled at you politely, because where she comes from that's
the custom . . . Snap to, Brandani, you're practically seventy . . .

Sexually unheard of. For him women had always been something strange & distant, as if they'd never formed part of his own
world. He'd attended all his schools in all-male classes, except for
third grade. Third grade was devastating, he fell in love simultaneously with Giusi and Alessandra. They wore white smocks with
a blue bow and he had a blue smock with a white bow. In class,
he kept his gaze fixed on the row of benches where he could see
the white. Strange, this distance from women: he had Mother and
two sisters, he had always lived in a house full of females. He could
clearly see the woman in Mother, but it was as if he were seeing
some female deity with attributes and powers different from the
others. Mother was a haven from injustice and sickness, in Her
presence were perennial protection and alliance, you could be
healed and freed of all ills. Sisters participated in Mother's same
nature but at a largely imperfect stage. They weren't like him,
because instead of fighting to become men, they were fighting to
become women, with all the uncertainties and inequalities, with
that continuous struggle to conceal anything that might seem
defective, ugly or poorly maintained in them—a tremendous effort.
To live with the Sisters was like observing a woman, only from the
wrong side, like entering a shop from the rear, instead of through
the front door. He never saw the Sisters' display windows from the
right side, always from the interior, when they were still being
dressed and staged. How could he consider them women in full?
He saw women—he still does—as something perfect, unattainable,
sweet-smelling, smooth, far away. Making love with them, though
it was never particularly difficult for him, was always *unheard of*.

Back then, to me, they were subliminal creatures, I believed
they were made of air and water . . . Back then, in the days of
Summer, the bikini was already in its classical phase: not too
skimpy, precise . . . It was the female body that was being liberated
. . . At first from clothing, and then from inhibitions, and we

witnessed the dawn of Sexual Liberation, with our fathers' old ideas in our heads . . . Those girls in skin-tight cotton trousers in pastel shades (pink or pistachio or Bordeaux red, or else bright yellow or black . . .), short above the ankle, with the slit on the side, a pair of pedal pushers with the white blouse—or yellow or pistachio green or watermelon pink—knotted over the belly, or else a cotton T-shirt, tight-fitting, and Capri sandals on their feet, pretty girls, their hair redolent of salt water and fresh air, a little mascara on the eyelashes and just a hint of eyeshadow . . . Christ . . . Those girls had their natural habitat on the beach, like gazelles on the savannah. They seized control of their territory in groups, moving from the cabin area to the beach umbrella area, to the water's edge and into the water . . . A supreme, adorable lightness, which transcended everything . . . The scent of a woman that emanated from those creatures, the occasional tuft of pubic hair winking from their bikini bottoms, their armpits, hardly ever shaven, dewy with the sweet-smelling sweat of youth, was . . . Overwhelming . . . And they *were willing*! Ivo, do you remember? They were astonishing . . . So different from me, from my filthy friends . . . They had this soft body, made of some indecipherable material, they were full of strangeness, secrets, their own particular demands . . . They had ambiguous reactions that were difficult to interpret . . . Always bound up with further conditions and checks—totally deranged . . . What you wanted was to touch them first thing, but they wanted to hear you tell them things, they wanted to have things said to them in a certain way, but it was never the same and what one of them might like could prove to be a disaster with another one . . . You had to know how to make them laugh, no vulgarities, no dirty words, but then you started to notice that many of them didn't mind them a bit, quite the opposite in fact . . . You couldn't be friends with girls, in fact, it was vital *not* to be: you were either on one side of that line or the other. Being friends meant ruling out any chance you might have had . . . I did the same as all the other males, I left open every possibility with practically all the girls I knew: first imperative, *do things*, as for the rest, it remains to be seen . . . There was this blinding sexual priority, that at first we didn't know exactly what it was, we just knew that we wanted it . . . You could always luck into it, girls were strange, they might even wind up liking an ugly, even a repulsive guy, or a cretin, they might discover an interest for a fatso, an old guy or someone much younger than them, they might like skinny guys or muscular guys, tall guys and short guys, stupid guys and intelligent guys, athletic guys, sedentary guys, the rich, the poor—there seemed to be a window of hope for everyone . . . But obviously things were that much easier if you were handsome, with some money in your pocket . . . It was Marcella who made that clear to me . . . But she was older than me, I was just a little boy, I had no real hopes—poor imbecile, such an imbecile that after she turned me down I started holding women in contempt . . . I felt contempt in particular for the women who were willing, because 'they took it', you understand? Talking among ourselves, we used to say that they liked cock, that is, that disgusting object we had between our legs . . . I was confused, if I think about it I'm still ashamed today . . . We felt contempt only for the girls who were into it, the ones who were 'loose', the ones who were 'a little bit sluttish'. The other girls, the ones who wouldn't let you touch their tits right away, who wouldn't let you put your hand between their thighs first thing, the ones who, at the very most, if they liked you, would give you a kiss, but just lips, no tongue, who at the very most might let you hold them close at a dance, the ones who checked you out, studied you carefully, before letting you have anything . . . Those girls, the administrators, they deserved our respect, pathetic imbeciles that we were . . . We were convinced that when we were with girls we couldn't be ourselves, we had to pretend to be different & better, we had to put on feelings and ideas we didn't actually have, we had to lie and lie some more . . . 'Do you love me?' 'Yes' (No, I don't love you, you just make me horny as hell, I like you well enough, but I find you boring, but still the tits on you, my God, what tits!). 'It's not like you're just interested in feeling me up, are you?' 'Of course not, I really like you a lot, otherwise why would I be here with you?' (I'm not just planning to feel you up, I'm also hoping to do stuff that's more serious than that, I'm hoping for some between-the-thighs work, I'm dreaming of a handjob, I'm theorizing, but I can't even really fully conceptualize it, a blowjob and, God! I'd like to fuck you . . . My hands are trembling, I'm feeling nauseous, I'm getting a stomach ache from how excited I am . . .). 'If we go to bed then you wouldn't go and tell everyone, would you?' 'Who do you take me for? Some gossipy housekeeper?' (Of course I'd go and tell everyone, you don't think I'd get to third base with a girl like you and keep that fact to myself, do you?)

It demanded patience, you had to learn to understand when a 'No' meant a 'Yes-No' or even a 'Yes', and instead when it really did mean a 'No' and it wasn't a good idea to insist. You had to understand when a sequence of 'No No No' could change into a 'Yes' and what method of persuasion should be used in that case. 'No No No . . . Yes.' At night, at the arena, you had to be able to figure out whether she'd crossed her arms across her chest to keep you from fondling her tits, or whether it was because it was cold, or for no particular reason at all.

Brush your hands over her breasts, see if she recoils, if she hits your hand away, touch her lightly on the thighs, as if by accident, to see if she clamps them together or leaves them in the same position, listen to her breathing as you kiss her neck and you stick your tongue in her ear (the bitter taste), to tell when she starts to pant . . . Then, late at night, on the beach, you try for the lunge, you try to slip her panties off . . . Once you get those off, you've taken one giant step forwards . . . The law was that you could never take back a step: if you let me touch your breasts today, tomorrow you won't be able to deny them to me and I'll try to see if I can get them to pop out of your blouse . . . If I can, then that means that I've scaled another section of the mountain and tomorrow night that's where we start over . . . Usually, it was no easy matter: a petting session could last for hours and in the end you emerged from it with your scrotum swollen and aching, with an urgent need of relief . . . Back then, no one talked about erogenous zones, female orgasms, the clitoris . . . These were things you'd learn in the field from these unforgettable girls who'd guide your hand gently towards the locations that were most interesting for them . . . It was a miserable existence, until they too learnt how to get sperm to squirt out of our overheated bodies. They were available but they always remained to me—and it's still true today—distant, unattainable . . . You grew older, you learnt, but the sensation of estrangement was still there, while sex became obvious, implicit, almost obligatory . . . Until, now, it has once again become that distant, inconceivable thing that it was at the beginning . . . You, Brandani, you're no longer in the game, but life doesn't stop: every day millions and millions of little new pussies emerge into the reality of the world, but they're not for you and they never again will be . . . The teensy newborn pussies, unsightly at first, but only for a short while, because soon they'll display all their seductive, natural & irresistible power. Even when they're little, they have wonderful eyes, like that little girl over there, her feminine mannerisms . . . To say 'feminine' wouldn't mean a thing, if it weren't for the difference from what we males are, pathetic incomplete variants on the feminine, with our erectile oversized clitorises, with our pussy that's been sutured along the axis of symmetry of the scrotum, with our dried-out, pointless nipples . . . I know perfectly well just how adorable a woman-child already is and what intolerable promises she carries inside her for the little snotnose toddler boys of today, who are going to grow into boys and young men long after I'm dead . . . The fact is that you're already dead, Brandani. You've long since set sail from anyone else's sexual horizon . . . These millions of elegant little girls with their big sweet shrewd eyes, their piping high voices, reflective, subdued and thoughtful, which ask you the reason for things, the sweet-smelling skin, firm as apricots, these little girls intently playing at their feminine games, to which they're inclined by genetic predisposition, all these women that you might say are under construction, if it weren't for the fact that every stage of construction has nothing transitory and incomplete about it, but instead presents itself as finished . . . Well, Brandani, there's nothing left but that last tragic stage before they blossom forth, when they start to gain weight, they become awkward, their T-shirts display growing breasts that pop up shameless and rapid as mushrooms in the underbrush . . . Their hips grow heavy without their waists narrowing, making them look like those big two-litre bottles of wine on the lower shelves of Italian supermarkets . . . It is in this period that they lose almost all of the gleam and wit of childhood femininity, the gaze dulls, turns torpid . . . And so they keep to themselves, chatting idly and continuously, when they laugh they display mouths crowded with orthodontic steelwork, and those too are provisional . . . And yet these graceless young girls are a seething & carnal programme, for those who know how to do read it, a promise but Not-For-Me, that the boys their age are incapable of glimpsing. The immense planetary mass of hormone-soaked female flesh, which grows and grows and increasingly configures itself to match the biological model of what we think of as woman . . . Well, this mass in the process of formation acquires, instant by instant, a brutal and irresistible force of attraction . . . Hips and asses and breasts, by now fully mature, that progressively deform the surrounding space-time continuum . . . It's a phenomenon that renews itself day by day, continuous, unstoppable . . . Every new generation of pussies that come to maturity begin their devastating work of *sexual modification* of reality, creating and falling victim to hallucinations, provoking tensions, anxieties, solitary spasms in the impure kidneys of the boys their age . . . Then the Darwinian struggle for power and, for their whole lives long, filthy thoughts in the minds of adult males . . . Adult, so to speak . . . A male *never* really becomes an adult as long as he has too much testosterone circulating in his bloodstream . . . Male adulthood coincides with the loss of sexual vigour and the humiliation of old age . . . I'm only beginning to become a *real* adult now. Every previous stage of life before this has been too steeped in sex to contain even a shred of mental lucidity . . . The human male is old when he starts clasping his hands behind his back . . . But it's only an apparent surrender, because deep in the bloody slipperiness of the loins there still smoulders, though now useless and ignored, the flame of possession, which lasts a whole lifetime . . . While the human male is shunted off onto the siding of old age, endless new brigades of women rise proudly and march defiantly across the earth's crust, making use of every means at their disposal to provoke stimulate excite the opposite sex, to propagandize themselves as promises of pleasure & reproductive pacification . . . The feminists hurl insults at advertising and the TV and the movies and the press . . . They accuse them of utilizing women's bodies for commercial ends—well, I'm not all that convinced . . . I'm tempted to wonder: 'Who uses whom and what?' . . . Of what use is a female body if not to be seen *first and foremost*? Might women's bodies not *also* be making use of advertising and TV etc., to constantly invade our imagination and take up a dominant position there? Might this not be the pussy's Darwinian strategy, after all?

A group of Peninsular families is getting in line at the gate to board a flight for the North.

Baby feet, fat as little bread rolls . . . The toes don't seem to have any reactive functions to the changes in posture . . . Children's feet stink, I know, more or less like grown-up feet . . . They aren't the jerks they're going to be when they grow up and already their chubby little feet stink . . . Northern European mothers are more relaxed, in their maternal biological inferno . . . You can spot Peninsular mothers immediately, they call their children in loud voices, they're *proud* to be mamas, that is, to have achieved this primary function to which all women seem to aspire . . . 'Say thank you to Baby Jesus, pray to the Little Virgin Mary and don't talk to children you don't know . . .' They're at the mercy of these ball-busting, spoilt little brats who grew up on cartoons . . . But they're contented all the same, proud to be serving a biological duty that is their whole life: the smaller the child and the more energy they devote, proud & slightly sweaty. The fathers, at least in the first phase, wish they were somewhere else . . . Look at that man . . . How old could his kid be? I'm no longer capable of judging a small child's age . . .

Brandani thoughtfully observes a man in his mid-thirties, in Bermuda shorts & flip-flops. He has tattoos on his arm and shoulder, it's a thoroughly aged ethnic design, by now fading, blurry.

An old piece of work, defective, low quality, with Maori overtones, cheap crap, long out of fashion, sooner or later he's going to have it removed . . . Or not, maybe he'll keep it, it'll remind him of the good times, the old ways, of when he was still a hunk going to rave parties.

Brandani realizes that he's hating a man he's never seen before in his life, someone who is a complete stranger to him. In the meantime the man busies himself with the little boy in the collapsible stroller, he picks at a clump of babyish rags stuffed into a piece of elastic netting behind the backrest of the device.

Maybe the little brat's mother has gone to the restroom . . . I hate him, but why? Let's see . . . Because he's still young, but not that young, because he possesses a culture dating from the Nineties, when I had already stopped approving of everything that was going on around me . . . When I was already practically out of the game, and he was living his blessed cock-driven youth, when he was fucking eagerly and often, tattooing arms and legs, pumping up his biceps . . . For sure his adolescence wasn't like mine: at age fifteen, he was starting to look at porn on the Internet, he grew up on videogames. He never gave a flying fuck about politics, he doesn't have the slightest idea of what dissent is . . . Now he probably wishes he was somewhere else, he feels like a prisoner, handcuffed to his wife, his baby, he feels like Christ on the cross . . . He doesn't have the paternal instinct, or at least he doesn't have it yet, maybe later on, when the baby is a little older, they'll be able to establish a bond, but for now it's sheer animal protective instinct . . . Here she is now, I wouldn't have imagined her so nicely put together, I expected her to be mousier: she's not bad at all . . . Yes, she went to the restrooms, she inspected the toilets . . . She's satisfied, or maybe she's not, maybe she's not at all . . . Maybe she has a job too, but from the way she takes care of herself, I'd guess she doesn't . . . She certainly was the one who wanted the baby . . .

He watches as she picks up a bag, while her husband, holding the boy by the hand, heads for the restrooms.

The little boy's still wearing a diaper, it needs to be changed . . . I wonder if that's actually his kid . . . By now it's been established that 30 per cent of all children aren't the offspring of their official father, but of some cuckoo-man who has impregnated his wife

. . . I inseminate, from there on it's your business . . . The mother knows it, whose child it is, that much is for sure . . . I'm hungry, let's go take a walk . . . The 'Peninsular' snack bar . . . Pizza by the slice . . . Panini . . . Salami and sausage and bell peppers, coagulated mozzarella on the slices of cold pizza, waiting to be revived in the oven, though never entirely resuscitated, because a part of the initial fragrance will inevitably be lost for ever in this hostile, oxygen-filled universe . . . The universe that refuses to allow pizza and everything else, even us, coral included, to survive and preserve itself intact . . . There's no inverting time's arrow, that's what I would say to these guys behind the counter . . . Everything has to go bad, rot, deteriorate, go to rack and ruin, until it's well and truly fucked up. Food becomes inedible . . . Human beings become no-longer-fuckable, just like you, O Brandani Ivo . . . Women look at me the way anyone would look at this cold pizza, actually, no, you can reheat the pizza, no matter what it still preserves a certain degree of appetizing desirability, but I don't: if you heat me up in the oven, nothing happens, except that I break out in an even worse sweat than normal . . . Anyone who doesn't hold on to a woman at the age when you can really bond her to you, accustom her to the way you think, make her become indifferent to your farts, etc., will be left to live alone . . . All there is for you now are old bags at your same level of desperation, mistrust, loneliness . . . At your same level of selfishness, people who by now are used to taking care of themselves alone, agreeing with themselves alone, finding their bathroom always available, the toilet lid unfailingly either up or down, making dinner by themselves for themselves, a shortlist of dishes, always the same . . . At night . . . When you're alone in front of a TV set in a hotel room, when the whole world around you seethes, completely indifferent to your fate, you just need to *make a home* . . . Make it there, in that hotel room, it doesn't matter whether it's for a few hours or a few days—it's still your home, with the television hearth flickering away, your virtual friends from the never-ending succession of American TV series, that they broadcast everywhere in all languages . . . Lieutenant Columbo, subtitled in Sinhalese . . . It's when you're stretched out on a bed, sprawled in an armchair, with your shoes off, and you can draw a straight line between your eyes and a television screen: if that line remains in place for more than ten minutes, well, as far as I'm concerned, all this constitutes *home* . . . This stuff is anti-matter, if it came into contact with my stomach it would produce a flash of annihilation, it burns me if I so much as look at it . . . My old gastric mucosa already screams at the terrifying threat of *salami, pepperoni, olives and motzarela* . . . They do sell salami, clearly this airport is already considered part of the West . . . They haven't taken the trouble though to inquire as to how you should properly write the labels . . . *Salsicia, fontina, rucheta and olive* . . . To make this pizza they must have summoned a chemist . . . They just slathered on the entire periodic table, every element known to man, all the possible combinations of ingredients . . . In the world history of the pizza, we are well into the rococco phase: from the mystery of an ancient archaic phase, to the classicism of the Neapolitan perfection of the model, to the North American baroque that was already quite a mess, until we reach the final phase, the porno-pizza of the globalized world, where everything is mixed together with everything else, and so you can put 'the whatever' on a pizza, as Mother used to put it . . . The cultural fall-out of the world's chaos is plainly evident on the pizza, where by now there no longer exists any criterion of compatibility between one ingredient and another, between the combination of the two or three and the human stomach . . . You would think that instead of human customers they are feeding nanny goats . . . And yet these people beside me are salivating, and those others are comfortably chowing down on one of those pizzas before boarding for a flight of who-knows-how-many hours with that junk in their gut . . . They're young . . . Pizza by the slice, *international style*, has a very specific *target*, which doesn't include people of a certain age, though there's nothing to keep them from making up a few well-turned-out portions of margherita pizza, pizza with mozzarella-tomato-anchovies (just a few and really first class), especially for the older travellers . . . It's not just a matter of my digestion, pizza has remained one of my few points of reference: if you globalize it, if you transform it and you kill its original form, if you scatter its genetic code to the four winds you wind up finding *salsicia, with chocolate and pepperoni everywhere you go* . . . Those are *panini al prosciutto*! *Sandwich with raw Parma ham*. It looks like genuine prosciutto from Parma, sticking out of the side, posing in every way as an authentic *prosciutto crudo* . . . Hmmm, better not to trust . . . But here we're not in Egypt, we're at the airport, which means we're in a world apart, the world of airports, which while it isn't properly occidental nor is it antiseptic, nonetheless remains something modern and air conditioned, connected by air routes to other airports around the world as if they were so many rooms in the same gigantic Airport-Home, a structure that envelops the globe in much the same way that, long ago, the fat meshed around the kidneys of the *fegatelli ribbudicchiati*, a dish they used to serve in the City of God with poached, pan-fried chicory, triggering Father's endless Sunday postprandial naps, naps that I can imagine as having been ruined by all sort of nightmares, by the vibration of his soft palate, something that is bound to carry me off just as it did him, in my sleep, from cardiac arrest . . . We aren't in Egypt, we're in the Airport-Home where anything can exist, even a prosciutto of Parma, even unsalted Tuscan bread, even fresh, though it's not all that likely that this is what it appears, maybe it's fake, maybe it was made by the Japanese technicians of Fakenature . . . Fake like everything else is, here and outside of here . . . Like the coral encrustations we're working on . . . Enough is enough, Brandani, make your choice . . . OK, ham and cheese, what else if not that? How could it be that a sandwich, a panino, a Certain Specific Panino, eaten at a certain hour of a given, long-ago day, in a place you've never gone back to, that you couldn't even find again and if you happened across it probably wouldn't recognize . . . how could it be that That Panino remains in your memory for so long and so vividly? It must have been nine in the morning, they'd left at five . . . It was all highway until a certain exit in a central valley of the Peninsula, then the state road up into the hills, an ancient, medieval region . . . Life was *open*, back then . . . We were supposed to survey a fourteenth-century church for an engineering exam ... Now that I think about it, life wasn't all that open after all, I'd already made certain crucial choices that I didn't even fully understand yet, decisions whose consequences I couldn't yet appreciate ... Yet I was inexplicably happy, happier than I'd ever been before or than I've ever been since, otherwise I wouldn't have remembered it, that Panino Al Prosciutto, that Ham Sandwich ... It was a stop in a little grocery store along the way, they laid out two slices of fresh bread, unsalted, stuffed with mountain prosciutto, dark red, very salty, rimmed with fat, thick cut ... It was cold outside, against the wall was a bench where I took a seat: there were a couple of my colleagues with me ... Who were they? I can see their faces before me, but I can't recollect their names ... I remember nothing but that bread and that ham, the fog that was lifting, the expanse of wooded hills reaching out beyond the edge of the state road, how hungry I was. Me and my Panino: nothing that can be forgotten, the absolute happiness of body and mind ... It's all engraved so deeply in my memory, that it comes back, periodically, and never leaves me ... Before I die I'll murmur a sibylline phrase in someone's ear, just like in *Citizen Kane*: 'Bread and Ham on the Solitary Hills ...' I'm not all that hungry after all, I decide against the sandwich entirely, I'll just settle for a simple globalized cappuccino, they'll certainly give me something to eat on the plane ... It's almost five o'clock ...

The City of God

There were glass doors in the flats. Pebbled glass in various styles, and if you had the time on your hands, you would stop and focus, trying to reconstruct the pattern. Weaves made up of repeating motifs, undulating lines, or else a single uniform and opaque surface, sometimes with sanded floral motifs. The glass doors were there to illuminate service hallways, corridors, front halls, vestibules. The light came in from a window, and there might not be that much of it, because the windows often overlooked the courtyards, or else they looked out of side or rear facades, and in that case the light glanced off the paint of the closest building, taking on its shade and hue. Once it entered through its main source, the light penetrated towards the humbler spaces of the interior, where a tiny side table might have a telephone perched on it, or else just the phone books, while the instrument itself was fastened to the wall, where there might be a few Swedish bookcases, hanging from hooks, slightly askew, a shoe rack, a coatrack at the front door, with the umbrella holder, a small shelf for keys, a mirror. Sometimes it was a console table, with its unfailing curved and gilded legs, scrolled woodwork with the customary attitude of period furniture, a style that to Ivo's eyes had something lewd and treacherous about it.

But this was true only of the homes of lawyers, notaries, engineers, businessmen, that is, for the residences of the age-old, unbudgeable, sordid block of families that had first settled in late-eighteenth-century neighbourhoods and that then scattered to other, newer quarters built in the second wave of the city's expansion. Families that clutched in their fists control of the City of God and who determined the nature of its everyday appearance, the way it was a city in the present, who indicated the most advisable shape and direction of growth, areas upon which they speculated undisturbed, making tidy sums of cash. But even in the homes of the newly risen people—the most recently built ones, on the top floors, drenched with light, and striking the pose of the Peninsular contemporary look of that time, which consisted of the 'stylizing' of anything that could be 'stylized', from the armchairs to the tables and the wall lamps and the kitchen chairs and the sofas, every object and conversation piece and accessory straining to seem like something new, up-to-date & rich—even in these homes there were vast glass doors, something of them sliding doors (or *'portes à coulisse'*, as Mother used to say, because she spoke French), or double glass doors, and in this case too the glass was translucent but stamped with a dense sequence of convex lenticular shapes, making it impossible to see through.

By the time the violent light of the City of God got to the mud-rooms of the flats it was already faint, dull, illuminating bookshelves with full collections of *Gialli Mondadori* detective fiction and *Urania* science fiction, of *Topolino, Monello, Intrepido, Tiramolla*. Packs of back issues of newsweeklies like *Epoca*, the *Settimana enigmistica, or Weekly Puzzler, Oggi, Gente, Selezione dal Reader's Digest, L'Europeo,* even folded copies of *L'Espresso, from back when it was an oversized news-sheet,* even copies of *National Geographic,* in English, the lovely photographs of Unspoilt Nature that he liked so well. When entering the home of any of his schoolmates, Ivo perceived in the air the typical whiff of domestic incubation, different from one home to another, but always with the same shared bouquet common to all families, describable as 'stale, closed air'. An odour that, after a while, you could no longer even perceive but which changed from room to room. In the bedrooms there often wafted a ham-like stench of wet dog, in the kitchen there was the odour of layered and stagnant frying pans full of minced vegetables, covered over in part by the fresher aroma of the last bout of sautéing, garlic and onions golden brown in the frying pan with canned tomato paste for meat sauce,

452

in the hallway there was an indistinguishable mix, sickly sweet, very distinctive, blending with the scent of fine dust burnt by radiators turned up too hot. To Ivo, in the first period after his return to the city, when they were staying in grandmother's Unheated Flat, that dry radiator-heated air would give him a headache and, once he'd finished his homework, he couldn't wait to get out and walk home in the chilly winter air which back then, even in the City of God, was quite nippy.

In those homes you could find an olfactory summary of the recent history of the Peninsula and of that family in particular, a sort of aromatic Play-Doh ball where you see everything merged into a final hue, an undefinable reek, the odour of the specific past of each family, but recognizable in what this family had in common with other families of the same period, same class, same quarter, same street, with children who went to the same schools, mothers who did their grocery shopping in the same stores.

The glass doors, small or large though they might be, sliding or otherwise, single- or double-panelled, brought light into the recesses odorous with human brooding, smells that seeped into the wallpaper, carpets and curtains, which remained in the clothing, where they mixed with the powerful stench of mothballs, the vaguely corrupt smell of fur collars that had once been alive—as witnessed by those small foxheads arranged in sequence to bite their tails, dreary around Grandma's neck at Sunday Mass—when it wasn't the pearl grey astrakhan overcoat with the matching bearskin hat, which made her look pretty much like a Cossack from the river Don, her nose red with the cold, her gaze lost in the distance like some uncomprehending bird.

In the Brandani family home there were a great many glass doors, and those that were not always open were always shut. The always-shut doors marked a threshold that could be crossed only for very sound reasons; behind them was the wall-to-wall carpeted *sancta sanctorum of* Mother's bedroom, but especially Father's, the place where he kept his Socks, the only possession of Father's to which Ivo, for some unknown reason, was given free access, which is why he frequently wore canary-yellow socks, the only eccentricity that Father ever allowed himself in his life, if you leave aside the occasional appearance of a bowtie. In that other bedroom, too large and too empty, behind a glass door and then behind a double door, which further sanctioned its special separation from the rest of the flat, Ivo knew that on the Sacred Dresser he would find Mother's Sacred and Succulent Purse, where for years he would find first spare change and then cigarettes, which Mother smoked in an absolutely Spartan manner: one after lunch and one after dinner. At that rate, a pack ought to have lasted her ten days, but when Ivo turned around sixteen or seventeen, they started lasting her much less. That glass door was assigned the task of defining a home within the home, because that had been Father's will, in the absolute regime of his dominance over all the other Brandanis who, by virtue of the vigour of his loins and the energy of his activities in the world, then lived there. Outside of there, that is, outside of that flat, that is, outside of the primary dialectical opposition between Father's Space / Space of His Subjects, there lay, in fact, the City of God.

A long strip of extinct volcanoes, apparently domesticated and cooled and extinguished now for hundreds of thousands of years, which runs from what is now known as Li Castelli up northward, right into the heart of Etruscan territory, until it reaches other grim and gigantic water-filled craters many millennia old, to great eruptive masses like the Conical Mountain: this is the territory, made up prevalently of soft, scratchable tufa stone, practically shapeable with the bare hands, carved by water in countless forested gorges, where the urban phenomenon that we now call the City of God manifested itself. Geology tells us of four long explosive cycles that, over a vast period of time stretching back to between 630,000 and 360,000 years ago, covered an expanse of 110 square miles with hails of dust, lapilli and cinders, lava flows of incandescent basalt. The Central Volcano, as this territory is now known, collapsed, revived and collapsed once more, while its secondary craters filled with water, creating deep-set lakes, which should be treated with great caution even today, shadowy and dreary, full of leaden water, also very deep. In short, a land dominated by the eroded and fossilized remains of immense geological monsters, covered by huge tufaceous plates, upon which even the most insignificant little river had all the time necessary to carve itself a canyon, and there you will still find lurking the primeval maquis. It was the forests, with large durmast oaks, holm oaks, cork trees, chestnuts and beech trees that, along with the tufa stone, laid the first savage foundations for the birth of, first of all, a landscape, followed by inhabitable caves, cities and villages perched high atop plateaus, immense necropolises carved into the yellow cliffs of soft rock. Starting from those effusive plates, the water had constructed, or, rather, deconstructed, a landscape that was, so to speak, inhabitable, defensible, fortifiable: all that was needed was to follow the form, already practically architectural, of the grand natural edifices in tufa stone, excavate their walls, build upon their summits. The classical dream of all this later produced a populace of lesser deities and nymphs, places inhabited by oracles, the remains of mysterious cities and temples, incomprehensible artefacts and ruins, all composing the first notion of the picturesque, as the fantastical coexistence of the natural given element with the human fragment, which was later, but only a very long time later, put into a complete and exportable form by French artists such as Claude Lorrain, Nicolas Poussin, Gaspar Dughet and all the others.

The roots of the classical here had little to do with the sunny soul that sprang from the dry and overheated blue of the Aegean, but were instead influenced by the dank radiations from the volcanic tufa stones, from the primeval blackness of the holm oak forests, thus building that ravenous, scowling, utilitarian character, the first foundation of the subsequent empire, which always remained something fundamentally loutish, right up to the most recent and most loutish Fascist revival. Before these, and before the preceding stock (which came from who knows where), and even before those, and earlier and earlier still, working backwards to the roots of Deep Time, before *Homo sapiens* came (it is said, to exterminate them), these lands were inhabited by Neanderthals, who 140,000 years ago inhabited this territory, hunkering down to eat snails along the twisting course of the Little River. And it was well before this riverine stream became a lurid sewer, long before these lands were covered with cities and hovels, before even its name was lost to memory among the apartment buildings large and small of the twentieth century: Saccopastore was a bend in the Little River with the shape of a haversack, or *sacca*, where sheep once grazed and that is why it was given this name. Here in the fourth decade of the twentieth century were still gravel pits where men delved rudely into land that was anything but recent. These were Pleistocenic deposits dating back 150,000 years, and indeed in 1929 an archaic section of female skull emerged that was thought to be 120,000 years old. Then, in 1935, two paleoanthropologists uncovered Saccopastore Two, an incomplete male skull: these were Neanderthals, but of a more archaic type than the classical Neanderthal. In other words, twelve hundred centuries ago, in the City of God, what had settled here was not the human species but something different. This was the territory of *Homo neanderthalensis*, a species that went extinct more or less forty thousand years ago, probably wiped out by *Homo sapiens*, namely by our forefathers, and therefore by us.

The water from some of those rivulets, which were later favourite subjects of seventeenth-century landscape painters—*pittura delli paesi*—now reduced to little more than collection basins for sewage water, their surfaces dotted with countless shreds of plastic tangled in the branches of the underbrush crowding the banks—by the whims of the configuration of the landscape, found itself hurtling off of cliff edges with thunderous roars, forming waterfalls and cascades that became legendary and remained so until the years in which Ivo, thanks to Father, first became aware of them, even though the spray that they pushed out into the air had already become an unbreathable E. coli–bacterial substance and the yellowish foam at the bottom of the falls was strongly indicative of the faecal nature of those fluids. There were few Christian deities with the time and interest to take root in these woods, no saints, Madonnas, sacred mountains, the only sanctuaries were primitive and few in number. It was as if the entire realm

456

of Christian sacrality were sucked away by the gravitational force of the City, there to be sedimented and concentrated in a density never seen before, so that the many locales of the larger territory could be left as deserted appanages of little goatish monsters, woollen and in constant states of feral arousal, on the hunt for modest, naked, non-existent and ready and willing sylvan females, to be tracked down with constancy and determination.

Due to a convergence of factors and events, given the concomitance of various interests or perhaps just divine whim—but perhaps merely by a case of fortuitous contradiction—at the centre of the residue of this paradisiacal pagan inferno, over time, the City of God came into being. It is said that in the very beginning it was the site of the bridge that marked its fate, that single mythical wooden bridge that joined the two banks of a river that was otherwise uncrossable, especially in the winter. This was the site of a discontinuity eliminated, of an obstacle boldly overcome in rash defiance of the sacrality of the water, hence the place in which a first technician, the *Pontifex*, maker of bridges, carried out the first profanation of the River, because he was able to see the two banks not as two separate things but as the two hems of the wound inflicted by that watercourse upon the continuity of the world. Which means that the City of God came into being with the technical profanity of the Bridge, by means of which the Northern territory became one with the Southern territory, to the benefit of travellers and trade, but also of armies. That is why the city was born and thrived on the river's left bank, the southernmost bank, because that was the side opposite the direction from which the enemy always arrived, before whose advance it was necessary to cut the Bridge. But also because there was more room to the south, and the hills were healthier, more inhabitable and defensible than those on the other side. Let us consider the rest of the story all too familiar.

Every place in its way forms the mind of the autochthonous inhabitant and marks it for all time: caught between the genetic marking on the one hand, pressed by the spatiotemporal, physical, economic, religious and cultural characteristics of our world-place

457

of origin, formatted by the original social placement and parental education, crushed by figures of mothers and fathers who often prove to be tireless in turning the handle of the family-qua-meat-grinder, in what manner and in what sense can we call ourselves *individuals*? The same as it is for us all it was also for Ivo Brandani: What resided in him that could be described as an autonomous production all his own? Of what could it be said that it formed an original part of his substance of animal matter, possessed of thought & emotion? What was there that could be considered unmarked, in direct or indirect manner, by the hand of others or public institutions or the chemical and physical state of the location? How to overlook the radioactivity of the tufa stones and basalts and cinders in the midst of which he had been born and lived, how to fail to acknowledge the force of that torpid city which, from his very first instant of life, held a rough paw pressed against his heart? How deny that the quarter where he was born and lived for so many years, after the postwar exile, might have left indelible signs on the interior of his cranium, first as a child, and later as a man? And what to say of all the rest? Of the puff of compressed air from the trolleybus that pulled up to the bus stop downstairs from his home, the mysterious sound emitted by the Red Ring Route, the more antique and screechy sound of the Black Ring Route, which was a transit line served by cars that were called *a stanga*, with a single trolley pole, hinged at the centre instead of broken up into two separate cars? What to say of the holm oaks with their foliage trimmed into a cube, of the pines, the river gravel scattered over the walkways in all the city's gardens and parks? How to neglect to speak of all the other things that had marked him, like the travertine carved into the shape of a crocodile in the fountain on the Central Piazza in his quarter, or the aroma of bread that wafted up from the courtyard in the early morning? Nor can we leave unspoken the colourful luminescences that the closed shutters projected onto the ceiling of his first bedroom on Sunday mornings, when the great church with its two redbrick bell towers pealed out clanging loudly, transforming those instants into something mystical and welcoming, made and constructed for him alone. And that promise of a future? Wasn't it for him? For *him alone*?

The exceedingly ancient city where he had chanced to be born and live, had little by little injected him with its distinctive drawling accent, of which he had never managed to free himself. A manner of speech that made him recognizable in much the same way that all those who, like him, had been parasitized by it, appeared equally and obnoxiously recognizable to him. In contrast with the relationship you might have with a city where you go to live as an adult, of which you might become an inhabitant, to which you can at the very most *feel* that you belong, it is the city where we are born, or where we have lived ever since we were small, that inhabits us, it is that city which uses us as a host-organism through which to reproduce, from individual to individual, one generation after another, for hundreds and hundreds of years. The array of acts, objects and words that have stratified in a single place, transmitted via language from mind to mind and from generation to generation, are more than just a local setting and dialect, it is thought, a way of existing and behaving, a conception of the world; and, however much you might struggle to keep it under control, it comes unexpectedly to the fore every time that your words leave your consciousness behind, abandoning the way you choose to be and appear, which is to say in those moments of anger, fear, joy, sorrow, etc. In that sense, the pressure of the City of God on Ivo Brandani's mind and body made itself felt immediately, nor did he ever have, small boy that he was, the slightest intention of putting up any opposition to it. Indeed, given the natural collective spirit to which he was subject as an ordinary human being, from the very first day of his family's return to the city, all he wanted was to adhere all in all to that impasto of breaths and bodies and objects from which for centuries the soul of the City had emanated.

So many have tried to say something that might help to understand the City of God, something that might define once and for all its peculiar and distinctive character. A great many have tried to capture its nature and meaning and set them down in words, but cities have no meaning, they are merely phenomena of human aggregation, confused masses of construction over time, irrational results of rational individual acts, where dominant powers rotate through, each attempting to leave its mark stamped unmistakably into the physical structure of the urban fabric, much as we do with calves. So much has been written about this city but nothing could render the idea of the place more effectively than its very name, 'City of God', which contains a certain amount of emphasis but never as much as the city itself contains in reality.

By night, as you approach the city along any of the ancient roads that run away from it like the spokes of a wheel, even when you're still many miles away, you can glimpse a reddish glow in the sky, diaphanous as some unknown threat that ventured slowly closer behind the dark needles of the pine trees. Ivo knew about that nocturnal luminescence that stagnated over the city's homes, the sirocco clouds that were tinged with it, because he'd watched it so many times from the back seat of Father's Car, during those starkly dramatic returns from Sunday outings, when, halted in long traffic jams of post-holiday re-entries on the state highways, his parents quarrelled ferociously, hissing unheard-of things at each other, brimming over with a hatred that only emerged on Sunday nights in the car, and the only escape was to be found in sleep.

City of God: How could any god of the standard variety, that is, endowed with normal human attributes, plus additional ultra-powers, love this city? It must therefore be some perverse entity, perhaps precisely that Unmoved Mover (or Unmoved Motor), that Primary Cause, which would later fill Ivo's mind during the summer of 1962. A black diesel engine, covered with grease and viciousness, but still, all the same, the Primary Cause. When that Causal Entity first chose to settle in the city, it had done so slowly, with a lengthy sequence of surgical acts, slowly explanting its ancient pagan vital organs, subjugating it to an insidious power that installs itself in your consciousness, demands its consent, and seizing possession of your mind from the earliest age, the same way a bodysnatcher would do. The city of the Great Temple and its priests was still home to a man who claimed the right to the ancient title of *Pontifex Maximus*, that is, Supreme Builder of

Bridges, a title bound up with the sacred maintenance of the legendary Bridge Primeval, of which we have spoken and which had already vanished far more than two millennia ago, but whose technical memory had been evidently incorporated into the dominant cult. The chief of the theocracy that had been ruling those territories for centuries had taken on that very title, indifferent to its roots in pagan engineering culture, perhaps doing so in search of legitimacy via roots that did not belong to him, nonetheless profound and ineradicable, sunken deep into the city's kidneys.

Ever since third grade, in the year when the Brandani family made its belated return from wartime evacuation, Ivo had lived in this very particular city and he had always perceived it as a sort of burden, as if, even when he knew no more than a tiny part of it, all those streets and piazzas, trolley-cars and trolley-buses, automobiles, coaches, trucks and taxis, all those apartment buildings and monuments were smearing themselves onto him every day, telling him: 'Careful now, this may be beauty but it isn't welcoming, it's not goodness, not brotherhood, not protection, not safety—this is only beauty, it will not take care of you, it will not show you any respect.' But at the time Ivo couldn't understand and he didn't understand for a great many years still to come, and maybe he never did understand.

On one of the first Sundays, Father had taken him to see a white monumental hulk, rigorously symmetrical, tall as a mountain, and they had climbed all the way up to the uppermost terrace, and Father was explaining everything and saying the names of the various domes and cupolas, the hills, the buildings, and he pointed out to him that great rock of the Great Temple and that population of enormous corroded statues. Ivo didn't really much like the building from which they were admiring the city, apart from the enormous fascinating bronze mass of the Equestrian Monument, the horse's great green belly, its enormous balls, the messy water stains on the relief of the veins beneath the skin. Taken as a whole, that enormous building reminded him of his school and all the things they taught at school, attention/at ease, standing/seated, absolute silence, the incomprehensible words, learnt by heart, of the National Anthem, jammed willy-nilly into an absurd piece of music that had always struck him as so oddly unserious, a sticky little military march: *Siam pronti alla morte! Sì!* (*Let us be ready to die! Yes!*)

To live in the City of God and not to love it were part and parcel to Ivo, who liked only the geometry and clarity of his quarter to the north of the Ancient City Centre, with its broad, tree-lined streets, the apartment buildings more or less all the same height, an orderly specification shared by that whole zone, from which often rose turrets, mysterious covered roof-terraces, loggias lost in space, perhaps drying rooms, washrooms or storerooms. But it is a gross simplification to say that Ivo didn't love it. He was captivated by it and, at the same time, he was mistrustful, perhaps because it was wrapped up with Father. At first it was a confused sensation, but over time the aversion became more specific and was reinforced and later, as an adult, it was transformed into open hostility—but if you had asked him why, he wouldn't have known how to answer. We were saying that Ivo lived all the rest of his post-war childhood, and then his youth, in a particular part of the city in comparison with which every other place or quarter, including the immense Ancient City Centre, seemed like a disorderly and confused swill, bound within the perimeter of ancestral city walls, devoid of that principle of geometry, order and perspective in which the quarter where he'd grown up was steeped, and therefore ambiguous, hostile and subtly repellent. Growing up in the order of the *forma urbis* would have serious consequences in terms of his *forma mentis*, on the way in which he would perceive the rest of the city and the world. What would later prove to be a sort of obsession for geometry, exactitude, the well made, probably originated in those years spent living in the certitude of form, measure and configuration which at first made him believe that the whole world was that way, that it simply had to be.

As a small boy, whenever he left his quarter he was always with Father and from the car windows he saw things that he could not approve: outside of his world of geometric harmony, the city was a thrown-together mishmash of buildings of which he could make neither head nor tail, both in the centre and in the outskirts. He didn't understand why people were always talking about the beauty of the Ancient City Centre, which struck him quite to the contrary as a shapeless mass of little buildings piled one atop another, broken by unexpected wide spots and roundabouts, patches of light on the jumbled, broken cobblestones, in the shade of looming grim churches black with dirt, with twisted, curving cornices. He didn't understand the beauty of the irregularity, of the patches of damp, the flaking plaster, the filth that accumulated on the facades, the leers of the sea monsters rising from the fountains, of those decorations in a reciprocal heaving grip, which from a distance just looked like an indistinguishable froth devoid of straight lines. Ivo Brandani was small back then, and he didn't approve of the insistence on the scrollwork motifs, the invasive presence of twisted seashells, the intrusiveness of the spirals, the faces of lions. And then there were the dolphins, the palms and palmettes everywhere, curled up in the pediments, beneath the cornices. Or else, as in a place-with-obelisk known as Mons Citatorius, he was surprised at the sight of travertines that seemed to have been left unfinished, the carving incomplete, with inexplicable inserts of unhewn rock on a smooth, rational facade: 'Bernini,' Father told him. Wherever there was something that Ivo Brandani couldn't approve in those days, something that he couldn't choke down without being able to say the exact reason, sooner or later someone was bound to say: Bernini. Or, though it happened less frequently, they'd say: Borromini. It seemed that in the Ancient City Centre, inside those eight and a half miles of city walls, there had never been anyone other than those two, it seemed that everyone else had been crushed, dominated, fascinated by them, until they all trooped along together, tracing along with them scrollwork and palms and tangles and seashells and trumpets and curving facades. It seemed to Ivo that, if you took away Bernini/Borromini, there was nothing left to talk about, nothing left to say. 'Baroque,' Father would say.

What astonished him about the outlying areas of the city, the *periferia*, in contrast, was the desuetude, the wreckage, the continual blending of objects, the presence of enormous blocks of affordable housing and tiny houses, the endless tenements and hovels, the empty lots, the railroads, the construction sites, the newly built broad and dusty roads, the endless lines of power poles and intertwining power lines, the ruins, mysterious & unexpected & black. Everywhere was slovenliness, slipshoddery, ramshackleness, garbage, confusion. It seemed to him that nothing had a comparable role to that of the Great Central Piazza of his own quarter, that dispenser of order, form, and regularity, to which all the other surrounding spaces appeared to be logically configured and subjugated.

But what caused him the greatest annoyance, to the point of inducing a full-blown state of idiosyncrasy in him in later years, were the countless ruins that the City of God prided itself on and gave pride of place. At first he was enthusiastic about them, when Father took him to see the Imperial Forum, the Great Amphitheatre, the Ancient Markets, and later to the immense Emperor's Villa, in the Port City. It was the allure emanating from the traces of vanished worlds, of places that many long years ago had been inhabited by people he struggled to imagine as similar to us.

'Were they like us?'

'Certainly, exactly like us . . . Maybe a little shorter . . .' Father replied.

All this made quite an impression on him, but the thing that had struck him hardest, to such an extent that he would remember it for ever, coming back to it and questioning the accuracy of the report, had been the traces, so the guidebook had said, left by a pile of coins on the floor of the Forum when they melted during the course of a fire. The notion of a Great Fire was intertwining in him with the idea of Antiquity, of the Ancient City Centre. He imagined cyclical infernos of flames, the arsonist emperor and all the rest of it, but it was especially the Wall of the Suburra that struck him, when Father read to him from the guidebook that in ancient times it had served to separate the Forum from the 'poor quarters built out of wood, thus keeping them safe from the frequent fires'. There was the disappointment of the Amphitheatre, when he realized that the arena floor was broken. He expected to see the space where the wild animals had once devoured the faithful, but instead the arena was gone, all you could see was a maze, a shattered ruin of walls.

'Is it broken?'

'It collapsed,' said Father, 'those are the cellar rooms where they kept the wild animals, the gladiators . . .'

'Why don't they fix it?'

'What do you mean?'

'I mean, why don't they put it back like it was . . . Why don't they repair it?'

'What are you talking about? WHAT ON EARTH ARE YOU SAYING? It would be a fake.'

Father had raised his voice, making him jump.

'. . . h-how, "a fake"?'

'I mean that you'd have to build something new that would be mixed in with the ancient structures . . . This is considered a sort of lie, you understand? You ought to think before you speak!'

That marked the beginning of his attitude towards the antiquities that pervade the city in all directions. It took some time for that distaste to seep into his mind. At first it was a faint discomfort, when for instance he happened to peer down into the central excavation of the square named Argentina, filled with incomprehensible ruins and rubble, rows of broken columns, weeds, cats and garbage. The few times that he took the train, the city welcomed him back with the black walls of the so-called Larger Gate, and then the ruins of the aqueducts and of a nymphaeum dedicated to the goddess Minerva. Leaving the city by car was a continuation of the same junk, an endless series of enigmatic objects, empty, damaged, useless, which stretched out into the distance in the vast rough meadows that surrounded the inhabited city, ruins encrusted with hovels and shacks or covered with vegetation, chaos within the chaos of the outskirts, where everything seemed piled up in wholesale heaps, the sudden gaps, the expanses of dirt, the cranes of the construction sites. Later, he started to wonder: 'But why do we have to keep them at all costs, preserve them like cadavers lowered into unlidded tombs, if they're already in such disgraceful shape and can't do us the slightest bit of good any more? Why do we have to cling to these filthy craters crawling with cats, weeds and garbage just because they contain a few stinking old walls built by the ancients?'

'You see,' Father was saying, expert builder that he was, 'this is *opus reticulatum* and this is *opus incertum* . . .'

Who the fuck cares, is what he would have liked to say, but saying it in front of Him would have been a fatal mistake.

'*Our* forefathers were great builders,' Father said proudly, 'and that's why their buildings are still standing today.'

'To me they're *too* broken, Papà,' he once ventured to say. He immediately rued his words, but nothing happened, because that was one of those mysterious and all-too-rare moments when Father proved not to be dangerous: boring, certainly, because invariably engaged in the manner of someone with something to teach but, for some unknown reason, not dangerous. All the same, he had better not relax, because Father could always go off without warning, unpredictably. For Ivo it was the usual reticence, the same caution as ever. He hated going out into the city, he wasn't interested in Father's lessons, much less in *opus reticulatum* & *opus incertum*, the two kinds of brickwork, he didn't like having to choke back what he really thought, always taking care what he said, walking on eggshells. Father's chief occupation was listening to himself, ready to fly off the handle at the slightest sign of contradiction, objection, one question too many, and yet he *had to ask* a few questions, otherwise he'd be irritated for the opposite reason: 'Aren't you listening to me? Aren't you going to say anything? Don't you give a damn?' That was Father, there was no changing him, no taking him back to the store where they got him. That was who he'd been assigned and that's who he'd have to keep. There was no reasoning with him, he was an airtight, armour-plated, impenetrable creature. All the same he was Father, he feared him but deep down he respected him and the moment was still far in the future when he'd dare to formulate thoughts for the first time such as: 'That asshole always spouts the same bullshit.' When that finally did come to pass, he was almost thunderstruck that he'd dared to think it, it was a profanation of the Sacred Indisputable Figure, but by then the dam had collapsed, the crack had widened: 'Bastard, asshole, imbecile, go fuck yourself. Drop dead, you piece of shit . . .' Ivo couldn't have known that this syndrome of rejection of much of the City of God would mark him for the rest of his life. When it would befall him that he had to live far away from the quarter where he grew up, he would suffer from it like an expulsion from an Eden of certainties. The Family Home, which seemed like an invulnerable fortress, had long since been sold, the family had been scattered, his parents were dead and lost in a distant cemetery of jumbled edifices, where the same senseless disorder reigned as in the outer city. It was the suffering of living in the privation of geometric order, in a diffuse ambience of inexactitude, in a disorder that everyone seemed used to and no one appeared to notice. Once the expulsion became definitive, he would return to his old quarter, to walking once again down those streets, those broad pavements, and every time it was a necessary return to clarity lost, in an attempt to rediscover the pleasure of a harmony between what he felt he was and what he saw. 'I envy those who were lucky enough to stay here to live,' he would tell himself.

All the same, in defiance of Ivo Brandani, outside of that schematic quarter arrayed in the shape of a star, there extended, chaotic, ignoble and beautiful, the City of God. Beneath it, concealed in the earth and protruding upwards, here and there, the City of Antiquity was intently eroding out from under the city above it, consuming its foundations, weakening its inhabitants with its radiations, forging their collective mind towards an exhausted and disenchanted approach, beneath a jaded cynical semblance. City of God was not just any ordinary human aggregate: a normal city believes in something, in a future, in the possibility of improving, City of God on the other hand believed in nothing. It was not the disenchanted and sceptical mindset of people who had seen it all and been through the mill, of people who've grown shrewd from an excess of History. It wasn't that, it was rather a matter of resignation, an inborn inability to conceive of

467

anything new, perhaps the subjugation of the social city to the excessive weight of the physical city, which generated in the majority of the people contempt and pity towards those who *still* believed in the possibility of a change for the better. The city was convinced it could not renew and modify itself towards greater beauty and rationality, it was convinced it could only grow upon itself, and nothing more. Indeed, the city wasn't convinced of anything, it took no interest in its own future, and so every modification was for the worse, for the uglier, for the shoddier, with the radiant exception of rare, glowing and usually misunderstood fragments of form, in fact, of utopia, that appeared here and there, by virtue of mysterious gaps, rents and tears in the mind of the city, only to seal up again promptly. The intelligence of the City of God had been for some time now wholly inert, overwhelmed by its own bitterness, but especially by its own willingness and complicity with the proponents of the worse, of the quick & dirty, who wallowed in the crumbs dropped by the compromise between, if not the actual coincidence of the powerful and the government. There is not a single error that doesn't reflect the responsibility of those who were unable to prevent it and the City of God was a master in this show, with its incredible number of reprises, the popularity that it enjoyed.

The city was enslaved not only by the Ancient, but also by God, as, for that matter, its very name suggested. It crawled at the feet of its own past and at the feet of the *Pontifex Maximus*. In order to provide a fitting abode for God, the decision was made to build a thing of gigantic size, equipped with two immense pincers arranged to simulate an embrace. It took more than a century and the work of a host of artists who were considered supreme in their fields to create the entire complex of the First Temple, in accordance with a plan for the exhibition of power that throttled the capacity for self-expression that the artists involved might be expected to manifest. With some exceptions, certainly, rare though they were. And when the poetry, in spite of everything, did appear, it did so in power and force, without any welcoming willingness to let itself be understood. Instead it remained there, on high, closed in its apocalyptic, admonitory beauty. All the same, with reference to this triumphal display of dominance, Ivo Brandani was told, and not by Father alone, that this was *beauty*, that this was the city's *glory*, and that he should be *proud* of it, that he should be contented. But he, perhaps because he was a young inhabitant of a quarter filled with order and light, clearly perceived the hostility and arrogance of those artefacts of God.

Ivo lived his childhood and youth at a crucial moment, when the city was tirelessly spewing up new urban material like a volcano, scattering it over the surrounding territory, over a landscape that had been devoid for many centuries now of all natural innocence, and yet over time had returned to a fascinating abandonment rife with arcane fragments, towers and nameless edifices, fragments of ancient barbarian sieges, traces of escapes, medieval conflicts, fires, murders left unpunished, grottoes, catacombs, hiding places, graves. And so the City of God overflowed the outer hills and invaded these ancient wastelands with immense lava-like flows of apartment buildings large and small, villas, all served by narrow roads, full of twisting curves, along earthworks with high retaining walls covered with scraps of tufa stone, holding up entire sections of the hillside. Instead of sections of the new city, it was something else, it was the mindset of the postwar *nouveau riche* translated into an infinite sequence of contrived buildings, with adorable little balconies, twee railings, cunning roofs, tiny mansard flats, garage ramps, small front doors, lobbies with decorative mosaics or blow-ups of archaeological views, lift and wooden handrails along the staircases, atop elaborately designed railings. It was the new soul of the city in search of a residence more in keeping with the latest social position attained. Even Father, with his little contracting business, was involved in that reckless expansion without rules, even He, in the end, fell prey to the age-old drive to attain some level of decorum in keeping with the tidy little sum he'd socked away. Father built for private citizens and cooperatives that sometimes had ridiculous names, such as *Swallows in Search of a Roof*, or more concrete and depressing, *Maimed in Service to the Country*, who all hoped to obtain their own little four- or five-storey apartment building, with two or three flats on each floor, central heating, lift, parking area or individual garages, shared terrace, cellar storage, boiler room, brickfront facade, travertine trim, oak doors, stairways with wooden handrail and brass door handles, porcelain bathroom tiles at the customer's choice. What is the right adjective to describe a city built scrupulously to deny and eliminate root and branch the very idea of the city? What to say of the culture and the mind of someone who willed, built and allowed square miles at a time of this junk, except that he was opaque to all civil ideas and perceptions of the necessity of order and design, of public space fit to be lived in and shared by one and all, with broad, tree-lined streets and squares, pavements and parking sufficient for the Fiats that were busily invading every square foot of asphalt? Who can say whether anyone can explain how it came to pass that a generation of human beings, in a city that was once a symbol and model for the entire planet, was able to built vast new neighbourhoods in sharp denial of any and all notions of urban space?

When Father dragged him with him to visit his construction sites, Ivo remained surprised every time by the speed with which those agglomerations of buildings grew, how they seemed to tumble down from the hillsides and low mountains, beyond the edges of which the city was overflowing in all directions. Muddy narrow streets, marked by the deep ruts of the trucks and the bulldozers that were continuously coming and going, by the wheels of the little Guzzi 500 three-wheeled trucks, everywhere the noise of the steam shovels, the cement mixers, the trumpeting of the pile-drivers, and then there were the scaffoldings which back then were still made all of wood, stacks of planks and unnailed lumber, piles of sand to be hand-sieved one shovelful after another, grinders and mullers busy mixing mortar and pozzolana, a continuous coming and going of workers and wheelbarrows up and down the stairs of the attics, bricks, stones, perforated bricks, hollow flat tiles and blocks, bundles of rebar in various gauges, rusting while awaiting the pouring of the cement, carpenters and metal benders at work, masons carefully following the angle of their plumb lines, the horizontal reference bars, their levels, slowly spreading the mortar on the wet bricks that the labourers below handed up to them, floor layers who could be heard singing and whistling from a distance in the echoing of empty rooms, damp with plaster, a continuous refinishing and breaking up once again, the swooping passages of the float trowel, until the laying on of the coats of plaster with the tool that Ivo loved best, the *americana*, even though the best name certainly belonged to the *maleppeggio*—literally, 'bad and worse'—a distinctive stonemason's hatchet, used to shape the tufa stone fragments for making rough-hewn walls for cellars, to be mortared over with cement. All this struck him as wonderful, the violence and determination of the act of construction left him open-mouthed every time. It was an inferno of labour unlikely anything that had ever been seen, not even at the foot of the Tower of Babel, not even in the construction sites of the Pyramids of Giza, of the Sphinx. And from a distance, a forest of cranes and block and tackle and hoists, with the Peninsular flags fluttering in the sirocco wind, above the rustics who had succeeded in record time in completing the last roof.

The City of God grew and built. Everyone was building, selling, and getting rich, buying a house on the coastline, or further north and further south, but always on the beach, they'd send their children to Catholic schools run by priests, they applied to become members of one of the sports clubs on the River. To be ushered in you had to present at least two existing members who would 'vouch' for you, they only rejected those who lacked the power and the money, and of course anyone who was a certifiable Jew, Socialist or Communist. But if the Kike and the Communist were sufficiently rich and powerful, some of the less prestigious clubs might be willing to turn a blind eye, and the new members would certainly have pretended not to hear the racist, sexist, Fascistic wisecracks that were the order of the day in the locker rooms. It's a shitty City, there's no doubt about it. The indolence of the wives stretched out at poolside, chattering idly, attractive enigmatic matrons with their drawling but opulent, respectable accents, their gazes turned attentively to monitor children who dived in and dived in, over and over again, constantly pestering—'We finally voted in the pool for the kiddies'—but also intensely and reciprocally observant of their surroundings, all of them ready to wield the switchblade at the drop of a straw hat. All of them, male and female, young and adult and elderly, checking and evaluating and eyeing one another, more or less openly, in search of the signals that might tell of the private matters being gossiped about, to pry and poke, to figure out who was getting richer and who wasn't. It was necessary to form an idea of who might be right for your daughter or son, who might be suitable to take as a lover this winter. Then there was the laughing and joking of the ladies among themselves, during the afternoon game of canasta, in the same rooms where later that night people would be playing hands of poker each worth millions of lire—thousands of dollars.

What Father aspired to, this master builder who wanted to be called an engineer, was to join these people. Not only, Ivo thought later, because he truly cared about it (a little bit he did care), but because he was tacitly obligated to do so by his need to establish relations with the moneymongers who were his peers and to become part of those wefts and warps that extended horizontally in all directions at his level, middle to low, a fabric of power and money, but then he was also being egged on by Mother, who wanted to be able to hold her head up in the face of her boasting sisters, so conceited about their husbands' economic and social conquests. These people truly were pieces of shit, the people who still lived in the parts of town built in the aftermath of the Risorgimento and the early decades of the twentieth century, who were now reaching out in camaraderie and friendship to the nouveau riche who had settled to the northeast of the city, people who had survived all the tempests and events of the Fascistic regime and war—though some of them hadn't made it out alive— citizens of a city that had been Fascist, 'but not all that much,' people would say, and was now Christian Democrat, 'but not all that much,' they'd add, that is, not enough to be really exposed, to emerge into the open and commit oneself, putting at risk business interests, concrete alliances, useful connections. Not so much as to attract the mistrust of one's brothers in social class, that is, a social group nestled like a flatworm in the principal nerve endings of the *urbs* and the *civitas*, the Eternal City, people who by their nature recoiled from all political passion, preferring to live as filter feeders, drawing in nourishment with every breath, capturing money along with every sort of impurity to be found in the environment. And so they were all apparently affiliated with the Italian Liberal and Republican Parties, right-leaning, though a few—dangerously tilting leftward—ventured so far as to root for the moderate Social Democrats. Then there were lots of *missini*, that is, Fascists affiliated with the MSI—the ambiguously named Italian Social Movement, and most of all, there were those who were secretly Christian Democrats, because it was embarrassing to be officially Christian Democratic, it simply wasn't done, even though everyone had to deal with them, with those people. Dark 'Humbertine' flats, dating from the reign of that king, assassinated in 1900, filled with oversized canvases and etchings, curtains and wall hangings and carpets, coffee tables and side tables covered with silver gewgaws, candy bowls, dark hardwood furniture with gryphon legs, neo-medieval furnishings out of the *The Jesters' Supper*, bookshelves crowded with leather-bound volumes with gilt lettering, the scent of ancient lives and dust. In these residences, Ivo would occasionally chance to visit, but these were only residues of long-past seasons, those who had come into more money had since moved to the north and the northeast of the Ancient City Centre.

But the recipe of the City of God consisted of other ingredients as well. While the central areas were expanding to cover and bypass the hills, in the meantime, far away, other human settlements had sprung up. Between the so-called *palazzinaro* city (to use the Roman terminology for speculative building) of the '50s and the '60s (or for that matter of the '70s, the '80s, the '90s, and every decade since, right up to the present day: that particular culture never changed, those people always remained faithful to their essence, just richer, more ignorant, more powerful) and these new inhabited spaces there frequently extended large gaps, vacuums, empty spaces that were eventually occupied by long multi-storey buildings and the tower blocks of the new subdivisions of public housing, which were a reflection of the official culture of the urban planners, in diametric opposition to the shantytowns on the one hand (for the very poorest and the more generally unfortunate) and high-rise blocks of flats on the other (for the non-poor and the wealthy). Over the course of the years, a populace of hundreds of thousands of human beings had washed up at the city gates from any number of different places. These were ancient, archaic, Apennine, peasant peoples, who preserved deep within a complete diversity from the city where they were now converging, burdensome and diverse cultural baggage that was soon destined to vanish, already with the generation of their children, things that would be lost, now and for ever. This population had, immediately & automatically, been downgraded to the suburban status of *borgatari*, residents of the peripheral settlements, known as borgatas, with their clusters of shacks clustering on the tablelands, or else nestled in the muddy bottom of some small tufaceous valley, clinging to the aqueducts, in the ancient, distant meadows, left untrammelled by the city and the countryside. And yet this too was city, nascent, larval city—nonetheless city. These were very extensive embryos of the subsequent formation of *strongholds*, in an archipelago of primordial & raggedy townships, which sprang up in accordance with archaic modalities of spontaneous aggregation, on highlands, in ravines and nooks of the Agro, the Ager Romanus, the sprawling rural region surrounding Rome, or else clinging to relics of Antiquity, such as of course aqueducts, the remains of villas, oversized tombs. The borgatas created cities in two ways: either by consolidating on their own, that is, resisting attempts at abrogation, or by prompting the intervention of the public powers to build new houses for the 'less well to do', who in their hovels were laying siege to the bourgeois and petty-bourgeois core of the city. Thus were born the new agglomerations, vast and planned from the top down, which also served as the bridgeheads for the subsequent joining of the outer areas with the central city.

It was not until much later that other masses of immigrants appeared, though this time not Peninsular, to besiege the city in a different manner, this time with a whiff of ancestral desperation, people who in time built their nests beneath bridges and the viaducts of the great beltways and ring roads, on the gravel banks of the two rivers, in tufaceous caverns and quarries, in incredibly rickety thrown-together temporary shelters, beneath jutting sections of buildings and overarching cornices, in niches raised only inches off the ground, in catacombs and archaeological grottoes, inside abandoned factories, for years and years constituting post-atomic communities, living off the by-products of a city that had in the meantime become rich, becoming servants and slaves and prostitutes, engaging in illicit trades. Some of them would take to panhandling, others would rummage through dumpsters and trashcans in search of scrap copper, others still would take to robbery, pimping, or simply settle for alcohol-comforted starvation, floating off on a last hopeless tide of forgetfulness. But most of them would get up every day and go off to work, furtively, unofficially, underpaid, in a system that redounded to the benefit of all sorts of other economic activities, first and foremost among them the evergreen sector of construction.

And so, for many years to follow, the City of God would serve as the setting for all and every human form of subsistence: from the hunter-gatherers picking through the trash, the troglodytes in the caverns, the nomads, the farmers, while central and unvaried the original herding of sheep continued on for decades still to come, even in centrally located green spaces, where it was still possible to see domesticated livestock grazing for what seemed to go on for ever. Still in the 2010s, when Ivo Brandani had thought as a child that the Future would have arrived in full, the city would continue to be inhabited by sheep and horses and pigs, cattle rabbits chickens, and in secret enclaves of nature foxes, wild boar and many other untamed species would long continue to run free and roughshod, unglimpsed. The Future of science fiction, which Ivo had dreamt about as a boy, would never ultimately arrive. What did instead arrive would have been impossible to imagine even for the professional imaginers who worked for *Urania*, who would *all* have committed the error of failing to predict just how much of the Past the Future would drag along with it, much less the consequences of those computer technologies, even then still relegated to the confines of the most advanced laboratories, inside huge cases full of reels and magnetic tape and punch cards.

About this new outer city, Ivo knew nothing. At the very most he might have caught a fleeting glimpse from the window of Father's car of rows of hovels shouldering up against the ancient aqueducts, or the columns of smoke rising from the hidden hamlets tucked away in the valleys of the Agro, along the various consular highways leading out of the city. All that reached his ears as a little boy were names uttered by other kids his age—strange and plebeian names he'd never heard before—along with hasty descriptions of sinister and mythical places, rife with danger, inhabited by violent people, places you weren't likely to come back from alive if you ventured there alone. This was the nomenclature of the borgata, episodes that surfaced in the feverish conversation of kids on the street, when all and every piece of nonsense becomes eminently plausible. Therefore, by the time he was fourteen, Ivo Brandani *knew* that the *borgata*s were places to stay away from, that they were inhabited by nasty folk, whores, pimps, thieves: that's what he'd heard from his schoolmates, even though he didn't know who whores and pimps really were or what they did. Every generation of the City of God had had its own mythical urban circle of hell where it was better not to set foot. Mother too had had *her* places of ill repute and they were all in the heart of the Ancient City Centre. She hadn't been to any of them in years, she still mentioned their names with dread in her voice, but by now all the bad guys had been gone for decades, their places taken by sharply dressed children of the middle class, intellectuals and faggots, while the old city resolutely continued in its metamorphosis into a theme park for tourists.

In other words, between that immense, rambling city of hovels and shacks in violation of every zoning regulation and the lava flow of middle-class apartment buildings vomited forth from the city centre, there was springing up a strip of working-class quarters built by the agencies for social welfare construction, all of them,

476

with only rare exceptions, made up of hulking six- or seven-storey bunkers, or ten-storey tower blocks, where Ivo would never have been willing to live, because they struck him as housing for the poor, which is exactly what they were. And then the sprawling four-lane high speed roads cutting through the endless succession of oversized built objects bristling with TV antennas, studded with windows and loggias, well spaced one from the other to leave room for neglected muddy wastelands, abandoned fields where kids played football, small roadside dumps where atop hillocks of trash the eternal Discarded Toilet enjoyed pride of place, whether intact or shattered, something you'll still see wherever you go, and which could rightly claim its place as an emblem on the national flag, much like the Cedar for the flag of Lebanon, or the maple leaf on the Canadian flag. Ivo had learnt to recognize it, the Discarded Toilet: you would find one anywhere there was an apparently abandoned expanse of land, even in his own quarter, in hidden corners where you might stumble across one while out riding bikes, or down along the banks of the River: the usual kibble of refuse from minor demolition projects, heaps of rubble consisting of fragments of plaster, shattered terracotta roof tiles, broken terracotta cinder blocks, old refrigerators, turds. The Discarded Toilet was a marker of a place's neglect and it signalled the mindset of the inhabitants of the City of God (and of the whole Country). Then one day, as he was heading past that same place, he found a corrugated metal enclosure that had just been thrown up, a stockade gate with a padlock, and inside he could glimpse machinery, pile drivers, bulldozers: it was another new construction site and it meant that a year and a half from then there would be another oversized apartment building, freshly mortared, not yet dry, with paint still damp. The same thing was going on where he lived too, certainly: every void was bound to be filled. The smell of wet mortar, fresh plaster, that is, newly finished buildings hovered for years, for decades, over the City of God. It would happen that he took the Red Ring Route bus in the afternoon and find it jam-packed with construction workers on their way home—where were they going? where were they coming from?—their faces like

477

leather, still spattered with plaster and washable paint, slaked lime, and everywhere the strong smell of bricklayers and hard work, the essence of a tired, mortar-speckled man, almost a scent, if compared with the fetid whiff of office clerk which so regularly disgusted him when he boarded public transportation. Masses of men at work moved every day from and to the city, men who were paid to build it, an epic migration of which Ivo, from his empty and silent realm of order, would have had no notion if Father hadn't told him, as he took him from one construction site to another, that many of these workers came from outside the city, from the depressed territories to the southeast of the capital, from as far as 60 miles away: if you were a labourer, you were still a construction worker, and if you were a construction worker, then City of God most certainly had a job for you.

The workers on Father's construction sites, men Father spoke ill of, though Ivo couldn't understand why, spoke the dialects that he had heard as a small boy, during the Postwar Exile, before their return to the city. He knew that every day Father's construction workers, with their creased peasant faces, were up by five, caught trains and coaches, travelled as much as 60 miles to be at the construction site by seven, ready with their cement trowels in hand, the mortar hod perched on their shoulders, a wheelbarrow full of bricks before them, trowelling pozzolana mortar, digging trenches in the mud, bending rebar, mixing lime and cement, chiselling trace lines in the partition walls, nailing planks and lumber into scaffoldings, floating plaster, laying floor tiles . . .

Some of these men, the younger ones, clearly came from the outskirts of the city, they weren't as shy as the others, they spoke with a heavy, drawling accent, they cursed, they had a provisional, frightening, cynical, detached attitude, and anytime that he went to the construction site, they paid him not the slightest fucking attention.

'Who are the construction workers?' Ivo wondered in the early days.

Once he asked Father. 'People who never studied and have no resources for their livelihood but their hands,' he answered flatly.

Then he added: 'Communists all of them, people with no interest in working . . .'

'Communists . . .' This was yet another thing for Ivo to figure out: Who were the Communists? He'd asked Mother—always ask Mother first and then, if she didn't know, or wouldn't tell him, then ask Father, but only if *absolutely necessary*—and she had replied: 'Ask your father.' OK. The circle had closed again, it was always on that door that he'd have to go knock, that dangerous, unpredictable door.

His friends knew less than he did. 'The Communists are sons of bitches,' said one of his friends, 'they don't believe in God, Jesus, the Virgin Mary, and in Russia they kill priests. If you try to go to church they'll kill you, if you don't do what they tell you they'll kill you, if you ask questions they'll kill you. The Communists burn churches, they'll take away everything you own, your home, your car, everything you possess, and they give it to those who have nothing or else they just keep it for themselves . . .'

Then there were the Fascists, about which even less seemed to be known. In the illustrated magazines Ivo had encountered several times the terrible and mysterious image of the Dictator hanging by his feet. 'The Fascists are all sons of bitches,' his friends from the street would say, while others said nothing and Ivo assumed that they too knew very little. Then he figured out that if a little boy said nothing when they were saying bad things about the Communists, it meant that his father was a Communist. The same thing must be true when they were talking about the Fascists. But *who are* the Fascists and, even more important, *where* are they? Once, when he was invited over to a friend's house for lunch, he had noticed a photograph of the Dictator hanging in the little dining room and had blurted out, 'That criminal . . .' only to notice, immediately afterwards, that a chill had descended in the room. No one said a word, but that was the first and last time he would set foot in that little boy's home. Since that day he had understood why, any time that someone in the group said, 'Duce-you-son-of-a-bitch-they-did-the-right-thing-when-they-hung-you-up-by-the-heels,' that kid remained silent. From that day on, Ivo could say that he had met a Fascist and he went around telling everyone that the kid's father was 'a Fascist', as if he was, say, a member of the Beagle Boys gang.

Father used to say: 'Communists and Fascists are the same, two sides of the same coin.'

'But the Christian Democrats are worse,' he added one time. Ivo, who felt a desperate need to know what was acceptable and what wasn't, yearned to ask him: 'Which ones do you like?' but he only asked him later, and that time Father replied: 'The Liberals are the ones I like.' And so it was that Ivo Brandani became a Liberal without ever really knowing what that might mean. And from that day on, he was able to tell his friends: 'My father is a Liberal.' No one else's father was a Liberal, being Liberal must be something special.

In the City of God, I'm not saying that you saw a lot of the Dictator, but he was still around, and there were places where he was mentioned quite frequently, especially as 'DUCE', or else as 'DUX'.

THE DUCE FOR US!

THE DUCE FOR US!

THE DUCE FOR US!

What could the meaning be of that exclamation repeated dozens of times in the mosaics of the Fascist Forum, where he went to skate? 'It means nothing,' said Father, 'it's just an exclamation, like "Eja eja alalà", it's meaningless, like a devotional prayer . . .' Ivo particularly liked the Sphere, the big marble Sphere that stood in the middle of what looked very much like a fountain, but was always dry. He also liked the obelisk with DUX written on it, so sharp, so full of sharp angles.

'It's a monolith,' Father said, 'and the tip is 24-carat gold.'

'Really! How much is it worth? What does "monolith" mean?'

'How would I know how much it's worth? It means that it's carved out of a single piece of marble . . .'

There was still admiration and pride in Father's words. You could tell from the Stadium with the Statues too that the Dictator liked things made of white marble, and so did Ivo; all those buttocks made him laugh, those peepees behind the large fig leaves, as if people were going skiing naked or played tennis naked. And then there were only men, all men with their hair combed back, Humbert-style, as people still said back then. Even the 1942 Expo, as Father called it, was all white, the buildings were so precise, with no second-guessing: where they ended, they ended, and there the blue of the sky began. No cornices, no heraldic crests, only cubes, spheres, cylinders immersed in a different light, which Ivo would later understand was reflected off the sea, the sea that was so much closer there.

'But were you a Fascist?'

'Yes,' Father replied. Then, almost automatically, as if to excuse himself—'Is he apologizing to me?'—he had added that in those days you really couldn't do anything else, that everyone had been a Fascist, that they'd grown up with it, with Fascism, that he had also been a Son of the She-Wolf, a Balilla, a Vanguardist, etc., that 'it's easy to say nowadays, but back then things hadn't been easy at all, we liked the Duce, we didn't see the danger . . . Then we were all shipped off to fight in the war . . .'

Now that matters political were finally clear, Ivo finally had an orientation, he knew what to answer.

First: Fascists and Communists were 'two sides of the same coin', negative.

Second: Never as bad as the Fascists and the Communists, but the Christian Democrats were negative too, because they were 'thieves'.

Third: He, Ivo Brandani, was a Liberal. Those who are Liberal want liberty, they want 'the smallest possible government' (those were Father's exact words), and they don't much like priests.

Fourth: It was best to call the Communists 'little comrades', because that way his friends in the street and the parish and the football field, his friends on bicycles, his schoolmates would all think that he was someone who knew what he was talking about. Likewise, he should call the Fascists *camerati* and the Christian Democrats *democristi*.

And so Ivo became a Liberal, and so he grew up convinced that the political aspect of life was already taken care of, that he wouldn't have to worry about it any more, even if being an Italian Liberal didn't help him all that much in getting an idea of the world and the different species of human beings.

Everything that had been built in the city had been made by men like the ones he'd seen working on Father's construction sites, Communists who didn't feel like lifting a finger, with ancient faces, different from his face and different from the faces of the people he knew, bronzed faces covered with a fine network of wrinkles and creases, peasants' faces, large dark hands with thick nails that were black with dirt and chipped, the pads of the fingers sliced and cut, the same hands that he'd seen attached to the wrists of the fishermen of the City by the Sea, as they handled that sort of wooden spindle they used to mend their nets. The city had been built and now it was continuing to be built—no one openly stated it—by inferior, ignorant people, who didn't know how to speak properly, who came from the provinces, from the surrounding towns, from the borgatas, from public housing, people who knew how to do that work, bricklayers, people who worked slowly and with precision, all of them identical, without any wasted motions, never once bending their back unless it was necessary.

Whenever he went to a construction site, Ivo watched them work, captivated. The one who knew he was the son of the engineer would give him a smile, or maybe a wink of the eye, but nothing more. No familiarity with him, except perhaps from the Assistant Gino, who was Father's 'trusted' right-hand man, and of whom Father spoke well but always with a hint of mistrust. Ivo didn't understand why, but every time the Assistant Gino and Father were together, he felt a sort of distaste, an uneasiness. It was as if he detected in Gino a servile, but ambiguous, attitude: he was constantly agreeing but anyone would have been able to tell that it was out of self-interest. Father and Gino: perhaps the two of them hated each other too, or perhaps they just mistrusted each other, but there was clearly something wrong and Ivo picked up on it. Gino gave orders to the workers, he hired and fired, he handed out the pay, he ran the construction sites from the bottom, as a sort of non-commissioned officer.

'Yes, engineer.' 'I'll take care of it, engineer,' Gino would say. 'He's someone I can trust,' Father always said, but even a little kid like him could see that there was no friendship between the two men, only utility. Ivo noticed that Gino too had his trusted men on the construction site, the ones he called and hired on each new job, and he could also see that there were other workers who seemed different, that they were pissed off and apathetic, that Gino treated them harshly, issued peremptory, brusque orders, scolded them.

On the other hand, if there was a city to be built, someone had to do it. It was work. And so in those years a provisional and infamous landscape gradually came into existence, made up of holes being excavated and heaps of fill dirt piled up beside them, building refuse and garbage as far as the eye could see, clumps of stacked lumber, sheds dotting construction sites, roads waiting for buildings, but to a far greater extent, buildings waiting for roads, sewer systems, light poles. A territory of ancient brown dirt, dug up, profaned, that when autumn came was transformed into a muck that could easily last into late spring, when it turned into dust. Even further off were weeds and reed beds, hidden shanties and ditches full of unholy filth that, Father had told him, were once filled with crystal clear water, water you could swim in, and he'd even gone fishing for lobsters in them. 'You could stick your hands under the rock and we'd just pull them out . . .'

Far away in the background, at the end of this landscape, were Li Castelli, foggy in the east, and to the north Mt Murale and the vague shapes of other mountains to the east, about which Ivo knew nothing, except that in the winter they turned white with snow and his cousins went there to ski. The only organizing event had been the great circle of the DRR, the Drain Ring Road, which Ivo had first heard about when he was more or less thirteen years old. All his friends knew what that name referred to, but he had no idea, even if he was careful not to give that fact away. It went on like that for several months, Ivo not knowing what the Drain Ring

Road was; he could certainly have asked Father but, who knows why, he never did and after all they never talked about the Drain Ring Road in his family, because there were a great many things that remained inexplicably unmentioned in conversation in the Brandani Home. The things that were known, that they talked about, that was something Father decided and so one day it was Father himself, at the dinner table, who said: 'Did you all know that the DRR isn't called that because it's actually a 'Drain Ring Road,' but because the last name of the engineer at the Governorship who designed it is Drain? That is, his surname is Drain!' 'Not really!' exclaimed Mother and Big Sister, even if there was no mistaking the fact that this piece of news left them completely indifferent (Mother and Big Sister never talked back to Father, not unless it was really necessary). Instead Ivo immediately took advantage of the opportunity to ask: 'What's the DRR?' 'It's a circular road, a beltway, that runs all around the city . . . Actually, it's not a closed circle, because there still isn't the northern section, but at least that's the plan,' Father replied.

This ring road ought to have been a perfect circle, at least that's the way he imagined it, but it wasn't. Ivo was disappointed when he discovered that it was incomplete, that its route actually resembled something much closer to the outline of a puffy potato, and once again his conviction grew that he lived in the only part of the City of God that could be considered right, orderly, and well made. It would take them time to finish the Ring Road, which would complete the city's ancient layout, supply a ring to fit the spokes of the ancient consular roads, each of which drove out in a different direction, towards each of the far-flung districts of the Ancient Empire, even though several of them actually came to a sudden end almost right away, in locations that weren't actually all that far away. The boundary between the inside and the outside of the City of God would now be transferred from the perimeter of the Walls, built at the behest of an emperor who had the same name as a boy Ivo Brandani attended school with, to the 41 miles of the DRR, built at the behest of Engineer Eugenio Drain, the general director of the Office of Public Works of the Governorship.

Ivo didn't know anything about consular roads. In the infrequent stories they told about Wartime, Father and Mother often uttered their names, as if they were talking about neighbourhoods where perhaps they'd lived when they were young, but he didn't know where they were, nor would he have had any way to place them, because he had no real idea of the city. With the passage of time these would always summon feelings in him of something at once intensely familiar and yet alien, places in outlying parts of the city, distant and ancient, but a more accessible, easy-going antiquity, more bound up with the people who had lived in it, who had lived during Wartime, with the black bread, the Germans who would round you up and cart you off to Germany, and all of that.

The City of God was marked to its very depths, that is to say, in its body and in its soul, by the centuries-old alternation—so age-old you might reasonably call it perpetual—of absolute powers: emperors & pontiffs, tyrants & temporal lords of all kinds, the last and most recent being that Duce invoked on the slabs of marble of the Fascist Forum. Every one of them, or very nearly, had taken pains to leave a mark of their own on the body, in the already highly stratified physical substrate, of the City. Many emperors were killed. We all know the end that the Duce met. Few, very few popes, on the other hand, have been murdered, perhaps on account of the sacral aura in which they generally wrapped themselves. An efficient reproductive system, which has developed over the course of a couple of millennia, ensures that they're still there, succeeding one after the other. A *pontifex* considered 'closed and conservative' is followed cyclically by another who is considered 'open and progressive', but it always turns out that it's nothing but the usual swill, all that changes is the way they cook it. All the *pontifices* wind up leaning on the city with all their weight, to persuade, direct, influence as heavily as possible, thanks to the highly sensitive tentacles, peduncles, sensors and receptors that have been deeply rooted for centuries into the vital nerve endings of the City and of the Country of which it is the capital. Since he was just a small boy, Ivo Brandani had always been taught to think of the Eternal City as synonymous with its Church, and even though he had only vague and confused notions concerning the hierarchies and existing forms of power in his country, he saw it as the chosen and natural dominion of the Pope, before any other earthly authority, before the carabinieri and the constabulary and the police and the teachers and even, perhaps, Father . . . If any evidence of this were needed, there was the enormous Dome, so immense that it became small and, in the end, what with its constant looming presence, disappointed, like everything and everyone that has been overblown, about which people sing such praise, like all the things that Father liked. Ivo wound up climbing up onto the dome, with Father, doing under obligation and without complaint something that he didn't feel like doing and especially with a person who, until shortness of breath stopped him, filled the entire ascent with pedantic lecturing.

Out of all that travertine there emanated a sense of uneasiness and betrayal, an all-too-worldly determination to attain domination that he could hardly miss—because kids understand everything—and in fact he didn't miss it, even though he was twelve or thirteen or so, even though he was religious, even though he went every day to Headquarters (as they called the premises of the local Parish), even though he feared Hell and was terrified of dying, any minute, in Mortal Sin without having time to repent . . . Outside, Bernini's gigantic Colonnade. Inside, every bit as gigantic, the bronze Helical Columns of Bernini's Baldachin. 'It's 100 feet tall, just think: a ten-storey apartment building,' Father had said. Then there were Bernini's tombs, with endless marble drapery that looked a stormy sea surging out into the aisles. Bernini everywhere. It was thanks to him and to others like him that that curvilinear off-kilter overloaded overemphatic city had been built, a city that repelled Ivo, because all that ornate decoration reminded him of the weltering octopuses in the wicker baskets of the seafood shops in the City by the Sea.

And yet, during the obligatory torment of the Sunday excursions, in spite of the boredom and the fear that he always felt in Father's presence, over time there formed in Ivo's mind an image of the City of God. That beauty was too unmistakable, obvious, proverbial, for it not to be hiding some deep piece of ugliness beneath it, grim and sempiternal, some sneaky imbroglio: the eye of a ten- or twelve-year-old boy, though clouded by the first surging sexual excitement, is still level, subtle, before being blurred once and for all. In the primary activity typical of those years, which is to squirrel away and process information about the world, Ivo gulped down data concerning his city in a stream of correspondences, as if in the many objects of various sizes, deployments and provenances that went to make it up, there might be something intimate that had to do with a truth, an essence, and that if he were able to seize it it could tell him important things. Perhaps it was a truth nestled in the ancient and fundamental Christianistic double nature of it: the city as a grand machine of indirect persuasion and occult propaganda—point a finger to God in order to produce earthly power, to make a strong impression on ordinary men, stun them with gaudy grandeur, dominate them with the force of fear, in order to direct them to specific purposes . . . In this way, then, by growing bored with Father, Ivo was obliged to observe the things and works that surrounded him, until he could ultimately feel the degree to which Bernini *was* the Eternal City, how profound a correspondence there was between the city and the work of that master sculptor, to such an extent that the one marked the other, and vice versa. The City of God owed some of the most significant passages of its form to the hand of Gian Lorenzo, such as the embrace, exaggerated and overlaid with emphasis, of the Colonnade, wholly striving and designed to astonish and admonish you: come ahead, draw closer O ye devout ones, your Church welcomes you and listens to you, over time you will learn that we too are no one to be trifled with.

A stupefying sculptor in the most literal sense, that is, a producer of unequalled stupefaction, but incapable of expressing any religious sentiment that might rise to the level of 'authenticity', that is, *true* and *heartfelt*, Bernini devoted himself to supreme mythological groups, monumental tombs, magnificent sculptural portraits of powerful men. Gradually, as Father showed him those artworks, Ivo got an increasingly strong perception from them of the spirit of the City of God: no desperation in the form, no real torment, but also nothing that could reach him in the *simple* form of a balanced, serene beauty. Always instead that determination to astonish with a deformation, that veil made up of an inimitable technical cunning and designed to conceal a void, a profound lack of conscious, adult seriousness. All this exhibition produced in him a sort of nausea, which was transformed over time into a subtle and subconscious disgust, capable of extending to the city as a whole— that is, to the few fragments of the city there were then known to him—and therefore also to the very man who was forcing him to go out and get a whiff of it: Father, of course. If Father, without any apparent inhibition, was willing to unload on his son his each and every bad mood and alienation, singling him out as the victim of his frustrations with life and with his profession, likewise Ivo silently reversed onto the city all the tension triggered in him by his status as a helpless creature caught in the grip of Father's abso- lute power. And so the boredom of all those eternal bolts of cloth in tumult around the hips of angels and saints, a sea of tempest- tossed fabric in which to drown the Virtuous Saint, who was in fact opening her mouth as she threw her head back in what looked to Ivo like nothing so much as a desperate gasping for air, or a strong stab of pain, somewhere. The same fate seemed to have befallen another Virtuous Saint, she too enveloped in a delirium of overabundant fabric, engulfed in a gusting wind; Father had taken him there too, to that church on the other side of the River. The same name as his literature teacher, Lucilla Albertoni, a small, petite woman, with strange iron spectacles, short raven-black hair; he thought she was pretty and he had probably fallen in love with her, because every time she quizzed him he felt his ears burn hot and in particular he was so completely intimidated when he met her out on the street that he unfailingly turned red as a beet and broke out in sweat, due to some mysterious unrestrainable embar- rassment that made him hide behind the parked cars. But she, Signora Albertoni, would spot him all the same, dirty and sweaty with the football between his feet, on the way home from the foot- ball field. Ivo knew it and for no good reason was ashamed.

Then there was the craggy heap of rocks of the Four Rivers, an entire savoury universe unto itself, where among the flowers and plants carved into the travertine there also grew real flowers and plants, where Ivo realized that there was something not quite right about the reciprocal dimensions of the various figures, the brawny bodies of the Rivers were too large in comparison with the lion and the horse and the crocodile, by now so eroded away by the water that it looked like a catfish. And that armour-coated monster that rose, the water up to its waist, in the chilly shadows of the north side, what was it? A demon? Father had replied: 'You'll never guess . . . Go on, take a guess!' 'It looks like a monster from outer space . . .' 'Ha, ha! You're miles off. Just think: it's an *armadillo*.' Ivo, who knew what an armadillo looked like from his Album of Animal Trading Cards, said: 'It's all wrong . . . Too big, it has the face of a crocodile . . .' 'Certainly, Bernini never actually saw a live armadillo, just illustrations from books about the explorers, I believe . . . But that's not even necessarily true, you know, he did as he pleased . . . Even if maybe someone had shown him a stuffed one, he went ahead and reinvented anyway . . .' In Father's words, the usual veneration for the Maestro. 'Why did he include it?' 'Because it's a South American animal and that statue up there must be the Amazon River, or the Río de la Plata, which is in South America . . .'

It was all lovely and surprising, the stone palm tree tossed by the wind, the travertine serpent twisting and coiling at the foot of the obelisk, the papal coats-of-arms stuck, slightly askew, as if that watery theatre had been forced to accommodate them unwillingly: a pagan exhibition in the City of God? He really liked the Fountain's vast Rock-World, and especially in the summer, when he happened to be on the piazza in the heat of the day and he observed those slender blades of icy water; it made him want to climb up there and jump in, the way he did off the low cliffs in the City by the Sea. Ivo understood that Bernini felt the same way about the water as he did, that is, thought it was the most beautiful thing that exists, the greatest wonder in the world, and that there was no getting used to it . . . 'Nowadays we live in a time of democracy,'

Father would say, as if talking to himself, as they wandered around the fountain, 'and that's why we can no longer create such lovely things . . . To make beautiful things, you need a dictatorship, you need tyranny, because they have absolute power and they can procure the best things and the best people . . . These really were the best . . . Where are they now? The last one who wanted the very best was the Dictator . . .'

In the years of Ivo Brandani's early adolescence, the years in which Father was struggling to emerge from the uncertain times of the postwar years, the law of the survival of the fittest among those who aspired to be builders of cities tended to reward squalid manoeuvrers in the construction business, those who gave the fewest headaches to politicians, administrators, investors and clients. The ones who slithered as slick as lamprey eels through the muck of the public offices, through the silty shadows where decisions are made, where the efficacy of the power of the few who controlled the city was tested, power that they knew how to transform with stunning dexterity into millions of cubic feet of parquet floors, double bathrooms, balconies large and small, basement garages, that is, apartment houses and blocks of flats and row houses and giant apartment buildings hotels skyscrapers. Anyone who under whatever pretext ventured to come into the system from outside, and in the beginning Father was one of these, needed to hurry to understand the rules of the game.

The new City of God that was springing up in the years of Ivo's youth was a piece of machinery spitting out personal fortunes and political power, a shapeless organism made up of payoffs and envelopes fat with cash: there was plenty to go around. The public functionary who dared to say no (that was something that did happen on occasion) was ostracized, if not openly derided with ostentatious acts of corruption, such as tossing an envelope full of cash through his open car window, after which the briber took to his heels and the corruptee chased after him, shouting, in the middle of the street. 'Listen, I don't want it, listen, I'm going to throw it away!' And the other guy: 'Do what you want with it, after all, now you've taken it, it's there in your hand!' That story was told over the dinner table in the Brandani household, Father had witnessed it, and he laughed about it with a disconsolate look on his face. But then, as time passed, certain hints, certain half phrases made it clear that he too had been forced to kick back a bribe or two. Ivo was always very careful to divine the hidden meanings, usually ineptly encrypted, the conversations between Father and Mother. For instance, Consignment of Bribe equalled Bad Mood of Father, that is, uproar, back of the hand, abuse, shouts at the drop of a hat, lips compressed and white with fury. Whatever the external challenge or difficulty, Father would vent his anger internally and take it out on him, the only male progeny and the inexplicable pole of attraction for his lightning bolts. When that was the situation, it meant brutal smacks with the back of his hand, sometimes bowls full of spaghetti with meat sauce would fly straight up to the ceiling. It was also thus that, indirectly, the New City of God, of which Father was the producer, dug deep grooves, day by day, into the construction of Ivo as a man.

Nauseating, unattainable, dangerous City, that recoiled from any and all ideas of order, of what is right, of the well made, just as in those very same years Order Precision Workmanship were installing themselves in Ivo Brandani's mind, where they were to remain, as categorical imperatives, for the rest of his life.

Bernini was one of that city's folk icons, an acknowledged and venerated genius. The Eternal City talked of nothing but itself all day and every day, nothing but Bernini/Borromini, Raphael/Michelangelo and all the others. Names that resonated through the groups of tourists being chivvied along by their guides, under domes, tiaras and heraldic crests featuring the triregnum, beneath statues and pediments, plastically curved cornices, slightly unsettling when viewed in enfilade, like weltering clusters of eels. Still, they came from all over the world to see it, the City of God, and then there were the movies, there were the Americans, that was a wonderful, special city. When he was older, towards age fourteen or fifteen, Ivo was dragged into the centre of town by Enzo, a friend more hardened to the realities of life than he was, someone he'd met one summer on the wharf of the City by the Sea: they had both been trying to catch the grey mullets that swam in the harbour with just fishing poles, hooks, bread and cheese, and instead committing great slaughter of a different kind of fish, small, silvery, dumber, but not particularly good to eat. And so he began to become familiar with the streets and piazzas of the Ancient City Centre. They would take the bus, or they'd go on long hikes, laughing and joking the whole time, if it rained they'd bring an umbrella and later return home with their trousers drenched, their shoes ready for the trash. This was how Ivo gathered a notion of the form of the city, places came back to him that he might perhaps have seen with Father and little by little he learnt to place one with respect to the other, he impressed in his mind the route to reach them. He was indifferent to maps for a long time, but even then Ivo understood that in certain places the city had a form of its own, that it was built in a certain way, such as for instance those three roads converging into the emptiness of a large piazza with an obelisk that was full of parked cars, and the choice, which struck him as logical, to build at that spot two twin churches, with slightly swollen domes, with pie-slice segments, like a leather football—you could see that someone had thought it through, had given it some application. Or else such singularities as the perspectival effect of Pope Sixtus Boulevard, at the end of which you could see another obelisk before the trilobate apse of a basilica, a complex thing that Ivo believed was very far away but instead seemed as if it were right there, within reach, very close—this was surely no accident, they'd worked on it. Or like the Monument to the Fatherland which, if it hadn't been for the layers of air darkened by the bus exhaust, would really seem to overlook the Initial Piazza, which was actually a mile and a half away. It was the stench of the compact city, the intoxicating odour of the Corso that suffocated him at the same time that it gave him a sense of an adult, complex, vicious, unknowable metropolis. Then, over time, he began to understand that the Eternal City manifested itself in three visual zones, three registers, three overlapping sectors that corresponded to the same number of different souls of the city, each of them with the duty of sustaining a distinctive and unique type of figures.

In the lowest register or sector, resting upon that sort of basalt mat that everywhere covered the central and ancient streets and squares, Ivo saw spurting out of the earth the savage and pagan world of water, populated with monsters and mythical animals, men and horses that were half fish, with long coiling tails, dolphins with vicious snouts that little resembled the actual rostrums of real dolphins, crocodiles, tortoises, nymphs, snakes, fish, human nudity and tangled welters of animals. Forms that sprayed water, dripped dampness, grottoes covered over with mosses and maidenhair ferns. He loved those masses of slobber-coated travertine, encrusted with rust and limescale, coated with mould and algae, because he could imagine them to himself as mountains and hills, he could see the basins of water as lakes, picture the splashing sprays as waterfalls. His curiosity was piqued by the tall pedestals of the chalice fountains, rising out of the centre of round, oval, square and octagonal basins, with soaring jets and limping dribbles, hobbled by the low pressure, occasionally dripping from aquatic micro-greenery. In the summer he liked to dip his hands in the water, drink from the streetside water fountains. Then Ivo began to discover the pre-Christian world of the great monumental fountains. The Acqua Paola, on the slopes of the westernmost hill, a universe of water-falls and cascades on a lake of churning water, stunningly beauti-ful, then the Trevi Fountain, where Father took him many times and which had left him breathless: he couldn't believe that there existed a fountain-world, so huge that a person could inhabit it, construct a hut, swim in the crystal-clear water, sail a boat among those gigantic rocks, so *rocky* that he was reminded of the tank of the polar bears at the zoo. In the City of God the mystery survived of a vast mythical and primordial world, a mystery that was not only tolerated but unquestionably desired, sought after, preserved, as if it had always been there, from time out of mind, snickering in a state of happiness primeval and pre-Christian. In short, the water of the City of God was *pagan*.

Looming above this weltering world of monsters, fins, nude figures, there was the layer of signs of the civic culture, the hierarchy of Palazzos & Apartments. Ivo couldn't really enunciate it clearly in his mind, but in his city he saw a principle of urban submission at work, where the residences of the dominated many lined up to compose a theatre, deploying themselves as a backdrop to the palazzi of the dominant few. The streets often came to a dramatic end, ending their line of perspective at a vanishing point that corresponded with a monument—old, less old, nineteenth century, Fascist—and at the centre of enormous aristocratic facades that had once belonged to citizens sufficiently powerful to deform the city's fabric at their whim and bidding. And so it was easy to see who had been in charge in that city over the course of time. But over the years in which Ivo Brandani chanced to live, that is, principally in the second half of the twentieth century of the Christian Era, the principle had been reversed: in a democracy those who mattered most were well advised to avoid notice, not to build palaces for themselves, not to straighten streets to run to the front door of their residence, if it was only to improve the view from the windows of the master suite. Even though these wealthy men of the twentieth century were as rich and even richer than the others, they were *less powerful*, since they were obliged at least nominally to comply with the ruling principle of egalitarianism. All the same, the city of the second half of the twentieth century was built by them, and they made it in the image and semblance of their own culture, in their own interests and to their own benefit. Hence the signs of those who commanded in the city could still be seen, but you would have to go outside of the Ancient City Centre to observe their imprint, their *modus operandi*, that is, you'd have to venture out to the far slopes of the hills, where the larger territory was being plundered and looted even now. In his walks with Enzo, Ivo began to grasp the way that the Ancient City Centre was actually put together: a continuous ping-pong of messages between ordinary buildings and monuments that were, in contrast, very special indeed, between what struck him as a chaos of ordinary constructions and the vast structural masses built by the powers of the ages, as one-offs, complete & dominant. The civic culture consummated its signals there, in this intermediate level: cornices, columns, capitals, pediments, plasters, various architectural members and decorations, heraldic crests. The Baroque, which you might say had seized church architecture by the throat, leaving it with no alternative, manifested itself in the palazzi with a certain timidity, with something approaching sobriety, as if the city's system of powers did not love the exhibitionistic quality of the detail, preferring to make itself known in size, in horizontal and vertical expanse, ultimately constructing for itself massive hulks. If we look carefully at the heraldic crests it is easy to understand that many of those families-with-a-palazzo had been families-with-a-pope and some with even more than one. 'Priests, nobility, and power are all the same thing . . .' Father had said once, speaking aloud.

With the advent of the twentieth century, with the progressive expansion of the urban fabric, the iconic civic sector of the Eternal City filled up with blocks of flats, large, intensive and working class, filled with 'little people', as Mother liked to call them, who had been born there and grown up there. The little people manifested themselves as a human group fiercely intent on minding their own fucking business, immersed in the domestic lives of families-as-coalitions, striking a tortoise formation towards the exterior, that is, shields raised and spears at the ready, the same families that every morning exuded stale smells of closed flats out the windows thrown open over the immense courtyard, with its cement tiles, palm trees, flowerbeds and potted aspidistra, in the apartment block known as Grandma's House, where Ivo was born and later lived for nearly a year after the family's return from its Postwar exile. That distinctive odour of mattresses draped over windowsills to air mixed with the scent of the steam oven downstairs, mingling with the wafting universal aroma of morning purification that could be perceived every day, until the smell of garlic & onion sautéing arranged to re-establish the proper organic perception of life.

A new apartment-building dreariness had taken root in the city in the wake of Italian unification and, later, in the early twentieth-century and Fascistic city, delineated, this last city, in accordance with the few pages of the Regulatory Plan, when the historic fabric of the city was butchered as freely as any pig in order to link together, in a more properly Fascistic fashion, the city's monumental presences. Thus, the Pagan Temple had to be connected to the Trevi Fountain and the piazza with the Staircase ought to be linked to the vast square, empty and white, that was going to surround the Emperor's Tomb, forcibly restored to its ancient splendour, that is, to a modern dreariness of black, depressed ruin, frightened by such inexplicable nudity. Ever since the City of God had gone back to loving itself to such a Fascistically excessive degree, that is, to seeing itself as sempiternal & imperial, it had engendered that tendency to enucleate every tiniest pebble and artefact, and terracotta bricklet and fragment of earthenware that ever belonged to Antiquity. By scraping away the living flesh, stripping bare its organism, in those times still hale and hearty, it was possible to get down to the dead tissues, to the bones of the preceding cities, neatly piled one atop the other, each of them marking with its own identity the one that followed, without any possibility of liberation and redemption from what had gone before. Then it was all left obscenely exposed to the public view, like a system of open wounds abandoned *en plein air* to rot right smack in the centre of the city, without knowing what else to do with them, other than simply to leave them there, so many black fetishes to broil under the dull gaze of the tourist masses.

Above the register of the images of civic power—by a long reach the prevailing imagery, but increasingly understated as you gradually made your way from the centre towards the outskirts— one would find the zone in which the signals of God were launched upwards towards Heaven, that is, towards spheres that you would have thought more properly fell under their jurisdiction, were it not for the fact that the representatives of Heaven in the city were also eagerly & indeed chiefly busying themselves with the things of this earth. Heaven, inasmuch as it is the headquarters of the divine, had always served as a target against which to ricochet the things of this world so that they might fall back down to earth in the form of a sacred, infallible edict, in the name of which pagan heads have been lopped off and individuals whose thoughts were judged untrustworthy burnt at the stake. Father, who was 'against priests', had told him the story of the Bronze Man who stood, head bowed and concealed beneath a cowl at the centre of that square hidden in the fabric of the Central City. This symbolic and spiritual relationship with Heaven was resolved in a concrete physical pro-jection into the atmosphere, which meant, practically speaking, domes. Dozens of domes, immense, great, medium, small, all to some extent or another flattened, to some extent spherical, to some extent ogival, mounted upon tambours of greater or lesser height, more or less endowed with windows, more or less decorated, more or less lavish. A forest of hurtling balls made of stone and brick, covered with lead or terracotta tiles or slate shingles, always mid-way between architecture and something else, since it had never been possible to solve—not even in Michelangelo's sacred hands—the dilemma of reconciling the tectonic configuration of the dome into the proper field of architectural form. All the same, what a show!

Father loved the terrace of the Big Fountain, way up there, whence you could look down upon the city's great aerostats, ready for their evening departure, swollen, turgid with Christian air and incense, yearning for a Reunification with the All-Highest who—in spite of the fact that these architectural apparatuses were there, and had been ready to lift off for centuries—still was slow to reveal Himself. An exception would have to be made for the dome of the millennia-ancient Pagan Temple, which instead appeared flattened, indifferent to the sky, directed rather towards the earth and solidly anchored, with concentric rings, to the earthly complex of which it formed part. He often took him there to watch the city below as it launched itself into the theatrical production of the sacred, if not the divine, to survey the forest of domes of this or that church. Among the domes they could see towers and campaniles, statues, pediments, the great outstanding volumes of the palazzi, covered roof-terraces, loggias, villas in the distance, on the far hill, still drenched in light. If you knew how to pick them out, you could identify the tip of this or that obelisk, but from there everything was where you least expected it, because the fabric of the city appeared flattened and mixed up in a way that formed a reddish magma without elevations or gaps, with strange and improbable juxtapositions of monumental masses that he knew were very far away from one another but which instead seemed to be set one beside the other, at least from up there.

It took time, the game of identifying monuments lasted as long as Father wanted it to, and therefore it depended on the mood of the moment, which could suddenly tumble out into the external world on the whim of an Absolute Power. An absolute power had reigned over the city at their feet, an Absolute Power could do as it wished with little Ivo Brandani, with his life, with the quality of every instant of his time, past & present, while what he could not know then was *just how much* that man would mark his existence and his future relationship with the world. But even then, in the moments of complete subservience to Father's power, he had begun to take refuge in a thought that was precise and, as far as was possible, solid: 'I'm not the same as He is!' He later ventured to think something else, totally unprecedented and secret: 'I'm better than Him!' But then, after more decades had passed, he would tell himself that this wasn't true, that had never been true, or at least not entirely.

The problem of the city in its entirety, in all its beauty, was one that Ivo never addressed in the whole time that he was a kid, that is, until he began to explore it on his own, but until that point what would remain important to him were the few streets around his home, those streets and no others. He had learnt to navigate them without getting lost, he'd never seen a map of them, but he knew that at the end of one of those streets Michelangelo's dome appeared, swollen and purple against the sunset, just as he knew about other important places in the immediate area: Grandma's House, the Two Barracks, the Post Office, the School, the large parish church with its two Bell Towers and the fresco in the apse behind the altar, an enormous and menacing Christ giving a benediction, with strange scraps of cloth tied around His arms. Further away, at the foot of the wooded hill, were the Tennis Courts, the horror of the Covered Pool, the Large Fascistic marble sphere, the obelisk with the gold tip, the white bridge, and the other bridge, the grey one.

In the formation of a direct Ivo-to-city relationship, that is, of a process of discovery that did not pass through Father's intermediation, what interested him at the very start was his quarter, and what he knew best of his quarter was the route from Home to School, which involved the Poplars and the 90 Bus—which was quite an experience to board, given the sheer physical work the driver had to do with that enormous steering wheel, and the noise of the engine contained in some kind of oversized case next to the driver's seat, and the puff of air that the doors made every time they opened/closed—and the route from Home to the parish football field, which involved the poplars, it is true, but also the square-cut holm oaks, with their black trunks covered with ants and with a dark and secret liquid, trees that turned those flowerbeds into pure dust, where not a blade of grass was permitted to grow, dust spangled with dog turds, invisible by night and therefore lethal. In the summer, to complete the triangle, you could get to the drinking fountain, and there that involved the pine trees of the Boulevard with Cookie, which were dizzyingly tall, aromatic, anomalous producers of resin and pine cones (the Cookie in question was none other than a large and continuous central flower bed, planted with specimens of *Pinus pinea, the stone pine*). While he certainly liked the poplars of the Boulevards without Cookie—especially in the springtime, especially during the afternoon, with a western wind—almost as much as he was disgusted by the square-cut holm oaks that seemed to infest his quarter, it was for the pine trees that Ivo had developed a feeling of respect, and in the summer that feeling matured into something more, a perceptual ecstasy, triggered by a scent of resin that was a promise of the sea and of summer.

In all the Fascistic places that Father took him, but also elsewhere, along the roads that ran out of the city, in the parks, on the sacred hills of the Eternal City, but also outside it, along the none-too-distant coast, which was then beginning to be covered over with structural encrustations—at first these were simply seaside shacks, later they were little houses and small, illegally thrown-up villas, their walls covered with marine-themed polychromatic ceramic wall inserts, with such motifs as seashells, octopuses, crabs, seahorses, that is, when they weren't mere appliqués, behind which might glow a light bulb to ward off the darkness of the nights in the midst of the dunes, nights that just a few years before that were still pitch dark and star spangled—in all these places and in others still, Ivo saw dizzyingly tall pine trees and smelt their perfume. It was especially during the sacred Summer that Ivo *sensed* the pine trees. In certain places it was the thick carpet of needles on the ground, the pine nuts scattered here and there, so difficult to open, and when you did, they'd stain your fingers with a dark brown powder, redolent of resin, and then the pine cones would come down with a crash—the woody petals, stripped and torn, were already dropping pine nuts before they fell—and explode as they hit the marble-chip floor tiles of the hidden gardens in the City by the Sea, launching pine nuts out in a starburst, like so many projectiles, with the occasional fallen scissors spider which lay on the ground stunned by the event and, before they had time to gain consciousness of the pitiless nature of the terricolous world, were crushed beneath the sole of some sandal. He liked all this, it was an integral part of Summer and he revelled in it. How tall were those pine trees? How old were they? Why did the bark at certain points ooze out that odd sticky honey-sap, wonderfully sweet-smelling, but if you touched it, it stuck to your hand and you couldn't get it off? Who had planted them? To get one to grow, was a single humble and downtrodden pine nut sufficient? And if that were the case, if all that was needed was a pine nut, then why didn't hundreds and thousands of pine trees spring up from all those pine nuts? Why weren't there a much greater number of pine trees to be seen?

To his eyes, the only defect of *Pinus pinaster* was its unclimbability: that dark crown of needles way up high, isolated like a world to itself, was unattainable, unlivable, uninhabitable, unlike the first bifurcation in the big plane tree behind the house, in the City by the Sea. Clouds, the crowns of the pine trees, full of aromatic pride, absent from the terrestrial and aquatic life of Summer, except as shade & crickets. And that certainly was no small matter.

City of God too was profoundly marked, as if stamped with some kind of vegetable tattoo, its own, highly original tattoo, made up of maritime pines. In the places of Fascism where he went with Father or on his own to roller skate, along with the marble, the travertine, the sequences of shameless, muscle-bound statues, most of all there were pine trees, large, tall, ancient—all leaning in the same direction, tilted in a single, possibly previously agreed-upon direction—or else of a smaller and more unassuming variety, which Ivo never did understand whether that was a separate species or else simply the youthful stage of the larger ones. This coordinated and synchronized bending could be handily observed in the pine groves by the sea, along the coastline, in Castelfusano and further on, in places that he would later reach on the strength of his own manly forces, by bicycle—tucked away in his pocket was bread spread with the Primordial Nutella, 'surrogate chocolate', though he didn't really know what a 'surrogate' was—on the dune-fringed plain towards the Sacred Mountain that for four months stood as a distant backdrop, pale blue, mythical, unattainable, to Summer in the City by the Sea. Then, one day, he even reached it, the Mountain. And he rode up it too, along a steep uphill path, with Father and Big Sister, until a humiliating urgency forced him to seek seclusion in the sweet scent of the dizzyingly steep under-brush alongside the path and there, clinging to a shrub, to release a turd that was indecent and historic in both size and profanatory capacity, in a place that was otherwise mythical.

There are conceptual institutions, in the life of a human being, that can form in an instant, or which require time to carve them-selves a niche, sink roots, then install themselves once and for all, for the rest of a lifetime, and from there *act*. Among Ivo Brandani's conceptual institutions, there was immediately Summer, with all its attributes, including in the front line pine trees and the perfume of the pine trees. But to him the Pine was also one of the attributes of Fascism and Fascism formed part of the dangerous subset con-stituted by Father, who also possessed his numerous attributes, almost all of them odious, including among them a face that Ivo Brandani, after age fifty, for no clear reason, suddenly started to see in the mirror every time he looked into it. Not that Father was the equivalent of Fascism: 'I'm a neoliberal,' he used to say. Fascism belonged to the legendary times in which Father was born and raised, the Regime for which he had fought in the War, the mental, political and physical site in which his education had sunk its roots, his mythical youth. A time during which—Ivo knew this, everyone knew it, even little kids—it had been necessary to collectively renege, abrogate, and fight with live ammunition, to keep from being Fascists any more. Without necessarily becoming— Father had never become one—anti-Fascists.

Later, much later, Ivo would hate the fact that his Father had never been an anti-Fascist. But how could he have understood that for Father, in spite of all his violence, it wasn't possible to deny his past without denying himself? That is, without abandoning for ever his youth, the Fascistic years that had given him the gift of the adventures of the War? That is, the years during which he really had tested himself, while his son, also a Brandani, would live his entire life without ever knowing anything about himself, only to succumb in the very few challenges to which he actually would be subjected?

Brandani the son dreamt, without knowing it, the dreams that the Fascistic fathers had already dreamt, he dreamt the Mediterranean light of the beaches, the locusts in the pine groves, he dreamt of seaweed and jellyfish dead on the wet sand, in the lapping waves, that smell of rot that filled the nerve endings in his nostrils, penetrating forcefully into his brain, etching his memory with an indelible signature: *Sea*. Throughout his childhood and youth, Ivo would yearn with every ounce of strength in his body to *purge* his life of Winter, abolishing it once and for all, along with the middle seasons, and to hurl himself into an endless, magnificent Summer, immense and odorous of pine resin and sailcloth, marked by the rhythm of the Tyrrhenian breezes in fine weather, with that powerful northwest mistral wind that sprang up around one in the afternoon only to sink entirely into a lull about six or seven in the evening, when the subsiding wind heralded the imminent triggering of the offshore breeze. A Summer like this, for the rest of his life, in fact, the entire length of his life. All this was summoned up unfailingly by the fatal pine trees of the Fascistic Forums and the boulevards of his quarter, a quarter that, although in June it became a physical paradise, for the entire rest of the year was instead a relational hell. And it was thus a bellwether, a non-trivial advance on what was normally going to befall Ivo as a human being living in the second half of the twentieth century of the Christian Era, that is, in Peacetime.

All the same, however much Ivo Brandani might dream of its abolition, every year a Winter unfailingly arrived, and those winters were harsh. A chill descended, a north wind blew sharp, but there was very rarely any snow. The City of God has always dreamt of snow and has almost always been given sleet. It happened that the sleet came down frequently, in the evenings of the years of National Poverty, when it turned dark early outside, and there was nothing out in the streets except for the trolleybuses and there was nowhere to go but Home: light bulbs burning that cast a warm yellow light, panes of glass that fogged up, especially those in the kitchen window, late, when dinner was starting to cook on the burners. Those were evenings when, coming home from a walk with Mother, or from a friend's house and maybe the wind was blowing, he could already smell the scent of his block of flats as he walked through the lobby under the watchful eye of the Doorman, even before crossing the courtyard and starting up Staircase B. And when it was really cold out, once he came in through the front door he could hear Mother saying: 'Tonight, may anyone without a home find one,' and that marked the end of the day, with that return home, that maternal decree, the dinner, the brief after-dinner interlude gathered around the evening radio shows, if there were any.

But things didn't always go that smoothly. A couple of times a week, in the late afternoon, there was always something to be done at Father's insistence, a course, some pointless lesson to be taken, like Swimming lessons. It was something strange and counterintuitive, something that struck Ivo as an act of violence against his hibernal desire *to stay inside*, to the point that he even sought out *the inside of the inside* in armoires, under beds, and when he could manage to put it together, in the cubbyhole of the closet at the far end of the flat, with an old sheet and a broom propped up on two chair-backs to make a sort of tent. But there was nothing he could do about it, he had to go, it was obligatory, off he went to the pool to 'learn to swim', in accordance with Father's unquestionable dictate. 'There's the Pool at the Fascist Forum,' he had said. 'I swim badly, overarm, with my head out of the water, I want you to learn how to swim right, I want you to know how to do the *crol . . .*' '*Il crol,*' he had said in Italian. Only much later did Ivo learn that it was an English word and that it was spelt *crawl* and that it meant swimming with your face in the water, turning to breathe, and making a tremendous ruckus by pounding and splashing with legs and arms. Raschio called it the *strisciata*, which was the literal Italian translation of that term.

The building housing the Pool was pozzolana red, with large plate glass windows overlooking a garden, between the massive semi-cylindrical marble pillars. The first time he was overwhelmed by all that steam, the damp floors, the enormous mass of water that occupied nearly all of the immense echoing space, the black-and-white mosaic floors, other figures impressed on the tremendously high walls all around it, the tremendous echoes of the coaches' whistles, their shouts reverberating, frightening, the bleachers with the family members, the mothers, the immense sloshing stupefying blue of the pool. And over everything the smell of chlorine, powerful, hostile, like the water itself that lay waiting for him, threatening. Put on his swimsuit, unwillingly leaving the warmth of his overcoat, his sweater, his shirt, his woollen undershirt. The odour of hidden filth, his own and that of the other boys, mixed with a stale scent of chlorinated swamp and bleach. From that moment on, Ivo Brandani felt like a newly shelled oyster, body and soul defenceless, stripped naked, under an acid rain of lemon juice, just seconds from death. That bit of a chill to the stomach gave him the same peristalsis he experienced when Schoolmaster Proia summoned him to the lectern, or when Father shouted in his face, his lips pale with anger, or when he was in line at school for a vaccination, or in the doctor's waiting room, or at the dentist. The same symptom he felt when entering the locker room grew more acute during the odious procedure of the sanitary pre-swim shower and then when he walked through the obligatory final rectangle of water. First the white porcelain tiles of the locker room, then the mosaic of the same colour, with black figures of chariots drawn by horses with the bodies of sea serpents. The diseased and foul-smelling blue of the pool waited to swallow him up, with its powerful stench of something hostile, negative, like all things desired by Father, by his inexorable and metallic will, impervious, like those slimy marble surfaces, damp with vapour, a will that emanated from an entirely autonomous Being, disinclined to negotiate, harsh and chilly, closed, impermeable, like the vast plate glass window that rose above it. Like Raschio.

Raschio was black-maned, his hair thick and curly, his chin darkened by the whiskers that were perfectly shaven yet always there, always on the verge of resprouting. An asshole, let's admit it, at one with that aquatic & stench-laden nightmare, at one with Father and Proia. He shouted, he blew his whistle with such force that the ear—in that instant and afterwards, in the extended aftermath of sonic reverberation—was incapable of perceiving anything else. The whistle penetrated into your spinal cord, it drove straight into your colon, it implemented peristalsis, the malaise of that scent of bleach, the fear of that expanse of water, so vast that you'd hardly be surprised to see a whale suddenly surface.

Raschio, the damned jerk, an agent working incognito for Father, had tossed him into the water. Picked up and thrown bodily into the deep water, on the third lesson. Without a handhold, Ivo, with nothing to grab onto, submerged up to his chin in an endless liquid expanse that smacked of betrayal and violence, the deafening incessant rumble of the pool, the enormous figures of the mosaic, high overhead, that were tossing javelins and diving. No one could or would come to his aid, not even the mothers in the bleachers. Nanny seated on the tiers of seats couldn't understand what was happening and didn't much care. The shame of being unable to conceal his fear, his head just bobbing above water, his chin quivering with tears, the water eager to suffocate him. At the edge of the pool, Raschio was shouting who knows what, but after a second he understood. Raschio was pointing him out to the others, mocking him, calling him a Scaredy-Cat: 'SCAREDY-CAT!

Careful, don't crap your britches or you'll dirty the water for the rest of us!' Then Ivo shouted louder and louder, in desperation, through his sobs: 'I want to get out! I WANT TO GET OUT!' The coach gestured and a young man, one of his assistants, swam over, grabbed him under his arms, lifted him out of the water and set him down at poolside in the grip of a bout of terror. Raschio looked at him indifferently, Ivo was trembling all over, the intestinal peristalsis was almost impossible to take. Naked, wet, bent over by the pain in his belly, he was sobbing helplessly: everyone, in that building inhabited by water and condensation, right then everyone was watching him and deploring what they saw. Everyone was looking at *something*, something that had been stripped naked, there in the fetid liquid of that enormous basin, something that should have been left crouched deep inside him, something he couldn't be proud of, something shameful that was best left unrevealed: fear.

Fear, which Father had never truly known, was there, undeniable, shameful, and even in peacetime it demanded its part, insisted on its existence, announced itself as an impossible-to-eliminate component of the substance that constituted Ivo Brandani. But the horror of that afternoon was not to repeat itself. Nanny told everything to Mother, and Mother took a firm stance with Father and strangely Father no longer mentioned the swimming pool or the imperative necessity of learning the crawl. The inexorability of Father, He-Who-Commands-and-Disposes, the horror of the Fascist Forum Swimming Pool, of Raschio's damp and perverse domain, were that one time finally defeated by Mother, She-Who-Understands-and-Defends.

But the hard part wasn't just at the swimming pool, or at school with Schoolteacher Proia, or at the tennis courts, tennis being the other thing that was obligatory for him to learn. The hard part was everywhere, and especially at the Parish Football Field, where he went every afternoon to play football.

The ones who had the right to choose were the two best, most dominant players. They were generally a little bigger, leaner and more muscular than the others, and they'd make up their two teams after playing a hand game of odds and evens to win the right to take first pick. The would-be players gathered round in a circle and the two captains chose according to the respect each player enjoyed, but not on that basis alone: friendship and reputation factored into it as well, that is, whether you were or were not someone who was thought of as a tough guy, in other words, someone who could fight. If the number of would-be players wasn't even, the last pick remained without a team and couldn't play until someone else came along to even up the numbers. This selection procedure, which Ivo experienced in that time of American trousers & marbles, was triggered by whoever was the first to *find* a football. The football, usually too small and quite misshapen, was something you you either found at Headquarters, or else it actually belonged to you. But no one had a real leather football all their own. There were those, however, that belonged to the priests, old, scratched up and full of dings, of various sizes, but only the Number 5 was the self-respecting grown-up & regulation-size used in Official Football, the size used in the Series A Championship. At Headquarters you generally found Number 4 and Number 3 footballs. The Number 3 was the smallest one. Number 4 was still acceptable but a Number 3 was used only as a last resort. Whoever managed to lay their hands first on one of these footballs had the right to play and to start the proceedings for the formation of teams. But even if you had possession of the football, it was always the strongest players who had the right to choose, and the strongest players were always a little irritable, intolerant and contemptuous. If once you got a football within reach of your feet you were an official piece of shit, that is, considered to be one by everyone else—and Ivo was in fact an official piece of shit—then you had only two shots at playing. The first way was to be chosen for one of the two teams, and that could happen only if, during the preliminary procedures for a game, there formed up an even number of would-be players: if the number was odd, Ivo was the first to be left out in the cold. The second way was to get hold of a football all your own, and with that football, the right to play. Therefore Ivo understood that for him, official piece of shit that he was, going down to the football field didn't automatically equate to a game of football.

Of course, that didn't apply to the strongest players and if you wanted to be considered one of the strongest players, you had to meet certain criteria. First of all, you had to be a striker, because there was no recognition of worth for any players not in a forward position; the good ones all played forward positions, further back, playing defence, were the pieces of shit. The pieces of shit would always be pieces of shit because, even in the case that they showed some potential skill as a fullback or a halfback, to the inborn prejudices of football, these were positions that were held in utter contempt, and there was no freeing yourself of that opinion. A strong player was by natural right a striker if he knew how to dribble and shoot goals better than the others and, most importantly, if he had no idea of what it meant to pass. A strong player hadn't the faintest idea of sharing-the-ball, he ignored the concept completely and had probably never once in his life passed the ball to a teammate. Once in possession of the ball, a strong player kept it poised at the tip of his foot for as long as possible, in defiance of the shouts showering down from all over the field: 'Pass it! Pass it!' until he could place it between the goalposts or, more likely, lose possession. The piece of shit player, on the other hand, did his best to pass the football to another player for fear of losing possession —which meant that on the parish football field the piece of shit players were the real *play makers*—whereas those who were actually good players, skinny and arrogant and pivoting, never dreamt of such a thing. Not because they were selfish or anything like that. Oh, of course, they certainly were, like everyone else, but the game was hierarchized: every time a team came into possession of the ball, it was passed strictly according to ranking, always forward, proceeding from the piece-of-shit players to the stronger players and finally to the strongest player, which was the one who was out in front of everyone else. If and when it got to the strongest player, the ball had to be treated, inner foot or outer foot, worked in repeated dribbling series, at the end of which it was sent flying towards the opposing team's goal, or else it was lost, but it was never ever passed again to a less strong player, who might be well placed, who might be entirely unmarked, he might even be alone-right-in-front-of-the-goal. To do so would have meant reversing the normal scale of values, and that was inconceivable, something that couldn't take place. It happened only if—something that was vanishingly rare—there was a parity of strength between two players, that is, if two of the strong players each considered the other to be at the same level.

Once he was out of the home, Ivo belonged to that society of Postwar boys, which was primitive, based on arrogance, the power of skill, talent, and strength, and being a piece of shit at football was no help in that context. It was an age with little or nothing that was happy about it, no friendship was truly peaceful and egalitarian, no game was truly carefree, or at least not back then, not at Headquarters, not in the street. Relations between those kids followed the secret rules of the state of nature, on the silent and semi-deserted pavements rules applied that were almost entirely extraneous to those that were foisted upon them in the schools, to the words that they recited in church as altar boys, to the prayers that the priest taught them in order to implore the clemency of God, that He might save them from Sin. At Headquarters, the gathering place for all the local kids, on the football field, in the few still-vacant lots covered with free-ranging weeds, on the gravel of the playgrounds outside of the school, in the two or three parish movie houses, beneath the Pine Trees and the holm oaks and the poplars, on the broad pavements of that apparently civil quarter, there existed a society governed by a primitive and ironbound hierarchic system. Or actually, a series of hierarchies, or rankings: there were at least three, plus a fourth, the most important one.

There was the hierarchy of football, the hierarchy of ping-pong, and the hierarchy of *ghergi*, that is, the game of marbles. These were the most important skill sets at Headquarters and on the Parish Football Field, even though there also existed sub-categories with their sub-rankings, never drawn up in official form, always provisional, but clear and present in the minds of one and all. In the game of marbles, there were some who were good at *spacca* and others who were good at *zibidì-zibidè*, but being good at *spacca* wasn't the same as being good at *zibidì-zibidè*, it was better to know how to play *spacca*, which was more difficult, and more prestigious—and needless to say, Ivo's only marbles skills were those that extended slightly to *zibidì*. But the most important hierarchy was the one concerning fistfighting. Being known as one of the boys capable of fistfighting offered a number of fundamental advantages, first and foremost, that you weren't bullied. In order to be considered A Guy Who Can Fistfight, you didn't have to pick on others, it might be enough just to know how to put up a strong defence when attacked, push back hard to the bullying that ran rampant among kids. The first clash was where it was determined which of the two was dominant, or whether by some chance you might actually be considered equals. New friendships in the street usually began with a certain administration of verbal pressure, an onslaught of provocative sarcasm, a pre-emptive and gratuitous denigration that served the sole purpose of attempting to intimidate the new arrival, to test his mettle. Who are you? What kind of person are you? Do you fight? Don't you fight? How hard do you fight? They'd make fun of you from the get-go to see if they could make you knuckle under, it was something natural, instinctive, totally in the order of life among savages. You had to know how to fight back, either with words or with deeds. If you were spontaneous with words and you had guts, you answered tit for tat: trading insults for insults, wisecracks with even sharper wisecracks. Otherwise you had to get aggressive, threaten to fight back physically and, once you headed down that road, it was tough to reverse course without losing face, which meant you had to be ready not to back down in case you ran into someone willing to fight fire with fire in a determined manner. Those who weren't capable of reacting in one of these two ways was bound to succumb and just had to get used to being in a subalternate position, a hanger-on, a soldier, not an officer, or else they opted out entirely and went their way. But those who gave in and stayed tacitly accepted that they were going to be insulted, derided, just because, for no good reason, and therefore had to expect that they would be told to their face that their sister was a blowjob queen, that their mother was a streetwalker, etc. And everything they owned would automatically become available to the dominant one. I need your bike. Give me one of your Stop cigarettes. Give me 10 lire. But if you managed to get them to see you as a hardass, that could make up for your other shortcomings, such as being a piece-of-shit football player. The problem was to keep your head screwed on straight and successfully overcome the initiation tests, which were bound to come sooner or later.

If you were respected as A Guy Who Can Fistfight and on the football field you screwed up, made some unforced error only a true piece of shit would make, then they might say to you something like 'what the fuck?' but they wouldn't add 'asshole'. If all they said was 'what the fuck?' then no problem, but if someone also added the word 'asshole', that is, if they said 'what the fuck, asshole?' then it was up to you, from the elevation of your status as A Guy Who Can Fistfight—an unwritten and unspoken standing, very solid and real nonetheless—to reply with the formula: 'Who-do-you-think-you're-calling-asshole?' If you failed to push back with that reaction, then you could expect to be attacked as part of a probing manoeuvre, something that might not happen instantly, that is, during the match itself, but to all intents and purposes it was a sure thing: you might even pretend that you hadn't heard the insult, but you ran the risk of planting the seed of doubt in the minds of bystanders that you had passively let someone call you 'asshole' without lashing back. At the parish football field, at Headquarters, and in the street, the words *asshole, go fuck yourself, fuck you*, etc. were grave offences, grievous irrevocable insults. Not part of the official language or even part of the semi-official sub-language, they weren't used at home, you'd never hear them at the cinema or on television—they were the secret words of the outside world. Father & Mother would never hear those words come out of his mouth, nor would he ever hear them uttered by either of them. On those Cartesian pavements there existed insults that were far more serious, that were unlikely to be uttered even in the primitive world of parish football fields. If you weren't A Guy Who Can Fistfight, you couldn't call someone a *son of a bitch*, because that would almost certainly lead to physical combat. Ivo had learnt this one chilly November evening, loitering with a hardened group of boys his age in the empty lot across from his building, where an unsightly ash-grey school would later be erected. Just to sound a little more grown up, he'd called Arcangelo, the Son of the Concierge, a *son of a bitch*. He'd said it with a laugh but Arcangelo's face had darkened instantly, and he'd come straight over and started shoving Ivo, hissing in his face: 'Who do you think you're talking to, eh? My old lady's not a bitch . . .' Ivo didn't know what to do, his legs were shaking and so was his voice, he tried to jolly Arcangelo out of it without losing face, without showing fear, amiably shortening the other boy's name: 'Don't take it the wrong way, Arcà, I was just kidding . . . Excuse me, come on . . .' Arcangelo was considered A Guy Who Can Fistfight, the hangers-on had all fallen silent, lusting to watch the impending clash, because it was obvious that Ivo was about to get pounded bloody. But Arcangelo, on the kind of whim that dominant boys can easily afford, suddenly brightened and it all ended then and there.

The persona of the hanger-on was treacherous and terrible: they accepted a subordinate status, but to make up for it, they enjoyed the clashes between those aspiring to leadership, they enjoyed themselves as hangers-on watching you beat someone else up or else watching someone else beat you up. For the hanger-on it was a delight to witness the symbolic tests of strength, chest to chest, the reciprocal nose touchings between ranking opponents, the conflicts during football matches, like when you would answer, 'who are you talking to, asshole?' and if the other guy said, 'to you', then that triggered the procedural preliminaries to a fistfight. Tribal customs of a small world of infamy. Father and Mother thought that at Headquarters everyone spent their time in the healthy amusements of childhood, they never even suspected the structural harshness of that pre-adolescent society.

Those were the days when Ivo was attending middle school, the most pointless and vacuous course of studies imaginable, designed strictly to keep a group of young human beings being tormented by their youth closed up in a random place. His class, which was entirely and depressingly made up of male students, reeked of filth and pheromones starting first thing in the morning, a herd of desperados afflicted with perennially stiff cocks, whose idea of fun was to lift their desks with pelvic thrusts, who knew nothing or practically nothing about sex or the female body, who told each other stories invented out of whole cloth, just because, to spout bullshit, stories that Ivo, mama's boy that he was, never knew if he should believe or not. Whole mornings spent studying Latin, Manzoni's *I promessi sposi*, the *Iliad* translated into Italian verse by Vincenzo Monti, an endless snore, the only decent teacher he had was a woman, who taught maths. Most important of all was the group of pariahs just like him, his consolation and his mirror, his fetid port in a storm, the deformed source of all the stories he knew about the mystery and terror of the world: his fellow schoolmates. They were liable to engage in primitive and brutal forms of expression, comprised of bullying, utter ignorance and obscenity. Some of them were already engaging in marathon bouts of masturbation, even jacking off in class and teaching their classmates the finer points of the art. And that was how, one early afternoon at the beginning of spring, Ivo returned home with the notion in his head, a new one for him, of Jacking Off, as a mysterious undertaking in the aftermath of which a Disgusting Liquid would be produced. And so, even though he was practically certain that he was engaging in Mortal Sin for the mere fact that it involved Self-Touching, as Don Filippo had explained to them, that very same afternoon, after lunch, he locked himself in the bathroom and *did it*, experiencing an almost unheard of pleasure, followed almost immediately by the tragedy of Repentance, so much so that he wound up slapping his still-hard and blood-engorged cock and rushing out that very evening to say confession. Father Capitani, the handsome young well-groomed and bronzed Father Capitani, discreet brusher-past of the bodies of girls and, the other kids said with a laugh, also of young boys' asses, Father Capitani who organized the Cinema Forum and who Big Sister liked so well, wasn't there. In the sacristy he found another priest, older and fat, humble and down at the heels, by the light of the candles for the evening service, his oily head was illuminated with gleaming reflections.

He heard Ivo's confession there, having him sit down next to him, putting his hand behind the back of his neck so he could press his forehead against him while the altar boys came and went, putting away paraments and vestments. In that awkward position, Ivo took a while before he managed to stammer out something about an Impure Act, but the priest had immediately understood what the matter was and with nonchalance and a certain haste he had breathed in his face the words not to do it again, advised him to take a run around his building when he felt the urge coming on, and assigned him three Our Father's, Hail Mary's & Glory Be's as penitence. Even though Ivo didn't even know what a Glory Be actually was—and he never would find out later what one is—in three or four minutes he had turned *pure again*, he had saved his soul! That night he could even die in his sleep and he'd go straight to Heaven! But it wasn't possible to forget the quiver that he'd felt somewhere, in a place buried deep between his legs, where the flesh had contracted irresistibly a number of times, making him nearly faint with pleasure, while the sperm squirted out with violence and smeared itself against the scratched porcelain tiles of the little utility bathroom, among the brooms and the tin bucket, with the cleaning rag stretched over it to dry. To achieve this all he had to do was *think* of the pictures he'd seen in the illustrated magazines of Brigitte Bardot in a bikini, of Mylène Demongeot, Marisa Allasio, with whom he still didn't know exactly what it was that a person could *do*, but who triggered inside him a desire for possession that could be so strong at times that it almost made him burst into tears as a sort of painful vacuum formed in his belly.

The human pursuit that subsequently, that is, many years after the end of the Dark Years of the '50s, would be generically identified as 'having sex', did not yet have an official name for him but only semi-official names, among which Mother seemed to prefer 'doing the filthy', while the bored priests in the confession booth would say 'impure acts'—'Impure acts? Self-touchings?' they would ask, with the same intonation in their voice as the concession-stand employee who, during the intermission of the movies shown in the parish auditorium would call out 'Orangeade? Beer? Coca-Cola? Chewing gum? Mostaccioli cookies?'—while on the other hand at school his classmates would use the filthiest imaginable images and words. And so in his mind the idea took hold that dick, pussy (what was that exactly?), shit, piss, fuck (?), fuck in the ass (??), blowjobs, on the rag, boogers, etc. were all things that clumped together to form a single, swinish, disgusting immense, inexorable mortal sin that was persecuting them all, his friends and his school-mates. All of them screwed, all them going straight to Hell. 'Did you know that your mother and your father *fuck*? That is, did you know that your parents *get it on*?' Mazzeo had once whispered in his ear, and then he'd added: 'Today my balls are tight, I think I'm going to need to jack off.' By which he meant he was going to do it in just a few minutes, in the back row, during the lesson, that he was going to ejaculate into a handkerchief that afterwards he'd stick in his pocket. Mazzeo, bigger, taller, dark-skinned, yellowish complexion, large black eyes that he'd level in yours, as if to ask you: 'What are you looking at, eh? Eh?' All of them, every last one of them were bound for perdition, they'd roast in Hell. Don Petacci, during religion class, said it loud and clear that God expected Purity from each of them, that every day they ought to feel they were being tested, that God wanted to see them struggle against Sin, at every moment. It was a crazy thing to think about. And, above all, *impossible* to do.

He fell back into Mortal Sin the next day and the day after that, too. Later, it happened to him several times over the course of a single afternoon, with the passing months that anguish dimin-ished, the confessions began to become less frequent, too: it was absolutely impossible to resist that temptation. 'If I die I'll go straight to Hell and stay there for ever. For ever means something that never ends!' Inconceivable that *for ever*, in comparison with the haphazard and hasty humbleness of those handjobs that he gave himself in the surroundings of the broom, the bucket and the floor mop, in the odour of dirty water, in the idea of dirtiness, cer-tainly, as was only proper for sex. But Ivo lived through terrible months and years in his obsession with Hell on the one hand and the impossibility of resisting Sin, on the other. 'Let's just say I get run over by a car, or I'm hit in the head by a meteorite, like what happened to that guy in America, who was killed on the spot, or say my heart just bursts without warning: with all this jerking off, no one is going to save me, no one. In fact, just one is enough to damn me . . .' And if after the first jack off he was damned anyway, then he might as well just have as many of them as he wanted, seeing that the number would have no effect on the final outcome. For one or for a hundred, you still wound up in Hell.

Ever since Ivo Brandani, around the age of five, had come into contact with his first priest, or actually make that with his first nun, the concepts of mortal sin and venial sin became extremely important to him, because they marked a narrow path beyond which lay the irreparable, the abyss of no return, the very gates of Hell. The only truly important thing wasn't whether he would go to Heaven—he didn't understand what that even was and what's more, didn't care—the only thing he really needed to worry about was Not Going to Hell. The torment began when he was flooded by a wave of Impure Thoughts, that showed up infallibly every time his mind stopped applying itself to something. It was a labyrinth with no way out of Guilt/Redemption, comprised of excitement and sexual fantasies mixed with outbursts of cosmic mysticism, attempts to imagine eternity, infinity, the omnipotence, the all-seeing eye of God, the everlasting suffering in Hell, the never-ending joy in Heaven. But what joy? Enjoyment of what? Father Capitani said, 'The joy of the contemplation of God', and it was clear that that particular form of enjoyment wouldn't be especially attractive without the threat of Hell. But if it was already difficult to stop his own right hand as it reached for his cock and began to masturbate, how could he possibly stop his thoughts? He'd never be able to do that, one thought could only be stopped by another thought, and his mind was wholly absorbed in just one thing, so how was it possible? It therefore meant that he was a Sinner, because the very fact that it was impossible was a manifestation of Satan, as Don Petacci liked to say, that is, a temptation, in the flesh. Which meant that he would *certainly* wind up in Hell. 'In that case, there's nothing to be done about it,' he started to tell himself, 'I might as well just give in . . . God can see me? Then what the fuck? What am I supposed to do about it, anyway? I certainly would have liked to be a saint myself, levitate, perform miracles, talk to wolves, to birds, but I can't seem to do it. So that's that.'

In that period of battles against Satan, boredom in school, jacking off and football matches that lasted for hours—until night fell and you could barely even see the ball any more and it was time to return home—in those first few days of June that marked the beginning of the marbles season when they wore American pants, made of heavy, stiff canvas, that you cuffed at the bottoms of the legs and that grew discoloured with sweat, in those times of continuous bike rides through the geometric layout of the quarter, Ivo entered—without wishing to—into the Who's Who of fistfighters, standing on the highest podium, the one reserved for whoever would one day beat up Nasini. Nasini, that's right, him and no other, The Guy Who Can Fistfight by definition, the Mythical Dominant Kid that no one knew how to stand up to. Nasini was an absolute bully and everyone was afraid of him. Ivo had heard lots about him before anyone ever actually pointed him out: You see that guy over there? *That's* Nasini.

He was a pale-faced, fair-haired, adrenalinic boy, his lips pressed white with the perennial fury that tormented him. He too was the son of a neighbourhood concierge, it was said that he lived in a basement flat, he moved in a nervous fashion, had a slightly paranoid-looking face, perennially covered with a fine film of sweat, which alone discouraged any impulse you might have had to kid around with him. He wasn't seen out and about much, and when you did run into him, perhaps in a knot of other little boys, he was the one who had the least to say, the one who didn't give a crap about anything, the one who, if he ever did say anything to you, it was bound to be said rudely and contemptuously. Nasini didn't play football, he didn't play anything, he never came to Headquarters or to the movies, either. It was said that he attended a vocational school far away, maybe he already had a job. It seemed as if something was always eating at him, everyone treated him with caution, no one contradicted him, they just smiled nervously and approvingly at the rare words he did utter. And, above all, they succumbed, that is, they never put up any opposition if

Nasini asked them for 10 lire, a loose cigarette, to borrow their bike. He didn't have a bike, but he'd take one from whoever had it at the moment and he'd keep it for as long as week, in rotation. Word had it that one of his victims had spilt the beans to his family and his father had had to go in person to retrieve the pair of roller skates that Nasini had borrowed. All these details only amplified his myth.

Ivo Brandani, without the slightest intention of doing so, became The Guy Who Beat Up Nasini and for a while he felt like Glenn Ford in *The Fastest Gun Alive*, a Western they were showing at the Vobis theatre: no one really knows who you are, until you're forced, against your will, to prove it. That's how Ivo felt and it was a thrill. But it had been no laughing matter: if he could have done it, if right then he had had a knife in his hand, Ivo would have tried to murder him, that's how blind he was with rage and fury. It was early summer, school was closed, he had this brand-new Lazzaretti Sport bicycle, with a three-speed Campagnolo gearshift, and he was pedalling through the quarter without a single thought in his head, enjoying the gusts of cool breeze as he moved through the shade of the buildings and the sweat cooled on his skin. The bike was a gift from that year, a sort of symbolic instrument of passage: it was tall, a grown-up bike, with the crossbar, a men's bike. He used to ride Big Sister's girl's bike, a ridiculous, ancestral conveyance, without gears and with straight handlebars, with push rod brakes, instead of cable-operated ones, which was the most embarrassing thing imaginable. In short: a beautiful June day, quiet, cool, the weather of full Summer lying spread out before him, endless; in a few days they would be leaving for the City by the Sea. He was wearing a pair of Lee denims with the cuffs rolled up over his white tennis shoes, which were stained with red dirt, 20 lire in his pocket, a small heap of marbles and a few stickers from his Animals album, which he was never going to be able to fill in completely because of the absolute impossibility of finding several of the stickers needed, especially the Proboscis monkey of Borneo, about which those few lucky individuals who had actually seen it had said that it was 'this monkey with a snout that looks like a damn banana'. With the sweat of summer, those jeans were dyeing his legs and underwear blue, so that he then stained his sheets with blue. Taking a bath? Not even open to discussion. That was something he did only under maternal pressure, he got in the bathtub only when and if he was forced to and, when he got out, he left on the porcelain tile a smear of dirt with a vague bluish tinge, the mark of his American trousers.

The plan was to cycle around the quarter in search of other bicyclists like him, with nothing to do, and maybe wind up at the little field to play marbles or organize a bicycle excursion along the banks of the River or somewhere else, where there wasn't much traffic, like the big open spaces and marble walkways of the Fascist Forum, maybe even go take a few spins around the white Great Sphere. But for a while now he hadn't been running into anyone at all. Around noon he left his bike on the pavement in the park beneath the strongly aromatic pine trees of the Boulevard with Cookie, near the Drinking Fountain, placing the pedal facing backwards on the travertine curb, to hold the bike upright, and went over to two punk kids sitting on the benches, next to their little kid bikes. He had met them at Headquarters, one of the two was strong like a bull, agile and muscular, and was good at ping-pong. At that point & in that moment of the world, everything was simple and normal, the ferocity concealed in everything was remaining momentarily at bay, the air was dry and silent, redolent of resin and pine nuts. Ivo stopped up the snout of the drinking fountain with one finger and drank from the violent upward jet, letting it slap against the vault of his palate, because he liked the feeling. Then with his hands cupped, he tried to get the two kids wet, who laughed without a single drop touching them, because they were so far away. The little bull said about the other kid: 'Did you know that they screwed him?'

Ivo spoke to the other kid, then: 'Did they really screw you? Flunked in full?'

'Yeah.'

'What class were you in?'

The kid said that he'd been in seventh grade and he'd had to do the year over.

'What about your father? Did he beat you?'

'Yeah, a little . . .'

Ivo always felt a shiver go down his back whenever someone told him about flunking a class. What would Father have done? Once he had told Ivo that if he flunked a class he'd make sure he spent the whole summer on a construction site, shovelling pozzolana mortar onto the sieve, hauling hods of mortar up and down ladders, pushing wheelbarrows. These were apocalyptic threats: 'If you flunk a class, this life you've lived till now of eating high on the hog without lifting a finger, you can forget about it . . . I'll send you off to work hard all summer . . . You'll study and work and no time at the beach, not even on Sundays . . .'

While Ivo is hanging around there, playing with the jet of water, Nasini shows up with two of his hangers-on. He has the usual ashen face, thin lips, chilly, remote, faded blue eyes. Ivo immediately registers the change in the situation: 'Holy shit! Nasini!' He respected and feared Nasini, like everyone, and it would never even occur to him to challenge him, in any fashion. The two punk kids sitting on the bench also stiffen at the sight of Nasini, they immediately stop joking around and fall silent. Ivo removes his finger from the spout of the drinking fountain and the water stops jetting out onto the stripes in the middle of the road, Nasini comes over, bends over to get a gulp of water, then straightens up and looks around. The Lazzaretti Sport bicycle is right there, gleaming, handsome and new, with the Campagnolo three-speed gearshift. He walks over to it and starts look at it with interest. It's clear that the gearshift is tickling his fancy, an indication that this is a grown-up bicycle. In other words, even if it's not a Bianchi, or a Legnano, it's still something an adult would ride. Ivo says nothing, he feels a surge of pride at all this attention, but he acts nonchalant, Nasini frightens him, he's scared.

Then Nasini, in that strange, distant way of his, asks: 'Is that yours?'

'Yes.'

At that point Nasini, without a word, as natural as you please, grabs the bike and starts to get on.

Ivo jerks forwards without a second thought, grabs Nasini by the arm and blurts out: 'What are you doing?'

At the very same instant that these words leave his lips, he realizes that he's just stepped across a dangerous threshold and he immediately feels his legs start to tremble, turn to jelly.

'I'm gonna go for a ride,' Nasini replies, turning to stare at him with the pale remote empty eyes in his head.

From up close, Ivo realizes that he's a little taller than Nasini, he notices that in order to look up into Ivo's face, Nasini has to lift his chin slightly.

'It's my bike . . .' Ivo replies, venturing down a path from which there is no return.

'So what?' asks Nasini and remains motionless, as if to say: 'And now what are you going to do, what are you going to say?'

Ivo has an instant of desperation, of terror. He's tempted to trust him, lend him the bike, but just for a short ride. 'But then what if he doesn't come back? I don't even know where he lives . . . And what if he takes it and keeps it? Or even sells it to someone? What am I going to tell Father? That I let Nasini take it away from me? That some guy came along, told me "give me your bike", so I gave it to him and said *ciao*?'

Nasini isn't *asking* if he can take it for a ride, he's *telling* him that's what he's going to do.

It's a blind alley, a road with no exit, Nasini is swinging his leg over his brand-new Lazzaretti Sport, his men's bicycle, and he's doing nothing to stop him.

And so he says: 'G-get off,' but it comes out in a suffocated, uncertain voice.

Nasini catches a whiff of his fear and gets up on the bike without paying any more attention to him, without another word. Once he's up on the bike seat he glances over at him, all pale and remote, and says to him: 'Why, if I don't, what are you going to do about it?'

All it's taken is those few split seconds for Ivo to be filled with a desperate fury and violence, ready to explode. If Nasini weren't a little stupid and overblown with his status as the neighbourhood hitter in the age group of kids from twelve to thirteen, he'd realize that this little kid is blinded by rage, that he's suddenly become dangerous.

Maybe a sort of doubt begins to bubble up, he hesitates, but he has no time to understand what he would need to understand before Ivo is all over him. They both wind up on the ground in a tangled welter with the bicycle.

Nasini never expected anything of the kind, so completely devoid of warning or respect for ritual. Usually physical combat takes place in accordance with a procedure that consists of initial insults, followed by shoving and nose-pressing and, in the end, but only if neither of the two decides to take a step back, a punch or two might be thrown. Instead, none of this happens, very simply Ivo wades in and wildly starts hitting him.

Nasini is stunned, he's underneath him, he's not fighting back. Nasini isn't fighting back!

'I'm *beating up* Nasini!'

He hits him in the face just as hard as he can, he feels his knuckles crunch into the hardness of his cheekbone and the bridge of his nose, the softness of his cheek, of his lips.

He's beside himself, as he hits he shouts at him in a choked voice: 'Wh-whose ... bike ... huff ... Are ... huff-huff ... Y-you t-taking? Huh?' But then he stops almost immediately, after just a few punches.

Ivo moves away from Nasini, keeping an eye on him, his breath coming in gasps, his legs wobbly beneath him, a sudden weakness demands that he sit down, but he necessarily must stay on his feet, while the other guy gets up, all dusty, shakes the dust off him, and leaves without a word.

Then once he reaches the far pavement, Nasini turns around shouts back at him: 'I know where you live ... I'll wait for you in front of your apartment building ... I'll bust your ass in half, you piece of shit!' His face is ashen as usual, but with red patches where he took Ivo's punches, and he has tears in his eyes. Nasini is crying! The hangers-on he showed up with aren't following him, they're just standing there, staring at Ivo with stunned expressions on their faces. They can't believe their eyes. This guy right here *just beat up Nasini*! And he beat him up good and hard.

Ivo is paralysed by the excitement and exaltation, he's shaking all over, he needs to sit down on the bench and catch his breath, while he mechanically shakes the dust off. The hangers-on, two little kids wearing shorts, start to say: 'Damn, he beat up Nasini!' 'Did you see that, he beat up Nasini!' 'He pounded his face!'

But he's too stunned to say anything, he just stands there in a trance, he relishes that moment of rebellion and victory, even if he knows there's always a chance of Nasini actually coming and hunting him down. In spite of the fact that he dominated Nasini without even realizing it, he's afraid of the boy, because he knows that the source of his own strength was all anger, he knows that if he went into it cold, he'd have been beaten up or, even worse, he'd have taken to his heels. In the end he climbs onto his bike without a word, putting on a show of nonchalance, while his heart pounds furiously in his chest and those kids remain behind, singing praise of his exploits, because that day witnessed something new, a shift in the ratios of strength on those pavements, in the unstated hierarchies: *Someone-beat-up-Nasini*.

Ivo quickly pedals down, first, one of the quarter's spoke roads, and then a ring road, gets home, eats lunch with his family in silence, goes to his bedroom, and stretches out on the bed. He sleeps fully dressed, practically all afternoon.

The next day, at the football field, he realized that his status had changed: when it came to football he was still just a piece of shit, but when they were forming up the teams, he was one of the first ones chosen because, whatever his football skills, he was A Guy Who Can Fistfight. 'I'm A Guy Who Can Fistfight,' thought Ivo Brandani, sensing a burst of pride, but also a tinge of fear. Satisfied, but with the shame of the victor, with the doubt that he might have become a-guy-like-Nasini, that he was now viewed as

Nasini was viewed, as a brute who instils fear. All the same, the pride prevailed and the world as it turned out wasn't all that hard to live in any more. What happened reassured him, it shored up the sensation that, all things considered, it might be possible to live in stability, in certainty, in solidity. That it might be possible to get by well enough after all, encouraged in this point of view by Mother, whose job it was to fight back against Father's effort to destabilize, with his scoldings, his unpredictability, his sudden bursts of violence. This idea that, deep down, life was nice and reasonably easy—leaving aside the nuns in nursery school and the priests and Schoolteacher Proia and Mazzeo and Nasini and mortal sin, etc.—had been inculcated in him by the usual grown-ups and, in so doing, they had lied to him, some of them perfectly well aware that they were lying, others on the other hand being entirely unaware of the Truth, that is, the absolute instability of all things. It would have been better to teach him a silent submissiveness from the very start, to renounce all and every form of self-affirmation, pride of any kind. And yet Father was pride in the very flesh . . . How could *he*, who was only a little kid, that is, a living being desperately seeking models to adhere to, how could he have ever protected himself from the incessant gusting wind of Father's influence? Who else would show him *what* to be? *How* to be? *How* to act? In what way could he avoid wounding and being wounded, with the overall balance already leaning frighteningly towards a preponderance of being wounded (though he *had* beaten up Nasini)? How could he avoid being hurt and dying?

5.16 p.m.

The cappuccino was good but now it's got his bowels in an uproar. Brandani asks the barista to give him a plastic cup, then he heads back to the same restroom where he urinated earlier. He pulls three or four paper towels from the dispenser, fills the cup half-full of water and goes over to the stalls.

The toilets here aren't bad, after all, even if they're already broken here and there.

Ivo is well equipped when it comes to having to shit while travelling, at the airport or, even worse, aboard a plane. He has a procedure all his own to ensure that he can wash every time. All he needs is a few paper towels, a plastic cup half-full of water to moisten them, it takes a little time and a bit of skill but he couldn't stand it otherwise. He was born and raised in the Peninsular culture of the bidet, which bestows that culture with its only secret superiority over all the other peoples of the earth: an asshole that's always as *clean* as possible. 'C'est vrai? Vous vous lavez *chaque* fois?' Lotte had once asked him.

The asshole, clamped spasmodically shut for an entire lifetime to hold in the outgoing shit, pounds and pounds and pounds of shit, hundredweights, tons of shit produced over the course of my existence, even though I have nothing to do with my own shit . . . I'm not responsible for it, I never asked to be given an intestine, a colon, a rectum, an asshole. These are things I submit to and despise, they've always disgusted me. 'It's all yours, after all,' the gastroenterologist told me . . . Not on your life: But you mean it's mine? I produce shit, no doubt about that, I can't deny it, but it was never *mine*. It's something I submit to, being a digestive tube doesn't mean that you made some choice, it means you were born ... At one end, the mouth, which slurps up food, savours it, a mouth that waters, drools, speaks, shouts, etc. ... At the other extremity, the foul, closed, hidden, rightly shameful, perennially stinky asshole, no matter how fastidious and scrupulous the ablutions ... The horrendous stinkhole, I have no choice about possessing one. Clenched like a fist your whole life long ... Then the owner dies and finally peace, rest, the definitive release, the faeces that issue freely forth into the light of day ... The last, unclean innocent excrements spread out, wafting into the air their final guiltless stench.

The odour of shit, which he finds horrid, contentedly expands in the plastic-coated stall of the toilet that he selected, rising up into his nostrils, pushed along by the warm breath emitted by his own faeces.

How disgusting, it's not my fault, it's the symbiotic bacteria, which live inside me, in my gut ... Billions of parasitic lives, unhurried, relaxed, which help me to transform everything I eat into shit. They are the ones that produce this stink. Every time it's different, it depends on the species of bacteria that happen to be prevailing over the others at any given moment ... I don't know who started it, whether it was us or them. We could have created a world-without-shit ... You'd have to ask the Burning Bush: What reason was there to create shit? Couldn't You have skipped that step entirely? What is it? An inevitable side effect? But of what? Of life itself? You're omnipotent, You can create anything You can think of, and what You think of is shit? What the hell kind of God are You anyway? A world population of seven billion, every one of whom wakes up every morning and takes a dump ... Which means, let's see here, a safe guess is half a pound apiece ... I'm going to need the calculator again ... Seven billion times half a pound gives us more or less 3.5 billion pounds, divide that by 2,000 and you get 1.75 million tons of shit every twenty-four hours ... The Earth spins around on its axis and, as the Sun rises progressively, human beings get up out of bed. And what is the first thing they do once they're up on their feet? They shit. It's a sort of planetary stadium wave that releases a vast wake of excrements, the fruit of an immense consumption of resources, both animal and vegetable, the fruit of an immense quantity of pain & death inflicted on other living organisms . . . Leaving out the bacteria, that is, the true masters of the planet, who remain invisible and are capable of taking our shit and using it as a comfortable habitat . . . Then how can we talk about the environment, nature and a natural equilibrium—think of it, Brandani: *natural equilibrium!*—in decent good faith? How is it possible to even use these categories if, say, in China there are cities that grow by *a million inhabitants a year?* There are hundreds of millions of people who want homes and schools, health care, electric appliances, food, cars and holidays and fun, who need a basic amount of energy per capita just like us, who want to consume products the way we do, the very same products we like so much . . . People who like the Maldives and the Laccadives and the Seychelles and the Caribbean and the Marquesas Islands, every bit as much as we like them and they want to go there and they'll wind up going there, the way they already come to Sharm in their tens of thousands . . . Here, where they too need fresh water, for showering and to drink, where they need water to cook and to sprinkle those stupid lawns around the hotels, where they need electricity, etc. . . . In other words, they consume energy & food and in exchange they dump, here too, hundreds of tons of shit, thousands and thousands of brownish turds that still contain fragments of crustacean carapaces, of *macadamia nuts* ingurgitated the night before during before-dinner drinks, of vegetable fibres brought here from who knows where else, since absolutely nothing actually grows here, except for that stupid bionic turf grass, imported and cut like an English lawn, except for palm trees propped up by a steady IV drip of chemical energizers . . . The Chinese tourists, who surge in waves into the restaurants that specialize in Chinese tourists in the City of God, where they are greeted at the front door by some guy dressed up as a warrior of the Ancient Empire . . . The Chinese, who already as biomass constitute a tidy business for the world trade in anything you care to name, even if that were the three-pronged

527

thumbtack, which nobody uses in this country any more ... How much steel do they need, they and the Indians and the people in Southeast Asia, and the Brazilians and the Russians? How much coal? Who will stop this mass of humanity in search of prosperity at any cost? Why fool ourselves into believing that the planet can withstand the impact of this great a blow? Where there's shit, there's life ... Those little reddish turds, all identical, that could be found up in the gorges and the high valleys of the Island were clear evidence of animals, but which ones? As long as I can keep producing this nauseating junk, I can say that I'm still alive ... Alive, in spite of the cervical arthrosis, in spite of the fact that the curvature of those four or five vertebrae is gone for ever ... Alive but with his vertebrae marked by periarthritis, alive with a hiatal hernia, chronic gastritis ... Alive like my inflamed colon, like the twists and turns of my intestine full of diverticuli, vital receptacles full of shit, full of bacteria that have never seen daylight, that have never known anything but shit ... Alive, with this aching shoulder, alive in spite of this herniated disk, the right leg that hits the ground with forty pounds more weight than the left ... Alive, but with high blood pressure, a pill every morning ... Alive, but with a cock that's now basically dead, with those deep shivers like a mummy reawakening, rising from the depths of my loins, telling me You're alive, let your dick have the news, find a way of procuring yourself a nice prostatic contraction, a fine strong spurt of dense and impetuous sperm like in the old days ... You're here, alive, in spite of the fact that all this is denied you by your aged appearance, by your placement at the ass-end of the world, as a residual individual, well out of the reproductive cycle ... Alive, in spite of the complete disinterest that all women feel towards you ... Alive but with aching feet, the soles burning, the orthopaedic insoles in ever larger sizes of shoes ... Alive but deprived by now of almost everything: no more sex, only occasionally paying for a blowjob, no more smoking, no more whisky, no more coffee, only a demitasse of espresso a day, only a little white wine, better if it's red, better if it's beer, better if it's water ... Alive but without hair, his ears getting bigger and bigger all the time, a series of wrinkles running out from the base of the lobes, bristling with white hairs

. . . Alive but with legs that for some unknown reason were almost completely free of hair, the heads of his thighbones that were beginning to scrape against the surface of the pelvic sockets . . . It's the skeleton that falls apart first, it starts little by little and then continues to deform and deteriorate, gathering speed: 'The lumbar section of your spinal cord is deviated, your right leg is longer than your left, your cervical vertebrae are covered with *ridges* . . .' At the Stockholm History Museum . . . Remember it, Ivo, remember the *ridges* on those Viking skeletons, elderly & ramshackle—you'd been brought face to face with arthritis! Finally you had a clear and heartbreaking picture of the bones of an old man . . . And yet I'm alive, I move, I walk, I eat, I chew, I swallow . . . I have practically nothing organic left in my mouth; the X-ray of my skull to see if there was some problem with the turbinate bones—such a great name: *turbinate bones*—showed whole rows, above and below, of extraneous objects and metal pins grafted into the osseous tissues, it looked like the skull of a cyborg . . . And in fact, I still shit, even if my shit isn't what it used to be, even if it seems more like the putrefied slime of an ancestral swamp than the healthy expulsions of a human in robust health . . . Now it's time to get washed up, come on, *à la guerre comme à la guerre.*

He takes off his trousers and hangs them on the hook on the stall door, he does the same with his underpants. Now he's naked from the waist down, in shoes and socks. The air conditioning makes him shiver, the band around his head torments him, he feels defenceless, humiliated, ridiculous, as he wipes himself off repeatedly with the paper towels that he dips one by one into the plastic cup. Right there, centre stage, placed at the median axis of his body, peeking out from under the convexity of his belly, he can see his penis protruding, a tiny shivery wrinkly cylinder, doing its best to conceal itself in an underbrush of sparse hairs.

How ugly you are, when you do like that . . . When you try to hide yourself inside my body . . . That's not a good sign, this fear of yours of existing, of being there in space . . .

Like every man, and practically from the day of his birth, Ivo has always had a complicated relationship with his dick. Whether or not he should say that it's *his* has never been clear to him, given the independent-mindedness that gadget has always shown, since he was a newborn, standing up and lying down as it chose and pleased, emitting unwanted spurts of pee, which from a certain point onward became quite a source of embarrassment. But this initial eccentricity was nothing in comparison with the behaviour that it would display in the years that followed. First of all, let's say that starting from age ten or twelve, it wasn't so much a matter of his dick getting stiff but of its changing size, and considerably so, the colour of the glans, and considerably so. It took practically nothing for it to stand up and then to pulsate in time with his racing heartbeat, the poor neglected pump doing all the work, including the job of building him—at the vaguest of lascivious thoughts, at the sight of anything less than a chaste female image— an erect cock. A boy in early adolescence and his erect cock—a cock that is already a grown-up's in size and shape but which still interests no one and which the boy, if he could, would dispense with entirely—are two inseparable entities but profoundly extraneous from each other. White-skinned and covered with infamous peach fuzz, subcutaneous eruptions, pimples, hints at a beard coming in, flakes of dandruff, red spots: the boy. Dark, wrapped in a fur as malevolent as the curls of a minotaur, bristly, like the hair of a warthog, filthy, foul-smelling and eager to disturb: the cock, ready to interfere in the least opportune moments of a young human creature's difficult existence, uncertain & indecisive, overwhelmed by waves of emotion and discharges of hormones, devoid of the faintest idea of himself and the world. Ivo's dick, like all dicks everywhere, became adult long before he did, and even before he had a chance to learn (in a raucous-confused-filthy way) how babies are made, his dick was already fully intentioned to make legions of babies, the fibres of his internal organs were already capable of producing quarts of sperm teeming with billions of male gametes. All of this was going on while he had his hands full with the *Iliad* in Vincenzo Monti's translation, which he was still playing football or marbles in the dust of the parish field, while he was wandering aimlessly through the streets of his quarter and blushing beet-red every time he crossed paths on the stairs with the little girl from the floor above—she was homely, had braces, wore knee socks and a pleated skirt over her bare, knobby knees, scuffed up and dirty. A man's cock attached to a boy's body, at odds with a mind befuddled by the suffering that comes with the gift pack of life, but at the same time capable of sudden intuitions and moments of lucidity, lightning quick, useless. A cock that at school would stay swollen for hours, that he could use to lift the writing surface of his school desk. To do it he just had to press it up against the wood from below, thrust with his pelvis, and pump it up, employing a mysterious muscle, concealed somewhere between his ass cheeks, nesting in the depths of his crotch, at the root of the tool itself—the tabletop would rise a good half inch. 'I wanted to be a perfect sphere, made of crystal,' he told Mother one afternoon after lunch while she sat in an armchair reading the newspaper and smoking a Peer, while Father, buried in the completely darkened bedroom, was taking his angry half-hour nap before getting back into harness.

'How could such a thing occur to you?'

'Today we learnt about the sphere, the volume of the sphere, you know. Mrs Figus is a good maths teacher.'

'And why would you want to be a sphere?'

'Because I'm foul, Mamma. A sphere is perfect, clean, transparent.'

'What are you talking about . . . Just take a bath, instead of talking nonsense.'

Mother was wisdom, reasonableness, moderation, affection, protection.

She added: 'We're human beings, made up of flesh, fat, sweat, poop, things that smell bad, in other words. There's nothing you can do about that, but you can wash more regularly—you just don't. A bath tonight? What do you say?'

'You don't stink, Mamma . . . You're not *foul* . . .'

As he was talking to Mother, kneeling down next to her armchair, he sniffed at her bare arms, the way he always did, to get a whiff of the scent of her skin, soft and dry, that smelt of air: Mother's Arms—there was nothing better, nothing as sweet-smelling & pure.

'If I don't wash I smell bad too, my dear boy, and stop rubbing yourself.'

'No. You never do, never never never, ever at all.'

As was customary in those Postwar years, Mother and Father had scrupulously abstained from giving him any information whatsoever about the use and function of his penis: nothing. They'd abandoned him to his problems, completely alone and confused. And so, for many years, Ivo had assumed he had some sickness that made his willy get hard at the sight of just, say, the Three Little Pigs tied up together with apples in their mouths, ready to be popped in the oven by the Big Bad Wolf. It was not until he started middle school—and found himself surrounded by a pack of desperados just like him, some of them accustomed to jerking off at least once a day—that he understood that having a penis & a pair of balls was a tragic but common fate, about which it was possible/necessary to joke, and he had felt slightly reassured. Now he's looking at himself in the mirror as he washes his hands. His linen suit is completely rumpled, his face with its eternal construction-site suntan has turned greyish, weary, bored. But that's not it, that's not it. It's Father, who increasingly emerges distinctly from that face and once again almost makes him take a startled step back.

He pursues me, he's coming after me, he won't leave me in peace . . . There he is, the same smirk that used to make his mouth tilt to one side, the eyes that become smaller and smaller, desolate, the flaccid cheeks with that web of tiny creases that don't look old so much as withered. He persecutes me, he got himself pointlessly hated for all the years he was alive . . . Now that he's been dead for almost thirty years—how many years has it been?—he reappears on me, in the bones of my cranium, and he makes me hate my/his own face, the way he made me hate everything about him. And yet until just recently I was different from him . . . I used to be a good-looking hunk, I had my own expression, but now there it is, *his* smirk, the one he used to wear stamped on his damned face . . . What was wrong with you anyway? What was bothering you? Why couldn't you just enjoy life? What were you lacking? You had to work? Who doesn't have to? You were forced to obey other people's instructions? To *obey*? What's wrong with that? Who is completely free to decide whatever they want? It was horrible for you, having to obey, wasn't it? It humiliated you and you made us pay for that . . . No, wait, you made *me* pay for it . . . It took me almost an entire lifetime to work up to contradicting you, to understand how stupid, and especially useless, pride really is . . . Courage & Pride, that was you in a nutshell . . . You were all physical courage, violence inflicted on minors, and pride . . . The problem, my dear stupid old turd, is that you made me believe that a person had to be like you, and I wasted more than thirty years before I understood that I needed to be different from you, that I needed to become your opposite, the anti-matter to your matter . . . But in the end I did it . . . Did you really, Brandani?

It's Father's face he can glimpse in tracery in the mirror, *inside* his own face. It's his voice, his words, his typical manners of speech that Ivo can detect lurking in his own way of talking. It's the fear of being like him, that reaches out and captures him even here, in this airport, at Sharm el-Sheik on the east coast of the Sinai Peninsula, even here Father's image reaches out to grab him, that sort of carnival mask that he wears over his face, that mask he wishes he could tear off.

Inside there, it's not him . . . It's me! Me!

He leans in closer to the mirror, he scrutinizes his face from up close, he tries to guess at the skull underneath the now-flaccid skin of his cheeks, but the only line that has remained distinct is the bottom edge of his jaw, beyond which begin to dangle the wattles of flesh on his throat, which then disappears into the unbuttoned collar of his shirt—he isn't Father.

I'm not Father, and yet, with every year that passes, Father appears increasingly clearly in my face, in my voice, in my way of acting, being, doing, using my hand, I can feel it from within that that's what's happening, he emerges from my skull like the silhouette of the pharaoh that emerges from the sand in that old movie . . . *The Mummy*. I recognize him, he's pushing for more room. I'm *not him*, but what emerges from the sand of my face, belongs to him / belongs to me, as if we were now a single thing, as if he were willing himself to live again in me, using me as a healthy carrier of his fucked-up face, a reproduction of Father reaching out for the future . . . But I don't have children, your genes end here, you old asshole.

Father's legacy weighs upon him, he's ageing the way the old man aged, he can feel it in the fibre of his own physical constitution. In his late years, Father had started to become bent, curved, hunched over, it looked as if he were shrinking, his protruding gut, his watery eyes, deceptively mild, were often bloodshot. But all it took was a few minutes of conversation and it became clear that, inside his head, inside that large hard hairless cranium—planted into the front of which, from time out of mind, from before Ivo was ever born, was a large & fleshy nose, strangely straight, which Father would blow like the blowhole of some vast cetacean— inside that tenacious bony capsule, nothing had changed: the same decrees and maxims uttered and repeated a thousand times, the same chestnuts and platitudes, the same blind determination not to understand any of what was going on around him, to cling to those few convictions he'd assimilated, you might say from his bones, in the dark & remote times of Fascism, when he too, even he, had given vent to his youth.

Even the skull resembles his, the flat brow, the marked frontal eminences, the faded, weak arch of the eyebrows, the square chin . . . But I'm better looking than him . . . At least I don't have his nose, that piece of inflamed flesh, the flaring, snorting nostrils . . . My nose is narrow and sharp like Mother's, I'm taller, my shoulders are broader.

Nonetheless, he can feel him lurking in the structural, constituent elements, in the very matter of which he's made. He has his same weaknesses, but without the strong points upon which Father stood his ground and from which he was capable of holding out indefinitely, long past any limit of which Ivo could conceive.

534

Father was irrepressible, indestructible, or at least that is how he had always seemed to Ivo.

He withstood the point load without bending, he successfully withstood the distributed load, he bore the concentrated load without swerving, but perhaps a dynamic load, and not even a particularly strong one, applied to one of his weak points, might have broken him.

But exactly what were his weak points? For the past several years Ivo has tried to compare him to a structure but without being able to picture exactly what kind of structure. If someone asked him to describe it, Ivo would express himself as an engineer, because it would be pointless to speak of Father today in natural language. And after all, if he tried to explain him: who would give a damn? Not even Big Sister would be interested, if she were still alive, nor would Little Sister, because Father was different with them.

By now he's fallen into the blackest and most complete oblivion, everyone who ever knew him is either dead or has forgotten him by now. Except for me . . . Maybe it even happened, that he finally broke, but if he did I never knew about it, even if I saw him stagger . . . He was weakened by the intrusions into the proud idea of himself that he'd built, all by himself, over the years . . . Me too, of course, who knows who I thought I was, before life pushed me to the proper state of ripening and softening . . . I'm made of the same material as Father, he sent me out into the world to recompense *his* sins, to correct his thoughtless actions, to mediate with others and with life and negotiate terms for an honourable peace . . . He sent me out into the world to settle his chapter and move on, to abolish the way he butted horns with everyone and everything, the way he burnt his bridges behind him, his extraneity from all and every social interaction, every friendship . . . I didn't ask for him, I didn't choose him as my father, but I had to pay for him all the same and I'm paying for it still, even now—there you go, dickface that you are. What's eating you, eh? And after all, when I sweat, I don't stink like him . . . I have Mother's velvety skin, I'm smooth as a woman to the touch . . . I'm not him, I have Mother's nose . . . But if I'm not him, or at least not entirely him, then who is this guy in the mirror, tired, depressed as a water buffalo? It's you, Ivo, you're Ivo Brandani, that's exactly who you are . . . In the end, the fathers resurface, they re-present themselves in the faces of their sons, in the way that they act and speak, in the way they think, the way they do. In our everyday, commonplace ethics, of each of us, our fathers are there . . . However much they may have said things to us, explicitly, however much they may have brutally imposed them upon us, however much we may have actively and dramatically opposed them, to the point of breaking off all rela- tions, until we could say: 'There, thank God, I've got him out of my hair, I never want to speak to him again, I never want to hear his name mentioned as long as I live,' the fathers always return, we exude them from our pores, they re-form like a thin film, a layer on our flesh, a sort of phantom hologram that overlays our persona, which we'd always thought of as autonomous & distinct . . . Until the day that someone meets you and says: 'You look just like your father!' 'What the fuck?' you feel like replying. 'I know that . . . I know it all too well, I know it without having to be told, without you coming along and pointing it out, and you might even think it's a pleasure for me to hear it . . .' Even his odour, which you didn't like, one day you wind up catching a whiff of it on your skin: the acid reek of Father's summer sweat when he arrives at the City by the Sea and gets out of the car with his wet shirt plastered to his back . . . it's Him knocking at the door from inside, from where you kept him hidden in the cellar, locked away like a bastard son, a shameful family monster, it's Him knocking to be let out into the open . . . And at last it's Father, self-evident, ineluctable, come back to ask you if you were really ever able to think of yourself as different from him, if you seriously tried to put up a fight against the will of the blood, the transmission of the soma and not only that . . . Who asks you whether you really thought you'd be able to get so far away from him that he'd never be able to find you again . . . It was his *being there* that counted more than his saying/doing/hitting/forcing/threatening/*forging* . . . What counted most was the daily osmosis of the contact, however much you might try to avoid it, however much you might recoil from him

. . . It was a silent, subtle, tremendously effective penetration when it came to changing you, granting that you even needed changing, that it wasn't already written in your blood . . . His violence is your violence, the violence that you conceal . . . He didn't conceal it, he did nothing to resist it, no one ever taught him how to do it . . . His pride is your pride, repressed & punished by life, a pride that proved so very dangerous: the thing that damaged you most, exactly as it damaged Him . . . You turned out much handsomer and more athletic than Father . . . Mother's beauty—what did she see in that man, she, so civil, so gentle, and intelligent? So lazy?—mitigated his nose, straightened in you his crooked legs, gave you blue eyes, and yet was not able to hinder his deepest imprint, the imprint that he carved into you with his blade . . . And all this in spite of the hatred that you nurtured for him. Think if you had actually loved him . . . Because you *never loved him*, did you? Or did you? And if you did, why? Only his courage, which instead you would have had great need of, that alone he didn't transmit to you, to make sure that the rest of your life you would feel less than him . . . That's what you always were: not-up-to-his-level . . . Behind that glass door there was another door and then yet another . . . He'd had them installed to be isolated from the rest of the house and do the only thing that he really did well: sleep, sleep for an hour every afternoon, go to bed early at night . . . In his sleep, he found what you find now: oblivion, forgetfulness, curling up in a room cut off from all the rest and wait for sleep there, while thinking about the usual things: how to build a raft in order to get off a desert island, how was Odysseus' bed built, how to jury-rig a water desalinator . . . Technical problems, the only problems that exist in and of themselves . . . And to think that on his nightstand there was always, for years, for decades, only one book, Gandhi's *Autobiography* or something like that . . . Gandhi, the nonviolent one, and He, the living monument to violence, kept it on his nightstand . . . My mouth has a bad taste of iron filings, I need to brush my teeth.

However many tubes of toothpaste and toothbrushes Ivo might buy, the tubes eventually get squeezed dry and the toothbrushes get worn out, the bristles bend outward and the whole thing winds up looking like something exhausted and out of sorts, useless, harmful. The same thing happens with soap bars. He'll buy three and then run out of those three. Even though, at the moment that he bought them, it seemed to Ivo that he was stocking up wisely, laying in a good supply of soap bars for the future, the soap bars are actually used up in the course of a few weeks, running out imperceptibly but inexorably.

If you believe that you have a nice fat package of toilet paper for the days to come, let's say a six-roll pack, you're living in a fool's paradise because either you die a short while later—and then you'll have no need of it—or else you'll go on living, in which case you'll soon use up all six rolls and then you'll use up the pack after that and the one that comes after that: for years and years you'll wipe your ass, day after day, you'll use up miles and miles of toilet paper . . . The same applies to the rolls of Scottex paper towels that from a certain point onward, from some unspecified moment in the century, changed the course of the twentieth century, replacing something, though what, perhaps cloth rags, though they still exist . . . After all, they're just made of cellulose, that is, tree trunks, plus a few macerated rags . . . And in order to make all this paper, Kleenex, for instance, the reams of extra-strong copy paper, and the enormous quantity of newspapers and magazines and books, that people somehow believe are ruining the planet, in reality the percentage of wood required is minimal, they say, the rest is rags and recycling . . .

Ivo buys shaving cream and before long it's used up, the blades lose their edges before long, you always need new ones, the hairs on his face keep growing and need to be cut . . . The shampoo quickly runs out, even if when it was new the quantity in the bottle seemed an infinite quantity, extending into the eons yet to come. The coffee and the tea run out, the sugar and the salt are used up. Pounds and pounds of sugar and salt and bread have passed through his body, thousands of quarts of water, quarts and quarts of olive oil, and this too, which always seems like such a substantial supply when you first buy it, eventually runs out. The petrol, first in the Moto Guzzi Trotter and later in the Lambretta, and then in the Fiat 600, and then in the Renault 4 and after that in all the other cars he'd ever owned, ran out quickly, burnt in the atmosphere to become carbon monoxide, etc. To say nothing of the pencils, the pens, the scotch tape, the scissors: all things that love to disappear, that hurry to conceal themselves in some secret place in the planet, long before they can ever really be used up. It is through the consumption and wear of dozens of objects and materials like these that Ivo obsessively measures the consummation of his own life, the irreversibility of every day that passes, its non-reproducibility. No instant will ever repeat itself, everything has to be approached as an imprint, performed to an extremely approximate and improvised script, full of gaps and traps and bloody ambushes. Bloody, as a manner of speech. Blood, the real blood, the kind that drips down into the earth, dense, in big drops, black with haemoglobin, splattering out into round stains, rimmed with the occasional residual spray that escapes the force of molecular cohesion, is something that Ivo had seen only rarely, in the street during demonstrations so many years ago, or in the foamy test tubes for his medical analyses, or those two or three times that he really hurt his head— all that red cream that oozed out of his scalp, which you would have assumed was a little less saturated with blood, so thin that to touch it it feels like nothing more than a leather sheath, a husk for the walnut of your cranium, and yet capable of bleeding quarts, blinding you, sending you into blind panic: oh Jesus I've shattered my head to the skull, this is it, I'm going to bleed to death. Living where and when he did, Ivo only ever saw other people's blood at the movies, he did see it gush out freely from the shattered heads of his comrades, he saw it seep into the improvised bandages of emergency first aid, spattering the asphalt after a car crash, he saw it gurgle, black, out of Mother's lips the night that she died; in other words, he'd never had truly bloody experiences, because he missed the war and he never took part in any guerrilla activity. As for the war, Brandani probably exists on account of it, that is, as a product of the great planetary coupling that swept over the men and women who feverishly reunited as couples as well as those who simply met for the first time, on the street, at a dance hall, at the movies, at a party at a friend's house, at the beach, on the job, or anywhere at all. They met and they resumed their lives, they caught their breath stretched out in beds, embracing naked, in the nights of those first summers of Peace, that reeked of rubble, the dust of ruins, motorcycle exhaust, but also peace and quiet, sex, clean sheets. After the blood, it was Bread & Peace that caused the birth of Ivo, like that of so many others his age, who overran nursery schools and elementary schools, sitting on the floor because there weren't enough desks and chairs. Then they overwhelmed the football fields of the parish oratories, the scout meetings, the middle schools and the high schools, the universities and the piazzas, the army barracks, the factories, the offices. A sea of young people, the children, like him, of the war, who grew up prosperous and florid in the boom years, when there was finally plenty for everyone to eat, when TB was finally subsiding, when there was hygiene and vaccinations against typhus, diphtheria and smallpox, and it was in those same years, more or less, that the nightmare of polio finally vanished, from one day to the next. It was when new brands of toothpaste and models of toothbrushes were continuously coming out, a strange abundance for such simple substances and tools, all of them with the same unkept triple promise: no more cavities, white teeth, sweet-smelling breath. Ivo grinds his teeth and, in the mirror, examines them: they're old, yellowed, crooked, patched, but still there.

For years my gums have been receding to reveal the roots of my teeth, leaving them bare, and what had always seemed to me to be tiny gleaming compact edifices of enamel proved in fact to be platforms rearing up on blackened pile works . . . Rather than teeth, they looked like mangrove roots at low tide . . . It's the low tide of his gums: the red flesh in which they had seemed to be so solidly bolted is going away, evaporating, it can no longer stand up, it's dying, I don't know . . . And it seems that the underlying bone is doing the same thing . . . You know what that means, don't you, Brandani? It seems that once the teeth have fallen out, after a while the dental alveoli, the sockets, close up, forming a single ridge for the entire length of the jaw's arc . . . I know that in a few years they'll find a way of stopping this tendency of the human mouth and bones towards self-destruction, this wearing out of muscles and tissues, the hardening of the blood vessels, the erosion of the joints from excessive rubbing, the deformation of the skeletal structure, the inflammation of the fleshy ligaments that hold the bone joints together, the general clogging up of everything, the disintegration of the sphincters, the entanglement of the mental circuits, the glazing over of the corneas, the appearance of those flashes and flying specks of something, some so dark and black that you'd think they were flies, the desiccation of the retinas in the back of the eyes, the aridification of the flesh, the weariness of the arms of the legs of the hands of the fingers, the aching in the wrists, in the elbows, in the ankles, the refusal of the feet to take even a few steps, the deterioration of the intestines into countless diverticuli, the weakening of the pump, the withering of the lungs, the surrender of the stomach, of the liver, of the pancreas, the flaccidity of the scrotal sack, the irreversible inertia of the dick . . . Sure I know that before long we'll be able to reverse the process, so the gums will grow over the roots, as will the jawbones, and even the teeth will be able to regenerate themselves, the various joints will once again become smooth and fluid, the withered musculature will appear to firm back up, pectorals and deltoids will reappear, the cock will once again be hard as steel whenever you catch a glimpse of a girl's ass, rebuilt stomachs will digest anything you care to name, even the House White Wine, even the Pasta alla Gricia, even the Spaghetti Cacio e Pepe, and your asshole will no longer burn when you poop out the red chili peppers . . . Everything will be brand new again, we'll become a repellent species of undead, made of red flesh, regenerated and revascularized, drooling with lust and eager to sin again and again, into the night of time . . . But I won't be there, for me it'll be like those soldiers who die in the last few days of the war, like the ones who kick off after the cessation of hostilities, like those children who caught polio when the vaccine was already in distribution but just hadn't reached them yet, like all those who happened to die at the threshold of the new therapeutic age of antibiotics, of pneumonia or just some stupid infection . . . I'm going to have to die, but if I think about how long my ancestors lived, well, I've had a pretty good time of it already . . . At age sixty-nine I'm still working, I travel the world, I'm hale and healthy, even if my back hurts, and so do my feet, my right shoulder, and my stomach, even if I suffer from anxiety attacks and all the rest . . . The abolition of infancy, of youth, will be a relief to the regenerated old people of tomorrow, we'll no longer need schools, we won't have to listen to wailing babies like this one in front of me and the women who look like fresh young unexperienced girls will actually be consummate, delightfully expert fuckers, they too regenerated, who've been around the block countless times . . . And so humanity will finally be able to celebrate, along with the disappearance of child-hood, the end of the most painful and serious childhood disease, innocence . . .

Bomb Crater

Bomb Crater has always been here, ever since the day Ivo first came up here with his family, since they moved into the little yellow villa—which soon in his mind will become the House on the Curve—atop this hill that is called Le Prebende, covered with stone retaining walls and other houses, narrow asphalt-paved streets, deserted scrubby fields with scattered bits of rubbish, foul-smelling weeds, black trees, high above an unknown old Postwar city, about which the only thing he knows is its name, while Ivo only sees all the rest from a distance.

Mother is unlikely to take him places, she teaches at the Big Grey School, she's never home in the mornings, she sleeps in the afternoons, corrects the schoolwork, only goes out to shop, sometimes comes home with pastries; Mother is soft and a sucker for sweets.

Before starting school and when he wasn't at the Nuns' Nursery School, Ivo had always been there, in the House on the Curve, playing in the garden, but then with the passage of time he was allowed to venture cautiously out into the surrounding area, no cars, back then, just the occasional motorcycle—Father's Norton was big, the distinct detonations of the engine, but that was *before* the Lambretta—and archaic undersized bicycles.

There had been a *before*, certainly.

Ivo remembered something from *before*-going-up-to-the-House-on-the-Curve, but nothing that dated back *before* that Getting Out of Bed, when he'd started walking again, wobbly-legged, after the Paratyphoid Fever.

That was the beginning.

He remembered nothing of the Limbo where they told him he had lived before his birth, he remembered that the Beginning, for him, was that foot set down on an uneven floor paved with terra-cotta tiles.

With respect to that initial act of getting out of the bed—how old had he been? two? three?—there existed no *before*, only an *after*: he knew that he had been born before then but his true birth was the Getting Out of Bed and the beginning of his convalescence from the disease.

Of the mental monuments that constituted the *after* of that event, at the time, that is, at the subsequent time of the House on the Curve, only ruins still remained: the Brazier, the Charcoal Grill, certainly the Paratyphoid Fever, the day of his recovery, while nothing remained of the months of sickness. In his memory there also remained the ceiling with the Wooden Rafters, and how when it rained they had to put pots on the floor to catch the leaking water, the Drops that resonated rhythmically in the silence of those Post-War nights, the faint glow of the Brazier.

Smaller, less momentous monuments, were the Little Bathroom, where he had learnt to sit on the potty, holding himself with both hands on the rim, the Baths that he took in the kitchen, in the zinc Basin.

But above all there was the Worm.

He couldn't remember when the Worm had come out but he'd seen it over the potty, dangling out of his asshole.

It happened a few days, or a few weeks or a few months, after the Fall into the Brazier, and therefore after the Getting Out of Bed.

It had happened, no one knew how and he didn't remember himself, that he fell backwards into a burning brazier, and was unable to get back out, because it was located between an armoire and a credenza, both of which had smooth sides, and even the embers had almost entirely subsided, he'd still been in there long enough to scorch his ass cheeks.

'The fear of the Brazier has kilt the Worm,' said Maria Muccetta, his nanny at the time, who had the creased face and the watery eyes of a tortoise. Maria had pulled it out of his bottom and in her distinctive dialect had said something that approximated to 'how disgusting'. In the days that followed, she would say that something bad had produced something good.

Then they all left that house with the leaking roof—'Damned place,' Father had always said, 'the quicker we get out of here, the better.'

They climbed all the way up there, to the top of the hill, a sort of Sinai, where Ivo was soon given the tablets of the Law of Father: just a few commandments but clear & not open to discussion.

First: I am the Lord, yours and all the Family's.

Second: Do not EVER knock over a glass at the dinner table.

Third: Be absolutely silent when I take my afternoon nap.

Fourth: No noise if I'm working at home.

Fifth: Do not, EVER, trust me.

Sixth: I work, you don't, so you need to be constantly grateful to me.

Seventh: From me you will receive Hard-Smacks-in-the-Face-for-No-Reason.

Eighth: You are my son, so from you I expect dignity & courage, along with everything else.

Ninth: You can't even begin to imagine what would happen to you if you got bad grades at school.

Tenth: From me you will NEVER receive a kiss or a pat on the head.

One of the first nights at the House on the Curve, at dinner, Ivo said: 'Back behind this house, there's a big, deep hole.'

'Yes, I've seen it,' Father replied, 'it was made by a bomb.'

'It's full of weeds and nettles. Just think if you fell in.'

'You just make sure you don't fall in,' said Father, giving a typical Father reply.

The idea of the Bomb, of a bomb falling right near home, was magical and hard to grasp.

The bombs that were the constant topic of conversation, the bombing raids that the young nanny who came after Maria Muccetta, Ersilia, talked about: 'We could hear the blasts in the distance, over the hills . . . We'd see the flashes . . . The following day we went there, on foot . . . *Madonna santa* . . . Everything knocked to the ground, everyone dead.'

Then Ivo had asked Mother about those bombing raids, about the dead people, and she had instructed Ersilia to stop frightening the children with those stories, but after a few days Ersilia resumed her storytelling, on the condition of a solemn promise to say nothing to Mother, otherwise she really would stop. It was stronger than her, the pleasure of summoning up the horror experienced, the pleasure of Peace, which including the Recounting of War.

The same day that Ersilia had arrived—guaranteed by the Broker—Mother had made her wash her hair with oil, to get rid of lice: 'I don't know if she has them or not, but if she does I don't want us all to catch them. Have you seen her hair? How long has it been since she washed it?'

Ersilia's hair was black as coal, long, swept up in a bun, I don't know how greasy, gleaming. Right after the washing of the hair, Ivo glimpsed the hatred for Mother in her gaze. She had a young peasant's face, an enormous skirt that smelt of burnt wood, as did her whole person. The smell of petrol throughout the house, the sandals on her feet, her bumpkin manner of speech, alluring. Ersilia was practically a pagan, enclosed in some kind of cultural capsule that made her untouchable. Ivo immediately, and involuntarily, began to imitate her accent, her figures of speech, her ironic harshness.

Ersilia often talked about the Moroccans, without Ivo being able to figure out much, to understand what she was talking about, except that they were an ineluctable menace, that they were invincible, pitiless.

The Moroccans 'did whatever they felt like doing', Ivo had understood.

'They grabbed you and *did whatever they felt like doing,*' Ersilia would say, 'male or female made no difference to them.'

This doing 'whatever they felt like doing' was sordid, from Ersilia's lips, it was exciting, even if he didn't understand exactly what it meant.

Ivo knew that maybe no one, and certainly not he, could *do whatever they felt like doing*. There was a jungle of prohibitions, directives, commands and threats that hung over his head. They came from all sides but especially from the most dangerous, the strangest looming presence of them all: from the large unpredictable creature that went by the name of Father, with his hairy hands.

Father came first, he was the supreme authority, He-Who-Gives-Hard-Smacks-in-the-Face-for-No-Reason. He who cannot be scolded for anything by anyone. The strongest of them all. The one who frightens everyone, even Mother. But she is courageous and sometimes she stands up to him. And she's always the one who knows how to bring a smile to his face, in spite of the fact that Father is always Worried-about-Work.

Father is at Work. He's away for Work. He won't be home tonight. He's Tired-from-Work.

Father is On Edge, he works hard to earn us a living, and if it weren't for him, we'd wind up in the middle of the street (this is what Mother says), so it's his right *to do anything to us that he wants*.

So if Father wants to give us a Hard-Smack-in-the-Face-for-No-Reason, he can do it whenever he pleases, just like the Moroccans during the War, like during the bombing raids and the evacuations and the Germans.

All of them on Father's shoulders, they should be grateful to Father who, as he puts it himself, 'hauls the wagon just like an ox every blessed day that the Lord creates'.

In fact, to be exact, he says, 'Oh well, it doesn't matter, you have someone to haul the wagon,' and inside him you can glimpse the admonishment and reproof, which are directed *at Ivo*, first and foremost, to ensure that he understands from the very start that a 'real man is independent' and doesn't live on the back of any father; Ivo understands the problem, but he is five years old and he doesn't really know how he can become 'independent'.

In the present and in the past—which still loomed everywhere, like Bomb Crater—there had always been someone who had done or was doing something *for Ivo*.

Like Mother and Father who do so much for him: 'Without us you wouldn't be here, you'd still be in Limbo.' Like Jesus, who actually *died for Ivo*: 'They nailed him to the cross for you too, certainly,' said the sisters at the Nuns' Nursery School, 'Jesus Christ *died for us*, for our sins.'

Our sins can be divided into two categories: Venial Sin and Mortal Sin. For a Venial Sin, you go to Purgatory, for a Mortal Sin you go to Hell. We all could die at any moment, or else the Angel might pass and say *amen*, and you stay there with that grimace on your face for the rest of your life. The Angel passes by and sees that you've sinned, reads inside you, blows the horn, plays the spy, if he decides that you die, then you die and you go to Hell: if you don't have time to repent, then that's where you go.

Still, there were at least two schools of thought on this point.

The other school of thought said that no Angel was needed, because God knew directly everything that happened, what you did or didn't do, what you thought, everything—impossible to escape Him: 'My son Jesus died *for you*, Ivo, don't forget it. So now I want to know, how are you going to behave?'

'But if for even a fleeting moment,' Big Sister would tell him, 'you say, or it's even enough just to think it, "*Forgive me Lord!*", then you're forgiven.' Boom! You no longer have to go to Hell.

If you were already tumbling in headfirst, if you were already fluttering in the darkness of the afterlife, all you had to do was think '*Forgive me!*' and God would hear you and save you, He'd haul you up to Heaven.

Better train yourself to say it fast: '*Forgive-me-Lord!*'

Are you run over by a car? You need to be quick enough to think: '*Forgive-me-Lord!*'

Do you get scarlet fever? '*Forgive-me-Lord!*'

Typhus? '*Forgive-me-Lord!*'

Do you get the Worm? '*Forgive-me-Lord!*'

Another point that needed clearing up concerned Purgatory, and especially Limbo. So there were four places: Heaven, Hell, Purgatory, Limbo. Limbo was for unborn babies, but especially for unbaptized babies, which didn't apply to him. It all depended on the kind of sin you were carrying inside you at the moment of your death—that's how the Nuns explained it, the ones that Mother called the Sisters. You died and you immediately found yourself at a fork in three paths, leading to three eternal fates; it was there, always present, waiting for you.

'Once you've chosen your path, you can never retrace your steps, dear boy. You can cry and plead and repent all you like, there's nothing left for you to do,' the nun used to say. Her eyeglasses, her red, scaly face, her bad breath.

Before you die, you absolutely had to think the words. Actually, better still, say the words, you never knew: '*Forgive-me-Lord!*' It was something *inexorable*. He'd heard that word who knows where, maybe he'd read it somewhere, on a movie poster, on the cover of a book.

He'd asked Mother. 'It means something you can't think through, something you can't stop from happening, that has no pity for you or anyone else.' Mother had been a schoolteacher, she knew Latin, she knew how to explain things better than Father.

That word became important for Ivo—now at least he had a word to assign to what seemed to be against him, what he couldn't defend against, and defending against it was worse than undergoing it: *inexorable*. Ivo understood that many of the things that exist, and a great many people, are inexorable, you can't bargain with them. However good and kind they might seem, even if they seem to be your friends, then they'll do like the Moroccans, like the Fox and the Cat in Pinocchio, like the Green Fisherman, like the Blue Fairy, the most inexorable of them all. Of course, there's Geppetto too, but more than anything else, you have to give him a hand, because he's too old and too much of a numbskull.

The nuns and the Schoolmaster are inexorable.

And then there's Father's inexorability, absolute, unappealable, intractable.

Equally inexorable was Bomb Crater, which had always been there, menacing. Ivo often walked around the edge of that crater, he liked the powerful repulsion that he felt for the dark bottom of it, covered with towering nettle plants, where you could glimpse crumbling walls, clumps of refuse, objects.

Who knows what's under there, maybe a Bomb, that is, another one. Like in the poster you see everywhere, the explosion, the child torn to shreds.

IF YOU FIND AN OBJECT THAT LOOKS LIKE THIS, DON'T TOUCH IT!
INFORM THE CARABINIERI IMMEDIATELY

Then there are the Carabinieri, inexorable like the ones that chase Pinocchio and set their dog on him, a dog that doesn't know how to swim and Pinocchio hauls the dog to safety on the shore and in exchange, out of gratitude, the dog saves Pinocchio from the Green Fisherman, who is totally inexorable.

Inexorable of the inexorables, God is at the top of any possible hierarchic scale.

The nun talks about Original Sin, which is what gets stuck to your back the minute you're born, like an April Fool's prank, and the only way to get it off you is with Baptism. But if you die before Baptism, then straight back you go to Limbo, which is a grey fog, and that's where you remain for ever.

Everything that has to do with the complex matters of Sin, God, Christ-Who-Died-for-Us, is For Ever.

For Ever is something inexorable, something you can't imagine, like Infinity.

Who could ever imagine Infinity?

Bomb Crater is very close to home, well within the precinct that is explorable outside of the garden fence. Inside the garden what triumphs is dust, light-coloured marble-chip floor tiles, and black trees, their trunks swarming with tiny, very fast ants that thicken on the skulls of the birds that have fallen out of the tree and are immediately stripped of all flesh to the bone.

The territory beyond the fence is made up of scattered institutions, some of them strange, others tremendous and dangerous. Others still, like Rex, inexorable & unbearable.

Strange is Loretta's Bridge, which joins the road to the front door of the building where she lives.

Loretta, one of Big Sister's girlfriends, dark-skinned, dark-haired, treats him with aloof benevolence, like a little boy, in fact, like Big Sister's little brother, like someone who doesn't matter, who doesn't understand, who sometimes it would be better if he weren't there, it would be better if he went and played somewhere else, because she needs to talk with Big Sister, undisturbed, about private matters.

The Bridge spans a kind of trench, overlooked by Loretta's windows, against a damp wall, green with moss. Loretta is strange like the bridge that leads to her house, opaque, ambiguous. It's clear from where she lives that Loretta's family doesn't have much money.

The friends, the people that they know, the schoolmates and, before school even exists, the other children at the Nuns' Nursery School, you can see right away whether they're poor or not, from the way they dress, from how they talk, from the complexion of their skin, from the things that they say, from what they bring to class for lunch, which if it's bread and meat sauce means they aren't living too well.

This thing is important, it's important how you talk, whether you know how to say things in proper Italian or in dialect. If your smock is clean, your bow is neatly tied, your collar is stiff with starch or not. It's important whether or not you have woollen socks, or else short cotton socks, tattered, broken-down shoes.

At school Ivo understood right away that these are things that matter, that it matters not to speak in dialect, not to have the already withered face of certain of his classmates, those fine creases under the eyes, that smell of dirt and woodsmoke, the high hob-nailed boots, legs blue with cold, hoarse-voiced, cigarettes in their pockets, that mocking, inexorable expression.

Loretta bears the marks of poverty, but not the same marks, because those are the marks that boys bear. She is poor in the humility of her thin sweaters and threadbare dresses, in her bony knees covered with thin skin and a patina of dirt.

While the Gandolfis bear marks that are diametrically opposed.

No one ever told Ivo what the marks are that tell these things, of people, of families, but he knows them all the same.

The Gandolfis wear light navy blue cardigans, the Gandolfi girls are fair-skinned, their knees are clean, their skirts are pleated, their kneesocks, in beige wool, are worn pulled high, their hair is smooth, blond. One of them has a soft, French pronunciation of the letter *r*, like her older brother, Ernesto. The littlest one lets you touch the open fontanelle in her cranium, the soft spot, a little hole beneath the skin, which makes your skin crawl.

'Does it hurt you?'

'No. Did you feel it?'

'Yes. Brrr . . .'

'That little girl's growth has been stunted,' Mother used to say.

But there were other physical marks, leaving aside the clothing of the non-poor, all it would take is Villa Gardenia to place the Gandolfis at the top of the social ladder of all the territory he could explore, filled as it was with neglected walls, rust-encrusted gates, and nameless fields where foul-smelling plants grow, wild figs. Villa Gardenia isn't far away, the gate, always swinging open in the day time, offers entry through a high wall, made of hard white stone, broken only by two rows of rectangular apertures, where a few small plants grow. It is from there that the Gandolfi girls emerge. Ernesto too comes out of that gate; he's big, tall, superior and inexorable, and he attends middle school. Ernesto is too far ahead, too well launched in life, too far beyond Ivo's minuscule position, for him to be able even to talk to him. He rarely even sees him. But Ivo can't say the same about Rex.

He always sees Rex, even from a distance. He's taller than Ivo, white with black spots, someone cut his ears and then taped them back together, he looks like an idiotic clown. A young and stupid Great Dane, with bloodshot eyes.

'What good is that dog? Is he a guard dog? Why don't they put him on a chain? Why do they let him out? Why doesn't anyone do anything?'

He'd asked these things at dinner one night, with tears in his eyes: 'Rex runs along next to me, I don't know what he wants, maybe he wants to bite me.'

'Who is Rex?' Father had asked.

'The Gandolfis' dog.'

'You're *afraid* of dogs?'

'It's a Great Dane,' Mother had said, 'the dog is taller than him. They ought to put it on a chain, even if Signora Gandolfi told me he's good as gold . . . Can't you just find a different way to go, so you don't have to go past their front gate?'

'How am I supposed to do that? The football field is that way. That's where we play . . . Can't they keep that dog inside?'

Father seizes the opportunity to deliver one of his lectures. He says that the dog needs to be faced without displaying fear, just as you would another person.

'If you're afraid of him, he's afraid of you too, remember that. Don't show him you're afraid, if you are. Stay motionless, look the dog in the eyes . . .'

'But it's too big . . .' Mother objects.

'Naaah . . . don't say anything, don't butt in,' Ivo wants to tell Mother, 'now he's going to lose his temper . . .'

Father whips around on her: 'Don't interrupt me!'

There, he's lost his temper. Now it begins. He's pale, his nose red because of a kind of pimple he gets a lot, right at the tip. He's snorting air out his nostrils, he heaves a sigh, exhales impatiently.

And he starts with the same old routine: 'A man works all day long to bring home the bacon and then if he wants to teach his son a lesson, he can't do it without being interrupted!'

Mother understands but doesn't give up: 'I just meant to say that if he wants to look that beast in the eyes, he'll have to do it looking up, because the dog's taller than him . . . That's all, Fede.'

'Well, OK, Christ, then he'll have to look up at the dog! But if he turns and runs, then it's much worse, do you or don't you understand that?'

Ivo says nothing, now it's an issue between Mother and Father, as is so often the case.

Mother says: 'I'm going over to talk to Signora Gandolfi, very politely . . .'

'No, you're not!'

'Why not?'

'Because that dog isn't hurting anyone, he's practically a puppy . . .'

'But Ivo's practically a puppy too, and he's smaller than that huge beast,' says Mother, protectively. 'I am going . . . If something happens to the boy, what are we going to do then? They ought to keep it on a chain, that dog . . .'

And so on, for a whole evening, with Big Sister keeping a low profile, saying nothing, eyes downcast. Father never takes it out on her. He's never so much as laid a finger on her.

The routine plays out continuously from there, expanding to take in Father's entire repertoire, which isn't really all that broad: the fulcrum of everything he has to say is that *he works* and he maintains the family, which means he has the right to say and do whatever he wants. He never actually says 'whatever I want,' but it's clear that that's what he thinks. Mother can't (entirely) accept this philosophical line and she stands up to him.

Every once in a while he flies off the handle and he's capable of smacking her. He's done it before. Ivo knows it, he's seen it, he's heard it: she was sobbing, she ran into the bedroom and Father chased after her, shouting: 'Where are you going? Where do you think you're going?' Father had gone in after her, he'd slammed the door behind him very loudly, then he'd heard Mother shouting: 'Don't touch me, you hear me? Don't you dare, you filthy animal!' Followed by the sound of two tremendous smacks. Then Mother weeping and screaming and cursing him. Ersilia had come and collected the two of them and locked them in the other room, him and Big Sister. Big Sister was crying too.

Inexorable, inexorable.

For some time now, Ivo has been split in two, right down the middle, along a vertical line that runs down the bridge of his nose, the centre of his chest, cutting his dick in half, along the longitudinal axis, and separating the Ivo who *listens* to Father from the Ivo who *reaches out to* Mother.

The first of the two has soon become the Inner Enemy who will probably accompany him for the rest of his life, gnawing away at everything that can be gnawed at from within, kicking into action automatically in the presence of any moment of self-evaluation or external evaluation: 'You don't know how, you're worthless, you're a chicken, a scaredy-cat . . .'

The half that falls under Mother's jurisdiction isn't capable of standing up effectively to the Inner Enemy, it will never be able to help him to construct an Inner Friend as strong as the other but of the opposite polarity, capable of neutralizing it every time it sets about its work of endogenous erosion. Mother is a consolatory & welcoming modality, in which he takes shelter every time that Father, by means of the Inner Enemy, unleashes his brutal blows.

And yet last Sunday had seen them work all day long to build a new Lampshade for the Standing Lamp of the Crackling Tripolinas, the two strange folding chairs that Father, in a by then long-ago Wartime, brought back from North Africa. She had even whipped up some homemade glue, with flour, and then they'd carefully cut the piece of parchment paper. When they rolled it up it became a conical frustum—Ivo had no idea of what it was called but it was technically a conical frustum—then they'd punched holes in it with an awl and then they'd fastened it to the framework with a fine piece of cord, out of the passementerie basket.

'It turned out beautifully,' Mother had said, though Ivo had thought instead that it was sort of depressing to make a lampshade for yourself, that is, something poor people might do, out of paper. Not cloth. And yet, in the evening, the living room was completely transformed, with that diffuse light, shafting both upwards and downwards. Even the odious Crackling Tripolinas, already worm-eaten, with that general impression of freshly skinned cowhides hung up by the hooves to dry on the framework, which had already broken once, but Father had cobbled it back together, who knows when, with a masterful embroidery of thin metal wire. There would be no way to get rid of the Tripolinas for many, many years to come. Those cows, or calves, or whatever they were, were part of the family; never had there been chairs more uncomfortable or stupider, none of his friends, past, present, and future, would ever have had them.

'We're the only ones who have to hold on to this old junk that creaks and stinks of leather and is worm-eaten, because Father forces us to . . . None of my friends has a father like Father . . . They all have normal fathers . . .'

The grandmothers of Ivo's friends are normal too, not like Father's Mother, who makes you spend a whole day at the Nuns' Nursery School, for punishment.

At noon Ersilia came up to the nursery school, with a basket. At first Ivo didn't understand, then she said: 'Here's the bowl with the pasta, Grandma Vittoria says your punishment is to eat here today, and to stay until tonight . . . There's an apple in here too . . .'

The bowl was tied tight to the plate covering it, with a dish towel.

'They're going to make me eat here? I have to stay at the nursery school? But why? What did I do?'

'This morning you slammed the door right on Grandma Vittoria's puss,' says Ersilia.

Ivo struggles to remember. That morning he might have been a little abrupt with her, sad old Grandma Vittoria, with her black hair pulled up in a bun, with her moustache. She too, never a smile, never a caress, always remote, always a lecturer, 'I Might as Well Be Her Son . . .'

Mother: there'll be no one to protect me until she comes back from the City of God.

'I have to get my appendix removed,' she'd said, she would be gone two weeks, Father too would leave with her, and would be gone for a few days.

'God, how wonderful . . . Me and Big Sister all alone, with Ersilia!'

'Grandma Vittoria will come stay with you, the whole time.'

'There, inexorable as always . . . Grandma Vittoria, who's ever even met her?'

It didn't take very long, maybe half a day, to figure out what Father's Mother was like, to figure out that Father wasn't an isolated case; in the world there were other creatures configured in accordance with the same format, with his same inexorable inclination towards punishment.

And so that day the Nuns' Nursery School welded itself to Grandma Vittoria's inexorability, producing the worst afternoon in Ivo's life: after untying the knot on the chequered dish towel, he was forced to eat a bowl of cold pasta with tomato sauce, then Ersilia peeled him the apple and then she left, leaving him behind and telling him she'd be back to get him at five o'clock.

By that time it would already be dark, a Postwar November night, cold and without Mother, with no protection, except for the distracted, indifferent protection of Big Sister.

After lunch it was obligatory, for the eight or ten children left there, to go back into the preschool classroom and sit down on those grey-green pew-like rows of desks, gleaming with enamel paint that stuck to the thighs. Then Mother Superior said that they had to keep their heads down, pressed against the hard bench top, and 'sleep for an hour—obligatory'.

After the shutters had been closed on the french doors leading out onto the garden, it was almost dark in the classroom of the preschool, and that was the longest hour of all his life thus far, because sleep wouldn't come even for an instant, and he lay there the whole time, the infinite time that it took for that hour to go by, tossing and turning his head on his arms and his hands, now this way, then that, endlessly, his mind flooded with thoughts full of menace, unthinkable things.

'Will Mother come back? Could she ... die? Could it be that no one actually told me the truth? What is Grandma Vittoria doing here? Will she stay here ... for good? Will we always be left alone with Father? Will I get sick with appendicitis too? Or scarlet fever? Diphtheria? Will I get tetanus? You've been vaccinated ... You won't get smallpox either ... They said that you can get it anyway ... No, only a sore-throat, when you stay in bed and Mother gives instructions for your care and comfort ... Mother ... But what if she never comes back home again?'

He'd almost started crying with his head on his folded arms on the preschool desk, before the nap hour was over and they were forced to pull out their notebooks and do their classwork, handwriting exercises, easy but as inexorable as forced labour ...

Then again at night—after Grandma Vittoria, the mother of Father, identical to Father, had said to him: 'That'll teach you to not slam the door in my face. Next time you'll think twice. I'm not your mother who lets you get away with everything'—he hadn't even eaten but had instead run to hurl himself onto Mother's bed, to bury his face in her pillow where her scent lurked permanently. Or actually, what Ivo believed was Mother's natural odour but instead was the smell of the perfume that she wore.

But the catastrophe was averted and a few days later, Grandma Vittoria had left. It was immediately after Mother's return—pale, skinnier, a faint smile when he'd hugged and kissed her, her smell there, entirely unaltered, long wavy blond hair, which she never again would wear like that.

For that matter, never again would life be like it was in the Postwar years.

Never again like the first Day of School, that October morning of the following year, when Ersilia took him down the hill, to the square Grey School, with the big windows with the white trim, the dark-blue curtains that you could see from outside.

There, outside the entrance, he felt as lonely as he had that Day He Had Eaten at the Nuns' Nursery School, only worse. Mother wasn't there. She was in his school too, but to teach. No one, except Ersilia, to protect him from the hostility of that place, those boys, the black mouth of that inexorable building. Mother had put a pair of knickerbockers on him. They were scratchy, they were too tight on his calves, like his knee socks. Then the dark-blue smock, with the white bow. The stiff, starched collar that was sawing at his throat. The basket made of something that looked like pressed carton, with a handle, air holes, two notebooks in the satchel, one lined, the other with graph paper. The wooden pencil case with a sliding cover and, inside, the ink dip pen, the pencil, the pencil sharpener, five pastels, the two-tone rubber eraser.

Ersilia put a wax-paper wrapping with a panino inside in the basket: out front there, in that first icy Post-War morning, alone with Ersilia, Ivo felt his guts twisting as if he was about to have an attack of diarrhoea.

Then inside to climb the big staircase with all the others, then enter the classroom, then discover that there weren't places for everyone to sit, that he's going to have to squat on the floor between the lines of benches. It strikes him as absurd. Will it be like this every day? The teacher is on a dais, at the blackboard.

His classmates with their hobnail shoes, their dirty hair, their strange faces, who would laugh and make and do, shoot paper pellets at one another. They all knew one another but Ivo didn't know any of them and none of them knew Ivo. After a while, the floor started leaking a chill into his ass cheeks, and so he tucked his legs underneath him. Then he crouched over. After the first hour he got to his feet, leaning against the far wall, against the enamelled green wainscoting. Then back on the floor again.

In the third-hour class, the teacher asked: 'Who among you knows how to draw?'

'Me,' said Ivo.

He said it because he couldn't stand it any more, he wanted to get moving, prove that he wasn't just an ordinary kid, that he knew how to do something that his classmates would never even have dreamt of. He would have liked to say that he had already attended the nuns' preschool, which meant that many of the things that the teacher was saying they'd need to learn during the year to come were things that he already knew.

'Then come do a drawing on the blackboard.'

Once again stripped bare, once again that intestinal sensation, a pain of peristalsis in his viscera.

He'd stood up and walked to the podium, walking through his classmates sitting on the floor.

Unintentionally he had stepped on one of their hands, though lightly, a boy with smooth hair who liked like a 'mouse dipped in oil', as Ersilia always said of people with smooth hair, a boy who looked older than him, his face like a dried chestnut, the same yellowish hue.

The boy choked back a shout of pain and hissed at him, 'Ouch! Somebody ought to murderize you!'

'Sorry,' Ivo replied, confused.

'We'll see you outside, on the street,' said the boy, in a grown-up's voice, 'I'll knock you silly.'

He continued his way, tripping and stumbling, climbed onto the dais, picked up the chalk and started to draw: the time had come to show them all a thing or two.

He liked to draw, it was the only skill of his that Father seemed to appreciate even slightly, even if he never once said to him 'good job'. Father, the most he could bring himself to say was: 'Well, take a look at that!' The very maximum he could muster was to call Mother and say to her: 'Rita, come take a look at your son.' Ivo had devoted a great deal of effort to drawing motorcycles and helicopters, it was a way to please Father, he had a notebook full of them. Lately, Father had said 'Well take a look at that!' specifically in reference to a helicopter, and so Ivo decided that what he would draw would be a helicopter. He put some serious effort into it, he wanted to blow the whole classroom away.

When he stepped aside to show off his finished work, the whole room exhaled a bored murmuring, then from the back of the room resonated like the crack of a whip the crucial question: 'What's that, a snail?'

Ivo was so chagrined that he was on the verge of tears. Then he'd told the teacher, as if to reiterate some unacknowledged position of pre-eminence to which he could lay claim: 'It's a helicopter. *I* went to preschool.'

'Cunt!' Dried Chestnut had called out, earning himself a smack on the back of the head from the teacher but making all the other kids laugh with that word that Ivo had never even heard before.

From that day on, for practically all the rest of the school year, all the other kids called Ivo *preschool*, or maybe *preeskie*, *snail*, *ellie-cop*, until he was forced into a fistfight with Dried Chestnut and managed to earn himself a little, but only a little, respect.

The day that Dried Chestnut had overstepped his bounds and had said to him: 'Your mother's cunt,' he knew that he was going to have to react and for the first time he experienced what he would always thereafter identify as an 'insane burst of fear': his legs were trembling, his mouth was dry, and his voice caught in his throat as he was saying, 'Enough is enough . . . Cut it out . . .' and he immediately regretted it. But the words were out of his mouth, and in fact Chestnut immediately shot back, aggressively, with the phraseology that you use when you're eager to get into a fistfight: 'Why, what'll you do if I don't?'

At that point there was only one possible response that would leave him with even a tattered rag of dignity, in the inexorability of that situation and of the world at large. That answer was: '*Watch out, I'll knock you silly.*'

Father's lesson for the problem of Rex was put into practice with Chestnut. All you had to do was take it, pretend you didn't care, just put up with it and eat your heart out: '*Watch out, I'll knock you silly.*'

'You said it . . . Smart boy, now *he'll knock you silly.*'

And in fact, the answer that came back in a flash was: '*I'll knock you silly, is what's going to happen!*'

A sudden flood of thoughts of how he could get out of it filled his brain and distracted him for an instant from what was inexorably happening: a fistfight with Chestnut.

'If you'd only waited until tomorrow . . . Today we might have wound up as friends . . . He might have just stopped without my having to say anything to him . . .'

But Rex and Chestnut, deep down, were the same thing: hostility, submission for no good reason.

'If I don't do something, they'll never stop . . . Even if you fight back, it's not a sure thing they'll stop . . . If you don't try, you'll never know . . . If every time I just let him insult me without reacting, without saying a thing, then he'll just keep it up, getting more insolent all the time . . . He thinks he can do anything he wants to me . . . He doesn't study a thing, he doesn't even know how to practise his cursive handwriting, he's flunking, he's bored . . . I'm just his puppet, he's using me as a toy . . .'

In spite of the powerful tension, Ivo understood that with Dried Chestnut it was only going to get worse and worse, that he might get beaten up, but there was no way to avoid the coming fistfight. His submissiveness with Chestnut was already inviting other aspiring persecutors, inexorably, to step forwards: he needed this fistfight. Immediately, right there, in the square downhill from the front of the school, beneath the holm oaks, he felt authentic terror and that sudden painful sensation that he knew so well, as if something were moving up and down in the twists and tubes of his gut . . .

And for the first time he felt himself split in two, a part of him was about to get into a fistfight with a schoolmate, big threatening alien, while another Ivo was watching and commenting on the scene to himself, without the first one being in any way weakened in terms of his focus, or his fear, or distracted by what he necessarily now had to do and that is, defend himself to the best of his ability, limit the damage that was about to ensue.

That was only going to be the first of a series of clashes, increasingly complex, and all the more cruel the less they involved physical violence, that he would be forced to confront every time his family moved to some new place, where he was bound to find territories already guarded as their own by other individuals his same age, who would demand of him tolls and submissions. All this formed part of the inexorability of the things and animals and people who surrounded him, who pressed in on him from all sides: from above (Father and Rex and Grandma Vittoria and the Nuns' Nursery School and Schoolteacher) and from all around him (Dried Chestnut—'Cunt! Somebody ought to murderize you! I'll knock you silly!'—and all *his* followers).

The fight only lasted a couple of seconds and, to look at it from outside, it was a sober, ferocious thing.

The guy did literally knock him silly, splitting his lip instantly, but before the blood could soak into his white bow and his smock, he managed to throw together a ham-handed defence, followed by an offensive of sorts, that is to say, a kick in the shins delivered with all his might, a blow that was taken with a grunt and was noticed by the onlookers: Chestnut scared everyone, so to give him a good hard kick was a remarkable achievement. Dried Chestnut paid him back with interest for that kick with a punch to the ear that was practically unbearable, but Ivo managed to hit him again, good and hard, right in the face.

Then it was all over, Chestnut's eyes were bloodshot, the punch he'd taken to the face was hurting him. Ivo unsuccessfully tried to choke back his tears. The blood from his lip filled him with horror, his ear ached terribly, but he wasn't retreating. Maybe one or two of the kids who had stayed to watch, if they hadn't come over to his side (an impossible thought), would at least now stop thinking of him as something less than the cowshit that perennially plastered itself to the hobnail work boots of the peasant children. Chestnut was muttering about future bloodbaths, but Ivo had done what he needed to, even though there would be no particular need for it: that same summer his family would be moving back to the City of God, and there they would remain.

Ivo walks around Bomb Crater, as he so often does, with a nice straight smooth stick in his hand, the kind you rarely come across, but the wood is green: a real club isn't green, it's not wet with sap.

Bomb Crater isn't one of the inexorable things. If anything, it's something he feels indifferent about it, or even friendly towards.

Sad, circular, sufficiently deep to swallow him whole, it limits itself to containing large nettle bushes and other filthy weeds, as well as mallow bushes, garbage, rubble.

That crater was made by the World War, a bombing raid, an inexorable bomb, dropped by an inexorable aeroplane, an explosion that Ivo can't imagine, tremendous, massively powerful, capable of excavating such a deep crater just like that, in a flash.

'Just think, on a house,' Elio says to him, 'ba-boom!'

They had arranged to meet around here, the field with the crater, the rusted wire fence, all torn up, easy to get through. Here you can imagine you're out in the wild, in the black *jungla* (it's pronounced *iungla*), which you have a bow and arrow to defend yourself with, to hunt animals to roast over the fire, or else you're a cowboy, in which case everything is different but the field still works fine.

Elio has a stick too and, more importantly, he's not wearing a blue-and-white checked smock like the one that Mother ordered him to play in: 'Without-wandering-off, without-crossing-the-street, without-hurting-yourself, and get-home-soon-if-not-you'll-catch-it-but-good . . .'

For Elio, apparently, none of that. He doesn't have a mozzarella panino in his pocket like Ivo does, but a thin loaf of bread with the chocolate spread that Mother says is no good for you, that it's 'ersatz', a 'surrogate' (what does that mean?). Elio is always out and about, he only goes home when he feels like it—where does he live?—he has dirt-blackened knees, thighs purple with the cold, but he doesn't seem to care, he pays no attention to anyone, no one can tell him what to do, he minds his own business, he doesn't talk much, he's not exactly a friend, but neither would you class him among the things of this world that are inexorable: you can play with him (where does he go to school?).

Elio is from around here, he was born here, and his manner of speech is local. He too has raven-black hair, smooth, combed back, greasy and hard with dirt and therefore never out of place, except for a slight stray quiff over his forehead. He wears the usual hobnailed work boots that all the kids seem to have and that Ivo wishes he had, if they'd only buy him a pair, but Mother says that they're hard, that they're bad for the feet, that they're only good for going into the countryside, that he's not a peasant, not a farmer, that already she's had to get him a pair of clogs to wear at home that the doctor prescribed against flat feet—the same inexorable doctor who also ordered the big bottle of yellowish cod-liver oil, which dominates the room from its cranny in the kitchen credenza, set on a plate, with its dutiful spoon sitting next to it: a dose every day, it makes you want to puke; it's good for you and there's no arguing, says Mother, as if this once she were Father.

Naturally, Elio possesses an excellent club-spear, long and flexible, made of genuine non-fig wood, the tip sharpened with a jack knife (to own a jack knife is the primary objective of the Postwar years, an objective that Ivo has not yet attained): 'Look out or I'll rip your gut open,' he says, and laughs, 'it wouldn't take me a second, you know?'

A genuine and wonderful weapon, Elio's spear, not like his own club of green figwood, certainly quite straight but inadequate in every other way: something that you can see is strictly for kids, whiney little punk kids, the kind that Ivo knows he is. A' *maschio*, the grown-ups call him, hey little boy, or *a' pisellé*, oh you young punk.

To be a young punk with an inadequate club, on an afternoon in late winter, cold but not even all that cold, on a small Postwar field, outside the fence, with Elio, peering down into the bottom of Bomb Crater: a *regazzino*, as they say, a young insignificant punk in a world that tends towards the inexorable, a world that hasn't wasted any time showing him what it's made of, that immediately made it clear to him just how guilty he should feel, how careful he should be about things, about people. But, above all, that he must take care to repent immediately before dying, because beyond, in the afterlife and far beyond that field and Mother and Father, there is stuff that's much, but much much more inexorable than this.

'You've got a sword and I've got a spear, look out or I'll rip your gut open.'

'Not fair,' Ivo replies, 'your spear is longer . . . Careful with the tip, you'll hurt me.'

'I'll be careful,' says Elio, 'it's not like I'm an idiot, you know.'

'Naaah, you're going to hurt me. If you do, my mother'll get mad and she'll give it to me good.'

'I'll go look for a stick and we can have a swordfight.'

'Will you lend me the spear?'

'No. It's mine.'

Elio goes away, outside the fence. Ivo isn't willing to follow him, he stays there to look at the bottom of Bomb Crater.

'One time or another, we ought to climb down there,' Elio told him, 'but we'll need another rope. Do you have a rope? All we need is one of those lines they hang out laundry on, Ivo . . .'

'Elio, cynical, disenchanted, knows things, knows how to do things, what it takes.

'"Better stay friends, he has a spear. He'll rip my guts open . . . Go down there: who knows what's there." At the edge of the crater, Ivo leans on his figwood club, he tries to bend it to see if there would be any point in using it as a bow. He pushes it into the dirt, soft with Postwar rain, dirt as black as mud, the club penetrates into the edge of the crater, Ivo pushes harder until a large chunk of dirt breaks away and plummets into the void, and Ivo, off balance, tumbles in after it . . .

' "I'm falling, I'm dying, *Forgive-me-Lord*!"

'I wonder what could be down there in the middle of all those nettles, with leaves as big as your hand, just think how bad it's going to burn before I die . . . I'm going to split my head open . . . Just like with that bicyclist, the mudguard on the bike, he was "coming down the hill and I was crossing the street, he hit me head-on . . . He fell off . . . So did I, just like this time, but without a chance to repent . . . It's just a good thing I didn't die, or else it would have been Hell, H-E-L-L, you understand? . . . Then the blood pouring down from his head, the cut on his eyebrow, dripping like the leaking rain gutter in the back of the house, splattering into the cracks in the asphalt, spraying more blood everywhere, onto his shoes, the white socks, my legs, aromatic with dust . . . The blood is dense . . . It seems like the paint that Father had applied to the gate in front of the house, dense . . . Just a burning sensation on my eyebrow, but all that blood, sweet Jesus . . . Blood without repentance, not like now, when at least I'm confident on that point . . . I'm not going to Hell, or to Limbo for that matter, maybe just a stint in Purgatory . . . A thousand years in Purgatory is what you do for a lie, the Nun at the Nursery School used to say, when I went to Nursery School and ate lunch, on the day of Grandma Vittoria's Punishment, inexorable she was . . . Getting hurt, all the time . . . Always pain, always courage to display . . . 'Are you afraid, kid? Are you about to wet your pants, punk? . . .' No . . . Of course I am, forget about fear, this is worse . . . Terror, Hershey squirts, stomach in knots, mouth dry, hiccups pressing from behind my sternum . . . What are you crying for? What is there to cry about? Are you a girl? Only little girls cry, boys don't, ever . . . Father never cried . . . There is no question about Father's immense strength, but he never protects us, ever . . . If anything, he's the danger . . . I'm his son, but he's the danger . . . He lashes out without warning, without rules, for no good reason . . . Will Father eventually go to Hell, I wonder? You mustn't, you can't want this . . . Burning in Hell, Father burning, naked, amid the flames . . . No! I've never seen Father naked. Maybe he can't even be naked . . . No one can strip Father of his clothing, that's impossible . . . You mustn't, you can't, it's not right to wish this upon him, it's a sin, repent immediately . . . Do it before you hit bottom . . . I'm going to shattered to bits, I'll fracture my skeleton, I'll tear out my innards, I'll break every bone in my body . . . But now I'm not afraid . . . I'm going to break my head again . . . Blood and more blood from my head again . . . Like that time with the sharp mudguard on the bicycle—"You could have gone a little slower yourself, sir," Mother had said to him, "didn't you notice that there were children?"—like the rock that Elio threw, he didn't want to hurt me, I was being the idiot with that club . . . I wanted to do something cool, like in baseball . . . You threw the rock and I'll hit it with the club and I'll send it back towards you, come on . . . Certainly, only you didn't manage to hit the rock, it caught you in the forehead instead, right in the middle where it left a mark that's still there . . . There was less bleeding, a lot less, but it hurt a lot more, that time . . . It hurt much worse than on the eyebrow . . . And there too, the scar is still there . . . Elio felt bad about it, he said it wasn't his fault, and he was practically crying . . . Getting hurt, dying, being brave and not crying, repenting your sins, doing it all right, one thing at a time . . . Most important of all, not showing fear, otherwise Father would mock you, whining and calling you Scaredy-Cat, he'd do it in front of everyone, he'd shame you in front of everyone . . . Father tells the Nuns that they can hit you, he says the same thing to the Schoolteacher in the Meeting of the Inexorables . . . (Then Mother, the minute they left, had said to Father: "What came into your head? What do you even have, in that head of yours? Why would you even think of saying such a thing to your son's teacher?" After which the fight, a terrible one, that went until evening and afterwards, up in their bedroom, you could still hear them shouting, then the sound of a smack, Father shouting and her sobbing . . .) You had to be courageous that time the Dentist took out your baby tooth that had a cavity . . . You didn't know how much it would hurt, a tremendous amount of pain, like nothing you'd ever felt before . . . It was fast, you didn't even have time to yell out before it was all over and your mouth was full of blood, blood pouring down your throat, a taste of iron, the smell of iron . . . A tremendous, retroactive rush of fear, but Father was contented: his courageous son! . . . "He was very courageous at the dentist's," he'd immediately said to Mother, who instead had kissed him and embraced him and tousled his hair and had then insisted he open his mouth and had peered inside: "There's a nice big hole in there, but you'll see, it'll grow back right away: did it hurt?" ". . . Yes . . ." "What are you talking about, did it hurt," Father had said, "he's practically a man already, these are bagatelles . . ." Father uses that word, bagatelles . . . Often I don't understand his words, but all the same, I don't like them, as if he were capable of ruining them, things that don't belong to him that are dirtied and ruined on his narrow lips, that turn white when he loses his temper, under that big nose, that nose he blows day and night . . . The anger that takes his breath away . . . Bagatelles of blood, blood that tastes of rust . . . It was coming out of my nose and dripping onto my lips, it was entering my mouth from within, from up my nose . . . Tremendous pain of that tin can that ricocheted back to hurt me, instead of sailing away forwards like a rock in a catapult . . . Damn that fig branch . . . It was nice and straight just like this, growing out of the ground, next to the trunk of the Fig Tree Atop the Wall, very flexible . . . *Sproinnnggg*! . . . Place an empty tin can on top of it, intuition of how a catapult works, all you needed to do was haul back on it and the can, *sproing*, would fly far away, in a high-arching trajectory, impossible for it to fail, and instead . . . It shot backwards, it slammed into my nose, luckily the edge didn't cut me, if it had cut me I was certain to get tetanus . . . With all that rust . . . And it would be the same as now: repent before dying, like now when I fall and I kill myself and I've repented and let's all just hope that I don't wind up in Hell . . . I'm a good boy, free of sin, except for the Nude Madonna . . . aahhh . . . What was the point of dragging out that whole story now? Now it's a sin again and you don't have time, you don't have the time to repent! Cretin! They just had to change it so they could carry it in the procession, that statue . . . They were starting to take the dress off it, in the sacristy—I was sitting there, nobody noticed me . . . Then they kicked me out, but I had an impure thought . . . I wanted to see what She looked like under Her clothes, Her at least . . . I don't know what girls are like under their clothes or even what Father looks like . . . Now I repent and I repent all over again and I don't think about it, I don't even think a tiny bit about the Madonna stripped bare: Lord have mercy! . . . I had committed a grave sin, perhaps a mortal sin . . . Blood from-a-tin-can-on-the-nose-that-drips-between-my-lips and the usual taste of a wound in my mouth . . . The usual pain, the fear of the cut . . . But there were no cuts, there was nothing at all . . . I was going home to wash off the blood, I was holding my hand over my nose . . . I'd gone the long way round, as usual, I didn't want to run into him and instead there he was, down there, enormous, with black leopard spots, bloodshot eyes that seemed to want to squirt out of his head, the ears bound together with a bandage, a filthy dirty bandage, his breath, the slobber: Rex!!! He'd broken into a run, my nose was hurting me, it was still bleeding, the blood oozed out between my fingers, you were crying, no one on the street, no one anywhere, no one could help you defend you . . . Turning to run away was *wrong* . . . Stay still, don't let him understand you're afraid . . . If I ran away it would only make things worse, he'd chase me, he'd bite me for sure . . . Still, I'm done for anyway, I'm lost, I repent of my sins . . . Better to stay here, standing still, motionless . . . He saw me and ran towards me and maybe he expected me to break into a run . . . Motionless you stood . . . I was sobbing but I stood motionless . . . He slowed down, then he stopped very close to me, he cocked his head to one side, he slowly drew closer, I could smell the stench of his breath, the odour of old ham, of dog . . . He didn't bark, he sniffled through his nose, like Father, no one to help me . . . He started licking the blood off the hand I was holding against my nose and then off the other hand, he was whining, he wanted something . . . He liked the blood, he was slobbering red, he was licking his chops . . .'

As everyone knows, Zeno of Elea's argument against motion is correct and at the same time wrong; Ivo tries to subdivide the space separating him from the bottom of the Bomb Crater into ever smaller intervals, but there's always an inexorable limit, everywhere and in every case and for everything.

He therefore hits bottom.

The impact wasn't that hard after the fall, which was endless & scary.

The filthy soil of the crater takes him in just as he's in the throes of his repentance, when Ivo falls among the nettles he is pure, ready for Heaven.

Beneath the nettles there is nothing but garbage, rusty tin cans, tame ones this time, sharp-edged, yes, but they didn't actually attack him: Ivo isn't dead.

The nettle bush is practically taller than him, it scraped him all over.

He looks up to see how deep the crater is, but the rim is right there, practically level with his eyes.

And now Elio is there, looking down at him.

'Now what are you doing down there?'

'I fell in, darn it.'

To say 'darn it' every now and then is a sin, but it's gratifying, it serves a purpose.

'Now how am I going to get out?'

'Grab holt of the spear,' says Elio, and explicates the process: 'Stick your feet in the mud, you can dig yourself steps and pull yourself up.'

7.47 p.m.

A clump of spaghetti with tomato sauce dropped in the dust. A ditch excavated in the arid dirt of some unidentifiable place, and full of spaghetti with tomato sauce, still hot, and splotched here and there with dust. Then the ditch grew bigger, a rectangular trench, the spaghetti with tomato sauce was transformed into food waste, you can smell it, you can glimpse the horror of it. What to do? Where to go? He tries to wrench his gaze away from that scene which turns his stomach and almost brings tears to his eyes.

'Sorry, sir, but you are snoring too loud, you are disturbing the other passengers.'

The hostess is leaning over from the aisle, reaching over the head of his seatmate, an Arab, dark and corpulent, and she's shaking Ivo by the shoulder. Ivo wakes up and is almost in time to perceive his own shameful snort, a sound that he's always emitted when he sleeps, and which earned him combat boots tossed into his face in the guardrooms of barracks in the distant past, during his national military service. The grunt of a warthog. He takes a deep breath through his mouth, his nose is stopped up by the dry cabin air, his breath is foul, his tongue dry. He was sleeping sitting up, he was suffocating, and he had been dreaming of spaghetti with tomato sauce in the dirt.

'Snort . . . 'skewssmee . . .'

We say *sorri*. No, *Sorry*. In English, in English . . .

'*I'm sorry, sir . . .*'

'*You are welcome . . . No problem, sir . . . I also have your problem . . . Me too.*'

It was the Egyptian who spoke, whose English is almost worse than his. The nausea continues beyond the vision of the dream, it seems to be increasing. He looks for the bottle of water in the seat pocket in front of him and grabs it, guzzling it until it's empty. The nausea subsides but only a little.

You drank too much water, wait and see, in twenty minutes you're going to have to go take a piss . . . The suffocating bathrooms on planes, the dim light, the stainless-steel toilets, the deep blue flush, beautiful, worthy of Giotto's backgrounds . . . The noise of the engines, that there you can hear so harsh and dangerous, like the snarl of something under strain, something that can't take it much longer . . . The fire that keeps us up in the air, the streak of flame that saves us at every instant, the infinitely divisible sequence of micro-falls avoided and postponed to the successive jot of time . . . That's how it's going to be for the rest of the trip: flight doesn't exist in any real sense, all that exists is a disaster continually avoided in a sequence of postponements . . . More or less, that's the way it is, an aeroplane flies because of its shape, it's the shape that keeps it up in the air . . . But the only way it's able to do that is on the condition that the speed never falls beneath a certain threshold, otherwise we all drop like a rock . . . Aeroplanes fly because they're beautiful . . . That's my thesis . . . And they're beautiful because they fly: it's their aeroplane body that flies . . .

It's the Xanax that kicked in and calmed him down, it's let him sleep almost the whole way, now, looking out the grease-smeared porthole he can see the land and the water joined in a largely regular stretch of coastline. He looks at his watch. It's been more or less two hours from departure. He hasn't managed to sleep for the whole flight, as he would have liked, his headache is still throbbing, and it's getting worse.

This is the southernmost point of the Peninsula, that's the sea, down that way is Greece, you can see something in the dark . . .

His right leg is completely numb, his foot seems to have expanded disproportionately in terms of sheer volume, it's a thing that always strikes him as grotesque, this time his right ass cheek

573

has also turned completely numb. He tries to reach down and touch it by insinuating his arm between the fabric of the seat and the cloth of his trousers, which are drenched in sweat under his thighs: cold on the back of his neck, scalding hot on the seat beneath him. He reaches up to adjust the air vent. He shuts it off, but he knows that he'll soon have to open it again.

It feels like somebody else's ass . . . Move his leg . . . Change position . . . How do the people who always travel in economy deal with it? It's too tight, it's brutally cold, the porthole is covered with the lard of everyone who's ever leant their forehead against it, the way I'm doing right this second . . . These Egyptian airlines . . . That time on Ethiopian Air the seat was actually caked with shit . . . So disgusting, I feel like throwing up . . . Don't think about it Ivo, soon you'll be home . . .

Since then, he's always tried to travel in business class, but this time there was no room, he would have had to wait another twenty-four hours in Cairo, and he just didn't feel like it.

When it's time to leave, it's time to leave: roller suitcase in hand, taxi, airport, ticket, check-in, take-off and go.

Ivo Brandani looks out his porthole at the wing's trailing edge, all the flat-headed screws, the tiny whirlpools of turbulence caused by the air flowing over the heads of screws that aren't perfectly continuous with the surface. The whole apparatus of the closed flaps creates the effect of a beetle's retracted wing sheaths, the joints not always seamless, here too pockets of turbulence. I love the flaps when they extend, vibrating, when you can loudly hear the buzz of the worm gear that deploys them before landing, the wing that disassembles into two or three sub-wings, it's the aeroplane as a flying body that seeks efficiency & lift, that effectively becomes a triplane. Flying is a scary thing, contrary to nature: however much Ivo has always adored aeroplanes as divinities and admired pilots as ultra-men, he's never got used to it. Every time, he has to take an anti-anxiety pill to stave off the surge of panic that washes over him upon take-off, when it feels to him that the plane has been rolling too long, that it can't manage to get into the air, that it's barrelling straight towards the end of the runway where it's bound to smash into a barrier, slam full speed into the mud that surrounds certain godforsaken and infamous airports.

I need to throw up . . . Strange, I've never had airsickness before . . . Stable flight, stomach practically empty, and yet this nausea, this headache . . . There's a screw missing! Right there, on the edge of that sort of camber in the wing, it looks like there's a screw missing . . .

A flush of cold sweat climbs up to his chilly head, a sign that the sublime effect of the Xanax is over and that the usual fear has found a way to raise its ugly head again. On earth the sun has already set, but from the windows on the opposite side of the plane shafts of blinding sunlight still sabre in. At 30,000 feet, it's still daylight. In the valleys between the hills and between the mountains, he can't say in what region of the Peninsula, pools of purple shadow are rapidly filling, but you can still see the terrain. What dominates are yellow and brown, as usual, but everything is darkening, even if the highest mountain peaks are still in full sunlight. Every time he's surprised by the inextricable welter of marks that humanity has left on the surface of the Earth. Seen from above, the Peninsula seems like a place that bears no comparison to any other country, given the massacre of the territory, the indecisiveness and the multiplicity of the traces left by the aboriginal inhabitants, for its chaoticity & its ruins, for the terrible chunks that the quarries have taken out of the mountain sides, for the irrational tangles of roads, the labyrinth of the land divisions, the shapelessness of the settlements, whatever their size and nature.

There's no doubt about it, that down below us is my Country . . . It's unmistakable . . . I couldn't be over Spain, the Iberian territory does vaguely resemble this mess, but there you have a semblance of order, not here . . . Much less could this be Germany or England . . . I'm surely flying over *my* Peninsula . . . There it is, the unmistakable trademark of my fellow citizens, of my birth culture, of the society that gave me my birth . . . There it is, the welter of individual wills that has never succeeded in rising to the level of a system, to say nothing of harmony, sharing, consensus, civilization, except in narrow restricted venues and, even then, in a concentrated, private manner, never public . . . 'You can gauge the quality of a culture from the sense of the borders,' Franco says. 'Notice it sometime, when you fly over a country. There are peoples that are very sensitive to lines of separation, that is, when one thing ends and another begins and there's something to mark it, a line, some device that contains the information that there is a break in continuity, which demands respect and must be marked. You could even call it a sense of order, but really it's an attitude that runs deeper and is more complex. It's something that's very meaningful, because it denotes a culture's determination, or a people's determination to oppose chaos.'

This discussion comes back into his mind in some vague way, along with the sensation of annoyance prompted by the sight of the territory below, a familiar distaste, the smell of home, dirty laundry never washed.

Certainly the boundaries, the sharpness and clarity of the separation, the 'determination to oppose chaos', the principle of geometry . . . Franco has a point . . . I wonder if he's still in New York? He was teaching at Columbia . . . Here everything is porous and detritic, a country where you can still empty a chamber pot out a window into the street below and, if you don't actually spill it on anyone, no one will say anything to you . . . This isn't complexity, this is just chaos and disorganization . . . Disorganization is never complex, it's a lack of rational collective thought, it's the result of the omission of organizing actions, it's the lack of rules and an inherent contempt for norms of any kind, it's a scarcity of governance, planning, design, and it's what you see now down below you, Brandani . . . All your life, this stuff has disgusted you: the disorderly and the poorly done, the ungoverned, the neglected, the non-thought-through . . . An entire lifetime spent waiting for something to change, for your fellow countrymen, those who shared your tongue, your culture, to change their views, for them to start assuming rules and planning and order and geometry into their way of life, that they might dedicate themselves to making distinctions rather than simply mingling opposites, instead of the quagmire and imbroglio of sets and subsets of objects and initiatives . . . It is the inability to choose, to assign priorities, to distinguish between what is important and what is not . . . It's the historical inability to manage a multiplicity of personal interests, all of them equally important . . . Never expect anything from them, from the inhabitants of this Peninsula . . . Never expect anything different from what they've always been capable of being and producing, that is, fragments of beauty in a sea of shit . . . Fragments of dignity & thought in a sea of baseness & stupidity . . . Always only fragments, never expect anything whole, anything complete . . . Only tattered rags, more or less clearly defined, bits of incomplete initiatives, objectives never wholly attained, pursued, carried to completion . . . Why am I even bothering telling you all this, Brandani? In all of this lurks the great unsolved mystery of why we are the way we are . . . And more importantly why, even though we know our nature to the point that we can depict unerringly, we do nothing to change it . . . Never anything held in common, never anything genuinely shared . . . Except perhaps that negative image that we have of ourselves and that can be seen so clearly from up here, from on high, because of the way it marks and deforms the territory . . . The lack of any real principle of reason that could hold us together . . . It would be worth the effort to set out to find the seeds of previous communities, smaller than the national community, whose boundaries you could track down and finally trace them . . . That is, finally *split up*, run away from each other, find ourselves in the small cultural enclaves that have nourished us for centuries, officially give space to the egotisms, the factions, the rivalries, the individual contrivances . . . Dismantle the Central State, stop posing as if it were a major industrialized nation . . . As if the fact of being industrialized were somehow an intrinsically good thing, leaving aside the issues of who is industrialized and the consequences of industrialization . . . A tribal, familialist country ought to have the courage to recognize itself as such, and openly base its own existence on families and tribes, on the unwholesome miasma that wafts over the whole sector of kith and kin, the clan . . . Because the only subject that is deserving of respect attention and care in our country does not concern what

577

we have in common and what represents us all but, rather, in minding our own fucking business, our private interests, in the stench
of what we refer to as 'our affections', in the stale air of our homes,
in our reeking bedrooms . . . And to think that the only real responsibility that we ought to have, as human beings, is to battle against
chaos, to ensure the separation of what is unduly mingled, the distinction of one thing from another, the re-formulation of the world,
delimitation, clarity, geometry, cleanliness, shininess . . . In other
words, *Order* . . . Which is of course first and foremost moral order
. . . But moral order doesn't spring from 'within', it is born of the
construction and management of 'what is outside of us' and it is
outside of us that it irradiates and penetrates the minds . . . It is
the norm that constructs the ethics and not the other way around
. . . And it is first and foremost the ordinative norm of the visible,
that is, the geometric, spatial norm, it is the cleanliness of common,
external things that engenders moral cleanliness, not the other way
round: Why should I allow myself to be constrained by the norm
if all around me what I see is an unbroken expanse of things that
are poorly made, disorder, filth, neglect, shabbiness? We must stop
thinking that things originate *first in the human soul* and then
propagate themselves into objects: that is the case only with a small
number of individuals . . . For everyone else it's only a who-the-
fuck-gives-a-damn . . . Whothefuck gives a damn where I dump
my broken toilet and refrigerator . . . Down the embankments of
the state highways: and where else, if not there? The philosophers,
the psychoanalysts and the religious leaders all nattered on about
the unplumbed depths of the human soul . . . The truth is that we're
simple, two-dimensional & followers, hangers-on . . . It's enough
for us to grow up in a given culture, it means that we're no longer
capable of sloughing it off. In fact, we become lifelong defenders
of it, convinced as we are that the broth in question, by the mere
fact that we were born in it, is *the best broth* . . . It is upon this
natural and idiotic sense of belonging that we have constructed
our idea of 'identity', and hence our identity is bound up with the
chaos that I can see down below me, where things are complicated,
but not *truly* complex . . . The brummagem myth of profundity, of

complexity . . . But it's only the congenital malfunctioning of our minds, like a poorly planned grid of roads, where there are continually traffic jams, slowdowns and crashes, but where there are stretches that are miraculously free, spacious, upon which you can drive without hitches, at speed . . . I don't know who invented the fairy tale of the profound, the complex, the unfathomable . . . I've always seen myself as superficial, simple, empty . . . That is, not empty in any absolute terms but empty of endogenous ideas, that is, devoid of the ability to produce concepts on my own: everything I've ever thought and now think comes from outside . . . In the end, even Father with his Three Precepts gave me an orientation . . . All right, now, let's sum up . . . the First was: *A tie is a piece of drapery, the knot should be loose* . . . The Second: *When you drive, the best thing you can do is to assume from the start that all the other motorists are insane and could do anything without a moment's notice* . . . The Third . . . well, the Third was: *When you have a physical set-to with another man and you're afraid of him, assume that he's afraid of you, too* . . . Maybe there was a fourth one, I can't remember . . . Oh, right! The Fourth Precept was simple, elegant and striking: *The right of way is a duty but not a right* . . . This is Father's entire legacy, leaving aside the genetic burden . . . But at least they were things he thought up himself . . . Maybe . . . Oh, right, it might not even have been original with him . . . And for that matter, love too was something I never thought of as 'profound'. Irresistible, sure, overwhelming, even, but 'profound'—what does that even mean? I fell helplessly in love with Clara, the very instant I saw her at that party, because of the curve of her hips . . . Because of the lithe arc of her spinal cord, because of her wonderful jutting butt, because of the promise of her beauty, in short . . . Was it something profound? Maybe it was, seeing that it lasted for more than eight years and that, even now, it endures inside me . . . That is, what is still lasting is a profound yearning for her body, her perfume, her skin, the smell of her breath, the sound of her voice, even . . . It gives me shivers . . . Since that night, nearly fifty years have gone by . . . I ought to call her, write her an email . . . To tell her what? 'The thought of you still makes me horny, so that means I love you still'?

The shadows in the valleys and on the plains grow deeper, the plane rocks and jounces a bit, it seems to have dropped in altitude, you can see the lights of cars lined up on the streets. The headache is still bothering Ivo, along with the nausea. His mouth is dry again, he asks a passing steward for a little water. A voice announces in English that the passengers must fasten their seatbelts because of turbulence. The water is cold, he drinks it slowly, he feels it slide down, it leaves an icy trail behind it, first in his oesophagus and then in the foam in his stomach. The gastric mucosa in his stomach that moves and contracts and slobbers phlegm like some mollusc: he saw it in the monitor while the gastroenterologist was giving him an endoscopy. 'You have a hiatal hernia . . . It's a very common thing at your age . . .' Since then he can't really help imagining the inner lining of his gut in that way. Down below he sees what would appear to be an enormous dump. A vast area surrounded by dirt roads, and which seems to be covered by an endless expanse of whitish material.

Garbage is white . . . I wonder if it can be seen from space . . . That's why extra-terrestrials steer clear of us: too much garbage . . . They must have us listed as one of the galaxy's garbage planets . . . Arid, covered with seas devoid of life, overwhelmed with trash . . . Or it's the dust that keeps them at bay, or the mud whenever it rains . . . Our water is rationed, our coasts are eroded, some of the lower areas are already being flooded and there's nothing to be done: the Northern Delta, the City of Water, a part of the territory to the south of the Agro . . . It doesn't rain much, but when it does, it's a universal deluge of water that sweeps everything before it . . . In the City of God, the retaining walls along the River had performed their duty admirably for more or less a hundred and forty years, before the Flood . . . Do you remember that, eh? An insane wall of devastation, the Apocalypse: we worked ourselves ragged for months and months . . . The water was coming up out of the manholes in the Piazza of the Pagan Temple, the Temple itself was the first to go underwater, the graves of the Founding Fathers inundated . . . I never should have signed that contract: it was the worst fuck-up in my life . . . Maybe not the biggest but one of the biggest . . . There was a tremendous blanket of mud left behind . . . It had to be removed before it could cake solid, before it could turn into dust . . . The Eternal City has never really covered, I got out of there as soon as I could . . . Why does it bother me so much? No one has been able to do anything about any of this . . . No inhabitant of the Peninsula, anyway . . . What good does it even do any more to be a nation if you can't put a halt to a process of fragmentation like this? What the fuck am I even thinking? What does it have to do with anything? Plenty, and I'll tell you how . . . Why does every negative planetary phenomenon, such as the deterioration of things that belong to everyone, including the soil, the city, the coasts, the sea, have to be felt so much more acutely here where we live than anywhere else? What's wrong with the very skin of this country, what's been poisoning it for centuries? Is there no more sense of belonging? No more class loyalty? Are culture and politics both over, kneaded together into a single dough and then spoilt by the disappearance of concrete rights and shared duties? OK . . . All right . . . If that's the way it is, every man for himself and fuck all the rest of you . . . In that case, we might as well continue the deterioration to its logical conclusion . . . Sanction it once and for all with a national referendum: Did we Unify the country and it turned out badly? Let it be, we'll try again in some other situation, when the time seems right . . . If that's all that was at stake, it wouldn't be such a tragedy . . . The problem is the more generalized massacre . . . That's right, the massacre of things objects cities, of the plains the hills the mountains the seas . . . In all these years we've gradually stripped ourselves of piece after piece of nature . . . We've turned our national territory into something senseless, which oscillates between general neglect and abandonment on the one hand and overcrowding on the other, between the void and the overstuffed, between absolute silence and a continuous roar . . . What appears 'natural' to us now is simply in a state of abandonment . . . It's nature that's already previously been tampered with, if not destroyed, if not reduced to the state of a dump, and abandoned to its own devices . . . But it's not true at all: what we have destroyed was nothing other than what was left over after other, countless prior waves of destruction . . . What we call 'nature' is nothing more nor less than something that's already been thoroughly domesticated and is mere residue . . . Previously modified when it hasn't been reinvented & falsified, based on something that used to be there . . . And then, whatever that was, in its turn . . . was just something from *before* that had been tampered with . . . And then so on, back into earlier time . . . Descending into the infinite depths of the Well of Time, where we glimpse the luminous glare of immensely long, silent, merciless eras, completely forgotten and erased . . . There, in that time, is when I would have liked to live! It is this need of prehistory . . . A yearning for the primordial simplification of the world . . . To live only in the present, with no past, no future . . . Careful, Brandani: *nothing has ever been simple* . . . Not the world, not the people in it, not the animals, not all the rest: nothing . . . Words will come to an end . . . The mind will dry up . . . The brain, like a dried chestnut, will bob in a yellowish broth of serum . . . It will be a sterile coprolite, devoid of connections, isolated in its container that consists of cranial bones . . . The damaged joints of the skull, like the welds of an old automobile, will start leaking liquid, oozing from the ears . . . 'It's not worth it,' people will say, they'll toss in the word, 'at this point . . .' Priests and nuns will come and go, they'll take custody of me, they've always been there, lurking patiently in the shadows, it will be up to them to get me to mumble prayers . . . *Our Father who art in heaven thy will be done* . . . All your pride, you will have long since shat it out beneath you, your teeth will have long since been lost, all gone . . . And beneath all this the anger, which will still gnaw away at your liver . . . The hatred for everything will smoulder behind your bloodshot eyes, in the inflamed hollow of your eyebrows . . . You'll be humble only in appearance, Brandani, but in secret you'll still be worm-eaten by the impossibility of approving, of going along with all that surrounds you, with the humans that you see . . . They robbed you of what this world . . . what your country . . . could have become . . . You had deceived yourself into thinking that Time's arrow was also the arrow of the Better, and yet so many had written that things aren't at all that way . . . They said that History has no objective, can't have one; it was only logical, but you never *really* believed it; it pissed you off to hear someone decree: 'The better is the enemy of the good . . .' So what about me? What about us, the people who build things, what are we even doing, if we're not trying to produce *the Better*? You used to say that your work served to improve, that the Good lay in the Improvement . . . You used to say that the *Good*, in abstract terms, meant nothing . . . You used to say that the *Good*, with respect to a river that cuts across your path, is a Sound Bridge, built with all the bells and whistles . . . You used to say that, if you need to cross the sea, the *Good* is a solidly constructed ship . . . You used to say that, for an infection, the *Good* is an antibiotic, that if you want to fly, the *Good* is a pair of wings . . . You used to say that for a ruined house the *Good* is someone who'll fix it up and live in it . . . But by this point . . . The one certainty is that the summation of all this partial, punctual, circumscribed good, doesn't construct a larger good, it doesn't improve the world, it merely domesticates it and kills it . . . A fine bridge adds nothing to a valley . . . You used to think it did, *before*, Brandani, when you wanted to be an engineer instead of a professor of philosophy . . . And instead *now* you think that a bridge subjugates and mortifies the valley beneath, it makes it invisible, it practically annuls it in terms of both form and function . . . I've got everything wrong, changing department was the biggest fuckup of my life . . . The motivation was ridiculous . . . The idea of a builder of bridges, the very idea of a bridge as a *philosophical action* . . . Laughable . . . I ruined my life . . . It's always better to say than to do . . . It's better to write and to speak, even about useless & metaphysical things, even about things that are stupidly hermetic and metaphorical and abstract, rather than acting in Concrete Terms . . . Concrete Terms means cement that has set up . . . It's not obvious to an Italian, but the English do call it *Concrete*, what we Italians call *Cemento* . . . To act means to fight, to carve tunnels through reality, move forwards yard by yard removing obstacles one piece after another, like a miner . . . If you're not willing to do that, people like me who have never learnt to do it, you never achieve a thing . . . In that case, you're better off devoting yourself to words, to philosophy, to art . . . A good schoolteacher, a good office clerk are worth much more than a hesitant, depressed technician, or a weak businessman like Father, with all his courage . . . A good country priest is better than an urban revolutionary, a guerrilla fighter on the Sierra Maestra, someone who knows how to use a submachine gun, someone who knows how to shake up History . . . To build something, a bridge, a dam, is to shake up History, it's hard work, it's a battle . . . And everyone, all those who acted against that particular type of Concrete that is the State, who killed crowds of people in the name of Communism—even you believed in it: 'I'm not the same as you are', remember?—what became of them, in the end? What is the result that they obtained? The Concrete has a greater mass than anything else, and therefore, whatever your purpose, whatever your objective, however marginal it might be, it will oppose you with an invincible inertia . . . Or at least for you, Brandani, it has always been invincible . . . To act concretely? It's not worth the effort, the world won't allow itself to be budged . . . It's never been worth the trouble, even just trying gives you nothing, is unrewarding . . . The Concrete continuously questions you, tests you to see whether you're willing to do what it takes to reach your objective . . . It all depends on that . . . You thought it would be easier, I know . . . I know . . . I know . . . The world didn't welcome you the way you expected at the beginning . . . You always found something or someone that blocked your path . . . They weren't against you, Brandani, it's more that they simply didn't see you . . . Simple matter: you happened to be between them and the things they wanted to attain, and that's why, when they didn't crush you, they shoved you aside or dodged around you, and in the best of cases they just used you . . . There were even times when they toyed with you: Do you remember De Klerk? He was a son of a bitch, that much is certain . . . But who of the two of you was the sucker? Who let his vanity lure him into the trap? In order to act, you have to be capable of opening a breach in the Concrete nature of things, many of your friends, many people your age knew it right from the start . . . How did they manage to figure it out? Who told them? You never really knew it, that's why you're here now, in a completely different world from the one you expected, working as a consultant for peanuts, with no more options, no prospects other than a decent pension . . . With no desire for anything more than enough health left to go out sailing again now and then around two in the afternoon, when the west wind springs up and the sea is covered with glittering scales of light . . . We technicians . . . For every single thing that we build it is necessary that some other thing be *destroyed* . . . As is the case with hillsides for cement quarries, or riverbeds that yield up their gravel, the mountains that yield granite . . . We wiredraw every resource through equations, we mathematize chaos . . . God, what a headache . . . Where is it, where does the disorder produced by the sacred Firth of Forth Bridge go to hide? Where are the galleries of the mines that spat up its iron? The quarries that gave the clay for its bricks? Where the forests chopped down for the scaffolding? Where were the coal mines to melt all that metal? Once the bridge was built, who bothered to take the trouble to tidy up, to restore all the devastation wrought to make all that order? No one, I'd have to guess: the wounds were left laid open . . . That is why from up here the territory appears so contradictory to you: precise, geometric, man-made marks and then dumps, gutted mountains, quarries, vast empty patches of dirt . . . I want to abrogate all this mess . . . I want an overall refoundation, totally bionic and false, I want every slightest trace of 'wild nature' to be swept away and remade, replaced with innocuous copies . . . I want everything that now has a 'natural' value to be carved up into significant artefacts and put in a museum, I want the world reduced to a diorama of itself . . . I want God in a bottle of formaldehyde, I want the spiders to be bionic, decorative, made of rubber . . . I want all of goddamned Amazonia to be remade in almond paste . . . Down there, you can see it, is everything that won't come back, it's as if it fell down a grate in the pavement, it's blurred, tangled, but still real . . . Real! Visible, but untouchable, unattainable . . . All that previous material, on the other hand, it reaches me whenever it wants to, it touches me, it tortures my memory until it bleeds . . . The memory of my life that twists out red from my larynx, I'd like to be rid of it, even vomit it onto myself, but I can't do it . . . All of that will remain buried in the nothingness of the past, which lies in layers deep at the base of my mind, comes out at night and insinuates itself

down my spinal cord, demands attention, cuts like a katana sword
... Every fragment, instead of fitting together with the other pieces
to form a coherent, legible picture, summons others still, profound
incongruous mysterious, capable of touching me in forgotten places
of my memory, as they say to me: 'You're done, game over . . .'
Everything that exists, that's sitting there, frozen for ever in time,
would be *for you*, only if you were able to retrieve it for yourself,
instead of being merely dazzled by it . . . Annihilated by the glare
of all those summers, those sounds, that wind, that light . . .

Another hot flush of panic forces him to pull out his wallet
where he keeps a blister pack of Xanax. The pills are marked off
three by three with a black Sharpie, each section holds a daily dose.
There are two unmarked tablets left over that he has set aside as
reserve doses. As he pulls one out he busily tries to work up a little
saliva in his mouth, then puts it under his tongue, but he knows it
will be at least twenty minutes before it takes effect. The headache
has become furious, he feels strapped to his seat, obligatorily
bound by his seatbelt, his knees pressed against the seat ahead of
him, if he could he'd throw himself out the porthole, just to get a
little cold air in his face. He shuts his eyes and throws his head
back, takes a deep breath to expand his diaphragm. He looks out
the aeroplane window again at the formless territory over which
night is falling, while the blades of absolute light flash like laser
sabres from the portholes on the opposite side of the fuselage; he's
drenched with sweat. He turns on the air vent, and it offers a slight
margin of relief. By now he is unable to recognize any aspect of
his country.

What city is that? What region are we flying over now?
Shouldn't we be lower? What approach route to the airport could
we be on? From north or south?

An unrestrainable burst of retching folds him over onto his
knees, his breath gasping out in a sort of rattle. The Egyptian
lurches to one side as if to dodge out of the way, but his belt
anchors him to the seat. He undoes it hastily and leaps to his feet.
Ivo hears a hostess asking the Egyptian to sit back down, he looks
up to say *sorry* in his broken English, but instead of words what
comes out of his mouth is another spray of watery vomit. The back

of the seat ahead of him is filthy and dripping. Ivo extends his hands in search of the sick bag in the seat pocket, but his fingers refuse to do his bidding.

. . . God doesn't exist . . . But if He does exist, he's hidden down there in the form of a Burning Bush, amid the mountains of Sinai . . .

He turns towards the Egyptian, who's on his feet and is gesturing to someone to come over. Ivo notices that the man has an absolutely insane comb-over and then loses consciousness without realizing that he's losing it. Or maybe he does notice. We can't say. Concerning the most frightening and curious human experience, we know nothing. Ten minutes later, the aeroplane is already on the landing strip. Belted into his seat, covered with a blanket with the Egyptair logo, is Ivo Brandani, unconscious, white as a sheet. He's sixty-nine years old, and in apparently good shape for his age. Five days in a coma, and then he dies in the hospital.

The anatomopathological report shows a finding of diffuse purulent meningoencephalitis, with cortical haemorrhage and edema. The examination found evidence of necrosis in the olfactory bulbs. The cerebrospinal fluid appears haemorrhagic and purulent. Testing for trophozoites in the cerebral material found positive results, pointing to a massive infestation of Naegleria fowleri. *From the information provided by his employer, it has been ascertained that the victim was returning from Egypt. For the transport of the cadaver, all the appropriate prophylactic precautions have been taken. The relatives have given their consent for cremation, as required, given the circumstances, by the health authorities. As is standard procedure, all the passengers on this flight are being questioned and examined, as they are considered at risk for infection.*

He'd come back when the War was over, in the summer of 1945. Who knows how, but he did manage to do it.

All he knew about her was that she had gone to stay with friends, in the country, twenty miles or so from the City of God, because there was still food to eat there.

She had this baby girl to take care of, the result of one of his leaves, when he was still a non-commissioned officer in Africa.

The city was steeped in the August heat. He got out of the train at the Big Station and started looking for a trolley to take him home.

The whole trip he'd inhaled the summery perfume of his country, which you could especially smell at night, when it came in through the open windows of the snail-slow trains, or sometimes standing motionless, for hours and hours, in the open countryside, and you could hear the crickets, you could see the fireflies floating through the air. The sweet smell of dry grass, the steam of cut hay, battled against the funk of humanity that filled the train, crowded with people that had been travelling for days, dirty sweaty frightened exhausted.

'Not yet.'

Now he could catch whiffs of the smell of the City of God, a mix of hot asphalt, dust, pine resin, hard to piece out the ingredients from the ordinary reek of life in that place—something that came to his nostrils, giving him an immediate signal of home, of age-old domestic familiarity.

He didn't know whether he should start to love that city again but the question wasn't a clear issue to him. Rather it was an uneasiness that he felt at the renewed sound of the way those people spoke, in their sleeveless T-shirts, ragtag, bitter wafting sweat under the crushing heat of that time of the day. He'd lost the habit of that disenchanted and disillusioned discourtesy. Suddenly he remembered that there, in his city, any display of kindness & empathy was considered a sort of weakness.

Just two years ago, they'd bombed a working-class quarter, right there, behind the Station. The city had writhed under the blows for an hour and a half, which is how long it had taken the formations of B-17s to finish the job. Five thousand human beings were killed, members of that heavy drawling spawn, the women in their light cotton flower-print dresses, wearing orthopedic shoes, when they weren't men's shoes or athletic shoes, their hair dark, dirty. A delegation of people commemorating the Event was passing through Piazza of the Imprint.

The trolley wasn't in service, not yet, or else not any more. The people at the stop told him about the van that was taking its place; it wasn't running exactly the same route, but still, it worked alright.

He waited in the sun.

'Not yet.'

In the city, for the past month, the Americans had arrived. There were also a few, in dress uniform, in the banner-draped contingent setting out on foot to pay their respects to the bombed quarter.

'Open City, my ass,' he thought, unable to dispense with the mental status of the War, the political contingency, even though for some time now he had felt entirely indecisive, like so many others, almost lost in his inability to say what side he was on, if there even were sides now. It had been hard, indeed impossible, to strike a balance between the desire for dignity and the wish to be on the side of the right.

'A betrayal is a betrayal,' he'd said it to himself a number of times.

And he had told himself every bit as often that you need to end a misguided war as quickly as possible, especially when you're losing it. Then his sense of dignity regained the upper hand and opened another series of pointless reflections.

'Who knows who these people took themselves for . . . While they were slaughtering on all sides, they demanded special treatment for the City . . . The Church, certainly, the Pontiff . . . They bombed their basilica anyway, even if it was theirs, property of the priests . . . And serve them right . . . That'll teach them to go to war with the first asshole that suggests it . . . They'll never fool me again . . .'

Coming away from Spain had also been a hard thing to think or do, but now he was here, at home. First a boat for the Island, then two weeks to find passage to the Peninsula, then a train to the City of God.

The van dropped him off around the block from home.

'Not yet.'

He was almost struggling to recognize his surroundings, the tenement where he lived. The concierge scrutinized him, as she gave him his keys and asked him questions that he answered with nothing more than yeses, noes, and of courses.

On the sixth floor, the rundown flat, which entirely overlooked the courtyard. The light, reflected in grey from the opposite wall of the courtyard, which came in through the windows, thrown wide after months of stale air. The faucet in the tub was leaking in a trail of rust down the porcelain-coated cast iron, the dreary wallpaper, the drawing room with the Tripolina chairs that he'd brought back from Africa, almost two years ago, the standing lamp with the shade dotted with fly shit.

He was home.

He got washed up and went out in search of something to eat. A black-marketeer sold him half a loaf of bread, some provolone cheese and a bottle of milk.

He ate sitting in the kitchen, then slept for the rest of the afternoon and, after that, the whole night through, until his hunger awakened him early the next morning. He made a bowl of bread-and-milk soup, and then another. Without sugar, there was none in the pantry.

He washed up again and soaked luxuriating in the cold water. He put on a suit of clean clothes, stuffed a small suitcase full, went out, and headed towards the Station.

'Not yet.'

He found a bus heading north, along the consular road. The trip took almost three hours, but once he got off the bus he reached the house in just a few minutes. 'She's not here,' Flavia told him, astonished to see him, 'she went for a walk with the little girl.'

'Not yet . . .'

He went to look for her and right away he saw her in the distance, coming home. Her light dress, with a low neckline, flower-print cotton, pleated skirt, narrow ankles, blond hair, high pert breasts, the smile, her steps hurrying at the sight of him. She ran with her daughter in her arms, her light blue eyes glistening with tears. She covered a few yards of terrain before those tears were already flowing down the freckles on her cheeks. A crushing embrace and immediately the scent of her and the little girl, practically crushed between the two of them.

A flush of heat was rising up his back and settled suddenly at the base of his neck, along the muscles at the back of his neck, where her hand already rested as she kissed him.

'Not yet.'